THE
FINAL
TESTAMENT
OF
THE
HOLY
BIBLE

Also by James Frey

A Million Little Pieces
My Friend Leonard
Bright Shiny Morning

THE FINAL TESTAMENT OF THE HOLY BIBLE

JAMES FREY

JOHN MURRAY

First published in Great Britain in 2011
by John Murray (Publishers)
An Hachette UK Company

1

A CIP catalogue record for this title is available from
the British Library

Hardback ISBN 978-1-84854-317-1
Trade paperback ISBN 978-1-84854-318-8

Designed by Graphic Thought Facility, London

Printed and bound by Clays Ltd, St Ives plc

John Murray policy is to use papers that are natural,
renewable and recyclable products and made from
wood grown in sustainable forests. The logging and
manufacturing processes are expected to conform to
the environmental regulations of the country of origin.

John Murray (Publishers)
338 Euston Road
London NW1 3BH

www.johnmurray.co.uk

He will come again
— The Apostles' Creed

This book was written with the cooperation of and after extensive interviews with the family, friends, and followers of Ben Zion Avrohom, also known as Ben Jones, also known as the Prophet, also known as the Son, also known as the Messiah, also known as the Lord God.

MARIAANGELES

He wasn't nothing special. Just a white boy.
An ordinary white boy. Brown hair, brown eyes,
medium height and medium weight. Just like
ten or twenty or thirty million other white boys
in America. Nothing special at all.

First time I saw him he was coming down the hallway.
There was an apartment across the hall from where
I lived that'd been empty for a year. Usually apartments in our project go quick. Government supports
them so they're cheap, for people who ain't got shit
in this world and, even though they always telling us
different, know we ain't ever gonna have shit. There's
lists for them. Long and getting longer. But nobody
would live in that one. It had a reputation. The man
who lived there before had gone crazy. He'd been
normal. Sold souvenirs outside Yankee Stadium and
had a wife and two little boys, real cute little boys.
Then he started hearing voices and shit, started rant-
ing about devils and demons and how he was the last
man standing before us and the end. He lost his job
and started wearing all white and trying to touch
everybody on their head. He got his ass whooped a
few times and his church told him to stop coming. He
screamed at his family and played this organ music
all night. Cursed the demons and pleaded to the
Lord. Howled like some kind of dog. He didn't ever let

his family leave. We stopped hearing the music and it started smelling and Momma called the cops and they found him hanging from the shower. Wearing a white robe like a monk. Tied up with an electrical cord. They found his wife and boys with electrical tape around their ankles and wrists and plastic bags over their heads. There was a note that said we have gone to a better place. Maybe the Devil got him or the demons got him or his Lord left him. Or maybe he just got tired. And maybe they did go to a better place. I don't know, and won't probably ever know, not believing what I believe. And it didn't matter anyway. Everybody heard about it and nobody would live there. Until Ben. He came down the hall with a backpack and an old suitcase and moved right in. He either didn't know or didn't care about what had happened before. Moved right the fuck in.

He was the only white boy in the building. Except for the Jews who owned the liquor stores and the clothing shops, he was the only white boy in the neighborhood. Rest of us was all Puerto Rican. A few Dominicans. A few regular old-school black mother-fuckers. All poor. Angry. Wondering how to make it better and knowing there was no answer. It was what it was, is what it is. A fucked up ghetto in an American city. They're all the fucking same. Ben didn't seem to notice. Didn't care he was out of place. He came and went. Didn't talk to nobody. Wore some kind of uniform like a pretend cop during the week that made everybody laugh. Stayed in his apartment most of the time on weekends, except when he'd go out drinking. Then we'd see him passed out on the benches out front of the buildings, right near the playground. Or in the hallway with vomit on his shirt. One time he came stumbling home on a Sunday morning and his pants were all wet and he was trying to sing some twenty-year-old rap song at the top of his lungs. My brother and his friends started going along with him, making fun of him and shit, and he was too drunk to even know. We started thinking we knew why he was living among us. Why he didn't care he was out of place, didn't belong. We thought he must not be welcome where he came from anymore. They didn't want him around. And we was right, he'd been kicked the fuck out by his people, we just had the reasons why wrong.

First time I talked to him was in the hallway. It was probably six months after he moved in and me and my daughter came walking out of our apartment on our way to chill in front of the building. He was standing there in his boxer shorts and a t-shirt with his door open, holding his telephone. My daughter was like a year and a half old. Just learning some words. She said hola and he didn't say nothing back. She's like her momma. I say something to someone, I expect they say something back. Everybody wants that. Some basic level of respect. Acknowledgment as a human being. So she said it again and he just stood there. So I said hola motherfucker, don't you know how to be a decent motherfucking neighbor and say something back. And he looked nervous and sort of scared and said sorry. And then my girl said hola again, and he said it back to her and she

smiled and hugged his leg and he laughed and
I asked him what he was doing just standing there
in the hallway with his drawers on and his door
open and the phone in his hand. He said he was waiting for a new TV, that he had bought one on sale and it
was being delivered. I told him he better have a good
goddamn lock, that there's motherfuckers around
here that'd kill a motherfucker for a good TV, no lie.
He just smiled, still seeming all nervous and scared,
and said yeah, I think the lock is good, I'll check and
make sure. And that was that. We left him standing
there. Waiting for a TV.

I know that damn TV came too, 'cause we started
hearing it. Bang bang bang. Some explosions.
Helicopters and airplanes flying around. Heard him
whooping and hollering, saying yeah yeah yeah,
gotcha you bastard, how you like me now, motherfucker, how you like me now. Could hear him
pacing, walking around. Got a little scared 'cause
he was sounding like the crazy man who killed his
family and I started wondering if that place really
was cursed. Made my brother, who dropped out
of school the year before me and was still around
then, go listen at the door. My brother got all serious
and listened real close and turned to me and said
this is bad, Mariaangeles, real bad, we got a honkey
playing video games across the hall from us,
I better round up some of my boys and take care
of this shit. I laughed, and knew I shoulda knowed
better. But that's the way it is in this life, you love your
own, and you don't trust people who ain't like you.

If I'd a moved into a white neighborhood and one of my neighbors'd started hearing gunshots and hollering, there'd a been a fucking battalion of cops kicking my damn door in. That's just the way it is.

My brother liked video games. He started spending all his time in that apartment with Ben. They got a basketball game and a driving game where the more people they ran over with their car the more points they got. They started watching Knicks games and drinking beer together and sometimes smoking weed. I told my brother to be careful 'cause white people could be tricky, and you could never know what they might want. I thought everything in my life that had gone wrong had been because of white people, and most of 'em looked Jewish. My daddy got sent to prison by some when I was little. My momma had to work cleaning their houses most her life. My teachers, who all pretended to care so much but was really just scared of us and treated us like animals, was white people. They're the cops, the judges, the landlords, the mayors, the people who run everything and own everything. And they aren't letting go of any of it or sharing any of it. The rich take care of the rich and make sure they stay rich, and they talking about helping the poor, but if they really did, there wouldn't be so many of us. And it was one thing having a white boy live across the hall and saying hi to him now and then or watching him get drunk or wear some silly uniform, but it's another having my brother spending all his time with him. I didn't think nothing good would come of it.

My brother didn't ever listen to me. Never did. Wish he had, he might still be with us. This time, though, he was right and I was wrong. Even before he knew, before he became what he became, before it was revealed, Ben was okay. Nothing more, nothing less, just okay. I first found out when my brother took me over there. He had got tired of me telling him all the time that the white boy was no good, so one day he says you either come with me and see he's cool or you shut the fuck up about me spending time over there. I ain't one to shut the fuck up, only a few times in my whole life, so I went with him. We made sure Momma was okay and we went across the hall and we knocked on the door and he answered in his boxer shorts and t-shirt with tomato sauce all over it and my brother started talking.

What's up, Ben.

Ben wiped some grease off his face and talked back at him.

What's up, Alberto.

This is my sister Mariaangeles and her daughter Mercedes.

Yeah, I met them once.

Ben looked at me.

How you doing?

I gave him a dirty look.

You gonna invite us in?

I guess.

He opened the door. Stepped aside. And we went in and I started looking around. Big TV in the living room. A grubby old couch with cigarette burns that looked like it was made out of old carpet.

Video game disks and controllers. Kitchen was nasty. Pizza boxes. Empty cans of soup and pasta with spoons and forks still in 'em. Garbage bags filled on the floor. I opened the fridge 'cause I was thinking of having a soda or something and all it had in it was some ketchup and that was it. Whole place smelled like old food and stale beer. Went to the bedroom and there was a mattress and a pillow. Some clothes on the floor. Closet had his uniform hanging up in it, and it was the only thing that looked cared for. Bathroom, the bathroom where that man was hanging, was worse than the kitchen. Stains in the toilet and sink. Tissues overflowing out of a little garbage can. No toilet paper to be seen and I doubt he had ever cleaned it once. Even by the standards we was used to seeing, his place was bad. And more than bad, or nasty, or disgusting, it was just sad. Real sad. Like he didn't know any better. Like he thought it was normal for a grown man to be living like that. Made me think he didn't have nobody in his life that cared about him. Like he was all alone. Alone in a place where he didn't belong because he didn't have nowhere else to go, and no one else to go to. They'd have done something if they was around. But they weren't. He was all alone. I went back into the living room. Bang bang bang. Him and Alberto shooting Nazis, throwing grenades at 'em. Mercedes sitting on the floor chewing her blankie, watching people explode on the TV. Too much. There's enough ugliness in the world already without pretending to do more. Too much I said, and I smacked Alberto on the back of the head. He got all mad, said you knew what we was doing here, you didn't have to come. I said play another game, play some game where you don't gotta see blood squirting everywhere, and Ben said we'll play the NBA game and changed the disk. While he doing it I ask him where he from, and he says Brooklyn, and I ask if he got family there, and he says yes. I ask him do he see them, he says no. I ask him why and he says I just don't. I ask for how long and he says a long time. I ask him how old he is and he says thirty, I ask where he been living before this and he says he don't want to talk about it. Answers made me sad. I always thought white people had good lives. Even the worst of 'em had it better off than me and everybody I knew. Just what I believed. But this boy didn't have it better. Worse. Just him and his video games and his shitty apartment that no one else would live in. I had my girl and my family at least. He had it way worse.

Their game started back up and I didn't like being there 'cause it was sad and depressing so I got Mercedes and we left and went back to our place. And that was it. For a long time. Six or nine months or something. Alberto played video games with Ben. I'd see him around. In his uniform if it was day, drunk if it was night, sometimes in the hall in his underwear while he was waiting for a pizza. I turned eighteen. Went out with some of my girlfriends from around the project and some girlfriends from when I was in school. They was all around my age, almost all of 'em in a situation similar to mine:

no diploma, a kid or two and a couple had three, boyfriend still around but not really there, no way to get out or move up. Just ways to make it through the day or the week or the month. One of the girls was wearing nice clothes and a nice watch and smelled good like expensive perfume and she started saying she was working as a dancer and making plenty of money. Said you had to be eighteen, but could make three, four hundred, maybe five hundred bucks a night dancing in clubs. We started saying she was hooking but she said no, she danced naked on a stage and gave men lap dances in a private room and they gave her cash. That it was easy. Men from Manhattan would come up, tell their wives they had meetings or was working late, or they'd come over after baseball games at Yankee Stadium. They was stupid and it was easy to make 'em think they was getting some ass and the more you could make 'em think it the more they would pay you. She said it wasn't a churchgoing job, rubbing her ass and tits all over white men, but none of us was churchgoing girls, and a good shower at the end of the night and she was fine with it, especially 'cause she was making so much money. She said maybe she was gonna leave the neighborhood. Find her a place where her kids would be able to go to a good school. Because even though almost all of us was dropouts, we knew the only way out for real was an education. Just none of us could do it.

Next day I called the girl. She took me to the club. I met the manager. Fat white man from Westchester.

He made me strip down to my panties and bra
and show him how I danced. Made me rub my ass
on his crotch and rub my titties down his chest and
whisper shit his wife wouldn't say to him in his ear.
His hands started wandering and I asked him what
he was doing and he said he test drove all the girls
before he let 'em out on the track. Made me sick.
But we needed the money. Momma wasn't working
and who the fuck knew what Alberto did. Made me
sick. But I let him. I let him do anything and everything. Took me for a test drive. Made me fucking
sick.

Started working a few days later. It wasn't hard
but I had to close up part of my heart, part of my
soul. I had been with three men before. One when
I was twelve. Mercedes' father, who I was with
from when I was fourteen until he left when I was
seventeen. The manager. Except for that manager,
I'd waited. Tried to make sure they loved me. I know
I loved them. Would have done anything for them.
Killed for them or died for them. Hit the cross for
them. I thought they felt the same, loved the same.
But love is different for every person. For some it's
hate, for some it's joy, for some it's fear, for some
it's jealousy, for some it's torture, for some it's peace.
For some it's everything. For me. Everything.
And to let a man touch me like that, or to touch a
man like that, I had always had to love. So I shut it
down. Closed it. Buried it somewhere. And I danced
and touched and whispered and got them hard
and took them as far as I could and took them for

as much as I could. They didn't know but they took
more from me. A shower at the end of the night
wasn't enough. Not even close. Didn't clean nothing.

Three nights a week I worked, sometimes four.
Started saving up. Got Mercedes some clothes
that hadn't been worn before, some of her own
shoes, brand new. Got my momma a sweater, and
new magazines every week. Didn't put none of the
money in a bank 'cause I know what happens
with white people and their banks. I put it away.
Where Alberto wouldn't never look. Where nobody
would look. A couple months, a couple more.
Making money but hurting. And changing.
Keeping myself closed and hard all the time started
taking it out of me. One of the girls gave me some
shit to smoke and it helped. So I did more of it.
And it helped. More than a shower or anything else.
But when it wore away it started hurting more so
I was taking more. Sleeping and working and
getting high. Starting to do things I would have
never done before because I didn't care, because
I was hurting so much that more of the hurt
wasn't nothing. And it brought more money.
One night I was working and Ben came in and one
of the girls smiled and said look who's here.
And I asked her what about him and she said he was
an easy mark. Would come in with his paycheck
and get drunk and give the whole damn thing away.
I told her he was living in my building and that
he was mine. She got in my face about it for a minute
till I told her how far I'd go. I was dipping into my

money too much and I needed more. Momma was
getting sick and Mercedes was getting sick and
I needed them to get to a doctor and I didn't have
no insurance. And I needed more.

I went over to him. He was already drunk. He
smiled and said hi and I said hey baby, nice seeing
you here. And I didn't even ask him. Took his hand.
Led him to the room where we did the dances.
And I went at him, giving him what all them men
wanted and whispering in his ear about what we
could do back at home now that I knew what kind of
boy he was. I told him I wanted to suck his cock and
I wanted him to fuck me, that I would ride his ass
all day and all night, that I was getting all wet thinking about it. And I kept ordering drinks and feeding
him. Just kept it going. And he took it. And was
wanting more. And after an hour he was gone.
His mind was gone and his money was gone. And
I felt bad 'cause I knew what he was and I knew
he wasn't bad. Just sad. And alone. Man without
anything or anyone, alone in that apartment where
no one else would live, with his TV and his games
and his pizza boxes and soup cans and his garbage
and his sad mattress and his dirty bathroom. That's
all he was. He passed out. Right in the chair with
my ass between his legs. The bouncers came and
took him out. He didn't have no ID or driver's license
or credit card. Nothing with his name or address
or nothing. I told them he was my neighbor and I
knew where he was living. They was gonna throw
him on the street, in the gutter. Leave him there.

Let whatever was gonna happen, happen. He'd
been there before, I know. And shit had happened
to him, I know that for sure. I told them I could at
least get him back to the building. I had just taken
everything he had and I was figuring I could do
that much. We got a cab and put him sleeping in
the backseat. I sat next to him. He was snoring like
a baby. And when we got to the projects the driver
helped me get him out of the cab. And I got him into
the building and into the elevator. Got him into
the hallway front of his door. And I left him there.
And I went back out and got high. Spent some of his
money on what I needed. And when I came home
later he was still there.

Next time I saw him was like two days later. He was
coming home in his uniform and I was going to
work. We didn't say nothing to each other. I don't
even know if he remembered. Just looked sad
and nervous like he always did. And the next time
I saw him after that was a long time. And he wasn't
the same no more. He had changed. Changed and
become someone else. He had become something
I couldn't even believe. And then I did. I believed.
I believed.

CHARLES

I felt sorry for him when I met him. He had come in
to apply for a security position at my job site. We ran
two guys at a time, on twelve-hour shifts. There were
weekday guys and weekend guys. Pay was minimum
wage. No benefits. It was a shitty job. You walked
the perimeter of the site, stood around for hours at
a time. We didn't have a security shack. You bring
one in and the guards end up never leaving. They buy
little TVs and drink coffee all day. Take naps. This
was a sensitive site. We were putting up forty stories
in a neighborhood where the tallest building was
twelve. There had been community opposition.
A couple protests, and a big petition. I needed guys
who were willing to work. To make sure that the site
was secure. It's harder than you think finding them.
Most people want something for nothing. They want
everything to be easy. When a job is hard, they
demand more money, more time off, they complain
to their union reps and try to renegotiate terms.
That's not the way it works. Life is hard, deal with it.
Working sucks, deal with it. I'd love to sit home and
collect a check every two weeks for watching baseball games and spending time with my kids. Doesn't
happen that way. You gotta work for everything in
this world. Scratch and claw and fight for every little
thing. And it never gets easier. Never. And it doesn't
end until you die. And then it doesn't matter.

Learn to deal with that. It's the way of the world.
You fight and struggle and work your ass off
and then you die. Deal with that.

He came in with a resume. It said his name was
Ben Jones, that he was thirty years old. He was wearing a button-down with the logo of a security guard
school on it. My first impression of him was that
he was very eager, very excited, and very nervous.
His hand was shaking when I shook it. His lips were
quivering. Aside from his basic biographical information, and an eight-week course at the security school
which made him officially qualified for the job, the
resume was empty. I asked him where he was from
and he said Brooklyn. I asked him if he went to
college, he said no. I asked him when he left home and
he said at fourteen. I told him that seemed young
and he shrugged and I asked what he'd been doing
for the past sixteen years and he changed, just a little,
but he changed, and something in his eyes came
out that was really sad and really lonely and extremely painful. It was only there for a second, and
normally I wouldn't notice anything like that, or pay
attention to it, or give a shit, but it was very striking,
and he looked down at his feet for a moment and
then looked up and said I've had hard times and
I'm ready to work and I promise I'll be the best worker
you have, I promise. And that was it. He didn't offer
anything else and I didn't push it. I just thought to
myself sixteen fucking years, what the fuck has this
guy been doing. And I still think about it, all the time,
what the fuck was he doing. And I imagined, and

still do, because of the flash of deep sadness and loneliness and pain that I saw, that whatever it was, and wherever it was, it had been truly truly awful.

So I gave him the job. He was very excited. Like a little kid at Christmas. A big smile, a huge smile. He said thank you about fifty times. And he kept shaking my hand. It was funny, and very endearing. It wasn't like he'd won the fucking lotto. He got a minimum wage job walking around a construction site for twelve fucking hours a day.

I put him on the five-days-a-week day shift. Thought that would be best. That he'd be proud to have that position. And he was. It showed in how he did the job. He was always on time. His uniform was always clean. He never tried to extend his breaks or his lunch. He never complained. He seemed fascinated by the process of putting a building up: knocking in the pilings, setting the foundation, the construction of the skeleton frame. He'd ask different people questions about what they did, or why they did things a certain way. He'd listen very intently to their answers, like he was gonna be tested on it or something. He was generally the happiest guard I'd ever seen or had on a job, and he became sort of the site mascot. Everybody liked him and enjoyed having him around. He knew everyone's name and would greet everyone in the morning and say goodbye at the end of the day. There were only two things that ever seemed off, and I dismissed them both because he did such a good job and seemed so happy. First was right after he got his first paycheck. He came and switched the address in our files to an address in the Bronx. The previous one had been in Queens. I don't know why but I was curious, so I looked up the address in Queens. It was a state-run transitional home, a place where they send men coming out of either prison, rehab, a homeless shelter, or a mental institution. I thought about looking into it more, but I had other things to worry about and Ben seemed fine. Second thing happened one day during lunch. I had a doctor's appointment and had to leave the site. On my way to the subway, I saw Ben sitting on a bench a few blocks away. He was crying. It was the middle of the day, and he had seemed like his normal self when I had seen him earlier. I did a double take because I couldn't believe it was him. But it was. He was sitting on a bench with his face in his hands and he was sobbing.

The day of the accident was a beautiful spring day. It was sunny, no clouds, slight breeze, in the mid-70s. A perfect New York day, not one I thought would fucking blow up. I had never had a major accident on one of my sites before, and it was a point of great pride for me. I believed there wasn't a building on earth that was worth sacrificing a life for, and I still believe it. Safety matters more than speed. Safety matters more than anything. It was one of the reasons I had been hired. Because the job was a sensitive issue in the community, and so many people were against it, the developer couldn't afford to have anything go wrong. Accidents are the best weapon community activists have against developers. While it would be nice to think developers care about safety, they don't. Like almost everyone else in America, developers are fucking greedy. They care about money, and activists with weapons cost them money. My job was to stay on budget, stay on schedule, and keep that site safe.

The skeleton was done. Forty stories of steel frame rising. We were putting in the windows, which were ten foot by ten foot mirrored panels. We had finished the first thirty-three stories without any problems, and we were installing on thirty-four. We'd lift seven panels at a time. Bundle them, secure them, rig them to a wire, bring them up with a crane. I'd done it literally thousands of times at job sites, and I had never had any problems.

I don't know what the fuck went wrong. Still don't. We had investigators from the city, the state, and the insurance company all look at the rig, and nobody could figure it out. To this day, the cause in all of the paperwork is listed as unknown. I could call them and tell them that it didn't matter what we did that day, that no rig would have held that glass, that there were other forces at work far beyond any that the city, state, or insurance company could muster, but they'd think I was crazy. And sometimes I'm not sure that I'm not. But that's part of faith. Believing and knowing despite what other people say, and despite what the world might think of your beliefs.

I was on the ground. Standing near our trailer, which was on the edge of the sidewalk. I was holding a clipboard, going over some budget numbers with one of our construction accountants. They blow an air horn right before any large load goes up, and the air horn went off. I looked up and the panels were slowly rising. We stop traffic when we lift panels, and there were no cars coming down the street. Most of the workers were standing around talking, which is what they did when work was halted. Ben was standing at the edge of the site, look- ing towards the stopped traffic, ready to stop anyone who might try to get around our traffic controller. Normally I would have gone back to the clipboard. But I felt something, something inevitable. If you can somehow feel fate, or destiny, or the power of the future, I felt it, very literally. And it made me watch. It forced me to do something that I normally wouldn't do. I couldn't turn away. I couldn't not watch those panels.

The panels continued to go up, and they drifted a few feet, just like they always did, like anything that heavy being lifted that high would drift. The crane was working perfectly. The rig was set perfectly. The panels were in wooden crates sealed with iron nails. At that point we'd lifted and installed hundreds of them. It was no big deal. Just part of our routine. Nobody was watching, and I'm the only one who saw. I saw the nails slip out of the crate. I saw the back of the crate fall. I saw the angle of the crates change. I saw them drift. I saw the panel fall out. A ten foot by ten foot glass panel. Probably weighed a thousand pounds. I saw it fall.

It hit him on the back of the head and shattered. There was a huge noise, an explosion of glass. He got flattened. A total collapse. Everything stopped, everybody turned. There was a moment, a long hideous moment of silence, of never-ending fucking silence. Then the screaming started. I dropped the clipboard and started running towards him. Pulled my phone out of my pocket and called 911. There was no way he was alive. I told the operator a man had just died on my construction site and gave her the address. I could see the blood before I got there. It was everywhere. And there was glass everywhere. All I could hear was screaming. People were getting out of their cars, running, calling 911. And above me, for a brief instant, I saw the rest of the panels being pulled onto the thirty-fourth floor. There was no way that one should have fallen.

When I got to him, I was positive he was dead. The back of his head was crushed. There was blood and something else, I assumed it was brain fluid, leaking out of it. There were shards of glass imbedded into his entire body. He was literally shredded, blood pouring from his arms, legs, chest, stomach, face. There was fucking blood everywhere. I couldn't really even see him. I didn't know what to do, if I should touch him, move him, try taking the glass out of his body. There was no way to try to stop the bleeding with a tourniquet, or ten tourniquets, or fifty tourniquets. And I didn't believe in God so I couldn't pray. I just waited for someone to come who would tell me what do.

A crowd started gathering. The other workers tried to keep them back. Sirens in the distance. A group of women kneeling in a prayer circle. People still screaming. As they got closer and saw what I saw, they turned away, covered their eyes, a few vomited. And the blood kept flowing. I was kneeling next to him, and it was running around my legs, soaking my pants. I took hold of two of his fingers where there was no glass, and I started trying to talk to him. I had no idea if he could hear me. I thought it might help him if he could, it might comfort him, give him some kind of solace as he died. No one wants to die alone, even though that's how it happens for all of us, even though we pretend there's some other way. I thought my voice might make it easier. Calm him, make him less scared. I can't imagine how fucking shocked and terrified he must have been, if he was aware of anything. I told him that help was on its way and that he was going to be alright. I felt sick to my stomach while I said it. I could see his brains through his shattered skull. Literally see his brains. I just held those two fingers and talked to him and watched him bleed away.

An ambulance arrived. The crowd parted and two paramedics came rushing through with a gurney. I heard one of them say Jesus fucking Christ, the other said no way this guy's alive. They dropped their bags and went to work. They started checking him, but they didn't seem to know where to start. One of them asked me what happened and I said a plate of glass fell on him. They checked his pulse, talked about how to proceed, leave the glass in him, get him out of here, let the surgeons deal with it if he's even still alive. He had a pulse, and they both seemed shocked. They lowered the gurney, asked me to step away. One took his lower body and one took his upper body. They lifted him onto the clean, white surface. Blood streamed off his body, stained the gurney, dripped to the ground. They started back towards the ambulance and I followed them. They asked me his name, I told them. They asked where he was from and I said he lived in the Bronx. They got him into the ambulance. I asked to come, told them I was his boss, that it was my job site. They said get in and I did and they closed the doors.

I sat on the bench near the door. One of them drove. The other worked on Ben. He put on a heart monitor, wove the wires around the shards of glass protruding from Ben's body. When it was on and working, he tried to stop the bleeding from cuts without glass in them, but there were so many of them it was almost useless. The monitor stopped, and the paramedic gave Ben CPR, and his heart started again. I don't know how long we were in the ambulance. It felt like ten seconds and it felt like ten hours, and Ben's heart stopped four or five times. He died in that ambulance four or five times, and the paramedic kept bringing him back. Something kept bringing him back.

Once the monitor stopped and the paramedic
didn't do anything. Just stared and shook his head.
I didn't blame him. It seemed like a lost cause.
Ten seconds passed, maybe twenty, it seemed like
forever. I just stared at Ben, or what was left of him,
and tried to figure out what the fuck went wrong,
how this could have happened. I started to say
I'm sorry, as if apologizing to a dead man would
mean something, though it seems that's how it works
most of the time; we say the things that matter to
people when it's already too late. Before the words
came out of my mouth, the monitor started registering a pulse again. Something kept bringing him
back. Something was not going to let him go.

We pulled into the hospital and they rushed him
away. I followed them into the emergency room.
I gave the administrators all the information I could.
I filled out all of the forms as best as I could. I called
back to the site and asked for a change of clothes
because the ones I was wearing were covered
with blood. Men from the site started showing up.
We were all in shock. Just sat and talked about
how we couldn't believe it happened, how awful
it was. Media started showing up and trying to
interview people. Nobody said a word. We knew
it wouldn't matter if we did, that the media was
gonna write what they wanted to write regardless of their so-called ethics, and their supposed
belief in truth. We just sat and waited to hear that
Ben had died. We assumed it was so. Though I
had seen what I had seen in the ambulance, at the

time I didn't believe it was anything more than coincidence.

More men from the site arrived. The crane operator and window installers came in. They were deeply and visibly shaken. I sat with them, asked what happened. They didn't know. They claimed the crate was intact. That there was no way that glass should have come out, or could have come out. I told them I saw the nails fall, and saw the back of the crate fall. They claimed that was impossible. That the crate was intact. There was tape around it, tape that had been applied at the factory, and that it was unbroken. The crate was empty. They could tell that by its weight. But it had never been opened. I figured someone was trying to cover their ass. Someone had fucked up and didn't want to take responsibility for another man's death. Ultimately the responsibility would have fallen on me. But it turned out they were right. The crate was unopened and empty. City and state accident investigators all agreed. The crate was fucking unopened. How the glass fell has never been explained. And Ben didn't die. Somehow he survived. More than survived. So much more. Something kept bringing him back. Something wouldn't let him go. Something, or someone, or I don't know what, wouldn't let him die.

ALEXIS

I was on break when the call came in, watching a
baseball game with some of the guys who work in the
cafeteria and were also on break. It was a Yankee
game, and I love the Yankees, and though my schedule tends to prevent me from seeing as many games
as I would like, I try to see two or three a week during
the season, and I always watch during my breaks. I
love the systems and the order of baseball, and I very
much appreciate the cause-and-effect nature of the
game. As a surgeon, my entire life is based in the
systems of the human body, the systems of the hospital and a surgical team, the order or orders under
which those things operate, and the cause-and-effect
nature of trauma, injury, and the surgical attempts to
remedy them. Though it often seems chaotic and
anarchic and spontaneous, all life is system, order,
and cause and effect. Try as so many do, it is impossible to escape them. I gave up at a fairly young age
and decided to dedicate my life to the service of
them.

The call was white male, late twenties or early
thirties, massive trauma, massive head wounds,
massive blood loss, and then the unusual part,
which was the first of so many unusual occurrences
with Ben and his case, hundreds of shards of glass
imbedded in his body. I'm a geek about my job,

and after doing it for many years—I was forty-one
when the case began—I still get excited when a
case comes in that sounds different or challenging
for some reason. At the time, I didn't even think
about the human element of it, that someone had
just undergone some horrific event and was experiencing feelings and emotions that are far beyond
anything within the realm of my experience. I just
thought about the potential medical and technical
challenges involved and how I would solve them.
Ben changed that for me. Now much of what I think
lies within the human realm of the surgical experience, what the patient is feeling, what the people
who love the patient are feeling, and how I can help
with those issues as well. I understand that all of
our lives revolve around what we are feeling at any
given moment. There is nothing more human than
emotion.

I got up and I said goodbye to my fellow Yankee
fans and I quickly made my way to the trauma suite.
Everyone was getting ready, the nurses, the assist-
ants, the residents, and I was the last to arrive.
At that point, and again this was before my experience with Ben changed me, because my position as
the head surgeon is one of authority, I tended not to
speak to any of the people I worked with unless
I needed something from them or needed to discuss
a specific aspect of the impending surgery with
them, both of which were rare. While I scrubbed
in and prepared myself for whatever it was that was
arriving, I was silent.

The moments while a team waits for a patient can be very tense. You stand at the ready. While you have a general idea of condition, you do not often know what the specific medical issues are, and you have no idea if you will be there for ten minutes or ten hours, though there is rarely anything in between. Different surgeons handle it differently. I think of myself as a batter in a baseball game, actually in the seventh game of the World Series, with the bases loaded, a three-and-two count, down by three runs, in the bottom of the ninth inning. I have one swing to either succeed or fail and the result entirely depends on what I do and how I perform. Unlike in baseball, though, I cannot hit a single, a double, or a triple. I either hit a home run or I strike out, and the patient either lives or dies.

As I mentioned, I was intrigued and excited by the call, and had no idea what a patient who had shards of glass imbedded in his body would look like or what I would need to do to make that patient survive. When paramedics enter the hospital with a critical case, they are greeted by ER doctors and members of the surgical team, and there is a transfer of information related to the patient: the circumstances of the trauma, issues, if any, during transfer, a preliminary diagnosis, if one is possible. Once the transfer is made, the patient is brought into the trauma bay, where I, and the rest of the team, go to work. It is usually a fairly seamless process, and it is one that is repeated with great regularity.

Not so with Ben. The EMTs were covered with blood,
as was the stretcher. They started to describe the
scene, and one of them kept repeating something
I myself said many times later, which was that there
was no way the patient should be alive, and that he
had no idea what was going on with him. The doctors
and nurses, who were incredibly seasoned and
experienced, and had seen all manner of horror and
gore after years in a public New York City emergency
room and trauma unit, were shocked almost into
paralysis, and one of the nurses vomited. Each looked
to the others for direction, which is not entirely
surprising. In life we often look to others for simple,
but difficult answers, despite the fact that we have
those answers ourselves. They needed to get him into
surgery, and they needed to do it as soon as possible.

One of them took the initiative and urged the others
to act, and they started moving towards me and my
team. We can always hear them as they bring
the patient into the trauma bay, hear the wheels
of the gurney, the various squeaking sounds it makes,
hear the nurses talking to each other, sometimes
the patients scream, cry out, or moan. As they get
closer, I tend to become calmer, more focused, and
more aware, and time slows down in a way that
makes those few brief moments seem incredibly
long and peaceful. I sometimes wish I could live
forever in that state, and believe that those who find
enlightenment, people like Ben, though he discovered so much more than that, live their entire lives
that way.

The doors opened and he was brought into the trauma bay, and for the first time in my fifteen-year career I heard an audible gasp come from every single person in attendance. It was a surreal, unbelievable sight, like something out of a Hollywood horror movie, something that shouldn't have been possible and isn't possible, but was right in front of my eyes. There was blood everywhere. There were huge, deep lacerations everywhere. When I heard glass shards, I expected small pieces of glass, maybe an inch long at their longest. What he had in his body were not shards, but actual pieces, some as tall as ten inches, some as wide as twelve inches, and we were only seeing what was visible above the level of his skin. The back of his skull had been crushed, and there were pieces of it that appeared to be missing. We could not see his face at all because it was entirely covered in blood. Everything was entirely covered in blood.

The first stage of treatment in any trauma situation is the stabilization of the patient. Death from blood loss was the obvious first concern. If a patient has lost more than 40 percent of their body's blood volume, they are likely to be in decompensated hypovolemic shock, which usually results in multi-organ failure. While we checked his blood pressure, which was at 40 over 20, the lowest I'd ever recorded in a living patient, and checked his pulse, which was 30, again an absurdly low number, we gave him injections of epinephrine and atropine to jumpstart his heart and get his blood pressure and pulse up.

Simultaneously, we tried to get heart-rate monitors and BP monitors on him, but it was incredibly difficult because we were weaving the wires around glass shards that had very sharp edges. We inserted a central venous line and transfused him with type O negative uncrossmatched red blood cells. Though we wanted, at some point, to take the glass out of him, we needed him to be stable first, and we needed to figure out which pieces to remove first, and in what order the rest of them would come out.

He shut down three times in my care, went into full cardiac arrest. We defibrillated him, which was difficult because of the glass, and on one occasion I absolutely know the defibrillation worked, but on the other two his heart appeared to start functioning again on its own, which was both surprising and confusing. We kept putting blood into him and he kept bleeding and we kept putting it in. I don't know the actual amount, but it became something of a game, a game where a man's life appeared to be at stake, and in which I and the other people in the room were working with incredible urgency and resolve, making sure we were transfusing more blood in than he was losing, a game that we knew would result in death if we did not succeed. What we could see of his skin was white, and I don't mean the Caucasian white, I mean truly white, alabaster white, like he was carved from marble. And no matter how much blood we put in, his skin didn't change, and his body showed no indication that it was actually maintaining the blood.

While we were stabilizing him, I also needed to
cover and protect his head. He had sustained
a comminuted skull fracture, which means it had
broken into a large number of small pieces, through
which I could clearly see his brain. I assumed there
was intracranial bleeding, most likely subdural,
epidural, or intraparenchymal, and even if I could
keep him alive, he would suffer from massive brain
damage. We applied compression dressings using
sterile surgical bandages, gauze, and surgical tape
and moved his head as little as possible. We found
pieces of his skull that were the size of nickels
and bagged them in case we might be able to use
them later.

Two extremely long and stressful hours after
he arrived at the hospital, his heart rate and blood
pressure were stable, or at least stable enough
for us to attempt to start removing the pieces of
glass from his body. I took a step back and took a
deep breath and looked at what was ahead of me.
There were three IV lines transfusing blood into
his body. We were applying pressure everywhere
we could, but blood was still coming out of him at
a rather alarming rate. We had been able to clean
him up and cut away his clothing, and his skin
was still deathly white. There was glass protruding from his legs, his arms, his abdomen and
chest, there were smaller pieces in his face, and
there were a number of large pieces that had been
deeply imbedded into his back when he hit the
ground.

I tried to identify pieces of glass that had nicked, punctured, cut, or potentially severed major veins and arteries: the jugular veins, carotid arteries, and subclavian arteries and veins in the neck, and the femoral arteries and veins in the legs. I wondered what I couldn't see, possibly damage to the aorta, the inferior vena cava, or the pulmonary vasculature, which are deeper in the chest and torso and were beneath my field of vision. While the conventional wisdom of a non-medical professional might say it would be best to remove the pieces of glass from those veins and arteries, there was the very real possibility that they were tamponading further bleeding and had sealed areas that had been damaged or destroyed. Getting through this part of Ben's treatment would be part luck and part strategy and, if successful, part miracle.

I had a vascular surgeon and his fellow join me and offer their opinions. I felt they might have something to offer that would help me, and help Ben, in some way. None of us had any idea where to start, or what to do, or what path to take, or what we might have in store for us when we started to actually remove the pieces. So I just started. I had three residents with me, and I had two of the residents prepared with suture in case sutures were needed, and I had the other prepared with a bipolar bovie, which is an electro-cauterization instrument. We had two surgical nurses with suction and another with an aspiration wand that delivered an anticoagulant. There were other nurses monitoring his vitals and continuing to transfuse him.

Once we started, we moved very quickly, because every movement, especially removing the largest pieces, resulted in blood loss, sometimes fairly significant blood loss. If we hadn't moved quickly, Ben would surely have died. There were a number of scares, and a number of times when his vitals dropped dramatically, and a number of times when we couldn't stop the bleeding in what I considered a timely manner. But Ben wouldn't die, and now, at this point, after everything, I believe that what we did that day probably didn't matter very much. Ben was not going to die.

Nine hours after we started, we tied the last suture. He had a total of 745 stitches, both internal and external, and an additional 115 external staples. We had used 40 units of blood, which is approximately double the amount any human has in their body at any given time. We also gave him multiple units of platelets and fresh frozen plasma. And for him, the day was far from over. There was a team of cranio-facial surgeons and neurosurgeons standing by to deal with his skull and brain injuries. As I stepped back from the table, I saw one of his hands twitching, which I took to be a good sign, and I stepped over and took hold of it, hoping that somewhere, on some level, he might find it comforting. To my great shock, his grip was very strong, very firm, and I immediately felt something similar, but deeper and more profound, to what I feel in those moments just before surgery, an intense calm and sense of peace and contentment. It was unreal, and obviously unexpected, and it ultimately changed my life in so many ways. I didn't want to let go. I didn't want that moment to end and I didn't want that feeling to ever leave me. But all things leave us, all people, all feelings, no matter how we want them to stay, no matter how tight we hold on to them. We lose everything in life at some point. I lost that moment the instant I let go of his hand.

After he was hemodynamically stable, he needed a CT scan of his head to determine the extent of intracranial injury. Moving a patient as critical as he was can be very difficult, very complicated, and very slow, so I knew I had some time to take a break, and I needed one. I went to our break room and took a shower and tried to take a nap but couldn't fall asleep. I was extremely awake, felt electric. I imagine I felt the way people feel when they take cocaine or ecstasy, though I have never used either of those or any illegal drugs. I got dressed and found Ben back in the OR, where the surgeons were now working on his brain, and I gowned up so I could watch the procedures. They had basically completed what was already a craniotomy, and evacuated both epidural and subdural hematomas. I watched the surgeons do some skull reconstruction using titanium plating, though they appeared to leave much of his skull as it was in case of cerebral edema, swelling of the brain, which can lead to brain herniation downward and death. Four hours after they started, Ben was taken to the post-anesthesia care unit.

He was later moved to the surgical ICU, and even
though he was stable, he remained on life support:
supplementary ventilation, intravenous therapy
with fluids, drugs, and nutrition, and urinary cath-
eterization. He was kept sedated using propofol so
that we could monitor brain swelling and function.
The ICU took over his day-to-day care, though
I would continue to treat him, as would the cranio-
facial surgeons and neurosurgeons. When I left the
hospital, I felt very good, given the extreme nature
of the situation and the trauma, about the care we
had provided and Ben's prospects for some type
of recovery. It was very early in a case like this,
and normally it takes quite a while for us to really
know how and if a patient is or is not going to recover.
I assumed that I would come back the next day
and everything would be more or less the same.
I should have known better.

When I arrived, there were no urgent cases, so I
went to the ICU to check on Ben and see if there
were any new developments. I picked up his chart,
and I noticed immediately that his name had been
changed from Ben Jones to John Doe, and that his
date of birth had been changed to unknown. I placed
the chart back into the wall file and went towards
the ICU offices, where I saw the ICU attending standing with two uniformed police officers and another
man who appeared also to be a police officer but
was wearing a suit. The attending introduced me to
the men and told them that I had treated the John
Doe when he had first arrived and had performed

the first surgery on him. I asked them why he was being considered a John Doe, and they proceeded to tell me that his name was fake, his driver's license was fake, his fingerprints did not show up in any city, county, state, or federal databases, and that they could find no records of a man named Ben Jones born on the date listed on his driver's license in any of the city, state, federal, or law enforcement databases at their disposal. Needless to say, I was surprised. I told the officers that I didn't know anything beyond what was on his chart and what I'd experienced with him in surgery, and I had no idea who he was or where he was from. I also suggested they speak to the men who had been gathering in the waiting room, who had said that they worked with the patient on a construction site. They said they had spoken to those men, and that all of them knew him as Ben Jones, and they had examined all of the paperwork the site manager had on file, and that all of it contained the same information that appeared on the fabricated driver's license. Again, I told them I knew nothing. They asked if anybody else had asked about the patient, or if there had been any other inquiries about him. I said not that I knew of, but that I had been either performing or observing surgery with him for almost twenty-four hours and normally didn't have that type of contact with individuals looking for information on patients. They said thank you, and they left.

I went back to Ben's room with the ICU attending and we started talking about his case, his prognosis, and started exchanging ideas about treatment.

He had ordered an electroencephalogram to test brain function and was hoping to get a quantitative electroencephalogram to fully map Ben's brain and see what areas had been damaged and how badly. When he left, I had a moment alone with Ben and I reached for his hand, the same hand I had held before, but there was no reaction. It was limp and cold and felt like the hand of a corpse.

I continued to follow the case over the course of the next week. There was a fairly significant amount of press related to the accident—it was a controversial building being put up by a high-profile developer—and it gave the newspapers and blogs a few days of salacious headlines. We had hoped the coverage would help with an identification, but no one came forward. I got harassed by a couple of reporters who waited outside the entrance of my apartment building and stuck tape recorders in my face, hoping to get me to say something they could write about, but I knew to keep quiet, and that despite the tape recorders, the reporters would write whatever they wanted and the newspapers would print whatever they felt like printing. My truth is in the life and death I witness at the hospital every day. Ultimately, life and death are the only form of perfect truth that exists in the world. Everything else is subjective, and subject to an individual's perspective. I don't look for truth in the media.

Aside from the mystery of his identity, Ben became a medical mystery. His lacerations healed in a remarkable, unheard-of amount of time; after a week we were able to remove all of the sutures, all of the staples, and his wounds were closed and starting to scar. He was weaned down on the respirator, and we continued to feed him intravenously. The electro-encephalogram results were erratic and unexplain-able. At times he appeared to have suffered brain death, where there is absolutely no activity of any kind registering on the EEG monitors. At other times he appeared to be in a persistent vegetative state, where cycles of sleep and some base awareness, but not cognition, were recognizable. Once or twice a day he went into a state of extreme brain activity, centered in two regions of his brain, the medial orbitofrontal cortex, which is one of our emotional centers, and the right middle temporal cortex, which is often associated with auditory verbal hallucin-ations. The activity was extreme to the point that it was almost immeasurable, and the neurologists working on his case had never seen anything like it, especially with someone who had experienced such severe brain trauma. The initial worries related to brain swelling, bleeding, and intracranial pressure disappeared, as his brain seemed to heal itself as quickly, and miraculously, as his body did. He would also, at times, twitch, shake, convulse, and make guttural noises, which should not have been possible with the levels of medication being used to keep him sedated. At the end of his first week with us, he had a second major craniofacial procedure, in which titanium plates were used to seal and close the re-maining open areas of his skull. The surgery went well, and he was returned to the ICU. Two weeks later we learned his real name, or rather, we learned the name he was given at birth. He was still in a coma, though no longer medically induced. It was some time after that, probably a year or so, that I learned who he was, and that his name, or any name any person could have given him, was meaningless. He was, and that is what is important. He was and he will always be.

ESTHER

My brother Jacob did not allow the mainstream
media to, as he said, infect our home. There were
no newspapers, there was no television, unless it
was Christian TV. We could only listen to Christian
radio stations, and our computers had filters on them
that prevented anyone using them from accessing
MSM websites. He believed, and still does, that the
mainstream media is anti-Christian and anti-family,
and promotes a liberal homosexual agenda in direct
conflict with the teachings of the Lord and Savior
Jesus Christ and God Almighty.

Jacob was head of our home. My father had passed
away when I was six and Jacob was sixteen, and
he had stepped into my father's role. A few months
after my father's death, Jacob was born again into the
Kingdom of the Christian God. Shortly thereafter, my
mother was also born again, and when I was eight, I
was as well. Life changed dramatically, and very very
quickly. We had been Orthodox Jews. My father had
always said we were part of an ancient family, that we
were Davidic, which meant we were direct descen-
dants of King David, that we were, in a way, Jewish
royalty. Life with him was tense, and he didn't, for
reasons I didn't know until later, have a good relationship with my mother. They fought all the time,
or my father didn't speak to her. I never knew why or

what she did, it was just the way it was. And when my
father wasn't at work—he was a kosher butcher—he
drank, read the Torah at the kitchen table, or sat in
our living room with our rabbi, and later with Jacob.
When the rabbi was over, all of the children were
required to go to our rooms and stay there until the
rabbi left. At the synagogue, the rabbi was always
happy and friendly and very welcoming. When he
was with our father, he was very serious and full of
intent.

I saw Ben on the front page of a newspaper. I was
walking to church for Bible study and was walking
past a deli. The headline said Miracle Man and there
was a picture of him lying on the ground with a man
in a hard hat holding his hand. There was glass
sticking out of his body and his head was bleeding.
There was blood everywhere. It looked like someone
had taken the picture with their cell phone. I stopped
and looked at the paper to make sure I was seeing
it correctly. I hadn't seen or spoken to or heard from
Ben in sixteen years, since my brother had told him
he had to leave. It was hard to tell exactly, so I went
inside to buy the paper. I was uncomfortable. I didn't
normally go into places like that, especially if they
sold any media other than newspapers, especially
magazines, which Jacob often said were the books of
the Devil. The man behind the counter asked me if
I had read the story and I said no. He said it was
pretty incredible, that the man had gotten hit by a
glass plate that fell from thirty stories and had lived.
He was a Muslim man. I had been taught to hate

Muslims, that they were evil. I gave him fifty cents, making sure not to touch him, and left.

Outside I read the article, and it said the man's name was Ben Jones, and that he lived in the Bronx. I knew then it was Ben, our Ben, our missing Ben, our exiled Ben. It said he was in a hospital in Manhattan in the intensive care unit. It was only a few miles away. I couldn't believe that after all this time he was only a couple of miles away. Jacob had tried for years to find him. He never said why he sent him away or why he wanted him back, but he desperately wanted him back. He talked to our church elders, and they hired a private detective who spent a year looking for him. They didn't find anything, not a single trace of him anywhere, and they looked all over America, and all over Canada, and even some places in Europe. So Jacob prayed and watched for signs. He hoped and believed that someday Ben might return.

I didn't know what to do, if I should tell Jacob or go see Ben myself or just let him be. Part of me wanted to obey and honor my brother as head of our home and as a pastor at our church. Part of me thought if Ben wanted to come back he would come back, and if the Lord and Savior deemed it so, then so it would be. Part of me was just scared, really scared, and I didn't know why, and normally I would have thought it was the work of Satan—that is what Jacob would believe and what they would have taught me at church—but for some reason it didn't feel like that was the case this time. I put the paper in a trash can, and after

Bible study I stayed at church and prayed to Jesus for some direction. I stayed all day, and I prayed all day. Normally if I stayed away from home Jacob would get angry with me and tell me my place was at home helping Mother with the cooking and cleaning. The exception was if I was at church, and especially if I was praying. Jacob believed that all things could be achieved through prayer, and at the time I believed that as well. I prayed real hard that day. I kept asking Jesus to show me the way.

I didn't see any signs or experience any revelations, so I decided I would continue in a similar way. I bought a newspaper every day and read about what was happening with Ben and I went to church and prayed for most of the day. It was hard on Mother because she was used to having my help around the apartment. And Jacob was very curious why I was praying so hard. I told them I felt like I needed some guidance from the Lord as I moved into woman-hood and was on my knees asking for it. They both approved of that and let me keep doing it. I saw it in the paper when they figured out Ben Jones was not Ben's real name. I read about how they were trying to find someone who knew him. I saw him when they showed his driver's license picture and I knew for sure. He looked just like he did when he left except that he was older, and I stared at the picture for a really really long time. Me and Ben had always been really close when I was little. My father and Jacob never liked Ben, and they were always mean to him. I didn't ever know or understand why, but they blamed him for everything that went wrong and yelled at him all the time. Sometimes my father hit him, and sometimes, when it was just the kids, Jacob would hit Ben. And as he got older, they hit him more, and they hit him harder. I would hear him in his room crying, and I would go in and give him hugs and tell him I loved him. He always said I was the only person in the family who loved him, and he would tell me I was the best little sister in the world. My father and Jacob mostly ignored me, and my mother was always worried about my father, and Ben paid the most attention to me, so I was closest to him and loved him most.

Each day there would be updates, and new stories. Ben was improving faster than the doctors had ever seen. He had another brain surgery. He was stable but still in a coma. There were protests at the construction site, and people were talking about lawsuits, and the developer was saying it wasn't his fault. I couldn't believe how much attention it was getting. I thought somebody who knew our family when we were Jewish, before we accepted Jesus Christ as our Lord and Savior, would recognize him and come forward, but no one did. The papers just kept calling him the Miracle Man. It was really the first time in my life that I had ever read newspapers, and I could see why people hated them. They didn't seem dangerous, though, just sort of silly.

I kept the same schedule and waited until the coverage slowed down. I was worried that if I went to see him before the reporters went away someone might figure out who he was and I would get into trouble with Jacob and the church. I was also waiting for some kind of sign from the Lord. I believed, at the time, that the Lord always provided those who lived by his word with signs that told them which way to go in life. One afternoon I heard one of the women in the church choir talking about how she had just gotten a letter from a brother that she didn't see any more because he drank and slept with women other than his wife. Her brother had found Christ and had been born again and had given up his evil ways and wanted to see her. She was standing beneath a cross as she was talking, and she was holding a Bible, and there was light streaming through a window across her face. I thought for sure it was a message from above. Now I understand there is no such thing, that there is no above and no one to send us super-natural messages. There is just coincidence or our individual interpretations of what we see around us, and if we do see something it's an accident, and it means nothing. That is truly the word of God.

At the time, though, I was convinced otherwise, and I decided to go and try to see Ben. I rarely went into Manhattan. If I did, I was with Jacob and my mother, and usually other members of our church. Our senior pastor preached that Manhattan was part of Satan's Empire. An island filled with sin and devoted to greed, where homosexuals and perverts were allowed to live freely and prosper, and where the word of the Lord was defamed and blasphemed. I was scared

of it. I was worried that if I went alone I would be
raped or forced into sin in some way. There were
temptations everywhere, on every block and in every
building, bars and restaurants and banks controlled
by Masons, stores that sold impure clothing, entire
neighborhoods devoted to homosexual sex. Satan's
hold was strong. I know now that it's a ridiculous
way to think, but I didn't know then. So I prayed for
strength, I prayed long and hard, and when I felt
strong enough I slipped out of the church and took
the subway under the river. I followed the directions
I had gotten from a church computer and got off
the subway and went straight to the hospital.
When I went in, I asked for intensive care and took
an elevator to the right floor. I was very scared. I was
shaking as I stepped out of the elevator and started
walking down the hall. I was holding a copy of the
Bible that had been printed in Israel and blessed by
the head of our church. I was wearing a cross that
Jacob had given me when I turned seventeen and
that he said would always protect me. I stopped in
the waiting room and I prayed. And when I felt the
Holy Spirit strong inside me, I went into the intensive
care and found Ben's room. I stood at the door and
looked inside. There was a woman, a woman dressed
like a doctor, sitting by his bed reading a clipboard
with some paper on it. She reached out and held
his hand for a moment, and I was scared, because
I believed women who weren't either related to or
married to a man should never touch him. I couldn't
do anything to stop it, though. I just stood at the door
and looked at him. He was lying in a bed and there

were machines all around him and there were tubes
coming out of his arms and there were wires attached
to his chest and his head, which also had a bandage
on it. I just stood there and said his name, the name
he was given when he was born: Ben Zion Avrohom,
Ben Zion Avrohom, Ben Zion Avrohom.

The woman looked up and saw me and started to
stand. I didn't want to talk to her so I left as fast as
I could and went straight back to Queens. I went
to church and I prayed to the Lord Christ for the
forgiveness of my sins because I had indeed lied to
my brother Jacob, and I prayed to the Lord and gave
thanks for his protection while I was in Manhattan,
and I prayed to the Lord and asked him to help my
other brother, Ben Zion, recover from his injuries.

Over the course of the next two weeks, I was able
to see Ben Zion almost every day. Our church was
going through its biannual fundraising drive, and
members of the youth ministry were expected to go
out and solicit funds. Our church had never been rich
in money, though all of the pastors, including Jacob,
said its coffers were overflowing with devotion,
worship, the fervor of the Holy Spirit, and the love of
the Savior Jesus Christ. Most of its parishioners were,
and still are, working-class people and immigrants,
mainly from Eastern Europe. While every member
of the flock was expected to tithe ten percent of their
income to the church, the fundraising drive was
very important. It usually paid for the church's
pamphlets and books, which were used to spread

the word of the Lord, and paid for expansion efforts
and church renovations. The senior pastor wanted
to triple the size of the congregation and find a much
larger building to consecrate and use as our place
of worship. The youth ministry was expected to raise
a large portion of the money. I would tell Jacob
that I was going out to solicit, preach, and spread
the word of the Lord, and I would go to the hospital.
The first couple of days, I would just stand outside
the door and stare at Ben with all of his wires and
tubes and listen to the noises the machines would
make. I gradually moved closer, to the chair near
the door, to the chair near his bed, on my knees next
to his bed. I prayed for him to recover and I prayed
for him to come home and I prayed for the pain
I imagined he was feeling. There were cuts all over
his body, these deep gashes with pink scars, and there
were bandages on some of them, and I could see the
little marks on others where there had been stitches,
or maybe staples. His head was wrapped in a big
bandage, a huge bandage, that made the back of his
head almost twice as big as it was. Sometimes
he would twitch a little bit or shake a little bit or
make some kind of noise, like growling or crying.
I assumed he was grappling with the spirits of
the Devil and prayed harder for him. At the time
I believed in spirits and in the Devil and that any
and all things could be achieved through prayer.
Now I know better.

Near the end of the two weeks, I was kneeling next
to Ben's bed. I had finished praying and I was telling

him about our life since he left. Our conversion, how we moved out of Williamsburg, into a part of Queens where there were almost no Jews, Jacob's schooling and his job as a pastor, Mother's sickness, our devotion to the church. I told him a little bit about my own personal relationship with my Lord and Savior Jesus Christ and how he was the only person I trusted and could talk to about problems in my life, how Christ was the only person who was always there for me and would always listen to me. At one point I said I love him so much, Ben Zion, I love Jesus Christ so much, and I heard someone behind me say what did you just call him? I turned around, and a doctor, the same woman doctor who had seen me before, was standing a few feet away from me. I looked at her, stood up, and tried to leave. She stopped me and said what did you call him? in a very firm voice. I was very nervous and very scared and didn't want to tell her anything, so I said I called him Ben, the name in the newspaper. She said no, you called him something else, and I just shook my head and told her I learned his name in the paper. She seemed very angry, and I didn't want to get into trouble. If I had to call Jacob and explain everything to him, he'd be angry, and he might hit me or lock me in my room or force me to do some form of penance that I didn't want to do. I tried to step around the woman, but she wouldn't let me leave. She asked who I was, and I said I was a member of the First Church of Creation in Queens and that I came to the hospital to pray for sick and injured patients. She asked me if I had permission from the hospital to be there, and

I said the only authorities I answered to were God and his only Son, my Lord and Savior Jesus Christ. She asked who Ben was, and I said that I only knew what I had read in the newspaper, and that I believed he was a man who might benefit from prayer. I stepped around her, and she let me go. I rushed out of the hospital and spent the subway ride home crying and shaking and asking the Lord for his forgiveness. I had lied and deceived, and though I believed I had done it for righteous reasons, I still believed it was a horrible sin and that I needed to ask the Lord in Heaven for forgiveness.

I ended up staying on the subway for a long time. I couldn't stop crying and I couldn't stop shaking and I kept asking for God's forgiveness, which usually made me feel better, but it didn't this time. I wondered if somehow I'd committed a sin that was unforgivable, and I was scared that I'd be damned to burn in Hell eternal. Eventually I calmed down enough to go back to the church. We were required to check in at the end of every day and turn in all of the donations we'd received. It was dark and getting near dinner, which I was required to help prepare every night. I knew I'd be in trouble because I didn't have anything, and I hoped that Jacob wouldn't be there. I would have prayed, but I was worried that praying for the absence of a pastor was some type of sin.

When I walked into the church, Jacob was waiting for me. He asked me why I was late and I said I was

out spreading the word of God to sinners and trying
to lead them to salvation. He asked how much I had
taken in in donations, and I told him I didn't get
anything today. He stared at me for a long time and
I got scared. He grabbed my arm and dragged me into
the back of the church. I told him he was hurting
me and he ignored me and kept pulling me. It hurt
my arm and I was scared and I knew that he knew
I was lying. He took me into his office and let go of
my arm and pushed me into a chair and stared at
me again and I was so scared and he looked so angry
and he spoke to me.
Where were you?
I was out trying to get donations.
He slapped me.
Where were you?
I started crying.
I was out.
He yelled.
Where?
I was crying, and he yelled again.
Where?
In Manhattan.
Why?
I was so scared. I tried to wipe my face, and Jacob
slapped me again.
WHY WERE YOU THERE?
And he slapped me again.
WHAT WERE YOU DOING?
And again. And again. And again.
And then he stopped and I was staring at the floor
and I was crying and he grabbed my face and forced

me to look at him and he was shaking he was so mad
and he said it again.
Why were you there, and what were you doing?
And I didn't want to say anything, because I was
scared and I didn't know what he would do when
I told him, but I was more scared about what he would
do if I didn't.
I found Ben Zion.
I started crying again.
I found Ben Zion.

RUTH

My life has been like all the lives, long and hard
and full of sadness and confusion and horror,
a frightening, difficult dream punctuated by brief
moments of joy. And as is the case with all people's
lives, the moments of joy are never often enough
and never long enough. They keep me going,
the same way a glass of water, or an idea of a glass
of water, might keep me going in marching across
the desert, except that the desert never ends,
it's many million miles long, and it never will end.

I was born in Israel. My parents had both survived
in the Holocaust of the Nazis, being in camps in
Poland. My father was a Polish and went in Stutthof,
and ended in Treblinka, and my mother, who was
a Slovak, was first in Theresienstadt, and later in
Birkenau. They met in Tel Aviv in 1949 and married
almost immediately. At the time Jews of their
ages were being encouraged to be married and
starting families in order to further populate Israel.
They didn't love each other truly, but on some level
they understood each of the other, understood
in ways that other peoples couldn't. Both of their
families had been put to death by the Nazis during
the war. Their entire families, parents, grandparents,
siblings, aunts, uncles, and cousins, had all been
murdered in the death camps. That was the basis for

their marriage. Their feelings of the extermination of their families.

I lived in Israel until I was twelve years. We had moved to a small settlement near what today is being called Gush Katif, on the southern part of the Gaza Strip. It was attacked by the mujahedeen of Egypt and my parents were both killed. I was in the school when it was happening and found them on the floor of our kitchen with their throats gashed open. Their closest friends had left Israel for living in New York a year before and took me into their home. They were childless and happy to have me with them, and like my parents, they were both survivors. Also like my parents, their marriage was without love and strained, the main common element of them being they had both been in the camps. Also like my parents, they had survived but didn't live through what had happened to them. They breathed and ate and spoke and went about their lives, but they didn't live, didn't truly be alive, because they couldn't after what they had seen and experienced. Trauma is survivable, but often not much more. It kills you while allowing you to still live.

They did the best they could with me and I accepted them as being my parents. Like my birth parents, they were being very protective of me, did not trust non-Jews, and were fearful of all the world outside our neighborhood, which was entirely Jews. My adopted father worked as cook in a kosher restaurant, and my mother worked being a laundress. We went to synagogue every week, observed the

Sabbath, ate kosher, and had a Shabbat dinner every Friday in the evening. We were happy, or as happy as we could be given the course our lives had all been taken, and we did not wish for anything more than what we had. In that way we were gifted. For if one knows nothing about what may be possible in the world, one will not yearn for it or be missing it.

When I finished yeshiva, I went to work with my step-mother being a laundress. I had hoped to be going to college and maybe becoming a doctor or a teacher, but we did not have the money for me doing that. When I was twenty, I started thinking about marriage and hoping for love. I got one of those when I met Isaac, who was to become my husband. He was working being a kosher butcher, and his family was said to be Davidic and had been in America since the early 1900s and owned their own family butcher shop. We met because the restaurant where my stepfather worked bought their meats from them and Isaac often was delivering it. My stepfather invited him to our home for Shabbat dinner and he came with his parents and we were sitting at the table across from each other. He was very handsome and very shy, with nice green eyes and blond hair, which are rarer among us, and I was very shy too. That first meeting we were hardly speaking and spending most of our time glancing at each other and hoping the other wouldn't notice even though we did. That night when I went to bed I knew he would be my husband. For my stepfather it was a good marriage and would improve his standing at the restaurant, and for Isaac it would be prestigious to marry an Israeli-born daughter of survivors because there were very few of us then. I believed we would love each other.

Our wedding was a simple and beautiful one and our wedding night was more complicated for us. Neither had ever in our lives been alone with a member of the opposite sex before and we were both scared and being nervous. I was very excited and waited for Isaac but he wasn't being ready and later he cried. We were both knowing we wanted children and it was expected for us. For six months Isaac was trying and not being comfortable about it and he was being more and more upset. One night he had too much to drink and we became truly man and wife and he cried again because of being happy. That night we were both very happy.

We tried for two years for me to be pregnant. Most of the time Isaac would be drinking but sometimes he would not be. We prayed and lived strictly according to our Jewish laws. When I became pregnant we were overjoyed, and our families too. We were finished choosing names for a boy or for a girl when I started bleeding. A few days later we put the names written on a piece of paper and we burned them and we never spoke of them again. For the worst things of our lives, it is sometimes the best way, to never speak of them again.

It happened three more times in our next four years, with two of the babies going to the full terms.

We stopped trying to choose names or even being thinking of names, always feeling we should only give names to the living. In our seventh year of marriage I was pregnant again and it stayed and our son Jacob was born healthy and right. We thought he was a miracle baby, and he was looking just like his father, and we didn't think we were going to be having any more children. Our families were tremendously pleased and we had two years of happiness, watching Jacob grow and learn, every day becoming more like his father. We never hoped for more childrens and we stopped trying to do it. One night we go to a wedding and Isaac has too much to drink and I have a little as well. The next morning we don't remember everything of the night before but I know I am pregnant and I know it will be okay and I know the baby will be a boy and I know this with all of my heart without any doubts at all, the same as I know I am alive and I breathe and that God, in any of God's forms, is all-powerful and all-knowing. There are no doubts in my heart.

Isaac had many doubts and he was always very confusing about the pregnancy. After I tell him about it he is very upset and angry though he will not tell why he is feeling these things. He sees our rabbi many times and then he is happy and ready for another child. When Ben Zion was born, there are some complications with him, and some things not normal, and he did not look like Isaac, for Ben has dark hair and dark eyes like me and my parents, and Isaac left the hospital very angry. Rabbi Schiff

examines the baby Ben and then comes to my room
and tells me it is a great day, a monumental day,
that baby Ben is truly a gift from God, and he stayed
by my bedside and read to me from the Torah,
and together for the rest of the night we prayed.

When I got to home, Isaac had been drinking and
waiting for me, and Jacob is with Isaac's parents at
their home nearby us. Rabbi Schiff is helping me
bring Ben home and took Isaac away while I settled
Ben Zion into a bassinet we have for him. Isaac also
went to his parents' home to sleep and Rabbi Schiff
came back with two other rabbis and they stayed
beside Ben for the rest of the night and the next day
as well reading the Torah and praying.

When Isaac came home with Jacob, nothing was
ever the same again. He was always very angry
and drinking and he did not like Ben Zion and
when I try to talk to him about it he would not do
any talking to me. He drank much more and
almost every day he was drinking and he wanted
to have another baby soon. He did not care that my
body was not ready and that I wanted time for
me to bond with Ben Zion. He wanted more babies
right away, I think to prove to himself that Ben Zion
was not a fluke. We started trying and it much hurt
me but it was my responsibility as a wife for my
husband.

We try for one years and it didn't work, which
enraged Isaac. He accused me of being with another

man and I said to him I have only been with one man in my life and it has been you. He did not believe me and he said I was with someone else, that Ben Zion did not look like him and could never be his child. He yelled at me often and would sometimes start to push me, and hit me, and call me a whore, even in front of the children. I went to Rabbi Schiff and he consults me and Isaac many many times and he often came over to see Isaac and talk to him and check on Ben Zion, who he said was a special boy, a gift truly from God. And that was our life. We try to have another babies, and Isaac would drink and yell and hit me, and Rabbi Schiff would try to talk to him and calm him down. The boys started to grow up and went to yeshiva and Hebrew school and learn how to be Orthodox men someday. We observe the Sabbath and have Shabbat and go to synagogue. And I would pray to God to make changes for me to make my life better. I would pray to God every day.

And then eight years later after still trying I am pregnant again by a miracle of God and I have a girl we give the name of Esther. She is a beautiful little girl who looks much like Isaac, with light eyes and light hair. I hope and pray that this child will make Isaac happy and return to the Isaac I married, but it did not. He became even more convinced that Ben was not his and he would start telling people at synagogue or at Shabbat that I was a whore who had a child with another man. Once he do it in front of Rabbi Schiff, who immediately take him away. They were gone for one day and almost two and when they come back

Isaac is different than he was before. He seemed
scared and upset and when I try to ask him what is
the matter he pushes me away.

Our lives were separate in the same house from
then to the end of our time with each other. He loved
very much Jacob and Esther but did not love anymore
me who was his wife or his second son Ben Zion,
who he would push away when Ben tried to hug him
or he would tell to shut up when Ben Zion would try
to talk to him. I would try to tell him that he was
my husband and I loved him and he would be polite
and say he loved me but I knew he did not love me.
I knew whatever he had been told by Rabbi Schiff
had changed him to make him different. The rabbi
still came by and took special care with Ben Zion and
would ask him all about his studies and his love of
God, and Ben Zion was such a good boy, a kind boy
who loved everyone, who was always smiling and
doing good things for people. It was Ben Zion who
got me through all those hard years. I had no longer
Isaac, and Jacob was his son and Esther was his
daughter and he told them not good things about me
that I think made them not love me the way children
should love a mother. And Ben Zion seemed to notice
and loved me more and made sure I knew he loved
me with his entire heart.

When he was thirteen, Ben Zion became a man with
his bar mitzvah. I never knew why but many rabbis
from New York and other places attended, and
they were not just Orthodox, but also Hasidic and

Conservative and Reform, and two came from Israel. He read the Torah in a way that made many of the members of the synagogue weep, which is not something I had ever seen before in my life. His voice was clear and pure and sounded so strong, almost like a thunder, but also his voice had care and love without trying. I had never heard this voice from my son Ben Zion, and I do not know where it came from inside of him. Sometimes I wonder, especially now, if it was even him speaking, or if it was the Lord God himself.

After the bar mitzvah things got worse again, with Isaac drinking and drinking and not going to work and beating me and Ben Zion every day. One morning after a year I go to our room to see why he is not awake and I discover that he would never wake again, that he had passed into the hands of God. The doctor said his heart gave way but no one in his family had that so I always wondered if it was so. Rabbi Schiff did the tearing of keriah and Jacob said the kaddish. We ate boiled eggs for dinner and there was much sadness in our family. For seven days we sat shivah. Even though the Isaac I loved was gone many years before, I grieved deeply for losing him.

At the end of shloshim, after we mourned Isaac for thirty days, Jacob was head of our home. On that very day he told Ben Zion he must leave and never come back again, that Isaac had died because of Ben Zion and that God would punish him. Ben Zion tried to speak to Jacob and tell him he loved him and loved his father, but Jacob beat him very badly and threw him out of the house and locked the door while he bled on the sidewalk. I could not watch and cried myself in my room, and I washed the blood away the next day. Rabbi Schiff was shocked and very stern with Jacob and said he had made a terrible, terrible mistake that he needed to right. But he did not make it right. And Ben Zion vanished. I thought he would come back or he would be at a home of someone that knew our family but he was not anywhere and nobody saw him or heard from him again. And every night I cried for him and it never became more easy for me. My beloved son Ben Zion was gone.

And then sixteen years later, sixteen years of terror, where I was forced to give up my God and pray before one I did not believe in, forced to leave my community for one I did not know, forced to live like a slave to my son who did not love me, Jacob came home with Esther from the church like every other day, but this day would change our life for all times. When they walked in, I could tell Jacob had been hitting Esther like he did sometimes to her and also to me, and I knew not to ask or defy him about it because then he hit more and harder. He was not, though, like he usually is when he is in one of those times hitting, he did not seem so mean and angry, and I asked him what was happening and he said Esther had found him, found Ben Zion, that he was alive, in a hospital in Manhattan, that she had seen him with her two own eyes and had prayed to her Lord and Savior Jesus Christ at his bedside.

Even though I always knew the day would come
when Ben Zion would return, I could not believe
it was today. I asked Esther who was crying if it was
true and she said yes. I asked her what hospital and
she told me and I asked her why he was there in
a hospital and she said he had an accident with
a glass falling on him and was in intensive cares and
she started crying. I went to her and held her and told
her she would be okay and Ben Zion would be okay
and I keep holding her until Jacob told me to let go of
her, that she will be fine. I told him she needs me and
he yells at me No She Is Not A Baby and he pulled
her away very hard and pushed her to the ground and
told her to stop crying. Then he turn back to me
and say Mother, we need to pray to the Lord for
guidance and I say no, I need no guidance, I only need
to go see my son who is in the hospital, my son who
I haven't seen in sixteen years. He said the Lord will
tell us when to go and I say the Lord has already told
me and I went towards the door. He reached for me
and I pushed his arm away and he grabbed me hard
with both his arms and pushed me against the door
and yelled at me We Will Pray Together Until The
Lord Gives Us A Sign. I try to struggle away because I
just wanted to go to the hospital so I can see Ben Zion
and Jacob hit me three times very quickly with his
open hand on the same side of my face and I know
I must pray with him, even though it is not for me
and will make no difference for me, I must pray. We
kneeled before a crucifix with me on one side of Jacob
and Esther on the other side and Jacob begin asking
the Lord for guidance. He said Jesus Christ I am your

humble servant please show me the way, please guide my actions, please give me a sign so that I may know your intentions for me and my family. And he go on like this for four hours, asking for a sign, for guidance from his Lord and Savior Jesus Christ, for strength from the Holy Spirit to be righteous in his actions. I did not need a sign, that Esther had seen Ben Zion is enough of a sign for me. I just wanted to leave.

After we pray Jacob says we should also fast and have no dinner and tells us we must go to our rooms and continue to pray on our own. I go and pack a small bag and get some money from a small amount I have earned for myself and wait until the house is quiet and I leave without anyone hearing me. I know Jacob will be very angry and he will punish me for leaving but I feel I must do this so I do it. I say to myself if you believe deeply in your heart you must defy, and if you are willing to pay for your defiance, you must always do it, even though the pain may be much. Too many times in our lives we do not do it, and we pay even more, so this time I do.

I did not know the hospital or where it was being located so I got a taxi and told the driver to take me there. The driver was a Muslim and had something in Arabic hanging from his car mirror. I was already nervous from leaving home knowing Jacob would be angry and the driver made me more nervous because I believe that if he knew I was Israeli he would hate me. I know it is not right for me to be thinking that way but it is also the real way of the

world. And it is the real way of the world that I hate
the Muslim for wanting me to die and for believing
I am not a human. Maybe if he was not what he
was and I am not what I am we would be friends in
our lives. But we are what we are, and humans will
always hate. It is the ruin of our world.

He drop me off and I give him money but do not touch
him. I go into the hospital and ask where my son
Ben Zion is and the lady tells me the visiting times are
over for the day. I tell her my son who I have not seen
in sixteen years is here and I must see him. I tell her
his name is Ben Zion Avrohom and she looks in her
computer and says there is no one here with that
name. I tell her my daughter see him here and that he
is hit by a glass and in the intensive cares. She looks
at me for a moment and picks up the phone and
makes call and tells me to sit down and wait for someone to talk to me about this situation. I became very
upset and said I just want to see my son who has been
missing for so long and the woman say she is calling
someone to see.

I sat and wait for someone to come and a lady arrive
in a doctor coat and introduce herself to me as a
surgeon who work on a young man she believe might
be my son. I say I don't believe anything, I know,
I know with my heart fully, that my daughter was here
and saw my son Ben Zion Avrohom, who has been
missing from me for sixteen years. The woman ask
me about Esther and I tell her what she looks like and
the woman nod and say I met your daughter earlier

today but she told me she was here to pray for the sick and injured as part of a church in Queens. I tell her my daughter is a Christian who lives in Queens and was praying to her Lord and Savior Jesus Christ for the welfare of her brother who she loves. The doctor asks me again what is Ben's name and I tell her and she asks me when I have seen him last and I told her it has been sixteen years that he has been missing and that every day I prayed to God for him to come back to me. She asks me why he has been missing and I start to cry and I cry for a long time and she sits next to me and holds my hand and it is the first time in many years I have felt any kindness from anyone other than my daughter, the first time in many, many years. I stop crying and wipe my face and try to make myself composed. The doctor tells me her name is Alexis and she tells me she did surgery on Ben when he came into the hospital and has been treating him for his injuries which are very much serious and threatening his life. She says it was a miracle that he was alive and that there was no explanation for it. I did not give her the explanation I know because she would not have believed if I did tell her it. She asked me if I want to see Ben Zion and I say yes and she leads me through the hospital. When we reach outside his room, we stop and I am feeling very nervous and scared and happy. She tells me to prepare myself and I say I believe Ben Zion will be okay no matter what has happened. She smiles at me and says please be prepared. There is, though, nothing that prepares us for the worst of things in our life. There is nothing you can do to stop the shock, or buffer the pain.

I walked into the room. Ben Zion was in bed on his
back. There were intravenous tubes in his arms
and a mask on his face and monitors on his head that
had no hair and on his chest covered with scars.
There were scars everywhere on his body where
he had been cut by the glass. Long terrible jagged
scars on his body everywhere. I was scared to go
closer to him, scared of my own son asleep in his bed,
my beautiful boy who I had loved his whole life,
even when he was not with me. My son with all of his
scars, with all of his pain.

I walked slowly to him and I started crying again.
I cry because of what happened to him, and for all
those lost years, and for why he was sent out of my
home, and for all the times Isaac and Jacob beat him
and are mean to him, and for the times I was with
him when he was a boy and a baby and he smiled
and laughed and for all the love I had for him.
I walk to him and I say his name and I start crying
very hard and it hurts my body and hurts me inside
like I am destroyed and I kneel by his bed and
I can't touch him or look at him, I just say to him over
and over I am sorry, I am sorry. There are no other
words, and even those words aren't enough for my
feelings. There are never words for the strongest of
our feelings. There is just the pain that we cannot
share. Pain we must all feel alone.

I stay at his bed for the whole of the night and when
the sun comes up I sit in a chair next to his bed
and I hold his hand and I tell him about the years he

has been gone and what has happened in our life.
I hold his hand and it's cold and there are scars on his
wrist and his hand and he does not move except for
breathing which is faint, and sometimes labored,
and sometimes he twitches or shakes a little amount.
At one point many doctors come in and ask me who
I am and I tell them and they say the chart still says
John Doe and it makes me cry to think of how long
my son has been lying here alone being called
John Doe. One of the doctors calls someone on
the telephone on the wall and more people come but
they are not doctors. Some of them work for the hospital and some of them are police and I tell them his
name and where he is from and I tell how long it has
been since I have seen him. They ask for my ID and
I tell them my son does not let me have ID or driver's
license because he does not believe in any authority
other than God. They take me to a room where they
say I must stay until they confirm me as who I say I
am.

It is a long time, many hours I sit alone. When the
door opens, it is Jacob and he says to come with him.
I ask him what happened and he say he talked to
police and tell them everything and show them
the driver's license he has for himself and they say
I can go. We go to Ben Zion's room and Esther is
waiting outside the door for us and we go in together
and we kneel and spend the day praying together for
the health of Ben Zion. And for many days that is
what we do. We kneel by the bed and together we pray
for the health of Ben Zion. Jacob and Esther go back

to Queens sometimes because they both have many responsibilities at church but I do not ever leave the hospital. I stay with my son. And I wait for him. And I know in my heart, because I have known all my life, and I have known all of his life, what he will become when he returns. I wait for him.

JEREMIAH

Jacob was like a brother to me and a father to
me and a spiritual guide to me and a true inspiration
to me. He saved me and believed he cured me and
I loved him and admired him, and in many ways
I wished I was him. When the MSM descended after
Ben's real identity was made public, he asked me to
stay in the hospital with his mother and help protect
them from the reporters and their tape recorders
and their cameras and their lies. He also wanted
me to take notes whenever the doctors were there so
he could have them for lawsuits he planned to
file on Ben's behalf against the city, the construction
company, the real estate developers, and the
hospital, which he hoped would provide him with
financial security and help to expand the facilities
and the teachings of the church. I was truly and
greatly honored, and I promised him I would take the
job very seriously and lay down my life if necessary.
Jacob said he knew, and that was why he chose
me. The hospital's policy was that only family was
allowed to stay, so Jacob told them I was his brother,
his real brother. And we believed that in the eyes of
God, the Holy Spirit, and our Lord and Savior Jesus
Christ, we were telling the truth, and that because
our aims were righteous, the sin of lying was not actually a sin. We did what people do all the time, we told
ourselves something we did was right and we found

a way to justify it, even though we knew it was wrong.
We told ourselves God would allow it, but not because
of the Laws of God, but because we wanted to do it.

I met Jacob when he was protesting deviant lifestyles
outside a club where I went to meet men. I had seen
him a few times before standing with three or four
other people, all holding signs that said God Hates
Fags, or Fags Will Rot in Hell, or AIDS is God's Cure
for Faggots, and he would yell verses from the Bible
at people smoking outside the club and hand out
pamphlets about his church. My story was the same
as a million others in New York. I grew up in a small
town, liked boys and dresses, got teased and beaten
at home and at school, ran away to New York at seventeen to be a model or a singer or an actor or whatever
I could be that was fun and easy and would make me
famous. It didn't work, and I got addicted to drugs
and sex and clubs and lived a sad empty life that
I pretended was fun and exciting. I always felt I had
a hole in my heart, this big black hole that made me
feel lonely and empty and worthless. I tried to fill it,
everybody tries in some way, and it just got bigger
and bigger. The night Jacob approached me I was
on a date with a man who gave me certain things and
expected certain things in return. He lived in the
Midwest and was in town for three or four days
a month. It was my second night out with him and
I was hurting really bad. The man wanted me to get
some meth, and on my way out of the club Jacob said
I can cure you as I walked past him. I stopped and
asked him what he would cure me of, and he said the

vile, soul-damning lifestyle of sodomy and homo-
sexuality. I asked him how, and he said the Bible
offers a message of love and hope, and the Lord and
Savior Jesus Christ will save you and show you the
way. I started crying. I was surprised. I hated religion
because of its treatment of me, and its absoluteness,
and I never would have believed I would believe in it,
but something opened inside of me, the Holy Spirit
opened inside of me, and it was lovely and fantastic
and the most powerful thing I'd ever felt, a sense of
joy and peace and love, and I believed at that moment
that for whatever reason God was calling to me and
telling me to follow this man. Two hours later I was
baptized and born again. The next day I moved into
a basement apartment in Queens in the house of one
of the church elders. It felt right and true and good
to me, and it was lovely and joyful and secure and
strong. To have the Holy Spirit inside of me and to
cultivate a personal relationship with the Lord and
Savior Jesus Christ. To have friends who called me
brother and wanted to take care of me instead of use
me. It was all I ever wanted in my life, all anyone ever
wants. To have someone love you. To have someone
tell you that they know the way and want to share it
with you.

I spent most of my time in a chair near the door of
Ben's room. We kept the door closed, and if it started
to open I would stand and ask whoever it was what
business they had in the room. It annoyed the doctors
and nurses because I made all of them show me
their credentials, even if I had met them before or

had seen their credentials before. Twice MSM reporters tried to sneak in as doctors. One of them even tried to show me bogus credentials. Everyone wanted to see the Miracle Man who had disappeared into thin air for sixteen years and survived what he never should have survived. Aside from the reporters, there were lawyers, photographers, psychics, healers, and women. I took the lawyers' business cards, but had everyone else removed as quickly as possible. And I couldn't believe how many women wanted to see him or touch him or marry him. He wasn't even awake and they didn't know what he would be like if he did wake up, if he'd even be able to speak or move or walk. I handed each of those women a pamphlet and said maybe the void they were feeling in their heart could be filled with the love of God and the love of his Son, the Lord and Savior Jesus Christ.

For the first ten days I was there, nothing happened. Mrs. Avrohom prayed by Ben's bed and I read the Bible. I went to the gift shop or cafeteria for food. We both slept in fold-down chairs, hers next to the bed, mine near the door. Jacob and Esther came by after breakfast and usually stayed until just before dinner. They spent most of their time kneeling by the side of the bed, praying, though Jacob often stepped into the hall to speak with the doctors, and on a couple of occasions with attorneys. Nobody seemed to know what kind of condition Ben was in. The machines they hooked up to his brain would give them all sorts of different results, and sometimes they were happy and said he seemed normal and sometimes they said he was going to be a vegetable and sometimes they said they were seeing things they had never seen before, extraordinary activity as one doctor called it, and most of the time they had no idea what was happening. When they took the breathing tube out of his throat, it was a big deal. They made everyone leave except for Jacob, who refused to leave, and they were really worried he wouldn't be able to breathe on his own. I waited outside the room with Mrs. Avrohom and Esther, and we were all praying to Jesus to give Ben the strength to live. We were praying really hard, and when we heard the doctors and nurses clap and Jacob yell Hallelujah, Lord, we knew our prayers had been answered.

For the next five or six days, nothing good happened. Ben was able to breathe, but he didn't move, and all the brain monitors indicated that there was absolutely no activity, and the doctors were saying that he was going to be a vegetable for the rest of his life. The timing was terrible because Jacob was finishing the church fundraising drive and was going to announce plans for the expansion of the church's facilities. He asked me to take notes on everything the doctors and nurses said and he'd come by at the end of the day and review them. He also asked me to pray extra hard, and I told him I'd pray my hardest, but I knew my connection to God wasn't nearly as strong as his was, and I was worried that I didn't have enough strength, and wasn't holy enough, to make a difference.

The doctors came and went. I heard terms like severe brain damage, without detectable awareness, Apallic syndrome, post-coma unresponsiveness, continuing vegetative state, permanent vegetative state. They tested his response to stimuli and there was no reaction. They tried to get him to track things with his eyes but he just stared at the ceiling, though I don't think he could really see anything at all. One of the doctors suggested something called bifocal extradural cortical stimulation, which sounded scary and evil, and I told Jacob that I believed that particular doctor, who looked like a Jew and had a hooked nose, might be in legion with the Devil.

On the seventh night, I sat reading my Bible. This particular evening I was reading Revelations 12. It is a powerful chapter, one of the most powerful in the New Testament, and one with a great amount of truth. It's about the woman clothed with the sun, with the moon under her feet, and the crown of twelve stars on her head, and the great red dragon with seven heads, ten horns, and seven crowns who draws the third part of the stars of Heaven with his tail, and how as the dragon prepares to devour the child of the woman, the child who is to rule all nations with a rod of iron, the woman is drawn into the wilderness of God for 1,260 days while the archangel Michael and his army of angels make war on the dragon. I had read the chapter many times, and I believed that the events of it were going to happen soon, as they had been foretold to occur in

the End Times, and I knew the End Times were
coming, and that I would bear witness to them,
and that I would be one of the 144,000 of the Lord's
anointed who would be saved and raised up into
Heaven. Mrs. Avrohom was kneeling next to Ben,
same as she did every night. This night, though,
this seventh night, she started praying in Hebrew.
Jacob told me she might do it, and he wanted to know
if she did because he had forbidden Jewish teachings, law, words, and language in his home, and he
would punish her accordingly for violating his rules.
I didn't know what she was saying, but I thought
I should put down my Bible and try to write down
anything I heard. As she was praying, Ben's mouth
started moving. She didn't see it, but I did. There
wasn't any noise coming out, but he was mouthing
the words, the exact same words she was saying in her
prayers. And then his eyes opened, and not like when
the doctors opened them for their tests, this time they
opened and they were clear and focused and alive,
and there was something about them, something
pure and heavenly, as if they were the eyes of the
Savior himself, and I was entranced by them. Mrs.
Avrohom was still praying, and didn't know
Ben was with her, and she was quietly saying the
Hebrew verses, and Ben started saying them with
her, softly, in a voice that sounded very old and
strong, and he matched her word for word, like he
knew what she was going to say before she said it,
and it sent chills down my spine. I tried to write what
I was seeing, and feeling, and what Mrs. Avrohom
was saying, and what Ben was saying, but I was

paralyzed, paralyzed with joy and freedom and
a lightness of spirit that felt like the moment I was
saved, when the Holy Ghost was so powerfully
alive inside of me.

Mrs. Avrohom became aware of Ben when he reached
out and put his hand on her forehead. I watched it
happen like it was in slow motion. His fingers started
moving slowly, slightly, each of them on its own, like
they were dancing. And then his hand and arm lifted
off the white sheet and his fingers stopped moving
and looked like they were stretching, like the fingers
of Adam reaching towards God. Mrs. Avrohom was
still praying, and Ben with her, and the sound of their
words in synchronization was simple and ancient
and had a beautiful rhythm to it and as his arm
moved towards her forehead he turned and looked at
her and it seemed like it took a million years for him
to reach her and it seemed like there was nothing else
happening anywhere else in the world, there was just
this one thing, this one moment, this lost, damaged
son reaching for his mother as they prayed to the
Lord Almighty.

When he did finally touch her, she gasped audibly.
I don't know if it was because she was surprised
or because of something she felt, but she looked like
she had had a huge bolt of electricity pass through
her. His hand was firmly on her forehead, and
she looked up, her jaw dropped, her body went limp,
her eyes were full of joy and peace and contentment.
And they both continued praying, there was no

lapse, no stopping, the words just kept coming.
Ben smiled, turned and started to sit up, and as he
did, the various monitors and IVs that were attached
to his body started coming off, and those that didn't
he pulled off with his free arm. The alarms started
dinging, shrieking, but he and his mother didn't seem
to notice. He sat all the way up and smiled, and it was
a beautiful peaceful smile, similar to so many of
the smiling images I've seen of the Lord and Savior
Jesus Christ, and his mother was staring up at him,
and he moved his legs off the bed, and they were both
still praying, almost singing, and his hand was still
on her forehead, and he stood up. He was wearing
a white robe. His body was hideously and terribly
scarred, you could see the scars running along his
arms and legs and on his face. His skin was so white,
and so pale. And there were alarms screaming.
And it was beautiful. He was so beautiful. If only
I could somehow communicate the feelings it
inspired in me. But that is the way it is with all of
the important feelings and emotions and moments
we have in our lives, words fail and don't express even
a fraction of what we actually feel. All I can say is
it truly did feel like I was in the presence of divinity,
in the presence of God himself. And I couldn't move
or speak or write or do anything but stare at him
and feel love, and awe, and humility. He was just
so beautiful.

The door flew open and a team of nurses and doctors
rushed into the room, though they stopped as soon
as they saw what was happening. Ben didn't turn

towards them or acknowledge them in any way.
He stared down at his mother, who was staring up
at him, and then he closed his eyes and lifted his hand
away from her forehead and raised it to the level of his
chest and held it there and stopped saying the
Hebrew prayers and took a deep breath and smiled to
himself as he exhaled. And as soon as he was finished
with the exhale, he collapsed onto the floor and had a
seizure.

I got pulled from the room, but what I saw of
the seizure was hideous. Ben shook, his whole
body violently shook, and fluids immediately started
coming out of his mouth and nose, and he made
these awful guttural noises. His mother stood up and
started screaming. The doctors and nurses immediately tried to hold him down and grab his tongue,
but he was strong, shockingly and unbelievably
strong, especially given that he had been in a coma
for the last several weeks, and it took two of them on
each of his arms and legs to hold him down.
As I stood in the hall, I could hear him struggling,
he sounded like an animal, like he was possessed by
Satan himself, and I could hear the nurses and
orderlies yelling for more help, and I could hear
Mrs. Avrohom, who was backed into a corner of the
room when I left it, screaming at the top of her lungs.

I don't know how long it was or what it took, because
it seemed like hours and hours and hours, but Ben's
seizure ended and everything calmed down and I was
allowed back in the room. Ben was on the bed,

either asleep or sedated, and his arms and legs
were in straps attached to the sides of the bed in case
he had another seizure. Mrs. Avrohom was in the
corner, quietly sobbing into her hands. I wasn't sure
what to do, but decided that if Jacob considered me
a family member, I should comfort his mother
as if I truly were one, and that things that might
normally matter for a Christian man, that I was
a single man and she was a widowed woman, that
she had been using Hebrew in prayer, that she had
been raised a Jew, didn't matter, and that if God
judged me, he would also forgive when I repented.
I moved over towards Mrs. Avrohom and I put my
hand on her shoulder and asked her if she was alright.
She looked up at me and between her sobs asked me
what had just happened, what had just happened
with her son. I told her that I didn't know, that God
always had a plan and that we should never question
it, but that I didn't know.

Jacob showed up later. The doctors had called
him because he was the family member listed as
a contact. In between the call and his arrival, doctors
came in and out of the room, checking Ben's blood
pressure and heart rate. I was no longer touching
his mother when he walked in, but he was upset
that I was sitting close to her. I told him what had
happened, with every detail I knew, and he didn't
seem surprised or upset. He looked at his brother, and
said let us pray, pray for the man who may be sitting
before us. I didn't know what he meant, and didn't
feel like I should ask.

Together we kneeled and we prayed, prayed silently until the sun rose and another of God's glorious days began for us.

In the morning, Jacob took his mother home. She didn't want to leave, but he felt she needed some time away, and she obeyed him because he was the head of their household. He asked me to stay and try to learn everything I could about Ben's condition. The doctors kept coming in and out of the room, but when they spoke they did so in hushed tones, so I couldn't hear what they were saying. Around lunch they stopped coming in. It was just Ben, who had not moved since his seizure, and me. I started reading my Bible, turning immediately to one of my favorite sections, Matthew 4:1-11, which is about the temptation of Christ by the Devil while Jesus was living in the desert, and about the food the angels of Heaven brought him after he resisted the Devil's offerings. I often imagined myself in the position of Christ, resisting the Devil's foul gifts, which I had spent so many sinful years indulging in, and someday having angels descend from Heaven, their wings shining with holy righteousness, to bring gifts for me. When I heard a voice, I thought my prayers had literally come true. I closed my eyes and I said thank you, God, thank you for rewarding my devotion to you. And then I heard the voice again and I stood up and I was scared to open my eyes, not knowing what to expect, and knowing that angels had extraordinary powers that humans could and never would understand. The voice again, and again. I opened my eyes,

and there were no angels, but Ben was looking at
me, which was almost like an angel was there.
He spoke.
Who are you?
My name is Jeremiah.
Where am I?
You are in a hospital in New York.
Why are you here?
I am here because your brother, Jacob, who is
my brother in the worship of God and his Son,
the Lord and Savior Jesus Christ, asked me to
be here.
Jacob?
Yes.
He looked away from me, laughed to himself,
looked back.
Is Jacob responsible for me being restrained?
No. The doctors did that because of your seizure.
My seizure?
Yes.
Take them off.
I can't.
Please, take them off.
He looked at me, looked right into my eyes, and there
was something about his eyes, which were black, jet
black, and so deep they looked limitless, that made
me feel weak and vulnerable, humbled me, and made
me want to do whatever he asked of me. I understood
why he was restrained, but also knew that there were
many doctors and nurses very close by if anything
happened. He said it again.
Please.

It wasn't desperate or pleading, just simple and direct.

Please.

I set down my Bible, stood up, and took off the restraints. He smiled and said thank you, and he didn't move, just closed his eyes and took deep breaths, one after another after another. I don't know how I expected him to act, or what I expected him to do, but not that, not just lie there as if he were still restrained. I just stared at him, waited. After a few minutes, he started slowly running his hands along his body, feeling the scars, running his fingers along the length of them. He put his hands on his face, moved his fingertips all over, moved them along his head and the back of his skull. When he was finished with the back of his head, he continued moving them over his body and his face and he spoke.

What happened to me?

You had an accident at a construction site. A plate of glass fell and hit you.

How long have I been here?

A couple months.

How did Jacob find me?

Your sister saw you on the front page of a newspaper and visited you and she told Jacob.

Why would Jacob care?

Jacob has been looking for you for many, many years.

Why?

I don't know. I only know he desperately wanted to find you.

You said he's a Christian?

Yes, Jacob was born again and baptized into the

ministry of the Lord and Savior Jesus Christ. He's a
pastor now, a holy man.
When did this happen?
Many years ago.
And my mother and my sister?
They're also Christians.
He opened his eyes and sat up and he turned to me
and put his feet on the floor. He looked at me and the
Bible I was holding, and again I felt this profound
sense of peace and joy and love and contentment and
humility. He reached towards me and put his hand
on my forearm, and as soon as he touched me, everything I had struggled with, and tried to leave behind,
my every urge and temptation, my need to sin and
behave in a deviant manner, came rushing forward
through whatever walls I had built to contain it.
I wanted him. I wanted him more than I had wanted
anything in my life, more than any man in my life.
I wanted to take him, and him to take me, and
I never wanted it to end. I closed my eyes and said
please protect me, Lord, please protect me, Jesus,
but nothing happened, nothing went away. His hand
was on my forearm and I wanted him in my mouth
and inside of me and on top of me and behind me.
I knew it was going to happen if he didn't let go of me,
I knew I would ask him to satisfy me. Then I felt him
lift his hand, and I opened my eyes and he was looking at me as if he knew, he knew what I wanted, and
he didn't judge me or hate me for it. He stared at me.
He took a deep breath. He smiled. And something
in him changed. His eyes were in the same place, but
he wasn't looking at me anymore. He was looking

beyond me, at something I could never know or touch
or comprehend.
And then he exhaled.
And then the seizure hit.

ADAM

I was certainly surprised when Jacob came to see
me in my office at the synagogue, very surprised
indeed. It had been many years since I had seen him,
though I had never stopped thinking about him,
or rather, I should say, I had never stopped thinking
about his brother, Ben Zion.

Ben Zion was extraordinary from the day he was
born, or more accurately, from the moment he
was conceived. The circumstances were unusual,
or confusing, or mysterious. There are a number of
words one might use to describe it, and all of them
would be appropriate. His parents had been trying
unsuccessfully to have a second child, Jacob being
their first, for several years. The night of conception,
or what is believed to be the night of conception,
they had been to a wedding together and had both
most likely, though Ben's mother claims not,
had a few too many alcoholic beverages, which,
as everyone knows, can affect behavior and memory,
along with a host of other things. Ben's father claimed
that he did not have marital relations with his wife
that night, while Ben's mother claimed they did. It
caused a terrible rift in the marriage, and in some
ways ruined both of their lives. Ben's father believed
his wife must have been with another man. She
hadn't been. But she did, I believe — though

I cannot definitively say — lie about having been
with Ben's father that night. He lived with a great
resentment and anger, which was transferred to Ben
Zion, and he never trusted his wife again, or loved
his child as a father should, and she lived with a lie
that she perpetuated for far too long. If both would
have accepted and acknowledged the truth, regardless of how unbelievable it may have been, and it was,
I believe, quite unbelievable, they would have had
dramatically different, and most likely happier, and
more content, lives. And I have always found that
to be the case: if you can accept the truth and live
with it, your heart will be at peace.

Jacob arrived in the middle of the day, when
I am often working on my weekly sermon, which
I deliver during services on Saturday mornings.
This particular sermon was focused on readings
from Exodus 13:17 to 15:21, which deals with Moses
and the Red Sea and the series of events that led
Moses to use divine powers to part the waters of the
sea, thus allowing the Israelites passage out of Egypt
on their way to Canaan. In today's world, I find this
story, and the story of the life of Moses in general,
to be particularly relevant, as so many people, people
of all faiths, are seeking an exceptional, perhaps
even divine, individual who might be able to lead us
into a place of greater safety, greater prosperity,
greater peace. I was asking myself, and ultimately
also asking the members of the synagogue, whether
this search is healthy and productive, whether
politicians should be mentioned in the same breath

as the Messiah, whether it is possible, despite the
ridiculous preening that so many engage in, and so
many people believe in, for a politician to really make
any significant changes, despite their claims, and
their promises to do so. There was a knock. I looked
up and said come in, and my assistant rabbi, Rabbi
Stern, entered and said a man named Jacob Avrohom
was here to see me. Rabbi Stern knew of the Avrohom
family, as I had often spoken about them with him,
and about Ben Zion in particular, and he knew that
a visit from Jacob might be of some significance.
I asked him to show Jacob in, and I put away the
sermon.

Though he looked like the person I once knew,
aged of course, by well over a decade of life, if I had
seen Jacob on the street I am not sure I would
have recognized him. He had very short hair, was
clean shaven, and wore tan slacks and a blue sport
coat. He carried a Bible with him, one that had clearly
been read with great regularity, and where one might
normally wear a tie, he wore a large gold cross on
a gold chain. I stood and smiled when he walked
into the office, and greeted him with an open hand.
He did not smile in return and didn't take my hand.
He asked if he could sit and I said of course, and
before I could ask if he wanted a beverage, water, tea,
or perhaps a cup of coffee, he spoke.
We found my brother.
I was surprised, but not shocked, for I had always
believed that Ben Zion would return. I believed that
he had to return, that God would impel him to do so.

I was very excited to have received the news, thrilled
actually, and extremely curious. Given, however,
Jacob's demeanor, and the fact that throughout the
entire time I knew him as a child he was a very angry
person, I thought it best to remain reserved.
Where?
He had an accident and is in a hospital in Manhattan.
What type of accident?
He was working on a construction site and a plate
of glass fell on him.
Oh my. Is he okay?
Yes, he is okay, or at least I believe he is.
How long has it been since you've seen him?
Sixteen years.
Your mother must be very happy.
Obviously. We are all very happy. We missed Ben
terribly, and we were all worried that we would never
see him again.
Is he still in the hospital?
Yes.
May I visit him?
He asked that I find you and ask if you would. Just so
you know, I was against it.
There's no reason for you to be angry with me,
Jacob. I tried...
He stood and interrupted me.
I'm not here to discuss anything with you other
than visiting my brother. If you would like to see him,
I can take you there. If not, I'm leaving.
I would very much like to see Ben Zion.
Come with me.
I stood and put my sermon aside, knowing that

this, the reemergence of Ben Zion, was more
important than anything I would ever write or speak,
and that if he was what some, including me, believed,
he would make all of my sermons irrelevant. Jacob
turned and walked out of the room. We walked to the
subway station, took the train into Manhattan, and
walked to the hospital. I did not, as I did not
feel it would be kindly received, initiate any sort
of conversation, and Jacob did not speak a word to
me, look at me, or acknowledge me in any way.
We entered the hospital, took an elevator up to
Ben Zion's floor, and walked down a series of long
white hallways, hallways of the type that, because
I visit any member of my synagogue who is in the
hospital, whether it's for a broken leg or terminal
cancer or anything else, normally depress me,
but in this particular instance greatly excited me.
Jacob was a step or two in front of me, and he stopped
in front of a door and motioned for me to enter,
and as I did I said a silent prayer of thanks to God
for who I believed I was about to have the honor and
privilege of seeing, speaking to, and being in the
presence of, if even for just a moment or two.

Ben Zion was lying on the bed, above the covers,
wearing a hospital robe and watching television.
A handsome young man was sitting in a chair near
the bed, reading the New Testament. Ben Zion looked
up at me, and I was hit with the full shock of how
he had changed, and the extent of the trauma he
had survived. His head was shaved and ringed with
deep, jagged scars. His skin was white, an unearthly,

almost inhuman white, and was covered with scars, some of which were thick, some of which were thin, some of which were long, and some of which were short, but which seemed to be everywhere. His eyes, which had been deep brown as a child, but definitely brown, were now black, a black so deep and thorough that it was almost something else, something without a name or word or label that would apply to it. He smiled and turned off the television and sat up and spoke to me.

Hello, Rabbi Schiff.

Hello, Ben Zion.

He stood.

Just Ben. No Zion anymore.

Hello, Ben.

And we shook hands. Jacob was now standing next to me. Ben looked at him and the young man, and he spoke.

Would you mind leaving us alone?

The young man stood and closed the Bible and left the room. Jacob spoke.

I would prefer to stay.

Please respect what I'm asking you, Jacob.

I don't trust him.

But I do.

You know what he did to our family?

I know what you believe, Jacob, and I respect your right to believe it, but I would like to speak to him alone.

Jacob stared and Ben met his gaze, but without hostility or anger, and Jacob turned and left, though it was clear he was not happy about it. Ben sat down

on the edge of his bed, and motioned for me to sit
in a chair across from him, which I did. He spoke.
Long time, Rabbi Schiff.
It certainly has been. I have often wondered
what became of you and if, or rather when, I would
see you again.
He smiled, didn't speak, so I did.
Where have you been?
Here.
For a short while, as I understand it, but what about
all of the preceding years?
Drifting.
Through greater New York, America, where? And
how did you live?
Doesn't matter.
Were you happy, or safe?
It doesn't matter. I'm here now.
And I'm very excited to see you, Ben Zion, or excuse
me, Ben, I was terribly shaken when you disappeared
and your brother did what he did with your family. As
you know, I have always thought you were extremely
special, and did everything I could to watch over you
as a child and...
He waved me off.
The past doesn't matter. People cling to it because
it allows them to ignore the present. I asked for
you because I need to talk to you about the present.
Something happened to me, or is happening to me,
and I don't understand it, and I don't want it,
and I'm scared of it.
You've had a terrible accident and...
I don't remember much about my childhood, but

I remember enough. You weren't visiting me
out of some sense of charity.
No, I wasn't, though I did care a great deal about
your family and its well-being, as I do about all of
the families who belong to the synagogue.
Tell me what's happening to me.
Only you can know, Ben, and at some point, if not
already, you either will or you won't, and you will
either be, or you will not be.
I'm not ten or twelve years old anymore, Rabbi Schiff.
Tell me what's happening to me.
You need to tell me what's happening to you, Ben,
and if I can inform you or help you in any way, I will
certainly do so.
He sat perfectly still, and stared at me in a way that
felt very soft, and very gentle, almost quiet, if it is
possible to stare quietly. I felt he was somehow looking into me, to see or learn my intentions. He took a
deep breath, but only through his nose, which gave
me the last piece of information I believed I needed,
and then he exhaled, and then he spoke, spoke the
words I had been waiting for thirty years to hear from
him, he spoke.
I think God is speaking to me.
And even though I didn't want to do it, and tried to
resist doing so, I smiled, perhaps as wide and true a
smile as has ever appeared in my life.
I have always believed this day would come.
I feel like I'm crazy, and I need to know why this
is happening.
First, tell me what he is saying.
God is not a man.

A woman?

No. God is not man or woman. Something beyond
that, beyond our humanity, our notions of male
and female.

If not a man or a woman, what does God sound like?

It's not some silly voice from above, like it is in the
books of the Bible or in the movies, or like it is when
delusional religious fanatics talk about it. It's not
even a voice at all. It's just this presence, this feeling, this state where I learn things, where I'm shown
things, where I see things.

What?

When I was in the coma, I was conscious. Not
conscious like I am now, but definitely aware,
definitely awake in a way. It was this state where
sometimes there was silence and blackness, this
infinite blackness, but other times I would see
and hear and understand things I shouldn't.

It was beyond individuality, or identity. I wasn't Ben,
not Ben Zion Avrohom or Ben Jones, or a man or a
human being in any way, I was just part of this greater
thing, or place, or force, or energy. I don't know.
That's why I wanted to see you.

I'm hesitant to comment, because this doesn't
sound like God as I know or understand God.
This sounds like something that might be organic
to your injuries, which I don't know the specifics of,
but were obviously rather traumatic and related
to your brain.

He smiled at me, pointed to a copy of the New
Testament sitting on a small table next to his bed.

Pick up that book.

I reached over and I picked it up.

Open it.

Where?

Wherever.

I opened the book.

Put your finger down, and tell me the chapter
and verse.

I followed his instructions.

Luke 12:5.

But I will forewarn you whom ye shall fear: Fear him,
which after he hath killed hath power to cast into
Hell; yea, I say unto you, Fear him.

You've been studying it, with your brother, perhaps?

Never read it. Never even held a copy of it. I can do
the same thing with the Old Testament, with the
Mishnah and Gemara, and the commentaries in the
Babylonian Talmud. I know, by date, every day of all
twelve cycles of the Daf Yomi, from today backwards
to the day it started.

And you knew all of this when you woke up?

Some of it. The rest has come with the seizures.
Every time I have one I know more.

You're going to have to excuse me, Ben, but this is
my first time seeing you in many years, and I'm not
familiar with everything about you anymore.

What type of seizures are you having?

The doctors think it's some type of epilepsy. They're
giving me CT scans, MRIs, all sorts of tests. I don't
know what I should tell them, if anything, but what
happens is that I feel them coming, I know a few
minutes before. It's this heavy calm that very gradually covers me. It feels like someone is pouring water

very slowly over my body. And when I'm covered,
I have this moment, just a brief, brief moment, an
instant, where I feel everything, see everything,
know and understand everything, and where the
world, or the universe, or whatever we are and are a
part of, feels perfect, and I feel perfect within it. The
only thing it's like is having an orgasm, but this is a
thousand times more intense, and it's beyond just
the physical. It's like a giant, unreal orgasm where all
the knowledge and wisdom there ever was and ever
will be is mine, but only for that instant. And then
the seizure hits. And I feel everything in the seizure,
and the pain of it is unreal, and as beautiful as the
moment before is, the seizure is its horrific comple-
ment, its terrible companion. Somewhere near the
end, everything goes black. And when I wake up, I
know more, like I've kept some of what I saw or felt or
knew.
I imagine you have capable physicians caring for you.
What do they say about this phenomenon?
I haven't told them. Just you and Jacob.
Perhaps you should.
They'll tell me I'm crazy.
I could speak to them for you. My position as a
rabbi might lend some credibility to what you're
saying.
Words of God mean nothing in the face of science.
I would disagree with you on that point, Ben.
Can your words of God cure cancer? Or AIDS?
Can your words of God save a dying child?
Some people believe they can.
They're delusional fools.

And if that is so, what are you, who is hearing the
words of God?
I might be a delusional fool as well.
The door opened and a doctor came into the room,
followed by Jacob and his companion, the young
man with the Bible. I stood and decided it was best
for me to depart, with the hope that I would be able to
return sometime in the near future. I said goodbye to
Ben, and remarked that I would like to see him again.
Jacob objected, but Ben said he would like me to come
back, the next day if possible. Jacob said his fellow
pastors from the church were coming the next day,
and Ben said he would like me to be there with them.
Jacob said absolutely not, and Ben leaned back onto
the bed and closed his eyes and asked the doctor to
begin doing whatever it was he needed to do.

I left the hospital and started heading home,
taking the subway, as I usually did when I moved
about New York, and especially when I was outside
of the borough of Brooklyn. As I rode the train,
I thought about Ben, who, while clearly the same
person, hardly resembled, physically, emotionally,
spiritually, or otherwise, the child and young man
I had known and tutored for so many years.
He was, I believed, or had been since the moment
I heard of his conception, the type of individual that
came along, depending on one's theological position,
once in a generation, once in a lifetime, once in a
millennium, or just once, once over the course of all of
mankind's existence. The signs had led me to
this belief, and while some of them were open to

interpretation, some were absolutely not, and I had
never questioned the signs, for I had no reason to
question them. This Ben, though, this new man,
this new incarnation of a person I had not seen for
so many years, and who refused to discuss what
he had done or where he had been for all of those
years, brought up a number of questions for me, and
certain things about him, including the extensive
knowledge, gained, he said, during a coma, of a book
not recognized as valid by my religious authority,
conflicted with some of the signs I believed would
confirm his identity. I had had tremendous expectations going into my meeting with him, some of which
I should have certainly tempered. I knew his brother
harbored great resentments towards me, which he
had extended out to include all Jews, and Judaism as
a religion, despite what I was told were his new beliefs
regarding God, Jesus Christ and the Holy Spirit,
the End Times, the Second Coming of Jesus Christ,
and Israel's required existence for those events
to come to pass. I wondered if this wasn't some
elaborate trick that would result in Jacob exacting
some form of sad, unnecessary, and ultimately
misguided revenge upon me, and if Ben hadn't
been convinced to play along in order to regain his
brother's, and thus his mother's and his sister's, favor.
On the other hand, something about him did seem
otherworldly, divine. His scars and his skin
and his eyes, which were remarkable, and the fact
that he had survived such massive trauma, it all
supported my initial reaction, and I had no real
reason to doubt what he was telling me, as it was, and

113   Adam

still is, my inclination to take someone's word as truth until I have reason not to. And that moment, just before he told me that he believed he might be speaking to God, when he took a deep breath, and the way in which he took that breath, was indicative of something astounding, and unless he had somehow gained knowledge that only I or another rabbi could have passed to him, he would not have known it would mean anything to me.

When I arrived home, I went directly to the dining table, where my wife and three children were waiting for me to have our nightly family meal. My wife could see I was preoccupied, which I rarely am, and tried to ask me why, but I didn't feel Ben Zion was an appropriate topic of conversation, and didn't want to discuss him or his family in front of the children. When dinner was over, I excused myself and went to my study, where I keep a small library of Jewish scriptures and sacred texts, which I use in my own continuing study, refer to when I work on one of my sermons at home, or share and use with my family, particularly during holidays and High Holy Days. I walked over to the Babylonian Talmud, which alone takes up several shelves. The copy I own is comprised of sixty-four tractates, totaling 2,711 pages, printed in twenty-four folio volumes. The cycle of Daf Yomi involves studying a single page of the Talmud every day, beginning on page one and continuing for 2,711 consecutive days. It was conceived by Rabbi Yehuda Meir Shapiro of Poland at the First World Congress of the World

Agudath Israel, held in Vienna in 1923, which was
the year 5684 on the Hebrew calendar, and the first
cycle began on the first day of Rosh Hashanah that
year. Each day, approximately 150,000 Jews around
the world study, contemplate, and discuss the page,
and there is a celebration at the end of each cycle
called the Siyum HaShas. The most recent Siyum
HaShas took place on March 1, 2005, known to us
as the year 5766. The idea that someone could know
the entire book, or even a single volume of it, was
inconceivable, and frankly, quite ridiculous. I chose
a volume at random and opened it. Its pages consist
of the Mishnah, or Jewish law, printed in the middle
of the page, with the Gemara directly below it. The
Gemara is a commentary on the law and how it
relates to the Torah, written by the Amoraim, a group
of ancient rabbinical sages. The Tosafot, a series of
commentaries by medieval rabbis, are printed on the
outside margins of the page. This incredibly dense
text, written in Hebrew, governs Orthodox Judaism.
One could devote one's entire life to the study of
it, and many do, and not even begin to fully and
completely comprehend and understand it, much less
have it memorized, which, if even possible, would be
a superhuman feat. I placed the volume back on the
shelf and went and kissed each of my children good-
night. I returned to my study and I prayed. When
my wife came into my study and asked me what was
wrong, I told her that Ben Zion had been found, and
I had spent the afternoon with him. Having been
with me for so many years, she knew what that meant
to me, and possibly to all of Judaism, and also the

world. Instead of spending time together, as we did most evenings, she left me in prayer, and I prayed for several hours before going to sleep.

The next day I went to the synagogue, where most of my thoughts revolved around Ben, and I found my daily tasks and responsibilities, which I usually so thoroughly enjoyed, to be a tremendous burden. I tried to finish them as soon as possible, and went immediately to the hospital. When I arrived at Ben's room, the young man who had been sitting near Ben's bed, and who was still clutching his Bible, was standing outside the door. When I tried to go into the room, he stepped in front of me and said that Jacob was inside with Ben's doctors and that he had been instructed not to allow anyone to enter. I told him that Ben had specifically asked me to return, and that I had been the family's rabbi before their conversion, and that as far as I knew, I was still Ben's rabbi because he had not converted to Christianity. The man told me he knew who I was, and that Jacob had told him not to allow me inside the room. I asked him his name and he told me it was Jeremiah. When I offered him my hand, he did not receive it.

We waited for a few minutes, and while Jeremiah was not physically imposing, something about him seemed off, as if he were very angry, very nervous, or very scared, or some combination of all of those emotions. He stood in front of the door, reading his Bible, and would occasionally either glare at me or nod to himself while saying Praise Jesus or

Hallelujah Lord. When the door finally opened and
several doctors stepped out of the room, one of them,
a tall thin man who appeared to have some authority,
walked over to me and addressed me. Rabbi Schiff?
Yes?
Dr. Wulf. Neurology attending.
Nice to meet you.
Ben is sedated right now. He's had two severe seizures
today. Last night, however, he both asked and author-
ized me to speak with you about his case.
Do you know more than you did yesterday?
We do. If you can come to my office, we can talk for
a few minutes.
That would be great. Thank you.
We went to his office, which was crowded with
papers, books, degrees on the walls, and a large
number of family photos depicting him and a woman,
I assumed his wife, and three young girls, I assumed
his daughters, on vacations, at ball games, in front
of a church. There was also a crucifix on the wall.
He sat behind his desk and I sat across from him,
and he spoke.
We've been working hard to diagnose Ben. It's
obvious that he's been suffering from some form
of seizure disorder, most likely as a result of his
accident. Jacob came to me last night, and he told
me about what Ben has been experiencing. That
information made it very clear to us that he is
suffering from temporal lobe epilepsy, and a rare
and specific type, called ecstatic epilepsy. Ecstatic
epilepsy is characterized by an aura, which is a
feeling the patient has right before a seizure. The

auras of someone with ecstatic epilepsy tend to be
extreme, often involving sensory hallucinations,
sometimes erotic sensations, and, more rarely,
religious or spiritual experiences. It can be, and was
in our case, difficult to diagnose because the onset
of the seizure isn't localized in a specific set point
in the brain, which makes it difficult to track using
EEGs, and because the experiences involved with the
seizures are so profound, and pleasurable, that the
patients don't tell their doctors about them because
they don't want them treated and stopped. Both seem
to be the case with Ben. I don't know what he has
spoken to you about, but he told Jacob he believed he
was communicating with God. As I told Jacob, that's
actually normal given this diagnosis, but unfortunately, it is entirely a function, or rather a malfunction, of his brain. It is not real, as much as someone
like you or Jacob or I would like it to be, and allowing
it to continue should not be encouraged. We need to
get Ben on a drug regimen and begin treating him.
I understand.
Has he spoken to you about his communications?
I don't discuss conversations between me and
members of my synagogue.
Even if it may affect their health?
I understand your position and your concerns,
and if they come up with Ben, I will address them
with him.
Thank you.
I stood and left and went back to Ben's room, where
his brother and Jeremiah were praying at his bedside.
He was asleep, on his back, and looked as if he was

at peace. Jacob looked up at me and I knew I was not welcome. Wanting to avoid an unnecessary confrontation, I decided it was best to leave. I said a prayer outside the door and went home.

After dinner I went to my study and turned on my computer and started researching epilepsy, and more specifically ecstatic epilepsy, on the internet, which I find a wonderful, though sometimes confusing and contradictory source of information. The diagnosis was perplexing to me. While Ben had clearly suffered major trauma to his head and body, and the epilepsy might have been a direct result of said trauma, if there wasn't a spiritual element, a true spiritual element to what he was experiencing, there was no way he would know the religious books he claimed to know. He had also, since before he was born, depending on who you believed, shown signs of messianic potential, which had grown stronger and more absolute following his birth and his childhood. On the other hand, I did not know if he actually knew the books, and he himself had stated that the words of God meant nothing in the face of science, and that he might well be a delusional fool. I found myself, until I knew more and spent more time with him and had more time for reflection and prayer, in the same place I was with God, which is a place of faith. I either had faith in Ben or I didn't. I either believed him, and in him, or I didn't.

My research proved to be very enlightening, and epilepsy turned out to be far more fascinating than I'd imagined it could or would be. Over the course of recorded time, some of the world's most important historical figures either were or are thought to have been epileptic, including Pythagoras, Socrates, Plato, Hannibal, Alexander the Great, Julius Caesar, Petrarch, Dante Alighieri, Leonardo da Vinci, Michelangelo, Isaac Newton, Napoleon Bonaparte, Ludwig van Beethoven, Lord Byron, Edgar Allan Poe, Fyodor Dostoyevsky, Vincent van Gogh, Alfred Nobel, Thomas Edison, and Vladimir Lenin. Many scientists and researchers believe that the genius these people possessed was either directly caused by, or most certainly related to, their epilepsy. The number of religious figures I found who are thought to have had it was astonishing, among them the Priestly source of the Pentateuch, Ezekiel, Saint Paul, the Prophet Muhammad, Joan of Arc, Martin Luther, Saint Birgitta, Saint Catherine of Genoa, Saint Teresa of Ávila, Saint Catherine of Ricci, Saint Margaret Mary, Ellen G. White, and Saint Thérèse of Lisieux. Among those who either definitely had or are thought to have had ecstatic epilepsy are Saint Paul, the Prophet Muhammad, Joan of Arc, Beethoven, and Dostoyevsky. The effects those moments, those brief moments before their seizures hit, had on their lives, and on the world at large, are astonishing: on the road to Damascus, Saint Paul had his vision of the resurrected Jesus, which led to his conversion to Christianity; the Prophet Muhammad is thought, by some, almost always non-Muslims, to have spoken to the archangel Gabriel and to have received the

Qur'an from him during those moments; Joan of Arc
is believed to have received the instructions from
Saint Margaret, Saint Catherine, and Saint Michael
that inspired her to lead the French Army into battle
and resulted in its victories against the English in
the Hundred Years' War; Beethoven is thought to
have conceived of his symphonies in their entirety,
which is perhaps how he was able to compose them
even when he was deaf; and Dostoyevsky is believed
to have conceived of his novels in their entirety. In
thinking specifically of Saint Paul and the Prophet
Muhammad, who, while I do not worship in the
same way as them or the followers of the religions
that one preached and one founded, are certainly
the two most important religious figures who have
appeared on earth since the death of Jesus Christ, I
was heartened in my belief that Ben might be divine,
that his visions might be of God, instead of a false
apparition of God, and that his condition might
be a requirement of his potential rather than an
impediment to it.

I returned to the hospital the next day, stopping
first at the synagogue to ask my assistant rabbi to
handle those responsibilities that are normally mine.
When I entered Ben's room, Jacob and Jeremiah
were sitting across from Ben, who was cross-legged
on his bed. They both had their Bibles open and
were giving him book titles with chapter and verse
numbers, and as soon as they finished saying them,
Ben immediately recited the text, in what I assume
was a word-for-word rendering, back to them.

Jacob looked up at me and started to speak, but Ben told him he wanted me to stay. There were no other seats, so I stood a few feet away from the foot of Ben's bed.

What I saw was absolutely amazing. Jacob was using an Old Testament, the first five books of which, Genesis, Exodus, Leviticus, Numbers, and Deuteronomy, also known as the Five Books of Moses, constitute the Torah, and Jeremiah was using the New Testament, the primary focus of which is the story of Jesus Christ. For over an hour they drilled him. They'd quickly flip through the pages, the book, chapter, and verse they landed on, and each time Ben would recite the corresponding text correctly. Near the end of it, while Jeremiah was visibly awed and excited, and I was silent and, in a way, very proud, Jacob seemed very anxious and nervous. He stopped Jeremiah, closed his Old Testament, and spoke.
How do I know you didn't memorize these while you were away?
Because I told you I didn't.
Why should I believe you?
It doesn't matter to me if you do or you don't.
Why won't you tell me what you did for all those years?
Because it doesn't matter.
Where were you?
I was drifting.
Where?
Doesn't matter.
It does to me.

Let's end our conversation. I'd like to spend some
time with the rabbi.
Tell me what you did and I'll end the conversation.
I lived and felt and learned and hurt and fell in love
once and most of the time I wasn't happy but some
of the time I was and I never stepped foot in a church,
a synagogue, a mosque, a temple, or any other kind
of religious establishment and I never picked up
a book of any kind, much less memorized one.
You didn't answer my question.
I just didn't give you the answer you wanted.
Jacob stood and said he'd be back in an hour,
and he and Jeremiah started to walk out of the room.
Ben spoke.
I love you, Jacob. And I appreciate how much care
and concern you've shown me.
Jacob stopped and looked back and he almost smiled,
which would have been the first time I had seen him
smile since he visited me in my office, and he said
thank you, and he and Jeremiah left.
Ben looked at me.
You spoke with my doctor.
Yes, I did. It was very interesting, and very
informative.
What do you think?
Words of science mean nothing in the face of God.
Ben smiled.
It could just be a malfunction of my brain.
What do you know about Messiah?
The Messiah?
Messiah. Not everyone believes it will be a person.
Many believe, as they do with large sections of the

Torah, that the story, and the prophecy, of Messiah
is symbolic, and not about an actual person who may
have lived, may currently be alive, or may at some
point walk among us, but about a period of time, a
Messianic age, when Jews, and the rest of the world,
will live in peace.

Is that what you believe?

No.

You believe in a person, an actual Messiah?

Messiah, or Moshiach, means anointed, or the
anointed one, in Hebrew. It is a word that has been
used to refer to many things and many people
in the Torah, including kings, prophets, priests,
and warriors. Some believe we may have seen many
Messiahs already, the most prominent being David,
Solomon, Aaron, and Saul. In at least three points
in our history, a great many Jews believed the
Messiah was among us. In 132 CE, a Davidic soldier
named Shimon Bar Kochba united the armies of the
tribes of Israel and led a revolt against Roman rule,
which freed Israel. He established a new government
in Jerusalem, and he started rebuilding the Temple
of Solomon. Rabbis made proclamations naming
him Messiah and stating that the Messianic age had
begun, which lasted for two years, at which point the
Romans returned, crushed the Jewish armies, and
killed a large portion of our population, including
Bar Kochba. Fifteen hundred years later, in 1648,
a Turkish rabbi named Sabbatai Zevi proclaimed
himself Messiah, basing his claim on a prophecy set
forth in the Kabbalah text of Zohar, which predicted
the Messiah's arrival in that year. Though he was

not Davidic, and possessed none of the requirements of Messiahship, by 1665, when he proclaimed himself Messiah again, he was able to convince eighty percent of the world's Jewish population at the time that he was indeed Messiah. He ultimately converted to Islam before Sultan Mehmed IV of Constantinople, humiliating his followers and embarrassing Jews around the world. Against all reason, there are people today who call themselves Sabbatians and believe he was Messiah, and that in order to herald the Messianic age, they pray for his return. The most recent individual thought to be Messiah was Menachem Mendel Schneerson, the seventh Rebbe of Chabad Lubavitch in Brooklyn, who lived from 1902 until 1994. He was undoubtedly a great man, and spent his life spreading Orthodox Judaism and working to unite Jews, but his call for prayer to hasten Moshiach was not a proclamation of his own Messianism, despite the belief of many of his own followers, which he neither supported nor rejected. You ask what I believe, and as you know, as an Orthodox Jew, and as a rabbi, I am required as part of my belief to subscribe to the thirteen principles of faith set forth by Maimonides. The twelfth principle states: I believe with perfect faith in the coming of the Messiah. How long it takes, I will await his coming every day. I also recite the Shemoneh Esrei, the eighteen prayers, three times a day, at morning, afternoon, and evening services, and in that prayer, I pray for the conditions of the Messiah to be met: the return of Jewish exiles to Israel, a return to religious courts and God's system of justice, an end to evil and the humbling of sinners and heretics, rewards to the righteous, the rebuilding of Jerusalem and the restoration of a king descended from David, and the building of the Third Temple of Solomon. And when that happens, the Messiah arrives? Or he arrives and then it happens, or some of it happens before and some after, no one knows, and the prophecies aren't specific about it. We only know, or believe, the Messiah will arrive, and that the arrival could be at any time, or it could have been and we missed it, or it could be now, or it could still be coming, and that's part of the beauty of Messiah, the fact that no one knows. There are, though, beliefs that specific events will herald the arrival of the Messiah: if every Jew on earth observes a single Shabbat, or if no Jew on earth observes a single Shabbat, if the world is good enough to be deserving of Messiah, or if the world is bad enough to need Messiah, if an entire generation of Jews is born innocent, or if an entire generation of Jews loses hope. None are likely, though, so instead of waiting for them, or trying to bring them into being, rabbis, or at least some of us, myself included, have looked for specific signs, which have been known for centuries, that Messiah, or the potential Messiah, will possess. Such as?

The Messiah, or potential Messiah, will have been born on Tisha B'Av, the day of the destruction of both the First and Second Temples in Jerusalem. The Messiah, or potential Messiah, will have been born circumcised, as were Adam, Noah, Joseph, Moses, and David, and some believe Jesus, though

Jews do not believe that particular myth. The Messiah, or potential Messiah, will be able to judge people, whether they are good or bad, whether they are honest or deceitful, whether they are deserving of Heaven or undeserving, with his sense of smell. The Messiah, or potential Messiah, will also perform miracles; though the exact nature is not revealed, the most common miracles are related to health and medical issues, and having the ability to heal either themselves or others. I watched Ben to see if he would react to what I said, as he knew he had been born on Passover. I knew, though I did not know if he did or not, that he had been born circumcised, which is one of the reasons I had tried, for the entirety of his life, to be close to him and his family, and to watch, guide, and counsel him when I could, and I believed, based on what I had seen, that he had acquired the ability to judge people using his sense of smell. The fact that he was alive, given his traumas, was an obvious miracle, though I did not know, at the time, whether he was able to heal others, or perform any other type of miracle. I doubted, because I did not, and do not, believe the Christ story as it is written, that he would ever have walked on water or turned water to wine. He did not react, which surprised me, because surely he knew he possessed three of the traits, and must have, given the difficult situation within his family, which had revolved around the circumstances of his birth for his entire life, suspected that he possessed the fourth and that he had been born as he was. He stood up and looked at me and spoke. I need to do something.

Shall I wait here for you?

It would probably be better if you went home.

Is everything okay?

He smiled and nodded.

Yes.

He turned and walked out of the room. He was
wearing his robe and a pair of hospital slippers and
I could see glimpses of the scars on his back, and
large scars on the back of his head. I think often of
that moment, if perhaps I said something wrong,
if I should have withheld some of the information
I gave to him, if I was too forward, or if perhaps
I should have sensed something when he told Jacob
that he loved him. I think often of that moment,
and I wonder if I should have known when he stood
and smiled at me, that he was going to walk out of
the room, and walk out of the hospital, and disappear again, and if I had known, would I have done
anything to stop him.

MATTHEW

Some people just ain't made for the world. Can't
fucking take it. Can't deal with Momma and Dadda
and school teaching you nothing and a fucking job
with some motherfucking boss going blah blah blah
and bills and neighbors and some kind of bullshit
church and having a good credit score and a mortgage and getting married with kids and some kind
of mysterious motherfucking retirement plan that
don't ever let you do nothing but put more in and get
none back. Lotta people ain't made for it. They the
people you see on the streets, in dirty clothes, talking to themselves, screaming on the corner like they
demonized, mumbling and crying, they the ones
in your family and your town you always scared of
and feeling sorry for and making excuses about, the
ones you don't even thinks is fucking human. They
is, they just ain't made like the rest of you and they
can't deal with it so they go to drinking and getting
fucking high and being criminal and getting locked-
the-fuck-up and just saying who gives a fuck to all of
it. People be thinking they're crazy and be needing
some kind of fucking help, but the help ain't nothing
'cause a motherfucking soup kitchen or some kind of
shelter that can't hold enough or a nuthouse where we
get beat or some charity that's really about motherfuckers' friends knowing how good they is and how
much they care ain't nothing but bullshit. And don't

even bring up that made-up motherfucker people
be calling God, 'cause that motherfucker don't even
exist, and don't be bringing up all these so-called
houses of God, 'cause they more about killing
and hating than they is about helping and loving.
Sorry to break the motherfucking news if you ain't
heard it, but that's it motherfucker, that's the
fucking news.

I been living underground for a long-ass motherfucking time. Living underneath New York
fucking City, where there's tunnels, and there's
tunnels underneath the tunnels, and there's
some more fucking tunnels under those tunnels.
Some of 'em empty, some still got trains rolling
through 'em, some of 'em got the subways and
some of 'em gots peoples. And then there's some
so dark, so goddamn dark, darker than the darkest
night, and blacker than what you see when your
eyes closed, that most peoples, even underground
peoples, won't go into 'em. And those are the tunnels
where miracles happen, where people like Yahya
and Ben go and come back something different,
where motherfuckers who got the gift go and in
the blackness they see. I know it be sounding crazy,
but the ones with gifts got to go into blackness,
'cause that's where they learn to see.

I was born in New Haven, Connecticut. My daddy
was a respectable motherfucker who had him a
college degree and worked his ass off as a bank teller.
My momma finished high school and spent her life

being his bitch. He wasn't never around when I was
growing up, saying he was always working to get
promoted and going out with clients and his boss.
When he was around, he was drinking and yelling
and ignoring me and my two sisters and telling my
momma she wasn't pretty enough or skinny enough
or dressing well enough or getting them invited to
the right parties with the right peoples and every
now and then if she talked back to him he'd hit her
in the fucking face. He didn't think nothing about
me 'cept that I was a piece of shit, which was fine with
me 'cause I didn't think nothing about him 'cept he
was a piece of shit too. They sent me to all sorts of
different schools, thinking the better name or more
of 'em would make a difference, but it didn't make
nothing 'cept them real pissed. When I was seventeen, I left 'em for good. Just walked the fuck away.
I was figuring I'd do fine on my own, and even if
I didn't, I'd rather be doing real bad my own way
than be an asshole doing what other peoples thought
I should be doing. I convinced myself I was breaking
out in the name of some kind of fucking freedom.
I hadn't learned yet that everybody's locked up some
way or another. That's how life is; we're all imprisoned by something.

I lived in a park for a while. Lived in a cardboard
box. Lived under a highway. Got my ass beat and
got robbed and got addicted and got locked up a
few times and got raped more than once or twice.
Learned what I already knew, that the world is
an ugly motherfucking place where people'll spit

on you and fuck you up before they'll be good to you. I found my way into the tunnels just wanting to get the fuck away, lived like a fucking rat, scrounging for food, eating fucking garbage, taking what other people didn't want and using it to survive. First time down was for three years. Just by myself. Living by the trains that went to Long Island. Had a sleeping bag and flashlight and a baseball bat. Then I got busted for being in a fight with a knife over some pizza in a dumpster and had some crack in my pocket and got sent upstate for three years. Got out and came back to my tunnel and found some other motherfucker in my sleeping bag and wasn't in no mood for fighting after fighting the whole time in prison and went further down and found me an old electrical closet on an abandoned IRT track and stayed there for three years. I got back on the rock and drinking again and spent my days begging and going through dumpsters trying to find some shit to sell. One day I came back from up top and I had me a couple nice rocks and a bottle of wine and I see two motherfuckers sitting on the ground outside my closet. They wasn't in uniforms and they definitely wasn't working with the MTA or Amtrak, so I figured it was some undercover pig motherfuckers coming to drag me back to prison 'cause I didn't never go see my parole officer, and I think about running away but figure they'd shoot me or some shit like they always do to poor supposedly crazy homeless motherfuckers.

So I just walked over to 'em and asked them what the fuck was up and when I was close I could see for sure they wasn't no fucking cops 'cause they had these

scars that was identical and looked liked someone
had put two long slices on each of their arms and they
said some motherfucker named Yahya wanted to see
me. I asked them what the fuck Yahya wanted and
they said to see me. I asked them who the fuck Yahya
was and where Yahya was at and they said they would
show me. And that's what they did. They fucking took
me down into the blackness and showed me.

I was there on that first day we saw Ben. We was just
sitting having some dinner and most of us was there,
sitting at the tables eating some macaroni and
motherfucking cheese. At that point I'd been with
Yahya for almost ten years, and it had taken a long
fucking time, lots of hard-ass work and patience,
but we had everything dialed up just fucking right:
electricity hijacked from the city power lines,
water hijacked from the city water pipes, a tunnel
that hadn't been used since the eighteen fucking
hundreds that was blocked at both ends, holes that
we could close that was going up to other tunnels
in four different places, and one passage that went
straight into a alley on the Lower East Side that we
could lock the fuck up to keep people out. We had
built little shelters for everyone out of scraps of wood
and siding that peoples up top threw away. We had
pots and pans and sheets and towels and beds and
old tape players for music and radios for when the
bad news started coming and we had thousands and
thousands of batteries. We had enough canned and
boxed food to keep us going for a year, and that was
if we didn't start eating any of the rats or the other

fucking animals that was living in the tunnels, which could keep us going for just about forever. And we had us a stockpile of weapons. Everything from old medieval-like shit, fucking swords and spears and shields we made out of scrap metal, to new-school shit like nine millimeters and assault rifles and tasers and mace. There was other tunnels that had peoples living in 'em, and there was other groups that had organized into some kind of community or something, but none like us. We was a movement, a fucking army, with a philosophy and a motherfucking plan. We was ready for what's coming. For what is going to befall humanity. We was prepared to survive when everybody else is gonna fucking die.

Yahya'd been telling us for a couple weeks he'd been having dreams about someone coming to see us. Yahya was a prophet, an old school holy man, like fucking Moses or Muhammad or some other motherfucker from the old books, so when he was telling us he was having dreams or visions we took that shit seriously. Yahya had been in the tunnels for thirty-three years. Came down when he was fourteen years old, living in some foster care fucking nightmare, getting beat by the other kids and raped by the man who was supposed to be caring for him. He got fed-the-fuck-up one day and lit the house they was living in on fire. The other kids got out but the man burned to a fucking crisp, just like his ass deserved, and as soon as he'd dropped the fucking match, Yahya walked into the nearest subway and hopped the fucking turnstile and walked off the platform and into the tunnels. He figured out how to live without being above, eating discarded food from the garbage cans of subway stations, finding clothes that people be leaving behind on accident, getting water from bathrooms at the big stations. He kept going down further and further, finding his own motherfucking way, like all the prophets and the great peoples of the world find their own fucking way, and eventually he found our tunnel we living in now, pristine and unopened for almost a hundred fucking years, and he lived in it alone for ten years, till he started building our society. He only been coming out one day a year for the whole time, just the day of the anniversary of the fire. He come out and he read a newspaper and he walk around the city and look at the shit going down, which ain't never any good, and been getting worse and worse every goddamn year.

So he'd been telling us 'bout his dream, that some motherfucker was going to find us, a man who'd wandered the world, suffered shit none of us could ever imagine, knew shit that none of us could ever imagine, that his arriving was a sign that the end was coming, the final motherfucking sign. And there we were, eating our macaroni and listening to Yahya preach, and this motherfucker comes walking out the darkness, skinny as fuck, white as paper, scars all over the fucking place, scars that made the scars we had, the scars Yahya cut into our arms as a sign that our life above was dead and we was in the tunnels for life, this motherfucker had scars made those scars look like little bandaid booboos I used to get when

I was a four-year-old shithead. Yahya, who preached
every night at dinner, just stopped, stared. If he
hadn't been having his dreams he'd a pro'ly killed the
motherfucker. But he knew, knew he was coming,
and knew who he was, knew why he was walking the
face of the fucking earth, and Ben just came strolling
up, not saying a word, just looking unhuman, but not
scary like a monster or shit, but unhuman 'cause it
looked like he was glowing, like there was some kinda
light coming out of him or something. He came to the
table, asked if he could sit down, and Yahya nodded.
We was all shocked and I personally was scared,
scared of the motherfucker who could silence Yahya.
So he sat down at the end of the table, looked at
Yahya, and asked him, real polite and shit, if he would
continue preaching. Yahya smiled, and he was not
the kind of motherfucker who smiled very often, and
said yes. And then he continued fucking preaching.
And I remember that sermon 'cause of Ben joining us.
Was about how the governments of the world leading
everyone towards death, disaster, ruin, and apocalypse. And how God and Jesus and the rest of the
motherfuckers and the dumbass prophecies in the
Bible had nothing to do with it. It was the greed and
folly of the men who running the world. Their belief
in silly religions that preach murder and hate and
division. Their need to control other peoples who's
different from them and kill them if they don't bend
to some motherfucker's will. That's what's gonna end
it all, some dumbass war over religion and money,
and that's who's gonna end it all, the motherfuckers
who believe and hold the purse strings.

Ben settled right the fuck in. He took a job like
everyone had a fucking job. Most of us went up top
to either beg for money that we used for buying
weapons and long-term supplies or look through
the garbage for food and building materials and shit
we could use down below. Some of us took care of
our business in the tunnel, working on the electric or
the water, managing supplies, doing maintenance,
cleaning the place the fuck up. The worst job was
cleaning the area around the toilets, two deep holes
that went into a tunnel down below us. We had
built little outhouses 'round the holes, and peoples
tried being hygienic and shit, but it was still nasty,
still a place where peoples pissed and took shits and
smelled fucking bad. Ben became the toilet man,
cleaning and stocking the paper and dumping
a bucketful of water down the hole to make some
of that foul shit go away. When he wasn't working
there, he'd help whoever else was needing help, doing
whatever they was needing doing. When we was
eating, he'd always sit at the end of the table, and he
didn't hardly eat nothing. Maybe two, three bites of
rice or pasta, maybe an apple or an orange or half a
banana, one glass of water, and that'd be it for the
whole fucking day. And when we was sleeping, we all
went into our shelters, some of 'em being pretty fucking nice, with mattresses and TVs and more than one
room, and some of 'em being more the simple way,
with maybe a sleeping bag or some blankets. Ben
would sleep on the ground at one of the dark ends
of the tunnel, all by hisself, nothing but his clothes,
'cept when it got real fucking cold, then he used this

thin-ass blanket that wouldn't keep a fucking cock-
roach warm. And he didn't hardly ever talk. If you
asked him a question, he'd either nod or shake his
head or smile. If it was needing more words, or was a
more complicated kinda thing, he would always say
just what he needed as quick as possible and then
shut up. And with the way he looked, he was making
all of us think he wasn't a person, not a real person at
least, he was something fucking else beyond, something that wasn't like the rest of us, not even like
Yahya.

About a week after he was being with us, his seizures
started happening. One lunchtime he just fell backwards from the table and his body went fucking
haywire. He was shaking and rolling 'round and had
shit coming out his mouth and was grunting like a
goddamn dog. People got up to help him but Yahya
said leave him be, the man is doing what the man
needs to do. So peoples left his ass alone. And the first
time it lasted something like two minutes. When it
was over we just left him alone, and at a certain point
he came back awake and sat back down at the table
like nothing fucking happened. Twenty minutes later
it happened again. He just fell back and freaked-the-
fuck-out. One of us was a doctor before he became a
crackhead and ended up in the tunnels, where Yahya
found him and saved him, and he was saying we
couldn't just leave Ben alone, but Yahya kept saying
this is what the man needs to do. And it was one
of Yahya's beliefs, one of the tenets of our fucking
society: a man does what he needs to do, he lives his

life how he wants to live it, other people ain't got no fucking right to impose. So even though we was all scared, and we be seeing that the seizures were fucking his ass up, we left him alone. He was doing what he needed to do.

In our world, in our society, our civilization, our culture, and I ain't talking 'bout yours, the one above the fucking ground, I'm talking about our nation, the one in the fucking tunnel, the underground empire, in that subterranean realm, there was rules. If you got brought down, if you got found by Yahya and chosen, you learned the fucking rules, and you lived by them, and if you became part of us, you was saved. Yahya believed the end of the motherfucking world was coming, and he was right, because it sure as fuck is, and it is coming soon. If he found you, you was one of the ones who couldn't live above, who wasn't cut the fuck out for it, and he believed you was capable of living below, and he believed you'd be capable of fighting. You'd get brought down, fucking blindfolded and shit so you wouldn't know where you was, most of us was addicted so we'd get taken the fuck off whatever the shit was, and we was indoctrinated. You had to work, fucking contribute. You had to submit your will to the good of the community. You could drink, use, fuck, gamble, read, play chess, cook, write, paint, build, do whatever the fuck you want, but there was no addiction, whatever you was doing had to be under control. You had to live and let live, but not like motherfuckers up top say that, you had to do it for reals. There was no stealing, no fighting, no judging, no hating. There was no God, no worship, no time wasting on made-up shit. You had to renunciate the fucking world, free yourself from the bullshit of it, accept that at some point there was gonna be nothing but what existed in the tunnel. And you had to be willing to die for that. And once you was fucking cool with all that, and was ready to make the commitment, you was fucking saved. And when you was saved, you was scarred. Yahya would cut you, two long gashes along each of your arms, symbolizing your death above and your birth below. And when the blood flowed, when you lifted your arms and it started running down your cheeks, your neck, when you could taste it, when you could feel it in your fucking shoes, you was free. Never going fucking back 'cept to get shit to live below. Never accepting their rules or expectations or so-called morals and so-called fucking standards ever fucking again. When the blood flowed, you was free.

When Ben came, there was thirty-two of us. It had been that way for two years. Even though Yahya had prophesized his coming, he had to follow the same rules as the rest of us, had to become one of us if he wanted to stay. His seizures made shit a little more complicated, 'cause he couldn't be doing most of the normal kind of shit the rest of us was doing. And who he was, why he was walking the motherfucking face of the earth, the gifts he was given or acquired or whatever you want to believe, though I know what I believe, that made shit more complicated too. Not every day a motherfucker like him comes strolling into the motherfucking lunch line. But he didn't seem to care. Yahya moved him to sweeping and garbage, which was sweeping the fucking grounds and taking the garbage out, which meant taking it to another tunnel that was also empty, 'cept for the fact we'd been dumping shit in it for years. When Ben would have a seizure, he'd just sit down and let it happen. Though Yahya noticed it the first time, the rest of us started seeing how Ben would go to another place right before those fucking things would blast him. His eyes would be real still, like he was looking at shit no else could see or had ever seen or would ever see. It would only be a second, maybe, or two or three, but somehow, those seconds seemed like forever. When someone asked Yahya what was happening, he said the man was speaking to God, seeing through to the eternal. Someone else asked how he was talking to God, if God don't exist? Yahya said God don't exist like people on this planet believe he exist, some big powerful all-knowing motherfucker sitting on a chair giving a shit about what's happening here on earth and planning our individual destinies, that's just stupid bullshit, but there was answers we didn't have, things we didn't know, things beyond the little minds of little men who was stupid enough to think that in the entire universe, infinite beyond human comprehension in size and energy and dimension, we was the only motherfuckers around, and that all the stupid little shit we did and fucking worried about mattered in some kinda way. Ben went to those places, those infinite places, and understood 'em, even though he couldn't or wouldn't talk about what the fuck it was he was seeing and feeling and experiencing.

The seizures got worse and fucking worse and fucking worse, and longer and fucking longer and fucking longer. They would last ten, fifteen, twenty minutes. Started lasting thirty minutes, lasting an hour, lasting three or four hours, shaking and convulsing and spitting up and grunting, you could see it hurting him while it was happening, and you could see him being in so much pain when it ended that he couldn't hardly move. The crackhead doctor said Ben was experiencing some shit called status epilepticus, a state of persistent seizure, and that he could be dying from it, that he would be dying from it if we didn't get him out to a proper hospital. But Yahya said leave him, that man is not going to die, at least not down here. Then he had him a seizure that lasted for a day, twenty-four fucking hours straight. It was scaring everyone and making us think Yahya was wrong, that Ben was gonna fucking die. On and on and on and on. Worse than we had ever seen. Don't know how anyone could live through it or be surviving something like that. And even if you could be living through it, how you wouldn't be fucking insane from the pain, just crazy outta your mind from the physical fucking pain. When it stopped, he just lie there, on his blanket, on the floor of the tunnel. Slept for like another two days. We was always going over to check him, make sure he was still breathing, and he always was, but it was real light, and you had to be looking real close to see it. When he waked up, we was all sitting around after dinner. Yahya had given us a fierce preaching, along the lines of his typical but real inspired, saying the world above us was dying, that greed corruption hate and intolerance was gonna lead to a war that would destroy it all, that the war was coming soon, that we got to renounce that world and prepare to survive, that we got to love each other and let each other live, and help each other live, and respect each other. Don't matter where we from or what we had before, don't matter our color or our religion, that nothing matter but living, and letting live, and loving. After he was done we got to listening to some old-timey jazz on the cassette deck, some of us having cocktails, some of us smoking some fine-ass weed, some of us dancing, mens together, mens and ladies together, just ladies, all of them cool down here, sharing their love and spreading their love however the fuck they want, nobody judging them. Ben joined all the people dancing, probably about twenty of us. Nobody saw him walk up, one second he wasn't there, the next second he was. And he was moving real slow, slow and in perfect rhythm, like he was part of the music, another instrument to it or some shit, tied directly into it. His eyes was closed, and he hadn't fucking eaten in so long, his skin was even whiter than normal, almost fucking translucent. His eyes was closed and he started moving to each person or couple, and he touched them, held them, moved with them, slowed them down so they was feeling the music same way he was, he was holding their hands, holding their faces in his hands, pulling them close so their bodies was real tight with his, and he was kissing them, men and women both, slowly and deeply kissing them, and you could see in their faces, in their bodies, that none of them had ever been feeling anything like it, nothing as pure, as sexual, as ecstatic, as fucking sweet and beautiful, and it was like he was fucking them, fucking them like they hadn't never been fucked before, even though he was just touching, kissing, moving, moving real slow, real real slow, he was fucking all of 'em. And those he wasn't with, who wasn't dancing, we was watching, and we was as turned on as the people he was touching, he was fucking. When I was a boy living in a world in my head to escape the world I was living in for real, I used to dream I'd be able to do anything I wanted to people and whatever I did they loved me, just loved and let me be free from all the shit in the world that I hated and that hated me. When I was older, I stopped dreaming that type of dreaming 'cause I realized that kind of shit just wasn't real or possible or ever going to be happening. But then I saw Ben, and I believed it was possible, that fucking anything was possible, because I saw it and felt and knew it and believed it and even though it didn't look real or feel real it was the realest thing I ever knew, that I ever saw on this fucking hellhole of an earth. That love was the realest motherfucking thing any of us ever saw. When he had been with everyone dancing, Ben stepped away and walked towards Yahya, who had been watching and feeling and believing too, sitting at the head of the table where he was always sitting, and Ben kneeled before him and offered his arms. Yahya always had his knife on him, or near him, and he picked it up and he took Ben's arms and he made the cuts. Normally takes longer, a year or so before you get them, and only when Yahya decides, but not with Ben. His blood flowed and he lifted his arms and the blood streamed down all over him. When he was covered and his clothes were soaked, and the ground beneath him, he stepped forward and he kissed Yahya. I hadn't never seen anyone kiss Yahya before, or even touch him, not outside of his room, which was the only place he did things with people, and only women. And Ben kissed him for a long time, and when he pulled away, Yahya's eyes was closed and he was breathing real slow and heavy, and he was looking like he couldn't move, like he was fucking paralyzed. And Ben just stepped away and turned and walked into the darkness.

It was a long time before anyone moved. And when we was moving again, we just went silently, not one fucking word outta anyone, back to our shelters, where most of us just laid there in our sleeping places and thought about Ben. Next morning we expected to see him, having breakfast or being in his sleeping area, but he wasn't nowhere around. Peoples started talking 'bout where he might be at, when Yahya tell us he gone, that he had him another vision last night, that Ben be gone into the tunnels, where he got some things that he need to do on his own, some fights he needs to be fighting on his own. Yahya say let him go, let him do what he needs to do, when he be finished with it, he'll be coming back.

A week went by and he didn't come back. Another week and still nothing. Peoples started getting worried a little bit. I started wandering the tunnels, looking for places I hadn't never been, places further down, places that got the true darkness, the black that don't ever see no light. I was thinking even though Yahya be having his vision, and even though Ben obviously got something special about him, he still a man, still flesh and fucking blood, still got him a heart that does its beating. And being a man, he vulnerable, and he wandering around somewhere with big-ass motherfucking gashes in his arms and some kind of medical condition that fucks him up worse than I ever seen. So I went looking for him, and looking for the places that are hidden, that ain't supposed to be found, the places where I say before that the magic happens, where in the darkness you learn to see.

After four or five days looking, walking through subway tunnels, trains blasting by me just a couple inches away, walking through Amtrak and LIRR tunnels, walking through PATH tunnels, walking through abandoned tunnels, the old IRT, tunnels that got started and never finished, just empty fucking holes, I come across a door in the lower tunnels beneath City Hall. Normally I don't bother with the fucking doors, 'cause they all be locked and breaking the locks just draw attention that don't nobody be needing, but something 'bout this door draw me in. I checked it and it was open, so I look inside and there's a hole with this ladder

going straight down, though I can't fucking see
where it's going or how far or where it ends.
Ain't nothing wrong with looking in life, looking
for new things and places and feelings and beliefs,
ain't nothing wrong at all, so I start climbing down,
looking to see what I find. I go down and it's black
and fucking silent and even though I'd been living
down there a long time at that point, I was real
scared, my heart thudding all fast and shit, taking
short breaths, wondering if something gonna
come out and get me, some fucking monster or
something, or if I'm gonna fucking fall and break
my damn neck. I was being real scared.

My foot hit ground and I could feel it wet and
slippery, which was telling me I must be somewhere
in the fucking sewers, which all of us stayed the fuck
out of because they was full of rats and disease and
lots of other shit no man don't want to spend time
in or around. I started climbing right back up but
as my foot start rising I heard me something that
was sounding like a scream. I stopped and stood
listening for more screaming and I heard another
fucking scream almost right away. I got down and
started walking towards where I was hearing it,
stepping real careful and moving real slow because I
couldn't see nothing. Even though my eyes was real
adjusted, I couldn't fucking see nothing.

Took me a long time to go a couple hundred yards
down that tunnel, long-ass time. All the while
I was hearing those screams, and the closer I was

getting to 'em, I was knowing it was Ben, 'cause
it was sounding like some of the noises I heard
him making during his seizures. When I was real
close I started hearing trickling water and started
knowing that the screams is coming from below me,
and that the water be running down somewheres.
My eyes had adjusted and I saw a few steps ahead
there was a huge hole, like some kind of fucking
sinkhole or giant pothole that happens in
New York once or twice a year, and Ben must
be down in that hole, maybe hurt, and can't get
himself out. I was about to call out to him, tell
him I was here and gonna help him, when I hear
him start talking, talking real slow and deliberate,
like he having a conversation with someone. So I
slide to the edge of the hole and look down, and
he be right there, maybe fifteen, twenty feet down
in some other fucking sewer tunnel, and he just
sitting on the ground like he Buddha, and I swear
on my fucking life his skin was glowing, and his
arms was already healed, the scars just blending
in with the rest of his scars, and he was talking to
the empty air right in front of him, and if I didn't
know him, and know how Yahya felt about him, I'd
a done thought he was plumb fucking crazy out his
mind.

I lied there and watched him. I was nervous he was
gonna see me, so I only just peeked over the edge of
that hole. I could hear him saying shit like yes or no,
yes or no, over and over again, saying why, saying
how, saying no, I will not, I will not. He talked for

like an hour or two hours and then I see him get real still and I know what that means and he starts seizing, worse than I ever seen before, his body literally coming up off the ground, he convulsing so fucking hard. And the noises he was making scared me, sounded like something I can only imagine hearing down in Hell, if there is one. And something felt wrong, like there was something else in there with him. Something dark and evil and old as the fucking sky, something with power that was beyond power, that was fucking so deep and black it was beyond power, and it made me shake and made the hair all over my body stick up and made me piss myself, right there I fucking pissed all over myself. Whatever it was, if it was anything at all, it scared me so fucking much I turned and got the fuck outta there fast as I fucking could.

I started going back to see Ben whenever I could. Didn't tell no one I had found him or knew where he was at. Most of the time he'd be in seizures, and they always bad. When he wasn't, he'd be talking or sometimes screaming, screaming into the blackness, screaming into the motherfucking abyss. Sometimes I'd go down and I'd feel that thing, that mean-ass evil fucking presence, and I'd turn and get the fuck out right away. Other times it'd come while I was there. Only once or twice it didn't come at all, and those was times when Ben was screaming, like he was keeping it at bay or some shit, like the sound of his scream had some fucking righteous power.

He was down there two weeks, three weeks, four weeks, six weeks. Down in that fucking nasty hole by himself. Far as I could see he never ate nothing, never drank nothing, never slept, never fucking left. And while he shoulda got sick or fucking died from fucking starving, it didn't happen. If anything I was seeing the opposite. He was seeming stronger, still skinny as fuck, but stronger. And it was looking like he could somehow be controlling the seizures. Like he could make himself go in and out of 'em when he wanted to go in and out of 'em. I'd hear him ask a question or say something, some heavy-ass shit like what happened before the Big Bang, or who were they, why were they, answer the problem of quantum gravity, can we unify the four fundamental forces. After he asked, he'd close his eyes and take a breath and open his eyes and be in that place, that place like eternity, and then he'd seize. And for the entire last week I went to see him, the seventh week he was in that foul fucking hole, he was seizing. And the entire time, that presence was with him, stronger, seeming somehow active, like it would ebb and flow, attack and retreat, made me wet my fucking pants every goddamn time, scared me to fucking death. At the end of the week, I went down and he was gone. Made me real fucking worried, scared something had happened, that the fucking evil had somehow got him. I went right back to our tunnel, was gonna get Yahya and take him back and tell him what I'd seen and what I'd been doing with myself and Ben and tell him we needed to find him and help. I went back as fast as I fucking could, ran in the darkness, ran from the darkness. And when I got back, Ben was there, with Yahya, looking just fine, like he'd never left, actually looking better than I'd ever seen him, skinny and shit, but glowing like some kind of fluorescent fucking lightbulb, even though I knew he hadn't had nothing to eat or drink in seven motherfucking weeks. He was back. And just like Yahya had seen in his visions, the end was near. The end was fucking near.

JOHN

I had heard there were people living down there.
They were called mole people. There had been a
book, a couple of documentaries. It was one of those
things people would talk about at parties. Frankly,
I didn't care at all. It didn't mean anything to me.
If people wanted to live underground, let them.
It relieved the taxpayer of the burden of them, and
it kept them out of institutions. As long as they didn't
cross my path in some way, I didn't give a shit.

The main function of my job was the tracking of
weapons that came into New York City, and the
apprehension and incarceration of those individuals
who chose to illegally possess them. It is forbidden
by law to own or possess a gun within city limits
unless you have a permit, and permits are very difficult to get. Whenever we recovered a weapon, our
first priority was discovering how it had entered
the city. A gun dealer in upstate New York led us to
the individuals in the tunnel. We came across the
dealer when a gang member in southeast Queens
arrested for murder was found in possession of an
illegal handgun. The suspect had not, as is stan-
dard procedure with gang members and murderers,
removed the serial numbers from the weapon, which
allowed us to trace it. When we arrested the gun
dealer for selling weapons to individuals who did not

have the required license, he made a deal with us to keep himself out of prison and started providing us with the identities of other individuals to whom he had sold weapons. At that point, he told us about the group in the tunnel, who had bought approximately sixty weapons from him, and thousands of rounds of ammunition.

It wasn't easy finding them. There are a large number of abandoned tunnels under the city, some of which haven't been entered in decades. We initially undertook a search of the tunnels, which was fruitless. The gun dealer had told us that the members of the group, who he described as apocalyptic wackos, made their money begging on the street, and that they all had long scars on their arms. We started looking for individuals who matched that description, and after eight months found two of them, one a male and one a female. We put them under surveillance and found the tunnel where they, along with approximately thirty other individuals, were living.

We knew very little about them when we executed search warrants on them. There was some worry we might be entering a situation similar to that of the Branch Davidians in Waco, Texas, where a group of heavily armed religious fanatics, followers of a messianic leader named David Koresh, engaged a federal task force, which held them under siege for fifty-one days, until the Davidians' compound caught on fire and eighty people, including seventeen children, died. Fortunately, that was not the case.

Approximately fifty law enforcement personnel entered the tunnel through four different access points. Almost all of the individuals residing in the tunnel were asleep, and the three that weren't were taken into custody without incident.

I met Ben when we were interrogating the suspects, who were being held at the MCC, the federal correctional center in lower Manhattan. We had found more than three hundred firearms and ten thousand rounds of ammunition in their compound, along with small amounts of cocaine and marijuana. They were also in possession of a large number of knives, swords, and spears. When we ran their prints, we were able to ascertain the identities of all of them except for two, and all of them had records, most for things like drug possession and theft, though a few also had assault convictions. Of the two we could not identify, one went by the name of Yahya and was recognized by all of them as their leader. The other identified himself as Ben Jones.

Yahya refused to speak. He literally did not answer a single question we posed to him, nor did he request a lawyer. He stared directly into the eyes of both myself and the other agent interrogating him, and never said a thing. We assumed it was a ploy to intimidate us, but having been in rooms with drug lords, serial killers, and terrorists, I didn't find him particularly frightening or off-putting. I did Ben on my own. As with Yahya, his prints and DNA came back clean, and there was no record of him in any law enforcement database. And though there had been extensive media coverage of the raid, we had yet to release pictures of any of the arrestees to any media outlets, and had yet to receive any public help in making a positive identification.

Before I entered the room where Ben was being held, shackled to the floor at his ankles and to the table at his wrists, I looked in on him through a one-way window. One of my colleagues was standing near the window, observing him. He sat absolutely still, his eyes closed. He was wearing a jumpsuit, so I could not see his arms or body, but his head and face were badly scarred. His hair was on the short side, black, dirty, and disheveled. He was incredibly thin, the veins in his neck and forehead and cheeks plainly visible. Usually people who are being interrogated for the first time are incredibly nervous and anxious; the only ones who are calm, as calm as he was, are usually extremely hardened criminals. I asked my colleague if he had observed anything unusual. He said the man looks like a fucking freak, and he hasn't moved at all in the last hour, and if I didn't know better, I'd say he wasn't breathing. I laughed and entered the room.

Ben did not move or acknowledge me in any way. I waited for a few moments, assuming he would, but he did not. He was absolutely still, eerily still, still the way large bodies of water can be still, the way they don't appear to be moving, don't appear to be alive, but you know they are. I spoke.

My name is Agent John Guilfoy. I'd like to ask you
a few questions.
He slowly opened his eyes. I hadn't had any contact
with him during the arrests and hadn't seen his eyes
when observing him, and I had never seen anything
like them. At least, not naturally. They were black,
obsidian black, the black of silence, the black of
death, the black of what I imagine it must be like
before birth. They startled me, scared me. I waited for
him to say something, and I waited until I was over
the shock of his eyes, and I spoke again.
Do you understand why you're here?
Yes.
Have you been treated well?
Doesn't matter.
I'm going to tell you upfront that the more coopera-
tive you are with us, the easier things will be for you.
He smiled, laughed to himself.
Is there something funny about that?
Go on with your questions.
We've been trying to identify you, and you haven't
turned up in any of our computer databases. I'm
wondering if you can help us in any way.
I gave you my name.
Is it your real name?
I consider it so.
Is there another one we should be checking?
There have been a few.
Such as?
None of them will be of any use to you.
Try me.
He smiled again, didn't say a word, waited for me.

I stared at him, tried to intimidate him. I might as
well have been staring at a rock. He was silent and
still and unmoving. I spoke again.
Do you understand the charges against you?
Yes.
You understand they are extremely serious?
If you say so.
You're looking at years, maybe decades in prison.
Yes.
That doesn't bother you?
No.
Why?
I can be free anywhere, just as someone can be
imprisoned anywhere.
Is that something your leader taught you?
I don't have a leader.
No?
No.
Yahya was not your leader?
My friend.
A dangerous friend.
If you say so.
He and his followers, amongst whom we count you,
were in possession of hundreds of weapons and
thousands of rounds of ammunition.
I possess nothing.
Did you know of the weapons' existence?
Yes.
Then according to the laws of the government of
the United States, you were in possession of them.
He smiled again.
If you say so.

Do you find this amusing?

Yes.

Why?

I think your laws are silly.

Why is that?

People should be allowed to live and act as they choose.

Not if they endanger or impose on other people.

No one in that tunnel was imposing on or endangering anyone.

I would disagree.

As is your right.

You were living illegally on public land and hoarding weapons designed to kill people.

If the land is public, why can't we use it?

Because it was designated for other purposes.

And how can the most heavily armed, most militarized government in the history of civilization tell its own citizens they can't arm themselves in preparation for the coming annihilation?

The coming annihilation?

Yes.

The apocalypse?

If you want to call it that.

You believe it's coming?

Yes.

The seals have been broken and the signs are appearing?

No.

The Bible says so?

It does, but those words mean nothing to me.

Christ is coming back to do battle with the Devil?

Is that what you believe?

What I believe is irrelevant. I want to know what you believe.

I've told you.

This have something to do with Allah?

It has nothing to do with religion.

Then how do you know?

Look around you.

And what will I see?

That it's coming to an end.

And you can see it?

In a way.

And it's coming soon?

Yes.

I took a deep breath. I wasn't sure if he was a fanatic or mentally ill. In either case, interrogation is virtually useless. Fanatics don't break unless extreme techniques are used, and those sorts of techniques were forbidden in my branch of the government, and whatever the mentally ill say is considered unreliable, and is usually unusable in court. He closed his eyes and started taking deep breaths through his nose. I asked him if he was okay, and he slowly nodded. I asked him if he needed something to eat or drink, and he slowly shook his head. He just breathed, and I waited. After a minute or so, I thought I'd leave him alone, grab a cup of coffee, and come back and try again. When I stood up, he opened his eyes, and he spoke.

I can take it away.

Excuse me?

I can take it away from you.

What are you talking about?

I'm sorry. Terribly sorry.

What are you sorry for?

For your loss.

What the fuck are you talking about?

You lost a child.

I was stunned. I was shot in the line of duty during my first year as an agent, shot in the shoulder with a .38 caliber revolver. The bullet entered my shoulder and exited my back. Ben's statement shocked, hurt, confused, and scared me more than that shot, more than anything in my life, except the event to which he was referring. There was no way he should have known. He had never seen or heard of me before I entered the room. I had asked all of my colleagues not to talk to me about it. We had not released an obituary, so it had not appeared in any sort of media. At the time, I believed there was no way he could have known, though that belief certainly changed.

I sat back down. I looked at him. He hadn't moved. He just stared at me and waited for me to say something. I couldn't speak, and if I had tried, I would have broken down. I stared at the table and clenched my jaw and thought about my little boy, about the first time I saw him, immediately after he was born, about the first time I held him, two minutes later, about a picture, which I could not look at until after I met Ben, of me and him and his mother, who I am no longer with, taken just after we brought him home. I think about his room in our house, about his first step, about his first word, which was Dadda. I replay his life in my head, and I think about how happy we were for the two years we were together. And then he started twitching, and having trouble walking, and he went into the hospital and he never came out and my life fell apart, except for my life at work, which was the only thing I could cling to in order to stay sane. I lost everything else when I lost my little boy. I lost everything that mattered to me.

Ben waited until I looked up. I can only imagine what my face must have looked like, certainly not the cool calm federal agent trying to be an intelligent, convincing, and intimidating interrogator. He spoke.
Release one of my hands.
I can't do that.
Yes, you can.
I won't do it.
You'll be able to walk through your front door without crying. You'll be able to sleep at night.
You'll be able to call her, and tell her you miss her, and you'll be able to love again, and live again.
Fuck you.
I know how much it hurts.
You don't know fucking shit.
Release my hand.
You don't know what the fuck you're talking about, you crazy fuck.
I wish I didn't, but I do.
You motherfucker.
I can take it away.
You're a fucking freak.
Call me whatever you need to call me.

I want to know how you knew.

By looking at you.

Tell me how the fuck you knew.

I did.

This is not some fucking joke here.

I'm just trying to help you.

You're gonna help me? You in shackles and a jumpsuit and twenty years hanging over your fucking head?

If you let me.

I stared at him. I didn't know what to say. I was confused and angry and in pain. He scared me. He scared me more than anyone I had ever been in a room with, anyone I'd ever met, anyone I'd ever seen. Most people, as dangerous or violent as they may be, are easy to figure out. They come from somewhere, and they have experiences that have shaped them, and they have soft spots, weaknesses, places inside where you can open them up.

Ben wasn't like anyone I'd ever met, watched, or interviewed, he wasn't like anyone I'd ever heard about. He was absolutely impregnable. At the same time, he wasn't putting up defenses, and didn't appear to have any. He made me think of something I read when I was in college about Buddha, something that described his physical presence and his state of being. It said he was soft as iron, hard as rain, quiet as thunder, and still as a hurricane. Our professor explained the paradox of the description, that iron is one of the hardest substances on earth but also malleable enough to be shaped into anything we want it to be, that water is fluid and yielding, but strong enough to carve canyons.

That while thunder shakes the ground we walk on,
a thunderstorm is also a peaceful and serene event,
and that while hurricanes are among the most
destructive forces we know of, the eye of the
hurricane is an incredibly calm place, an eerily and
almost otherworldly calm place. Ben stared back
at me. He didn't move, and if he blinked, I didn't
see it. He just took me in with his eyes, those bottom-
less black eyes. And our session as agent and suspect
ended, and our conversation as two men, two men
trying to live and be alive and find their way, which
is all any human being can really do in this life,
began. He spoke.

Despite your earlier statements, you believe in God?

Yes, I do.

And you have sought God out in order to deal with
your grief?

I have.

You have gotten down on your knees and cried,
and pleaded, and begged for relief, and for answers?

Yes.

Has your God answered you?

No.

What version of God do you believe in?

I'm Christian. Episcopal.

Your priest has counseled you?

Yes.

And he is well-intentioned, but he has left
you empty?

Yes.

Has he spoken to your God about you?

What do you mean?

Has he spoken to him, the way I speak to you,
the way you speak to other people?
No one speaks to God that way.
And yet you keep trying, because you believe at
some point your God will answer your prayers?
I hope.
Hope is an illusion, a carrot dangling.
Hope keeps me going.
Going towards what?
I don't know.
Your God offers you hope. Hope offers you nothing.
You should seek another way.
What would that be?
I've told you.
Let you go.
I don't care if you let me go. I don't care if I'm in
a cell for the rest of my life. I'm telling you, if you
release one of my arms, and believe in what I tell
you, and trust me for a brief moment, I can do
what your imaginary God, your fairytale God,
a God no one has ever seen or spoken to and who
has not relieved your pain or provided you with
the answers you seek, cannot do.
I could lose my job.
If that's more important to you.
He sat there and waited. I looked away, towards
the glass, and wondered if my colleague was
watching us or listening to us. We also record all
interrogations, so video was a concern. Agents are
given a certain leeway with suspects. If we think
giving a suspect space or room to move might help
them open up, we are allowed to do it. If we think

giving something to eat or drink will motivate them, we are allowed to do it. This, though, wasn't anything like that. This was entirely personal. And it involved physical contact, which was expressly forbidden. It was against regulations. But I had been in so much pain for so long. I had been haunted and terrorized and destroyed by images of my dying child, of the pain he felt as he went, of the fear he must have experienced as his body failed, of the horror of the moment when he stopped breathing, with my wife and me holding his hands. I knew I would never recover from my boy's death, and I doubted the pain would ever subside, but I decided that if Ben could relieve me of it for a minute or an hour or a day, it would be worth whatever penalty I would have to pay.

I reached into my pocket and took out a key. I leaned across the table and unlocked the shackle that kept his right arm bound to the table. He did not move as I did it, but once his arm was free, and I was still leaning over the table, his arm shot up and he grabbed me and pulled me towards him with a strength that no one who looked like him should have possessed. I felt my feet leave the ground. He held me with my head on his shoulder, and he started whispering in my ear. I don't know what language it was, though I believe it was either ancient Hebrew or Aramaic. I was terrified, and I didn't know if he had tricked me and was going to hurt me, or if he was actually doing what he said he could do. And in a way it didn't matter, because he was so strong that I couldn't have gotten away if I had wanted to.

He kept whispering, and my body went limp. It felt like someone had just emptied it of everything, like what I imagine people who die and come back say they feel while they're dead and drifting towards the light. My emotions, my soul, and my physical strength, my pain and sorrow and struggle, it was all gone. I felt completely empty. I felt like I had always wished I could feel: peaceful, and simple, and uncomplicated. I wanted to be that way forever, to stay with him forever, my head on his shoulder, his voice in my ear. I heard the door open behind me and I heard people come rushing into the room. Someone had been watching us and assumed he was hurting me and I knew it was going to end. Ben stopped speaking whatever language he had been using and just before I was pulled away he said I love you.

I was carried out of the room. The last image I have of him before the door slammed shut is of one of my colleagues spraying mace into his face. I was later told he was also shot with tasers and beaten with billy clubs, and when the beating was over, he was carried out of the room, bleeding and unconscious. I was taken to a hospital, where I checked out normal and went home a few hours later and slept easily for the first time since the day my son went into the hospital. I was transferred off the case and Ben was bailed out two days later. I never saw him again, though I did try to find him. I wanted to thank him for doing whatever he had done, and for giving me a new chance at life, for teaching me to love as he had loved me. I wasn't surprised when I heard what happened to him. We live in a cruel and unfortunate world. The longer I am in it, the more I believe he was right. Hope is an illusion, a dangling carrot, something to keep us going, but going towards what? It all is ending. His end, cruel, unnecessary, and cloaked in a veil of religion and righteousness, like so much of what's wrong with what we've built, will be but the beginning.

LUKE

I'm a white man, brothers and sisters. From the
great state of Mississippi. Born a Christian white man
and raised with a strong sense of my Southern
heritage and the belief that I was part of a God-
given few: the few who founded this country, who
built this country, and who run this country, even
when it appears someone else might be doing it.
I was raised in Jackson, Mississippi. A beautiful
town, brothers and sisters, a beautiful town.
My family had been in the state for two hundred
years, and most of us had never seen a reason to go
anywhere else. We'd been settlers, soldiers,
plantation owners, slave traders, slave owners.
We'd fought for the South in the Civil War, and
a good many of us had died for her. We'd been
gamblers, farmers, Indian hunters, sheriffs, thieves,
lawyers, bootleggers, congressmen, and senators.
My daddy was an oilman. Spent his life searching
for the black gold, that thick, dark, elusive money
juice. He bought and drilled some land in Laurel,
Mississippi, and he struck it, brothers and sisters,
struck it deep and made himself a bundle. When
I was a youngster, he lived in Laurel during the week,
working and spending his nights sleeping with his
black mistress. My momma and I lived in Jackson,
and my momma spent her nights sleeping with the
golf pro, the tennis pro, the local police, and just

about anyone else who wanted to sleep with her. On weekends my momma and daddy got drunk and pretended they loved each other. They went to cocktail parties and horse races. They played golf and went to events at the club. Occasionally they threw things at each other, and occasionally my daddy hit her. I didn't think it was anything but normal. Even after my momma killed herself, my brothers and sisters, I didn't think it was anything but normal. I just thought maybe my momma had got got by the Devil, or that she had had a bout with some kind of female insanity. Lord knows how many believe those kinds of things happen. Lord knows.

Back to me. I must declare that I grew up like a little prince. I had fancy clothes and fancy food and went to the fanciest schools in Jackson. I did whatever I wanted and acted however I wanted and I got whatever I wanted. I had black women who cooked and cleaned and cared for me, and though my momma claimed to be raising me, it was really them. And that was the way it was with all the white kids I knew, and we just thought it was the way of the world. When I finished high school, I went to Oxford to attend the University of Mississippi, where I lived like a gentleman prince. I didn't hardly ever go to class, because I knew I had a job waiting for me. I was the president of my fraternity, where we drank beer and played cards every night and flew the Confederate flag right outside our front door. And when I wasn't drinking and gambling, me and all my friends did whatever we could to get coeds to sleep with us, including forcing them to do it. It was four years of what I thought was bliss, brothers and sisters, before I knew what bliss was. There was no responsibility to myself, my family, or any sort of higher authority. My loyalty and faith resided within my own ego, and within the bonds established at the fraternity house, where, by the way, we had black women working for us cleaning our clothes and cooking our meals. And yes, brothers and sisters, occasionally we'd try to sleep with them, and if by God they said no, we'd force them to do it.

At the end of college, I went to work for my daddy, supervising his wells. I married myself a nice young blonde girl, whose daddy was in the oil business in Louisiana and had known my daddy for twenty years. We had ourselves a big wedding at her parents' plantation house, where everyone got drunk and ate too much and generally acted like we were Southerners before we lost the war. We settled in Gulfport, 'cause it was closer to her family, and in six months' time she was pregnant. We had ourselves a little girl, and then another. They were cute little things, brothers and sisters, believe me, they were pretty as buttons the both of them. I settled into a pattern like my daddy's. I was working in Laurel and coming home on weekends. Though I said I wasn't going to do some of the things my daddy did, I did them anyway. I found myself a black ladyfriend and spent my evenings in bars with her and in bed with her. I played some cards and lost some money. I drove a big fast car and yelled at the people who worked for me, even if they didn't deserve it, and I fired 'em when I felt like it, even if there wasn't a good reason. I was living a bad, bad life, and I didn't know any better. Some would say, and I have said at times myself, that I was singing with Satan, running with the Devil, walking down the dark dirty path of the demon Beelzebub. But I thought that was the way life was supposed to be led by a man of my type, brothers and sisters, a rich white man from the South.

As it is in life, what rises must fall. The mighty become the meek. Giants are stricken and empires razed. And even though nobody ever thinks it's ever gonna happen to them, it sure as shit does, brothers and sisters, and I can attest to that. My fall was swift and pitiless, like a box of rocks falling off the back of a wagon. I started smoking crack, which was a newfangled thing, with one of my ladyfriends. I could not for the life of me stop smoking it. Simultaneous to that little bit of nastiness, my daddy's wells ran dry and he had a falling-out with my father-in-law. Simultaneous to that, my daddy's stockbroker disappeared to Brazil with a mistress and all of our money. I stayed in Mississippi under the auspices of helping my family navigate the turbulent and troubled waters of financial Armageddon, while actually spending all my time in a cheap motel with a pipe and a torch and a stream of hookers. Upon returning home, I was greeted by my father-in-law, who had hired himself a private investigator, with a shotgun and some divorce papers. He told me my wife and beautiful daughters were in Louisiana, and if I tried seeing

them or contacting them again I'd be strung up and
castrated. Brothers and sisters, if you had seen the
look in his eyes, you'd have known that was no joke.

So I went back to Laurel and smoked away everything
I had left. And then I smoked away a whole bunch
of what I didn't have. And then I started stealing
things that weren't mine and smoking those.
Brothers and sisters, I descended into the depths of
Hell, where I laughed with Lucifer and made love
to his dastardly disciples. I stayed there for three
years, smoking and doping, hooking and whoring,
wheeling, dealing, and stealing. When I was near
a point where I believed I was shutting down and
about to leave my earthly body, I had a revelation,
brothers and sisters, a tremendous revelation, and
I was born again, born again into the heart, soul, and
spirit of the man who became my best friend and
mentor, the man I believed to be the power and the
glory, the mighty Almighty himself, the Prophet and
the Son, our Judge and Redeemer, the Lord and
Savior Jesus Christ.

It happened in a rotten old basement of a rotten old
abandoned shack that a bunch of crack smokers used
to hide out in and get high. We were like a bunch of
rats. Gray and stinky and dirty, greedy and hungry,
willing to crawl through a world of shit just to feed
ourselves. I had been having some pains in my chest
from lack of proper diet and too much of the drug and
had been in a fight with another man over rocks
he claimed I owed him. He showed up angry and

fixing for a fight. I didn't want to fight, so I tried
to ignore the man, which made him angry as a
cut snake. He picked up a brick and smashed it
right against my head, knocking me literally and
figuratively right into kingdom come. When I woke
up, brothers and sisters, there was light streaming
through a broken window and coming right across
my face. I heard the words, in a deep, strong pure
voice, you must be born again. I didn't know who
it was so I said who's that and the voice said
Jesus Christ and I said how do I know it's you and
he said look into your heart, my son, and I said what
do you want me to do, Lord, what do you want me
to do and he said you must be born again. I said I am,
Jesus, I am, what do you want me to do now and
he said spread the word of God the Father, preach
the truth of the Gospels of the Son, and fill the
hearts of sinners with the spirit of the Holy Ghost.
I said I will, Jesus, I promise I will.

The light went away and I stood up and brushed
myself off and walked out of the hellhole and went
straight to the nearest church and got down on
my knees and prayed. I spent two days praying.
No food, no water, and no sleep. When approached
by the clergy of the church, I waved them off and said
I'm conferring with the Lord, brother, I'll talk to
you when I'm done. Sometimes it felt like the Lord
was sitting right there next to me, chattering in
my ear. Other times I wondered why the silences were
so long. Near the end, I believed the Father himself,
the omnipotent one, the creator of all that we know,

told me that I was to go to the one city on earth
that held the greatest number of sinners, and the
greatest amount of sin, and start a church and start
saving souls. So there I went, brothers and sisters,
to New York, New York.

I walked the entire way. Walked with the shoes
on my feet and the clothes on my back and a Bible
in my hand. I was depending on the kindness of
strangers to sustain me, and, brothers and sisters,
as cruel and ugly as this world can be, there is much
goodness still to be found in it. Within a day I had
a full belly. Within two I had new shoes and new
clothes. Within three I had a couple of dollars in my
pocket. On the fourth I got a haircut and a shave.
Everything was given to me by blessed strangers,
all of whom I considered angels in disguise, angels
from Heaven sent to aid me and guide me, sent,
brothers and sisters, to insure my mission was
successful. Every night I prayed for several hours,
slept for three or four, and walked the rest of the time.
And while I was walking, every few minutes, I said
in a manner I would call and consider loud and
proud, Lord, I love you, I'm a humble man and a
humble servant and I love you with my whole heart.
After twenty-two days on the road, I walked across
the George Washington Bridge.

It was worse than I expected. I thought it a sinners'
paradise, brothers and sisters, a giant whorehouse
being run by the Devil. I found myself a place at
a homeless shelter. I stood on street corners and

preached the gospel of the Lord. I went to Central
Park, which at the time was a sinners' field, where
drinking and drugging, robbing and stealing, all
manner of sodomy and sexual perversity were practiced with impunity, and tried to convert people to
the ways of the Lord. I preached in Union Square.
On Wall Street. In Greenwich Village. I stood in the
center of Times Square, brothers and sisters, and
shouted the word of the Lord at the top of my lungs.
I felt like there were so many souls to save, so many
sinners, perverts, homosexuals, and Devil worshippers that needed turning or needed to be brought into
the flock of Jesus. I preached all day, every day, and
I have to say, brothers and sisters, because I believed
what I was saying with all of my heart, it was quite
wonderful.

I started wandering into the other boroughs of
New York, looking far and wide for people ready to
be born again. I got beaten in Staten Island by some
men in a Cadillac and threatened with my life if I ever
came back. Nobody in the Bronx spoke English,
and if they did, they looked at me like they wanted
to kill me. With all the Jews in Brooklyn, I didn't feel
like there was a place for me. So I stayed in Queens,
and saved a man, and then two, and then three.
Brothers and sisters, within a few months I had
my own flock. A fine flock. People who believed in
the righteousness of my words, and believed that
I was preaching the one true word. We started
meeting in the back room of a dry cleaner owned by
a man I had brought into the arms of Jesus. I started

collecting money after every sermon to start a real church. People started telling other people about my relationship to God and his Son, the Lord and Savior Jesus Christ, about how I knew his words and his Gospels, about my personal connection to Heaven above us, and my flock grew until the dry cleaner couldn't hold us anymore. And it wasn't just the numbers, brothers and sisters; it couldn't hold the power of our worship and devotion to the Holy Spirit, and it couldn't hold our love for God and his Son, and it couldn't hold the prayers we were sending on high. Lord have mercy, those were righteous days.

So I moved the church. We got our own building, one that used to hold an auto supply store. It wasn't pretty, but worshipping the Lord isn't about beauty, it's about spirit and devotion, and that was not lacking, brothers and sisters, we had worship and devotion in abundance. Around that time is when I met Jacob and his family. Jacob was a seeker, a searcher, a man trying to find his way into the heart of the Savior. He just didn't know how or where to go or have anyone to show him. He had been raised Jewish, and being a Jew had left his heart empty and his soul in turmoil. We met when I was preaching on a street corner. He walked up and asked for a pamphlet and I gave him one on the Second Coming of Christ, which I told him I believed was nearly upon us. He asked me how I knew, and I said no one but the Father knew the day or the hour, not even the angels of Heaven or the Son himself, but that it was my duty as a Christian to keep watch, and that my heart told

me I would see something soon. Jacob asked me if
I wanted to meet the Messiah, because he knew him.
It was like a lightning bolt struck me, brothers and
sisters, like the hand of God reached into my heart
and said yes, yes, yes, like the mission of my life and
my church had suddenly been revealed to me, the
way the missions of their lives had been revealed to
so many of the Bible's holy men. I asked him
who this Messiah was, and he told me his brother.
I asked him how he knew, and he said since birth
his brother had been identified by Orthodox rabbis
as the Messiah, and that he met all the criteria and
fulfilled all the signs. I told him the Jew Messiah
and the Christ returned were different things,
and his response was that Christ was the King of
the Jews and that it would make sense that when he
returned, he would return as the King of the Jews.
The logic was simple and sound, and I knew he
was right, in my heart, because God was telling me
so. Christ would return as he lived and died and
was resurrected by the Holy Father, as the King of
the Jews. I asked him where this brother was, and he
said he didn't know, that he had disappeared, but that
he would come back someday. Most people in
my position would have thought this kid was crazy.
But I was a believer in the Father, and his messages,
and his history of choosing prophets, and I believed
he worked in mysterious and unknowable ways.
So I believed, brothers and sisters, and I opened my
heart to Jacob, and took him and his family into
my church, where I taught them traditional Christian
values, and helped them rid themselves of their

Jewish faith and their Jewish traditions. He became
like a son to me, my closest advisor and my partner
in the church, which continued to grow, and continued to save souls from the Hell of eternal damnation.
And for years, we searched for Ben Zion Avrohom.
We searched all over New York, all over America,
and a few times we believed we had found his trail
overseas, once in India, once in Africa, and once in
China. We never lost hope, and I never believed the
Father and his Son, Jesus Christ, were sending me
on a journey that would not have an ending. I knew
we would find Ben Zion, or that he would return to his
family. And I believed he would lead us towards
righteous glory.

And he did return. He returned, and Esther found
him. And it was a glorious, glorious day. Only the
church elders knew of our belief in and quest to find
Ben. We had prayed daily for almost sixteen years,
and yes, brothers and sisters, we believed our prayers
had been answered by the mighty Father himself.
The Messiah had arrived. Jesus Christ, our Lord and
Savior, had returned. First time I saw Ben, I knew
what he was and who he was. Oh my, he was a powerful thing to behold. It didn't matter that he was on life
support, and had wires and tubes coming out of him
everywhere. He was glowing, brothers and sisters,
he had the glow of God upon him, the glow of angels,
the glow of Heaven, the glow of the Holy Ghost, the
glow of eternity. I fell to my knees and I prayed and
I thanked the Lord God for including me in his plans
and I asked him for the strength to carry out his

wishes. And when he survived the accident the way
he did, which only a divine being could have done,
and when he started having his seizures and speaking to who we believed was the Holy Father himself,
and when he started reciting Bible verses and
knowing the most ancient of the holy languages,
and not speaking in crazy tongues, like the Holy
Ghost makes some people do, but speaking in the
holy languages themselves, brothers and sisters,
how could there be any doubt? When something is
staring you in the face in your life, and you see it
with your own two eyes and feel it within the beating
of your heart, only a fool doesn't believe it to be true.
And my momma might have raised a lot of things,
but she didn't raise no fool.

We prayed for Ben to recover, though there was
never any doubt that he would. We allowed the
Jew rabbi to visit him, because Ben insisted on it.
We believed Ben would leave the hospital and return
to his family's home and would join the church,
as we believed the Father had destined him to do.
Both Jacob and I had had conversations with
God about it, and believed God's word to be true.
When Ben disappeared while meeting with the
Jew rabbi, we believed that the rabbi had taken him
somewhere. There was no reason for the Messiah,
Christ returned, the Lord and Savior himself, to
flee the arms of a loving family and a loving church,
unless someone forced him to do it. Jews had been
trying, and in many cases succeeding, to control
the world for two thousand years. They killed our first

Messiah, had him nailed to the cross and killed him, though thankfully he did it to redeem us of our sins. I believed that in their hands the power of Christ would most likely be used for a diabolical end. At the same time, every good Christian worth his salt knows that Christians are dependent on the Jews to bring about the End of Days. They have to be living in Israel, and Israel has to exist, for the End of Days to happen. The Temple of Solomon must be rebuilt. The war of Armageddon will take place on their lands. The trumpets will sound, and the four horsemen will ride on across the desert plain, and the Rapture will occur. Jews are necessary for all of it. Evil, I believed, but necessary. So we watched the Jew rabbi. We had people follow him. We tried to tap his phone, but we couldn't make that happen. There was nothing out of the ordinary. He went about his business in a seemingly normal way. We prayed extra long, and extra hard, and we asked the Holy Father for a sign to help us find his Son, and we promised that if we got him back, we would not let him go again. We read MSM newspapers and watched MSM news shows, even though we knew they were full of lies and propaganda, even though we knew they were controlled by Jews and homosexuals, hoping for a clue.

I saw the newspaper article on the black man's apocalyptic tunnel cult. The idea of it made me sick to my stomach. I believed that human beings were the product of God's glory and created in his image, and I can tell you, brothers and sisters, God would not approve of men and women living like worms in the dirt, even if they were sinners. After it came out, though, the Jew rabbi started acting different. He went to a bank, had long meetings with a lawyer, and went to the federal correctional center. The private investigator we had tailing him did some research and found out there was a man being held with the crazy black man that fit Ben's description. We believed that it had to be the work of the Devil, who never sleeps, never rests, and is always working to foment sin and evil in the world. The black man was surely an agent of Lucifer, meant to capture the Son and hold him in an attempt to pervert him, and when that failed, because no one and nothing can pervert the Messiah, the Son of God, the Lord and Savior, to kill him.

We immediately went to a bail bondsman. We had been raising money for a new church, in part to celebrate the coming of the Lord, and knew it would be irrelevant if the Lord were in prison. We also believed that when the lawsuits Jacob was filing on behalf of Ben were settled or went to court, our coffers would be overflowing. So we pledged our money, and the building we owned that held the church at that time, as collateral for a bond. A couple of the elders were worried, but I told them, if money can't be used for the glory of God and his Son, what can it be used for? And we wanted and needed to beat the Jew rabbi, who we believed was doing the same thing, though his sources had identified the issue before we did. That's the way I believed it was with Jews. That they knew everything first. And that was one of the ways they sought to control the planet.

So we went to the federal correctional center downtown, which is a cesspool of sin and degradation. We went with a lawyer and asked for information about the prisoner they were calling John Doe #4. Can you imagine, brothers and sisters, calling the Messiah, the Son of God, Christ returned, John Doe #4? It was a disgrace. It was an abomination. And though we could not tell the authorities, who I believed were evil and in legion with the Jews and the Devil, who Ben was, I certainly let them hear some of my righteous fury. We first saw Ben in a visiting room. Jacob and I and our attorney, Caleb, a fine Christian who believed in the words of the Father and the Gospels of the Son. He was led in with his legs and arms shackled, like he was some slave. His face was bruised and swollen, one of his eyes was black, and his lip was cut. He looked like he hadn't had a meal in a month.

We tried talking to him. He was very polite, but very distant. I assumed he was on some type of mind-control drug, which the government is known to have and use against people they believe threaten them. And the Messiah would certainly be a threat. The Messiah is going to bring it all to an end, or at least herald the end. Jacob hugged him and said we were going to take care of him. Ben said he was fine to take care of himself. Jacob said we were going to get him out of there as fast as we could, and Ben said he was perfectly happy where he was. Jacob told him how worried we were and how we had been searching for him, and Ben just closed his eyes and smiled. When I asked him if he wanted to pray with us, he told me I was free to pray, but it wasn't something that he did. I asked him if I had heard him correctly, that he didn't pray, and he said yes, you heard me correctly. It was mystifying. We were expecting a glorious reception from a holy man anxious to get into the world to spread the word of God. A holy man in the tradition of the biblical holy men. A holy man like Moses, or Isaiah, or John the Baptist. I was expecting to see Jesus before me. That ain't what I got.

We bailed him out anyway. I went to court, and we pledged all of the church's funds, along with the deed to the church property. Some of the other church elders thought we were risking too much, but I believed that if you can't risk everything for the Lord, and I mean everything, brothers and sisters, your life and money and family, then you must not truly believe in the Lord. For if you truly believe in anything in this life, be it God, be it love, be it money or greed, be it anything, you will risk all for it. And I did, hallelujah I did, I believed and pledged it all. I did not hesitate, not for one second, and in doing so, I thanked the Lord Almighty for giving me the opportunity to serve him. The judge issued a decree stating that Ben would be released into my custody and the custody of his family. He required that an ankle bracelet be attached so that Ben could be tracked. I objected, because I believed

the tracker would be used by the Jew and his allies
to track and capture him, that surely the device
must be part of the Jews' plan, and by association,
Lucifer's plan. Caleb told me to keep quiet, that the
judge was also a Jew. I knew then that keeping Ben
safe was going to be a battle. Jews, blacks, sinners,
and perverts, we were going to have to fight all of
them.

When we actually took possession of Ben, in a small
room at the correctional center, I was with Caleb.
Caleb was also a good Evangelical man, a member
of our church, a man of Christ who believed in
traditional American family values. He had been
an Episcopalian, but had left what I believed to be
a perverted faith, a faith that allowed women and
homosexuals a say where they did not deserve one,
a faith that was not in line with the real values of
the Lord and his Son, and found the true Christ.
He had become an alcoholic, despite attending his
perverted church's services every week, which to us
was a testament to the weak and blasphemous nature
of his church's faith, and started hitting his wife and
children without cause. He was born again after
he had a car accident. He was driving and turned
around to discipline one of his children. As he was
reaching for the child, he lost control of the car and
slammed into a tree. He woke up in the hospital
and thankfully, brothers and sisters, his wife and
children were fine. He was better than fine.
He said the Lord had spoken to him in the second
before he hit that tree. And the Lord Almighty,

in all of his grace, wisdom, and mercy, had told him
he would spare him if he devoted his life to his one
and only Son, the Lord and Savior Jesus Christ.
Devote he did, brothers and sisters. He left the firm
he was working for in Manhattan, what we called
the Devil's Island, and opened a practice devoted
to Christian causes. He fought for the unborn
children murdered in abortion clinics, he fought
against laws granting queers and faggots the rights
normal, healthy people deserve, he fought for prayer
in school and for creationism to be taught in science,
he fought for the right of Christian men to bear
whatever arms they choose in order to protect their
families. He was a nightmare for the ACLU, which we
believed did nothing but promote sin and perversity
and sought to control and subvert Christians for the
good of the Jews.

Ben walked in, shackled. Both Caleb and I fell to
our knees and bowed. We bowed before the Messiah,
as one always should, brothers and sisters. We had
met Ben before and had not bowed before him.
We weren't sure, before our first meeting, what he
would be like. No one, not even the holiest of the
holy, not even the most righteous and pure of the
Lord's flock, had met the Son of God before. He was
not what we expected, and when we talked about it
later, we realized that we should not have expected
anything. God is God. Omnipotent and almighty.
The creator of Heaven and Earth. The Judger and the
Redeemer. We did not know God's ways and intentions. We did not know God's plan. Only he could

know. And he revealed what he wanted to reveal. And we believed, and I still believe, that Ben was his beloved Son. And we also looked back, brothers and sisters. We looked back to Jesus Christ, the Lord and Savior, the man who sacrificed himself on the cross for the sins of humanity. We looked back to the man we believed had been reborn in the holy vessel of Ben Zion Avrohom. Christ was beloved by twelve men, twelve believers, twelve disciples, twelve apostles. He wandered the Holy Land, preaching the word of God. His message was unlike anything the world had heard before. His message was pure and beautiful and true, and straight from the Holy Father himself. His message was the future, and the world isn't always ready for the future. The world isn't always ready for the truth. He was a radical, brothers and sisters. A radical unlike any the world has seen, a radical sired for man by the ultimate authority on man. Christ was thought of as crazy by many. He was mocked and scorned. The rabbis of Israel laughed at him and dismissed him. His message was misunderstood and misinterpreted. There were only twelve who knew him in their hearts while he graced the earth. It took thousands of years for his true followers to find him, brothers and sisters, thousands of years. For people like me and my flock to be born again into the bosom of his love. Thousands of years and untold numbers of false churches with deviant messages. Thousands of years of popes and preachers and ministers and reverends and pastors spewing aberrant, heretical sermons and issuing meaningless edicts. They may have meant well, and their intentions may have been pure, but that does not relieve them of their roles as apostates. We determined, after much counsel and many days of prayer, and after untold numbers of conversations with God and with Christ, and after any number of intimate experiences with the Holy Spirit, that Ben was indeed the Messiah. We needed to accept him as such, and treat him as such, and protect him as such, and covet him as such, and worship him as such.

So he entered and we kneeled and bowed. I have never been so humbled, brothers and sisters, not even at the moment I gave my heart and soul to the Lord and was born again. As the guards took his shackles off, both of us prayed, and thanked the Father for his Son, and thanked him for the opportunity to serve him. The guards left but told Ben to stay and wait for the ankle bracelet. He stood above us, both of us still on our knees, still bowed. He spoke.
You posted my bail?
I spoke.
Yes, my Lord.
Thank you.
We are humbled and honored, my Lord.
Why are you kneeling?
We kneel before you, the Prophet, the Son, the Messiah, our Lord and Savior. We kneel before you, Christ reborn.
Please stand up.
We both looked up and stood. And there he was, brothers and sisters, the Prophet, the Son, the Messiah, our Lord and Savior. There he was, Christ

reborn. I could use words to describe him, but there aren't any that would mean anything. For the most profound experiences in our lives, and in the world, words are worth nothing. Can you describe love? Or death? Can you describe what it really feels like the first time you see your child? Or the first time your heart gets broken? You can try, brothers and sisters, but it won't come close to describing what it really was, or what it really felt like. And it was like that with Ben. He stood in front of us, scarred and beaten, sick and starved, the Lamb of God, the Light of the World, Ruler of the New Covenant, King of Kings, and we were awed. I spoke.

We are here to serve you, Mighty God.

I am a man.

As was Christ.

Yes.

Are you born of God?

We all are born the same.

Are you not the Prophet, the Son, the Messiah? Are you not our Lord and Savior?

Do you believe I am?

I do, my Lord. I do.

He stared at me, a slight smile on his beautiful face, his eyes black and motionless. It was a peaceful smile, still and calm, like the smile I had seen on so many images of Christ. Before I could say anything else, two men came in with an ankle bracelet and asked Ben to sit. They fitted the bracelet and explained how it worked, told him that the court would approve areas where he was allowed to be, and that the brace- let would track his movements. If he strayed from the approved areas, he would be arrested and his bail would be revoked. I was sick to my stomach. Outraged and offended. The idea that the government and the Jews could restrict the movement of the Messiah, the man the world had waited two thousand years to see, could track his movements like he was some dog? It made me want to kill someone, brothers and sisters, and it made me look forward to the reckoning of the Rapture. They would all burn. Burn in Hell, where they belonged. Burn while I sat at the right hand of the Lord Almighty. Burn while I enjoyed the spoils of Heaven as the pastor who saved the Messiah from death in prison at the hands of God's enemies. I believed they would all burn.

The men left and we were alone with Ben. He was wearing rags. Loose black pants and a black t-shirt and black plastic sandals. Rags I wouldn't want to see on the worst sinner, regardless of whether they deserved it or not. We had brought him a fine white suit. One we had purchased with church funds from the best suit maker in Queens. He refused to wear it, said he would wear the clothes that he had. I told him his family was waiting for him. He smiled and said nothing. I told him we were at his disposal, and that we wanted to help him spread the word of God on earth. He stood and asked if we were ready to leave. We opened the door and motioned for him to lead us. He stepped forward, and we walked down a hallway and took an elevator to the ground floor. Ben said nothing. As we walked out of the correctional center, three men stood outside the door.

One was in a shirt and tie. He wore a gun, so he must
have been some type of federal agent. The other
two wore the uniforms that all of the correctional
officers wore. They were clearly waiting for Ben.
I immediately thought they must be assassins. I was
ready to defend and die for the Messiah. Ready to
demonstrate my love for him and for his Father.
Ben smiled at them, and walked towards them.
He stopped in front of each of them and hugged
them. They held him tight. Like you hold someone
going to war, or going into prison and not coming
out again. Like you hold someone you love and you
know you are never going to see again. He spoke
softly to each them. Softly, so only they could hear
what he was saying. And I swear, brothers and
sisters, I swear on my life, I saw them change. They
physically changed. Like they went from being
weighed down to floating on air. Like they had been
sick and were suddenly well. And when Ben pulled
away from the last of them, he left them, and he did
not look back.

We had a car waiting. We had gone first-class.
A long black stretch limousine, with a driver in
a uniform and a hat. Just like my daddy used to ride
in sometimes. We had three Bibles inside and hoped
to read with Ben as we drove back. We had chilled
water and juices. It was first-class all the way, but
Ben did not want to get in the car. He wanted to walk
back to Queens. He wanted to walk across the Devil's
Island and breathe its polluted air and mix with its
deviant citizens. We tried to talk him out of it, but he

just walked away. There was no choice but to walk with him.

It was a mighty powerful thing, brothers and sisters. Walking the streets of the Devil's playground with one of the two men ever created powerful and pure enough to do combat with him. He walked slowly. He didn't say a word. We walked on either side of him. He moved his eyes slowly as he walked, looking back and forth. He was clearly seeing everything, hearing everything, knowing everything. Every now and then he would close his eyes and take a deep breath through his nose. Every now and then he would take a step in the direction of someone, usually someone who was poor and dirty, more than one of them a homeless drunk or drug addict. He would lift his hand very slightly towards them. I saw him do it towards a crying woman. A man in a suit on a cell phone. A cop in the middle of the street. A woman in a nurse's outfit running down the sidewalk. An Arab hot dog vendor and some Africans selling fake hand-bags. He would do it to children. He did it to all of the children he saw.

It felt like hours and hours we were walking. Brothers and sisters, my feet and legs were hurting. We went up the east side of the island. We went through Chinatown, the Lower East Side, the East Village. There were freaks and sinners everywhere. Drug addicts and homosexual perverts. Caleb and I each held our Bible in our right hand. We wore crosses around our necks. We stayed close to Ben.

He did not speak, so we did not speak to him.
We walked through Union Square, up Park Avenue,
through Grand Central Station, where hordes of
sinners got off trains to indulge in their foulest
fantasies. He kept lifting his hand, just a little bit.
Always towards people who made me sick, who
were clearly in legion with Lucifer. People I would
have avoided; people I believed the Lord would have
condemned. I was happy when we came out of the
station, which felt like the bowels of Hell. I was
overjoyed when I felt God's light on my face again
and could breathe God's air.

We turned east and started walking towards the
Queensborough Bridge. There was a big wind coming
off the East River, as if it was keeping the fumes of
evil away from Queens and Brooklyn. We entered the
walkway to the bridge on Second Avenue and started
crossing. It runs along the south side, facing all of
lower Manhattan, the towers rising with all of Satan's
menace. The walk is a simple sidewalk. There's a
stone wall three or four feet tall, with a chain link
fence built into the top that is about ten feet tall.
The wind was blowing fierce, brothers and sisters,
whistling. Caleb said he believed it was the echo
of the Lord's trumpeters announcing the return of
his Son to the one true church, our church. And that
was what it felt like. We were crossing the river.
The Messiah, the Son of God, who we had just saved
from the clutches of the government and the Jews,
and who had walked through the city, a newer version
of the valley of the shadow of death, spreading

blessings and grace, was leading us. Of course the
Heavenly Father, the Lord Almighty, the Ruler of
all there was and ever will be, was heralding our
return. It was a righteous moment, a truly righteous
moment. One of the most powerful any man, woman,
or child on this earth has experienced. I can't imagine
anything greater. Praise be to the glory. Praise be,
brothers and sisters.

As we got close to the middle of the bridge, and the
stench of Manhattan was fading, and the Lord's
trumpets were blowing, Ben stepped towards the
wall. Before we could say a word, he had climbed to
the top of the chain link fence. I swear I saw him jump
onto the wall and climb the fence, but later, after
everything else, Caleb said he floated up, like a gust
from Heaven lifted him and placed him there. And
there he stood. On a wire a quarter of an inch thick
running through the top of the fence. He was a couple
hundred feet above the river. His hands were at
his side. He closed his eyes and he just stood there.

We didn't know what to do. I was terrified he
would fall, though I also believed that if he did he
would not die. Caleb got down on his knees and
started to pray, saying Father God, I kneel humbly
before you in Jesus' name, thank you for allowing
me to serve you, Father God, and please show
me a sign, Father God, so that I may serve you as
you wish. He stared at Ben, said it again and again.
The wind started gusting, and I joined him on my
knees, and Ben just stood there. He shouldn't have

been able to stand on that fence. He shouldn't have
been able to keep his balance. The wind should
have taken him away. The sky was blue above him,
clouds drifting slowly past. Cars were blowing by
behind us on the bridge and we could hear them
honking and people yelling from their windows.
The quiet drift of the river was whispering beneath
us. And the wind, still there, was heralding his presence. It was the most beautiful moment of my life.

I don't know how long he stayed there. It could
have been two minutes or two hours. I joined Caleb
in prayer and I lost myself in the power of the
Holy Spirit, which we could feel around us the way
you can feel joy at a wedding or pain at a funeral.
When he came down, he didn't say anything;
he just started walking again. We stood and followed,
and neither of us said anything. Like I said, brothers
and sisters, sometimes words just don't work.

His family was waiting for him at their apartment.
Our brother in Christ Jeremiah was with them.
The women, as was their duty, had prepared a meal.
A simple meal. A meal just like what we thought
the Big Man, JC himself, would have eaten: rice,
fish, bread, water, and wine. Caleb and I were dead
tired when we got there. Ben didn't seem any different; he was fresh as a daisy. I wished he was in nicer
clothes, or cleaner ones, but the Savior makes his own
choices. I did not believe I was one to question them.
He reached for the door, which was always locked
with three locks, and it opened. He stepped inside.

It was the first time he had been inside his family's
home in sixteen years. His mother immediately
started crying. He stepped forward and put his arms
around her and said I love you, Mother. She started
sobbing. She put her head on his chest. He put his
hands on the sides of her face, and lifted her face
and looked into her eyes. He said it again, I love you,
Mother, and I am happy to be home. He stepped away
and towards his sister. She was looking very, very
nervous. Her hands were shaking and her lips quivering. He smiled and said hello, Esther, I love you.
He kissed her on the forehead and gave her a long
hug. He stepped away and looked to Jacob. Jacob was
very somber, and very serious. He looked very much,
brothers and sisters, like the young man of God that
he was. He was wearing a suit and a tie. He knew he
was greeting his brother, his flesh and blood, but he
also knew he was greeting the most important person
to walk the earth in two thousand years. He was
greeting the Son of God. Ben stepped forward and
hugged him and said hello, Jacob, I love you. Jacob
put his arms around him and hugged him back.
Hugged him strong and tight, like a man should
hug the Lord. It was the first time, in all the years
we'd prayed and worshipped and studied the Bible
together, in all the years, brothers and sisters,
that Jacob and I had been preaching the gospel
together, that I ever saw him show affection for
anyone other than Jesus Christ. Ben pulled away
and asked if he could take a bath. His mother
said of course and went to show him the bathroom.
Jacob led us into the living room, where me and

him, Caleb, and Jeremiah sat down. We related the
events of the day to Jacob, and then we got down
on our knees, arranged ourselves in a circle, and we
prayed.

Ben came down a little while later. He was wearing
the same clothes. I know Jacob had had his mother
and sister buy some new ones for him. We rose when
we saw him. Jacob asked him if everything was okay.
He smiled, and said yes, it is, thank you. He walked
to the dinner table and sat down.

Everyone followed him. Mrs. Avrohom and Esther
started placing the food on the table. Jacob insisted
he sit at the head of the table. Ben said it wasn't
necessary, that he was fine where he was, at the
end on one of the sides. When everyone was seated,
I stood and spoke.
Seven thousand years ago, the Almighty God created
Heaven and Earth. He made man in his own image
and placed Adam in the Garden of Eden. He made
Eve from the rib of Adam, and the first woman
arrived in Paradise. Satan tempted them, and man
fell. For five thousand years, the world was filled
with misery and sin. Two thousand years ago, the
Almighty Father sent his firstborn Son, the Lord and
Savior Jesus Christ, to earth, where he died on the
cross to redeem us of our sins. He was resurrected,
and took his place at the right hand of his Father.
For two thousand years, we have waited for Christ
to return to us, and to do battle with the Antichrist
for the salvation of humanity, and to bring about

the Rapture, where 144,000 of God's true followers will be lifted into Heaven. It has been a long wait. And there have been many, the Jews, the corrupt, lying Catholics and their Pope, the Lutherans, the Presbyterians, and the Baptists, there have been so many who believed and still believe they are part of the holy family. They are not, never have been, and never will be, and they will all be sent to Hell for their blasphemy, which is where they belong, for all eternity. For true Christians, for those of us who truly live by the word of God in the Holy Bible, for those of us who live by the example of the life of the Lord and Savior Jesus Christ, for those of us who have the Holy Spirit inside of us, the wait is over. Christ has been reborn, and the Messiah has arrived. And the Heavenly Father has been generous enough to have given this woman, a proud member of our church, the privilege of carrying his Son, and this young man, a pastor at our church, and young woman, another member of our church, the glorious gift of living with him as a child. And to us, brothers, he has given the responsibility of protecting and guiding his Son as he spreads the message of the Gospels, and the true word of God, as found in the books of the Bible. Let us rejoice. Let us praise the Lord. Let us pray. Everyone bowed their heads and prayed. Ben did not. I was surprised, but then thought it was logical that the Son of God would not pray to himself. After a few minutes of silent prayer, I raised my head and spoke.
Ben, would you like to say a prayer before we eat?
He spoke.
Would you like me to say a prayer?

Yes, we would all be honored.

Everyone was looking at him. He reached up and took the hands of his sister and mother, who were sitting on either side of him. The rest of us followed his lead and took each other's hands, and we were an unbroken circle of faith and love and belief in the Holy Father. Ben smiled, and he spoke.

Thank you all for being here to share this meal with me. Thank you, Mother, and thank you, Esther, for preparing it for us. I love you both, and I always have, and I always will. Let us enjoy.

There was a long silence while we waited for him. I was, and everyone else was, expecting something more. He didn't thank the Lord, didn't thank the Holy Spirit, didn't thank anyone but his mother and sister. It was shocking, brothers and sisters. We were all shocked. He smiled and pulled his hands away. I opened my eyes. I looked at Jacob, Caleb, and Jeremiah. We all seemed to be waiting for something. Ben stood and reached for the plate of fish and asked if he could serve us. I laughed, said the Lord certainly does work in mysterious ways. It was all I could say, brothers and sisters. Now I know it's just life. Life happens in mysterious ways. Ben served each of us. He acted like he was some kind of waiter. He asked us how much we would like and put the fish on our plates. He did the same with the rice and the bread. He hardly put anything on his own plate. Not enough for a small child. Two bites of fish, one or two of rice, no bread. It was like he didn't need food. He was beyond food. What he did eat, he ate out of a sense of manners. So that his mother and sister weren't

offended. Everyone watched him. He did not appear
to notice. When he looked up from his plate, he would
slowly chew his food and smile. No one spoke. I know
I had a million questions for him. This was the man
who spoke to God, was of God, knew things no one on
earth had known for two thousand years. I figured I'd
start easy. Always good to start heavy things real nice
and easy, brothers and sisters. Start with the small
and work towards the big. I spoke.

How are you feeling, Ben?

Alive.

That's good. Better than dead, that's for sure. Bless
the Lord for giving us this life.

He smiled.

Is there anything you want or need?

No.

We're very excited to have you see our church
tomorrow.

He smiled again. Nothing more.

Do you mind that I'm asking a few questions?

Ask whatever you'd like.

What does it feel like?

What?

Being the Son of God.

I'm a man, like you.

But divine.

If you say so.

You can speak to him?

Him?

God.

In a way, yes, I speak to God.

What's it like? What is his voice like?

He smiled.

It's not what you would expect. It is not what
is written in the antiquated books you read.

The books of the Bible?

Yes.

Antiquated?

Yes.

The Bible is eternal, brother. As relevant today as
the day it was written.

The Bible was written two thousand years ago.
The world is a different place now. Stories that
had meaning then are meaningless now. Beliefs that
might have been valid then are invalid now. Those
books should be looked at in the same way we
look at anything of that age, with interest, with an
acknowledgment of the historical importance, but
they should not be thought of as anything that has
any value.

Brother, do you hear what you're saying?

Yes.

It's crazy.

What's crazy is living your life according to some
book written by someone who couldn't imagine what
your life would be like.

I respectfully disagree. I feel the world is very much
the same.

Do you live in a two-thousand-year-old mud hut
with no electricity, no heat, no running water, pissing
and shitting in a hole in the ground? Do you go to
an open-air market in a wooden carriage with stone
wheels, being pulled by an ox? Do you pay for your
food in trade with whatever you've grown in your

backyard? Do you cook your meals over an open fire made of wood you collected and started using a flint? Look around you. This world is not that world. That world is dead. Those books were written for that world. Those books are dead. They should be taken out of every church on earth and recycled, so at least they might do some good in this world. The oldest and most beautiful copies are historical curiosities and should be put in museums.

There was silence at the table. We were all shocked. Brothers and sisters, it was beyond shocking. It was blasphemy. Straight from the mouth of the Lord and Savior himself. Ben sat calmly, waited for one of us to say something. Nobody said a word. It felt like the moment after someone dies, and just before everyone in the room starts wailing. Heavy, brothers and sisters, extremely heavy. Finally, Jacob spoke.

And this is what God tells you?

God tells me other things. This is what common sense tells me.

Common sense is nothing when placed against the word of God.

And you think the word of God is found in the books of the Bible?

I know it is.

Did God write those books?

They are his word.

They are the word of writers. Men telling stories. No different than writers today who craft mystery stories, or adventure stories, or war stories, or stories of the apocalypse. Biblical stories were written decades, and sometimes centuries, after the events

they supposedly depict, events for which there is
absolutely no historical evidence. There is no such
thing as God's word on earth. Or if there is, it is not
to be found in books.
Then where is it to be found?
In love. In the laughter of children. In a gift given.
In a life saved. In the quiet of morning. In the dead of
night. In the sound of the ocean, or the sound of a car.
It can be found in anything, anywhere. It is the fabric
of our lives, our feelings, the people we live with,
things we know to be real.
I have faith the books are true, and I believe I will be
rewarded for that faith.
That is your choice.
I have faith that the stories in the books are true.
And that is also your choice, but it is the choice
of fools.
Faith is something for fools?
Faith is the fool's excuse.
Faith is a gift from God.
Faith is what you use to oppress, to deny, to justify,
to judge in the name of God. Faith is what has been
used as a means to rationalize more evil in this world
than anything in history. If there were a Devil, faith
would be his greatest invention. Get people to believe
in that which does not exist, and have them use
that belief to destroy everything of value in the world.
Get them to buy into an idea of something false, and
use that idea to create conflict, violence, and death.
If you opened your eyes, you would see that the end
is coming, that our world is going to end. And it
is coming, and it is going to end, because of faith.

It is coming because God has forewritten it.
Because man will cause it.
Because you have been sent to hasten it.
I will announce it, but not as the consequence
of a false prophecy, or the wild imagination of a man,
or many men, writing a book in a stone age society.
I will announce it because I see it before me. Because
all of the conditions for it exist. There is hate, aggres-
sion, pride, a lack of love and patience, a lack of
understanding, and there are weapons, weapons that
can end it all, weapons that can kill millions of people
in a second, and there are men, leaders of nations,
who are willing to use them. Apocalypse will happen
because of man, not because of a nonexistent God.
So you are not the Messiah of the Bible? You are not
Christ returned?
Do you believe I am?
I do not want to believe you are, but you have been
given gifts. You claim to speak to God. You are
Davidic. Born under circumstances which indicate
divinity. Born circumcised. You survived the unsur-
vivable. You are able to speak the ancient languages.
You know all of the words of the holy books without
having read them. And I have heard that you perform
miracles. Ben looked at him, same as he always was,
simple and direct, calm. Jacob waited for a response
and got none. He spoke.
Is it true?
Yes.
Then show me.
I don't think you'd like the miracle I would
perform here.

Let me tell you one I'd like to see.

If that makes you happy.

He held up his glass.

Turn this water into wine.

And after, I'll walk on water, or make my face glow,
or turn the food and drink on this table into my flesh
and blood.

If you can.

Those are parlor tricks, not miracles.

Christ did them.

He did, or so your holy book says. And every casino
magician in Las Vegas can also do them. A miracle is
changing someone's life. Freeing them from whatever
bonds tie them. Giving them the gift of being able to
live the way they dream of living.

So show me.

Ben smiled. He looked around the table. He stayed
on each of us, like he was trying to decide what
he was going to do, and who he was going to do it to.
We were all nervous. One of us was going to be
changed forever. I believed one of us would be blessed
by the Lord with a miracle from Heaven. Graced
by the power of God Almighty, through his one and
only Son. I wanted it to be me. I wanted to feel
the beauty of the Heavenly Father inside of me.
I wanted to be changed in whatever way God,
and Ben, wanted to change me. I silently prayed
for deliverance into God's hands. I had never
wanted anything more in life.

He stood and pushed his chair out and walked
around the table. We were all watching. We were

all waiting. And we were, brothers and sisters, all
hoping. He stopped in front of young brother
Jeremiah, who was the last person I would have
thought he would choose. Jeremiah was looking
up at him. I could see his lips quivering and his hands
shaking. He looked terrified. He was about to be given
the greatest gift a man could ask for in this life. He
was about to be given a miracle. Ben reached
out and put his hands on Jeremiah's cheeks.
Jeremiah smiled. Ben stood with his hands on
his cheeks and stared into his eyes. He didn't move.
He just stared at him. Stared right into his eyes.
Did it for what must have been ten minutes.
Not moving at all. Just staring. And we waited.
And it should have been boring, but it was beautiful,
and fascinating, and I swear on my life, brothers
and sisters, as Ben stared at him, Jeremiah changed.
His skin became flush. His posture improved.
It was like he changed from a kid to an adult, from
a boy to a man. We all knew something more was
going to happen, though. We just didn't know what.
Frankly, I wouldn't have been surprised if Ben and
Jeremiah had risen from the floor and started flying.
That's not what happened, brothers and sisters.
Not even close. Ben stood there staring, and then he
started leaning down. He leaned very slowly, staring
into Jeremiah's eyes the entire time. There was no
hesitation and no uncertainty. He went right in there
and kissed Jeremiah. Kissed him right on the lips.
And it wasn't the kind of kiss you give your grandmother. It was a real kiss. It started slow but got real
heated, real fast. Within a couple of seconds, they

were making out like drunk teenagers. Ben put his
hands on Jeremiah's shoulders and pushed his chair
back and sat down on his lap. And they were just
going at it. We were all too shocked to do anything.
At the time, I didn't understand what was happening
or why. To me it was just a shocking and disgusting
display of homosexual perversity and deviancy.
One man in another man's lap, kissing like they were
in love. Like the Holy Bible, the word of God, the
truest of the true, the most divine of the divine, said
was wrong.

I heard a fist slam down on the table. It was loud,
brothers and sisters, sounded like a gun. Everybody
turned except Ben and Jeremiah, who didn't seem
to notice and didn't stop what they were doing. Jacob
was standing up. He yelled stop at the top of his lungs,
but they didn't stop. In fact Ben's hands were now
running over Jeremiah's chest, and moving down to
parts inappropriate for a dining room.
Jacob yelled stop again, and Ben pulled away.
He turned towards Jacob and spoke.
Your miracle, brother.
You're a pervert.
If you say so.
Jacob started coming 'round the table.
You're not divine. You're not a man of God. You're a
foul pervert who is going to burn in Hell. Ben stood
and turned towards him.
If you say so.
Jacob moved towards Jeremiah, who was still sitting.
And you. I pulled you out of a den of sin, out of the

depths of Hell, from the grips of queers and sinners. I saved you. Brought you into the loving arms of the Lord and Savior Jesus Christ.

The closer he got the angrier he looked. His jaw was clenched and his veins in his neck were bulging.

How dare you faggots? Disgusting perverted freaks.

He rushed Jeremiah, hit him like a football player. He knocked him straight back over his chair and started choking him and slamming his head against the floor. Esther and Mrs. Avrohom started screaming. Caleb and I stayed where we were. We knew there was no stopping Jacob when he got something in his head. And for a second I thought Jeremiah was a dead man. That Jacob was going to kill him. Then Ben grabbed the back of Jacob's shirt and pulled him off. He dragged him a few feet back and pushed him down. Jeremiah was bleeding and had choke marks on his neck and stayed on the ground. Jacob got up and started after him. Ben pushed him back. Jacob screamed at him.

Do not touch me.

Ben looked at him, very calm.

Do not touch him.

I'll do whatever I want to him.

No.

Jacob went after him again, and Ben pushed him back.

You want to hurt someone, hurt me. He's walking out of here to live the life he was born to live.

Jacob pushed Ben. Jacob was breathing heavy, raging. He's going to die of AIDS and burn in Hell. You both will.

Love's going to kill us?

Jeremiah was up, crying, bleeding, breathing heavy. Esther and Mrs. Avrohom were tending to him. I looked to Caleb and back to Ben and Jacob, as if we should do something. Caleb shook his head. Jacob took a step towards Ben. God's gift to you and the rest of your kind will kill you. He pushed him. Ben just smiled.

You can't hurt me, Jacob. No matter what you do. Jacob pushed him harder. Jeremiah was on his feet, still crying. Esther and Mrs. Avrohom were moving him away. Ben spoke again.

You've always hated me. This is your chance. Let Jeremiah walk out and I won't resist. Take out what you feel about him on me. Unleash your mighty God's wrath.

Jacob pushed him harder. Ben glanced back, saw Jeremiah being led from the room. He looked back at Jacob, smiled. Jacob pushed him again.

That's it?

He did it again, and harder.

That's not much from a powerful man of God.

And again, harder.

Seems more like a faggot's push. You sure you aren't ...

And Jacob attacked again. He threw Ben on the ground and climbed on top of him and started punching him in the face and on the head and on his body. Ben did not resist at all. From what I could see, he almost looked like he was smiling. Jacob was screaming faggot at the top of his lungs, and just kept hitting him. Caleb and I both stood, knowing we'd have to stop Jacob at some point or Ben would die. We came around the table and Ben was clearly out. His body was limp and his face was covered in blood. It was also all over Jacob and all over the floor. And Jacob kept hitting him. Brothers and sisters, a man can only allow so much. A man can only watch so much. Whatever Jacob was doing wasn't about God anymore. I didn't understand or endorse gay behavior. Frankly, I found it sickening and wrong. But Jacob was killing his brother over a kiss. And kissing, and loving, whatever kind it may be, is not something the Holy Father would condemn someone to death for doing. At this point in my life, I believe—actually, brothers and sisters, I know—that God believes love, even between men and men, and women and women, is still love. And it is something beautiful, the most beautiful thing there is in this world. Let more of it exist. In every form. I say hallelujah. So we pulled Jacob off of him. His hands and face and shirt were dripping. He was still screaming, and we were struggling with him. He was yelling he deserves to die, I am God's soldier, he deserves to die. We took him out of the room and to his bedroom and convinced him that the best thing for us to do was pray to the Lord above for guidance and strength. I knew Ben was going to be needing a doctor. So I left the room to use the telephone. Caleb and Jacob were on their knees, holding hands, praying. The phone was in the kitchen, and I had to walk through the dining room to get there. I was going to check on Ben, make sure he was still breathing. When I came into the dining room, it was empty. There was a silhouette on the floor. And where the feet would have been, there was the ankle bracelet. I picked it up and it was still functioning. Wasn't broken and hadn't been cut. It was supposed to be impossible to remove it. But it was removed, brothers and sisters, it was lying there on the floor. I started to go back towards the other rooms to see if Ben had gone into one of them. As I did, I glanced at the table. And brothers and sisters, I am telling you, brothers and sisters, I am telling you because I saw it with my own two eyes, every glass on the table, glasses that had been filled with water a minute before, were filled with wine. They were filled to the top, and they were filled with deep red wine.

II MARIAANGELES

I was at home. Mercedes was watching TV. I'd just
got back from the hospital, where my momma was
dying. Alberto was in Rikers for killing some motherfucker. I heard a knock on the door. Figured it was
the cops or some bitch from child services. Either
way it'd be the same thing, some white person
making threats on me and my baby, some white
person saying they had the authority to tell me how
to live my life and raise my girl. Like they could do
better. With all their power and government money.
Look what they done to the world. They couldn't do
no better.

I opened the door. Ben was standing right there.
Or some fucked-up version of Ben. I hadn't been
seeing him for over a year. When he left we was
wondering what happened. One day he was there
being drunk and playing his video games, coming
in to the club all fucked up, the next day he was
gone. We didn't know where he went to. Figured he
got tired of living with black folks and took off.
It happens. People get tired of living with people
that ain't like them and they go back to their own.
And sometimes it's best. Sometimes I be thinking
black folk and white folk ain't meant to be together.
And you can give all the motherfucking speeches
you want, it ain't gonna change.

He smiled at me. Said hello. Some of his teeth was broken and he had blood all over him. His face was all cut and swollen, his eyes turning purple all around them. And underneath the blood and swelling, I could see there was scars everywhere, like he'd been in a knife fight with twenty men. And his clothes was nasty, something I didn't even see 'round here with people who can't afford clothes. He reached up and put his hand on my cheek and said it's nice to see you, Mariaangeles. I had men's hands on me all the fucking time. Men grabbing my ass, my titties. Men trying to put their fingers everywhere inside of me. Never had a man put his hand on me like that. Just being gentle. Just being kind. Most men looking for some pussy and someone to take care of them, cook their meals and do their laundry. That's what they think love mean. Ben just touch my cheek and say it's nice to see you, Mariaangeles. Nicest thing any man had ever done for me.

I was wondering what he was doing. His apartment wasn't his apartment no more. After he left it stayed empty for a few months. My brother broke in and stole the TV and the video games and all the beer in the fridge. Said he'd give it back if Ben came 'round again and ended up selling it all to buy a gun. After a while white people with clipboards and phones on their belts came 'round and opened it up. Some old man moved in and died like two months later. Went to sleep and didn't never get back up. Then some family moved in. Woman and six kids and her husband, who didn't do nothing but yell and

beat the shit outta all of 'em and blame all his own
shit on the Jews. He got arrested for something, don't
even fucking matter what, 'cause he just another
brother in the pen, and the woman and them kids
went back to Puerto Rico, where they from. Now
there was some girl like me. Eighteen and three kids
with three different daddies, none of them giving a
shit. Didn't think she'd want him coming in there,
and she could have pro'ly whooped his ass, specially
looking like he was looking. I was thinking what to do
when he smiled and spoke.
I need somewhere to stay.
And you wanna stay here?
Yes.
Why you thinking I'm gonna let you stay here?
Because I love you, and I can help you.
What the fuck you talking about, Ben?
Trust me.
I looked at him. More than anything, I was feeling
sorry for him. He was clearly fucked up. More fucked
up than me, more fucked-up looking than anyone I'd
ever knowed. He was all beat-the-fuck-up and skinny.
I wasn't worried about him hurting me. And I was
feeling a little guilty about taking all his money that
time at the club. So I opened the door. He smiled
and said thank you and stepped inside.

My place was bad. When I wasn't working, I was
getting high. When I wasn't working or getting high,
I was trying to be taking care of Mercedes. I didn't
have no time for cooking and cleaning. I tried sometimes to straighten up, but it didn't happen.

There was dishes in the sink, trash in the kitchen. Didn't have nothing but milk and water and old macaroni and cheese from the deli in the fridge. I kept my drugs and my pipes in Momma's old room, and kept it locked so Mercedes couldn't get at it. Me and her was sleeping in the bedroom I used to be sharing with Alberto my whole life. I hadn't done no laundry in a long time so there was clothes everywhere. Mercedes was sitting on our couch, watching some TV show about crime, which she was doing all the time. Ben walked in and went to the couch and kissed her on the forehead. She didn't pay him no attention. He turned to me and asked if there was somewhere he could sleep. I told him he could sleep wherever he wanted.

He walked over towards Momma's room. I told him not to go in there. He asked where my mother was and I told him she was in the hospital. He asked why and I told him she had some cancer that was killing her. He said I'm sorry and he reached for the door and I told him it was a private place and he shouldn't be going in there. He opened the door and he stepped into the room.

I didn't know what to do. If I should be stopping him or if he was gonna be taking my shit or if he was just fucking crazy. I walked to the door. My shit was on my momma's dresser, where I always left it. Ben was in the bathroom, turning on the sink and starting to wash his face. I could see him doing it real soft because he was all beat to shit. When he put some water in his mouth and spit it out, everything was red. When he took off his shirt, he was so skinny I could see all his ribs and veins and his whole body was covered with bruises, all purple and black, like someone went at him with a baseball bat. He looked over at me standing near the dresser, where I had me a vial with one rock I was trying to save and a pipe and torch. He smiled and said it's fine, Mariaangeles, I will not judge you. After he was done with his cleaning, he come back into the room and took off his pants and layed down on the bed and closed his eyes. He didn't do no moving at all.

He slept for two or three days. I kept checking on him 'cause he was looking like he was dead. Only time I saw him moving was a few times I came in and his eyes was open a little and he was laying on his back twitching and shaking and doing some kind of grunting, but it was real soft like a baby. I started getting high in my room and just leaving him be. I knew he'd be waking up or dying at some time or another, and I thought either way it happened he'd be outta my apartment.

Thursdays sometimes I'd work a double shift. All the white boys from Manhattan would come up 'cause it was right before the weekend so they could get drunk but they could tell their wives and girlfriends that they was out for business dinners. They'd start rolling in right after lunch, looking for black girls, all of them thinking we was gonna fuck them. After the shift I'd stay and get real fucked up, smoking just to forget the day, and then I'd be coming home. I'd have my neighbor watch Mercedes and I'd pay her and then she'd put her to bed and lock the door. I told her about Ben being sleeping in Momma's room and told her to pay him no mind.

This shift was worse than most of 'em, and they was all bad. Had a man who knew the manager and was old friends, some rich white man wearing a suit and living in a big house in Connecticut or someplace. The manager gave him a private room for free without any champagne tip, and I had to go back there, wasn't no choice in it for me. Man was mean and cheap and I had to do everything he wanted. Sucked his dick, let him fuck me, putting his fingers where they didn't belong. Went on for four hours, and when he finally left there wasn't nothing to do but go out and hustle and try to make up for the money I didn't make while I was with him. I went into the back room three more times. Let them men do whatever they wanted and got fucking paid for it. When I was done, I left and found a quiet place behind a dumpster and spent the next six hours getting fucking high.

I came home knowing Mercedes was going to be crying, like she always was when she was hungry and alone too long. I wasn't in no mood for it either. Just wanted to drink me some water and go to sleep. When I put the key in the door, I could hear some laughing. I didn't know what the fuck was going on.

I opened the door and went inside, and it wasn't
even looking like my apartment. Whole place had
been cleaned. Like it was all shining. There was
some spaghetti cooking in the kitchen. And Ben
and Mercedes was both all cleaned up too, and they
was standing in the middle of the living room,
laughing and dancing together. Ben looked over
at me and smiled.
Welcome home, Mariaangeles.
What the fuck is going on here?
I'm teaching Mercedes to dance.
She know how to dance already. I taught her
how to dance.
Then I'm teaching her to laugh.
She know how to do that too.
No, she doesn't.
And what the fuck happened to my apartment?
Your life is going to change, Mariaangeles.
I don't want it to change.
Yes, you do.
No, I don't.
Yes, you do.
He walked over to me, holding Mercedes' hand.
I wasn't sure what to do. He was just smiling at me.
And my little girl was smiling at me, smiling real
wide. I hadn't seen her smile like that in a long time.
In a long long time. Broke my fucking heart.
And nothing in the world more beautiful than
a child's smile. And there was my little girl, smiling
all wide at a mother that didn't deserve nothing
like that. A mother that was feeling like she didn't
even deserve to be living this life that she had

been given. A life she know now can be something she want, so full of moments like the smile of a beautiful child. Ben was right, even though I didn't want him to be right. Life was going to change.

As they walked to me, Ben leaned over and whispered something in Mercedes' ear. She smiled and went running right up on me, and I bent over and took her in my arms and gave her a big hug, a big hug like I didn't ever give anybody, not even her. And as I was holding her, she said I love you, Mommy. And I said I love you, baby, and even though I didn't want to be doing it, I started crying. And then Ben came over and put his skinny-ass arms around both of us. And he said I love you, Mariaangeles. And for the first time in my life, when a man said I love you, I believed it. I believed it with my whole heart. And he just stood there, holding me, while I held my daughter and I cried.

When we stopped hugging, Ben walked me to my bedroom and told me to get cleaned up and get ready for lunch. I took a shower and stayed in there a long time, thinking 'bout my night, thinking about what Mercedes made me feel. When I come out, I'm wearing my best sweat suit and the table is set all nice as it can be and there's spaghetti on plates and my pipe and three vials of rock I had are sitting next to my plate. Ben and Mercedes are sitting waiting for me. I look at the pipe and the vials and look at Ben. Why you putting that out like that?
Is there a reason you don't want it out?

I sat down and put everything in my pocket.
My daughter don't need to be seeing that.
Why?
You a fucking fool, man. Why you think?
You think she doesn't know.
She ain't old enough to know nothing.
If you say so.
I do.
You ashamed of it?
What do you think?
That you should stop.
You don't know shit, white boy.
He smiled and didn't say nothing. We started eating.
He was helping Mercedes using her fork. I just
watched her, and watching him with her made me
hate myself more, knowing what I had in my pocket.
I could feel it there. Heavy and bulging out. I was
always pretending Mercedes thought I was just
a regular momma. That our life was a regular life.
Or at least regular for where we was living, for where
we was from. I was just another girl with a kid trying
to do my best and struggling. And in a way it was that
way. But I was also knowing it was wrong. Knowing
I could do better. Even in the way that we was.

We finished our lunch and Ben told Mercedes it
was time for her to go napping and he took her into
Momma's room. I sat at the table and thought about
what was in my pocket 'cause it's all I wanted even
though it was hurting to think about it and I heard
Ben singing some kind of lullaby to Mercedes.
It made me remember when I used to sing to her,

before I was working at the club, before Alberto
got arrested, before Momma got sick. When he was
finished, he closed the door and came out. I was still
sitting and he sat down across and just stared at me.
His eyes was looking different from when I used
to know him. More black. Blackest things I ever saw.
And he had been healing when he was sleeping.
The bruising on his face was almost gone and his cuts
was healing good. It made the scars stick out more.
Made me be seeing them more. Made me really be
understanding how much he changed. He must have
been thirty or forty pounds skinnier. And he was
whiter. Most white people I don't notice. They all
be looking like they got the same skin. Just white.
Ben was white white. Paper white. And them scars
was even whiter. Like glossy paint over regular paint.
And he just stared at me. Them black eyes calming
me down so I could actually be feeling my heart
slowing down. And when I was real calm, and not
even wanting to smoke no more, I spoke.
What happened to you, Ben?
I changed.
No shit there. What happened?
It doesn't matter.
Does to me.
What matters is what I have become.
What's that?
Someone who loves you.
You don't know me well enough to love me.
One must know oneself to love, not know others.
You sound like a preacher.
I'm not.

You gonna try to save me?

You're going to save you.

How I'm going to do that?

Give me your pipe, your drugs.

What you gonna do with them?

Put them on the table.

They're mine.

Yes.

I need them.

No.

I do.

Why?

Because I fucking do.

Put them on the table. I'm going to show you
something.

You try to use them and I'll fuck you up.

He smiled, stared at me, waited. If I saw him on
the street, I'd think he was a crackhead for fucking
real. But sitting with him and talking to him, I didn't
think it. I didn't have no reason to trust him, 'cept
how he was looking at me, but I did. Trusted him like
I had never trusted no man or no white person ever.
So I took my shit outta my pocket and put it on the
table. Ben didn't even look at it. Just kept looking at
me. And then he stood up and walked around the
table and leaned over and started kissing me. Real
slow at first, real light, just brushing his lips right
against mine. And it felt good, felt right. So we started
kissing more, using our lips like we was meaning it,
using our tongues. Kissing like we meant it, like we
was in love. And he lifted me outta that chair, like I
weighed nothing. And he took off my clothes. And

he put me on the table. And he licked me, and sucked me, and fucked me till I couldn't see straight. Lying right next to my drugs. He showed me how to get high. He showed me what it felt like to feel good. He fucked me, and he loved me, and when he came inside me, it fulfilled more than any person, school, church, book, or God had in my life. He whispered I love you in my ear and he came inside me and it felt like I was right inside. It felt like what it was supposed to feel like to be believing in all those other things.

When we was finished that first time, he stayed inside me a long time. Just stayed inside and kissed me and held me. And then he picked me up, still inside me, and carried me to bed. And he put me down on that bed with his arms around me and we went to sleep. I didn't think about being poor. I didn't think about what I was doing for money. I didn't think about my brother rotting in a fucking cell. About my mother dying in a fucking hospital where nobody cared. About being black in a country where it means I ain't got no chance. About my daughter who wasn't gonna have no chance either. About a life stretching out in front of me where it never gets to be any better. The feeling of arms around me, of love in my heart, it was more powerful than any of the negativity I knew was existing in the world for me. That feeling of love killed it all.

When I woke up, he was gone. I went in to be looking in on Mercedes and she was still sleeping. I was supposed to be working so I started getting ready.

Taking me a shower and doing my makeup in the bathroom. When I went out to the kitchen, my shit was still there on the table. Made me fucking sick to see it there, made me sick to be thinking that's what I'd been doing for the last year. Made me sick to be thinking why I'd been doing it and why I was just getting ready. For money. For money that didn't make a difference. Didn't get me or my daughter out of anywhere or anything. Didn't change how I felt in my heart or how I was feeling when I looked in the mirror. Was just something I could hold in my hand. Money don't mean nothing when your heart is empty.

So I picked that shit up and threw it out the window. Figured some crackhead would find it and have a surprise, there was enough of 'em around. And I didn't go to work. Didn't even bother calling. They wasn't gonna miss me. They might not have even been noticing I was gone. Was gonna be easy to find another girl, 'cause they always too many out there willing to throw it around for the money. I ain't judging, 'cause I did it. It's the way of the world. You use what you got, and that's all that too many women got.

I waited for Ben. Mercedes woke up and I got her and gave her a big long hug. We went out and started playing in the living room, singing songs and tickling. I started getting a little sick, was starting to realize I might be needing the crack I throwed out. I went over to the window and looked down and it was still there. Was some kind of miracle it hadn't been picked up. I know in the Bible they be saying miracles is withering some motherfucking fig tree or some shit, but in the world I live in, the real fucking world, a miracle is a vial of crack lying on the ground in an American housing project unclaimed for more than three fucking minutes. But there it was. Tempting me. Calling to me. Not even calling, it was screaming at me. I could hear Mercedes behind me. I started telling myself love stronger than drugs, stronger than anything, love stronger, but telling ain't always believing. You can tell yourself anything you want, but until you believe what you're telling yourself, you're wasting words. I was ready to go down there. Ready to go. So I turned and walked towards the door. When I opened it, Ben was sitting on the floor. He smiled. I started talking.

What you doing?

Sitting.

How long you been sitting there?

A while.

Doing what?

Just sitting.

I looked at him. Just sitting there on the floor.

He smiled at me, spoke.

You want to go back inside.

I smiled.

Yeah.

May I come in?

Yeah.

He stood up and followed me back inside. We played with Mercedes for a long time, singing and playing with her toys, and the whole time I was wanting to smoke. Dinner come around and Ben serve us more

spaghetti. We eat at the table. When we finished I'm
feeling really sick, shaking, wanting to jump out the
fucking window. Ben have me put Mercedes to sleep
and when I'm done I come out and he waiting for me.
He take me to my room and lay me down and spend
the rest of the night licking and sucking and fucking.
And every time I got to feeling sick he do it again, till
I finally fall asleep.

And that's the way it stay for a few days, maybe
a week. Ben go out in the morning while I sleep
and find food somewhere. When I wake up he with
Mercedes, and whenever she nap or sleep or whenever I feel sick he take me in the bedroom or on the
floor or the table. And he was always telling me
he love me. That I'm beautiful. That I can live
however I want to live. That life can be beautiful.
That Mercedes love me and I can be a good momma.
And I stop hearing it. I start believing it.

And then one day I wake up and know. Know that
I'm okay and going to be good, or as good as I can
be where I'm at. And I tell Ben and he smile. And
I stop thinking just about me and ask him more
about why he here with me. He tell me about living
in the tunnels and being arrested and he tell me how
he leave his family. And how he skipped on his bail.
He tell me about his being able to speak to God.
He tell me that he know things about the world,
and that he know the world going to end if we don't
change it. That man is sick. That the leaders of the
world killing us all. Making us think we progressing

while killing us. And it ain't like there be some big grand plan, they just ignorant. And greedy. And thinking about themselves. And thinking about their Gods. Christians thinking they got God. Muslims thinking they got God. Jews thinking they got God. Everybody thinking God on their side. That God want them to kill and judge and dominate. And all of them wrong. All of them doing what they do in the name of something that don't exist like that. That fairy tales ruling the world. That God ain't part of the world that way. That God don't judge. God don't give power. That God something beyond the understanding of men or women on earth. That God ain't giving no gift of eternal life. The gift is the life we got, and when it's over, it's fucking over. No Heaven. No parties with relatives and people we love while the angels sing and play harps. No seventy-two virgins waiting for us to teach them how to fuck. No nothing. No God like we believe. Just the end. And all we got in the world is other people. And all we got with them is love. And not love like some dumbass pop song. Love is just taking care of each other, and fucking each other, and letting each other live how we want to be living. And protecting each other from all the shit that life throws us. That comes at us because that's fucking life, not because some fake silly God is trying to test us, or prepare us for the afterlife, or because he thinks we strong enough to deal with it. Bad shit just happens. Ain't no reason for it 'cept that it's life. It ain't no fucking God. And everything he say making sense to me. Making more sense than everything else I hear in the world. Making more sense than the

bullshit politicians and preachers and popes spewing
out every day. Making more sense than the bullshit
in textbooks and newspapers and on TV news shows.
Making more sense than the bullshit laws our government be trying to make us live by. The government
that says One Nation Under God, but under what
God? The old white man God with a beard who say
blacks ain't got rights, Hispanics ain't got no rights,
women ain't got rights, gays ain't got rights, and no
one who ain't like him and believe like him ain't got
no rights. Fuck that. And fuck that God. And fuck
all the fools believing in that God. They can come
kiss my black ass, 'cause that ain't no kind of Nation
Under God, it's just fucking bullshit.

Life settled down for me and Mercedes and Ben.
I started taking me some GED classes and got
Mercedes in a daycare program in the project.
It wasn't all daisies and bunnies and hugs, but it was
better than sitting and watching TV. Ben would leave
for the day. Said he would just wander around New
York. Walk or get on the train and get off wherever
he felt like it. Said he would just see people and talk
to them and help them and love them. I know he was
fucking some of them, 'cause I could smell it on him
when he came back. Sometimes I'd ask him who
and sometimes it was a woman, sometimes a man.
I'd ask how he'd be helping people and he'd say
however they needed it. I asked him how he loved
them and he said however they needed it. I know he
talked to some of them about how he could speak to
God, about what God really is, about the way he

saw the world. About how it going to end. And people
believed him. They started showing up at my apartment. Sometimes they brought gifts, brought food or
clothes, sometimes they brought money. Sometimes
they'd be crying. Sometimes they'd be fucked up
on drugs or drunk. If he was home he'd let them in.
Some of them he'd take in his arms and whisper
in their ear. Some he'd sit with on the couch and take
their hands and stare at them. Sometimes he'd
stand by the window with them and talk real soft.
Some he'd take in the bedroom, men and women
both, and he'd close the door, and I know he'd be
fucking them, and loving them, and making them
better, same as he did to me. Some he put his hands
on their cheeks and he'd kiss them real light.
I don't know what he was ever saying or doing
to them people, but they'd leave better. They'd leave
different. They'd leave with that true belief in their
heart. And they'd be telling other people. So Ben
started having people saying things about him.
That he had powers. That he could perform miracles.
That he could save you or change you or make
your life better. That he was a prophet. That he was
a holy man. That Christ had come back. That he
was the Messiah. The Messiah the world been
waiting for and praying for and worshipping for,
that he was the man come to save us or let us all die.
He never said nothing about anything of that.
People would say things to him about it and he'd
smile and say nothing at all or say if you say so.
What he told me was important was him loving all
the people and making them so they was leaving

better than they was when they came. That was what
God was. Making people still living their lives in
this world feel better. All the rest was just made-up
fantasy stories.

When it was just us, it was like we was married,
but not hating each other like most married people
being. Was like we was a couple. He didn't seem
to be loving me any more or any different than
anyone else, but we was together, and he always
came back, even when he'd be gone for a night or two,
and I was always knowing he'd come back, never
doubting nothing. It didn't matter I was only nineteen and he was thirty-one, and it didn't matter
we was different colors and had been raised different
or that our parents was from different countries,
speaking different languages and believing in
different Gods. We just loved each other. Didn't want
each other to be no different. Didn't bitch about what
we didn't like 'bout each other. Was accepting of
each other as human fucking beings. Who felt the
same shit. Knew the same kind of pain. And knew
that love was the only weapon against that pain.
Nothing else can end it or stop it. That's what
Ben taught me more than anything. That we got this
gift of life and we got it one time and we gonna get
hurt in it and be hurt going through it and the only
thing that'll make that hurt better or hurt less is love.
And part of our love was fucking. Ben loved to fuck.
He loved to kiss me and lick my body and suck on
everything I got. When Mercedes was sleeping
and no one was knocking on the door, we'd spend all

our time fucking. Fucked for hours and hours.
He never got tired of fucking. Said coming was the
closest thing any human on earth would ever know
about Heaven. That there wasn't no pearly gates,
no trumpeters, no man waiting with some book 'bout
all the good shit and bad shit we supposedly done in
our lives, 'specially when most of what we do ain't
good or bad, just boring. That there ain't no one
gonna judge us and decide we can be in that all-time
never-ending party or get sent to burn. That there
ain't no party like that, just like there ain't no ball
for Cinderella and her sisters, or prom for Barbie,
or labyrinth with a bull that gonna eat your ass up.
But there's the feeling you get when you cum.
When everything disappears. When your body
tells you it loves you and everything in the world is
perfect and secure and safe. When you feel better
than you ever feel any other time in your life.
That feeling you wish wouldn't never end. He said
people that try to say it's wrong is just stupid. That
people who say fucking is wrong is just stupid. That
say you got to fuck under certain conditions laid out
by God are just fucking stupid. No one should tell
other people how to fuck. Said people who take vows
not to do it are denying themself one of the greatest
gifts we got in the world. That men in silly robes singing songs in dead languages who ain't never fucked
in their life certainly got no right. That maybe if they
fucked, they'd understand God in a way no book and
no cardinal and no pope could ever be telling them.
He said if everyone who went to church or temple or
mosque spent all that wasted time fucking instead

of praying to made-up shit, the world wouldn't be ending soon. And he right. And you know he right. If you look in your heart, and if you've ever cum in your life, you know he absolutely right.

After my classes and before I'd get Mercedes and go home, I'd go see my momma. They had moved her to some place where people watched her and tried to make sure she was comfortable and she lied in a bed and her body was just wasting away. She was hurting real bad. Her body eating itself. Eating all its organs and eating all its bones. Cancer everywhere and no way to do a thing about it. There wasn't ever a thing to do about it. Most days I was strong and I'd hold her hand. Some days I'd just sit by her bed and cry. They'd just be giving her more and more drugs. Drugs that make her someone she wasn't, make her something not even a person. Just some flesh lying there breathing. You ever sat by the bed of someone dying you know what it's like. There ain't nothing you can do. You just sit there feeling pain like nothing else on earth. You sit there feeling help-less and empty. When they awake, every second you sit with them you know that they gonna die soon. Every word you say got this weight on it 'cause you know there ain't gonna be many more words. Everyone comes into the room do their best to be happy and seem cheery. To be talking about shit that ain't got nothing to do with death. But it's always there. The sickness. The death. The fact there ain't nothing to do about it. The fact that they won't be no more. That they gonna go in the ground and rot.

And that you gonna go on living. And you can say whatever you want and tell them you love them and do everything in the world to make their passing easier, but it don't change. They feel the pain. And the only way to stop the pain is load up on so many drugs that you a vegetable, or die. And in the meantime, everyone that loves you just feels the pain. The worst pain you can know.

Momma was getting worse and worse, but not dying. Just being in pain. The doctors wasn't even around anymore. Just nurses and people doing their best to have her be comfortable. She started telling me she wanted to die. Every day she tell me she don't want to go on, that it hurt too much, that she ready. I tell her she gonna be okay, that she got to keep fighting, but she tell me she don't want to fight no more. That her whole life been a fight. Growing up in a shack in a broke shitty country was a fight, coming to America thinking her life would be better was a fight, being in New York and realizing that nothing gonna be better, that the American Dream only for people with the right skin and the right accent was a fight. That raising two kids without no husband or man and without no money or family or help while she cleaned the houses of people who seemed to be getting everything real easy was a fight, that watching those kids drift and watching her dreams for them die was a fight. That getting cancer and not being able to afford to do anything about it was a fight. It was all a fight, from the moment she came screaming outta her momma 'til she ended up where she ended up, in some run-

down place with cockroaches and rats and crack-
heads outside and gunshots every night, what they
call a peaceful place where they send poor people to
die. She was done. She didn't want it no more. I cried,
wailed, sobbed, begged her, told her I didn't want her
to go. She smiled and said she loved me. And then
they gave her more drugs and she passed out.

When I went home I was doing terrible. I couldn't
stop crying. Mercedes come over to me, say it's okay,
Momma, it's okay. And it make me cry harder 'cause I
wish I could tell my beautiful little three-year-old girl
that I love so much and that I want to have whatever
she want in the world and that I would die for that it
ain't okay, that the world is fucked up, that pain and
suffering everywhere, that people hurt each other
and hate each other and kill each other for no good
reason, that we live and then we die and when we die
that's it, we gone, just fucking gone. I wish I could tell
her that she would be okay. That she gonna have a
great life, but I know I'd be a liar. She gonna grow up,
get hurt, and someone gonna break her heart and she
ain't probably gonna have what she want in life and
she gonna get treated like dirt and she gonna bust
her ass alone and then she gonna die. There ain't no
beauty in that, there ain't nothing but pain. So I cried
harder. For Momma and me and her and everyone
else in the world that ain't got and never gonna. I
cried and I couldn't stop. It wasn't gonna be okay.

Ben came in and saw me and asked me what was
wrong. I couldn't even be talking for a long time.

Just cried. And he put his arms around me. I wanted
some of whatever he did to other people to make their
pain go away. I waited for him to make me free.
He didn't whisper nothing in my ear. Didn't put my
face in his hands and stare at me. Didn't talk. He just
held me and had Mercedes come over and he put his
arms around both of us. And he just hold the both of
us. And I didn't stop crying for a long time. And then
I did. And Ben ask me what's wrong and I tell him
and I start crying again. Momma's in pain and she's
dying and there ain't nothing to fucking do. She don't
want to be living no more, say she ready to go, that
she love life but she in too much pain. And I got to sit
there with her knowing it, and feeling it, and hurting
so much it make me want to die, and there ain't
nothing to fucking do.

Ben waited for me to stop crying again. He looked
into my eyes for a real long time, then spoke.
You would die for her?
Momma?
Yes.
Yeah.
You love her that much?
Yeah, her or for Mercedes. I would die for them.
And you know that without doubt or hesitation.
Yes.
He smiled. He took my hand and he standed up and
he took Mercedes in her room and he put on her
best dress and her best shoes and he make her hair
pretty with some ribbons and barrettes. He tell me
to get dressed in my best clothes so I go to our room

and I put on the nicest I got, a dress I bought when I was first starting working at the club and was thinking that maybe church every Sunday would make me feel better. It was before I learned that crack was stronger than God. At least that God they be praying to on the cross.

We left the project and went to the place where they had Momma. She was awake when we went into her room, lying there, and we could hear her moaning as we came down the hallway to her. Ben stood aside and let us into the room first. Momma had her blanket pulled down so we could see how thin she was, how there wasn't nothing left of her, just skin hanging off her bones. Mercedes went running over to the side of the bed, saying Abuela, Abuela. Momma lifted her hand just a little bit, put it right on her head, said hello. I went over to kiss Momma and she try to touch my head but she couldn't be lifting her hand enough. I ask her how she doing and she shake her head. Mercedes give her a kiss and she try to smile but she couldn't really even be doing it, so sick she couldn't even be smiling at her granddaughter. I told her Ben was there, the white boy used to be our neighbor. Ben step behind me so she can see him. She look at him long time, like she trying to recognize him, and I'm thinking it's probably being hard for her 'cause he looking so different. I see her looking real close, and he just staring at her, right into her eyes, just staring. She smiled and say real soft I know who that is, thank you for bringing him, Mariaangeles. I ask her what she talking about and she try to smile again, and do it a little better. Ben put his hand on my shoulder and ask me real soft if I'm ready and I look at him and ask for what and he say to say goodbye. I look at Momma and she still trying to be smiling at me all skin and bones just lying there in pain and dying. Dying too slow. Dying without no dignity or peace. Dying misery and shit in a bed that's held way too many other people who died in it. Every time I looked at that bed I was thinking about how many people died in it, and how my momma was just another one.

Ben told me to go around and take Momma's hand, so I did it. He had Mercedes take her other hand. He whispered in Mercedes' ear, and Mercedes kiss Momma and say I love you. He looks at me and smiles and I know what he wants me to be doing and I lean over and kiss her and tell her I love her and I thank her for doing the best she could be doing. I hold her hand real tight and I tell her how much I'll be missing her and how I'm going to do the best I can to be a good momma to Mercedes. I start crying again. I know what's going to be coming. And even though it's what Momma wants and is the right thing, I start crying.

Ben stepped around Mercedes and sat himself down on the edge of the bed. Momma smiled at him, first real smile of the day. He leaned over and kissed each of her cheeks and her forehead. He took her cheeks in his hands and started

whispering to her, real quiet, and I couldn't hear
what he was saying. She was occasionally answering yes, and after he finished he pull back and look
her right in the eyes. He kiss her one more time,
and he tell her he loves her, and she says I love you,
too. He continue to stare at her, right into her
eyes, and I see her eyes start to slowly close. I start
crying harder. I know when them eyes close they
ain't going to open again. Mercedes is saying Abuela
over and over again, like she think her grandma is
going to be able to say something back. And Ben
just stared at her, and she stared back at him, and
just before she went, before her eyes closed for good
and she went into the blackness, I saw peace in 'em.
I saw calm. I saw happiness. And I saw that little
thing you see in someone's eyes when they got love
in their heart.
More than anything else.
I saw love.

MARK

One of my parishioners came to my office and told
me someone was having a seizure in the restroom.
It was the third or fourth time that this exact
situation had come up, someone telling me about
a seizing man in the restroom, except whenever
I went to check, the restroom was empty. Despite this,
I immediately went to the restroom to check again,
concerned for the individual's safety, if in fact there
was an individual. We had had an elderly parishioner
die of a heart attack in our lobby a year or so before,
and he was there, alone and on the floor, for at least
two hours before someone found him. Though I
believed that a church would, in some ways, be an
almost ideal place to pass on, I did not want another
death on the premises. The first one had brought
the diocese a fairly significant amount of unwanted
negative publicity, and had generated a storm of
paperwork. Given all of the controversies of the
past years, and my love for the church and desire to
protect it, I hurried to see if it could be avoided again,
or if I could be of any aid to the man who was sick.

I entered the restroom, the men's restroom, and
saw a man standing at the sink, washing his hands.
I immediately thought he was Jesus Christ. I gasped
and I was frozen and I could not speak. He had long-
ish black hair, a short black beard, and alabaster

white skin. He was extremely thin, wearing ragged clothes that hung off his body, and he was covered in scars. And he was glowing. Literally glowing. The restroom has no windows, as is proper for a restroom, and only one ceiling light, and I would swear on a Bible, or anything else I hold or held dear, that the walls were illuminated, and that he was glowing.

He looked at me in the mirror and smiled. He continued to wash his hands, very slowly and deliberately, very peacefully, if it is somehow even possible to wash your hands in a peaceful manner. I can only imagine what I must have looked like, standing before the Son of God, a man I had worshipped every day of my life, a man I had spent countless hours praying to meet. I couldn't move, and he just stared at me in the mirror. When he was done washing his hands, he turned and walked towards me. He put his arms around me, and I whispered My Lord into his ear. He held me for a moment and kissed me on the cheek and turned and walked out of the bathroom.

I stayed in the restroom for several minutes, standing exactly where I was when he left me. I was trying to reconcile what I had just experienced, which was, I believed, then and now, that I had been in the presence of Jesus Christ, the Son of God, the Messiah, the Savior, the earthly embodiment of the Lord God. He had smiled at me, and held me, and kissed me. He had placed himself within the sphere of my life, and my church, and my worship. I thought about how many people on earth could say that they had

had this profound experience, or could say that
they had been literally touched by the Lord?
Though billions and billions had prayed for it, and
continued to pray for it every day, Christ had not
appeared, or had not made his appearance known,
for over two thousand years. It was a miracle.
The greatest miracle. He had returned to save us and
redeem us. He had come back to bring about the glory
of the End Days. There are no words for what I felt at
that moment, knowing what I knew, or what words
there are, are inadequate. If forced to try to charac-
terize it, I would describe a feeling of great peace,
humility, and serenity, a deep sense of hope for both
myself and for humanity. A feeling of enormous satisfaction in that all I believed in had been validated.
And to be completely honest, there was something
electric in it, something ecstatic, something I had felt
only once or twice in my life, but never so strongly.
It was something that scared me because it felt like I
could lose control of it. And loss of control is always
the source of fear. It is also, however, always the
source of change.

After leaving the restroom, I went about the rest of
my day. I met with one or two parishioners during my
office hours, older women who attended mass most
mornings and whose husbands had passed away.
I went to a local hospital, where I pray for patients
two days a week. I had a simple dinner in my quarters,
which are in the rectory behind my church. I prayed
to and thanked God for blessing me with his Son's
presence. I read the Bible, focusing on the book of

Matthew, where the Second Coming is addressed in some detail. I prayed again and tried to sleep, but was unable to do so. So I stayed up, thinking about my life and how I had arrived at that moment, praying to a God I had met earlier in the day.

My childhood was, to say the least, troubled and difficult. My parents were Russian immigrants who had escaped from the Soviet Union in the '50s. Neither had believed in the Communist system, and both had dreamed of a life of freedom in America. In many ways, this is why they fell in love, or it was, in some way, one of the primary reasons they ended up together, for never in my life did I ever see any real love exchanged between them. Their fathers both fought in and died in World War II. My mother's father was taken prisoner near Raseiniai and died in a German POW camp, and my father's father froze to death outside of Leningrad. Their mothers both worked in factories near Daugavpils, and both were brutalized by German occupiers in the early stages of the war. My mother's mother had a child by a German as a result of a rape, and my father's mother was branded a sympathizer as a result of being forced to work as a prostitute servicing German soldiers. After the war, they were shunned by their neighbors and constantly harassed by the KGB. They were often taken in and held for indeterminate amounts of time at local prisons, and were denied the same rights as others who had suffered during the war. Also, because of this situation, neither of my parents was allowed to attend a decent school, or had a chance to become anything more than a basic service worker. They held jobs as cleaning people at a tank factory, where they met, and six months later they fled to Finland, initially leaving with four other workers from the factory. Though neither would ever discuss what happened during the actual escape, I know that all four of the other people they left with died during it. Once I heard mention that my father was somehow responsible for their deaths. I also know that they learned that as a result of their escape, their remaining family members were rounded up and sent to a gulag in Siberia.

Once in Finland, they went to the u.s. Embassy and asked for asylum. Because they had worked in a tank factory, the u.s. government believed that they might have valuable intelligence and flew them to a military base in Germany, where they were debriefed. Aside from knowing how to sweep and mop floors, neither of them knew anything. They were, however, given residency and sent to Detroit, and given jobs similar to the ones they had held in Russia, though this time in an auto-parts factory. They married, more because they knew no one else and had become dependent on each other, and I was born, though during my birth there were complications that prevented my mother from being able to have any other children, which she reminded me of almost daily for the rest of her life. They brought me home and continued on with their sad lives. They worked at the factory, and when they were home they drank and fought. My father beat my mother, and when I was relatively young, two or

three, he started beating me. We both learned to leave
him alone and not speak in his presence, though that
made little difference. As I got older, the beatings got
worse. At different times, both my mother and I had
our noses broken, our arms broken, our ribs broken,
and our teeth knocked out. The neighbors knew
what was going on, but none called the authorities.
It was a different time, and that was thought of as
the correct way to handle such a situation. People
at school knew I was from a troubled home and they
spurned me. I had no friends, and no teachers who
cared about me or believed I would ever do anything
with my life. When I was sixteen, my father went over
the edge. He saw my mother talking to a neighbor,
a man, and believed she was having an affair.
When she came home, he beat her with a wrench,
and when I tried to stop him he beat me. When I woke
up in a hospital room six days later, I learned he had
beaten my mother to death, and had hung himself
in his jail cell after being arrested for murder. To be
completely honest, I wasn't upset at all. I felt bad that
they had lived such miserable lives, but I felt relieved
that their lives were finally over. My only concern was
what I would do, or how I would take care of myself.
I had no other family, and I was entirely alone.
Soon, though, I learned I was not. A Catholic priest
came to see me and told me he had spent several
hours a day praying at my bedside. My parents were
both atheists, and I knew nothing of God. I did,
however, feel that this man was kind and pure and
interested in helping me. He gave me a Bible and
started talking to me about God, and about Jesus

Christ and the manner in which he gave his life
for the sins of man, and about the power of prayer.
I was in the hospital for several weeks, and over
the course of that time he indoctrinated me into
the ways and beliefs of the Roman Catholic Church,
and I became a Christian. He was the first person
to ever pay attention to me, and show me love, and
I came to love him in the manner I believe many sons
love their fathers. When I finished high school,
I entered the seminary and began training for my
life as a priest. When I finished, I took my vows and
entered the priesthood, believing I would devote my
life to the Father, and the Son, and the Holy Ghost,
and to what I believed was the one true church.
I believed I had found my true home, and that I had
found my true family, and that what I was doing was
the work of God, based on his word.

As I lay in my bed, reflecting on my life and praying,
I eventually fell asleep, though not for long. I woke
at five the next morning and prayed the Liturgy of
the Hours from my Breviary, as I do most mornings.
After praying, I would normally write the homily
for the morning mass, but I was feeling God so powerfully, and feeling so strong in my faith, that I decided
not to write anything and say whatever I was feeling
in the moment. I was very excited to celebrate mass,
which I do on most days, and which can be something
of a grind, especially on days when the church is
empty. On that particular day, I knew it wouldn't
matter if there were any worshippers or not. I didn't
believe I'd be celebrating with anyone but God

himself, who had blessed me so profoundly the day before, and I believed that none of the church's problems were relevant anymore, and that we were about to enter the greatest era in our long, distinguished history, an era when we would be proven righteous, and our glory would be confirmed by the Second Coming of Jesus Christ. The dwindling numbers of church members, and the aging of the remaining membership, would no longer matter. The controversies related to our policies towards women and homosexuals would cease to be. People would stop blaming us for the spread of AIDS in developing countries because of our stance on the use of condoms. And the never-ending scandals caused by the sexual abuse of children would end. We would be righteous.

I got dressed and left my quarters and walked to the church. I prepared the service with the deacon and the two altar servers and walked towards the altar to begin the introductory rites. I looked out into the church, and I saw four people, three elderly women and one elderly man, and the man appeared to be both homeless and asleep. Although this was typical of a morning mass, normally it would have disappointed me. This morning, though, it did not at all, for I knew at least three of these people were here to worship, and that at some point soon, along with the rest of God's true followers, we would all be in Heaven together. I began the service, and greeted them by saying In the name of the Father, and of the Son, and of the Holy Spirit, and my voice sounded pure and strong and true. When the people answered amen, I felt chills down my spine, and I thought yes, my Lord, amen, yes, my Lord Almighty, amen.

Normally, and according to tradition, during the Liturgy of the Word, I would read one passage from the Old Testament and one from the New Testament, but on that day I read two passages from the same book of the New Testament, Matthew 24:42-44, [42] Keep awake therefore, for you do not know on what day your Lord is coming. [43] But understand this: if the owner of the house had known in what part of the night the thief was coming, he would have stayed awake and would not have let his house be broken into. [44] Therefore you also must be ready, for the Son of Man is coming at an unexpected hour, and Matthew 25:31-34, [31] When the Son of Man comes in his glory, and all the angels with him, then he will sit on the throne of his glory. [32] All the nations will be gathered before him, and he will separate people one from another as a shepherd separates the sheep from the goats, [33] and he will put the sheep at his right hand and the goats at the left. [34] Then the king will say to those at his right hand, "Come, you that are blessed by my Father, inherit the kingdom prepared for you from the foundation of the world." Nobody noticed my indiscretion, not even the deacon, so I kept going, believing that God had endorsed my choices, and that he understood I was trying to alert people that his Son had arrived. The rest of the service was simple and beautiful, and as is the case sometimes with the things we do in life, whether they are part of our life's work, or simple tasks, or recreational events, everything felt right, and it was easy, and the time, which could sometimes pass slowly, seemed to speed up and move more quickly. After the mass, when I would normally go to my office and return mail and deal with administrative tasks, I decided to go for a walk through the neighborhood.

The church was in the Midtown area of Manhattan, on the west side of the island, in a neighborhood referred to as Hell's Kitchen. Directly to the east was Times Square, which, when I first started at the church, in the late '80s, after working first at a church in Newark, New Jersey, was a cesspool of sin, filled with pornography parlors, the streets teeming with prostitutes, drugs for sale on every corner. In the '90s, it was cleaned up by the mayor, a man I believed to be a fine, moral, righteous Catholic, a man who was holy without being part of the clergy, a man who was a warrior in the name of God and God's values. Hell's Kitchen, which had been an extension of Times Square, and a receptacle for the residual overflow of sin emanating from it, benefited greatly from the changes that the mayor imposed on the Square. Where it had once deserved its name, it became a neighborhood filled with actors, musicians, and young professionals who liked the idea of living near their offices in Midtown, and filled with restaurants and cafes and theaters that served them and provided them with venues. When I first started working there, I loved taking walks. While many of the neighborhood's residents were not Christians, or were lapsed Christians of some denomination, my clerical collar and position at the church commanded a certain respect. Shopkeepers were kind to me, and often went out of their way to help me. Policemen greeted me, and I often stopped and chatted with them. Mothers and their children would smile and wave to me. Even the prostitutes and drug dealers would greet me, saying things like hello, Father, how's the Big Man doing today? My walks made me feel good about myself, and about my choice to devote my life to God and service. I was proud to be a Catholic priest, and proud of my church.

Over the years, though, all of that had changed. My collar, for many, had become a symbol of shame and outrage. The press that resulted from the sexual abuse scandals had permanently altered the image of the church, and regardless of our individual positions on the issues, or our individual involvement in any of them, they had permanently altered how people viewed the men who served it. Inside the church, the most obvious effect was the number of parishioners who stopped attending our services. Outside the church, on my walks, I became something of a pariah. Shopkeepers were openly hostile towards me, and would sometimes ask me not to shop in their stores. Policemen looked at me in suspicious ways. Mothers and their children went out of their way to avoid me. I often heard people yell pervert or child molester after I had passed them. Once I was attacked and beaten. As I lay on the ground, being kicked and punched, I heard my attackers slurring me and slurring the church. I decided not to report them. And on more than one occasion, the doors of the church were spraypainted with epithets. I scrubbed them off myself.

All of this was heartbreaking for me. I had entered the priesthood in order to serve God, serve society, and do my part to make the world a better place. I had done everything in my power to live a life devoid of sin, and when I had sinned, I had confessed it and atoned for it. To know that, because of the actions of others, deplorable unforgivable actions, my life and work had been debased and tarnished was very difficult. It got to the point where I rarely left the church, and often when I did, I went out in civilian clothing so that I would not be identified as a Catholic priest. It was a nightmare. And not just for me, but for many of us in the church, or at least those of us who believed that some of the indiscretions had actually occurred. For those who didn't, and there were many, including Pope John Paul II and Pope Benedict XVI, there was no shame, just denial, confusion, defiance, and rage.

There was no nightmare, though, not on that day, that day after I had met the Messiah, the Son of God, Jesus Christ himself. There was only excitement and pride and tremendous optimism. I went out without an agenda, in my finest clothing, wearing my collar. The dirty looks I received did not bother me. The remarks I heard meant nothing. The way I saw parents hold their children's hands a little tighter when I passed was meaningless. I walked for three

hours, and saw the glory of God everywhere, in everything. The city had never been so beautiful, despite
the trash and squalor and desperation I saw, despite
the fact that most of what went on in the city was
done for the glory of money. I knew that soon everything would change. That soon, everything would
be done for the glory of the Son, and of his Father,
the Lord Almighty.

For the next several days, I followed the same routine.
I would take care of my duties at the church, and
celebrate mass, and in my spare time I would walk.
During every service, regardless of the number of
worshippers, I would scan the pews, hoping to
see him again. With every step I took during my
walks, I was filled with anticipation, and with every
corner turned, I thought he might appear. I stared
at the restroom door, and sometimes went into the
restroom, hoping I would find him again. I knew
it was only a matter of time. Jesus Christ would not
appear in my life once and vanish. I knew in my heart
that he would be back.

I saw him the next week during Sunday morning
mass. The church was about half full. I was performing Communion, and the parishioners from the
middle pews were at the rail. I glanced up and he
was there, sitting alone, dressed in rags. It was a
dreary New York day, cold and wet, and there was no
sun coming through the church windows. There was,
however, light coming from him, and light around
him, in the same way you see light surrounding

Christ in classical depictions of him. I froze for a
moment, and smiled, and was immediately flooded
with a deep sense of love, and forgot that I was in the
middle of mass, until the parishioner asked me if
I was okay. I looked down and said yes and continued
with the Communion, though I wanted to stop, stop
everything, and tell everyone in attendance that God
was literally in the room with us, that the Messiah
had arrived, that all our prayers had been answered.
As the service came to a close, I saw him stand
and leave. Part of me was crushed, but a larger part
of me told myself to trust God's plan, because
I believed God would take care of me, take care of all
of his people, and that all of what was happening
was happening for a reason.

He was back again the next morning. And two mornings after that. And then he was gone for a week, and
then reappeared again on a morning when there was
no one else in attendance. Each time I saw him, I felt
the same overwhelming sense of love. I felt the same
ecstasy and electricity. The same peace. And each
time I saw him, he stood and left just before the end
of the service. And each time I believed he would be
back, that it was part of God's plan, and that it would
unfold before me as it was meant to be.

He came again during a Sunday mass. And this time,
he didn't leave. As the rest of the parishioners left
the church and I stood at the door and said goodbye
to them, he stayed in the pew, unmoving, staring
straight ahead, the light still emanating from him.

I was not the only person to notice him. A number of people approached him, all of them clearly feeling something similar to what I felt, as I saw them kneel before him, at which point he would motion for them to stand or sit next to him. As each of them left him, I saw him hug them in the same manner he hugged me the day we first met, and I saw them change, physically change, as if something had been taken from them, something sad or unpleasant, something tormenting, something that had prevented them from living or feeling or believing in the manner in which they wanted to. It was striking and beautiful, watching the touch of one man immediately change someone, watching whatever their burdens were lift and vanish. It was something that only God, or the Son of God, could possibly have the power to do.

When everyone had left, and the church was empty but for the two of us, I walked towards him. He was still sitting, silent and unmoving, and with every step I felt my heart beat faster and harder, and my hands started shaking. I stopped at the pew, and he turned and looked towards me. I spoke.
My Lord.
He smiled.
My name is Ben.
I kneeled before him.
Please get up.
The Bible says let us kneel before the Lord, our maker.
And I say no man should kneel before another.

I didn't move, couldn't move. I closed my eyes and
held my hands in prayer in front of my chest. I heard
him move and felt his presence come towards me.
When I opened my eyes, he was kneeling in front of
me, his face inches from my face. He spoke.
You like this?
He smiled at me.
You think it's required?
I spoke.
I am not God.
He spoke.
No man is God.
Are you not the Son?
Do you believe?
Yes.
He smiled again.
Sit with me.
He stood up. I couldn't move. He moved back to
where he had been and sat down. I looked at him,
but still couldn't move. He smiled.
Come, Father. Sit with me.
I stood slowly. My legs were shaking and my hands
were shaking and I was both thrilled beyond
description and absolutely terrified. I took three
steps towards him and sat down. He smiled again
and turned away, looking towards the altar of the
church, above which was a statue of Christ hanging on a cross. I had a million questions for him, a
million things I wanted to say, but I couldn't speak.
I just stared at him, and he was beautiful, and he
was God. I thought of Psalm 34:5, They looked unto
him, and were lightened: and their faces were not

ashamed. I don't know how long we stayed that way, it might have been five minutes, and it might have been thirty, but once again, seeing him made me believe that my life's work had been worth it, that my commitment to God and the church had been worthwhile, and right, and just, and that God's light and glory would soon flood the world. He turned to me, and spoke.

You going to say anything?

I don't know where to begin, my Lord.

He laughed.

You look up there...

He motioned towards the altar, towards the crucifix hanging above it.

And you look at that piece of dead wood, beautifully carved, and beautifully painted, but still just a piece of dead wood, and you think it represents someone, and you think that someone is me.

Yes.

I'm not him.

You are.

I am not.

Is this a test?

No.

I know that God tests our faith every day, that being tested is part of faith.

God does no such thing.

And I believe this is exactly the type of test I would expect from him.

He laughed at me.

And I want to pass the test. I want to prove myself worthy of whatever God has in store for me.

God doesn't know you exist, and doesn't care about you.

I don't believe you.

So be it, but it is true.

How do you know?

Because God speaks to me.

Literally speaks to you?

Not with some silly voice, as it happens in the Bible.

Then how?

How doesn't matter. What does.

And what is that?

That this is all a fraud. This church, every church. That the world's religions are bankrupt and meaningless. That the world itself is bankrupt. That it's all going to end.

As has been foretold.

I know every word of every holy book ever written. None of them foretell what is coming.

Revelations does.

Revelations is a stone age science fiction story.

If that's so, who are you?

Who do you think I am?

Despite what you say, I believe you are Christ reborn.

I'm a final chance.

You're here to redeem us and forgive us.

There will be no redemption, and no forgiveness.

You're here to resurrect the dead, redeem the living.

I'm here to warn humanity that it is going to destroy itself in the name of greed and religion. That there is no God to save any of us. There is no Devil to take us to Hell. That man's only enemy is himself, and only chance is himself.

You're here to bring about the Kingdom of God
on earth, and to show that the Catholic Church
represents the one true faith.
Your perverted church has done more than any other
to bring this about.
If you feel that way, why are you here?
I've been going to churches, synagogues, and
mosques, trying to understand why people still
believe, despite the fact that what is said in these
places is ridiculous.
It's because God is real, and people know it.
It's because they're scared of death, and want
to disbelieve it.
The promise of eternal life is God's greatest gift.
The promise of eternal life makes people forsake
the life they're given.
Worship makes one's life better.
Love and laughter and fucking make one's life better.
Worship is just the passing of time.
I stared at him, and he smiled at me. And even though
I disagreed with everything he had said, or wanted
to disagree with it, his overwhelming physical pres-
ence, and the undeniable and unassailable feeling
that he was divine, and that, despite his denials, he
was the Son of God, made his words penetrate to
the core of my being, and the core of my faith.
He spoke again.
Stare at your cross.
I looked away and towards the crucifix hanging
above the altar. It was a realistic depiction of Christ.
Both the cross itself and Christ on top of it were
carved out of wood from an olive tree. The nails could

be seen through the hands and the ankles, and the look on Christ's face was one of peace, calm, and serenity. A crown of thorns could be seen on his head, and his eyes were open. Christ himself was painted in what I would call a realistic manner, giving one the sense that it was a close representation of what the real Christ must have looked like during the Crucifixion. I had seen it a countless number of times, and had stood beneath it while celebrating mass for many years. I had prayed to it, asked it for advice, begged it for help, and sought it out in times of strife and sorrow. And while it was, to me, a representation of the Holy Trinity and the Catholic Church, I would be less than honest if I said that it held my attention the way the man next to me did, or if its presence had the same power his presence had. After two or three minutes, during which the only sound I heard was the two of us breathing, he put his hand on my thigh. I felt an immediate, and extremely powerful, rush, unlike anything I'd felt in my life, something that was in my blood, my bones, my heart, and my soul, something that literally took my breath away. And as I turned towards him, he stood and leaned over to me and gently kissed me on the cheek, holding his lips on my cheek. I closed my eyes, and I felt myself become erect, a sensation I was not entirely comfortable with and had always resisted with the fear that it would lead towards sin, but that felt wonderful, absolutely and stunningly wonderful. He held his lips against my cheek for a moment, and then ran them slowly towards my ear, where he whispered.

Life, not death, is the great mystery you must
confront.
And he stood and he walked away.

Needless to say, I was stunned, and unable to move
or think, and I stayed in the pew, in a heightened
state, my heart pounding, my face burning,
my skin tingling, and my penis erect, for a long
time. When the physical sensations faded,
I started thinking about what had happened,
and felt a deep sense of conflict and confusion.
While I had never felt so good before in my
life, or felt love so powerfully, both physically and
emotionally, everything I knew, and had been
taught, and thought I believed, told me that what
had just happened was wrong, terribly wrong,
at best a sin and a transgression of my duties and
responsibilities as a priest, and at worst blasphemy,
heresy, and something that could result in my
spending eternity burning in the fires of Hell. In
my worship, I had never actually conceived, in a
real way, what it might be like to stand in Christ's
presence, to hear his voice, to speak with him,
and to have him touch me, to feel his love flowing
through and affecting every cell in my body and
every aspect of my soul. My thinking had always
been abstracted, about what it would mean to meet
Christ, but not what it would feel like to meet him.
And while I could not reconcile all of his words and
actions with those of the Savior, or what at the time
I believed might be the words and actions of the
Savior, the feelings I had felt when he spoke, and sat

with me, and touched me, and kissed me, and was
left with after his departure, felt very pure to me,
and very true to what I now believe Christ must have
made his believers feel. It was, more than anything,
an overwhelming and very profound sense of love,
innocent, unconditional, deep, and true. And it
was after feeling it that, for the first time in my life,
I truly knew what it meant to be close to God. Not
the Catholic God, or the Jewish God, or the Muslim
God, or any other God, but the true God. The God
that is life, and the God that is love.

When I could, which was at least an hour later,
and probably longer, I stood and left the church.
I asked the deacon to handle my remaining
responsibilities, and I went to my quarters in the
rectory, where I kneeled before a small crucifix
on my wall and tried to pray. I wanted to say
a prayer of examination and contrition, which is
something I said most evenings before I went to
sleep, in which I examined my thoughts and actions
and asked the Lord to make me a better person,
and a better priest. As I stared at the crucifix,
I kept thinking about what Ben had said, about
the cross being nothing but a piece of dead wood,
and I kept thinking of the feeling of his hand, and
his lips, and the difference between what Ben
made me feel and what the crucifix made me feel.
I recited the traditional prayer of contrition,
O my God, I am heartily sorry for having offended
you, and I detest all my sins, because I dread the loss
of Heaven and the pains of Hell; but most of

all because they offend you, my God, who are all
good and deserving of all my love. I firmly resolve,
with the help of your grace, to confess my sins, to
do penance, and to amend my life, amen, but I did
not feel any better, or any different. I kept trying,
and tried to put more spirit into the prayer, but
nothing changed, so I started praying, and speaking, directly to the Almighty Father, telling
him about the conflicts I was having, telling him
about the potential sins I had committed, and
begging for his forgiveness. Nothing changed,
and if anything, the fact that prayer was not helping
me made me think more about Ben and what he
had made me feel.

Whenever I was in crisis, or felt lost or confused,
or needed earthly guidance, I reached out to the
man who had brought me to Christ, and to the
church, a man I considered my father here on earth,
who had loved me more than my biological father,
and who had brought me to the Holy Father.
He had excelled in the priesthood because of his
devotion and piety, and had become an archbishop
of the diocese in Michigan where I grew up. I felt
like I needed him that day, and though Sunday is
obviously a busy day for a Catholic bishop, and
normally I would never expect him to take time
from that day, God's day, and a day when his
diocese needed his leadership, I believed I truly
required his counsel. It took two hours to get him
on the phone, during which I only grew more
confused and upset. When I heard his voice, and

heard him tell me that he would always be there
for me in my time of need, I felt better. I proceeded
to tell him the entire story, from the moment I first
saw Ben in the bathroom until the moment he left
me sitting alone in the pew, and I included all my
personal thoughts and emotions. When I finished,
he told me that he was happy that I had reached out
to him, and that my mortal soul was at great risk.
The first issue he addressed was the church, and
my feelings regarding some of its recent scandals.
He said that while priests were human, and thus
vulnerable to the same temptations as any human,
the sexual abuse scandals were, in large part, a
creation of the media, which was controlled by the
Devil. He said that many of the allegations were
invented as part of a smear campaign, and that the
church protected the priests because they had done
nothing except serve God, the church, and their
parishes. He said that the campaign against the
church was designed to destroy it, and was similar
in conception to the Holocaust. And though the
church did know of some transgressions, it had
always handled them appropriately, and had
done everything in its power to protect priests
from unfounded accusations. He said he also
believed that a large part of the campaign had to
do with depleting the church's wealth through
frivolous lawsuits, and he believed that if something
truly bad had been happening, God would have
stopped it. God, he said, always looked after the
interests of the one true universal church. God, he
said, would not have allowed anything so perverted

to exist within it. He reminded me that he believed God chose each of the priests who became ordained within the Roman Catholic Church, and that God did not make mistakes.

We moved from there to my specific experiences with Ben. He said he wholeheartedly believed that Ben was an agent of Satan, most likely a demon in human form, sent specifically to tempt me and destroy me. He told me that God obviously must have something greater in store for me if Satan was sending someone so powerful, and that I should continue with a strict prayer regimen, which would give me the strength that I needed to fight. He also said that if the situation got further out of control, the Vatican had a staff of approximately ten exorcists who worked exclusively in the United States. They could be called upon to confront the demon directly, and had the power to send him directly back to Hell. He directed me to alert the other priests in my parish to the demon's presence, and said that all of us should keep holy water on our persons at all times, and that when the demon returned, we should splash him with it. I thanked him for his advice, and he told me he was proud of me, and that he was excited to see what the Holy Father had in store for me. I thanked him and said goodbye.

I spent the rest of the evening in prayer. I slept for a couple of hours and woke the next morning and resumed my duties and worked according to

my normal schedule, celebrating mass, advising
and comforting parishioners, and doing paperwork
related to my church. Every free moment I had,
I spent either reading the Bible or praying, hoping
that God would respond to me in some way.
I wanted, more than I had wanted anything in
my life, to receive some sort of sign from the
Holy Father, some sort of indication that all of the
time I had spent on my knees and before the cross
had not been wasted. Because of what I believed
to be the gravity of the situation, I hoped to receive
something quickly, and though I had been taught
that God works in his own ways, ways that man
does not and should not understand, I was upset
when nothing came. A sense of loneliness, which
in some way had always been with me, but through
study, prayer, and activity I had always been able
to ignore, deny, or control, began to overwhelm me.
I had always felt that I was missing something,
or had lost something, or misplaced something,
and I assumed that that was a normal state of being,
part of the pain of being human. Within a few days,
however, the feeling became one of complete
emptiness, hopelessness, and horror. I started
weeping while I prayed, and weeping before
I went to sleep. I wept when I woke up, and I wept
whenever I was alone, and I had to force myself
not to weep in the presence of other people.
I didn't want to get out of bed and didn't want to
see anyone. The job that had meant so much to me
for most of my life had lost all meaning. It got to the
point where I started thinking about killing myself.

I knew it was considered a mortal sin by the church, that it was believed I would damn myself to Hell for all eternity in committing it. I also didn't know what else I could do. I had no one to talk to about the situation. I knew that my fellow priests would tell me to continue to pray and that through prayer I would find my way. I had no other friends, and no family. I no longer felt close to the Holy Father or Jesus Christ. I was absolutely alone, doing something that no longer had any meaning for me, and I wanted to die.

I tried to identify why this was happening, and it was obviously tied to meeting Ben. This led me to a startlingly simple conclusion, which was that in my entire life, as a child, in the seminary, and in all my years in the priesthood, I had never felt real love. I hadn't received it from my parents, my teachers, or my fellow priests, and, despite what I wanted to believe, I had never got it from prayer, from the church, from Jesus Christ, or from my supposed relationship with the Holy Father. I realized that the most powerful form of love could only come from another human being. That the love that was spoken of in the Bible could only exist in a person walking the earth, and could not come from a representation of that person, regardless of how beautifully it was made. That love was something real if it was coming from a real person. I realized that I loved Ben, that even after my limited inter-action with him, I loved him in a way that I had never loved anyone or anything. I also realized that, in some way, he loved me, that in his divinity, he expressed love for everything and everyone he came into contact with, and everything and everyone he touched. And for the first time in my life I understood Christ, and his importance, and I understood why I believed Ben was Christ reborn, and was the Messiah, as I still do. Like Christ, Ben loved unconditionally and without judgment; he loved men and women equally, and did not make distinctions between loving men and loving women; he made everyone who met him feel his love, and feel it in a way that was unlike anything they had ever previously felt; and he understood that religion as it was practiced had little to do with love. Love is something we must feel in our hearts, and in our bodies, and something we must express without fear of judgment or damnation. Love is something beyond rules and dogma. Love is beyond good and bad, or right and wrong. And love is beyond people who know little of it and have no experience with it deciding how it can be felt or expressed or who has the right to feel it or express it. I believed Ben would come back, and I decided to wait until I saw him again before I made any decisions about my future, though I already knew what I was going to do.

A week passed, and I continued to perform in my role as a priest, though it was entirely ceremonial for me. The words I spoke were empty, and I no longer viewed the blood and flesh of the Eucharist as anything other than what they were, and what

they are, which is cheap wine and bad wafers.
I spent most of my personal time sitting in the
church, which was almost always empty, staring
at the door, waiting for Ben to walk inside and
sit down, but it never happened, and I thought
constantly about what he had said to me the last
time I had seen him, how he had whispered life, not
death, is the great mystery you must confront in my
ear. And he was right. I had spent my life worshipping death, fearing it, obsessing over it, and living
my life according to what a book says will happen
when it comes. I had functioned as a missionary of
death for a dead church, praying to a dead man, and
I came to understand that it's no way to live, and
that living is all we have, and all we will ever have,
and that it is not to be wasted. That love is life.
That life isn't worth living without love. And that
the Catholic Church, filled with celibate men who
have no experience with it, has no right telling other
people how to love or who to love or what kind of
love is right or wrong.

I was faced with a choice, a very simple choice:
I could continue to worship a God who promised
me some kind of life after I died, or I could go live
the life that I have been given. I could kneel before
a statue, or I could find real people who might
actually hear me. I could preach judgment and hate
or experience love. It was an easy decision, and one
morning, three weeks after my meeting with Ben,
I took off my collar, and wrote a short note resigning
my position, and thanked the men I worked with

for their service, and walked out of the church.
I walked into the street, a street where I knew he
had walked, in a city where I knew he lived, and
I started looking for him.

JUDITH

I'm a light sleeper. A very light sleeper. I always
have been. As a little girl, my parents used to have to
turn off the television and the phones after I went to
sleep because if I heard them I'd wake up. And if
I woke up, I always believed it was because something
bad had happened, or was going to happen. I was very
skittish. Everything scared me. At school and later,
when I started working, even in my car, I was always
scared. I didn't like being that way, but I couldn't
help it. It's just how I am, I guess. Or it's how I was.
How I was until Ben. After Ben, everything changed
for me.

I've led a quiet life. Lots of people would say it
was boring, and they're probably right. I was born
in a small town in upstate New York. My dad was
a farmer who grew potatoes and raised goats.
My mom helped him and took care of me. I was an
only child. My parents both wanted a large family,
but there were complications when I was born and my
mother couldn't have any more. My mother blamed
my father for not getting her to the hospital early
enough, and my father blamed my mother's body. I
know neither of them really ever got over it because
they used to tell me about it. The fact that
I was such a disappointment didn't help.

I met Ben in New York. I love musicals and used to
go into the city once a year to see a show. I would save
all year and get a special outfit and a hotel room in
Times Square and go by myself for a fancy dinner
and a show. The next day I'd walk up and down Fifth
Avenue and look at the windows of the fancy clothing stores. I knew I'd never be able to afford any of the
clothes, and I knew they didn't make them for women
my size, but I loved doing it anyway. I always dreamed
of going into one of the stores and buying something,
a bag or a dress or some shoes, but knew I'd never
do it. Dreams are for people who can afford to make
them come true. For someone like me, and for most
normal people, dreams are just things that keep us
going.

I was sleeping when I heard him. I usually stay
in rooms on the first floor because they're cheaper.
And because elevators scare me, and I don't like
to use stairs. I had eaten a sandwich for dinner.
It was roast beef and cheddar cheese, which I love.
I had brought it with me from home, along with
a bag of chips and some diet soda, and I had had some
doughnuts for dessert, which are my true favorites.
I had watched a couple of TV shows. One of my favorite shows is a dance competition show. The men are
really handsome and always smiling, and the women
are graceful and wear the most beautiful dresses.
It's really like a fairy tale. And even though I loved
the show, and never missed it, it hurt me every time
I saw it. In some way, I know my parents loved me,
even though they had trouble telling me, but no one

else ever had. I'd never been on a date. I'd never
danced with a man. I'd never really even had a man
talk to me, at least not in a flirty way or anything.
And it was what I wanted more than anything.
Really, more than anything. To dance like one of
the girls on the show.

After the show, I had gone to sleep. I had even put
in earplugs because New York City is always so noisy.
But I woke up right away. First I heard a rustling.
Like an animal or something. It was a sound I knew
from living on a farm. My dad had all his goats, and
we had a couple of pigs, and there were lots of animals
living in the woods near us. Animals aren't so scary,
especially if they're not in your house. I thought I'd
wait and it would go away, but it got louder. I thought
whatever kind of animal it was, it was really loud. So I
got out of bed and I walked to the window and peeked
around the curtain.

At first I couldn't tell what I was seeing. There was
a dumpster right outside. The lid was open, and
there was tons of garbage in it. Something was
moving around. Really moving around like crazy.
I didn't want to open the window because I was
scared whatever it was would come after me.
And I didn't want to call the front desk because
I could tell when I checked in that they didn't like me.
I just stood and watched and hoped it would stop.
I thought maybe even it would die. It was banging
against the side of the dumpster, making really loud
noises. I knew it must really hurt. And even though

people try to pretend that pain doesn't do anything
to them, none of us can really handle it. Everything
bad we do in our life is because of pain of some kind.
I couldn't imagine what it must have felt like. Twice
I walked away from the window. I got into bed and
put in my earplugs and put my pillow over my head.
I closed my eyes real tight. I even balled up my fists.
I just kept hearing it, though. A banging sound
against the side of the dumpster.

Finally it stopped. It sure seemed like it took
a long time. I went back to the window and peeked
outside again. I saw a man lying in the dumpster.
He was pale, and his clothes were really dirty and
gross. He wasn't moving at all. He looked like
he was dead for sure. But he didn't look scary dead,
or mean or angry dead. He looked very peaceful.
And normally I would have been very scared.
I would have yelled or screamed. I might have hidden
somewhere. I wasn't scared at all, though. I actually
felt sort of wonderful. I just stared at the man lying
in the dumpster. I forgot about everything. I even
forgot I was me, which was something that had never
happened. After a few minutes, the man started
moving his hands and legs a little bit. I opened the
window and talked to him.
Hello?
He looked up at me.
Hello.
You okay in there?
Yes, thank you.
You were banging around a lot.

He sat up and turned towards me.
Yes.
What were you doing?
I was looking for food.
In a dumpster?
Yes.
That's gross.
He laughed.
There's lots of good food in dumpsters.
No lie?
He laughed again.
No lie.
What do you find?
What other people don't want.
And you eat it?
Of course.
Is it good?
People throw away wonderful things.
Did you find anything wonderful tonight?
He smiled.
Maybe.
I smiled.
In there?
No, I got interrupted.
By me?
By God.
Excuse me?
I was speaking to God.
Like God, God?
Yes.
God from Heaven?
No, the real God.

Who's the real God?

If a bird dropped a pebble in the same spot once every thousand years, the time it would take for that pile of pebbles to grow to be the size of the largest mountain on earth would be equal to one second of infinity.

Yeah, so?

He laughed again.

God is infinite. And like infinity, too vast and too complicated for us to understand.

Then why do people worship him?

They've been tricked into believing something that is wrong but that they can understand. Humans cling to what they can understand, even if it's wrong.

If that's true, then how does God talk to you?

The sound you heard was me having a seizure, and my arms and legs and head hitting the sides of this dumpster. In the second before I have the seizures, I see things, and I hear things, I know things, and I am told things.

How do you know it's God?

Because of what I'm told, what I'm given.

Which is what?

I speak languages I've never studied, some of which are no longer spoken. I know the contents of the world's holy books, word for word, even though I have never read them. I understand general relativity, quantum mechanics, string theory, astrophysics, quantum gravity, physical cosmology, and black hole thermodynamics, even though I dropped out of school when I was fourteen.

What's all that got to do with God?

The first things allow me to understand

God as God has been written, and portrayed,
and worshipped. As people believe in God.
The others allow me to understand how close we
are to understanding the real God, the God that
doesn't need to be worshipped, that does not
exist as we do, that does not judge us, that does
not offer us anything more than what we have.
You sound crazy.
He smiled.
I haven't told you the crazy things.
Things crazier than going into dumpsters for food
and ending up having a conversation with God?
Yes.
I'm not sure I want to hear them.
He stood up, and in the dumpster he was almost
at the level of my window.
Give me your hand.
Why?
I'll show you.
Show me what?
He held out his hand. I stared at him. He was very
thin, skinny like he was starving. And for the first
time, I saw his eyes. They were jet black, and they
should have been scary, but they weren't. They were
beautiful. And when I saw them, for some reason
none of the crazy things he was saying sounded crazy.
They sounded right, and I saw everything he was
talking about in them.
Give me your hand.
Why?
To let you feel some of the things God tells me.
I reached out the window, through the bars that were

covering it. As I watched myself do it, I couldn't even
believe it. I didn't like touching people. I knew they
didn't like touching me. Not only that, I knew people
didn't even like the idea of having to touch me.
I always believed I was a good person, and I always
felt I was kind and honest, but I knew what I looked
like. I had to face myself in the mirror every day.
I was, and I am, fat and ugly. It hurts to say it, but
I know it's true. People have told me all my life what
I am. They did it when I was a child, and all the way
through school. They do it at work, even though
I always smile and say hello. They do it as I walk
down the street, like they think I can't hear them or
something. And it always hurts. No matter how many
times I hear it. It always hurts. So I couldn't believe
this man was asking to take my hand. No man had
ever done it. Part of me should have been scared.
Once he had my hand, he could have done anything
to me. But I guess I didn't care. His eyes told me he
was something beautiful and eternal. And even if he
had hurt me, I would not have regretted it. Just to
have had it happen once. To have a man ask for my
hand, and to have a man want my hand.

It was a little cold. There was a slight breeze coming
into the alley. The dumpster smelled like bad meat.
I could hear traffic out on the streets of New York.
I could hear someone yelling the word tickets over
and over. The alley was lit by two streetlights.
They were yellow, and one of them kept flickering.
The shadows were moving with the flickers.
People walking the street were moving into the

shadows. I remember the moment very clearly.
More clearly than anything, ever, because it's the
moment my life changed. My hand went out between
the bars of the window. The bars were round and
painted black and some of the paint was flaking off
and my skin became cold, even though I was wearing
a long-sleeved nightie. He took my hand and held it
between both of his, and he smiled, and he spoke.
My name is Ben.
I had hoped to feel some kind of awesome romantic
electric charge, like from a TV drama or a romance
novel or even a Hollywood movie. What I actually felt
was even better. It was the best feeling I had ever had
in my life. My insecurity disappeared. My self-doubt
disappeared. My self-hatred disappeared. My sense
of disappointment in myself disappeared. The feeling
that I was bad and wrong and ugly and nothing, that
I was a fat, ugly failure, it just disappeared. That feel-
ing of being alone, always alone, truly and deeply and
horribly alone, disappeared. He held my hand and
smiled and looked at me. I smiled back and spoke.
God.
Yes.
I let go and smiled.
Thank you.
He smiled and stepped back.
I don't want you to go.
I need to find food.
I have food in here.
It's not just for me.
Who else?
My friends.

Who are they?

People who want to be loved.

What's that mean?

You know what it means. You felt what it means.

Can I get it for you?

No.

I have a little bit of money.

No, thank you.

I would like to give it to you.

I don't need money.

Why not?

Because I find what other people throw away.

And that's enough.

More.

He started to step out of the dumpster. I didn't want him to go. Ever. I knew that when he did, I would feel the way I always felt. The way I felt before him.

Don't go.

He stopped.

I don't want you to go.

He turned around.

Will you come inside, and sit with me?

Yes.

I'll meet you in the lobby?

Yes.

He turned and climbed out of the dumpster. I closed my window. I met him in the lobby a couple of minutes later. I was really nervous before he arrived. People were staring at me and laughing. I couldn't blame them, really. If I wasn't me, I would have been laughing too. When Ben walked in, everyone stopped. I was worried that they would stop him, or call the police, but everyone just stopped talking and laughing and everything. They just stared at him.

He smiled at me and took me by the hand and we walked to my room. I opened the door and we stepped inside. He closed the door and told me to lie down on the bed. I was really excited. Really, really excited. Super excited. I had no idea what was going to happen. Whatever it was would be great. And as excited as I was, I was also calm in a weird way. Much calmer than I would have thought. I wasn't shaking or feeling like I was going to cry or scream at all.

He turned off the TV and lay down next to me. I couldn't believe it was happening. He started asking me questions. My name, where I was from, what my parents were like, and what they did. As we talked, and I answered his questions, he moved closer to me, and put one of his arms around me, and took one of my hands. He was so close to me that he started whispering. He asked me about my child-hood. I told him it was unhappy. He asked me about school, and I told him it was always easy for me, but that I failed on purpose, because I didn't want to give kids another reason to hate me. He moved closer, and his hands started moving around my body. It was beautiful. Totally the best time I had ever had. And it wasn't dirty or perverted. His hands felt like they were part of my body. Everywhere he touched felt like it was absolutely the right spot, and the spot where I would have had him touch me if I could have asked him. We kept talking, and I started asking him questions. The same type of things he asked me. And he told me about his childhood, and growing up in Brooklyn. He told me his father hated him and beat him, and his brother hated him and beat him. He told me that his mother coddled him and that his sister worshipped him. He told me that he was Jewish. I had never met a Jewish person before, or at least not one that I knew was Jewish. He said his Jewish rabbis where his family went to pray had great expectations for him, and believed he would do great things, and maybe even change the world. I told him that must have been hard, that it was the opposite of my life, where nobody expected anything. He said it wasn't hard, because they were right about what they believed, but wrong in thinking about what he would do, and how he would do it. What was hard was waiting for it to happen. Spending all of his life alone, knowing it was going to happen, and just sitting around and waiting.

We fell into some kind of talking trance. He kept touching me and feeling me. He took off my nightie. And he took off my panties. And he whispered in my ear, and I felt him move inside of me. And it wasn't like some thunderbolt hit me, or like some passionate kiss in a rainstorm. It just felt full, and complete, and quiet. I felt like I could die at that moment and I would be okay with dying. I felt like however I had wasted my life, and whatever terrible things I'd seen and heard and felt, it didn't matter anymore. This man was inside of me and he was holding me and I was feeling love. True

love. The kind of love that really could change
the world.

We stayed that way for hours. For the whole night
even. He stayed behind me and inside me. He was
moving the entire time. Very slowly and gently.
Sometimes so slowly I could hardly feel him moving.
Sometimes a little faster. We talked the whole time.
I told him everything about myself and my life. I told
him how I lived alone on my parents' farm, which
was overgrown and crazy. How I worked as a cashier
at a superstore and tried to be nice but had people be
mean to me all day. How I lived in a dead town filled
with churches and bars and husbands beating their
wives and children. How I spent all my nights alone
in front of the TV, eating canned food and potato
chips and ice cream. How I cried every night because
I didn't believe anyone would ever care for me. I told
him about all my best hopes and biggest dreams and
my scariest fears. I told him all I wanted in my life
was a friend who I could call sometimes and say hi.
How I always dreamed about having someone tell me
I was beautiful, or even pretty. How I was scared I'd
die someday all by myself and no one would find me
until a long time after I was gone. I told him that there
hadn't been a time in my life that I hadn't been lonely
and that I didn't want to feel it anymore.

He told me how he lived with a woman and her child
in a small apartment. How he had been in jail and
knew people were looking for him because he had
jumped bail. How he spent his days touching people

and helping people and teaching people about
how to live in a world that is falling apart and dying.
He talked about love. How love is the only thing in
the world that is worth living for, the only good thing
that we have left, and the only thing we haven't
destroyed. That true love, God's love, isn't about
beauty or perfection or man or woman. That love isn't
about declarations made before false idols. That love
isn't what a bunch of hateful old white men decide it
is. That love isn't something that can be written into
laws by corrupt governments. He said love is something shared by two people, any two people, man and
woman, or man and man, or woman and woman, in
whatever way makes them feel perfect and beautiful
and peaceful in their hearts. He said love is what
I was feeling as he held me and touched me and
moved inside of me. He said that if I wanted to see
God, see God as he did, and in God's true form, he
could show me. He told me to close my eyes, so I did.
He moved his hand onto me and moved his body a
little more and he stopped talking to me and I could
feel his breath on my neck and my cheek. It built
inside of me. God built up inside of me. And the more
he moved, the more it built. And his breath felt hot
and smelled sweet. And he kept moving, real slow,
and moving real deep inside, and it built until I saw
it and felt it. It was love, and joy, and pleasure, and
every part of my body sang some song I had never
heard but was the prettiest, most beautiful song ever,
and it was blinding and pure and my brain went
the whitest white ever, and I saw infinity, forever
and ever, I saw infinity, and even understood it, and

understood everything else in the world, all the hate
and rage and death and passion and jealousy and
murder, and none of them even mattered. I felt one
hundred percent secure. I felt nothing bad. I saw
the past and the future. It was the greatest second of
my life. Really the greatest, and I knew in that one
second I was experiencing God. The real God.
The true God. The eternal God. The God that can't be
in a book or in a church or on a Sunday TV show or on
a cross or a star. The God that can't be explained or
described or written about or taught or preached.
The God that can't be forced upon people or used to
damn them. And I loved that God, that perfect
amazing unbelievable true God. And I knew that
none of the other Gods meant anything.

When that moment ended, Ben kept moving and
breathing very slowly. I didn't know what to say
and I guess I didn't want to say anything. Nothing
I would have said would have meant anything or
even mattered. So I just kept my eyes closed and
listened to him breathe and felt him. And it just
kept going, for the whole night, him inside of me.
His hands moving all over me. The two of us loving
each other. He kept speaking but I don't know what
he was saying. All I know is what I felt. God, God,
and more God. God all night. When the sun came up,
he stopped moving but stayed inside of me and just
held me. Finally I said something to him.
Ben.
Yes.
I don't ever want you to leave.

I'm going to leave in a little while.
Please.
Come with me if you want.
Where?
I have to find some food and go back to the Bronx.
What will I do?
Whatever you want.
What will your woman say?
She's her own woman.
What will she say?
She'll say hello, and welcome you.
He kissed me softly on the cheek and pulled away
from me. I felt him come right out of me. And not just
physically. I felt it right in my heart too. And I felt
like I had lost something. But not something silly,
like my keys or my gum. More like my arm or my foot
or something, something that really mattered.
Like something that I could live without, but would
make life much harder if it were missing. And life is
hard enough. Life is hard enough with everything
we're given. With what I used to think God gave us,
before I knew the truth. Before I realized that all that
Bible nonsense is just silly. That Bibles are just books,
like any book is just a book. Except maybe Bibles are
more boring and more ridiculous and harder to read.
And even though they say all sorts of things,
and make all sorts of promises, they're full of lies,
or lies if you're foolish enough to believe they contain
something real. I know that God doesn't give us
anything in life. So God can't take anything away.
But a real person can give, and can take away.
And when Ben was no longer inside of me, I felt

something was gone. Something that was more than anything I'd ever known. Something greater than a made-up God in an old dusty book.

He stood and I watched him get dressed. I felt sorry for him in his raggedy clothes. I wanted to get him some new clothes. Not that I could get him anything fancy, but I could get a discount on some clothes at the store where I worked. Simple clothes for a regular person. And I noticed his scars for the first time. Long thick scars over his whole body. They were really scary. Like someone had taken a white marker and drawn lines everywhere. Except I knew they weren't from a marker or anything. He had been really hurt. And I tried to imagine what it must have felt like to be hurt like that. And I could imagine it. That really truly awful terrible pain. The kind that can only be felt alone, and that no one can help you with. I really could imagine it.

As he was putting his shirt on, he smiled at me.
I knew if he left I would never see him again. I didn't want that. I couldn't even think of it. Of not having the feeling of being with him, or even near him again.
So I spoke up. For the first time in my life. A life spent not talking and hiding and being scared and alone.
He changed me away from it, and I spoke up.
I want to come with you.
He smiled.
Okay.
Really?
Yes.

No lie?

He smiled again.

No lie.

I stood up, and even though I look the way I do,
I wasn't even embarrassed. I started getting dressed
right away.

What should I bring?

You don't need anything.

Clothes?

He laughed.

What you're wearing.

Money?

Doesn't matter.

It will take me just a minute to get packed.

You don't need those things.

Will I be back?

If you choose.

You sure I don't need anything?

We don't need most of what we have.

I smiled, and pulled on my pants and put on my
jacket. He smiled at me while I got dressed, and
his eyes stayed on my body, and he made me feel
beautiful, which is something I had never felt,
not once, in my entire life. Once I was ready,
I grabbed my wallet and we left.

It was a crappy day. Cold and really rainy. It was the
kind of rain that hurts your skin when it hits it. It felt
like little needles. Ben didn't have a good coat. His
was an old brown sport coat like a librarian would
wear. It was really funny. And I don't think it kept
him warm or dry. He didn't seem to mind, though.

The rain hit him and he smiled. We walked along the street and he smiled. Everywhere we walked, he just smiled. He didn't talk at all. Sometimes he would take my hand. Like when there was a big crowd, or the cars were blocking the crosswalk. And sometimes I would get out of breath or have to slow down. He never seemed to even care. He would slow down and make sure I was okay. He was so nice and kind and gentle. It seemed like that was all that mattered to him. And it made all of the terrible things that had tortured me my whole entire life just go away. Kindness and love can make any pain go away. It's true. I know it.

After we walked a long time, Ben cut off the street and we went into the subway. I had never been in it before. I had always been scared to go under the ground. I thought I'd get mugged or bit by a rat or fall in front of a train. Or maybe I would just get lost and never find my way out. Or maybe people would point at me and make fun of me. I was just scared. Really scared. But Ben took my hand and we walked right down, and we waited for one of the exit doors to open and then we walked right through it. And we walked right to the platform and waited. I could feel people staring at us, but I realized they weren't staring at me. They were staring at Ben. Nobody was talking. And they weren't looking at their phones or little email machines or newspapers or the floor or even each other. They were looking at him. All of them, just silent and staring at him.

The subway train pulled up and we stepped on. There were empty seats and we sat down. I had no idea where we were going, and Ben and me hadn't said a word to each other since we'd left the hotel. There were a few other people in the car, and a few more got on with us. Everybody was sitting down. Ben closed his eyes and smiled and started breathing very deeply and slowly. It wasn't dramatic or anything, like some actress trying to calm down after being hysterical. It was just simple and pure. Just a man breathing. And people were staring at him again. Like they couldn't believe what they were seeing. Like their lives were all so busy that they had forgotten what a still silent man looked like. And as he breathed they all seemed to calm down. As if he were giving them what he had, or what he was feeling. Some of them closed their eyes and started breathing just like him. Some just smiled and stared at him. A few stood up and walked towards us to be closer to him. And at every stop more people got on the car. And whatever he was doing, he would do to every one of them. And even though it was roaring down the tracks at some crazy speed, that car was the most quiet and simple and beautiful and peaceful place in the world.

We stayed on the car for thirty or forty minutes. Nobody got off at a single stop. It got really crowded, but didn't feel that way. People were just breathing and smiling and being happy. I had never seen so many different kinds of people, black people and white people and brown people and all different kinds, smashed together in one place without looking suspiciously at each other or avoiding each other.

Without hating each other, or at least not liking each
other at all. And it was just because of him, because
of the way he sat and he breathed and smiled.
Because he just looked like love, like peace, like he
was content with things, even though he was dressed
like a bum. As the car started to slow down before
one of the stops, I felt Ben's hand on my leg. I looked
at him and he smiled and motioned towards the door.
When the car stopped, we stood and walked off.
Everybody watched him go, and no one moved.
They just stared at him and kept breathing. And as
we were walking away, I looked back at the car.
People were standing at the doors and the windows,
staring. Watching Ben and me walk away. They were
all smiling.

We came out of the subway into another part of the
city. It was not very nice. I could hear sirens and
cars honking and loud rap music and people yelling,
mostly in Spanish. It smelled like meat was cooking.
There were people everywhere on the streets, and
none of them were white. The buildings were all big
and rundown and looked the same. There was trash
in the streets. Ben seemed the same as he was everywhere. Comfortable and calm. Like he wasn't scared
at all. I was scared, though. Really scared. There were
no black people in the town where I lived. Once or
twice a week I might see a black person in the store
where I worked. When people talked about them, it
was mostly because they were on TV or on a sports
team or something, or because they had seen them
in the city being loud and were scared of them. I was

scared of them, for sure. Me and Ben were the only
white people I saw. It was like I was one of them where
I'm from. It didn't feel nice.

We walked towards a group of big brown buildings.
I guessed it was some kind of housing project.
It looked dangerous to me. Nobody stared at us
or even paid attention to us. Ben just walked along.
And he didn't look so poor anymore. Lots of the
people we saw were wearing old clothes that weren't
so nice. Lots of the people looked poor. He just looked
like one of them. Or like a white version of one of
them. A beautiful scarred white version. But he was
obviously still poor. And poor people are poor people,
regardless of the color of their skin.

As we crossed the street and stepped onto the curb
in front of the buildings, a large black man came
walking up to Ben. I thought we were dead, for sure,
and I wished I had a whistle or some mace or something. I thought about running, but knew I wouldn't
get very far. Ben just kept walking and said hello to
the man and the man said hello back. They hugged,
and the man started whispering in Ben's ear. I was
relieved, for sure, but something seemed wrong.
Ben nodded as the man talked. The man looked real
worried, and I could see his eyes looking around as he
whispered. When he finished, Ben hugged him again
and turned to me.
We need to go.
Why?
It's not safe here.

I know that.

Not for the reasons you think.

I could tell this was a dangerous place.

It's a poor place.

Yes.

Poor people are desperate, not dangerous.

Let's leave.

My friend is going to take us somewhere safe.

I'm scared of him.

You're scared of the color of his skin, not him.

That's not true.

Yes, it is.

He took my hand and nodded to the man and we started to walk away from the buildings. We were following the man and we were walking fast and I was still scared, but not as much. What Ben said hurt me, but mostly because it was true. I was extra scared because the man was black, and black people scared me. I knew it was wrong, but it was also just what I felt. I'm sure if he was walking around where I lived, he might be scared too.

We went around the corner, and the man opened the doors of a big SUV. We got inside and he started driving us away, but not too fast. As we came around another corner, I saw a group of policemen standing near their cars. All of their lights were flashing. Standing with them was another group of men in blue suits, and some had bulletproof vests. They all looked very serious, and they looked really mean. They were holding photocopies of a picture. I couldn't really see it very good, but I knew who it was. I knew that they were looking for Ben. He watched them as we drove past. He didn't look nervous or scared or anything. He just looked at them like he looked at everyone else, like he was best friends with them or something. I couldn't imagine looking like that at people with guns who were hunting me. But he did. He looked at them like he loved them with his whole heart, even though they wanted to get him.

We drove for a few blocks until we reached another set of big buildings. They looked exactly like the other ones. If I had been shown pictures of them, I would have thought they were all the same. The man parked the car, and we got out and started walking. We went into one of the buildings. It was dirty. There was trash in the entrance. A man was sleeping on the ground right outside the door. He was snoring and his pants were dirty. We waited for the elevator. I could hear it creaking on the wires. The big man who drove us was still standing with us. He and Ben weren't even talking. The elevator arrived and the door opened. We got inside and went up. It stopped at the seventh floor. The man got out first and Ben smiled at me and motioned for me to follow him and I did it. I stepped right out and followed him. And I should have been scared, but I wasn't. I was with a black man who looked like a killer and a homeless man who ate garbage. And I wasn't scared. I was just walking along with them like we were going to the mall to get some new pants or a computer game or something. What Ben had said before was right. I was scared

of that man's color. What matters is what's in a man's
heart.

We walked to the end of the hall and the man took
out some keys and opened a door. He held the door for
me and Ben and we went inside. It was a small apartment. It wasn't anything fancy, but it wasn't bad.
There were five or six people sitting at a table, listen-
ing to a police scanner. They were all black. They
were drinking water and eating fruit. They looked
right at us. I didn't know what to say. A young girl, a
really really pretty girl, with long curly hair
and beautiful caramel skin, stood up and laughed
and walked over to Ben. She started talking.
You know the trouble you cause?
He smiled and kissed her.
I'm happy to see you.
They kept kissing and talking.
They got an army out there trying to find you.
Michael got us first.
You lucky.
I know.
They catch you they taking you away.
I know.
I don't want that.
Neither do I.
We can't go back.
We'll find somewhere else.
We gotta leave everything behind.
That doesn't matter to me.
He put his arms around her and hugged her and
kissed her neck and her cheek and her lips again.

And even though he seemed to love everyone,
and make everyone feel loved, I could tell he loved
her differently. Like he knew that no matter what he
did or where he went he would always come back
to her, and she knew the same thing. It was real sweet
the way they held each other and kissed each other,
really the sweetest thing I'd ever seen, including
all the sappy stuff on TV and in the movies. There
were no barriers between them. Like they accepted
each other completely, and loved each other truly.
I guess that's the way it's supposed to be between
everyone. Love without conditions, love for the
sake of love, love even though we're different. But
it's never actually like that. Most of the time love is
closer to something like hate. But with them it was
beautiful.

They separated and the girl looked over at me.
Ben introduced us and the girl, Mariaangeles,
smiled and said hello. The people over at the table,
an older woman who was fat like me, and a younger
woman, and three men, including the one who
had brought us here, were all still listening to the
police scanner. One of the men looked over and
smiled and said they're leaving, motherfuckers are
leaving, and everyone started laughing. Ben smiled
and walked over to the woman and kissed her on the
cheek and said thank you. I asked Mariaangeles what
had happened, and she said the woman monitored
the scanner for some people in the projects and let
them know when the police were coming. She had
heard they were coming for a white man in his early

thirties, with dark hair, who was heavily scarred.
The only person who fit the description was Ben.
She said Ben was known in the area because he was
the only white person living there, and because he
helped people, and gave them food and money.
She said some people believed he could make sick
children well and make drug addicts and alcoholics
stop taking drugs and drinking. That people called
him the Prophet, and believed he was a holy man,
and they loved him and watched out for him. So the
lookouts, who were normally there for other reasons,
which I didn't ask about, had come to their apartment and brought her away, and watched for Ben to
make sure he didn't get caught. I asked why the police
and FBI were looking for Ben, and she said because
he skipped bail after he got arrested for living in the
subway tunnels. I asked if that was really something
they would need all those guns for, and she said it was
because Ben was living there with a black man who
had a bunch of guns. I asked her where they would go
now, and she said they'd figure something out, that
there were people who would help take care of them,
people who loved Ben, and they would give them
somewhere to live.

I looked over at Ben, who was sitting with the people
at the table. They were all speaking Spanish, which
he seemed to speak just like them. The word policia
kept being used and they were laughing a lot.
Watching them, they looked like a family, a really
really happy family. I was a little bit jealous, because
they looked like the family I had always wished my

family was, smiling and joking and being nice to each other. It didn't even matter that they all looked different from me. I wanted to be one of them. I had been living alone for a long time, and I had my parents' whole house and whole farm all to myself. It was not a happy place and never had been. It hadn't been awful or violent or scary, it was just empty. An empty house and empty fields. And I was empty. And I was tired of it. Tired of being sad and alone. I wanted to know what it was like to smile there and be happy there and to know love there. I wanted to hear someone laughing in my house. I couldn't remember ever having heard it, unless it was me laughing at a TV show that I was watching alone while I ate dinner or something. I wanted to come home from my job, which really stunk, just standing checking people out at a superstore all day, and feel like there was something or someone at home waiting for me. Who might even be happy or excited to see me.

Mariaangeles came out of a bedroom with a little girl. A beautiful little girl who looked just like her, though she sure seemed young to have a child. The girl ran over to Ben and gave him a hug and sat on his lap. Everyone was still talking in Spanish. I didn't know what they were saying at all, but I imagined they were talking about where they were going to go and what they were going to do. I sat down at the end of the table, in the only empty chair. I felt happy to sit down and be part of the table. And I had an idea. It was a great idea, I thought. A wonderful, really fun idea. I raised my hand, but nobody noticed, so I raised

it a little higher, and waved it a little. Ben looked over
at me.
You don't have to raise your hand.
I don't speak Spanish, so I wasn't sure about
the rules.
There are no rules.
I didn't want to be rude.
You're not.
I have an idea.
About what?
About where to go.
We're okay here.
But those men, they're going to come back.
Yes.
And they'll keep coming back until they get you.
Probably.
I have a farm. It's upstate. There's a big house
and land, and it's just me. I live there all by myself.
It's not just me.
Whoever you want could come. I'd like it a lot.
They might come for me there as well.
Oh man, if you think you have a good system here, we
could really have one there. Our nearest neighbor is a
mile away. We'd know for sure if someone was coming.
He smiled.
You're sure you want us.
I smiled.
Yes. I'd love it. It would be so fun.
And the yard would be awesome for the little girl.
We could get her a wagon or a bike or something.
Her name is Mercedes.
I smiled at her.

Hi, Mercedes.

She smiled at me. He tickled her.

You want to move somewhere with a yard?

She laughed.

Yes.

He looked at Mariaangeles, smiled.

She smiled at him.

She seems okay to me.

He breathed through his nose and nodded.

She is.

I ain't ever lived anywhere but here. Be nice to
get out.

Yes.

She looked at me.

You sure?

I nodded.

Yes.

She smiled.

Let's go.

I smiled.

No way.

You asked for it, white girl, you got it. I hope you know
what you in for.

I laughed and she laughed and I stood up and hugged
her and she hugged me. The man who drove us asked
when we wanted to leave and Ben smiled and said
let's go now. The man stood and said cool with me
and the old woman gave all of us hugs. One of the
other women asked Mariaangeles when she'd be
back and Mariaangeles said if she was lucky, never.
We took the elevator back down from the seventh
floor and we left.

I didn't even go back to the hotel and get my stuff. The man put my address into the computer in his car, and off we went. The drive was real easy. And it was fun too. We listened to the radio and sang along with some of the songs whenever we knew the words. Ben could sing beautifully if he wanted to, like an opera singer or something, but mostly he just sang for laughs. He'd make faces and do little disco dances and pretend to be crying during the love songs. He'd take Mercedes' hands and make her laugh and laugh over and over again. During a duet, he and Mariaangeles took the separate parts and sang to each other. We stopped a couple of times for food and bathroom breaks and stuff, but Ben didn't really eat anything. He would drink water and stand outside, staring up at the sky. I asked one time if he was looking at God or talking to God or something, and he just laughed and said no, he just liked looking at the stars and that he couldn't see them in the city. I looked up, and the stars were just coming out, and I have to say, they were pretty cool.

The drive took five hours. When we arrived, the house was dark and there were no lights. Mariaangeles said she'd never been out of the city before and Mercedes started crying. Ben held her and whispered in her ear and she stopped right away. The house was big and white and old. It had six bedrooms and four bathrooms and was sort of falling apart a little bit. There was a barn and the fields were overrun with weeds and little baby trees. When we pulled up right in front of the house, Ben got out and smiled and looked up at the sky again. I went right inside and turned on the lights. Mariaangeles brought Mercedes in and I told them to take whatever rooms they wanted, and the man who drove came in and I made him some food I had in the fridge. Ben stayed outside. I got a little worried and looked out the window and saw him walking into one of the fields. The moon was only out a little bit, and before I could go out to him he disappeared.

I waited up for him and watched TV. There are so many good shows on late at night. He never came back, though, and I fell asleep on the couch. When I woke up the next morning, I could hear Ben standing near the front door with the man, and I heard him say:
It could be tomorrow, or it could be in five years, but there's no stopping it. Protect the good around you. Love the good you know. Keep them safe.
How do I know who's good?
You know.
I can't tell the way you can.
We all know good and bad in our hearts. We can see and feel it. Trust yourself.
You sure you gonna be okay up here?
Yes.
What if they come for you?
Then they come.
They gonna lock your ass away if they get you.
They won't get me unless I let them.
You gonna?

Live your life. Love your children. Don't believe
what you're told. Forget the lies of religion and
government. And don't worry about me.
You need money?
No.
Anything?
No, thank you.
Get in touch if you do.
Go, my friend.
Ben hugged the man, and the man turned and got
in his truck and pulled out. Ben came inside and
smiled at me and kissed me. He asked how I was and
I said great and he said thank you again for having us
here, it's a beautiful place, a perfect place. I said
sure and he hugged me and it felt great. When he let
go of me, I missed him right away, even though he was
right there. He asked what I was going to do for the
day and I told him I had to go to work. He asked
if I minded if he did some work around the house
and I laughed and told him to do whatever he wanted.
He smiled and said thank you, and walked away.
I got dressed and went to work. The store I worked in
was the biggest store ever, the size of a whole bunch
of football fields. It sold everything you could ever
imagine, though the most popular things were steaks,
beer, and guns. I just rang things up all day. I sat on a
little stool when I could, but mostly I was standing up,
which isn't easy for someone like me. On my breaks,
I went to the break room and ate. I had a couple of
people I talked to at work, but mostly I didn't talk to
anyone. I sat by myself and watched TV. On the first
day with Ben and Mariaangeles and Mercedes, I

could hardly sit at all. And I didn't mind being alone.
I kept wondering what they were doing, or thinking
about them walking around the house and the yard. I
always tried to be cheerful with customers, but I was
extra cheerful. And it didn't even bother me when
they ignored me.

When I came home, I couldn't even believe it.
The whole house was clean. Really really clean.
Everything had been wiped down and the floors
were all mopped. Even the kitchen was clean
and the fridge was scrubbed. The yard, which
I only had done three times a year, was totally cut.
We had a push mower, so I knew it must have been
hard work. I started looking around the house for
everyone. I found Mercedes in her room, playing
with a doll. I don't know where they'd found it, but
it was one of mine from when I was a little girl. It was
cheap but pretty cute, with a little pink dress and
plastic hair, and I hadn't seen it in years and years.
I went in and started playing with her. And she
wanted to play with me. And it was awesome.
Just playing with this little girl. Who didn't look at me
and think bad things about me and wasn't scared of
me. She was just happy. We played dance and
nurse and singer. We played going to the grocery store
and ice cream summer day. And the rest of
the world disappeared. The rest of the world didn't
even matter. I felt like I felt with Ben. Like what was
important was right now, not sometime in the past
or sometime in the future. It felt like life was what
it is supposed to be.

We played for a long time, and near the end I heard
some noise down the hall. I hadn't seen or heard
Ben or Mariaangeles, but figured they must be
around somewhere in the house. I stood up and told
Mercedes I would be right back and went down the
hall. The noises were closer. They were clearly hanky
panky noises. They made me nervous and scared, but
also pretty excited. The door was sort of open and
I peeked around the edge. Mariaangeles was on top
of him and she was really moving her hips. It looked
like she was dancing or something. Ben was watching
her, and smiling, and his hands were moving up and
down on her body. I started to move away but Ben saw
me. He smiled wider and motioned for me to come
into the room, but I was too embarrassed and ran
back down the hall and went back in with Mercedes.
I kept hearing the noises for another half an hour
or so. I had always thought of sex as dirty or bad.
Something you weren't supposed to be open about
with other people. Something that was against the
rules of the church and God and that laws were made
against. But they sounded happy. And when Ben was
inside me, it was the best feeling I had ever had in
my whole life. I had been in churches with my parents
many times. And I had never felt anything in them.
It was just boring. And it seemed old and silly.
But when I felt that feeling with Ben, when I saw the
light, and saw forever, and felt them, that was God.

When the noises stopped, Ben and Mariaangeles
came into the room. Mercedes was really happy to see
them, and we all went and had dinner together.

I wasn't sure how to act after what I had seen, but
they just acted the way they always seemed to act,
which was really happy. Dinner was great, my favorite, macaroni and cheese. After dinner, Mariaangeles
took Mercedes upstairs to give her a bath and put her
to bed. Ben smiled and walked over and kissed me.
It was a long kiss. A real French kiss. I wasn't sure
what to do so I just did it back. And it kept going.
We kept going. Kissing like teenagers or something.
And he pulled me out of my chair and started taking
off my clothes. Thinking back, I can't even believe
it, but at the time I couldn't think at all. I was just
feeling so awesome. He took off my clothes right there
in the dining room. And we went down on the floor.
And he started going over my whole body. He was
using his hands and his mouth and his tongue.
Everywhere on me and in me. And I just closed
my eyes and let him do whatever he wanted. It was
wonderful. Like the best thing ever. He was whispering while he did it. And I tried to listen but it took
me away from what he was doing to me. But what
I could hear was about God. That this was God.
That what I was feeling was God. That God in books
could never make me feel like this. That I would
never feel this way if it wasn't right, if it wasn't
natural, if it wasn't part of God, the true God.

As he was doing all those things to me, I heard
Mariaangeles come into the room and laugh.
I opened my eyes and I was really embarrassed.
Ben was the only person except for my parents who
had ever seen me naked. I started to get up but she

shook her head and smiled and kneeled next to me
and put her hands on my shoulders and held me down
and started kissing me. Something in me said it was
wrong, but it wasn't. It felt as good as it did with Ben.
And I did it back to her. Even though I had always
been taught that being gay or doing gay sex things
was against God's way, it didn't feel that way. God
doesn't care if a man kisses a man, or a woman kisses
a woman, or a woman and man kiss. God doesn't care
at all. It's just love. Kissing or touching of any kind is
just an expression of love, and it doesn't matter who is
doing it. Anybody who says God believes something
else doesn't know what they're talking about at all.

We were together for the rest of the night. On the floor
in the dining room and then upstairs in my bedroom
and then in the bathtub. What a night it was. My
oh my, I saw God over and over, and I saw eternity,
and I felt complete peace and understanding, and I
felt loved, boy, did I feel loved, more loved than just
about anybody on the whole earth that day, I think.
When it was over, we all fell asleep together, right in
the same bed. Ben was in the middle, and me and
Mariaangeles were on either side of him. I slept really
great and didn't even have any bad dreams. When I
woke up in the morning, Ben was gone. Mariaangeles
was still sleeping, but Ben was gone.

I got up and went to work, same as I did every day.
When I came home, more projects had been done,
like there was some wood stacked up and the barn
was being cleaned out. Ben and Mariaangeles

and me and Mercedes all had dinner together,
and Mariaangeles put Mercedes to sleep. When she
was done, we all went to my bedroom and did the
same thing we had done the night before. We touched
each other and we kissed each other and we licked
each other. And we made each other feel wonderful.
And we loved each other. That was what it was all
about. What life is about. Loving each other. A man
who was Jewish who could talk to God and a black
Dominican girl from the Bronx and a fat white
cashier from the middle of nowhere. We didn't care
about color or religion or money or what kind of
school we'd gone to or what kinds of jobs we had had
or what our families were like or even what our bodies
looked like. We didn't care that we weren't married.
Or that we were sinners. Or that some people would
even say we were damned to Hell. We just loved each
other. For what we were. Which is how it's supposed
to be. True love isn't about anything other than how
it makes you feel. And if it makes you feel good, keep
doing it, regardless of how other people may think of
it or feel.

We fell into a routine. I would go to my job. Ben and
Mariaangeles would work around the farm. We would
have dinner together and go to bed. He was never
there when I woke up. I asked one day where he went
at night all alone. He said sometimes he went into the
woods or the barn and had seizures, and sometimes
he laid in the grass and stared at the stars, and he said
sometimes he walked to town, which was three miles
away, and went looking for things other people had

thrown away, like food and clothes and stuff. I told
him he was being silly and that he didn't need to
do that anymore because I could buy everything we
needed at the store with my employee discount.
He said he didn't want bought things. That buying
things just fed the system that was destroying the
world. I asked him if he really thought the world was
being destroyed and he smiled and said yes, it is, and
it will be final soon. I asked him if he was mad that
I worked at the store and he laughed and said of
course not. He kissed me on the cheek and said that
it wasn't his place or anyone else's to tell me how to
live. I told him I wouldn't mind quitting my job and
he said I should do what I wanted to do, that my life
was my own, and when it was over, it was over, and
that I should do and see and try and feel and experience everything I could and everything I wanted to.
I told him I didn't know what I wanted, and he smiled
again and said yes, you do, we all do, we just need
to be honest with ourselves about it, and stop being
scared of it. Fear, he said, ran all of our lives. Fear, he
said, after religion, was the most destructive force in
the world.

Other people also started coming to the house.
At first it was just one or two a week. I don't know
how they knew Ben or how they knew where he was.
They would be there when I came home, or they
would knock on the door. They all seemed crazy or
sad or sick or on drugs. Ben would walk with them.
He would go walking into the fields where my daddy
used to farm. The fields were overgrown and scary.

Even though I knew better, and I was grown up, I was always sure there was something evil in them, like a monster or something. Ben would walk in there with people, and sometimes they would come back in five minutes and sometimes they would come back in five hours, but the people were always better. I didn't really know what to think about it. Something was going on out there, but it was hard to really think about it for real. Miracles were something people talked about, and I would read about in the newspaper, and people would pray really super hard for, but they never really seemed to happen, or if they did it was like one in a billion times. But people kept praying for them, millions of people did it, every single day they did it. Some of them were going to get lucky. And that was really all it was for them, and for their praying for miracles, just dumb luck. Something good is bound to happen like one in a billion times. Really most of the people who prayed for miracles were just wasting their time. It was silly. They begged and pleaded for some kind of help that never came. They should have spent the time having fun or something. Especially if it was for health reasons. They could at least have some kind of fun before they died instead of praying. And when these not really real miracles did happen, there wasn't really any reason for them. Like the people involved couldn't say what had happened or why it had happened. Not for real, at least. But with Ben it was different. Sick people would walk into the fields with him, and they would walk out healthy. Drug addicts would walk in with him and come out without wanting drugs anymore.

People on crutches would come out running. I saw
a couple of people with sunglasses and white canes
come out smiling and blinking. A man in a wheelchair skipped across the lawn. It was crazy. And
beautiful. It was miracles for real. Not praying to
some thing that wasn't even there and couldn't even
listen. Not praying for some promise in a book that
never made any of its promises come true. But having
someone actually do something that changed someone. Knowing that because you met this one person,
and he did something, that your life was totally different and totally better. That was a miracle. And Ben
could make miracles happen. He could make prayers,
which really are pretty useless considering how many
there are and how little they actually do, he could
make prayers actually come true. I don't know how he
did it, except to say that he was the Messiah, and he
had the same powers that that Jesus Christ man had,
if that man was even real. He could make miracles.
I've never heard of anyone else who could do it. But
he could, for real. And it wasn't like it was easy or
just some little thing. After he did it, he would always
come out looking worse than when he went in. Like
whatever he did took something from him. Like he
was giving something of himself to the people so they
could be better. Sometimes he didn't come back at all.
The people would say he'd told them he was going
to have a seizure and they should leave him. Or he'd
walk out of the field and just have the seizure right
in the yard. They were really terrible scary ones. He'd
shake and grunt and spit and stuff would come out
of his mouth. I'd get really worried and want to go

help him, but I knew he wouldn't want that, so I'd usually just bite my nails on the porch. Once I asked why he did it, gave people the miracles. He said he did it because he loved them, and that miracles aren't done, miracles are given. And that anyone could do it. If people were willing to love enough, and to give enough, that anyone could change someone's life. And that that was the easy way to describe God on earth. People changing other people's lives. Not some heavenly being, or some made-up superhero, but people changing other people's lives.

After they were done with Ben in the fields, most of the people would leave. Some of them, though, would stay with us. It was pretty funny. They weren't like normal people. Or at least that's what I thought at first. They were men who dressed up like ladies, and ladies who looked like men, and they were people who were gay and people who liked men and women. They were homeless people who were on drugs, and they were black people and Hispanic people and Asian people and Arab people and people who were so mixed up I didn't know what they were. There were women who had definitely done some dirty things, and maybe even sold themselves for money. There were men who were the same way, even. There were criminals and drug dealers and beggars and people who had nowhere else to go. If I had seen these people on the street, I would have definitely been scared of them. If I had seen them in my town, I would have hoped the police were some- where really close. All the God-fearing, church-going

people I knew would have said they were damned to
Hell for being sinners. They would have said these
people were going to Hell for sure. But when they
were in my house I loved them. And I loved them
because I saw Ben loved them. I saw him hug them
and kiss them. I saw them cry in his arms. I saw him
spend hours listening to them and talking to them
and laughing with them. I saw him heal them and
change them. I saw him treat them like they were real
people, which almost all of them said hadn't been
done in a really long time. I saw Ben have sex with
them, and all of them wanted to have sex with him,
and he with all of them, and saw him marry them.
Some of them came to the farm together and were in
love or fell in love while they were with us. Men and
men and women and women and men and women,
every combination you could imagine, gay ones and
straight ones. Ben told them that marriage wasn't
about a man and a woman being together, it was
about people in love being together. And he said that
laws and restrictions against love and marriage,
regardless of who was in the marriage and who
they loved, weren't the way of God. God didn't care
about those things. God was beyond those things.
Marriage is a human issue, and all humans should
be allowed to participate in it, regardless of how
they love. And I followed his example. I talked and
laughed and listened and hugged and kissed and had
sex. I went to the weddings and cried and cheered,
I was so happy for everyone, and I danced after,
danced until my legs and feet hurt like crazy. I didn't
think about anything except that I was loving

313   Judith

people.That that was what mattered. That we were all human beings and we were loving other human beings. And that's God. Not some silly man with a beard wearing a robe, sitting in a gold chair in the clouds. Not some angry man who knows everything and says what is right and wrong. Not some old man in Italy talking nonsense, or some crazy man in the American South judging everyone. Not some man in Pakistan who thinks he has the right to kill, or some man in Israel who thinks he has the right to oppress. God is not a person or a man or even a being of any kind. God is loving other human beings. God is treating everyone you meet as if you love them. God is forgetting we're all different and loving each other as if we're all the same. God is what you feel when there's love in your heart. It's an awesome feeling. And it's the real God. The only real God.

People kept coming. And some who seemed to know Ben from before. A lady doctor from the city who said she had treated Ben in the hospital. A man who used to be his boss when he was working at a construction site. A sweet gay boy who was as pretty as any girl and who used to live with Ben's brother and who loved Ben and who Ben loved, and they kissed a lot and spent a lot of time in bed. An FBI agent who hugged Ben and cried and said thank you over and over again. Some people would stay for a day or two days, some would come and go, and some never left. Pretty soon people filled up all the bedrooms, and the attic, and the basement, and the living room, and the TV room. They were everywhere, really. And then they started sleeping outside. In the barn and in tents. Over the course of a couple of months, we went from the four of us to thirty or forty people, all living on my farm, and even more kept coming. I couldn't believe it. It was super fun. The house had never been cleaner. We started growing vegetables. And some of the people brought money and I'd buy things like food and blankets and fruit with my store discount. All day people would do jobs. Some would clean or make dinner or plant food in the garden. People would take care of Mercedes. People would go into town at night and go through dumpsters. And at night we would all sit around the front yard and Ben would talk to us. I wouldn't say it was preaching. Preachers are always trying to convince you they're right. Preachers are always trying to make you believe what they believe. Preachers are always trying to tell you if you don't listen to them you're going to pay some price. Ben didn't care if we believed. He said everybody should have the right to believe whatever they wanted. He didn't need to convince anybody. All anybody had to do to be convinced by Ben was look at him. When you saw him, you knew he was different from the rest of us. You knew he was special, or even something really beyond special. He was divine. He was what people prayed for and begged for and spent their whole lives worshipping. He was the real Prophet. He was the real Son of God. He was the real Jesus Christ born again. He was the real Messiah. He was everything all of the crazy religious people all over the world had been praying for and waiting for for all of these thousands of years. He was God. He was God.

And even though he told us all, every single one of us, that we didn't have to believe what he said, we did believe it, we believed everything he said, even when it was kooky. I remember the first night it happened. The sky was clear and there was no moon and it was warm. There were millions and billions of stars out, so many I couldn't even begin to count or guess how many there were. Ben had been in the house, having a seizure. Everyone knew to leave him alone when that was happening. Even if it had been happening in the kitchen or where we could see him, he told us all to leave him alone. He was having this seizure in the living room that night, right on our old carpet. He had been talking during it, talking in some weird language that sounded really old and scary and serious. Everyone had left the house and gone out to the lawn. We were just sitting on the grass, looking up and not saying anything because it was so beautiful we couldn't even believe it. It was when there were only eight or nine of us at the house. Me and Mariaangeles and Mercedes sleeping in her arms, and a gay man and two transvestites and a woman who had been a crack smoker when she came but wasn't anymore, and maybe someone else. Ben walked out and sat down with us. He took the crack lady's hand because she was having a really hard time being off her drugs. He kissed her on the head, and she smiled. One of the men asked him if he was okay, and he said yes. He asked if he knew he was talking when he was having his seizure, and Ben said yes. The man asked if he knew what he was saying, and Ben said yes, I was speaking to God. Everyone was quiet for a couple of seconds. Like they couldn't believe it, or maybe like they could believe it and did believe it but it was awesome and there was nothing to say. Me and Mariaangeles both knew already. The others looked at each other and one of the men smiled and said I told you, that's what I heard, that's why we're here. The other man asked Ben what God said to him, and Ben smiled and said God wanted to tell you hello, and to make sure you know you are welcome to stay here for as long as you like.

We all laughed. Ben laid down on the ground so he could stare up at the stars and brought the woman down with him and held her in his arms. It was really super sweet. She had been shaking before, her hands and her whole body and even her lips had been twitching and shaking. Ben just held her and ran his hand through her hair over and over and she got really calm and peaceful. We all laid down on the ground like him, like we wanted to see whatever it was he was looking at, and because he looked real comfortable. And Ben just looked up at the stars, and so did everyone else, and they went on forever and ever and ever. Nobody said anything for a long time. We just stared. And I saw stars that twinkled, and stars that looked like they moved, and really bright stars and stars that I could barely even see at all. I tried to count them, but there were too many, so I tried to count them in just one little square in the sky, but there were too many to do even that. Eventually I just got lost in them. I wasn't even thinking about anything. I was just staring at the wonder

of the sky and stuff. And everyone else was the same
way. We were lost, and when we had all forgotten
he was going to, Ben spoke.

God isn't what you think, or imagine, or have been
taught to believe. Much of what you have been taught
to believe about everything in this world is wrong,
but so much of it is tied to notions of God that it's
easiest to start there first. We are animals. We were
not created in the image of anyone or anything. We
are a biological accident, and we are what we are
now because of a long process of natural selection,
and occasional spontaneous genetic abnormalities
that made us stronger, and eventually became part
of us. We started as single cells in swamp water, and
rose from there, became fish, amphibians, reptiles,
mammals, apes. It happened over the course of
billions of years. The idea that this planet, this solar
system, this galaxy, and this universe were created
five thousand years ago is ridiculous. We know better.
We might not have then, but we do now. And even
then, when the stories were created, regardless of
what culture they came from, they weren't created
because the people creating them actually believed
them, they were created in order to consolidate
power, and to enslave people. They were created
because a few men understood that if they claimed
some direct relationship with God, some unique
understanding of God, and that God was a God that
created all life, and judged life, and knew everything
everyone did at any given moment, and if that God
was a God that controlled fate, and decided who
would live and when we would die, and after death

granted eternal life in either Paradise or Hell, they
could use that power, that supposed relationship, that
supposed understanding, to make people live
as they told them to live, and make them do what
they wanted them to do. They could use that power
to make people slaves. Religion. It's remarkably
simple. A beautiful con. The longest running fraud
in human history. I know God. God created all,
knows all, and is all-powerful. Do what I say God
tells me you should, which also happens to make
you subservient to me, or you will burn forever.
The Christians are the masters of it. They have built
empires with their scam, murdered, tortured, and
terrorized literally billions of people. All in the name
of their bearded superhero, in the name of their crucified fiction. In today's world the Roman Catholics,
American evangelists, and fundamentalist Muslims
are particularly good, though all are guilty: the Jews,
the Christians, the Muslims, all the leaders of all
the various sects and denominations, anyone on
earth who thinks there is one God with the power
to know and judge all. They're all wrong. And they
are either slave masters, or they are slaves, worshipping things that don't exist. God is not a man. God
is not a reflection of man. God is not a being or
a spirit or a consciousness. God does not live in
some place with a staff who does God's work. God
is not a he or a she. God does not have an army
of angels or a mortal enemy who was cast out of
his kingdom. In terms that mean something to us,
God is nothing. God plays no part in our lives. God
doesn't care about earth or about humanity. God

doesn't care about the petty dramas that mean so much to us. God doesn't care what we say or who we fuck or what we do with our bodies or who we love or who we marry. God doesn't care if we rest on Sundays or if we go to some building to sing songs and say prayers and chant and listen to sermons. God doesn't care if we kill in God's name. God doesn't give a fuck. God does not give a fuck. Look up. There are twenty-five hundred stars visible in the night sky. Twenty-five hundred. Not that big a number. In our galaxy, our little galaxy, there are three hundred billion more that we can't see. Three hundred billion. We don't know how many galaxies there are because we don't have the technology to know, if it is even possible to know. There are estimates, guesses, darts thrown at a board. Some say a hundred billion, some say five hundred billion, some a trillion. Some say the universe is infinite, which is a concept we pretend to understand, but is beyond our minds. Humans worry about eating, finding shelter, fucking. We worry about jobs and money. We worry about class and status and what other people think of us. We worry about rules imposed on us by men who know nothing. We worry about death and when it is going to find us. We can't conceive of infinity. We can't grasp the idea of something that has no boundaries and no end. And that's where God is. That's what God is. Beyond our minds. Beyond our understanding. Beyond anything we can categorize or write about or preach about or place into one of our systems of rules. God is infinite. An infinite number of galaxies, an infinite number of stars, an infinite number of planets. Look up. Try to imagine infinity. Your mind shuts down and moves back to some number you can understand, some image you can grasp. Look up. Beyond what you see, beyond what lies behind what you see, beyond what lies behind what lies behind. What stretches out forever. That's God. All of it is God. An infinite God that we can't understand. That does not care about our little lives. That is beyond caring about anything, anywhere in this infinite universe. Look up and see God. Look up. Look up.

And we did. We looked up at all those pretty stars, and they were there shining and blinking and maybe moving around a little, but that was probably my eyes playing tricks on me. I tried to imagine all those numbers of billions and trillions and think about things just going on forever and ever and I couldn't do it, just like he said. My brain would come back to stars I could see and to the little sliver of moon glowing and the grass I was lying down on that was tickling my arms and the sounds of crickets playing and bugs winging real fast and a sweet little breeze moving through the trees and the other people around me breathing, just looking up and breathing.

After that we started doing it every night. It wasn't like it was required or anything, not like school or church, nobody was going to get in trouble, but almost everybody did it. We'd have dinner and go outside and lie on the grass and Ben would talk. He'd talk about life, about what he thought of it, and

how he lived it, and about our world, about how we
had allowed it to be destroyed, and about how it was
going to end soon. He said life was simple, we were
born and we were going to die. There was nothing
for us before we were born, and there would be
nothing for us after we died. While we were here we
had choices. While we were alive we had choices.
We could choose to be and do whatever we wanted.
We could choose to become part of society, and follow
its rules, which were mostly designed to control us
and keep us in whatever place we were born into, or
we could make our own rules and live our own lives.
For him, he'd say, life was about love and fucking
and helping other people. Life was about feeling
everything he could and experiencing everything he
could. Life wasn't about the accumulation of money
and possessions, but the accumulation of friends.
He'd talk about living simply. That the more
complicated our lives became the more miserable
we were. The more we had the more we wanted.
The harder we worked the less we lived. He'd talk
about patience, and say that there was nothing in life
that was made better by being anxious or nervous
or aggressive. He'd talk about compassion, how we
should have it for ourselves and for other people and
for the earth, and that if he could stop people from
inflicting pain on everything around them, that the
world might have a chance to survive, and that we
might have a chance to survive. He said we needed
to let go of the idea of death. That death was the end,
very simply, and nothing more. That when death
came it was blackness and silence and peace, but

nothing we could experience. That our obsession with death was killing us. That our obsession with life after death, which did not exist, was destroying what we did have, which was consciousness and all of its gifts, the greatest of which was love. He said life, not death, was the great mystery we all must confront. He said it over and over again. Life, not death, was the great mystery we must confront.

When he talked about the world, it was usually about how we had destroyed it, or allowed religions and governments to destroy it, and how it was all going to end soon. He said religions and governments were never about what they claimed to be, which was helping people and making their lives worth living, but were simply instruments of greed and power and death. That none of them were worth a shit. That even the best of them were evil, and existed solely to control and exploit humanity, and control and exploit the earth's resources. That he couldn't, over the entire course of recorded history, find a single example of a government that didn't exist in the name of power, that didn't kill in its own quest for power, and that didn't use its citizens as servants of its greed. Though he said he didn't know how the world would end, it was obvious it would, that there were too many ways, and that one of them would happen, and it would happen soon. He said that too many people had too many weapons. That once the big weapons started flying, they wouldn't stop. That once one crazy man pushed a button, all of the buttons would be pushed. That too many people wanted to be right. That too many people wanted to control. That too many people wanted their God to be the only God, their system to be the only system. That Democrats and Republicans, and Capitalists and Communists, and Liberals and Conservatives, and Fascists and Anarchists, and Nationalists and National Socialists, whatever they called themselves, were all the same, and that they were no different than people who worshipped God. But that instead of pretending to believe in a supernatural God, they pretended to believe in Gods called social justice, and equality, and freedom, but that their real goals were no different than the religious people, that all they were truly interested in were money, and power, and control. That between them, they would destroy the world. That they would start a war that they wouldn't be able to stop, and that would have no winner. That the war to end everything would be coming. And that even if the war didn't come, everything would end anyway. There were too many people. There were no more resources. The earth itself couldn't support everything on it anymore. Soon all of its resources would be gone. And when we realized it, we would tear each other apart while we starved. And he said it was too late to try and stop it. That there was nothing anyone could do at this point. That no leader, no religious figure, no man, no woman, no nothing, could do anything about it. That we had jumped off the cliff, and that at some point soon we were going to land. And it was all going to end. And we were all going to die. And that it was best. It was the best thing that could happen. That destroying all of it, razing it, burning it to the ground, was our only chance. And that after it happened, he hoped, though he doubted it, that whoever was left would be smart enough to start again and forget all of it. And start something that revolved around the worship of love instead of the worship of God and money. God and money brought nothing but death and war. Love might bring something worth living for.

And he wasn't angry or mean when he talked. He didn't scream or shoot spit out of his mouth like lots of people did when they said stuff. He said it just like someone would say they were going to buy some milk or fill their car with gas. Just like it was something that was going to happen. He said we had choices about how we were going to live before it happened. We could either accept it and live as beautifully as we could before it happened, or we could not believe it and keep wasting our lives doing things and chasing things that didn't make us happy and make us feel good. He said his choice was to love as much as possible, and give as much as possible, and feel joy and happiness and ecstasy and pleasure as much as possible. Life was hard enough, he said, without denying ourselves the things that brought us into a state of bliss. Those who thought we should deny ourselves were fools. Our bodies were built for it. We should allow them to do what they were made to do.

After he finished speaking, he would always kiss someone. He did it with Mariaangeles the most, but sometimes it would be someone else, and sometimes it would be a man, and sometimes a woman, and sometimes a man that looked like a woman, or a woman who looked like a man. He would kiss them and touch them and love them. Most of us would follow his example and start kissing and touching and loving. Some of us would go into the house or into the barn or the fields, but most of us would stay on the lawn. It didn't matter who you were or what you looked like or what your background was or what color your skin was or if you had an accent or if you had money or no money or if you had gone to school or not gone to school or anything. Everyone loved everyone else. And everyone had sex with everyone else. And everyone came with everyone else. When we first started, it was just a few of us, but near the end there were lots of people staying all over the place and more would come or would be visiting for the day and people would be everywhere. And there was so much love. And we were all happy. And nothing else in the world mattered at all. Not one single bit.

Seven months after we all came to the farm together, after all of the space in the house and barn were taken up, and people were living in tents in the fields and the woods, and there were seventy-seven people living there, a girl came to see Ben. I was sitting on the porch when she came walking up, and I could tell something was wrong. She was young and sad and her face was bruised and her clothes were not in good shape. It was pretty normal for people like her to show up, but I could tell somehow that she was different. She asked if Ben was around, and I said he lives here but isn't around right this minute. She asked if she could have something to drink, and I said yes, of course, silly. She sat down on the porch stairs, and I got her some water and gave it to her. I tried to be chatty with her, but I could tell she didn't want to be chatty, and really she looked like she was going to cry in a sad way so I left her alone. An hour or two later Ben came walking out of the fields with a young couple who had been trying to have a baby but couldn't and they were smiling and I could tell the woman had been crying in a good way and Ben put his hand on her stomach and put her husband's hand on top of his hand and they both just looked so happy, like they knew everything was going to be fine for them. As they walked away towards their car, Ben turned towards us. The girl saw him and stood up and Ben smiled and she immediately started crying. He walked over and put his arms around her, and she just cried into his shoulder, really cried, like her whole body was shaking and sobbing. I could tell it was something really serious, so I left them alone there in front of the porch and went inside and read books to Mercedes.

Later everyone at the farm met outside for dinner. Ben seemed really happy and really sad at the same time and the girl was still there. She was sitting with Mariaangeles and they were holding hands. It wasn't unusual for women to be holding hands, but they were holding hands really tight. We had a really awesome dinner, and afterwards, instead of talking, Ben kissed every single person at the farm. He kissed everyone really nice, and everyone different, like he could tell what kind of kiss they liked and what kind of kiss they wanted and what kind of kiss they needed. When it was my turn, he kissed me real soft on the lips but not really sexy or anything. Just really nice and soft for like ten seconds or so, and then he pulled away and whispered I love you in my ear. After he kissed everyone, he took Mariaangeles by the hand and took Mercedes, who had dinner with us lots of the time, by the other hand, and they walked into the house with each other, and the girl walked with them, right alongside of them. It was really cute. Like he was Mercedes' dad and Mariaangeles' husband and the girl was part of their family somehow and it was really super cute. For a minute nobody was sure what to do, but then people started kissing each other just like we did every night when Ben was with us. And then we loved each other. And the sky was clear and it seemed more clear than ever and the stars were out and they seemed brighter than ever and it was a beautiful night, a perfect night, the most awesome I had ever seen and still have ever seen. And everybody loved each other. We all loved each other in some perfect way even stronger than before, like somehow the night made us better than ever and gave us more love. It gave us everything and it was beautiful. The most beautiful thing in the world. Love.

The next morning, when I woke up, Ben was gone. The girl was gone too, and Mariaangeles didn't come out of her room for the whole day. And when she did, she wouldn't say where Ben had gone or who the girl was or what had happened. All I knew was that Ben was gone.

II ESTHER

I think about my suffering. My sadness, loneliness,
the fact that my family has been destroyed, that
I've been beaten and tortured and forced to worship
a God that is not mine, and live a life that is not mine.
I think about the suffering of others in this world,
this ugly, ugly world. I think about all of the violence
and war, the poverty and hunger. I think about the
addiction and abuse and oppression. I think about
all of the sickness and disease and physical misery,
and I think about all of the suffering of the soul,
which is greater and more profound than any of the
physical ailments that befoul us. I think about all
of the pain that everyone feels every minute of every
day. There is so little joy. So little freedom. So little
security. So little that makes us feel as if this is all
worth it. And what there is that makes us think
it's worth it is love. Love is the only way to alleviate
suffering. Love is the only way to find freedom.
Love is the only place in all of humanity where there
is security. And even love doesn't work for very long.
Love always disappears or vanishes. Love is always
killed or destroyed. Love always changes into something that isn't really love. Moments of true, pure,
unconditional love are the rarest and most valuable
things on earth. If we have two or three of them over
the course of our entire lives, we're lucky. Most of us
have none. Most of us live with the illusion of having

love or seeking love or knowing love, but what we have or seek or know is desire and possession and control. What we know as love doesn't really make us happy. If anything, it makes us suffer more. It makes us more unhappy and more violent and more oppressive and more miserable. It increases our suffering. But if we could learn. If we could learn what Ben Zion learned. If we could live as Ben Zion lived. If we could feel as Ben Zion felt. If we could love as Ben Zion loved.

I always believed we would see him again. I hoped it would happen before our mother died. After he first left again, after his fight with Jacob, I prayed for his return. I prayed for hours a day. When I was supposed to be praying for other things, when I was supposed to be praying for things that Jacob wanted me to pray for, and told me to pray for, I prayed for Ben Zion. While I was praying, I thought about what it had been like seeing him again. I thought about who he was and what he had become, which my parents, and everyone in our family, and our rabbis always believed he would become. I thought about what he could do, how he could perform miracles, how he could make people feel, and how he could change lives with a word or a touch. I thought about all of the languages he could speak without having studied them and all of the books he knew without having read them. I thought about how he could speak with God. I thought about all of the signs of divinity that were recognized when he was born: his Davidic blood, his birthday on the day the Temple of Solomon was destroyed, his circumcision at birth. I thought about the burden he must have felt for most of his life. Being raised and educated as someone who might be the Messiah. What that must have been like for a little boy. A three-year-old who should have been playing with trucks. A five-year-old who should have enjoyed playing at a playground. A seven-year-old who should have enjoyed school like a normal child. A nine-year-old who should have been allowed to have friends. I thought about what it must have felt like for him to know what he was, or what he was believed to be, what made his father and brother jealous and scared and made them hate him. I thought about what it must have been like for him when he was thrown out of our home. He was still a child, barely a teenager. I wondered what he did for all of those years we searched for him and could not find him. I wondered where he was, who he met, and what he felt. I wondered if he was waiting to become what he became. If he believed it. If it was a burden. If he woke up every day in terror, wondering if today was the day he became Moshiach. If he ever spoke to anyone about it. If he had any friends or anyone who loved him. If he cared. If he knew how it would end, and I suspect that he did. I don't have answers, but I believe it must have been some kind of hell. To know that you were Moshiach, the Messiah, the Son of God, Christ reborn, the earthly incarnation of God on earth, even though his God was not the God propagandized on earth for thousands of years. It's a miracle he survived knowing. It's a miracle that he accepted it and waited for it, wherever he

was, whatever he did, whatever he felt, however he
suffered. It's a miracle. My brother was a miracle.

And while I thought about all of this, I let myself
doubt it. Any faith, any true faith, involves doubt.
If you say your faith is unshakeable, you have no
faith. If you say you have no doubt, then you have no
belief. The struggle of faith, the worthiness of faith,
the value of faith, is holding true to that faith in the
face of doubt. If you are to believe in God, you must
allow yourself to doubt God. If you are to believe
in anything, you have to doubt it. I believed in my
brother. In his power and his divinity. In his righteousness. In his mission, which was to show us the
folly of our beliefs, to show us the danger of our religions, to show us the stupidity we exhibit by placing
our hopes and dreams in the hands of politicians,
and to show us the value of living our lives believing
in love, and living with love, not the false, judgmen-
tal love we have been taught, but a love where every
human on earth is given equal value, and granted
equal rights, and provided equal care. I believe that
he was who he was born to be, and that he was the
man that had been prayed for for thousands of years.
I believe that in his death, in his sacrifice, he gave us
a chance to redeem ourselves. He died willingly in
order to redeem us of the sins of religion, the sins
of our Gods, the sins of placing our lives in the hands
of politicians who have defrauded us. He redeemed
our humanity by showing how and why the humanity we have been sold is wrong. That the Gods we
worship don't exist and don't care. That the systems

we have been forced to exist in are destroying us.
In the same way that Christ supposedly sacrificed
himself for our sins, sins that are a natural part of our
humanity, as natural as breathing and eating, sins
such as love and sex and choice, Ben Zion sacrificed
himself for our belief in the Christ story, and for all
the stories like it, stories that enslave us, and oppress
us, and destroy us. If we realize Ben Zion was right,
and if we learn from what he taught us, we have a
chance to save ourselves. I don't, however, believe we
will take it. He was prophetic in that he knew the end
was coming. He was Moshiach in how he showed
us how to avoid it. He showed us we are all asleep.
He screamed, and he kept screaming it until it led
to his death. We have a chance if we remember that
scream, if we listen to it. I don't, however, believe
we will take the chance. It will all end.

And while I believe what I believe, there is doubt,
there is always doubt, and there has to be doubt.
Was Ben Zion just a man? Was he a child poisoned
by religion and convinced to believe in ancient
prophecies that will never come true? Did he become
what he became because he was told he would?
Was he mentally ill? Did his epilepsy destroy his
sanity? Was he a criminal who deserved what he
received? Was he an egomaniac serving his own
self-need? Was he delusional and sick and dangerous?
I allow myself to ask the questions, because when
I think about the man I knew, and the life he lived,
and the words he spoke, and the example he gave, and
the miracles he performed, and the love he shared,

and the sacrifice he made, the answer, to all of the
questions I ask myself, is no. Or the answer is no to
all the questions but one. He was dangerous. He was
absolutely dangerous. Dangerous because if we listen
to him we will wake up. If we listen to him, we will
stop buying the bad goods that are sold to us, and we
will stop falling for the cons of preachers, popes, and
presidents, and the disease of religion will be cured,
and the lies of politicians will no longer be believed,
and everything that has been built, all of the sick,
diseased institutions that rule us and control us, and
deceive us, will crumble, and they will fall. He was
absolutely dangerous. And they killed him.

After he left, after his kiss with Jeremiah and after
Jacob beat him, and after he turned our water
to wine, the priority became finding him again.
When Jacob saw the wine, he immediately believed
he had made a mistake, a major mistake, an irrepar-
able mistake. He ran from our house into the street,
but saw nothing. He got into his car and drove
around the surrounding streets, but saw nothing.
He went into local churches, believing that might be
where Ben Zion would seek refuge, but saw nothing.
He called the local precincts and hospitals, but
nobody had seen anything. He searched for days,
and when he wasn't searching, he was on his knees
praying at the church, or talking with Pastor Luke,
who, after meeting Ben Zion and hearing him speak
and witnessing his miracle, was convinced that Ben
Zion was Christ reborn. Jacob did not find him, or
even any sign of him, and Ben Zion did not come

back, or offer any clue as to his whereabouts, or contact us in any way. After Jacob realized Ben Zion was really gone, he started disbelieving what he had seen and claiming that Ben Zion had kissed Jeremiah only to upset, and had hid a bottle of wine somewhere in the house, knowing that he might get an opportunity to replace the water with it when he was alone in our dining room. He also started to become angry and say that Ben Zion had mocked him, and mocked God, and that what Ben Zion knew, the languages and the holy books, was something anyone could know if they studied long enough, which was what he must have done. When Ben Zion's court dates were coming up and he did not appear, thus jeopardizing both our home and the church, Jacob became enraged. He restarted his search for Ben Zion, and with greater vigor, and he also started screaming at, and eventually abusing, our mother, whom he believed knew where Ben Zion was living. Our mother knew nothing. As had always been the case, she became the focus of Jacob's rage. He screamed at her. He spit on her. He took all of her money and refused to give her any food. He would push her into our front closet and lock the door and spend time kicking it, and whispering through the door to her that she was the mother of the Devil, and telling her that our father had never loved her and regretted marrying her. Eventually he threw her out of the house. He let her leave with the clothes on her back and nothing more. She tried to go to other church members for aid, for they were the only people for years that she had interacted with, but they would not help her. She went back to Brooklyn, where we had lived as Jews, but the people we had known there would not forgive her for forsaking them. She lived in a shelter until her time there ran out. She went to another one. After a couple of months, she ended up on the streets, begging, hoping each day to get enough money for a meal. I tried to help her. I would bring her small amounts of money, blankets, clothes. Jacob caught me and beat me, breaking three of my ribs and three of my fingers, and quoted Ecclesiasticus 26:25, A shameless woman shall be counted as a dog; but she that is shamefaced will fear the Lord, after he was finished beating me. He told me if I did it again, he would beat me worse, and throw me out as well.

As the days went on, and Jacob became more desperate, and our mother became more desperate, I also became desperate. At the time I believed in the church, in Jesus Christ, and in the Heavenly Father as depicted in the Old and New Testaments of the Holy Bible. I knew nothing else. I had never been given the chance to learn anything or believe anything else. I did not want Jacob's church to fall apart, or to be taken by the government. Obviously I did not want to lose our home, as it was the only thing of value that my family owned. I started looking for Ben Zion on my own. I asked Jacob's permission before I started, and he initially said no. After Pastor Luke left, saying he could no longer reconcile his belief in Jesus Christ with what he had witnessed in Ben Zion, and he could no longer preach a gospel that he did not feel in his heart, Jacob granted me permission. Not only was he in danger of losing the physical building that held his church, but the congregation was losing members, as people felt the chaos, and saw the instability in the leadership, and started going to other churches.

I started by asking my mother, but she knew nothing. I went to the Bronx, where Ben had been living before his accident, before he came back to us, but no one would speak to me, and one large man recommended that I leave, that no one there would tell me anything, and some might hurt me if they thought I would hurt Ben Zion, who they knew only as Ben. I went to the construction site where he had worked, but the workers there had not seen Ben Zion, and the foreman of the site would not see me. I went to the jail and tried to speak to some of the people who had been in the tunnels with him. I saw three men and one woman. As soon as I told them who I was, they stood and walked away without speaking a word to me. I did what Jacob did, called police precincts and hospitals and homeless shelters. I went to the hospital where I had found Ben, but the doctor was not available. I went back to my mother, hoping maybe Ben Zion had contacted her, but I couldn't find her. I went everywhere she had been, or where I knew she had been, but she was nowhere to be found. I stayed home and at church for two days and prayed, and still nothing. On the third day, I decided not to go to church and not to pray. I was tired, and I did not like being around Jacob, who was becoming increasingly

desperate and irritable and rageful. I stayed home.
I listened to the radio. I put on a station that was not
a Christian station, which would most likely have
resulted in a beating had Jacob known or come home
and discovered it. I listened to a pop station, like a
normal girl my age might have done, like normal girls
my age all over New York City were probably doing at
exactly the same moment. I heard songs about falling
in love, about being in love, about going to parties
and dancing, and about losing love and mourning
love. I heard songs about beautiful kisses and songs
about sex. I heard songs about big dreams and people
going after them and sometimes losing them and
sometimes finding them. I had never known any of
these things. I had never experienced anything like
them. My life had been church and prayer and school
at home and Bible study. What boys I knew were off-
limits until marriage, and contact between us was
strictly controlled and supervised. I had never walked
out the door of our house knowing I was going to see
a boy, a boy who might like me, who might kiss me,
who I might fall in love with and laugh with and
dance with, a boy who would make me happy. I loved
the songs I heard, and they made me smile. And
they made me hope. And they made me dream. I had
dreams I had only dreamed of having. Maybe someday I would know something real about them. Maybe
someday some of them would come true. After two
hours of songs and dreams and smiles and some
awkward dancing, the phone rang. Jacob answered
the phone when he was home, and it was my job to
answer it while he was out, though no one ever called

for me. I immediately turned off the radio, assuming it was someone for Jacob, and knowing that if they heard the radio, I would pay for it later. I picked up and said hello, and a man asked me if I knew Ruth Avrohom. I told him she was my mother. He said he was a social worker from a hospital in Brooklyn, and that my mother was there, and that they needed someone to sign some forms related to her. I asked him what had happened, and he said he could not share details, but that he would discuss it if I came to the hospital. I asked him if she was okay, and he said she was in critical condition. I got the address and hung up.

Without thinking, or without thinking of the potential repercussions, I left immediately. I took the subway and found the hospital. It was in a poor section of Brooklyn, and I was the only white person there, at least among the patients and visitors. I asked a woman where to find my mother. She sent me to the critical care unit. When I got there, I had to speak to another woman, who gave me my mother's room number, but told me I had to wait for a doctor to speak to me. I sat down and I waited.

I waited for a long time. I was very scared. People looked at me like I didn't belong there, in that hospital, and I felt the same way. No one else was white. Lots of the people didn't speak English. I knew people who weren't white or didn't speak very much English at church, but there we were all united by our belief in God. At the hospital we weren't united by anything. I had no idea what they believed. I didn't trust them. I could tell by the way they were looking at me that they didn't trust me. One asked me if I was a police officer. Another asked me if I worked for the state and was there to take away someone's child. Most just stared at me for a minute or sat where they didn't have to be too close to me. Finally a doctor came to see me. He asked to see my ID and I showed it to him. He walked me to a room down the hall, where my mother was lying in a bed. Her face was hideously swollen and there were large bruises on it. There were tubes and wires going in and out of her arms and a tube going into her mouth and bandages all over her. Her eyes were closed.

I didn't know what to do, what to say. I was scared to step into the room. The doctor told me she had been attacked outside a homeless shelter. There were no real details as to what exactly had happened, but he had heard that there had been a dispute regarding food with a man at the shelter. The supervisor at the shelter had seen her leave, and she was found an hour later in an alley two blocks away. She had been raped and beaten. Her nose and cheekbones were broken and her skull fractured. She was stable, and would most likely live, but she was in poor condition. The police had taken a report, but there were no real suspects and they didn't expect to arrest anyone. He said that for the immediate future my mother could stay at the hospital, but that she would have to leave fairly soon. He asked if I could take her in. I started crying.

I stayed with her for a couple of hours. I sat at her bedside and tried to apologize to her. I knew she couldn't hear me but I did it anyway. When I got home, Jacob was waiting for me. I tried to tell him what had happened but he said he didn't care. Our mother was no longer our mother to him. I tried to talk to him about it and he hit me, and he kept hitting me. When he stopped, I went to my room and I stared at the ceiling until I heard Jacob go to sleep. I waited for an hour after that, and I got up and I got dressed and I left.

I went to Manhattan. The subway was empty. It was the middle of the night. My plan was to go back to all of the people I had seen and ask them again if they knew where I could find Ben Zion. I would explain the circumstances and why I needed to see him, believing if I could find him and bring him back, Jacob would allow our mother to come home, where I could care for her. I came out of the station into the city. The sidewalks were deserted. The shops were all closed. There were no cars on the street. It was quiet and still and beautiful. The long, straight blocks stretching out to the horizon line. The buildings in shadows, in black. The electric storefront signs were glowing red, yellow, blue. The streetlights were flickering. The blacktop was deserted. The closest location was the hospital, so I started walking towards it. For fifteen minutes I saw no one, though I did occasionally see shadows moving behind lit windows. As I got closer to the hospital, I started to see cars, and a few people. Hospitals are one of the few places in

the world that never sleep, never stop, never have a
chance to breathe, to be alone or quiet, to be deserted.
The closer I got, the more people I saw, some in scrubs
or white coats with badges on the front, some just
sad or upset, some who looked sick and lost. I went
to the emergency room, where the doctor worked.
There were a few people in the waiting room. All of
them looked scared, almost guilty. A young woman
and a young man, both dressed like they had been
somewhere fancy, looked like they'd seen a ghost. A
little boy held his father's hand. An old woman sat by
herself and stared at the floor. A couple was sitting
together, the woman sobbing into the man's shoulder.
As I walked to the reception desk, I saw the doctor
standing in an office behind it. She was on the phone.
She seemed very serious. The receptionist asked if
she could help me and I told her I needed to see the
doctor. She asked why and I told her it was about
my brother. She asked if my brother was a patient at
the hospital and I told her he was but not anymore.
She asked why I needed to speak to the doctor and I
told her it was very important, that it was about my
brother. I asked her to give the doctor my name and
tell her I needed to see her. She said she would and I
sat down.

I waited for an hour. Every time a doctor or nurse
would come in, everyone would look up, some
mixture of great fear and great hope on their faces,
knowing that at any minute they were going to be
either saved or ruined. The fourth time, the woman
doctor came in and looked at me and smiled and sat

down next to me. She said hello and asked me what had happened. She could see fresh bruises on my arms and neck, and assumed I was there for some kind of care. I told her about what had happened with my mother and the situation at home, though when she asked if Jacob had beaten me, I said no, and I told her I needed to find Ben Zion, and that I had been searching for him for several weeks and couldn't find any trace of him, or anyone who would even talk to me about him. She asked me if I thought Ben Zion would be in any danger if I found him, and I said no, we're his family, we need him, we love him and we miss him and we need him. She smiled and said she'd be back, and she hugged me and walked away. She came back a little while later with a sticky note in her hand. She said he was living on a farm upstate and that she'd called the farm and spoken to him. He told her to give me the address and that I should come see him, and that he loved me. I took the sticky note and she hugged me and I left.

I walked to the bus station. I had enough money to buy a ticket most of the way there, but not all of the way. The station was disgusting. And frightening. It was dirty, and there were lots of homeless people and men who stood around waiting for something, or someone, and never seemed to leave. More people seemed to be coming to the city than were leaving it. As I watched them get off their buses, I wondered how many of them, if any at all, would end up happy, or would think they had made a good decision. I found my bus as fast as I could and got on and sat down in the seat directly behind the driver, so that if anything happened, I'd be near someone who could help me.

The ride was a few hours. The bus was mostly empty. An old couple sitting together holding hands. Three girls with shopping bags. A teenaged girl who looked tired and sad. A teenaged boy who looked like he was going to explode. I stared out the window at the green blur and the endless gray line stretching out in front of us. Three hours later I got off in a small town in upstate New York. It looked like it had been nice at some point in the past. The houses were clapboard Victorian, and many of them were very large, though most were now decrepit. There was a main street lined with shops, almost all of which were now closed and boarded. There were liquor stores and churches. Three gun shops. A discount clothing store and a thrift shop. A used car lot full of pick-up trucks, and crumbling factories at the edge of town. Most of the people I saw were sitting on their porch, or their lawn. Nobody seemed to be working. I stopped at a gas station and asked how to get to the town where Ben Zion was living. The man laughed at me when he asked me how I was getting there and I said I was walking, but he gave me directions anyway. He told me it was about seventy miles away. I started walking down the road. It was a two-lane country road with garbage and weeds along the sides. When I saw cars, I would step deeper into the weeds so that no one would see me, even though I knew they did. I was tired and my body still hurt from Jacob, and I was ashamed to be walking along the side of the

road. I didn't have running shoes or walking shoes.
Just my church shoes, cheap black leather flats with
plastic soles. And I was wearing what I always wore,
a long skirt and a long-sleeved blouse and long socks.
I started sweating almost immediately, and I hadn't
eaten or had anything to drink for a long time. I'd
walk for a while, and then I'd sit down and rest. I was
making some progress, but seventy miles seemed like
a thousand. I could not imagine walking the entire
way. And I knew that at some point I'd need to sleep,
and find some food. I knew that at some point I'd
need to find shelter of some kind.

I started praying as I walked. I was talking to Jesus
and the Holy Father, and asking them for aid and
guidance. I told them I was scared and needed help.
I told them I was devoted to them and believed in
them and would do whatever they asked of me if they
helped me. I begged them for a sign, for something
to let me know they could hear my prayers. I held my
hands together, above my heart, as I walked, and
I looked up towards where I believed Heaven was,
and I asked for the angels to come down to me.
I believed, because I believed in and lived by the
word of God as expressed in the Bible and had a
personal relationship with Christ, that help would
come in some form. I prayed so hard. I kept walking,
and I prayed so hard.

I don't know how far I got the first day, probably ten
or fifteen miles. I slept in a park in a small town that
looked exactly like the first one. All of them looked

like the first one. I was woken by a police officer's boot. He was pushing me with it. Not in a violent or angry way, but enough to wake me. He asked me who I was and what I was doing. When I told him where I was going, he laughed at me and turned and walked away. I got up and got back on the road.

It was a long day. The longest day of my life. I drank water from gas station bathrooms. I ate food from garbage cans. I walked for hours and hours. My feet and my body hurt. I kept praying. I kept asking Jesus Christ and the Holy Father for help. Twice cars pulled over and I believed my prayers had been answered. Both times men offered me rides if I would do things with them, if I would defile myself for them. Both times I ran off the road into the woods to hide. When they pulled away I came out, and I just kept walking.

Three days after I got off the bus, I found the entrance to the farm. My feet were burning and my throat was burning and I felt like I was going to vomit. I thanked God for giving me the strength to make it. I literally got on my knees and looked to where Heaven is supposed to be and thanked Jesus Christ and God. I thanked them for guiding me and keeping me safe and showing me where to sleep and where to find water and where to find food. I thanked them for allowing me to recognize non-Christian predators and avoid them. I thanked them for allowing the doctor to tell me where to find Ben Zion. I thanked them for Ben Zion himself, and for the gift of having him as my brother. I stayed on my knees for an hour, praying and thanking Jesus and the Heavenly Father. I stayed on my knees until the urge to vomit disappeared and until I felt like they had given me my strength back.

The walk up the drive was easy. The road was long and straight and there were woods on both sides. It took about ten minutes. When I came to the end, there was a large white farmhouse and a barn, and huge overgrown fields behind them. There were people around. Some were working a garden, some just sitting around. They all looked happy. A large woman asked if I needed help. I told her I was looking for Ben. She said he was out and she wasn't sure when he'd be back. I asked for a glass of water and she got me one. She tried to talk to me but I asked her to leave me alone, and she did.

I watched the people around the farm. There were all types of people, all colors, different ages. Some of them were definitely strange, or what Jacob would call perverted or deviant. Men were holdings hands. Women were holding hands. I had been taught for my entire life that homosexuals were evil and damned to Hell. That they spread disease. That they were mentally ill. I was scared of them. I didn't want them coming near me, and although I had seen Ben kiss Jeremiah, I thought that was more just to anger Jacob than because he accepted them or their lifestyle, and I couldn't believe he was living with them.

I sat on the porch for an hour or so. Once I stopped moving, my fatigue caught up with me. I had trouble keeping my eyes open. It took a great effort to bring the glass to my lips, though the water was wonderful when I did. It felt like my chest was weighted down, and each breath was work, and with each I could feel my strength dissipating. The woman who had gotten me my water checked on me occasionally. The rest of the people, and they were coming in and out of the house, coming down the road with bags that appeared to be filled with food and clothes, people going out to the barn, seemed not to notice me, and when they did, they were very friendly, and seemingly normal. Finally Ben came walking out of the fields. He was with a couple, and they looked happy, and he hugged each of them. He turned towards me and saw me and smiled. He looked thin, and his hair was longer, and he was still pale, and his scars looked worse than I remembered them, or they seemed to jump out more. He walked towards me, and I started smiling. He sat down with me and took my hand and put his arms around me and said hello. I immediately started crying, sobbing, into his shoulder. I couldn't say anything, I just sobbed. And it felt wonderful to do it. I felt secure and strong. I wasn't scared anymore. I felt comfortable and calm. I felt like what I wanted to feel like when I was praying to Jesus and the Holy Father. I felt loved.

He took me by the hand and led me to a room. He told me I should lie down, and the bed was big and the sheets were clean and I was so tired. I tried to tell him about what had happened in New York and why I was there and how our mother needed him and how Jacob was going to lose the church and how Pastor Luke had left. He just smiled and said I should sleep. I told him he would only have to come back for a few days and he could leave again and come back here or go anywhere. He said once he left he'd never be back, and I asked why and he said because we both know what is going to happen when I get back to New York. I told him we'd get our mother home and he'd talk to Jacob and everything would be fine. He smiled and told me he loved me and would come get me later, after I'd slept, and he left the room.

I fell asleep almost immediately. I woke to Ben Zion sitting next to my bed, his hand on my arm. It was dark, and there was no light coming through the window. He smiled at me and said it was time to go. I got out of bed. He had a pair of shoes for me. Not new new, but someone else's shoes that were in better condition than mine, and were better for walking. I asked him why we were leaving in the middle of the night, and he said it was easier to walk because it was cooler, and there were more trucks on the road, which would increase our chances of getting a ride. He walked out the door and motioned for me to follow him.

We walked through the house. It was silent and dark. As we came down the stairs, I saw people in the living and dining rooms. There were five or six in each room. Most of them were nude, and they were

entwined with each other. I saw two of them kissing,
and moving, and I immediately looked away.
I believed that whatever they were doing, it was
wrong. Whatever they were doing, it was against
the ways of God. Whatever they were doing was
a sin. Ben didn't pay any attention to them.
We left the house.

The yard was the same. It was warm out and people
were sleeping on blankets in the grass, and some of
them were still awake. The moon was high and
half full, so I could see them better, and they were
doing the same sorts of things, and some of them
were making noises. I saw two men kissing, their
arms around each other, and I looked away again.
I must have tensed up, because Ben took my hand and
spoke.
It's okay to look.
I spoke.
It's wrong.
Why?
It's a sin.
Why?
It goes against the word of God as expressed in the
Holy Bible.
Two people making each other happy isn't wrong.
They're both men.
They're both human beings.
Leviticus 18:22 says you shall not lie with a male as
one lies with a female; it is an abomination.
I can see that they're happy, and they love each other,
and they're making each other feel good.

Their souls are damned.
You hate them for how they live?
Yes.
Your Bible also says, in 1 John 4:20, if anyone says,
"I love God," yet hates his brother, he is a liar.
For anyone who does not love his brother, whom he
has seen, cannot love God, whom he has not seen.
In God's eyes, as I have been taught, because of what
they are, they are not my brothers.
You've been taught wrong. We are all the same,
regardless of who and how we love.
That's not what the Bible says.
The Bible is a book. Books are for telling stories.
They're not for denying people the right to live
as they choose. Live by what you feel, and what
feels right to you, not by what some book of stories
tells you.
I can't look at them.
You don't have to look, but it's no different than a
man and woman in love, and you wouldn't look away
from that.
If they were sinning I would.
There is no such thing as sin. Only control and guilt.
We walked away from the house, down the drive.
He kept holding my hand. We turned off the drive and
started walking down the road. I asked him where we
were going and he said the highway.
We walked for thirty more minutes. We didn't speak,
but it wasn't awkward. Ben Zion made me calm,
made me feel safe, made my insecurities and anxieties disappear. He just held my hand and walked next
to me. And as ridiculous as it may sound, sometimes

all any of us needs in life is for someone to hold our hand and walk next to us.

We made it to the highway and started along the side of it. There were lots of trucks, and very few cars. They would drive by us and the wind they created would move me a little, and I was scared because they were so close. Ben just walked and didn't appear to be scared at all. He told me that he had done this a number of times and that usually someone would stop and offer a ride, though it might be harder because there were two of us. And even though I had had some sleep, I was tired and couldn't imagine walking all the way back to New York.

After an hour or so, a truck pulled over. It was an eighteen wheeler with the logo of a grocery store on the side. The driver rolled down the window and asked where we were going and Ben said New York. He said he could take us to New Jersey, and we climbed into the truck. The cab of the truck had a small area behind the seats with a small cot mattress and a blanket. I went back and lay down. I tried to stay awake to hear what he and Ben Zion would talk about, because I was curious what the Messiah would say to someone he had just met, but almost as soon as we started moving, I fell asleep. When I woke up, we were in New Jersey. The truck was stuck in traffic, and we were barely moving. Ben and the driver were telling each other jokes. Silly one-liners and knock-knock jokes. They would tell a joke and laugh and laugh and laugh. I didn't really get the jokes, and when Ben heard me he turned around and said hello and put his hand on my head. Though I had been a bit sleepy still, I was immediately awake, and my heart was beating really fast, like I had just been running or something, or like what I imagined it must be like to be on drugs. All of the worries and fears and insecurities were gone. This weight I had felt my entire life, that I think every person feels, this weight that is our existence, or our soul, or the bad things that permeate our souls and infect us and make us do bad things, was gone. I didn't know what to say, so I said hi, and Ben Zion laughed and he told me we were almost home. I smiled and said good, and the trucker turned around and looked at me and said hello, and I smiled, but wasn't sure what to say. I rarely spoke to men outside of church. He told me my brother was a funny guy, and a good travel partner, and I smiled and said yeah. He asked me if I was shy, and Ben Zion said yes, she's shy, she's a good Christian girl, or she used to be before I came around, and they both laughed and I was a little confused by what Ben Zion meant and why the trucker would laugh. I did, though, feel different, felt better and lighter, felt the way I had felt before when I had been sick and woken up better, like my fever had broken or something, like I wasn't sick anymore. The trucker turned back around and Ben Zion told another joke and they laughed again and we kept moving slowly towards the city. That was it for the next ten or fifteen minutes. They told more jokes and the trucker called another trucker to ask about traffic and he called his destination and told them how far away he was. He pulled off an exit and to the side of the road and I could see the skyline of New York in the distance. The sun was coming up between the skyscrapers and streams of light were pouring through the spaces between them. And even though I had lived there for my entire life, I hated New York, and was scared of it, and thought of it as a cesspool of sin, a modern-day Gomorrah, a place where the Devil took the souls of innocents every day. This morning it was beautiful. The buildings were all shining. The Hudson was calm and there were ferries moving slowly across it, small wakes trailing behind them. I could see the George Washington Bridge, and cars streaming on both levels, full of people going to their jobs, or to see friends, or shop, or visit the sights, or do whatever they were going to do, and I felt happy for them, like the bright shiny beautiful place they were going was somehow going to help them, or make them better, or make them happy. And I didn't resent them for it. I guess growing up in an environment where I was told everyone was wrong and we were right and everyone was going to Hell and we weren't had me scared and hateful, and resentful, in a way, of people who didn't think like me or live like me. But for some reason this morning, all of it was gone, all of it was gone.

We got out of the truck and the trucker got out with us and he gave Ben Zion a big hug and said thank you over and over, and Ben Zion said no, thank you for the kindness of the ride, and the man started crying. I don't know why, but he did, he just stood there and cried and Ben Zion held him against his shoulder and let him do it. The sun was still rising behind them. And the light was still streaming. And the ferries and cars were still moving. And all of the people in the city and going to the city were alive and living their lives and I loved them all. And I don't know why, but I did. And I know Ben Zion did. And I know that trucker did. And I don't know why or what Ben Zion did to me or to that man while I was asleep and before they were telling silly jokes and laughing, but it's never left me, and while I may have wondered before, I didn't after. I didn't anymore.

The trucker watched us walk away. Ben Zion took my hand again and he smiled and we walked towards the bridge. It took an hour or so. Walking along empty sidewalks next to roads packed with cars. We crossed the bridge, and the closer we got to the city, the more beautiful it looked, the brighter it seemed. We were the only people walking on the bridge; everyone else was in cars or trucks, and almost all of them were alone. Tens of thousands of people, all of them going to the same place, all of them alone. We came down off the bridge and into the city. We were in upper Manhattan, where it's mostly long blocks of low-rent apartment buildings, and empty factory buildings, and warehouses, and where some of the subway trains run on elevated tracks. I asked Ben Zion where we were going and he told me the subway and I told him I didn't have any money and he told me we didn't need any. He led me into a tunnel where one of the trains came out of the ground, and it went from being bright and

beautiful to being pitch black and terrifying. I told
him I was scared and he said don't be, and I asked
him if he knew where we were going, and he said yes,
he had come across the bridge and into this tunnel
many times.

We walked right down the middle of the tunnel, in
the area between the two tracks. Occasionally there'd
be an overhead light, but mostly it was black.
I could hear dripping water and rats, and once or
twice I heard some yelling. When the trains would
come by, I'd put my hands over my ears, and the wind
was really strong and the girders holding the tunnel
up would shake a little bit. The trains were only
a few feet away, and the people in them were a blur.
Even though Ben was with me, I stayed scared.
I felt like we were walking into Hell and the trains
were full of souls of the damned, rushing towards
eternal fire and pain. And though I would have
once thought, having seen what I saw with Ben Zion,
and having disobeyed Jacob, and having forsaken
my mother, that I was going to join them, this time
I didn't. If I was walking into Hell, I knew I'd walk
out. Or if I felt like we were walking into Hell,
I believed that there was no such thing. There is only
life. This life that we live. If it is Hell, it is because
we make it so.

I saw lights ahead of us, and we came to a platform
and we climbed up and waited for the next train.
There were a few other people on the platform, but
they paid no attention to us and didn't seem to be

bothered by the fact that we had come walking out
of the tunnel. We got on a downtown train and
switched to one going to Brooklyn. Nobody on the
trains spoke or really even looked at each other.
Ben held my hand and closed his eyes and leaned his
head against the window and breathed through his
nose, and though he looked like he was asleep, I don't
think he was. Once a thin white man in a nice suit
got on with a briefcase, and Ben immediately opened
his eyes. The man was sitting across from us and
further down, and Ben stared at him. He didn't give
him a dirty look or a mean look, just stared at him.
At the next station the man got off the train.

It took an hour or so. We got off and walked
to the hospital. When we arrived, our mother was
sleeping. The doctor said she was fine but not good.
Ben Zion took me to the waiting room and left.
I asked him where he was going and he said
for a walk. I asked him where and he just smiled
and walked away.

He came back three hours later. I had tried to pray
while he was gone, but had had trouble doing it.
It seemed strange to be talking to something that
wasn't there, or that I didn't know was there, or that
I believed was there but had no evidence was there.
And I saw other people in the waiting room who were
praying. I watched them carefully. Two of them
were praying to a Christian God, and I know because
one had a Bible with them and the other made the
sign of the cross before prayer, and another was a

Muslim, and had a copy of the Qur'an. They were
praying very hard, and they were very focused.
I was used to praying with other people, sometimes
many other people, especially at Bible conventions
and Christian Youth meetings, so that wasn't it.
I just couldn't do it at that moment, and wanted to
see other people do it, and wanted to see what,
if anything, happened. There were magazines in the
room, magazines with movie stars on the front of
them and silly headlines and bright pictures of pretty
people in fancy clothes. I picked one up and looked
at it. While I looked at it, I watched the people
praying. If the outside of the magazines seemed silly,
the insides were worse. The stories were about people
who were very concerned with how they looked and
dressed, and how much money they made, and the
houses they lived in. And while I could understand
worrying about those things on some level, they
seemed incredibly insignificant in a hospital, a place
where people were sick and diseased and dying,
and where the people who loved them came to watch
them suffer. At the same time, what the people
praying were doing seemed equally insignificant.
They were all begging for help, for aid, for some way
to relieve their suffering, and to relieve the suffering
of whomever they were praying for, begging to characters in books, characters that no one had ever
met or seen or spoken to and was sure even existed.
They were praying to whatever God or Savior
they believed in to save them, and in the same way
that some people worship the silly people in the
magazines, who we at least know are real, they

worshipped the people in their books, who we don't
know anything about. I watched a doctor come in to
see one of the Christians, and he had some type of
bad news, because the person immediately started
sobbing. A family member of the other Christian,
or someone who I assumed was a family member
because they looked exactly alike, came in to take the
person away, and the family member had clearly been
crying. The man with the Qur'an saw what I saw, that
the prayer had clearly done nothing, but kept clutching his book and praying anyway. I wondered, and
I still wonder, if I had replaced their books with the
silly magazines I had been looking at, and if they
had worshipped the silly people in those magazines,
if they would have gotten the same result.

When Ben Zion came back, he smiled and told
me to come with him. I stood and we left the waiting
room and walked to our mother's room. When we
went in, she was awake and she smiled at me.
The tubes were out of her mouth, but there were
others still in her arms, and she was still covered in
bandages. I sat next to her and took her hand and told
her I was so sorry and that I loved her and I started
crying. She pulled me towards her, and though
she was too weak to really do it, I understood what
she wanted, and I stood and put my arms around her.
I kept telling her I was sorry and that I loved her,
and she put her hands on the back of my head and
held me against her chest. Ben Zion stood a few feet
away and watched us. After a minute or two, our
mother let me go and I pulled away and sat back

down, though I still held her hand. Ben Zion walked over and kissed me on the forehead, and leaned towards my mother and whispered something in her ear, though I did not hear what it was. She smiled and kissed his check, and he stepped away and sat with me. He stayed until she feel asleep, and when she did, he stood and kissed her forehead and turned and started to walk out of the room. I asked him where he was going, and he stopped and turned around and looked at me and spoke.

I'm leaving.

Where to?

I'm going to see Jacob.

Don't.

I'm going to make sure you never have to see him again.

Don't hurt him.

I wouldn't hurt anyone.

Then why go?

I want you to be free.

I'll be fine.

Fine is no way to live. Take care of Mom.

You call her Mom?

When I was little I called her Mommy, when I got older it was Mom. Only when we were alone. It was our little thing, away from the rules and formality of our home.

Is she going to be okay?

I don't know if she wants to live anymore. She's had a long, brutal life.

She didn't deserve it.

None of us deserve it.

He turned and walked to the door.
Don't let him hurt you, Ben Zion.
I love you, Esther.

PETER

I met Ben at his arraignment hearing. It was at the Queens County Criminal Courthouse. He had been arrested and charged with attempted murder and arson. I am an attorney and work for the criminal defense division of the Legal Aid Society. In simple, layman's terms, I am a public defender. I literally drew his file out of a basket. In doing so, I have been irrevocably changed. In almost every way for the better. Except for the rage I feel when I think about what was done to him.

I became what I am because of my father. He was a drug dealer. He was not a drug lord or anyone of importance in the drug trade. Rappers have not glorified him in their songs. Writers have not written books about him. Hollywood has not made his life into an award-winning drama. He was, like many black men, both now and in the '70s, when he was active, a street-level drug dealer. He literally stood on a corner and sold drugs. He did so because he believed there were no other options. He was not well-educated. There were no jobs available to him. He did not have parents who were able to support or nurture him. We lived, and still do, in Harlem. He and my mother were married, and still are, and they had three children, me and my twin sisters, who are a year younger than me. We lived in a fifth-floor walk-up. My mother worked as a checkout

clerk at a grocery store but made very little money.
My father looked for legitimate employment but was
unable to find anything. He did what he had to do.
He took the only job that was available to him.

As I said, he was a street-level dealer. He stood on a
corner and sold heroin and cocaine. His customers
were mainly whites from the suburbs and the more
economically privileged areas of Manhattan, though
there were plenty of local customers. In 1973, New
York State passed a series of statutes known as the
Rockefeller drug laws. The purpose of the laws was
to stem the flow of drugs into the state by institut-
ing harsh penalties for the sale and distribution of
them. If an individual was caught with more than two
ounces of either cocaine or heroin, and there was the
intent to distribute, they faced a minimum sentence
of fifteen years to life, and a maximum sentence of
twenty-five years to life. When my father was arrested
after selling cocaine to an undercover narcotics officer, he was in possession of a total of 2.5 ounces of
cocaine. The cocaine had been processed into crack.
It had been placed into small vials that held doses he
sold for ten, twenty, fifty, or one hundred dollars. It
was 1984. I was three years old, and my sisters were
two. After a two-day trial, my father was convicted
and sentenced to twenty-five years to life. While
I don't condone what he did, the idea that he was
given a harsher sentence than many murderers, than
almost all child molesters, than the rich white-collar
criminals who have bled this country and its people
dry, than corrupt politicians destroying our cities,

makes me absolutely sick to my stomach. My sisters and I were left without a father. My mother was left without a husband. My father was sent to a maximum security prison, where he still resides, and where he believes he will die. My sisters and I spent the rest of our childhood visiting him on his birthday, and on Christmas, and on the Fourth of July. It wasn't until I was older that I understood the irony of the July visit. Let us celebrate life in the Land of the Free and the Home of the Brave.

Having lost my father, my mother was determined to keep me from following in his footsteps. She took a second job, also working as a cashier, at a second grocery store. She enrolled us in a preschool at our church. She was able to dress us in secondhand clothes that looked firsthand, and she drilled into us that the system, the system of opportunity in America, and everywhere in the world, was rigged against us. We would have to work twice as hard to get half as much. We were poor and black and we lived in a ghetto. The schools we were supposed to attend were not going to educate us in a way that would prepare us for success. No doors would open for us because of the color of our skin or because of our last name. We would have to behave twice as well, work twice as hard, achieve twice as much. And if we could do those things, we had a chance. If we could not, we would end up like her, and almost all of the women in our neighborhood, working eighteen hours a day to support her family in a single-parent home, or like our father, and a large number of the fathers of children in our neighborhood, in prison for taking the only job available to him.

Though I do have happy memories, it was not a happy childhood. I studied most of the time. I was mocked and beaten by the other boys in my neighborhood, boys destined to follow my father's path. I started working part-time when I was fourteen in anticipation of college. The job was at one of the grocery stores where my mother worked. I took a weekend job picking up garbage in Central Park. I graduated third in my class in high school and got a partial academic scholarship to a large state school. I worked in the school cafeteria to cover what the scholarship didn't. I went straight into law school, which I did in New York, also on a partial academic scholarship. I worked in the school library at night and went back to my weekend job picking up garbage in the park. As soon as I finished law school, I became a public defender. And while I am not always successful in helping people like my father, or women who might have been my mother or my sisters, who both became doctors by working as I worked, I fight like a motherfucker to do what I can. I scream. I yell. I try every trick in the book, because I know the government is going to use everything they've got. I spend most of my free time studying areas of the law that I believe might apply to my work. I seek out experts in other fields who might have applicable knowledge to share with me. I don't bother speaking to young men to warn them of the evils of the drug trade, or of crime. They know the evils, and they know the potential consequences. They know the system has been rigged against them since the moment they were born. They know the world is rigged against them. If you aren't born with a silver spoon in your mouth, regardless of your race, religion, or sexual orientation, you might as well have been born in shackles. I'm not bitter about it. I accept it as it is. But I fight like a motherfucker against it.

As I said, I met Ben at the Queens County Criminal Courthouse, where I go to work every day. After an individual has been arrested, he or she goes to a precinct holding cell. From there, a prosecutor in the intake bureau of the DA's office looks at the case and files charges. The offender is booked and fingerprinted and sent to central booking. A criminal history, also known as a rap sheet, is brought up, and the Criminal Justice Agency looks at both the charges and the criminal history and makes a bail recommendation. All three are then put together in a case file. The case files are put in a basket when the individual is brought to court for their arraignment hearing. We, the public defenders, draw the files out of the basket, and the individual whose file I draw becomes my client. I meet them in an interview booth behind the courtroom. The interview booth is basically a Plexiglas box, where I communicate with my client through a partition. After briefly reviewing their file, I talk to them about their potential bail options. In the best-case scenario, there is a chance I will be able to get them out. In the worst, I can do nothing.

Looking at Ben's file, I knew he wasn't going anywhere. He had been charged with the attempted murder of his brother. The prosecutor claimed that he had also burned down a church and had charged him with arson. He had jumped bail on a long list of federal charges. I remembered reading about the federal case in the newspapers. Some kind of heavily armed apocalyptic cult in the subway tunnels. A large number of arrests. The leader of the cult had been killed in prison while awaiting trial, after supposedly attacking a guard. There were a number of questions surrounding the death, including whether he had actually attacked anyone, and even if he had, whether the force used in subduing him, which killed him, had been justified. Ben was facing life sentences in both the state and federal cases. He was considered violent, and an obvious flight risk. There was mention in the file of potential mental instability. He had been booked in Queens, but transferred for three days of treatment to a local hospital that had a secure wing. He had been taken into custody with severe facial swelling, multiple facial lacerations, nine broken ribs, a punctured lung, and a broken arm. Normally I would have assumed that the police had administered the beating. The file, however, said that he had been taken into custody in that condition, and that he had been injured by witnesses trying to subdue him after his alleged offenses. I saw him as I was walking to the interview. Needless to say, his appearance was startling. He was sitting in a hospital robe, chained to a chair. He was absolutely still, motionless. And he looked like he was in bad shape. Stitched gashes across one of his cheeks. Black eyes. A nose that had clearly been broken. One arm in a cast. And if he hadn't had his ass beaten recently, he would still have been startling. He had jet black hair and marble white skin. He was covered with the most severe scars I had ever seen, and I had seen plenty of them. He was extremely thin, though he did not look unhealthy. Actually, despite his wounds, quite the opposite. He looked like he was glowing in the way people some-times describe pregnant women as glowing. He was staring straight ahead. Did not acknowledge anyone or anything around him. As I got closer, he started following me with his eyes, though he did not move in any other way. It was unnerving. Like I was being stared down by a statue. I sat down across from him. I set the open file down on my lap.

I spoke.

Hello.

He smiled.

Hello.

I've been assigned to be your public defender.

Thank you.

You've been charged with attempted murder, assault and battery, and five counts of arson. Do you under-stand these charges?

Yes.

Do you want to tell me what happened?

It doesn't matter.

If you want to try to stay out of prison it does.

What happens to me at this point is beyond anything you can do.

You're facing a life sentence. I'd like to try to help you avoid it.

Do you know why I'm really here?

I don't know anything except what's in this file, which is very basic information, and lays out some very serious charges.

Whatever's in that file is meaningless to me. And it doesn't actually have anything to do with me.

It has absolutely everything to do with why you're in court today.

I don't recognize that this court has any authority over me.

Unfortunately, you're going to have to.

No, I'm not.

I need you to work with me on this, Mr. Avrohom.

He didn't respond. He just sat there, staring straight ahead. It isn't unusual to have a client who won't speak. Or a client who has no respect for the legal system. There are times, quite often, that I too don't have any respect for the system, which is one of the reasons I do the job. Unlike other offenders I'd encountered who didn't speak, or seemed potentially belligerent, though, he didn't have a perp stare. A perp stare is an offender's attempt to appear strong, intimidating, and fearless in the face of their charges, in the face of the system aligned against them, a system that often destroys them. There is always fear in a perp stare. That's actually all that it is. Fear. An attempt to control fear. His stare was quite the opposite. It was soft. Almost gentle. If I had seen him sitting somewhere other than where he was, I might have thought he had just received good news. He

seemed happy. And calm. Remarkably still.
He, and his expression, were absolutely devoid of any
fear. I believed, in that moment, and still do, that if
I had put a gun in his face, he would not have moved.
If I had told him there was an electric chair in the
room next to us and it was being prepped for him,
he would not have moved. If I had told him he was
going to be burned at the stake or crucified, he would
not have moved. He was beyond it. He was the first
and only person I've ever seen or met who was truly
beyond fear. I literally did not know what to say.

We sat there for a minute. Maybe two. We did not
have much time. We should have been talking.
I knew, though, that regardless of what I said, he was
not going to cooperate with me. He smiled at me and
lifted his hand. He placed it on the glass partition and
held it there. He stared at me. Looked directly into
my eyes and held his hand on the partition. Although
I wasn't sure I wanted to do it, I raised my hand and
placed it directly opposite his. And I don't know how
it happened, but I knew absolutely and unequivocally
that he was innocent. I knew it as much as I had ever
known anything in my life.
You didn't do it.
Does it matter?
What happened?
I was brought here.
I don't think I'm going to be able to get you bail.
I don't need bail.
You'll probably be sent to Rikers.
I'll be safe there.

Nobody's safe there.

They don't want me in prison.

What are you talking about?

Do what you can to stop them.

He took his hand down. His name was called, and
we went into the courtroom. It was a large venue.
Very busy. People were, rightfully, concerned about
themselves. They rarely, if ever, paid attention to
anyone else. Ben silenced the room when he walked
into it. Everyone turned and stared. The glow I had
seen at the interview seemed brighter, more real.
His skin was whiter. His scars more visible. And his
presence. The presence beyond the physical. It was
unlike anything I have ever seen. Before or since.
Hardened lawyers, hardened criminals, bailiffs,
and cops. They were all silenced. By his calm and
stillness. By the glow.

When the judge entered, Ben refused to stand.
He refused to acknowledge the court in any way.
He just stared straight ahead and smiled. The judge
threatened him with contempt. He just kept smiling.
A pure, simple smile. Mouth closed and cheeks
drawn. Staring straight at her. She asked him to
stand again. He slowly and calmly shook his head.
Normally she would have charged him immediately
with contempt of court, but she didn't. She turned
to me and asked if I was willing to waive the reading
of the rights and charges, and I said yes. She turned
to the prosecutor who gave grand jury notice, which
meant that he would take the case to a grand jury for
an indictment, which is required by law in New York.

The prosecutor then asked for denial of bail based on the seriousness of the crime and the defendant's background. I requested bail of ten thousand dollars. She looked again at Ben. He was still staring at her, and she was clearly unnerved. Most offenders are either deferential to the judge or belligerent towards her. He just stared and smiled. She asked him one more time to stand. He did not move. She denied bail. When the bailiff came towards him, Ben stood and allowed himself to be led away.

I had a full day, with a number of other cases. I took Ben's file with me when I left. I started reading it on the subway home. It seemed fairly simple. His brother was a pastor at a church in Queens. When Ben was incarcerated on the federal charges, his brother had put up both his home and his church as collateral for Ben's bail. Ben had disappeared shortly after being released, though how he had disabled his ankle bracelet was unknown. No one had heard from him for seven months. He had reappeared at his brother's home four nights earlier. He had a rabbi with him. They had dinner together, and the next morning went to services at the brother's church. The brother claimed they were going to the service so that Ben could repent before turning himself back over to federal authorities. There was some type of altercation at the church. Ben was beaten and taken to the office of the church. He was locked inside while they waited for the police. While in the office, he lit it on fire. When Jacob, his brother, came to the office after smelling smoke, Ben attacked him and said he was going to kill him. Once again Ben was beaten and subdued, and shortly thereafter, he was taken into custody.

There was nothing to indicate that anything was wrong with the case. It seemed airtight. Multiple witnesses. Physical evidence. The officers at the scene followed proper procedure. When I first get a case, I always look for holes in it. Look for spaces of doubt where I can move in and create openings. Look for small cracks that I can turn into fucking canyons. There were none in Ben's file. Nothing even close. Granted, sometimes it takes time to find them. Sometimes a witness will change their story. Or the evidence will prove to be something other than what it initially looks like. But Ben seemed to indicate, for whatever the reasons, that there weren't going to be any this time. And given how he made me feel, and what he made me feel, I believed him.

I thought about him at Rikers. Wondered what he was going through. A thin white man in his condition. He was out of medical and in general population. For the hardest men, the conditions are brutal. There's violence and rape. There are gangs, almost always divided by race, and if you're not affiliated with one, you're a target. People go in as petty criminals and come out as vicious predators. I doubted he would last long. Or if he did, he would be beaten and raped. Essentially enslaved. I stayed up with the file. Read it over and over again until my eyes hurt. Until I literally fell asleep with it in my arms.

I woke up. Got dressed. Went back to the courthouse, where I had a number of hearings scheduled. I kept thinking about Ben. About Rikers. About what I imagined was happening there. Midway through the morning, my phone rang. The prison's phone number showed on my caller ID. I took the call, expecting bad news. It was the warden of the prison. I was shocked. I had never spoken to him or had any contact with him. It was extraordinary to hear from him directly. He told me there was a problem. Asked if I could come to speak to him. I asked what the problem was, and he said he'd speak to me about it when I got there.

I took the subway to the bus and went over the Rikers bridge. I got through security and went to admin. The warden was waiting for me. I sat across from him. He spoke.
What do you know about your client?
Only what's in the file.
You ever hear of Yahya?
Heard of. Yes.
Know anything about him?
Very little.
He was a murderer. Killed his foster father when he was a kid. Disappeared for thirty years. Started some religious group in the subway tunnels. Preached about the evils of government and organized religion. Typical wacko shit. Scarred his followers, most of whom were drug addicts and petty criminals. Said the scars liberated them from society, freed them from its laws and obligations. They had their own

little world down there. Electricity, water. They did drugs and had orgies. Really fucked up. Near the end of their time, they built up a huge cache of weapons. Yahya said the apocalypse was coming. That the Messiah would arrive, heralding the end of the world. And when it came, he and his followers would be safe in the subways. I know all of this, more or less. They all got arrested. They were all held at the MCC. Yahya refused to acknowledge the authority of the court. Tried to reorganize his followers in prison. Got sent to solitary. Went on a hunger strike. Prosecutors got an order to feed him intravenously. When the guards opened his cell, he attacked them. As he was being subdued, he hit his head on the floor. His brain bled and he died. His followers went fucking crazy, and all of them ended up in solitary. Some got sent to other institutions, including this one. Everywhere they went, they preached the gospel of Yahya. And they preached the gospel of Yahya's Messiah, who had indeed arrived, and was the one member of his group who got bail and immediately disappeared.

My client.

Yes.

He's the Messiah.

He's a fucking lunatic that thinks he's the Messiah, and that some other lunatics think is the Messiah. Anything happened since he arrived?

It took a day or so for people to figure out who he was when he got to our medical facility. As soon as they did, the inmates started talking. We had him isolated so there were no problems, though we tried to listen to the chatter. When he came back yesterday, he entered general pop. I was watching when he went to the yard, where a group of inmates were waiting for him, which usually means someone's gonna get fucked up. As he walked out, they all stared at him. No one moved. The ones who weren't waiting for him stopped whatever they were doing and turned towards him. He went straight into the middle of the yard and sat down. First ones over to him were the ones who'd scarred themselves like Yahya. There are four or five of them. They have a few who follow them, who were all part of the initial group waiting for him. They followed. And then everyone in the yard, black, white, Hispanic, Blood, Crip, Latin King, DDP, Trinitario, fucking Hells Angels and mobsters, all walked over and sat down around him. I've never seen the yard so quiet, so still. Usually when it gets quiet it means there's gonna be a fucking war. It's the calm that descends before the killing starts. But not this time. Somehow he made men who literally spend most of their time trying to figure out how to murder each other sit around in a big circle. He started talking. We don't know what he said, and no one will tell us. We wanted to go in and break it up, but they weren't violating any of our regs, so we couldn't do a thing. He spoke for ten or fifteen minutes. At the end of it he stood up and walked around and put his hand on people's heads. Didn't say a word. Just put his hand on their foreheads and smiled. He walked back to where he had been and sat back down. Almost immediately, he had some kind of seizure. A fucking crazy, body-shaking, spitting, eyes-rolled-up-in-his-head seizure. Normally we would go in immediately and get the prisoner and take him back to medical. There was no fucking way this time. I knew absolutely, without any shred of doubt, if we had tried there would have been a riot. And men on both sides would have died, and this prison would have fucking exploded. So we left him there, left all of them there, and let him have his seizure. And waited for it to end. Ten minutes later it was still happening. Twenty minutes. Forty minutes. He just kept seizing. And the men stood up and started mixing with each other. All over the yard, men who a couple hours earlier were deadly enemies were talking, laughing, shaking hands. And Avrohom was still in the middle of the yard, having his seizure. And even though everyone had seemingly left him alone, it felt like they were all still watching him, watching everything he did, and waiting for it to end. The time passed when we would have normally brought everyone inside. We weren't sure what to do, so we left them out there. Two hours later the seizure stopped. Quickly as it started, it just stopped. He was still for a minute or two, looked dead. Then he stood up and walked towards the gate back inside. We opened it and he came in, and everyone else followed him. He went back to his cell, where he is right now.

The yard covered by cameras?

Of course.

Can I see the tapes?

You don't believe me?

I want to see it.

Fine.

We went to the control room where all of the surveil-

lance feeds come in and are monitored. He showed
me the tapes, which showed more or less exactly what
he had described. When they ended, when the last of
the prisoners had reentered the prison, he spoke.
I can't have him here.
He hasn't done anything wrong.
If he can do that, he's a profound threat to the safety
of this facility, and to the people who work here.
It looked more to me like he might be able to help you.
I don't know what the fuck he did out there, but
sooner or later it will turn.
How do you know?
Because I've been working in prisons for most of my
life and I've never seen anything remotely close to
what I saw earlier today.
You can't punish him if he hasn't done anything
wrong.
We're gonna recommend that the prosecutor have
him declared incompetent and ship him to a maxi-
mum security mental institution.
That's fucked. I'm not going to let you.
Most attorneys would be happy to get their clients out
of here.
I'm going to fight you.
Why?
He doesn't belong in a mental institution.
He thinks he's the Messiah.
He say that?
Enough other people have.
You can't hold things he hasn't done against him,
and you can't hold statements he hasn't made
against him.

He's fucking dangerous and I want him out of here.
He stood and shook my hand. I asked him if I could
see Ben, and he said no. I left and went back
to my office. By the time I arrived, I had received
notice that the assistant district attorney had filed
an Article 730, which was a motion to declare Ben
incompetent to stand trial and to have him examined
for mental illness. Normally Article 730 was something used by defense attorneys. If they could have
their client declared incompetent, they could avoid
a trial, and their client would be sent to a mental
institution for treatment instead of going to prison,
which is obviously a better result for someone who's
mentally ill. I had never heard of an ADA using it
before. Normally they want the conviction, and the
offender to be held in prison. Following its procedures, Ben would be examined by two psychiatrists.
They would write reports. We had the right to have
him examined by our own psychiatrists. They would
write reports. All of the reports would be submitted
and the judge would make a ruling. If he was deemed
competent, he would stay in prison and face trial. If
not, he would be sent to a mental institution.

I could not ignore or displace my other clients or
cases, so I went back to the courthouse. As my day
moved along, I was informed that Ben had moved
into solitary. The next morning he had another
seizure and was moved into the secure medical unit.
Over the next several days, he seemed to move in and
out of seizures. None of the drugs that were given to
him were able to stop them. They would stop for a

few minutes, start again. He had had no food and no sleep. Psychiatric examinations were scheduled and cancelled. I spent all of my free time trying to find a way to stop the 730, but there didn't appear to be one. I met and interviewed his mother. She was still in the hospital. She told me about the circumstances of his birth. About his immediate identification as the potential Messiah. About the pressure it had put on her, her husband, her family. About his childhood, where he had appeared normal but was expected to be anything but, and how those expectations had weighed on everyone in the family. I met and interviewed his sister. She told me about the relationship between him and his brother. His brother's hatred and fear of him. His resentment of him. His feelings of jealousy towards him. She told me about the farm and the life he appeared to be living there. I met his rabbi. He told me about the accident, how he had survived it, the condition he had acquired because of it, and the gift within that condition. He told me about the unreal amounts of knowledge Ben possessed, the languages he spoke, the books he knew word for word. He told me Ben could never have learned all of that through studying, or from school, that it would have taken five lifetimes, maybe ten. I met and interviewed his doctor, one of his lovers, three people who lived upstate with him. I met and interviewed the federal agent who had arrested him, a former preacher who had left the church after meeting him. All of them said the same thing: Ben had changed their lives. He could perform miracles. They believed he was the Messiah.

Normally I'd laugh at the things these people told
me. Had I not met him. Had I not seen what I saw
and felt what I felt. I would have laughed. Dismissed
them as crazy. But they weren't. None of them were.
They were reasonable. They believed. And he wasn't
asking them for anything. He didn't want people
to worship him, or pray to his God, or to follow
the rules of a book, or give him anything. He didn't
have a big church. Or a weekly television show.
He didn't want publicity. He told them that he loved
them. And that they should love each other. And that
nothing else mattered. That God was something
beyond our understanding. That we should live our
lives in a way that made us happy. And not follow
rules simply because we're told to follow them.
Or worship a God that no one has ever seen, or had
any contact with. He was telling them things all of
us know. We can be redeemed through love. Do not
let imaginary characters dictate how we live our
lives. Within the context of religion, these ideas were
warped. Manipulated. Fucked. And he showed
them that.

I checked on his status every hour or so. Called the
prison to see if there was any change. After three
days he stopped seizing. He was asleep for twenty-
four hours after that. When he'd been stable for a
day, the court scheduled his exams. It was a much
faster process than normal. I tried to stop it, slow it
down, but to no avail. The court and ADA were being
pressured by the prison. The warden thought Ben
was a danger to both himself and other prisoners.

He also said the prison's hospital facility was unequipped to deal with his epilepsy, the source of his mental illness. Ben's brother supported the action. He told the ADA that he thought Ben was, at the very least, profoundly mentally ill; at the most, a homicidal and suicidal maniac. The situation at the prison was becoming tenuous. Other prisoners were demanding he be released into general pop. Those who saw him at the medical unit all walked out claiming he had changed them. That he could heal people. Make their rage disappear. Make their addictions disappear. Give them peace. What normally might have taken months took days. And I had no defense. Ben would not speak to me about the case, or provide me with any information that would help him. And the witnesses I had interviewed would have worked against him. They would have supported the notion that he could speak to God. That he was the Messiah. That he was somehow going to change, and/or end, the world.

The exams took place at the prison. I was allowed to attend them, but not to participate or interfere in any way. I sat in the back of the room. Ben was shackled to a chair. He refused to answer any questions. He did not acknowledge the psychiatrists in any way. He just sat and stared at them. They asked basic questions. Do you understand why you're here? Do you understand the charges against you? Do you know who your lawyer is? Do you know what state you're in? They got nothing. Between sessions, I told him that if he didn't answer the questions, he would be declared incompetent. He told me that it wouldn't matter what he said. That he did not believe the court had any rights over him. That by answering the questions, he would be acknowledging that it did. That the system was designed to do what it did. That it would kill him as it had killed, or was killing, millions of others. I also brought in a psychiatrist for an examination. I hoped that Ben would come to reason in some way. He would not speak to my psychiatrist either. I kept asking him to see reason, to be reasonable, to act reasonably. He smiled and told me that he, in his defiance, was the only reasonable person in the entire situation. That no one with any reason would submit to the court, or acknowledge the authority of the criminal justice system.

The hearing itself was swift and merciless. The state brought three witnesses: the two psychiatrists and Ben's brother. The psychiatrists both said the same thing. Ben would not speak to them, and would not acknowledge the charges against him. They both stated they believed he was incompetent and unfit to stand trial. His brother spoke about Ben's life. Said there was a long history of addiction, delusions, sexual perversity. He said Ben had believed for most of his life that he was the Messiah. That Ben believed he had powers. That Ben believed he could perform miracles. He said that as a pastor he had been offended by Ben's beliefs. That he had denounced God. And believed in free love and orgies. He said that as a man he felt sorry for him. That he had tried to get Ben help for many years. That he had prayed for Ben and tried to bring him into the arms of God, Christ. Ben had spurned all of their efforts. He thought he was better than God. Beyond God. He thought he was God. An hour after it began, Ben was declared incompetent to stand trial. The judge was a Christian who sat beneath an American flag and swore people into testimony using a Bible. He ordered that Ben be moved to Bellevue, where he would be evaluated and treated. He also ordered that his brother, Jacob, become his guardian and be responsible for decisions related to Ben's treatment.

As Ben was led away, he looked at me and said thank you. Those were the only words he spoke that day. He started seizing in the back of the cruiser as they were transporting him to the hospital. He didn't stop for seven days. Seven days of continuous seizure. When he stopped, he would not speak or acknowledge anyone who worked at the facility. He was put on a unit with other patients. He seemed to calm them, and was seen whispering to them. Fearing some type of issue similar to the one at the prison, hospital staff moved him into segregation. Essentially a rubber room. He was diagnosed as a paranoid schizophrenic with Messianic delusions. He was given massive amounts of psychotropic drugs, but none seemed to have any effect on him. He started seizing again and was given massive amounts of antiseizure medication, but none seemed to have any effect on him. He was kept in segregation and forced to undergo electric shock therapy. It had no effect on him. After three weeks, the physicians at the hospital recommended he be given a temporal lobe resectioning, a relatively common procedure and not particularly dangerous within the scope of brain surgery. They believed that by cutting out part of his brain they would be able to stop the seizures. Again he was strapped down. He was wheeled to a surgical suite. He was given anesthesia. He was given extremely large doses because of his resistance to previous drug treatments. An hour into the surgery, as one of the surgeons was about to begin the resectioning, Ben opened his eyes. His skull had been opened and was literally lying on the table next to his head. His brain was exposed. The surgeon had a scalpel in her hand. The scalpel was just above the surface of his frontal lobe. From her account of the incident, he looked directly at her and he spoke. It is finished.

III MARIAANGELES

Ben used to talk about our souls. Said the idea that
we had souls was something silly. Ridiculous.
Like something a child would think up. Said people
who believed we had these spirits inside of us that
would survive after we died was fools. That people
was living their lives for something we didn't even
have. Something that wasn't even possible. He used
to say we had brains. It was all in our brains. And
more and more and more, doctors and scientists and
people who be living in the real world were coming to
understand that everything we is, everything we feel,
everything we know and experience, every emotion
we got and every thought we got and all the pain
we got and all the love we got, it all comes from our
brains. There ain't such a thing as a soul. You believe
in that shit, you just stupid.

I don't know exactly what happened. Doctors tried to
explain it to me but nobody could ever get their story
straight. They was all worried, nobody wanting to
take the blame, nobody wanting to just admit that
what happened is what happened. That's how it is in
America today. Everybody blaming everybody else.
Even the fucking president do it. Used to be the buck
stop here. Now it's always somebody else fault, don't
blame me, I'll take your money and fuck you but it
ain't 'cause of me. All I know is the end result.

One of them killed Ben. They cut his brain and they couldn't stop it bleeding and when they did it was already fucked. It was fucked beyond fixing. It was fucked beyond anything. Like he said, we ain't alive 'cause we got souls, we alive 'cause we got brains.

When they finished with that surgery, he was gone, but there was enough of his brain left that he kept breathing. It was the most fucked thing I ever saw. This beautiful man, this man who knew shit nobody for thousands of years had known, this man who could change your life and change the fucking world, he was gone, but his body was still working. They laid him down in a bed and he stared at the ceiling. You sat him in a chair and he'd stare straight ahead. You'd turn him on his side and he'd stare at the fucking wall. He didn't move. He couldn't move. He'd blink but nothing else. They gave him all these tests. Testing his reflexes and whether he felt pain or whether he could hear somebody or know what they was saying. All negative. He was a shell. A body that could breathe and be alive but nothing else.

They moved him out of Bellevue. Said they needed more room for more of the crazy motherfuckers that was crazy for real. Sent him to some home in Brooklyn where he could be cared for. Cared for meant making sure his feeding tube was hooked up and his diapers was changed. It wasn't hardly more than that. Sometimes they'd turn the channel on the TV they kept in the room. Sometimes they'd move him a little bit so his bedsores wouldn't get infected. It was him and two other men in that room. One of them was a vegetable like Ben. Had been in a car wreck. Some drunkass had hit him. His wife would come every day and hold his hand and talk to him. She'd read him the Bible like she thought it was gonna do some fucking good. She'd get down on her knees and pray for him. The other man might as well have been a vegetable. He was a gay man who'd got beat for being gay. Nobody ever came to see him. Most of the time he was staring too, but every now and then he'd start groaning, trying to move. It was almost more sad 'cause he had some inkling he was fucked. Some inkling of what he used to be. Some inkling that he was alone and he was gonna be alone for the rest of his fucked-up miserable life. Most days the orderlies would just line the three of them up in front of the TV. They'd shit their pants and piss on themselves. If they was lucky, somebody would turn the channel. In some ways it wasn't much different than how half the people in the fucking world lived. And whether they believed it or not, none of them, not Ben or the other two, or all the rest of the motherfuckers in the world, had a choice.

I came twice a week. I'd moved back to the Bronx. Back to the same apartment. After everybody heard what had happened, we left the farm. Maybe a few people stayed, but most of us went back to whatever we had been doing before we went there. We didn't stop believing in what Ben taught us, or how we lived with him, we just spread back out. Decided to take it back to the real world. That's how it always started.

There was one person. One person who understood. Who could see. Who knew. And that person would share what they had, and it'd just spread 'cause everybody touched by that person would be sharing it. In Ben's case there were enough of us. Enough to help each other and maybe some others. Enough to know what it felt like to feel real love. To see real love. To live with real love. To share real love. Love that wasn't about hating or judging or where you was from or what color you was or where you grew up or who you loved. There was enough of us that had been changed that we could change some others. Change them over before all this shit goes fucking boom and explodes.

Mercedes had plenty of people helping out with her. She was growing up real sweet. She'd always ask if she could come see Ben 'cause she missed him so much. I'd kiss her goodbye and tell her some other time and ride the subway over and come and sit with him and hold his hand. I knew he couldn't feel it, but I did it anyway. And I'd talk to him. Nothing like all that God bullshit the other man's wife would talk about. Just tell him what was going on in my life. I was working at a clothing store. I was doing school at night to get my GED. I was starting Mercedes on letters and numbers so I could get her into a better school. And I was pregnant. I was pregnant with Ben's baby. I knew he wouldn't know, but I'd tell him anyway. I was gonna have his little baby.

It wasn't the first time I'd been pregnant with him. First time was when we was at the farm. I'd known right after we got there and Ben and I talked about what to do and he said it was my choice. I asked about what God would say to him about that and he laughed and said God didn't make choices about what women did with their bodies. Women got that right. Only women got that right. No man, no God, nobody else did. And he said if I didn't want the baby, he would go with me, and hold my hand, and love me, and make sure I was okay when it was over. And we went, and he did what he said he would do, and it was the hardest moment of my life, but sometimes you got to make hard choices. And at that point, being on the road and not having no money and not having no idea about what the future would be doing, I couldn't have that baby. I remember when we was walking in. All these people had signs about God and us being killers and was yelling at us. They had verses from the Bible on their t-shirts. Ben just smiled at them. And that got them real mad, even madder, and he just kept smiling. One of them got real close and called him a murderer and said he was going to burn in Hell. Ben took the man's hand and kissed it, kissed it real soft and long, and it looked like that man was going to die, and his friends was all shocked. Ben let go of his hand and whispered something in his ear and the man smiled and hugged Ben and walked away. I ain't got no idea what he said, just what I saw. Ben loving another man. There ain't nothing wrong with a man loving another man. It's all the same. It's love.

I was keeping this baby, though. I wasn't expecting it to be no Messiah or nothing like that. All I wanted was a healthy little baby. A healthy little child that was part me and part Ben, this man I loved with my whole heart, and this man that loved me, loved everyone he knew. I would tell Ben about how I was feeling, what I was feeling, what I was eating, the names I was thinking about, had some for if it were a boy, and some for if it were a girl. I'd tell him about my dreams, about how maybe we was gonna go back to the farm after I got my GED, about how maybe I hoped I'd fall in love again sometime. I'd tell him about how people was still showing up at the apartment sometimes looking for him and people was still talking about him in the ghetto and the jail. When I got sad, and I always did get sad, looking at that shell where there was once a beautiful man, looking at the vegetable where there was once the man I loved, I'd tell him how much I missed him and loved him and wished he'd come back to me. I'd ask him to perform one of his miracles on himself, to make himself better, to heal himself so he could get up and walk again, and talk again, and smile again, and hold my hand again, and kiss me again, and say my name again, just one more time I wanted to hear him say my name, and I wanted him to love me again, and make me feel perfect and beautiful and peaceful and safe again. I'd ask him, and say do it Ben, please do it for me, but he wouldn't do nothing. And even if he could, I knew he wouldn't. Thing about him that made him what he was and who he was, if he had one more miracle, one more hiding in his back pocket, one more hidden in his cheek, he'd use it on someone else. If he had two, he'd use both on other peoples. If he had three, there'd be three lucky motherfuckers out there. He wouldn't ever do nothing for himself. He'd always give before he take. He was giving until it all got took.

After a couple months, my belly was getting real big. The people at the place knew me enough to let me take Ben outside sometimes. They'd put him in a wheelchair and strap him all up so he wouldn't fall out, not that it would make a difference. I'd bring a blanket to put under him to help with his sores, which would be seeping blood and pus and looking like they hurt real bad, even though I knew he couldn't feel nothing. I'd just push him around the neighborhood. Tell him what I was seeing and smelling and hearing. Make up little stories and shit about the people that'd walk past us. The facility wasn't far from the water, and sometimes I'd go down to the boardwalk along the ocean and I'd sit on a bench and put Ben's chair right next to me and hold his hand and watch the waves come in, one after another. And they kept coming, one after another, just like they'd been doing since billions of years before there was any people on this planet, and just like they'd be doing billions of years after we had killed each other and was gone. It made me feel small, watching those waves, realizing how little a mark we made on this world, and how we was just one little planet in a universe so big we couldn't understand it, and how short we was alive in this life that we got, and how we got to take it and use it the best we can. Not to do anything but love, like I was loving Ben by holding his hand, and he had been loving me by changing my life.

Summer turned to fall turned to winter. I was almost
ready to have our baby. Mercedes kept asking about
Ben so I decided to bring her along one day. I also
had pictures of our baby still inside of me, sonogram
machine pictures that I wanted to show Ben and put
up on the wall behind his bed. We got to the hospital,
and they had him all ready to go. I had asked if we
could take him out to the boardwalk, even though
it was cold and had snowed a little the night before.
He was wearing a winter coat and a cute little hat
and some gloves that was worn down but would still
keep his hands warm. Mercedes was all excited and
a little confused about why Ben looked the same but
couldn't move or talk or do anything. I thought about
what to tell her, but she wasn't ready for the story, for
the whole story, for the story of Ben's life, and who he
was and what he did and what he meant and why they
killed him, their courts and their orders and their
surgeons with their scalpels. Why they killed him,
with their bullshit laws and religions. I thought about
what to tell her, but she wasn't ready, so I said Ben
was just being quiet for a little while and left it at that.
We went to the water. The waves were still breaking.
There was an inch or so of snow over everything. We
were the only ones making tracks. A newspaper blew
by us, and I could see all that was in it was bad news.
People dying, people killing, governments lying and
starting wars, corporations robbing and thieving.
Same as the news had always been, same as it would
always be. We went to a pier that went out into the
ocean, and it was a little windy and a little cold and
the waves were louder, breaking right underneath

us, just like they had been doing for four or five
billion years, and just like they would be for four or
five billion more. All those waves, one after another,
one after another, just rolling along, rolling into the
shore. We got to the end of the pier and stopped. I was
going to turn around but my phone rang. It was someone calling about a job I had applied for and they
was wanting to schedule an interview. I took the call.
I was holding the phone with one hand and Mercedes
with the other. I didn't think Ben would be going
anywhere. He didn't have no brain left. He couldn't
walk or talk or move or think or feel or do anything.
I didn't think nothing. I turned around and took the
call. It lasted like a minute or so. Wasn't nothing, just
bullshit about time and place, shit that we all deal
with and think matters but really don't at all. When
I turned back around, Ben was gone. His chair was
empty and the clothes was sitting on it and he was
gone. The cute little hat was right there, and the
gloves. He was gone, though. I didn't know what to
do, whether I should scream or cry or laugh or what
to do. There was no possible way what was happening could be happening. I didn't hear no splash and
there weren't no tracks anywhere except mine and
Mercedes' and the ones that got made by the chair.
And later, after the cops came and they looked at
the videotapes made by the security cameras, there
wasn't nothing to see. One second Ben was sitting
there. The next second he wasn't. And I didn't know
whether I should be crying or screaming or laughing
or what, but I felt love, I felt the same kind of love
I had felt when he was with me, when he was alive, it

was inside me still, and I picked up the hat, and it was
still warm from where it had been on his head, and
I looked out across the ocean, and I looked out across
the sky, and I took my daughter's hand who I love so
much, and I took a deep breath of cold winter air from
the sea, and the sun was warm on my face, and
I smiled and I thought of him, and real quiet-like
I said it, and not just to him, but to everyone, to everyone everywhere, 'cause that's what it's really about,
what it is really all about.
I love you.
I love you.
I love you.

Thank you Ben Zion Avrohom for your life. Thank you Mariaangeles Hernández, Mercedes Hernández, and Ben Zion Hernández. Thank you Charles Kelly Jr. Thank you Dr. Alexis Donnelly. Thank you Esther Avrohom. Thank you Ruth Avrohom. Thank you Jeremiah Henry. Thank you Rabbi Adam Schiff. Thank you Matthew Harper. Thank you John Dodson. Thank you Luke Gordon. Thank you Mark Egorov. Thank you Judith Cooper. Thank you Peter Wade. Thank you David Krintzman. Thank you Eric Simonoff. Thank you Jenny Meyer. Thank you Courtney Kivowitz. Thank you Ari Emanuel, Christian Muirhead, Alicia Gordon. Thank you David Goldin. Thank you Andisheh Avini. Thank you Richard Prince. Thank you Ed Ruscha. Thank you Richard Phillips. Thank you Dan Colen. Thank you Terry Richardson. Thank you Gregory Crewdson. Thank you Larry Gagosian. Thank you Jessica Almon, Britton Schey, and Aaron Rich. Thank you Roland Philipps. Thank you Olivia de Dieuleveult and Patrice Hoffman, Sabine Schultz, Claudio Lopez de la Madrid, Job Lisman. Thank you Melissa Lazarov, Alison McDonald, Nicole Heck, Sam Orlofsky, Jessica Arisohn, Rose Dergan, Kara Vander Weg, Darlina Goldak, Andres Hecker, Paul Neale, Julie Van Severen, Jennifer Knox White, Sarah Lazar. Thank you Carter Burden III. Thank you Dr. Alexis Halperin. Thank you Mariana Hogan. Thank you Rabbi Adam Mintz, thank you, thank you.

THE
FEMALE WITS

WOMEN PLAYWRIGHTS ON
THE LONDON STAGE 1660-1720

FIDELIS MORGAN

Virago

Published by VIRAGO Press Limited 1981
Ely House, 37 Dover Street, London W1X 4HS

All rights whatsoever in these plays are strictly reserved,
and application for permission to perform them etc. must
be made in advance to Virago Press, Ely House,
37 Dover Street, London W1X 4HS before rehearsals begin.

Set in IBM Journal by 𝍫 Tek-Art, Croydon, Surrey.
Printed in Great Britain by Lowe & Brydone Printers Ltd.
of Thetford, Norfolk.

British Library Cataloguing in Publication Data
Female wits.
  1. English drama — 17th century
  2. English drama — 18th century
  3. English drama — Women authors
  I. Morgan, Fidelis
  822'.4 0809287   PR1265.3

ISBN 0-86068-231-5

SULLEN   Oh this is a lady's!
CRITICK   How's that? Audetque; viris contendere virgo?
RAMBLE   See how Critick starts at the naming a lady.
CRITICK   What occasion had you to name a lady in the confounded work you're about?
SULLEN   Here's a play of hers.
CRITICK   The devil there is: I wonder in my heart we are so lost to all sense and reason: what a pox have the women to do with the muses? I grant you the poets call the nine muses by the names of women, but why so? not because the sex had anything to do with poetry, but because in that sex they're much fitter for prostitution.
RAMBLE   Abusive, now you're abusive Mr Critick.
CRITICK   Sir, I tell you we are abused: I hate these petticoat authors; 'tis false grammar, there's no feminine for the Latin word, 'tis entirely of the masculine gender, and the language won't bear such a thing as a she-author.

A Comparison Between the Two Stages (1702), attributed to Charles Gildon

CONTENTS

PREFACE

The female wits, the first women playwrights on the English stage, have before now been the subject of books and essays, some scholarly, some speculative, some scurrilous. Although I am indebted to several of these studies for whetting my curiosity to inquire further, it has not been my aim to add to their number. Instead, in the collection of plays gathered here, I have set out to present a representative selection of the best of their work, to make accessible, both to theatres and readers, plays which otherwise are available only to scholars in research libraries.

My introductory chapters summarise these authors' lives, so far as these are known; much of the biographical information comes from early documents, some of which have not so far been studied. Even in outline, their lives were fascinating but I have given them as a context for the plays, not an explanation. Few authors oblige anthologists by writing only a single masterpiece; I have therefore included in the synopses of their careers some scenes from further plays to convey more of the range and variety of their achievements.

Even though poems and novels may be composed in lonely isolation, plays are rarely written in a vacuum, and belong on the stage for which they were produced. So long as Restoration theatre was forgotten, its plays shared its oblivion. Recent productions have successfully revived Restoration drama, but its background is still widely misunderstood and swamped in fanciful legend. Interested readers will find some of the more valuable recent studies listed in the Further Reading section. My opening chapter provides a brief background survey intended to cut through the more distorting legends attached to the subject.

I have followed modern dating, and for transitional years have always taken January 1st as the first day of the new year.

I wish to acknowledge kindness and assistance from the staff at The British Library, The Bodleian Library, Oxford, The Special Collection of Glasgow University Library, Birmingham University Library, The Victoria and Albert Museum, and the Wandsworth and Westminster Lending and Reference libraries.

My love and gratitude go to the friends who helped me, to Mavis, Jackie, Zoe, Stewart, Jocelyn, Christine, Paddy and Celia.

BACKGROUND

In one popular comedy, when his nieces suggest that a visit to the theatre might cheer him up, an old gentleman grumbles that he 'can never endure to see plays since women came on the stage; boys are better by half'. That his name is Snarl suggests he is the butt of satire, to be mocked rather than believed; by the end of the play it has emerged that his complaints against the pleasures of the age only mask the pleasure he takes in visiting a whore-house which specialises in flagellating old gentlemen — as one character delicately puts it: 'Your landlady in German Street is a schoolmistress, is she not?'[1] That it had become laughably ridiculous to object to women on the stage indicates a major development which had occurred in English theatre during the late seventeenth century, for, as Virginia Woolf lamented, 'it would have been impossible, completely and entirely, for any woman to have written the plays of Shakespeare in the age of Shakespeare'.[2]

Even though the obvious competence and independence with which Elizabeth I ruled undermined the notion that women had somehow less than men to offer, the only place in the theatre for a Tudor woman was in the audience: the plays then performed were all written by men and both male and female parts were played by men or boys. Elizabeth's successor, James I, was Mary Queen of Scots' son and, whether because he needed to live down his mother, or whether in violent and uneasy response to his own bisexuality, his reign discouraged women from enterprise. Winds of change blew from France, and were fanned by Charles I's French wife, but when a French company employing actresses visited England they were, as the Puritan Prynne gleefully reports, 'hissed, hooted, and pippin-pelted off the stage'.[3] With the closure of the theatres under Puritan edict during the Commonwealth, theatrical opportunity was limited to opera and masque. With the Restoration of the Monarchy in 1660, all this changed.

Returning from France, where he had passionately enjoyed plays and women, Charles II's Royal Warrant, licensing new theatres in London, specified that only women should play women's parts. And hot on the heels of the first actresses came the women playwrights.

The advent of the actress marked revolutionary change in the position women held in the theatre. For instance, female title roles and leading parts now became immensely fashionable and whereas the early seventeenth-century stage had seen Marlowe's *Tamberlaine* and *Dr Faustus,* Jonson's *Sejanus* and Shakespeare's *Hamlet* and *Henry V,* the latter half preferred Lee's *The Rival Queens,* Settle's *The Empress of Morocco, Pope Joan — The Female Prelate,* Shadwell's *The Woman*

Captain and Hopkins' *Boadicea.* Although there had been a fashion for
female leading roles in the era of the male actresses, these women, like the
Duchess of Malfi, had much less control over their own fate than, say,
Roxana in *The Rival Queens,* or Homais in Mrs Manley's *The Royal
Mischief.*

Because theatrical reputations are sustained by memory, they are
easily distorted. The achievement of these early actresses has had a
particularly unjust press in later generations. Nell Gwynn is usually
remembered as one of the royal mistresses, or as an orange-seller
(which, indeed, she was — for a few months before she became fourteen). She was, however, most admired by her contemporaries for her
brilliance as a comic actress, well before Charles II fell for her. The
leading writers of her time, including John Dryden, wrote starring roles
for her, and she saved weak plays by the wit and panache with which
she could deliver a prologue or an epilogue. The way posterity now
celebrates her is as gross as it would be for future generations to remember of Glenda Jackson only that she worked as a counter assistant for
a high street chemist, or that Grace Kelly's major achievement lay in
marrying a minor European prince. The test of time also proves a
crooked and unreliable yardstick when applied to the work of the
women playwrights. As theatres became larger in the eighteenth century, managements had to attract larger audiences, and to do this they
had to please rather than take risks. These new theatregoers came from
a rising bourgeoisie, conscious of themselves as *arrivistes,* seeking to
establish social credentials and so unsure of their own tastes that they
settled for what they deemed 'polite' and 'proper'. The notion of
'politeness' came to insist on much that Puritans protesting against the
theatre had proclaimed, including Jeremy Collier's view that 'modesty
. . . is the character of woman'.[4] Although plays were adapted to
comply with this taste, Restoration plays appeared less and less in the
repertoire as moralists acquired more and more power to direct society.
By the Victorian period, the gusto of Restoration plays had well nigh
disappeared from the English stage, which had no real place left for it.

It is sometimes claimed, untruly, that Restoration plays passed into
oblivion because they were frivolous, entertaining an audience that was
riotous, noisy, and more interested in paying attention to each other
than to the play on the stage. But in fact there is evidence that Restoration audiences frequently cried during particularly moving scenes.[5]
Because the theatres were small and intimate — an average Restoration
theatre in its entirety could be built on the stage of the present Theatre
Royal, Drury Lane[6] — they allowed intense concentration and the
attention demanded by fast-moving, intelligent dialogue. Our nearest
equivalent today to such a convivial and attentive audience might be a
group of people watching television at home, who chat when bored and
then can suddenly be held, riveted and hushed. And like people watching

television, the Restoration audience was lit almost as brightly as the performers in front of them. It is true that there are contemporary references to riots and to strange occurrences in the Restoration theatre. There is a newspaper report of an incident at the Duke of York's Theatre when a popular comedy was brought to a standstill as a couple in one of the boxes, who were having sexual intercourse, reached a climax. This appears in the *Sun* newspaper for 15 July 1975,[7] and illustrates that the basis for such reporting is that the situation is unusual. An occurrence is not worth reporting unless it is a departure from what is customary.

Late seventeenth-century theatregoers delighted in novelty, and it was this that opened the way for women to act and then write for the theatre. But, as novelty wears off, tolerance often diminishes. In the closing years of the century, opposition increased. As my account of her career shows, it was the last of the writers I have included, Susannah Centlivre, who got most stick for being a woman. Her death may be seen to close a chapter: by that time, women writers had another medium open to them: the novel. Theatre managers were already exercising more and more control over what was written and presented in playhouses, newspapers and novels were then coming into being and, as well as the scope for enterprise and experiment a new medium can offer, it gave writers more control over their material than they enjoyed in the theatre, an advantage Mary Delarivier Manley seems to have understood particularly well.

This does not mean that novelty was all the female wits had to offer. The plays included here reflect not only their variety and vitality, but also show the considerable understanding of stage-craft which made their plays as successful with audiences as the plays of male dramatists. What has delayed their revival has been a particular kind of conservatism in the revival of Restoration drama this century. When Nigel Playfair presented his season of plays at the Lyric, Hammersmith, in the 1920s, including neglected plays by Congreve and Farquhar, he was bringing to the public plays that had already been rediscovered in Oxford student productions, in literary circles, and in Bloomsbury. These were first taken up for their literary rather than theatrical merit − indeed, reviewers were often surprised to find they could actually enjoy what they considered 'good' plays when they saw them on stage. Risk has not been a trademark of English theatre-managements, and when further Restoration plays have come to be chosen for revival they have, in the main, been plays that seemed safely similar to the successful selection which Playfair pioneered. These plays were all, as it happens, by men.

It is also worth noting that, in all of London's theatres during the sixty years from 1920 to 1980 (a time which boasts huge social and political advances for women) fewer plays by women writers have been performed than were played by the two London companies which held the dramatic monopoly from 1660 to 1720.

PART ONE

The Playwrights

KATHERINE PHILIPS—THE MATCHLESS ORINDA

> Silence were now a sin.
> *Upon the Double Murther of King Charles I*

Katherine Philips was the first woman to have a play professionally produced on the London stage and yet she does not even receive a mention in *The Oxford Companion to the Theatre*. But she has had honourable notice from others who have known unjust neglect:

> The world, and especially our England, has within the last thirty years been vexed and teased by a set of devils, whom I detest so much that I always hunger after an acherontic promotion to a torture, purposely for their accommodation; these devils are a set of women, who having taken a snack or luncheon of literary scraps, set themselves up for Towers of Babel in languages, Sapphos in poetry, Euclids in geometry, and everything in nothing . . . The thing has made a very uncomfortable impression on me. I had longed for some real feminine modesty in these things, and was therefore gladdened in the extreme on opening the other day . . . a book of poetry written by one beautiful Mrs Philips . . . and called 'The Matchless Orinda' — you must have heard of her, and most likely read her poetry — I wish you have not, that I may have the pleasure of treating you with a few stanzas . . . You will not regret reading them once more. The following to her friend Mrs M.A. at parting you will judge of.

I have examined and do find
Of all that favour me
There's none I grieve to leave behind
But only, only thee
To part with thee I needs must die
Could parting sep'rate thee and I.

But neither chance nor compliment
Did element our love;
'Twas sacred sympathy was lent
Us from the quire above.
That friendship fortune did create,
Still fears a wound from time or fate.

Our chang'd and mingled souls are grown
To such acquaintance now,
That if each would resume her own
Alas! we know not how.
We have each other so engrost
That each is in the union lost.

And thus we can no absence know
Nor can we be confin'd;
Our active souls will daily go
To learn each other's mind.
Nay should we never meet to sense
Our souls would hold intelligence.

Inspired with a flame divine
I scorn to court a stay;
For from that noble soul of thine
I ne'er can be away.
But I shall weep when thou dost grieve
Nor can I die whilst thou dost live.

By my own temper I shall guess
At thy felicity,
And only like my happiness
Because it pleaseth thee.
Our hearts at any time will tell
If thou, or I be sick or well.

All honour sure I must pretend,
All that is good or great;
She that would be Rosania's friend,
Must be at least compleat,
If I have any bravery,
'Tis cause I have so much of thee.

Thy leiger soul in me shall lie,
And all thy thoughts reveal;
Then back again with mine shall fly
And thence to me shall steal.
Thus still to one another tend;
Such is the sacred name of friend.

Thus our twin souls in one shall grow,
And teach the world new love,
Redeem the age and sex, and show
A flame fate dares not move:
And courting death to be our friend,
Our lives together we shall end.

A dew shall dwell upon our tomb
Of such a quality
That fighting armies thither come
Shall reconciled be.
We'll ask no epitaph but say
Orinda and Rosania.

In other of her poems there is a most delicate fancy of the Fletcher kind.

John Keats to John Hamilton Reynolds, 21 September 1817

Although little of her work is of extraordinary literary or theatrical value, Katherine Philips' place is important in dramatic history. Her pseudonym 'The Matchless Orinda' is offputting, but in fact it conceals much more fatuous comedy than might at first be apparent.

Katherine Philips was born on 1 January 1631, in the parish of St Mary Woolchurch. According to John Aubrey: 'When a child she was mighty apt to learn . . . she had read the Bible thorough before she was full four years old.'[1]

Her father, Mr Fowler, a prosperous merchant, sent her to Mrs

Salmon's fashionable boarding school in Hackney when she was eight years old. During her time there she met and struck up a close friendship with Mary Aubrey, the Mrs M.A. of the poem Keats sent to his friend. Mary Aubrey's relationship with Katherine Philips was to prove a lasting one and of fundamental importance to her career as a writer.

After her father's death, Katherine's mother soon married Richard Hector Philips, and the family moved to his home in Wales. In 1646 Katherine met James Philips, a son of her step-father by a former marriage. The banns for their marriage were published on 23 August 1648, and a few weeks later they were married. She was seventeen, he was fifty-four.

The following year saw the outbreak of the English Civil War. James was a staunch Parliamentarian who played a very important role under the Commonwealth, while Katherine's friends were mainly Royalist. She trod a delicate path between the two. At the Restoration of the Monarchy in 1660, Mrs Philips added her voice to the general clamour to hail the return of his most sacred majesty King Charles II. Her husband tried to stand as an M.P. but first had to stand trial to ascertain his involvement in the illegal High Court of Justice death warrant on Colonel John Gerard. He won his case, but on his second attempt to stand the election was declared void by the Committee on Elections because of a technicality.

In 1651 Katherine adopted the *nom de plume* Orinda. She rechristened her husband Antenor, and Mary Aubrey her Rosania; other friends were given similar names, and Katherine Philips' Society of Friendship was born.

She held a postal discussion on friendship with Dr Jeremy Taylor, the Bishop of Down and Conner, Palaemon in her circle. He directed to her his 'Discourse of the Natures, Offices and Measures of Friendship', under three headings: '1. How can it be appropriate . . . who is to be chosen to it. 2. How far it may extend, that is with what expression signified. 3. How conducted?'[2] I think some of his opinions on the friendship of women are worth quoting in full:

> I cannot say that women are capable of all those excellences by which men can oblige the world; and therefore a female friend, in some cases, is not so good a counsellor as a wise man, and cannot so well defend my honour, nor dispose of reliefs and assistance, if she be under the power of another; but a woman can love as passionately, and converse as pleasantly, and retain a secret as faithfully, and be useful in her proper ministries, and she can die for her friend as well as the bravest Roman knight. A man is the best friend in trouble, but a woman may be equal to him in the days of joy; a woman can as well increase our comforts, but cannot so well lessen our sorrows, and therefore we do not carry women with us when we go to fight; but, in peaceful cities and times, virtuous women are the beauties of society and the prettinesses of friendship.[3]

From Katherine Philips' point of view her friendship cult, the inner sanctum, was exclusive to women. She had noted how 'men exclude women from friendship's vast capacity',[4] and in her own way tried to make up for that.

Her friendships with women were florid in their intensity. Her first obsession was Rosania, Mary Aubrey, and to her she wrote some of her best poetry:

> Thou shed'st no tear but what my moisture lent,
> And if I sigh, it is thy breath is spent.[5]

Another poem 'To Mrs M.A. Upon Absence' is worth quoting in full.

> 'Tis now since I began to die
> Four months, yet still I gasping live;
> Wrapp'd up in sorrow do I lie,
> Hoping, yet doubting, a reprieve.
> Adam from paradise expell'd
> Just such a wretched being held.
>
> 'Tis not thy love I fear to lose,
> That will in spite of absence hold;
> But 'tis the benefit and use
> Is lost, as in imprison'd gold:
> Which though the sum be ne'er so great,
> Enriches nothing but conceit.
>
> What angry star then governs me
> That I must feel a double smart,
> Prisoner to fate as well as thee;
> Kept from thy face, link'd to thy heart?
> Because my love all love excels,
> Must my grief have no parallels?
>
> Sapless and dead as winter here
> I now remain, and all I see
> Copies of my wild estate appear,
> But I am their epitome.
> Love me no more, for I am grown
> Too dead and dull for thee to own.

From these poems, and Orinda's eloquent but intellectual opinions on platonic love between friends, we could easily accept that her special friendships were as innocent and cloyingly sentimental as she would have us believe. In 1652, however, when Rosania married William Montague, an up-and-coming lawyer, the resentment and disappointment that is evident in Katherine's work suggests that, even if not physical, these friendships were far from humdrum. The poem 'On Rosania's Apostacy and Lucasia's Friendship' withdraws from Mary Aubrey all rights to a special place in Katherine's heart, and welcomes Mrs Anne Owen ('Lucasia') to fill the space:

> Hail, great Lucasia, thou shalt doubly shine;
> What was Rosania's own is now twice thine;
> Thou saw'st Rosania's chariot and her flight,
> And so the double portion is thy right.

An even more telling example of the strength of her passions came ten years later when Anne Owen married Colonel Marcus Trevor, Lord Dungannon. Mrs Philips wrote 'I alone of all the company was out of humour; nay, I was vexed to that degree that I could not disguise my concern, which many of them were surprised to see, and spoke to me of it; but my grief was too deeply rooted to be cured with words.'[6] In 'To my Lord and Lady Dungannon on their Marriage' her enthusiasm is non-existent. The poem is formal and polite. Then, when Lucasia planned to honeymoon with her husband on his estate in Ireland, Mrs Philips went too.

From the Dungannons' house she wrote home to her friend Sir Charles Cottrell, Charles II's Master of Ceremonies, known in her circle as Poliarchus: '[I am] press'd with such a load of sorrows that I despair of ever finding relief.'[7] Of her host, Lord Dungannon, she wrote: '[he is of] humour stubborn and surly enough . . . silly and clownish . . . I see no alteration either in her husband's humour or mien, but in my opinion he behaves himself more despotically towards her than becomes him',[8] and, to her surprise and obvious misery, 'She [Lucasia] tells all of us she is extremely happy, and that all that love her ought to take part in her happiness.'[9]

Her expectations of friendship were obviously, beneath all her academic analyses, as naïve as Lady Wishfort's in Congreve's *The Way of the World* when she says to her dissembling friend, Mrs Marwood, 'You are enough to reconcile me to the hard world, or else I wou'd retire to deserts and solitudes; and feed harmless sheep by groves and purling streams. Dear Marwood, let us leave the world, and retire by ourselves and be shepherdesses' (act V, scene i). And Mrs Philips used the mannered *précieuse* jargon just as Lady Wishfort does, to be as appallingly possessive as that demanding stage harridan. In July, realising the hopelessness of her situation, Mrs Philips moved to Dublin to act on her husband's behalf in a land claim. Disgruntled, she wrote to Sir Charles:

> I now see by experience that one may love too much, and offend more by a too fond sincerity than by a careless indifferency, provided it be but handsomely varnish'd over with civil respect. I find too there are few friendships in the world marriage-proof; especially when the person our friend marries has not a soul particularly capable of tenderness of that endearment, and solicitous of advancing the noble instances of it as a pleasure of their own, in others as well as themselves; and such a temper is so rarely found, that we may generally conclude the marriage of a friend to be the funeral of friendship; for then all former endearments run naturally into the gulf of that new and strict relation, and there, like rivers in the sea, they lose themselves forever. This is indeed a lamentable truth, and I have often study'd to find a reason for it.[10]

And further: 'But oh! that there were no tempests but those of the sea for me to suffer in parting with my dear Lucasia!'[11]

Resigned to the failure of her principal friendship, Mrs Philips threw herself into a new project, translating a scene from the third act of

Corneille's *Pompée* from the French, 'to divide and cure a passion that has met so ill a return'.[12]

The Dublin of 1662 was an elegant city, thriving on business and crowded with members of the English aristocracy. In October of that year a theatre was completed in Smock Alley, at a cost of £2,000. Mrs Philips wrote: 'It is finer than D'Avenant's . . . We have plays here in the newest mode, and not ill acted.'[13]

In Dublin she became friendly with Roger Boyle, Earl of Orrery, himself a successful if appalling playwright, 'a man of great parts and agreeable conversation'.[14] Orrery was responsible for turning Mrs Philips into a fully-fledged dramatist.

> By some accident or other my scene of *Pompey* fell into his hands, and he was pleased to like it so well that he sent me the French original, and the next time I saw him so earnestly importuned me to pursue that translation that, to avoid the shame of seeing him who had so lately commanded a kingdom become a petitioner to me for such a trifle, I obeyed him so far as to finish the act in which that scene is; so that the whole third act is now English . . . He no sooner had it than he enjoin'd me to go on; and not only so, but brib'd me to be contented with the pains by sending me an excellent copy of verses . . . You will wonder at my lord's obstinacy in this desire to have me translate *Pompey*, as well because of my incapacity to perform it as that so many others have undertaken it: But all I can say or do is to no purpose, for he persists in his request, and will not be refused.[15]

When the translation was complete, Orrery pressed Philips to write songs to link the acts. On their completion in January 1663 she wrote:

> I think they have been the reason that has made my lord Orrery resolve to have *Pompey* acted here, which notwithstanding all my intreaties to the contrary he is going on with, and has advanced a hundred pounds towards the expense of buying Roman and Egyptian habits. All the other persons of quality here are also very earnest to bring it upon the stage, and seem resolved to endure the penance of seeing it play'd on Tuesday come sevennight, which day is appointed for the first time of acting it. My Lord Roscommon has made a prologue for it, and Sir Edward Dering an epilogue . . . so that all is ready, and poor I condemn'd to be expos'd unless some accident which I heartily wish but cannot foresee kindly intervene to my relief.[16]

The play was presented with such success that King Charles II demanded a copy.

At about the time of the Dublin staging a London publisher gathered together a collection of Orinda's poems for publication. Mrs Philips was very unhappy about it: 'This is the most cruel accident that could ever have befallen me . . . it has cost me a sharp fit of sickness since I heard it.'[17] She had taken great care to ensure that the name Katherine Philips, or even her initials, were nowhere in any version of her *Pompey*. When Sir Charles Cottrell proposed its printing Mrs Philips wrote: 'I consent to whatever you think fit to do about printing it, but I conjure you by all our mutual friendship not to put my name to it, nay, not so much as the least mark or hint whereby the public may guess from whence it came.'[18] Some 500 copies of the play were printed under the name Orinda. But even in the guise of Orinda she did not want her private verses, written for her friends, available to anyone who could spare the shilling. She wrote: 'I never writ a line in my life with intention to have it printed . . . sometimes I think that to make verses is so much above my reach, and a diversion so unfit for the sex to which I belong that I am about to resolve against it forever.'[19] The poems were eventually withdrawn from circulation.

According to the *London Stage* calendar for 1663:

> It is possible that Katherine Philips' *Pompey* which was given in Dublin in February 1663 may have been presented in London in the late spring of 1663. Sir William D'Avenant's *The Playhouse to Let* which apparently appeared in London in the late summer of 1663 has in Act V some elements of travesty upon *Pompey*. It is unlikely that its appearance in Dublin would make satire upon it have much point to London audiences without a performance in London.[20]

A group of court wits, led by Sir Edmund Waller, had produced a rival translation of *Pompée* which was presented at Court in January 1664, and by D'Avenant later in the year. Mrs Philips, upset that D'Avenant preferred their version, especially after Orrery had been 'so partial as to speak of [her] translation of *Pompey* with preference to the other',[21] wrote: 'I wonder much what preparations for it could so prejudice William D'Avenant when I hear they acted in English habits, and yet so appropriate that Caesar was sent in with his feather and muff, till he was hissed off ye stage.'[22]

Gerard Langbaine, in his *Account of the English Dramatic Poets* (1691) claims that Mrs Philips' *Pompey* played on the London stage as late as 1678. Baker's *Biographia Dramatica* states that 'it was frequently presented with great applause'.[23] But as there is no documentary evidence of any specific performance, and often references are made which confuse Philips' and Waller's versions, it is impossible to state categorically that Mrs Philips' version was ever professionally produced in London.

Eventually she returned to the ageing arms of Antenor (i.e. her husband) and the peaceful solitude of his estate in Cardigan. But she soon grew restless. While secretly working on a translation of Corneille's *Horace*, she tried to persuade her friends, chiefly Cottrell and Mary Aubrey (now Montague), whose husband had become one of the most prominent lawyers in the country, to use their influence in getting Antenor a job in London, in order both to restore his fortunes and to house her near her friends. She bade Cottrell to compose his reply to her request in Italian so that her husband would not suspect what she was up to.

In the spring of 1664 she came to London. While there she wrote a poem 'On the Death of My Lord Rich, Only Son to the Earl of Warwick, Who Died of Smallpox, 1664':

> That fierce disease, which knows not how to spare
> The young, the great, the knowing or the fair.

Ironically, smallpox, 'that murtherous tyrant, with greater barbarity seiz'd unexpectedly upon her, the true original, and to the much juster affliction of all the world violently tore her out of it and hurry'd her untimely to her grave, upon the 22nd of June 1664'.[24]

Eulogies flooded in, from Cowley —

> We allowed you beauty, and we did submit
> To all the tyrannies of it.
> Ah cruel sex! Will you depose us too in wit?

and other poets and wits.

But the translation of *Horace* was incomplete. Mrs Philips had got as far as act IV, scene vi. The final scenes were prepared by Sir John Denham and the play was presented at Court in February 1668 by amateurs, including the Duke of Monmouth (speaking the prologue), Henry Savile, the younger brother of George Savile, Marquis of Halifax, the Duchess of Monmouth, and Charles II's mistress, Lady Castlemayne, who was 'adorned with jewels to the value of £200,000, the Crown Jewels being taken from the Tower for her . . . None but the nobility [were] admitted to see it.'[25]

Then, in January 1669, the King's Company, under Sir Thomas Killigrew, presented the play at the Theatre Royal in Bridges Street. Pepys attended on 19 January:

> To the King's house, to see *Horace*. This is the third day of its acting — a silly tragedy, but Lacy hath made a farce of several dances — between each act, but his words are but silly, and invention not extraordinary, as to the dances, only some Dutchmen come out of the mouth and tail of a Hamburgh sow.[26]

Unfortunately Mrs Philips was not around either to witness the production or to prevent the mess the company made of it. Her songs for *Pompey* 'were added only to lengthen the play and make it fitter for the stage'.[27] For instance, at the end of act III, Cornelia, Pompey's widow, lies asleep on a couch, and the ghost of her dead husband sings to her as in a dream:

> *I come . . . to visit my Cornelia's dreams . . .*
> *There none a guilty crown shall wear,*
> *Nor Caesar be dictator there,*
> *Not shall Cornelia shed a tear.*

> (After this a military dance, as the continuance of her dream, and then Cornelia starts up, as waking in amazement, saying)

What have I seen? And whither has it gone?
How great the vision! and how quickly gone!
Yet if in dreams we future things can see,
There's still some joy laid up in fate for me.

And after act IV Cleopatra sits on stage listening to a song (sung by an off-stage voice) which points out to her the precariousness of her situation. The *entr'actes* designed for *Horace* served no such purpose; they were pot-boilers, having no connection with the main dramatic offering.

In her defence it must be said that Mrs Philips followed in every detail the disciplines she set out for translators: 'The original [should] appear in its own true undisfigured proportion, and yet beautify'd with all the riches of another tongue. Adding, omitting, and altering the original as they please themselves I take to be a liberty not pardonable in translators, and unbecoming the modesty of that attempt.'[28]

She made as good a job of translating French alexandrines into English heroic couplets as any of her contemporaries. Perhaps her translations would not stand up today, but neither, I think, would any of the other heroic-verse translations from the Restoration period.

In her lifetime Roger Boyle wrote of her:

When I but knew you by report,
I fear'd the praises of th'admiring Court
Were but their compliments; but now I must
Confess, that I thought civil is scarce just:
For they imperfect trophies to you raise,
You deserve wonder, and they pay but praise.[29]

Two centuries later Sir Edmund Gosse ventured to revive interest in her, in his *Seventeenth Century Studies*, 'because of the personal charm of her character', and because unlike

so many of her contemporaries [she was not] an absurd, or preposterous or unclean writer: her muse was uniformly pure and reasonable, her influence, which was very great, was exercised wholly in favour of what was beautiful and good, and if she failed it is rather by the same accident by which so many poets of less intelligence have unexpectedly succeeded.

In her letters and poems Katherine Philips wrote out her problems and anxieties, and her anxieties are to us now perhaps more interesting than those games born of her self-delusions, which men like Gosse chose to consider charms.

Katherine Philips had two children, a son, Hector, born in 1649, who lived but forty days, and a daughter Katherine, born in 1654, of whom all we know is that she outlived her mother, and married a Lewis Wogan of Boulston, Pembrokeshire. John Aubrey leaves us the only physical description: 'pretty fat, not tall, red pumpled face'.[30] Good, bad, ugly or fair, Katherine Philips was the first, and had created a position for women that was soon to be filled by the indefatigable Mrs Aphra Behn.

APHRA BEHN – ASTRAEA

A Devil on't, the woman damns the poet.
Preface to *The Lucky Chance*

Continually in her plays we encounter hostile references to marriage, and particularly to marriage without love . . . It is also significant that in so many of her plays the theme should be a forced marriage . . . while the theme of marriage to old men appears almost as frequently . . . It should further be noted how often city merchants . . . are held up to ridicule . . . I therefore suggest that Aphra Behn may have been married, more or less against her will, to a city merchant very much older than herself.[1]

Miss Scarlet, in the billiard room, with the candlestick? This passage from a reputable biography is characteristic of the Sherlock Holmes approach almost invariably taken in studies of this writer, because of the scarcity of documented facts. Here are the few sure facts we have.

After John Dryden, Aphra Behn was the most prolific writer of the age, with at least eighteen plays and many poems and prose works to her credit. Four of her plays were performed at Court, a feat excelled only by Dryden with ten, and equalled only by Roger Boyle (Earl of Orrery), John Crowne, and Nathaniel Lee.

Mrs Behn was born in or around 1640. Her birthplace is generally acknowledged to be Kent, near Canterbury. Her maiden name is argued convincingly as Amies, Johnson and Cooper.

During her youth, Aphra Behn and her family set sail for Surinam, where her father, or a relative of her father, was to take up the post of Lieutenant-General of the colony of Guiana. The family probably arrived in the colony in the autumn of 1663. The Lieutenant-General-to-be had died on the voyage, but Aphra Behn stayed in Surinam, at the house on St John's Hill, long enough to study the treatment of the Indian slaves on the local plantation, under the management of John Trefry, before returning to London in the early spring of 1664.

She brought back with her 'some rare flies, of amazing forms and colours . . . some as big as my fist, some less',[2] which she presented to His Majesty's Antiquaries, and an Indian costume made from 'feathers . . . and glorious wreaths . . . whose tinctures are unconceivable',[3] which she gave to the King's Theatre. This was the dress worn by the 'Indian Queen' in Dryden and Howard's play of the same name.

It was during this time in London that Aphra Behn married Mr Behn. Who or what her husband was we do not know, but in 1666 she was persuaded by Sir Thomas Killigrew, the licensee of the King's Theatre, to leave the country and act as a spy in the Dutch wars. It is generally accepted that Mr Behn died during 1665, possibly a victim of the Great Plague. Whatever the cause, Aphra Behn was an independent woman when she left Gravesend for Ostend in July 1666. The harbour at Ostend was closed, owing to plague, so Mrs Behn landed in Bruges on 28 July 1666.

Her instructions were to seek out William Scot, son of Thomas Scot, the regicide, and pump from him information concerning the Dutch naval and military activities, and also details of the activities of exiled Englishmen in Holland.

Aphra Behn had probably got to know Scot in Surinam. He arrived in Antwerp on the morning of Sunday, 5 August. He would not talk in her rooms, and Aphra Behn 'was forced to get a coach and go a day's journey with him to have an opportunity to speak with him'.[4] They met again two weeks later at a house two miles outside Antwerp. She dutifully transcribed reports sent from Scot, together with information provided during their meetings, and sent them to Whitehall. Unfortunately for Mrs Behn, Scot's information was of small value, and this made her worth less, too. Consequently the English government failed to pay her even her expenses, and she was forced to borrow money in order to survive. Her letters to Whitehall are full of pleas for financial assistance: 'I protest to you, sir, I am and was as frugal as possibly I could be, and have many times refused to eat as I would only to save charges.'[5]

> I do therefore intreat you, Sir, to let me have some more money . . . Pray, sir, be pleased to consider me very speedily for the longer I stay without it the more time I waste in vain for want of it, and if I did not really believe I should accomplish my business, I would not stay here, it being no delight at all for me so to do, but much the contrary, pray sir, let me not want the main and only thing that is to further my design.[6]

And

> I confess I carried no more upon bill but fifty pounds, and I have not only spent all that upon mere eating and drinking, but in borrowing of money to accomplish my desires of seeing and speaking with this man. I am as much more in debt, having pawned my very rings rather than want supplies for getting him hither.[7]

No money was forthcoming, and by 11 March 1667, when she returned to England, she was forced to borrow £150 from Edward Butler, to help pay her debts.

The London which greeted her return was very different from the one she had left eight months earlier. An enormous area, from the Tower of London to the Temple, bounded on the south by the Thames and stretching north to Moorgate had been destroyed in the Great Fire. Hundreds of people, having lost their homes, were forced to live in tents and huts, which were found in clusters as far north as Highgate. Many were 'without a rag, or any necessary utensils, bed or board, who from delicateness, riches, and easy accommodation in stately and well

furnished homes were now reduced to extremest want and poverty'.[8]
The situation had not been helped by one of the coldest winters
London has ever seen, when even the Thames froze over.

Edward Butler started pressing Mrs Behn for repayment, and she
filed two petitions to the King. In October Butler threatened her with
imprisonment unless she paid within a week. In desperation she wrote
to the man responsible for the whole episode, Sir Thomas Killigrew.

> Sir, if you could guess at the affliction of my soul you would I am sure pity
> me. 'Tis tomorrow that I must submit myself to a prison the time being
> expired, and though I endeavoured all day yesterday to get a few days more,
> I cannot because they say I am dallied withall, and so they say I shall be for-
> ever. So I cannot revoke my doom. I have cried myself dead, and could find
> it in my heart to break through all and get to the King, and never rise till he
> were pleased to pay this. But I am sick and weak and unfit for it, or a prison.
> I shall go tomorrow, but I will send my mother to the King with a petition,
> for I see every body are words, and I will not perish in a prison, from whence
> he swears I shall not stir till the utmost farthing be paid. And, Oh God, who
> considers my misery and charge too, this is my reward for all my great promi-
> ses and my endeavours. Sir, if I have not the money tonight you must send
> me something to keep me in prison, for I will not starve.[9]

Even this piteous appeal failed, and Mrs Behn sent another petition to
the King from prison.

When and how she was released is uncertain, but in 1670 she began
her career as a writer. She was then the first English woman to be a
professional writer, that is to say, to earn her living by her pen, quite
simply because she had to. It was the only course open to her if she did
not want to, or could not, find a man and marry him. What makes
Aphra Behn remarkable here is not her circumstances — other women
had known such poverty — but the decision she took. The tragicomedy
The Forced Marriage was performed by the Duke's Company at
Lincoln's Inn Fields late in that year. The cast was led by Betterton and
his wife, Mary Saunderson, and included Thomas Otway, the young
playwright, who played the first night only, 'he being not used to the
stage, the full house put him to such a sweat and tremendous agony,
being dashed, spoiled him for an actor'.[10] The play ran six nights. Not a
brilliant, but a promising first play, *The Forced Marriage* includes the
verse

> Hang love, for I will never pine
> For any man alive;
> Nor shall this jolly heart of mine
> The thoughts of it receive;
> I will not purchase slavery
> At such a dangerous rate;
> But glory in my liberty,
> And laugh at love and fate.

Aphra Behn's second play, *The Amorous Prince,* a comedy, was produced at Lincoln's Inn Fields between February and May of 1671. The

play is notable for its risqué opening scene, in which a half-dressed man and a woman in her nightclothes have just risen from bed, and a scene in which a young man meets a woman disguised as a boy, and offers to set himself up as the 'boy's' favourite.

Her next play, *The Dutch Lover*, a busy comedy of intrigue, was prefaced by an epistle to the reader to end all epistles to the reader. It begins 'Good, sweet, honey, sugar-candied reader, which I think is more than anyone has called you yet', and goes on to explain how the play

> was hugely injured in the acting, for 'twas done so imperfectly as never any was before, which did more harm to this than it could have done to any of another sort, the plot being busy . . . and so requiring continual attention, which being interrupted by the intolerable negligence of some that acted in it, must needs much spoil the beauty on't.

This play contains the line: 'I never made love so well as when I was drunk. It improves my parts and makes me witty; that is, it makes me say anything that comes next, which passes nowadays for wit.' And another song:

> *Ah false Amyntas, can that hour*
> *So soon forgotten be,*
> *When first I yielded up my power*
> *To be betrayed by thee?*
> *God knows with how much innocence*
> *I did my heart resign*
> *Upon thy faithless eloquence,*
> *And gave thee what was mine.*
>
> *I had not one reserve in store,*
> *But at thy feet I laid*
> *Those arms which conquered heretofore,*
> *Tho' now thy trophies made.*
> *Thy eyes in silence told their tale*
> *Of love in such a way,*
> *That 'twas as easy to prevail,*
> *As after to betray.*

First performed in February 1673, it failed, and it was perhaps owing to this failure that Aphra Behn had no plays performed until the late summer of 1676.

Her next work, *Abdelazer,* a tragedy full of murder and treachery, opens with her most famous lines:

> Love in fantastic triumph sate
> Whilst bleeding hearts around him flowed,
> For whom fresh pains he did create,
> And strange tyrannic power he showed;
>
> From thy bright eyes he took his fire,
> Which round about in sport he hurled;
> But 'twas from mine he took desire,
> Enough to undo the amorous world.

From me he took his sighs and tears,
From thee his pride and cruelty;
From me his languishments and fears,
And every killing dart from thee.

Thus thou and I the god have armed,
And set him up a deity;
But my poor heart alone is harmed,
Whilst thine the victor is, and free.

The play is drenched in unbridled sexual passion. The title role, a sexual savage, was taken by Betterton, and Isabella, a villainess as colourful as a Disney wicked queen, was played by Mary Lee.

This play was quickly followed up with a funny but uneven comedy, *The Town Fop*, which includes hilarious scenes in a brothel, where two lovers having an evening off from each other meet up as wench and client.

In March 1677, Dorset Garden produced her most celebrated play, *The Rover*. Revived often, it stayed in the repertoire until late in the eighteenth century. Dealing in a sympathetic way with the problems of arranged marriages, this comedy perfectly depicts the callousness which pervaded London society during the reign of Charles II, and includes the much quoted line: 'Come away; poverty's catching.'

Her next play *Sir Patient Fancy*, based on Molière's *Le Malade Imaginaire*, was produced at Dorset Garden in January 1678. In her introduction to the edition of 1678 Mrs Behn explains:

I printed this play with all the impatient haste one ought to do, who would be vindicated from the most unjust and silly aspersion woman could invent to cast on woman, and which only my being a woman has procured me: that it was bawdy, the least and most excuseable fault in the men writers, to whose plays they all crowd, as if they came to no other end than to hear what they condemn in this, but from a woman it was unnatural.

The epilogue is again a defence of a woman's right to write:

MRS GWIN (*looking about*)
    I here and there o'erheard a coxcomb cry,
    Ah, rot it, 'tis a woman's comedy,
    One, who because she lately chanced to please us,
    With her damned stuff will never cease to tease us.
    What has poor woman done that she must be
    Debarred from sense and sacred poetry?
    Why in this age has Heaven allowed you more,
    And woman less of wit than heretofore?
    We once were famed in story, and could write
    Equal to men; could govern, nay, could fight.
    We still have passive valour, and can show,
    Would custom give us leave, the active too,
    Since we no provocations want from you.
    For who but we could your dull fopperies bear,
    Your saucy love, and your brisk nonsense hear;
    Endure your worse than womanish affectation,

Which renders you the nuisance of the nation;
Scorned even by all the misses of the town,
A jest to vizard mask and pit-buffoon;
A glass by which the admiring country fool
May learn to dress himself *en ridicule*,
Both striving who shall most ingenious grow
In lewdness, foppery, nonsense, noise and show.
And yet to these fine things we must submit
Our reason, arms, our laurels and our wit.
Because we do not laugh at you when lewd,
And scorn and cudgel ye when you are rude,
That we have nobler souls than you we prove,
By how much more we're sensible of love;
Quickest in finding all the subtlest ways
To make your joys, why not to make you plays?
We best can find your foibles, know our own,
And jilts and cuckolds now best please the town;
Your way of writing's out of fashion grown.
Method and rule you only understand —
Pursue that way of fooling and be damned.
Your learned cant of action, time and place
Must all give way to the unlaboured farce.
To all the men of wit we will subscribe
But for your half-wits, you unthinking tribe,
We'll let you see, whate'er besides we do,
How artfully we copy some of you:
And if you're drawn to th'life, pray tell me then,
Why women should not write as well as men.

A year later *The Feigned Courtesans*, a comedy dedicated to Nell
Gwynn, was produced at Dorset Garden. Montague Summers, the
editor of the fullest edition of her works, claims this to be 'one of the
very best and wittiest of her sparkling comedies'.[11] Slick and packed
with intrigue, it follows the escapades of two sisters who disguise themselves as courtesans for a night.

In the autumn of 1679, *The Young King*, a tragicomedy, was performed at Dorset Garden. Cleomena, the leading woman in this play,
is 'bred up in war', an Amazon queen, and through her Mrs Behn continues her feminist arguments. It is generally thought that Mrs Behn
started writing this play while in Surinam, and held it back until this
time.

The second part of *The Rover* was her next dramatic offering,
performed by the Duke's Company in April 1681. Like most follow-
ups, it was not as successful as the original; nonetheless it is a very good
play, notable in that, in the last scene, one couple decide not to marry,
but make vows to live together.

Mrs Behn claims that she wrote *The False Count* (1681) in five
days. It is a comedy full of disguise and mistaken identity, with
people dressing as Ottoman pirates, sultans, a chimney sweep as a
nobleman, etc.

A careful blend of fact and fiction made up her next play, *The Roundheads*, a comedy about the last days of the English Civil War.

The City Heiress, a comedy lampooning Shaftesbury and the Whigs, was performed a few months after *The Roundheads*, in March 1682. 'This play had the luck to be well received in the town.'[12]

Her next play, 'Like Father Like Son' (1682), was not printed and only the prologue and epilogue survive. It was obviously a failure and this, together with rising anger about *The Roundheads* and *The City Heiress*, led the Whig playwright, Shadwell, to write:

> Such stupid humours now the gallants seize
> Women and boys may write and yet may please.
> Poetess Aphra though she's damned today
> Tomorrow will put up another play.[13]

Tomorrow, or five months later, Aphra Behn did not put up another play, but wrote the prologue and epilogue to the anonymous play *Romulus and Hersilia*, which was performed on 10 August. Two days later a warrant was issued for the arrest of the actress, Mary Lee (now Lady Slingsby), who had spoken the epilogue, and for Mrs Behn for her sedition in writing it. They were accused of making 'abusive reflections upon persons of quality, and have written and spoken scandalous speeches without any license or approbation of those that ought to peruse and authorise the same'.[14] The offending lines were:

> And of all treasons, mine was most accurst;
> Rebelling 'gainst a king and father first.
> A sin, which heav'n nor man can e'er forgive . . .[15]

which were taken as comment on the Duke of Monmouth's uprising against his father, King Charles. There is no evidence of the women being punished, and it is generally thought that they got away with a warning.

In 1683 Aphra Behn started writing prose works: three *novellas* which were not published until after her death, and *Love Letters between a Nobleman and his Sister* which was published in 1684. This collection of letters is based on the relationship between Forde, Lord Grey, and his wife's sister, Lady Henrietta Berkely. The couple had eloped in 1682 and were subsequently caught, brought to trial, and found guilty.

Also in 1684 she published *Poems on Several Occasions, with A Voyage to the Island of Love*.

The following year she published her *Miscellany*, which includes poems by herself, of which this is a fair sample:

> While, Iris, I at distance gaze,
> And feed my greedy eyes,
> That wounded heart, that dies for you,
> Dull gazing can't suffice;

Hope is the food of love-sick minds,
On that alone 'twill feast,
The nobler part which love refines,
No other can digest.

In vain, too nice and charming maid,
I did suppress my cares;
In vain my rising sighs I stayed,
And stopped my falling tears;
The flood would swell, the tempest rise,
As my despair came on;
When from her lovely cruel eyes
I found I was undone.

Yet at your feet while thus I lie,
And languish by your eyes,
'Tis far more glorious here to die,
Than gain another prize.
Here let me sigh, here let me gaze,
And wish at least to find
As raptured nights, and tender days,
As he to whom you're kind.

The year 1686 saw not only a prose work, *La Montre: The Lover's Watch,* but also a return to the theatre with one of her best plays, *The Lucky Chance.* Described by Genest as 'too indecent to be ever represented again',[16] it was prefaced by a defence of her right to write as freely as men:

When they can no other way prevail with the town they charge it with the old never failing scandal — That 'tis not fit for the ladies, as if . . . the ladies were obliged to hear indecencies only from their pens and plays . . . Celebrated plays have entertained 'em with things that are never taken notice of, because a man writ them, [but] they . . . blush at [the same] from a woman.

She closes her preface with a threat:

If I must not, because of my sex, have this freedom . . . I lay down my quill and you shall hear no more of me . . . for I am not content to write for a third day only. I value fame as much as if I had been born a hero, and if you rob me of that I can retire from the ungrateful world, and scorn its fickle favours.

She did not lay down her quill. She went on to produce, in March 1687, one of the most successful plays of the seventeenth and eighteenth centuries, *The Emperor of the Moon.* This was a farce, incorporating the Italian *commedia dell'arte* characters, Harlequin and Scaramouche, and it was regularly performed for foreign dignitaries visiting London, among them the Moroccan Ambassador, an African prince, and His Excellency Hodgha Bawhoon, envoy from the great King of Persia, who could enjoy jokes which were primarily visual rather than verbal; it was also popular with the English royal family. It was often chosen for performances which fell on Friday, the 13th, because it never failed. This was the last of her plays that Mrs Behn was to see performed.

In 1687 she published many of her non-dramatic works, among them translations from Fontanelle and Aesop, and the novel *Oroonoko*, which was inspired by her life in Surinam. This novel, it has been argued, makes her the precursor of Harriet Beecher Stowe, anticipating the theories of Rousseau and the anti-slave movement. It was later dramatised successfully by Thomas Southerne in 1695.

On 16 April 1688, five days after the coronation of William and Mary, Aphra Behn died. She was buried in Westminster Abbey on 20 April under a black marble slab, inscribed with the couplet

> Here lies a proof that wit can never be
> Defence enough against mortality.

In the autumn of that year, her play, *The Widow Ranter*, was produced at Dorset Garden. It was a failure. This was partly due to the casting of Samuel Sandford as the juvenile lead, a dashing handsome officer. Sandford's 'figure . . . was diminutive and mean, being round-shouldered, meagre faced, spindle-shanked, splay-footed with a sour countenance and long lean arms'.[17] In the dedication, written by G.J., probably her friend, George Jenkins, it is claimed that 'had our author been alive she would have committed it to the flames rather than have suffered it to have been acted with such omissions as was made and on which the foundation of the play depended'.

In February 1696 Charles Gildon produced another of her plays, *The Younger Brother*, at Drury Lane. Gildon defends the play in his dedication, and describes

> the unjust sentence this play met with before very partial judges in the acting
> . . . so that I may reasonably impute its miscarriage to some faction that was
> made against it, which indeed was very evident on the first day, and more on
> the endeavours employed to render the profits of the third as small as could
> be.

Aphra Behn left a number of non-dramatic works, too, that were published after her death.

Throughout her career Aphra Behn had had an intense relationship with John Hoyle, the son of Thomas Hoyle, the Alderman, Lord Mayor and M.P. for York, who had hanged himself the same hour that Charles I was beheaded. John Hoyle was known to be 'an atheist, a sodomite professed, a corrupter of youth and a blasphemer of Christ',[18] and was regularly involved in brawls and duels. Mrs Behn described him in her poem 'Our Cabal'

> Next Lysidas, that haughty swain,
> With many beauties in a train,
> All sighing for the swain, whilst he
> Barely returns civility . . .
> His eyes are black, and do transcend
> All fancy e'er can comprehend;

And yet no softness in 'em move.
They kill with fierceness, not with love:
Yet he can dress 'em when he list,
With sweetness none can e'er resist.
His tongue no amorous parley makes,
But with his looks alone he speaks.
And though he languish yet he'll hide,
That grateful knowledge with his pride;
And thinks his liberty is lost,
Not in the conquest, but the boast.
Nor will but love enough impart,
To gain and to secure a heart:
Of which no sooner he is sure,
And that its wounds are past all cure,
But for new victories he prepares,
And leaves the old to its despairs:
Success his boldness does renew,
And boldness helps him conquer too,
He having gained more hearts than all
Th'rest of the pastoral Cabal.

After her death some of her songs and poems were retitled in order
to point them at him, among them this 'Song to Mr J.H.':

Amyntas led me to a grove,
Where all the trees did shade us;
The sun itself, though it had strove,
It could not have betrayed us:
The place secured from human eyes,
No other fear allows,
But when the winds that gently rise,
Do kiss the yielding boughs.

Down there we sat upon the moss,
And did begin to play
A thousand amorous tricks, to pass
The heat of all the day.
A many kisses he did give,
And I returned the same
Which made me willing to receive
That which I dare not name.

His charming eyes no aid required
To tell their softening tale:
On her that was already fired,
'Twas easy to prevail.
He did but kiss and clasp me round,
Whilst those his thoughts expressed,
And layed me gently on the ground;
Ah, who can guess the rest?[19]

Her *Love Letters to a Gentleman*, published with the 1696 collection of her novels, is generally agreed to be her letters to Hoyle. From
these we can gather that he did not treat her very well:

You may tell me a thousand years . . . of your unbounded friendship, but after

so unkind a departure as that last night, give me leave . . . to doubt it; nay, 'tis
past doubt: I know rather you hate me.[20]

When shall we understand one another? . . . I have a great mind to say a
thousand things I know will be taken in an ill sense. Possibly you will wonder
what compels me to write, what moves me to send where I find so little welcome? Nay, where I meet with such returns, it may be I wonder too.[21]

I conjure you to consider what resolution I took up, when I saw you last . . .
of seeing no man till I saw your face again, and when you remember that, you
will possibly be so kind as to make what haste you can to see me again.[22]

[I] grow desperate fond of you, and would fain be used well; if not I will
march off. But I will believe you mean to keep your word, as I will forever do
mine . . . For God's sake, do not misrepresent my excess of fondness, and if I
forget myself, let the check you give be sufficient to make me desist.[23]

My charming unkind, I would have gaged my life you could not have left me
so coldly, so unconcerned as you did, but you are resolved to give me proofs
of your no love . . . Tell me no more you love me, for 'twill be hard to make
me think it, though it be the only blessing I ask on earth. But if love can merit
a heart, I know who ought to claim yours. My soul is ready to burst with pride
and indignation, and at the same time, love, with all his softness assails me,
and will make me write, so that between one and the other, I can express
neither as I ought. What shall I do to make you know I do not use to condes-
cend to so much submission, nor to tell my heart so freely?[24]

Just before her death Hoyle was arraigned before a grand jury at the
Old Bailey, on a charge of sodomy with a poulterer, and discharged
with a verdict of 'ignoramus' (equivalent to the Scots verdict 'non-
proven'). It is highly probable that Hoyle carried on *affaires* with both
men and women while he was with Aphra Behn. A lawyer with chambers in the Inner Temple, Hoyle wrote a set of articles for the maintenance of their relationship. Nevertheless, Aphra Behn seems to have been
devoted to him for most of her life.

The works of Mrs Behn have been attacked ever since they first
appeared. In 1686/7 *The Epistle to Julian* described her:

Doth that lewd harlot, that poetic queen,
Famed through White Friars, you know who I mean,
Mend for reproof, others set up in spight,
To flux, take glisters, vomits, purge and write.
Long with a sciatica she's beside lame,
Her limbs distortured, nerves shrunk up with pain,
And therefore I'll all sharp reflections shun,
Poverty, poetry, pox are plagues enough for one.[25]

At the end of the eighteenth century Dr Kippis wrote an article
about her in the *Biographia Britannica*:[26]

The wit of her comedies seems to be generally acknowledged, and it is equally
acknowledged that they are very indecent, on which account I have not
thought myself under any obligation to peruse them. It would have been an
unworthy employment, nicely to estimate a wit which, having been applied to
the purposes of impiety and vice, ought not only to be held up in the utmost

detestation, but consigned, if possible to eternal oblivion. It is some consolation to reflect that Mrs Behn's works are now little regarded her novels excepted, which, we suppose, have still many readers among that unhappily too numerous a class of people who devour the trash of the circulating libraries.

In the nineteenth century Dr Doran wrote of her in his *Annals*, 'no one equalled this woman in downright nastiness save Ravenscroft and Wycherley . . . With Dryden she vied in indecency, and was not overcome . . . She was a mere harlot who danced through uncleanness and dared [the others] to follow'.[27] And Julia Kavanagh, a woman of letters herself, wrote, 'Even if her life remained pure, it is amply evident her mind was tainted to the very core. Grossness was congenial to her . . . Mrs Behn's indelicacy was useless and worse than useless, the superfluous addition of a corrupt mind and vitiated taste.'[28]

Others have come to her defence. Swinburne and Blake were impressed with her poems and songs, Colley Cibber's son, Theophilus, wrote in 1759, 'Mrs Behn suffered enough at the hands of supercilious prudes, who had the barbarity to construe her sprightliness into lewdness, and because she had wit and beauty, she must be likewise charged with prostitution and irreligion.'[29] In her own century Gildon wrote, 'She excelled not only all that went before her of her own sex, but great part of her contemporary poets of the other.'[30] Even when her works were well-nigh forgotten, Aphra Behn continued to matter, the way pioneers do. Because writing was, in the nineteenth century, such an acceptable pastime, women writing might pass as amateurs, girls with hobbies, but it became a source of difficulty once you wanted to be taken seriously. Virginia Woolf, who voiced the difficulties faced by a woman wanting to be taken as a professional writer, saw it as Aphra Behn's achievement that she established this: '. . . here begins the freedom of the mind . . . For now that Aphra Behn had done it, girls could say . . . I can make money by my pen'.[31]

CATHERINE TROTTER

*Passion is to be the noblest frailty of the mind, but 'tis a frailty, and
becomes a vice when cherished as an exalted virtue.*

Dedication to *The Unhappy Penitent* (1701)

Aphra Behn's translation of a French short story, 'Agnes de Castro',
was adapted for the stage by Catherine Trotter, a girl of sixteen, and
appeared at Drury Lane Theatre sometime in late December 1695, or
January 1696.

Catherine Trotter was born in London on 16 August 1679. In 1683,
her father, Captain David Trotter, attended Lord Dartmouth as Com-
modore in the English navy's demolition of Tangiers. As a reward for
good service King Charles sent Captain Trotter from Tangiers to convoy
the fleet of the Turkey Company. It was understood that he would
make his fortune in Turkey. At the time of his arrival in Scanderoon,
the town was stricken with plague. David Trotter, instead of the fortune he expected, only gained a fatal dose of that disease and died,
along with all the officers on his ship, in January 1684. The purser made
off with Captain Trotter's effects on board ship, which were considerable, and his family in England were further impoverished when the
goldsmith, in whose hands the greatest part of his money was lodged,
went bankrupt. King Charles II advised the Admiralty to bestow a pension upon Captain Trotter's widow, Sarah Ballenden. The pension was
paid in 1684, but, when the King died the following year, the pension
stopped, and Mrs Sarah Trotter and her two daughters were obliged to
depend on the charity of their relations and friends.

Catherine Trotter 'gave very early marks of her genius, and was not
past her childhood, when she surprised a company of her relations and
friends with extempory verses on an incident which had fallen under
her observation in the street'.[1] She taught herself to write, and learned
French without the aid of a teacher, although she was assisted in Latin
and logic. 'The most serious and important subjects, and especially
those of religion, soon engaged her attention.'[2] Despite her upbringing
as an Anglican, she chose to follow the Roman Catholic faith.

In 1693, at the age of fourteen, Catherine Trotter wrote a set of
verses to Bevil Higgons upon his falling prey to, and subsequent
recovery from, an attack of smallpox. Bevil Higgons, 'greatly esteemed
at that time for his wit and poetical talents',[3] had written a tragedy,
The Generous Conqueror, and the prologue to Congreve's first play,
The Old Batchelor, earlier in the same year. No one knows whether
Mrs Trotter knew Higgons or whether she sent him the verses out of the
blue, but Gosse[4] surmises that writing to Higgons may have led to
introductions with Congreve and Dryden.

Her first play, *Agnes de Castro*, 'met with good success'.[5] In her introduction to the edition of 1697, Mrs Trotter ('A Young Lady') admitted that the play was 'indeed a bold [attempt] for a woman of [her] years, but . . . would not offer [her] little experience as a reason to be pardon'd for not acquitting [her] self well'. Gosse finds the play 'rather extraordinary for nimble movement and adroit theatrical arrangements . . . It is a bad play, but not at all an unpromising one.'[6]

In 1697 Catherine Trotter sent verses to William Congreve on his tragedy *The Mourning Bride*. He replied in a letter of genuine gratitude:

> I can never enough acknowledge the honour you have done me . . . It is the first thing, that ever happened to me, upon which I should make it my choice to be vain. And yet such is the mortification that attends even the most allowable vanity, that at the same instant I am robb'd of the means, when I am possessed with the inclination. It is but this moment, that I received your verses; and had scarce been transported with the reading them, when they brought me the play from the press printed off . . . and all the satisfaction that I can take, and all the sacrifice that I make to you, is only to stifle some verses on the same barren subject, which were printed with it, and now, I assure you, shall never appear, whatever apology I am forced to make to the authors. And since I am deprived of the recommendation you designed me, I will be obliged to no other, till I have some future opportunity of preferring yours to every body's else. In the mean time, give me leave to value myself upon the favour you have done me; and to assure you, it was not wanting to make me more ready than I have been in my inclinations of waiting on all your commands.[7]

The following year her second play, *The Fatal Friendship*, was brought upon the stage at Lincoln's Inn Fields, where Congreve acted as chief writer and literary adviser. 'This tragedy met with great applause. and is still thought the most perfect of all her dramatic performances.'[8] Even the cynic Charles Gildon wrote, 'I need say nothing of this play, the town has prevented my approbation; and I can only add that I think it deserved the applause it met with, which every play that has the advantage of being clap't, cannot get from the severer and abler judges.'[9] *The Fatal Friendship*'s plot is extraordinary, for a tragedy, in its ingenious obsession with money, its advantages, and the problems resulting from the lack of it.

George Farquhar's 'passions were wrought so high by representation of *Fatal Friendship*, and since raised so high by the sight of the beautiful author'[10] that he sent her a copy of his play *Love in a Bottle*, which 'had been scandalously aspersed for affronting the ladies'.[11] Mrs Trotter had sat through his play on its third night, but she left nothing to indicate whether she approved of it or not.

On 1 May 1700 John Dryden, the Poet Laureate, died. Catherine Trotter was engaged to write a verse tribute, along with eight other women poets. The poems were published in September 1700 under the title *The Nine Muses; or, poems written by so many ladies, upon the death of the famous John Dryden esq*. As 'Caliope' she gives directions how to deserve and distinguish the muse's inspiration:

> Let none presume the hallow'd way to tread,
> By other than the noblest motives led.
> If for a sordid gain, or glitt'ring fame,
> To please without instructing be your aim,
> To lower means your grovelling thoughts confine,
> Unworthy of an art that's all divine.

In November 1700, Mrs Trotter's first, and only, comedy, *Love at a Loss,* or: *Most Votes Carry It,* was performed at Drury Lane. It was published in May 1701,

> but her absence from London during the impression occasioned many errors in the edition, some things marked in her copy to be left out, being inserted, and others absolutely necessary to the sense, omitted; the whole being by this means so altered and disguised, that she would gladly, if possible, have called in and suppressed the edition.[12]

In her handwritten dedication to Lady Piers she wrote that: 'she had never thought of making any pretence to a talent for comedy . . . till some leisure hours inclined her to amuse herself in piecing it up, with little care or concern for the success, not intending to establish her fame upon a work of this kind'.[13]

On 4 February 1701 *The Unhappy Penitent* was premièred at Drury Lane. Genest dismisses it as 'an indifferent tragedy by Mrs Trotter'.[14] More interesting than the play itself is the preface, in which Catherine Trotter gives an interesting assessment of English playwriting, in which 'the inimitable Shakespeare seems alone secure on every side from attack'.

At the age of twenty-two, with four plays behind her, Mrs Trotter left London. After spending some time at the home of her patron, Lady Piers, in Kent, she settled in Salisbury, Wiltshire, in the house of Dr Inglis, her sister's husband. There she became very friendly with Bishop Burnet, and formed a close relationship with his second wife, an active theologian, of whom Trotter wrote, 'I have not met such perfection in anyone of our sex.'[15] She also struck up a friendship with a relative of the Bishop, George Burnet, who shortly after left England on a religious mission.

In 1690 the *Essay Concerning Human Understanding* by John Locke had been published in London. Seven years later various attacks, or animadversions, were published against the work. These were, in the main, by Oxford University reactionaries. John Locke

> indulged in no soaring flights. Content with more modest aims, he made no attempts to scale the mountain tops of truth, satisfied with such relative verities as our puny hands can grasp . . . The prudent Locke will . . . put you on a quiet road leading to the foothills of certitude, a smooth and level road, without any sudden twists or turns.[16]

This low-key common-sense philosophy appealed to Catherine Trotter, who was so enraged at the attacks on Locke that she sat down to refute them. She showed her *A Defence of Mr Locke's 'Essay of Human Understanding'* to Mrs Burnet, who showed it to the Bishop and to John Norris of Bemerton, the author of an anti-Locke essay. The *Defence* was published anonymously in May 1702. In June 1702 a copy reached Locke himself. Old and ill, he sent his cousin Mr Peter King, with a present of books and a letter for his fair defender:

> Give me leave . . . to assure you, that as the rest of the world take notice of the strength and clearness of your reasoning, so I cannot but be extremely sensible, that it was employed in my defence. You have herein not only vanquished my adversary, but reduced me also absolutely under your power, and left no desires more strong in me, than those of meeting with some opportunity to assure you, with what respect and submission I am, Madam, Your most humble, and most obedient servant, John Locke.[17]

Soon afterwards she heard that Lady Mascham, Locke's companion, writing to the philosopher, Leibnitz, implied that Trotter's thoughts were not her own. Indignantly, Catherine Trotter defended herself:

> Women are as capable of penetrating into the grounds of things and reasoning justly as men are who certainly have no advantage of us but in their opportunities of knowledge . . . I see no reason to suspect [Lady Mascham] would pretend to write anything that was not entirely her own. I pray be more equitable to her sex than the generality of yours are who when anything is written by a woman that they cannot deny their approbation to, are sure to rob us of the glory of it by concluding 'tis not her own.[18]

Catherine Trotter returned to the exercise of her dramatic talents in 1703 with a tragedy, *The Revolution of Sweden*. She sent a copy of the play to Congreve for criticism. He replied:

> I think the design in general very great and noble; the conduct of it very artful, if not too full of business, which may either run into length or obscurity; but both those . . . you have skill enough to avoid. You are the best judge, whether those of your own sex will approve as much of the heroic virtue of Constantia and Christina, as if they had been engaged in some belle passion: for my part, I like them better as they are. In the second act, I would have that noise, which generally attends so much fighting on the stage, provided against; for those frequent alarms and excursions do too much disturb an audience. The difficulty in the third act is as well solved by you as possible; and certainly you can never be too careful not to offend probability, in supposing a man not to discover his own wife.
>
> In the fourth act, it does not seem to me to be clear enough, how Constantia comes to be made free, and to return to Gustavus; the third act intimating so strongly, why we might expect to have her continued in the viceroy's power. This act is full of business; and intricacy, in the fourth act, must by all means be avoided.
>
> The last act will have many harangues in it, which are dangerous in a catastrophe, if long, and not of the last importance . . . You see, Madam, I am as free as you command me to be; and yet my objections are none but such, as you may provide against, even while you are writing the dialogue.

I wish you the success, which you can wish, and that, I think, will hardly be so much as you deserve, in whatever you undertake.[19]

Mrs Trotter spent the summer and winter of 1704 in London, studying and revising *The Revolution of Sweden*. George Burnet wrote to her there upon his arrival at the Court of Berlin. He told how he had discussed Trotter's work with Sophia Carlotta, Queen of Prussia, who was 'charmed with the agreeable picture which he had drawn of the new Scots Sappho, who seemed to deserve all the great things which he had said of her'.[20]

The Duke of Marlborough's victory at Blenheim inspired Catherine Trotter to compose verses in his honour,

but being doubtful with respect to the publication of them, she sent them in manuscript to his grace; and received for answer that the Duke, and Duchess, and the Lord Treasurer, Godolphin, with several others, to whom they were shewn, were greatly pleased with them; and that the good judges of poetry had declared that there were some lines in them superior to any which had been written on the subject. Upon this encouragement she sent the poem to press; but it was not published till a month after it was written.[21]

In February 1706 *The Revolution of Sweden* was produced at the Queen's Theatre, Haymarket. It expired after the sixth day. In the preface Catherine Trotter declares:

I . . . could never allow myself to think of any subject that cou'd not serve either to incite some useful virtue, or check some dangerous passion. With this design I thought writing for the stage a work not unworthy those who would not trifle their time away, and had so fix'd my mind on contributing my part towards reforming the corruptions of it that no doubt I have too little consider'd the present taste of the town.

The play is written with Trotter's usual care for language, and is well constructed, but because of the subject matter as much as anything else, certainly leaves a distinct impression of dullness.

Soon after this Mrs Trotter left Salisbury for Ockham Mills, near Ripley in Surrey, where she lived as companion to a Mrs de Vere. While she was there she abandoned her Catholic faith in favour of the Church of England, and wrote *A Discourse concerning a Guide in Controversies*, discussing the whole problem of denominational Christianity.

In Ockham, Mr Fenn, a clergyman, declared his love, but Catherine Trotter (intent on marrying a clergyman), chose Mr Cockburn, with whom she had engaged in friendship and correspondence. They were married early in 1708.

From this moment her life was dependent on the decisions of Mr Cockburn, for better or for worse. The couple settled in his parish at Nayland, Suffolk. Before the end of the year they moved to London, where Mr Cockburn took up the position of curate of St Dunstan's in Fleet Street.

The Stuart age ended on 1 August 1714 with the death of Queen

Anne, and the accession of the Hanoverian George I. Mr Cockburn had scruples about taking the Oath of Abjuration (renouncing the Stuart claim to the throne through the Pretenders), which was obligatory to public employees, and he was therefore sacked.

He took a position as Latin teacher at a school in Chancery Lane. He, Catherine Trotter, and their young son and two daughters, were reduced to great poverty for twelve years until, in 1726, after discussions with his father Dr Cockburn, 'an eminent and learned divine of Scotland',[22] and Peter King, Locke's cousin, who was now Lord Chancellor, Mr Cockburn was reconciled to taking the oath.

The following year Mr Cockburn was appointed Minister of the Episcopalian Church in Aberdeen. Soon after settling in Aberdeen, the Lord Chancellor presented him to the living of Long Horseley, near Morpeth, Northumberland. He accepted the income from Long Horseley, and for a while the Cockburn family lived in relative prosperity. The congregation at Long Horseley never saw their minister, who remained in Aberdeen.

Mrs Trotter rewrote her comedy *Love at a Loss* under the title *The Honorable Deceivers*, or: *All Right at the Last*, and also penned *Vindication of Mr Locke's Christian Principles from the Injurious Imputations of Dr Holdsworth*, for which she could not find a publisher (and it was not published until two years after her death). In August 1732 she wrote *Verses Occasioned by the Busts in the Queen's Hermitage*, which was later printed in *The Gentleman's Magazine* (May 1737).

In 1737 the Bishop of Durham caught up with the vicar of Long Horseley, and summoned him to take up the duties for which he had been accepting the stipend over nine years, and the Cockburn family had to leave Scotland for Northumberland, and learn to live on one income.

Catherine Trotter did not write for money but turned her pen to another philosophical tract, *Remarks upon some Writers in the Controversy concerning the Foundation of Moral Duty and Moral Obligations*, in the winter of 1739. Her eyes were growing weak and, unable to sew, read or write by candlelight, she 'amused herself during the long winter evenings in digesting her thoughts upon the most abstruse subjects in morality and metaphysics'.[23] These works remained in manuscript form until 1743 when they were published in *The History of the Works of the Learned*. In her letter of dedication to Alexander Pope, which was never sent, she wrote: 'Being married in 1708 I bid adieu to the muses, and so wholly gave myself up to the cares of a family, and the education of my children, that I scarce knew whether there was any such thing as books, plays or poems stirring in Great Britain.'[24]

Despite fading vision and acute asthma, she next set out to confute Dr Rutherford's *Essay on the Nature and Obligations of Virtue*, which had been published in 1744, and 'having finished it with a spirit, elegance and perspicuity equal, if not superior, to all her former writings',[25] she submitted the manuscript for publication in April 1747. Its success induced her friends to encourage her to collect her writings together and publish them.

Mr Cockburn died on 4 January 1749, 'after having long supported a painful disorder',[26] and Catherine, his wife, followed him to the grave, four months later, on 11 May 1749, aged seventy. The edition of her works was incomplete.

She was buried at Long Horseley, near her husband and youngest daughter. Her tomb bore the inscription, 'Let their Works Praise them in the Gates. Prov. xxxi.31'.

Thomas Birch M.A. took on the job of completing the compilation of Mrs Trotter's works, and the two volumes were published in 1751. Unfortunately he decided to include only one play, *The Fatal Friendship*, as space was limited, and Birch felt that her prose works were 'of more general and lasting use to the world'.[27] Most of the papers he did include are described by Edmund Gosse as 'so dull that merely to think of them brings tears into one's eyes'.[28] It is hard not to agree.

Birch does include some of her poetry, which is, on the whole, more concerned with morality than versification:

'The Caution'

Soft kisses may be innocent,
But, ah! too easy maid beware;
Though that is all thy kindness meant,
'Tis love's delusive fatal snare.

No virgin e'er at first design'd
Through all the maze of love to stray;
But each new path allures her mind,
'Till wand'ring on, she lose her way.

'Tis easy e'er set out to stay;
But who the useful art can teach,
When sliding down a steepy way,
To stop, before the end we reach?

Keep ever something in thy pow'r,
Beyond what would thy honour stain:
He will not dare to aim at more,
Who for small favours sighs in vain.

'The Vain Advice. A Song'

Ah gaze not on those eyes! forbear
That soft enchanting voice to hear:
Not looks of basilisks give surer death,
Nor sirens sing with more destructive breath.

Fly, if thy freedom thou'dst maintain.
Alas! I feel th'advice is vain!
A heart whose safety but in flight does lie,
Is too far lost to have the power to fly.

claims to have been 'born in Hampshire, in one of those islands which formerly belonged to France',[3] it seems more likely that she was born between 1667 and 1672, when her father, Sir Roger Manley, was Lieutenant-Governor and Commander of all His Majesty's castles, forts and forces within the Isle of Jersey. The editor of the posthumously published second edition of *Rivella*, Edmund Curll, claims that she was 'born at sea between Jersey and Guernsey'.[4] If this is true the most likely date is 1672 when the Manley family were leaving Jersey for Portsmouth, where Sir Roger was to take up a new commission.

Sir Roger Manley fought for the King in the Civil War, and went into exile in Holland in 1648. In addition to his military ability, Sir Roger Manley published a few history books and translated *A True Description of the Mighty Kingdoms of Japan and Siam* from the Dutch.

After their mother's death, Delarivier Manley and her two sisters, Mary Elizabeth and Cornelia, were tutored by a governess in their father's garrison, while her brother Francis was educated for a naval career.

In February 1680 the family moved to Landguard Fort, Suffolk, where Sir Roger took up the post of Governor of the garrison. In 1685, following the death of King Charles II and the accession of his brother James II, a new company of soldiers came to Landguard Fort. Delarivier Manley fell madly in love with a young subaltern officer, Captain James Carlisle. He was in love with someone else but she was enraptured: 'His voice was very good; the songs then in vogue amorous, and such as suited her temper of mind; she drank the poyson both at her ears and eyes.'[5] Her father did his best to divert her attention but her passion continued until Carlisle's removal with the rest of his garrison, a few weeks later.

Delarivier Manley was sent to a 'Huguenot minister's house on the other side of the sea and country about eighteen miles farther from London'.[6] Ill health forced her return, but not before she had learned to 'speak and write French with a perfection truly wonderful'.[7] It was hoped that her education would be completed by a stint as maid of honour to Queen Mary of Modena. The flight of King James and the Queen in 1688 and the subsequent Glorious Revolution put an end to this, and the death of her father at about the same time plunged her headlong into real life.

Her elder sister, Mary Elizabeth, had married Captain Braithwaite, an officer briefly stationed at Landguard Fort, after a whirlwind romance. Delarivier Manley describes her as 'unhappily bestow'd in marriage . . . on a wretch every way unworthy of her, of her fortune, her birth, her charms or tenderness',[8] and claims that Captain Braithwaite was 'so ill-natur'd and disobliging that our family no longer conversed with theirs'.[9] That is the last we hear of Mary Elizabeth.

Delarivier and Cornelia Manley were left to the care of John Manley.

John's father was Sir Roger's younger brother John, who had gone against his Cavalier family and fought in the Cromwellian army. Sir Roger had brought up and educated his nephew as though he had been his own son. Nonetheless, John Manley did not want the burden of the two young Manley sisters (he was twenty-three years older than Delarivier), particularly as he was married to an old woman. He put the girls in charge of 'an old out-of-fashion aunt, full of the heroic stiffness of her own times; who would read books of chivalry and romances with her spectacles',[10] which Delarivier claims 'infected' her and made her 'fancy every stranger that [she] saw ... some disguised prince or lover'.[11]

It was not long before the aunt died, and John Manley came to fetch the girls. Delarivier describes what followed:

> He was in deep mourning . . . he told us for his wife. We congratulated him for his deliverance from an old uneasy lady, that we remembered enough of to hate, ever since we had been children . . . My cousin-guardian immediately declar'd himself my lover, with such an eagerness that none can guess at who are not acquainted with the violence of his temper. I was no otherwise pleas'd with it, than as he answer'd something to the character I had found in those books that had poyson'd and deluded my dawning reason. However I had the honour and cruelty of a true heroin and would not permit my adorer so much as a kiss from my hand without ten-thousand times more entreaty than anything of that nature could be worth . . .
>
> I fell ill of a violent fever, where my life was despair'd of. [John Manley] and my sister never quitted the chamber in sixteen nights, nor took any other repose, than by throwing themselves upon a little pallet in the same room. In short, having ever had a gratitude in my nature and a tender sense of the benefits upon my recovery I promis'd to marry him. 'Twas fatally for me performed in the presence of my sister, one maid servant, and a gentleman who had married a relation of ours. I was then wanting of fourteen, without any deceit or guess of it in others. 'Tis true I had formerly heard [John Manley's] lady repeat, in the violence of her rage, the base methods he had took to gain her, producing writings to a good estate, when he had but the expectation of a small one, and that not 'till after the death of his father . . .
>
> He brought me to [London], fix'd me in a remote quarter of it, forbad me to stir out of doors or to receive the visits of my dearest|sister or any other relation, friend or acquaintance. I thought this a very rough proceeding, and griev'd the more excessively at it, since I had married him only because I thought he lov'd me . . .
>
> I was uneasy at being kept a prisoner, but my husband's fondness and jealousy was the pretence . . . Soon after I prov'd with child, and so perpetually ill that I implor'd [him] to let me have the company of my sister and my friends. Having first tried all the arguments he could invent, then the authority of a husband, but in vain, for I was fix'd to my point and would have my sister's company; he fell upon his knees before me, with so much confusion, distress and anguish, that I was at a loss to know what could work him up to such a pitch. At length . . . he stabb'd me with the wounding relation of his wife's being still alive! conjur'd me to have some mercy upon a lost man, as he was in an obstinate, inveterate passion, that had no alternative but death or possession . . .
>
> My fortune was in [his] hands, or worse, already lavish'd away in those ex-

cesses of drinking and play, that he could not abstain from, though he had lately married me, a wife of whom he pretended to be fond . . . What could I do? forlorn! distress'd! beggar'd! to whom could I run for refuge, even from want and misery, but to the very traitor that had undone me? I was acquainted with none that would espouse my cause; a helpless, useless load of grief and melancholy! with child! disgrac'd! my own relations either impotent of power or will to relieve me! . . .

Thus was I detain'd by my unhappy circumstances and his prevailing arts, to wear away three wretched years in his guilty house, though no intreaty, no persuasion could ever again reconcile me to his impious arms. [12]

John Manley returned to his first wife in the country, leaving with Delarivier 'a fam'd piece that was newly wrote in defence of polygamy and concubinage'. [13] We do not know what became of Mrs Manley's son except her regret that 'whenever I cast [my] eyes upon him, [he] was a mortal wound to [my] repose'. [14]

By 1693 Mrs Manley was living in Arlington Street at the home of Barbara Villiers, the Duchess of Cleveland, a mistress of the late King Charles II, who twenty-five years earlier had worn the Crown Jewels to play Camilla in Katherine Philips' *Horace*. The Duchess believed that Delarivier Manley brought her good luck at cards, and kept her as a mascot.

Within a year Mrs Manley was accused of seducing the Duchess' son, and discharged. (The Duchess' replacement mascot was a Madame Beauclair 'a kitchin maid . . . [who] had been refug'd with King James in France . . . [and] made gaming her livelihood, and return'd into England with the monstrous affectation of calling herself a French-woman; her dialect being thence-forward nothing but a sort of broken English'. [15] Now Mrs Manley's 'love of solitude was improv'd by her disgust of the world', [16] and she left London for Devon where she could live more cheaply and escape the gossip of the Town. In Devon she started to write.

Two years later, in 1696, she returned to London with *Letters Written on a Stage Coach Journey to Exeter*. She had this published and then immediately demanded its withdrawal, claiming she had not intended the work for publication.

At about the same time she started a liaison with Sir Thomas Skipwith, the manager of Drury Lane Theatre, who at the same time kept another mistress with whom, he openly boasted,

he never had the LAST FAVOUR, though she lov'd him to distraction, for fear of consequences, yet she never scrupled to oblige him so far, as to undress and go even into the naked bed with him once every week, where they found a way to please themselves as well as they could. [17]

Mrs Manley wrote him a poem:

Ah, dangerous swain, tell me no more
Of the blest nymph you worship and adore;
When thy fill'd eyes are sparkling at her name
I raving wish that mine had caus'd the flame.

If by your fire for her, you can impart
Diffusive heat to warm another's heart;
Ah, dangerous swain! what wou'd the ruin be,
Shou'd you but once persuade you burn for me?

which he had set to music and he 'sung himself in all companies where he came'.[18] What was intended as a lover's reproach he used to his own advantage, and 'his flatterers . . . gave him the title of the dangerous swain, which he prided himself in'.[19]

Delarivier Manley included the song in her first play, *The Lost Lover, or: The Jealous Husband*, which was performed at Drury Lane in the early spring of 1696. *Jacob's Poetical Register* says that 'the dialogue of this play is very genteel, though it did not succeed in the representation'. This is not surprising: according to her preface for the play, Mrs Manley wrote it in seven days, and her 'design in writing was only to pass some tedious country hours'. The failure of this play convinced her that 'writing for the stage is no way proper for a woman, to whom all advantages but mere nature are refused . . . I think my treatment much severer than I deserved; I am satisfied the bare name of being a woman's play damn'd it beyond its own want of merit.'[20] Charles Gildon, in *An Account of the English Dramatic Poets,* agrees with her, but *The Lost Lover* does contain two scenes worth quoting in full.

WILMORE *is presenting love to* LADY YOUNG LOVE, *'an old vain conceited lady', and has gone so far as to propose marriage in order that he may secretly marry her daughter,* MARINA. WILMORE'S *father,* SIR RUSTICK GOOD-HEART, *thinks that he is to marry* MARINA *at the double wedding ceremony. On the eve of the marriages* WILMORE *comes upon* BELIRA, *his ex-mistress, in the garden*

WILMORE   Here so late Belira?
BELIRA   I come in search of you, the bride expects you.
WILMORE   Tonight! It must not be.
BELIRA   The same thing as tomorrow, the sooner 'tis over the better, for in these cases our fears are the worst part of our punishment. Was not Marina with you? She is wanted. Sir Rustick has drunk himself into a matrimonial temper, and Mr Priest-Craft swears twelve at night is as canonical as that at noon.
WILMORE   Belira, have you loved me?
BELIRA   Has not my ruin told you?
WILMORE   Then do you love me?
BELIRA   Yes, to see you happy. But the mask is off, and thou canst cheat no more, and I no more believe.
WILMORE   You never loved, but now abhor me.
BELIRA   You reproach me with what I would be; do not, do not rouse the woman in me, I would be calm tonight and see you married.
WILMORE   You never loved, but now abhor me.
BELIRA   Perhaps so. Could the remembrance of my wrongs but sleep with thee, I would not envy thee a quiet grave.
WILMORE   Farewell, we part forever, I'll leave the town this minute.
BELIRA   At least, sir, if you will not marry yourself, but unkindly leave

your bride thus in the longing moment, do your father the honour to grace his marriage.

WILMORE   What have I done, that you should wish to make me wretched?

BELIRA   What hast thou left undone to make me such?

WILMORE   Your reputation yet stands fair, and unless your own indiscretion betrays you, the secret shall be such, with me forever.

BELIRA   But thy heart, traitor, thy perjured heart; tell me, how shall I get it back?

WILMORE   Never this way, I assure you.

BELIRA   'Tis given for gone, then. Go. Live as wretched as I can make you, I'll think no more upon you.

WILMORE   Where, Madam, are you going?

BELIRA   To a wedding, sir, Marina's wedding; you say we must not dance at yours.

WILMORE   Rather of the two, Belira, but why tonight?

BELIRA   All bridegrooms are not as backward as yourself. Your father has the start of you, in desire as well as years, he is impatient of his happiness.

WILMORE   You are peevish, Belira, does your love make you jealous?

BELIRA   I have none, the Moor has taught me better; no longer doubting, away at once with love and jealousy.

WILMORE   Then 'tis spite disturbs you. In what have I deserved it?

BELIRA   Look in thy false perfidious heart, and take my answer thence.

WILMORE   That speaks of nothing you can quarrel with.

BELIRA   Then I will stay and argue with thee, how often hast thou told, thou could'st for ever love me?

WILMORE   I told you that I could, not that I would.

BELIRA   Poor caviller, those who can jest with oaths can play with words. You'll come after and wish the bride joy.

WILMORE   We must not part thus, you were not used to fly my arms.

BELIRA   By all that's good, he has got the sorry cunning of our sex. Just so does a wife when her husband has caught her false, the guilting creature cries: 'Do you believe it, spouse? You do not use to be so unkind.' Ha, ha, ha. Let me laugh, though 'tis maliciously. Go on, I'm in the vein of audience. Let me hear some disagreeable truths, and how well thou canst turn woman. Marina is at stake before you. Do it handsomely; I would be fortified in my aversion, and have my hate implacable.

WILMORE   'Tis barbarous to insult, where you should rather pity.

BELIRA   I do. Let all the world else judge else. Nay, do more than pity, I would prevent your ruin, and stop the passage up to your undoing; would save you from the ills, nay, scorns of poverty, keep your friends such, and put it in your power to be one by still preserving you the world's opinion, who judge of merit but by fortune's favours.

WILMORE   We know the extent of your generosity. But serve me as I would be served, Belira.

BELIRA   I thought this was your way. I mistook you for him that was to marry my Lady Young Love. But I'll go look for certainties within.

WILMORE   Come back, Belira, 'tis my last call. I would satisfy thy womanish revenge, and let thee see me curst by any other way than fatal marriage. Take my sword. Thy malice can supply thy want of use, despite can furnish strength, and too often thou hast found the way to my unhappy heart to miss it now.

BELIRA   Ha, ha, ha, in love to dying! By all that's good, turned hero. Your mistress, sir, is much obliged. Keep your sword, it may be a fortune better worth than all your father's lands. There's wars abroad you may employ it in. 'Twill keep your wife from wanting here at home.

WILMORE   Am I indeed your scorn, proud, fantastic woman? Thy liking
was foul lust, not love. That gentle name brings happiness, but thou . . .
Let me not think upon thee, for fear it force my tongue to something
worse than should be said of ladies. I've served it seems, as long as you
could like, and now you choose another.

BELIRA   Would it were come to that. I would exchange thee for the last of
men, and think the bargain cheap; would part with all that goodly form for
honest ugliness, and think it fairer; thy youth for age, and doat upon his
dotage, so in return I found but truth, mark well that word, that word has
charms thou never knewest, and which out-weighs thine.

WILMORE   Belira, thou hast power to read my soul. Thy magic spells are
irresistible. How hast thou found this failing in my virtue, which I not
knowing of, my wants could never miss 'till now?

BELIRA   Thank my wit, nature's best gift. I've seen your shuffling, poor,
designing arts to waive this marriage and promote another. Your care, too,
of Marina's fortune, falsly gilded with the weak pretence of generosity;
'twas not doubled thick enough for me. But because doubts never should
condemn the man I loved, I would not seem to doubt 'till I was certain.
Therefore no more dissembling, 'tis vain. Marina never shall be yours, and
if you could not think it an unhappiness, I fain would keep you mine.

WILMORE   Give me this night to think in. I'll promise nothing but this: I'm
grateful where I am obliged.

BELIRA   To show your power I will. My Lady Young Love, through my
persuasion, designed this the marriage night. I'll excuse you to her. But not
one word or thought of Marina, for in that moment she shall be bestowed
upon another. I would divide the world rather than you should meet. I
hope tomorrow we may give you joy. This night I find but little.

Exit BELIRA

WILMORE   Less thou hast left behind. Oh, the curse of lewdness! What
woman's fair after we find her faulty? What lady innocent when no longer
chaste? Or who so vain to hope for honour, or for pity from that soul
who wants it for herself?

Act IV, scene ii

The discussion is resolved in a later scene:

WILMORE   Do you remember our last discourse, Belira?

BELIRA   Can I ever forget anything where you're concerned?

WILMORE   Then I must tell you, I'm resolved to marry where I best can
like, not for conveniency alone, 'tis sinful, and you, and I, and all must
live to die.

BELIRA   So godly, one would think your time were come. You have forgot
sure, Marina is to marry your father.

WILMORE   She never will Belira, therefore, if you have loved, show it in
this only proof I ever asked, and let me marry her.

BELIRA   How dare you think the question, much less to ask it? I only live
for you, in hopes of you, and when those hopes are gone I've done with
life, the heavy load will not be worth the bearing, the very thought has
loosened it, and I want power to answer.

WILMORE   No tears, Belira. We will always be friends. Your honour will be
safe, and you my chiefest care.

BELIRA   What can pay love, but love? Marina's arms will make you cold to
mine. Nor can I stoop to share your hurt. Oh, yet consider! E're it be too
late, think on the wreck, the ruin of your fortune, the flowing tides of
poverty, that ruins all it covers, and, lastly, think on an unhappy wretch,
whose only fault is desperate love of you.

WILMORE   I've thought on all, and nicely weighed the sense. The consequence is this: I love Marina, and rather than not marry her, would be
undone. Therefore if you can save me 'twill be noble, and like the love you
promised.
BELIRA   What generosity canst thou hope to find, where only injuries are
given? What suffering, tame, deluded monster dost thou think me? My
wrongs have waked that rage which wonder had becalmed, and I am now
prepared to dash thy hopes, and prove thee traitor to thy vows and me.
WILMORE   Be wise, Belira! We live not now in those romantic constant
days, where their first mistress was their last. I used you once, and still
esteem you, but vows that are made in love are writ in sand. It's impossible
to recall a lover's heart, when once 'tis made a present to another, should it
return 'twould sooner love a third.
BELIRA   Thou needst not seek for arguments to kill my hopes; thus I blow
them from me: farewell for ever, both to thy love and them. Thou hast
loved me little, but thou knowst me less. Vengeance is due to thy mistake.
I only live to wish, and hope to see it take your minion. Love her as long
as you are used to love a woman, and then let want of wealth and liberty
pursue you. Be poorly wretched, and wretched poor, and may you hate the
cause as bad as I do curse, for her sake, the very name of woman. Yet think
on me, and sigh for such a friend, but may no friend be found, 'till scorned
at home thou seekest abroad some wretched death unknown.

Act V, scene iii

There were quarrels within the Drury Lane company over the pro-
duction of this play, and Mrs Manley took her next play, *The Royal
Mischief*, which was already in rehearsal at Drury Lane, to Betterton at
Lincoln's Inn Fields, and it was produced there in the late spring of
1696, with a cast including Mrs Barry, Mrs Bracegirdle, Kynaston, and
Betterton himself.

The play 'was acted with great applause; the rules of Aristotle being
observed and the mataphores, and allegories are just. The diction of her
tragedy is purely dramatic.'[21] Mrs Barry in the leading role, Homais, 'is
concluded to have exceeded that perfection which before she was justly
thought to have arrived at'.[22]

The main objection to the play seems to have been against the
'warmth of it'.[23] In her preface to the play Mrs Manley points out that
the same members of the audience 'sit attentively and unconcerned'[24]
at equally passionate moments in plays written by men, and suggests
that 'when the ladies have given themselves the trouble of reading and
comparing it with others, they'll find the prejudice against our sex'.[25]
The Royal Mischief had a good run of six days.

In December 1696 Catherine Trotter asked Delarivier Manley to
save her friend, John Tilly, from the consequences of a Parliamentary
investigation into his activities as Deputy Warden of the Fleet prison,
by interceding with her husband, John Manley. Delarivier Manley saved
Tilly, and soon they were lovers. 'His face was beautiful, so was his
shape, 'till he became a little burly.'[26]

Tilly, a married man, confessed to Mrs Manley that Catherine
Trotter was 'the first lady that had ever made him unfaithful to his

wife'.[27] Mrs Manley was amused, because Mrs Trotter had 'given herself airs of not visiting [Delarivier] now she was made the town talk by her scandalous intrigue with [Tilly]',[28] and she describes Mrs Trotter as 'the most of a prude in her outward professions, and the least of it in her inward practice',[29] her charms 'the leavings of the multitude'.[30]

Mrs Manley's *affaire* with Tilly continued and, six years later, in December 1702, Tilly's wife died. At this news Delarivier Manley tells us she burst 'forth into tears, she cried: I am undone from this moment! I have lost the only person who secured me to the possession of your heart.'[31] She was correct: Tilly began to court a rich widow, a Mrs Margaret Smith, and he married her to get himself out of debt. Following Tilly's marriage, Delarivier Manley left London for Bristol to recover her spirits.

In 1704 she returned to London, and to writing. During the election campaigns of 1705 she made her first attempt at political satire with *The Secret History of Queen Zarah and the Zarazians*, directed against Sarah Churchill and the Whigs.

In December 1706 her second tragedy, *Almyna*, appeared at the Haymarket Theatre. Mrs Barry was in the title role, supported by Betterton, Mrs Bracegirdle and Colley Cibber.[32] Like all Mrs Manley's work, the play has strong feminist undertones, and the plot revolves around her own pet grievance: that it is possible for a man 'after accumulated crimes to regain opinion, when [women] though oftentimes guilty but in appearance are irretrievably lost'.[33]

In 1706 Mrs Manley published *The Lady's Paquet Broke Open*, her first epistolary novel, its title promising spice and scandal.

Mrs Manley caused further stir with her *Female Tatler*, started on 8 July 1709, in which she wrote, under the name 'Mrs Crackenthorpe, a lady that knows everything'.

Then in May 1709 she brought out *Secret Memoirs and Manners of Several Persons of Quality, of both sexes from the New Atalantis, an island in the Mediterranean, written originally in Italian*, which went into a second edition two months later. *New Atalantis* is a clever blend of fact and fiction, romance, politics, scandal and autobiography. The follow-up to *New Atalantis*, which forms the second volume of the collected *New Atalantis*, was published on 20 October 1709. Nine days later the publisher and printer were arrested, 'as also Mrs Manley, the supposed author'.[34] The publisher and printer were 'examined touching the author Mrs Manley'[35] on Tuesday, 1 November. They were discharged, but Mrs Manley was only admitted to bail the following Saturday. The case against her was heard on Tuesday 14 February 1710 at Queen's Bench Court, and Mrs Manley was discharged. It seems that no one would believe that a woman could have written this book, and

they used several arguments to make her discover who were the persons concerned with her in writing her books; or at least from whom she had received information of some special facts, which they thought were above her own intelligence . . . but after several times exposing her in person to walk across the court before the bench of judges . . . dropped the prosecution though not without a very great expence to the defendants.[36]

Among the thwarted readers eagerly awaiting their copies of part two was Lady Mary Wortley Montagu, who wrote:

Saturday came and no book. God forgive me, I had certainly wished the lady who was to send it me hanged, but for the hopes it was to come by . . . Monday, but after waiting Monday and Tuesday, I find it is not come . . . But do you know what has happened to the unfortunate authoress? People are offended at the liberty she used and she is taken into custody. Miserable is the fate of writers! If they are agreeable they are offensive, and if dull they starve. I lament the loss of the other parts which we should have had . . . but now she will serve as a scarecrow to frighten people from attempting anything but heavy panegyric with names at length and false characters so daubed with flattery that they are the severest kind of lampoon.[37]

Undeterred, Delarivier Manley brought out third and fourth parts, entitled, *Memoirs of Europe Towards the Close of the Eighth Century, written by Eginardus, secretary and favourite to Charlemagne, and done into English by the translator of the 'New Atalantis'* in 1710, and in the following year an associated volume, *Court Intrigues, in a collection of original letters from the island of New Atalantis . . . by the author of those memoirs*.

Also in 1711 Jonathan Swift sent Mrs Manley his notions about the stabbing of the Tory Chancellor, Harley, by a Frenchman, Antoine de Guiscard. Guiscard was a friend of, and had been granted a government pension by, John Churchill, the Duke of Marlborough. The political implications, smearing the Whigs, were very much to Mrs Manley's taste, so she cooked the story 'into a sixpenny pamphlet in her own style'.[38] entitled, *A True Narrative of what pass'd at the examination of the Marquis de Guiscard*. She began to collaborate with Swift on *The Examiner* and she took over the editorship on his retirement in June 1711. On 9 November 1711 he wrote, 'I got a set of *Examiners* and five pamphlets, which I have either written or contributed to, except the best, which is . . . entirely of the author of the *Atalantis'*.[39]

She became very ill in the winter of 1711/12. Swift wrote:

Poor Mrs Manley, the author, is very ill of a dropsy and sore leg; the printer tells me he is afraid she cannot live long. I am heartily sorry for her; she has very generous principles for one of her sort; and a great deal of good sense and invention: she is about forty, very homely, and very fat.[40]

But she pulled through, and in 1714, after the death of Queen Anne, and the resignation of Harley, offered her services to Harley and the Tory party. She received £50 from him, the only known direct payment for her political services. She wrote *A Modest Enquiry into the reasons of the joy expressed by a certain set of people upon the spreading of a report of Her Majesty's death*, and virtually retired from the political arena.

Until her death she lived with the printer, John Barber, in Lambeth Hill, near Old Fish Street. Barber started out as a barber, became a printer in 1705 and went on to become Lord Mayor of London.

On 11 May 1717 Delarivier Manley's play, *Lucius, the First Christian King of Britain* was premièred at Drury Lane, with an up-and-coming company, including Booth and Mrs Oldfield. It was a financial success. She was paid 600 guineas on delivery, and it ran fifteen nights with a good profit.

Three years later, she published *The Power of Love, in seven novels*, the plots being taken from the popular sixteenth-century source book, Painter's *Palace of Pleasure*.

The same year *Lucius* was revived and the earlier tragedy *Almyna* went into a second edition.

After this, Delarivier Manley is remarkably silent.

John Barber started an affair with 'an ignorant and insolent country wench . . . This creature he hired in the country and brought her up to town to attend Mrs Manley in the lowest degree of servitude . . . His behaviour to this Dulcinea soon broke Mrs Manley's heart.'[41]

In 1724 Barber left for Rome with £50,000 in bills of exchange for the Old Pretender, James Francis Edward Stuart. He did not confide in Mrs Manley, but instructed his country wench to meet him in Calais and help him in his plot. Mrs Manley was mortified.

> She died at Barber's printing house on Lambeth Hill. Her corpse was very decently interred in the middle aisle of the church of St Bene't, Paul's Wharf, where on a marble grave stone is the following inscription to her deserving memory, viz:

> Here lieth the body of
> Mrs Delarivier Manley
> Daughter of Sir Roger Manley, knight
> Who, suitable to her Birth and Education,
> Was acquainted with several parts of knowledge,
> And with the most polite writers, both in the
> French and English Tongue.
> This accomplishment,
> Together with a Natural Stock of
> Wit, made her Conversation agreeable to
> All who knew Her, and her Writings to be
> Universally Read with Pleasure.
> She died July the 11th, 1724.[42]

Delarivier Manley is perhaps the most fascinating of the women playwrights of her time. At once an example of decaying gentility and of a sort of swashbuckling feminism, at the same time as she snubbed her nose at popular opinion she was upset that people did not approve of her behaviour. Although not the first, nor most prolific, nor perhaps the best, she combines in both her life and her work naïvety and energy, strength and vulnerability.

She is described in a Victorian literary journal as 'this demi-rep, to give her a name exactly as much above her deserts as it is below those of an honest woman'.[43] From an age that firmly believed a woman's place to be in the home this is a fitting epitaph.

But perhaps the last word should be left to her most thorough and entertaining biographer and critic, Mrs Manley herself:

I might have entertain'd you much more agreeably . . . together with songs, letters and adorations, innumerable from those who never could be happy. Then to have rais'd your passions in her favour; I should have brought you to her table well furnish'd and well serv'd; have shown you her sparkling wit and easy gaiety, when at meat with persons of conversation and humour: From thence carried you (in the heat of summer after dinner) within the nymph's alcove, to a bed nicely sheeted and strow'd with roses, jesamins or orange-flowers, suited to the variety of the season; her pillows neatly trimm'd with lace or muslin, stuck round with jonquils or other natural garden sweets, for she uses no perfumes, and there have given you leave to fancy yourself the happy man, with whom she chose to repose herself, during the heat of the day, in a state of sweetness and tranquillity: From thence conducted you towards the cool of the evening, either upon the water, or to the park for air, with a conversation always new, and which never cloys . . . the only person of her sex that knows how to *live,* and of whom we may say, in relation to love, since she has so peculiar a genius for, and has made such noble discoveries in that passion, that it would have been a fault in her, not to have been faulty.[44]

MARY PIX

Applause that food of scribblers, were it mine,
would not satisfy my ambition.

Dedication to *The False Friend* (1699)

Mary Pix was born in 1666, the daughter of the Reverend Roger
Griffith and his wife, Lucy Berriman, in Nettlebed, Oxfordshire.

Her father had died before 24 July 1684, when she married George
Pix, a merchant tailor six years her senior, at St Saviour's Benetfink.

The couple had one child, who was buried in the cemetery at Hawk-
hurst in 1690.

Her first play *Ibrahim, the Thirteenth Emperor of the Turks*, was
produced at Drury Lane in late May 1696, a month after Mrs Manley's
Royal Mischief first appeared at Lincoln's Inn Fields. Mary Pix had to
apologise in her preface for the 'gross mistake' of calling it *Ibrahim the
Thirteenth* when the play depicts the story of Ibrahim the Twelfth.

As the prologue says:

> Here's nor poignant repartee, nor taking raillery,
> Nor feast for critic pit, or graduate gallery . . .
> This play on solid history depends,
> Old fashioned stuff, true love, and faithful friends.

A slice of heroic Turkish delight, the play tells of the wicked Emperor,
Ibrahim, and his harem, led by Sheker Para, his favourite mistress and
pimp. At the end of act III Ibrahim sets his lustful eye on Morena, 'a
free born maid', and Sheker Para attempts to arrange a tryst against the
will of the virtuous Morena. The chief of the eunuchs (played by a
woman — which could bring a kind of conviction, difficult for an uncas-
trated man) offers himself in her place, and is consequently stabbed by
Ibrahim. Morena interposes, and catches the blade of the Emperor's
scimitar in her bare hand, refusing to let go. Ibrahim, furious at the
delay, 'draws it through her hands'. Thus bloodied, Morena challenges
Ibrahim:

> MORENA   See, Emperor, see are these hands
>   Fit to clasp thee? Judge by this
>   My resolution. Death hath a
>   Thousand doors; Sure Morena, cursed Morena,
>   May find out one . . .
> IBRAHIM   Slaves, why dally ye thus?
>   By heaven, rage is mixed with love,
>   And I am all on fire!
>   Drag her to yond appartments . . .

MORENA   I will not stir, fixed upon earth
   I'll rend obdurate heaven with piercing
   Cries, till I have forced their mercy!
   Help! Help! Open thou earth to hide me!
   Have my woes not weight enough to sink me
   To the centre? At length 'tis come;
   My spirits are decayed, Oh Amurat
   Where art thou? And where (alas) am I?

She swoons

VISIER   She faints. Convey her in quickly,
   Your majesty has [charms]
   Will soon revive her.
IBRAHIM   Threatening danger shall never bar my way,
   I'll rush through all, and seize the trembling prey,
   Rifle her sweets, till sense is fully cloyed
   Then take my turn to scorn what I've enjoyed.

Mary Pix, in her dedication, wrote 'I am often told, and always pleased when I hear it, that the work's not mine.' In the 1699 edition of Langbaine the compiler wrote that the

> play, if it want the harmony of numbers and the sublimity of expression, has yet a quality that at least balances that defect, I mean the passions, for the distress of Morena never failed to bring tears into the eyes of the audience, which few plays if any since Otway's have done.

How long the play ran we do not know, but it was successful enough to be revived in 1702, 1704 and 1715.

At some time in 1696 Mrs Pix wrote her only novel, *The Inhuman Cardinal, or: Innocence Betrayed*.

In August of the same year *The Spanish Wives*, 'a most damnable farce',[1] was performed at Drury Lane. Mrs Pix, in her dedication to Colonel Tipping of Whitfield, who 'have known me from my childhood, and my inclination to poetry', claims that the play was 'kindly received by the audience'. The epilogue tries to assuage the judgement of all sections of the audience:

> Some will think it too cold, others too full of fire.
> With submission our author still appears,
> Counts your indulgence, and your judgement fears,
> Lives on your smiles, and at your frown despairs.

This bustling comedy of intrigue has some amusing turns. Eleanora, wife of the jealous Marquis of Moncadas, who locks her in their house, has realised that 'complaints won't break locks', and sends her maid, Orada, to 'get me the song I love, the succeeding tedious. Imprisoned wretches thus count the succeeding hours, and groan the melancholy time away.' Her beloved song is then performed:

Begone, begone thou hag despair,
Begone, back to thy native hell.
Leave the bosom of the fair
Where only joys should dwell.
Or else with misers, willing revels keep,
And stretch thy wretched lids from sleep.
But hence be gone, and in thy hated room
Let hope, with all its gentle blessings, come.

Again we know nothing of its initial run, but this play too was revived early in the eighteenth century.

The Innocent Mistress, 'a diverting play . . . met with good success, though acted in the hot season of the year,' and prompted the author of *The Lives and Characters of the English Dramatic Poets* (1699) to write, 'As a lady[2] carried the prize of poetry in France this year, so, in justice, are they like to do in England, though indeed we use them more barbarously and defraud them both of their fame and profit.' Presented at Lincoln's Inn Fields in June 1697, it had the actors Betterton, Barry, and Bracegirdle in the leading roles. Sullen in *A Comparison Between the Two Stages* complains, 'Though the title calls this innocent, yet it deserves to be damned for its obscenity.'

The Innocent Mistress is thought to show the influence of Congreve, who was at this time also writing for Lincoln's Inn Fields. Congreve played a large part in the troubles that surrounded Mary Pix's next presentation, *The Deceiver Deceived*.

Mrs Pix had sent the play initially to Drury Lane, who had declined it. Then the Drury Lane company opened their 1697 season in September with a very similar play, *The Imposture Defeated*, by actor/playwright George Powell, who had played Amuret in Mrs Pix's *Ibrahim*.

The mighty man of wit [Congreve] . . . at the representation of this play [*The Imposture Defeated*] . . . was seen very gravely with his hat over his eyes among his chief actors and actresses, together with the two she-things, called poetesses, [Mrs Pix and Mrs Trotter?] which write for his house, as 'tis noble called, thus seated in state among those and some other of his ingenious critical friends, they fell all together upon a full cry of damnation, but when they found the malicious hiss would not take, this very generous, obliging Mr Congreve was heard to say We'll find out a new way for this spark, take my word there is a way of clapping of a play down.[3]

The prologue to Mrs Pix's play exclaims in her defence:

Deceiver Deceived, and Imposture cheated!
An audience and the devil too defeated!
All trick and cheat! Pshaw, 'tis the devil and all,
I'll warrant ye we shall now have cups and a ball;
No gallants, we those tricks don't understand;
'Tis t'other house best shows the sleight of hand . . .
Our authoress, like true woman, showed her play
To some, who, like true wits, stole't half away.

Mary Pix showed this play to Queen Mary, and 'Her Royal Highness showed such a benign condescention as not only to pardon [her] ambitious daring, but also encouraging [her] pen.'[4]

'A heavy English tale'[5] was Mrs Pix's next production with the Lincoln's Inn Fields company — a blank-verse tragedy about Queen Catherine, relict of Henry V:

> this warlike queen
> Who wealds herself the sword, and gives the distaff
> To the effeminate and Holy Henry'
>
> Act I, scene i

and her battles with the House of York under Edward IV. It appeared some time in June/July 1698.

In May 1699, Mary Pix's tragedy, *The False Friend*, was performed at Lincoln's Inn Fields. John Hodgson spoke the prologue, which announced:

> Amongst reformers of this vicious age
> Who think it duty to refine the stage,
> A woman to contribute does intend,
> In hopes a moral play your lives will mend.

Although it is set in Sardinia and ends in a colourful frenzy of madness and death, this play is rather dull.

A very funny comedy, *The Beau Defeated*, was Mrs Pix's next offering. Performed by the Lincoln's Inn Fields company in mid-March 1700, the play opens with a scene between Mrs Rich, played by Mrs Barry, and her maid, Betty:

BETTY   What's the matter, madam? What has happened to you? What has anybody done to you?

MRS RICH   An affront! Ah! I die. An affront! I faint. I cannot speak. A chair quickly.

BETTY   An affront! To you, madam, an affront! Is it possible!

MRS RICH   But too true, my poor Betty. Oh! I shall die. To disrespect me in the open street! What insolence!

BETTY   How, madam! Not to show respect to such a person as you? Madam Rich, the widow of an honest banker who got £200,000 in the King's service? Pray, madam, who has been thus insolent?

MRS RICH   A duchess, who had the confidence to thrust my coach from the wall, and make it run back above twenty yards.

BETTY   A very impertinent duchess! What, madam, your person, shining all o'er with jewels, your new gilt coach, your dappled Flanders with long tails, your coachmen with cocking whiskers like a Swiss guard, your six footmen covered with lace more than any on a Lord Mayor's day? I say, could not this imprint some respect in the duchess?

MRS RICH   Not at all. And this beggarly duchess, at the end of an old coach drawn by two miserable starved jades, made her tattered footmen insult me.

BETTY   S'life! Where was Betty? I'd have told her what she was.

MRS RICH   I spoke to her with a mien and tone proportionable to my equipage, but she, with a scornful smile, cried 'hold thy peace, citizen!', struck me quite dumb.

> BETTY   Citizen! Citizen! To a lady in a gilt coach, lined with crimson vel-
> vet, and hung around with a gold fringe!
> MRS RICH   I swear to thee that I had not the force to answer to this deadly
> injury, but ordered my coachmen to turn and drive me home a full gallop.

This incident leads Mrs Rich to the decision upon which the plot
hangs:

> MRS RICH   I am resolved, and I will be a countess, cost what it will, and to
> that intent I'll absolutely break all commerce with those little cits by
> whose alliance I am debased. And I'll begin with Mr Rich.
> BETTY   Mr Rich, madam, your brother-in-law?
> MRS RICH   My brother-in-law! My brother-in-law! Thou simple wretch!
> Prythee know better!
> BETTY   Pardon me, madam, I thought he had been your brother-in-law
> because he was brother to your deceased husband.
> MRS RICH   That's true, my husband's brother. But my husband being dead,
> fool, Mr Rich is now no more kin to me than my footman. Nevertheless,
> the fellow thinks himself of importance, and is continually censuring my
> conduct, and controlling my actions. Nay, even the little minx, his
> daughter, when we go in my coach together, places herself at the end by
> my side.
> BETTY   Little ridiculous creature!
> MRS RICH   But that which angers me the most is that with her little smiling
> mimicing behaviour, she attracts the eyes of the whole town, and I have
> not so much as a glance.

The first thing she does in her climb up the social ladder is to change
Betty's name:

> MRS RICH   And from henceforth let me call thee de la Bett; that has an air
> French, and agreeable.

Later she censures her niece, Lucinda:

> LUCINDA   Pray, don't be angry, Aunt.
> MRS RICH   In the first place, leave off that word Aunt, and make use of
> Madam, or stay at home with your father.
> LUCINDA   But Aunt, since you are my aunt, why may I not call you Aunt?
> MRS RICH   Why, I being a woman of quality, and you but a citizen's
> daughter, I cannot, in decency, be your aunt, without disgracing myself in
> some measure.

The play also has a sub-plot about women gamblers, led by Lady la
Basset and her footman, Vermin, and ends with a poem spoken by Mr
Rich:

> The glory of the world our British nobles are,
> The ladies, too, renowned and chaste and fair,
> But to our citizens, Augusta's sons,
> The conquering wealth of the Indias runs.

Genest wrote of her next tragedy, *The Double Distress*, 'This is a
poor tragedy by Mrs Pix. It is written partly in rhyme and partly in
blank verse. Mrs Pix should have stuck to comedy, and not have
meddled with tragedy.'[6] Mary Pix admitted in her dedication 'this play

is not wholly mine, because I thought it done and revised by abler hands'. It features some interesting scenes demanding great ingenuity from the designers and scene-builders, in particular the Temple of the Sun in act III, scene ii, which calls for 'several pyramids of light'.

This speech of Leamira's from act V, scene i, gives the general impression of the play:

> Oh misery on misery! Cleomedon!
> Oh royal sir! All is undone again.
> Poor Cytheria's lost, for ever lost,
> Your daughter wretched, and Tygranes ruined!
> Think of a sin too horrid to be named
> And call it incest, that which starts the gods.
> Of that they are both guilty.

As it turns out, advised by a 'mournful voice, as from the silent tomb' (act IV, scene iii) the couple have not committed incest, and the play ends happily. It was performed in March 1701.

Within days a tragedy attributed to Mrs Pix, *The Czar of Muscovy*, was performed by the Lincoln's Inn Fields company. It is another tedious tragedy, concerning the dictatorial reign of Demetrious, an imposter to the throne of Muscovy.

However, a hilarious comedy, *The Different Widows,* was put on in November 1703. Intrigues and amours abound. The only trouble is that they all seem to occur in the house of Lady Gaylove, a woman obsessed with her 'decorums'. Lady Gaylove desires to be *à la mode,* but not to be implicated in anything scandalous. Her sister, Lady Bellmont, asks one day to see her sister's children:

> LADY GAYLOVE   Fy, fy, is anything a greater indecency than to talk of one's children? How can you raise such odd, out of the way discourse?
> LADY BELLMONT   Now I am convinced the report was true we heard in the country that you conceal your children as you do your wrinkles, and for the same reason, you'll pardon my freedom, for I have resolved to see them.
> LADY GAYLOVE   (Devil on her, I shall go mad).

Eventually the 'children' are produced, dressed in children's clothes, having left the tops and other toys which are their only possessions in the nursery where they have been immured for at least two decades. Lady Gaylove tries to explain their size and maturity: 'Though they are shot up so, I assure you the eldest is not fifteen, and I was barely that when I had him.'

In 1704 Mary Pix translated the eighth novel of the second day of *The Decameron* into verse, and published it under the title, *Violenta, or: The Rewards of Virtue.*

The new Queen's Theatre, Haymarket, presented her next work, *The Conquest of Spain,* in May 1705. 'It had not the life of a stock play, for it expired on the sixth day.'[7] A wordy play about the war between the Spanish and the Moors, it was published with no name, and the prologue talks of the author as a man.

Mary Pix's last play, *The Adventures in Madrid*, a comedy, was performed by the Haymarket company in June 1706. This play contains a Shakespeare-like speech on the virtues of money,

> Money is that philosopher's stone, the grave-studying fellows meant, and the new hunt in vain after, for there is no proof against its power. It makes the young old, it conquers towns without soldiers, alters the decrees of senates, raises towers from the dust that touch the skies, in fine it is that golden elixir, that spirit of life the old dons kept such a work about.
>
> Act I, scene ii

and some interesting lines on love *affaires*:

> LAURA   I find an Englishman true to one woman, nay even before he has had her is a miracle.
>
> Act II, scene ii

and

> GAYLOVE   Oh the affairs of love begin quite different from those of war. We yield to all conditions before the engagement, but end alike, for, when we have taken the town, we seldom keep them.
>
> Act III, scene ii

It is a pity that Mary Pix devoted so much of her time to tragedy. She herself expresses an ill opinion of the heroic play through the character of Lady Landsworth in *The Beau Defeated*: 'I know you dote upon heroic. I have been reading three whining plays this morning that I may love in your strain.'

During her own lifetime it was said 'in this poetic age, when all sexes and degrees venture on the sock and buskins, she has boldly given us an essay of her talent in both, and not without success, though with little profit to herself'.[8] Later references imply that she made little money from her writing:

> The first that took coach, and had often took ———
> Was the famed Mrs B. with P-x at her a ———
> Who was said to write well, because well she could treat,
> And for her sake had written her husband in debt.[9]

We know little about her life, but can assume from *The Female Wits* that she was fat.

We do not know when Mary Pix died, but it must have been some time before 28 May 1709, when 'at the desire of several persons of quality'[10] a benefit performance was held on behalf of the executor of Mrs Pix's will. The play performed was *The Busy Body*; the writer, Susannah Centlivre.

SUSANNAH CENTLIVRE

Let men pursue their strictest jealous care,
We women still can match 'em to a hair.
The Perplexed Lovers, Act II, scene ii

Susannah Centlivre was born between 1667 and 1677. J.H. Mackenzie[1] has claimed that she was the daughter of William Freeman and Anne, his wife, and baptised on 20 November 1669, in Whaplode, Lincolnshire. But the opinion of her early biographers is divided over the name of her father. Giles Jacob[2] supports Freeman, but Abel Boyer[3] suggests that she was born Susannah Rawlins. Similarly some biographers think that she was born, not in Lincolnshire but in Ireland, where Freeman, 'a zealous parliamentarian . . . was necessitated to fly'[4] at the Restoration.

It is possible that Mrs Centlivre left home before she was sixteen, and joined a troupe of strolling players. If gossip is to be believed, having left home,

> she had not travelled many miles, but fatigued with her journey and filled with a thousand perplexing thoughts, she sat down, with tears in her eyes, on a bank by the side of the road, bewailing her lamentable condition, when a young gentleman from the University of Cambridge [Anthony Hammond Esq] . . . chancing to come that way, could not but take notice of our weeping damsel . . . Having enquired into the cause of her distress, he was so much moved with her story . . . that he could not think of parting with her, and of suffering her to pursue her painful journey in the condition she was in; he therefore entreated her to put herself under his protection, which after some modest but faint reluctance she consented to.[5]

Hammond then dressed Susannah Centlivre in boy's clothes and introduced her to his friends at the university as a relation called 'Cousin Jack'. After a few months, during which she learned to fence, and studied grammar and the terms of logic, rhetoric and ethics, Hammond thought she was being watched a bit too closely and advised her to resume her own gender and move on to London.

Mottley and Jacob agree that 'she was married or something like it'[6] to Mr Fox when she was sixteen, but that this relationship, 'whether by death or whatever accident',[7] lasted less than a year. Shortly afterwards she was married to an army officer named Carroll, who died within one and a half years of the marriage.

Whether it was disillusion with these marriages, or lack of money, or both, that drove her to writing, we do not know, but her first play, *The Perjured Husband*, a tragicomedy, was produced, with help from Abel Boyer, at Drury Lane in September 1700. According to her preface to the play, which was published under her married name of Carroll

during October 1700, 'it went off with general applause, and 'tis the
opinion of some of our best judges that it only wanted the addition of
good actors and a full town to have brought . . . a sixth night'. But it
was not a successful production, and was attacked by some moralists
for its indecent language, and particularly for the part of Lady Pizalta.
Although Lady Pizalta's marriage is unsatisfying, she is far from joyless,
and can remark, while waiting for her lover to visit: 'Oh, the pleasure of
hearing my husband lie coughing and calling me to bed; and my answering, I'm coming, dear; and while he imagines me in the next room undressing I'm happy in the arms of Lodovico.'[8] Mrs Centlivre defended
her work simply by arguing that it was unrealistic to want to put
prayerbooks into every woman's hands. Another reason for the play's
failure was the clumsy intermingling of a blank-verse tragedy plot and a
bawdy comic one.

Her second play, *The Beau's Duel*, was presented at Lincoln's Inn
Fields in June 1702. This comedy, which satirised the beaux and fops,
and made humorous allusions to the popular craze for astrologers and
philomaths, was the first of many which she centred round a woman of
sense, morally and intellectually independent, as much the pursuer in
love as any man.

The Stolen Heiress, a tragicomedy, had its first night at Lincoln's Inn
Fields on 31 December 1702, and was published anonymously in
January 1703. It criticised the law which made it punishable by death to
marry an heiress against her father's wishes. Interestingly, the printer, Will
Turner, thought it best not to admit the play's female parentage, but he
printed a list of the other plays he had in stock at the back of the
edition: two plays by Catherine Trotter, one Aphra Behn, one Mary
Pix, and one by Jane Wiseman.

Susannah Centlivre's next play, *Love's Contrivance*, was performed
at Drury Lane from 4 June 1703, and published ten days later. Bernard
Lintot, the printer, 'put two letters of a wrong name to it, which
though it was the height of injustice to [Mrs Centlivre] yet his imposing
on the town turned to account with him, and thus passing for a man's
it has been played at least a hundred times'.[9] (This includes provincial
performances by strolling troupes.) Mrs Centlivre, understandably,
incensed, put a statement into *The Daily Courant*: 'Whereas the last
new comedy called *Love's Contrivance*, or: *Le Médecin Malgré Lui*, has
the two letters RM to the dedication. This is to give notice that the
name of the author (who for some reasons is not willing to be known at
present) does not begin with those two letters.'[10] In her preface
Susannah Centlivre claims that 'writing is a kind of lottery in this fickle
age, and dependence on the stage as precarious as the cast of a die'.

She was undeterred, though, and her next play appeared at
Lincoln's Inn Fields in February 1705, with an all-star cast. Published
anonymously, *The Gamester* was an enormous success, and was used to

open the new Queen's Theatre, Haymarket, on 27 April 1705. Sometime later, a bookseller told Mrs Centlivre that 'a spark had seen [*The*]
Gamester three or four times, and liked it extremely. Having bought one
of the books [he] asked who the author was, and being told a woman,
threw down the book and put up his money, saying he had spent too
much after it already, and was sure, if the town had known that, it
would never have run ten days'.[11] In her preface, Mrs Centlivre claims
that 'the design of this piece were to divert, without that vicious strain
which usually attends the comic muse . . . There is nothing immodest or
immoral in it.' But this play, too, was attacked by the religious zealots.
Although it set out to criticise gambling, her critics were upset that the
gambler, although reformed, came out of the play with the heroine and
a fortune.

Susannah Centlivre stuck with gambling for her next play *The Basset
Table*. This very funny comedy dealt with women gamblers, and was
'designed to correct and rectify manners . . . and by the main drift of it
endeavoured to ridicule and correct one of the most reigning vices of
the age'.[12] It digresses from its main topic, and produces one of her
most interesting characters, Valeria, a young woman preoccupied with
scientific experimentation. Her interest in science has not been encouraged by her father, who threatens to 'throw all the books and mathe-
matical instruments out of the window', and is totally disapproved of
by her proposed husband, who thinks 'she's fitter for Moorfields than
matrimony'. Valeria's first appearance is very interesting:

Enter VALERIA, *running*

LADY REVELLER   Why in such haste, cousin Valeria?
VALERIA   O! dear cousin, don't stop me, I shall lose the finest insect for
     dissection, a huge flesh fly, which Mr Lovely sent me just now, and open-
     ing the box to try the experiment, away it flew.
LADY REVELLER   I am glad the poor fly escaped. Will you never be
     weary of these whimsies?
VALERIA   Whimsies! Natural philosophy a whimsy! Oh! The unlearned
     world.
LADY REVELLER   Ridiculous learning!
MRS ALPIEW   Ridiculous indeed, for women. Philosophy suits our sex as
     jack-boots would do.
VALERIA   Custom would bring them as much in fashion as furbeloes, and
     practice would make us as valiant as e'er a hero of them all, the resolution
     is in the mind – Nothing can enslave that.
LADY REVELLER   My stars! This girl will be mad, that's certain.
VALERIA   Mad! So Nero banished philosophers from Rome, and the first
     discoverer of the Antipodes was condemned for a heretic.
LADY REVELLER   In my conscience, Alpiew, this pretty creature's
     spoiled. Well, cousin, might I advise, you should bestow your fortune in
     founding a college for the study of philosophy, where none but women
     should be admitted, and to immortalise your name, they should be called
     Valerians, ha, ha, ha.
VALERIA   What you make a jest of, I'd execute, were fortune in my power.
Act II, scene i

Later, Lovely, the handsome young man with whom she falls in love, tries to make love to her in her laboratory, but she is too interested in showing him a tapeworm (which she found while dissecting a dog, and which she keeps in a cardboard box), to respond. Love and Lovely do win in the end, but only when they support Valeria's feminism.

In 1706 Mrs Centlivre took her next play, *Love at a Venture*, to the strolling players, the Duke of Grafton's servants, at Bath's New Theatre. The play had been rejected by Colley Cibber and, the following year, scenes from it appeared in his play, *The Double Gallants*. He later admitted that his play was 'made up of what little was tolerable in two or three others that had no success'.[13] After being rejected by Cibber, on behalf of one of the only two theatres in London, a play had little chance of success.

According to Mottley, while in Bath Susannah Centlivre joined John Power's troupe of players as an actress, and

> she attended them to several parts of England, and about the year 1706, the Court being at Windsor, she there put on her breeches again, and acted the part of Alexander the Great, in the tragedy of that name. She played this part it seems to great perfection. How much she was admired by the rest of the Court is at this time uncertain, but she so greatly charmed one courtier, of inferior rank indeed, Mr Joseph Centlivre, one of Her Majesty's cooks, that he fell in love with, and married her.[14]

The Centlivres' wedding was held on 23 April 1707 at St Bene't's Church, and the couple lived from this time at Mr Centlivre's house in Buckingham Court, Spring Gardens. According to the local registers, the Centlivres (St Livers) paid higher rates than anyone in the area except the Admiralty. Joseph Centlivre's official position was Her Majesty's Yeoman of the Mouth, and his annual salary was £60 a year. Susannah Centlivre now had financial security, but continued to write for the theatre.

A comedy, *The Platonic Lady,* had appeared at the Haymarket during their courtship, in November 1706. It ran only four nights, and Mrs Centlivre defended herself in the 1707 edition of the play, which she dedicated 'to the generous encouragers of female ingenuity': 'My muse chose to make this universal address, hoping among the numerous crowd to find some souls great enough to protect her against the carping malice of the vulgar world, who think it a proof of their sense to dislike everything that is writ by women.'[15]

The play features another of Mrs Centlivre's women who know what they want, Isabella. Isabella's maid, Toylet, confronts her with the line:

> I should guess your ladyship may have some small pulse for the handsome young officer that Mrs Dowdy is so much afraid you should see, and thrust you into the bedchamber when he came into the dining room. I remember with what fury you catched up the red hot poker, and burnt a hole through the door to look at him.
>
> Act I, scene ii

The play also contains a very funny scene sending up trend and fashion. Mrs Dowdy, 'a Somersetshire widow, come to town, to learn breeding', is meeting Mrs Brazen, the matchmaker, Mrs Wheedle, the milliner, Mrs Turnup, the mantua-maker, Mrs Crispit, the tire-woman, and Peeper, her maid:

They all seem talking to her

MRS DOWDY   We'l, we'l la you now, la you now. Shour and shour you'll gally me.

TURNUP   Here's your ladyship's Mantua and petticoat.

MRS DOWDY   Ladyship, why what a main difference is here between this Town and the country. I was never called above Forsooth in all my life. Mercy on me, why you ha' spoiled my petticoat mun, zee, Peeper, she has cut it in a thousand bits.

PEEPER   Oh, that's the fashion, these are furbeloes, madam, 'tis the prettiest made coat.

MRS DOWDY   Furbelows, a murrain take 'em, they spoil all the zilk. Good strange, shour London women do nothing but study vashions, they never mind their dairy, I warrant 'em.

TURNUP   Ladies have other employment for their brain, and our art lies in hiding the defects of nature. Furbelows upwards, were devised for those that have no hips, and two large ones, brought up the full bottomed furbelows.

WHEEDLE   And a long neck and a hollow breast, first made use of the stinkirk. And here's a delicate one for your ladyship . . .

MRS DOWDY   Oh, sirs, Peeper, what swinging cathedral hedgeer is this?

PEEPER   Oh, modish French night-clothes; Madam, what's here? All sorts of dresses painted to the life. Ha, ha, ha! Head-clothes to shorten the face, favourites to raise the forehead, to heighten flat cheeks flying cornets, four pinners to help narrow foreheads and long noses, and very forward to make the eyes look languishing.

MRS DOWDY   Ay, that, Peeper, double it down. Oh, I love languishing. (*She puts on an awkward languish*) . . . I shall never ha' done, shour, zeeing all my vine things. (*Tumbling her things over*) Hy day, what's these two pieces of band-box for?

TURNUP   'Tis pasteboard, madam, for your ladyship's rump.

MRS DOWDY   A rump, ho, ho, ho! Has cousin Isbel a rump, Peeper?

PEEPER   Certainly, madam.

MRS DOWDY   If cousin has one, as I hope to be kissed, I'll have it, Mrs Turnup.

CRISPIT   Will your ladyship sit down and let me shape your eyebrows?

CRISPIT *nips her eyebrows*, DOWDY *flies up and roars out*

MRS DOWDY   Ods flesh, the devil's in you, I think. What, will you tear all the hair off? A murrain take ye, an this be your shaping.

WHEEDLE   Be pleased to put on the addition, madam.

MRS DOWDY   What does she mean now? To pull my skin off mehap next. Ha, Peeper, are these your London Vashions?

PEEPER   No, no, addition is only paint, madam.

MRS DOWDY   Paint, mistress, od I've a good mind to hit you a dows o'th'chops, zo I have, what de ye take me for a whore, because I'm come to London, ha? Paint quotha.

PEEPER   Fie, fie, Madam, women of the first rank think it no crime to help nature in the complexion.

MRS DOWDY   Zay you so? Nay, my skin was ever counted none of the best. Well we'll zhut the door then.

WHEEDLE   There you are in the wrong again, Madam, our ladies make no scruple of letting all the world see 'em lay it on.

MRS DOWDY   Well, in my conscience and zoul, they care not what they zhow here.

PEEPER   Madam, your dancing master.

MRS DOWDY   O lack, get all you into the next room, and stay for me there.

BRAZEN   Madam, you promised to hear a word from me about Sir John Sharper.

MRS DOWDY   Zo I will by and by.

Enter CAPER, *the dancing master*

CAPER   Will your ladyship please to take a dance?

MRS DOWDY   Pshaw, I hate your one, two, three, teach me a London dance, mun.

CAPER   I'll lead you a courant, Madam.

MRS DOWDY   Ay, a rant, with all my heart, I dan't understand the names, let en be a dance, and 'tis well enough. (*He leads her about*) Hy, hy, do you call this dancing? Ads heartlikins, in my thoughts 'tis plain walking. I'll show you of our country dances. Play me a jig. (*She dances an awkward jig*)

CAPER   Oh dear, madam, you'll quite spoil your steps.

MRS DOWDY   Dan't tell me that. I was counted one of the best dancers in all our parish, zo I was.

PEEPER   Ay, round a Maypole.

Act III, scene i

On the first day of her next play, *The Busy Body*,[16]

there was a very poor house, scarce charges. Under these circumstances, it cannot be supposed the play appeared to much advantage. The audience only came for want of another place to go, but without any expectation of being much diverted. They were yawning at the beginning of it, but were agreeably surprised, more and more every act, till at last the house rung with as much applause as was possible to be given by so thin an audience.[17]

This comedy went on to be one of the most successful plays of the early eighteenth century. It was acted over 450 times before 1800, and became a stock piece through the nineteenth century. Steele praised the play in *The Tatler*: 'the plot and incidents of the play are laid with that subtlety of spirit which is peculiar to females of wit'.[18] George, Prince of Wales, cancelled the scheduled performance of *Othello* on 22 October 1717, and commanded a performance of this play in its place. His father, King George I, commanded performances in December 1719 and March 1720. In 1796 an article in *The True Briton* described the play as 'sterling stuff' and thought it a relief to the town from 'O'Keefean trash', and Hazlitt in 1816 described *The Busy Body* as an 'admirable comedy'.

But the play met with opposition from the actors when in rehearsal for the first production. The actor Robert Wilks 'in a passion threw [his script] off the stage into the pit, and swore that nobody would bear to sit to hear such stuff . . . it was a silly thing wrote by a woman',[19] and the players 'had no opinion of it'.[20] Nonetheless, it played for thirteen nights that season, and by 1884 demand for the play in print had led to the production of more than forty editions.

The Man's Bewitched, a pastoral comedy, performed at the Haymarket Theatre in December 1709, was dogged by another quarrel between the actors and Mrs Centlivre. An article appeared in *The Female Tatler*[21] in which the 'ingenious Mrs Centlivre' was supposed to have told the editor that this play 'had a better plot, and as many turns in it as her celebrated *Busy Body*, and though the two first acts were not so roared at as the rest, yet they were well wrought scenes, tending to business . . . not to offend the nicest ear, with the least double entendre'. The actors were, understandably, offended by the following section:

> Mrs Centlivre told 'em that 'twas much easier to write a play than to get it represented; that their factions and divisions were so great, they seldom continued in the same mind two hours together; that they treated her (though a woman) in the masculine gender; and, as they do with all authors, with wrangling and confusion . . . that to show their judgement in plays, they had actually cut out the scene in the fifth act . . . that the audience received with that wonderful applause, and 'twas with great struggling the author prevailed to have it in again. One made faces at his part, another was witty upon hers. But as the whole was very well performed at last, she has condescention to pass over the affronts of a set of people, who have it not in their natures to be grateful to their supporters.

The play was cancelled on the second day, and withdrawn on the fifth. In her preface she denies being responsible for the article.

In March 1710, Mrs Centlivre's first after-piece, *A Bickerstaff's Burying*, a one-act black comedy, was performed at Drury Lane, in a double bill with Vanbrugh's *The Mistake*. Set on an island where there is no divorce and custom requires the burial of the whole married couple when only one partner dies, the play is scattered with hilarious ingenious episodes between couples who wish to be single but not dead.

A follow-up to *The Busy Body*, *Mar-plot*, was performed at Drury Lane in December 1710, and despite 'an entire set of a pleasant wood, painted by Mr Boul after the Italian manner'[22] the play suffered the fate of most follow-ups and its run ended after six nights.

In 1711 she took a sabbatical, but made a comeback on 19 January 1712 with *The Perplexed Lovers*. In this play she aggressively displayed her Whig politics: it ran only three nights. The main problem was the epilogue, which praised the Duke of Marlborough's exploits on the Continent. 'The managers of the theatre did not think it safe to speak it'[23] unless it was licensed 'so that at last the play was forced to conclude without an epilogue',[24] and instead, Henry Norris, 'who is an excellent comedian in his way'[25] spoke six lines extempore. The audience thought that this was the intended epilogue and hissed. By the second day, 21 January, Mrs Centlivre had managed to get a licence for her epilogue, but Mrs Oldfield, who was to speak it, had been advised to refuse as it was Whiggish. Instead Norris went on in mourning and spoke an epilogue claiming that the original epilogue had not been granted a licence.

In its preface Mrs Centlivre does 'not pretend to vindicate the following scenes about which [she] took little pains'. She apologises for an excess of business, and explains that as the play is set 'from five in the evening till eight in the morning' there are 'four acts in the dark, which though a Spanish audience may readily conceive, the night being their proper time of intriguing, yet here, where liberty makes noonday as easy, it perplexes the thought of an audience too much'.

Her next play did not appear until April 1714. A comedy, *The Wonder!*, she daringly dedicated to the Duke of Cambridge, Prince George Augustus. At this time he was very unpopular at Court, but within months he was King.

Despite a first run of only six nights, the play had been performed more than 250 times by 1800. The leading male role, Don Felix, became Garrick's favourite part and, despite his feeling that the play was a bit racy (and his cutting it accordingly), he not only played it more than sixty-five times between 1756 and 1776, but also chose it as his last performance before retiring on 10 July 1776. It was a favourite play, too, of the later Hanoverian Kings. George II commanded it often, both as Prince of Wales and King, and George III commanded it at least five times. Even Queen Victoria commanded a performance at Covent Garden on 24 March 1840. Hazlitt described the play as 'one of our good old English comedies which holds a happy medium between grossness and refinement. The plot is rich in intrigue and the dialogue in *double entendre* . . . The plot is admirably calculating for stage-effect and kept up with prodigious ingenuity and vivacity to the end.'[26]

In 1715 Mrs Centlivre wrote two more short farces, *The Gotham Election* and *A Wife Well Managed*. *A Wife Well Managed* was never performed as 'it was said there would be offence taken at the exposing of a Popish priest'.[27] 'Good God!' cries Mrs Centlivre 'To what sort of people are we changed?'[28]

A Gotham Election was written 'to shew their Royal Highnesses the manner of our elections, and entertain the town with a subject entirely new . . . But the Master of Revels did not care to meddle with it, and the players act nothing without his licence.'[29] The play makes fun of exorbitant pre-election promises, nepotism, and the buying of votes, and ends with a riot. Not surprisingly, the play was suppressed. The passage from Stuart to Hanoverian rule was not an easy one. In 1714 the clergy were ordered to refrain from political sermons, and the violence of the election in January 1715 led to the passing of the Riot Act in June 1715. In tackling a current socio-political problem head-on, this play was well ahead of its time. Prologues and epilogues discussed these sensitive areas, but plays rarely more than touched on them. It was eventually performed at the Haymarket Theatre in March 1724 after Mrs Centlivre's death.

Susannah Centlivre had another stab at the tragic strain in *The Cruel Gift*. The prologue, by fellow playwright George Sewell, promised

> Intrigue and plot and love enough.
> The devil's in it if the sex can't write
> Those things in which they take most delight.

Unfortunately for Mrs Centlivre the play had more talk and less action than was expected of plays of this type, and the characters marked for death did not actually die. The anonymous *Satire Upon The Modern Times*[30] complained:

> *The Cruel Gift* has won the town's applause
> But we are always pleased without a cause.

The play opened on 17 December 1716, was performed seven times, and of those three were benefit performances. No other play, however, had more than seven performances that season.

Mrs Centlivre introduced the phrase 'Simon Pure', meaning 'the real or genuine person or article',[31] into the English language in her next play, *A Bold Stroke For a Wife*. This comedy, like *The Wonder!* and *The Busy Body*, became a stock piece throughout the eighteenth century. John Philip Kemble kept the play (as he did *The Wonder!*) to bring out when nothing else was ready for performance. *A Bold Stroke For A Wife* was severely criticised for mocking religion through its satire on the Quakers, and for encouraging children to disobey their parents. Nonetheless, it was performed more than eighty times by 1750 and went on to be even more popular during the second half of the eighteenth century.

Mrs Centlivre's last comedy was her coarsest. *The Artifice* began rehearsals on 20 September 1722 and opened on 2 October. It ran only three nights. An advertisement for the first printing of the play[32] rails against the author of *Advices from Parnassus* who 'having set himself up for a dramatic critic, roundly asserts in the arrogant style of his brother Collier that "the whole scope of *The Artifice* is to encourage adultery, to ridicule the clergy and to set women above the arbitrary power of their husbands, to exert their natural rights for the preservation of their lusts"; with many other invectives, as "That this comedy is, at best, a scurrilous, impious, monstrous performance, without any beauty to recommend it except the principles of genuine Whiggism".

The play contains one of her most amusing characters, Widow Heedless, who stamps around, shouting and boxing people's ears, and is determined not to marry below a lord. In act III, scene i, she discusses the servant problem:

I would not keep a town-servant, my Lord, if they would live with me for nothing. Their whole attention is drunkenness and pride. The dirtiest trollop in the town must have her top-knot and tickin-shoes. This city spoils all servants. I took a Welsh runt last spring whose generation scarce ever knew the use of stockings. And, will you believe me my Lord, she had not lived with me three weeks before she sewed three penny-canes round the bottom of her shift instead of a hoop petticoat.

Unbeknown to her, her servant, Fainwell, is a young ensign in disguise. She is entertaining Sir Philip Moneylove, and instructs Fainwell to wait on them:

Go bid the cook set on the tea-kettle and cut some bread and butter. But d'ye hear, don't you bring it dangling in your fist, as you did yesterday, sloven. If you do, I shall throw it at your head, sir. Remember to bring me nothing without a plate, d'ye hear?

She then sends Fainwell to fetch Misha, her dog. A few moments later he returns empty-handed.

WIDOW HEEDLESS   Well! Where's Misha?
FAINWELL   By mess, I can't bring her, not I.
WIDOW   How so? Is she so heavy?
FAINWELL   No, she's not so heavy. But I can't make her lie upon a plate, for the blood o'me, so I can't.
SIR PHILIP   Ha, ha, ha! Ridiculous enough! ha, ha!
WIDOW   A plate, a blockhead! A plate! Did you ever see a dog brought on a plate, clod-hopper? Did you? (*She follows him about*)
SIR PHILIP   Pure innocence, faith!
FAINWELL   Nay, how do I know your London vashions? You bad me but now, I am zure, to bring you naught without a plate, so you dud.
WIDOW   What! Living things? Ha, did I say living things?
FAINWELL   Living things! S'blead, the devil would not live wi'you. The cobbler wants six-pence for mending your clogs, Judith bod me tell yow.
WIDOW   These wretches will distract me! Is that a message to be delivered to me in public? Ha, thickskull! But since you had no more wit, let me see what he has done for the money. My Lord, you'll excuse this piece of economy.

Exit FAINWELL . . . FAINWELL *returns with the clogs upon a plate*

WIDOW   Did you ever see the fellow of him, Sir Philip? I protest he puts me into a agony! Why, you thick-skulled rascal! You unthinking dolt! You senseless idiot! Was ever a pair of dirty clogs brought upon a plate, sirrah? Ha! Was there? Was there? Was there? Hedgehog?

She follows him about and beats him. SIR PHILIP *interposing*

FAINWELL   What d'ye strick me vor? The clogs arn't living things too, are they? By the mess, I'll take the law of you, so I will, an you thrash me about at thick same rate. S'blead, an yow were a man, I'd dress your jacket for yow.
SIR PHILIP   Fy, fy, cousin, this is not like a fine lady.
WIDOW   That's your mistake, Sir Philip. My Lady Flippant beats her whole family, from her husband to her coachman.

                                                                                                   Act III, scene i

On 1 December 1723 Susannah Centlivre died, at her home in Buckingham Court, and was buried four days later in what is now the actors' church, St Paul's, Covent Garden.

She was a very successful playwright; her plays lived longer than any of the others written by the women and most of those written by the men of the Restoration theatre.

She was a keen supporter of the Whig party, but limited her political writings to the general bias of her plays, some outspoken prologues and epilogues and a number of eulogistic poems dedicated to her Whig heroes. Her career was summed up with admiration by Mottley, for whom brass was brass:

> If she had not a great deal of wit in her conversation, she had much vivacity and good humour. She was remarkably good-natured and benevolent in her temper, and ready to do any friendly office as far as it was in her power. She made herself some friends and many enemies by her strict attachment to Whig principles, even in most dangerous times . . . She lived in a decent clean manner, and could show (which I believe few other poets could who depended chiefly on their pen) a great many jewels and pieces of plate, which were the product of her own labour.[33]

But it had to be suggested that success made a female 'unfeminine' in one of the oldest kinds of slur — 'She had a wen on her left eyelid, which gave her a masculine air',[34] and it says much about the commentators on her success that what most pre-occupied them was her squint:

> While Carroll, her sister-adventurer in print,
> Took her leave all in tears, with a curtsey and squint.[35]

THE OTHER WOMEN PLAYWRIGHTS

> From her own sex something she expect,
> 'Tis women's duty women to protect.
>
> Prologue to *The Northern Heiress*
> by Mary Davys (1716)

Eighteen months after Katherine Philips' *Horace* was performed at Court, and about sixteen months before Aphra Behn's first play, *The Forced Marriage*, was premièred, a tragicomedy called *Marcelia, or: The Treacherous Friend*, appeared at the Theatre Royal in Bridges Street. Of the writer, Frances Boothby, so little is known that by 1691 the compiler of the *Account of the English Dramatic Poets*[1] had no idea whether she was alive or dead. The play itself is unremarkable, and presumably, as Mrs Boothby did not continue writing, it did not succeed in the representation.

In May 1677 a troupe of French players visited London and performed an operatic comedy at Court. Although the writer, Mademoiselle La Roche-Guilhen was something of a celebrity in her native France, having already published a novel, *Asterie ou Tamerlan*, her opera, *Rare En Tout,* did not please the English taste. The production was 'most pitifully done, so ill that the king was aweary on't, and some say it was not well contrived to entertain the English gentry with a lamentable ill-acted French play, when our English actors so much surpass'.[2] *Rare En Tout* is an amusing little diversion, set in countryside in the middle of which we find the Palace of Whitehall. The prologue is a discussion between the Spirit of the Thames and Europe, and the main body of the piece is interspersed with *entr'actes*, the first an amorous dispute between Tritons and Nereids on the banks of the Thames, watched by astonished fishermen, the second a discourse between lovers, women, and the Heart. The play closes with a pastoral scene in which shepherds and satyrs sing and dance:

> *Que l'amour est charmant,*
> *Qu'il est doux de le suivre.*
> *Un cœur indifférent*
> *N'est pas digne de vivre.*

Mlle La Roche-Guilhen went on to write a number of romantic and historical novels, and translations into French. Her most important work is probably *Histoire des Favorites*, published first in Amsterdam in 1699, and frequently reprinted in French and other languages well into the eighteenth century. Mlle La Roche-Guilhen was born in the early 1650s, and died in 1710.

Anne Wharton, born in Oxfordshire in about 1632, was the daughter of Sir Henry Lee, third baronet of Ditchley. She married, on 16 September 1673, Thomas Wharton, the eldest son of Lord Wharton. Thomas Wharton was sent to the Tower in 1676 for his attempt, with Buckingham, Salisbury and Shaftesbury, to prove that Parliament was in effect dissolved, as it had been prorogued for over a year. He was released in 1677. Three years later he was a ringleader in a riot at the Duke's Theatre, in which 'some gentlemen in their cups entering into the pit, flinging links at the actors, and using several reproachful speeches against the Duchess of P.[3] and other persons of honour, occasioned a prohibition from farther acting till His Majesty's farther pleasure'.[4] The marriage was childless and unhappy, and Anne Wharton would have left her husband in 1682, had not Bishop Gilbert Burnet persuaded her to stick it out. She wrote many poems, which were praised by Burnet, Waller and Dryden, and one play, 'Love's Martyr'. There is no reference to any specific performance of this play, but it was entered in the Stationers' Register for February 1686, and then never published. A handwritten copy of the play, dedicated to Mrs Mary Howe who, Anne Wharton wrote, 'alone makes the happiness of my life',[5] is in the manuscript collection of the British Library.[6]

The play describes Ovid's love for Julia, Caesar Augustus' daughter. It is a self-indulgent work, and Anne Wharton obviously used the play to express feelings which were not in the scope of her marriage. The word 'love' occurs approximately six times each thirty-line page. Anne Wharton could be the 'Love's martyr' of the title.

'Ariadne', a young lady who confessed that she was 'altogether unacquainted with the stage, and those dramatic rules which others have with so much art observed',[7] was also not given enough encouragement to write a second play, although her first, *She Ventures and He Wins*, performed at Lincoln's Inn Fields in September 1695, is brisk and amusing.

The plot concerns Charlot, played by Mrs Bracegirdle, who, in order to find a man suitable to be her husband, dresses in boy's clothes, 'for they are so used to flatter and deceive our sex there's nothing but the angel appears though the devil lies lurking within, and never so much as shows his paw till he has got his prey fast in his clutches'.[8] In and out of disguise she drags her projected spouse, Lovewell, through trial after trial before deciding that he is the man for her. In the sub-plot Squire Wouldbe, who lives with his wife, Dowdy, and her mother, Beldam, tries to carry on an intrigue with the happily married Urania (played by Mrs Barry). Urania, in league with her husband, manages to put the Squire through a series of humiliations, including a soaking, being covered in feathers and believing himself to be dead, being carried off to Pluto by devils, who in fact drop him naked at his mother-in-law's feet. Eventually he is tricked into bedding his own wife, thinking it to be Urania, as the plot's strands are brought together in the last scene.

A play by another anonymous woman, writing as 'A Young Lady', was performed at Lincoln's Inn Fields at the end of 1697. The play, a tragedy, *The Unnatural Mother*, was printed the following year.

In 1701 the tragedy *Antiochus the Great* was performed at Lincoln's Inn Fields. The author, Jane Wiseman, was a friend of Susannah Centlivre. The play depicts the consequences of the fickleness of King Antiochus. Leodice, 'seduced by the King and now forsaken', opens the play, as the Queen approaches:

> She comes, she comes, the hated Berenice comes,
> And I must fall to make my rival way.
> Curse on all cowards, those slow dregs of phlegm,
> For treason was not what the rout disliked;
> Mischief was ever welcome to their wills.

Act I, scene i

Later, Leodice goes to Antiochus in disguise, to plead for justice:

> LEODICE   Oh, save me, save me from approaching ruin.
>   I love the foe that has procured my fall.
>   Let him restore me to his dear embrace,
>   Return my passion and forget his hate.
>   So may eternal joys reward your aid,
>   And every god consent to what you wish.
> ANTIOCHUS   Name me the man, and he shall do thee right,
>   By the imperial majesty of kings,
>   By all that's great above, and just below,
>   I swear he shall.
> LEODICE   A thousand blessings on that welcome oath.
>
> *(She throws off her disguise)*
>
> See here Leodice.

The King then goes through a number of rethinks. He decides to ignore Leodice's plea. She produces their child. He says he'll keep the child, but not Leodice. Then, jealous of a suspected romance between his wife, Berenice and Ormades, an Egyptian prince, he decides to keep Leodice, too. Once Leodice is set up as his partner, he rushes off in pursuit of Berenice and, finding her, sends to Leodice to remove herself, which she does, by taking poison. Rejected by Berenice he returns to Leodice, by now in her death-throes. She manages to make him join her in a cup of poison, and meanwhile Leodice's brother accidentally kills Berenice. So all ends satisfactorily with everyone dead.

Although the play is that of a writer learning the craft, Jane Wiseman did not get enough out of the experience to tempt her to write another.

On 27 April 1716, *The Northern Heiress*, or: *The Humours of York*, by Mary Davys, the widow of the Rev. Peter Davys, Master of the Free School of St Patrick's, Dublin, was performed at Lincoln's Inn Fields.

The performance 'was attended with only two single hisses . . . The one was a boy, and not worth taking notice of, the other a man who came prejudiced because he expected to find some of his relations exposed'.[9] The play is funny, with amusing characters, among them Lady Greasy, who belches and stinks, and always comes up with the prettiest ways of putting things: 'Love is like a bug, the longer it sticks in the skin, the harder it is to pluck out.'[10] She is apt to go in for malapropisms: 'Come no more salivating under our windows'[11] she instructs a young boy who has been serenading her outside her house, and later complains that she is afflicted with 'certificate', by which she means sciatica. The play ran for three nights, and Mrs Davys' other play, *The Self Rival*, according to the fly-leaf, 'should have been acted at the Theatre Royal, Drury Lane, but wasn't'. It was printed in her *Works* of 1725. She went on to write 'a surprising novel', *The Reformed Coquet*, which must have been one of the more popular works peddled by the circulating libraries of the eighteenth and nineteenth centuries. Mary Davys started to write after the death of her husband in 1698, and kept a coffee house in Cambridge, after spending some time in York. Of her two plays she wrote: 'I never was so vain as to think they deserved a place in the first rank, or so humble as to resign them to the last.'[12]

On 22 May 1719, a mock-opera, *Harlequin Hydaspes,* by Mme Aubert, was scheduled at Lincoln's Inn Fields. The performance was postponed until 27 May, owing to the unexpected arrest of the actor, Christopher Bullock, who was to take the part of the Doctor. A burlesque on Mancini's popular Italian opera, *Hydaspes, Harlequin Hydaspes* satirises the medical world, and in particular the goings-on at Gresham College, with innumerable scenes depicting the administration of emetics, purges, clysters, vomits and oil of anything. Nothing is known of the author.

A few other women put their names to plays which were published but probably never performed. A mysterious Elizabeth Polwhele is referred to in Halliwell's *Dictionary of Old English Plays* as being the author of a manuscript comedy, 'The Frolic', written apparently in 1671. I can find no references to it in performance, but it has been the subject of a recent American scholarly exhumation, and is currently in print. An unsigned manuscript of *The Faithful Virgins* in the Bodleian has now been identified as by the same author.

The poet, Anne Finch, Countess of Winchilsea, left two plays, *Aristomenes*, a tragedy, printed in 1713, and *Love and Innocence*, a tragicomedy, which remained in manuscript until printed in Myra Reynolds' 1903 collection, *Poems of Anne Finch, Countess of Winchilsea*.

Ironically, it is Margaret Lucas, later Margaret Cavendish, Duchess of Newcastle, who wrote at least twenty-six plays, none of which has ever been performed, who has attracted more biographical coverage than

any other writer in this book. This is possibly because she fulfils the
popular fantasy that a woman writer is necessarily slightly demented.

Langbaine wrote of her, 'I know there are some that have but a
mean opinion of her plays, but if it be considered that both the language
and plots of them are all her own, I think she ought, with justice,
to be preferred to others of her sex, which have built their fame on
other people's foundations.'[13] Genest concludes that her plays are 'very
bad. The Duchess in general writes sensibly, but her scenes are so
insipid, so dull, so deficient in the essence of drama that one is almost
tempted to say

> Of comedies I've seen enough,
> Most vile and execrable stuff,
> But none so bad as thine, I vow to heaven.'[14]

Born in the mid 1620s in Colchester, the youngest of eight children,
three boys, five girls, Margaret Lucas became lady-in-waiting to Queen
Henrietta Maria from 1643 to 1645, and accompanied the Queen to
Paris during the troubles in 1645.

It was in Paris that she met and married William Cavendish. He was
fifty-two, she was twenty-two. The couple lived abroad, in Paris, Rotterdam
and Antwerp until the Restoration.

The Duchess wrote and wrote. In 1668 she wrote in her own defence,
'malice cannot hinder me from writing, wherein consists my chiefest
delight and greatest pastime, nor from printing what I write, since I
regard not so much the present as future ages, for which I intend all
my books'.[15] She was very specific about what constituted a suitable
pastime. Tennis, for instance, she thought

> too violent a motion for wholesome exercise, for those that play much at
> tennis impair their health and strength by wasting their vital spirits through
> much sweating, and weaken their nerves by overstraining them. Neither can
> tennis be a pastime, for it is too laborious for pastime, which is only a recreation,
> and there can be no recreation in sweaty labour.[16]

Apart from her prolific literary output, the Duchess became famous
for dressing peculiarly. Sir Charles Lyttleton saw her in 1665 'dressed
in a vest, and instead of courtseys made legs and bows to the ground
with her hand and head'.[17] Her dress-sense was not accidental. She
declared that she 'took great delight in attiring, fine dressing and
fashions, especially such fashions as I did invent myself, not taking that
pleasure in such fashions as was invented by others'.[18] John Evelyn's
wife was not at all impressed writing: 'I was surprised to find so
much extravagance and vanity in any person not confined within four
walls';[19] and Pepys almost broke his neck racing around London trying
to get a glimpse of her. After a few distant sightings he eventually
tracked her down at a meeting of the Royal Society in 1667, where she
was shown experiments with colours, acids dissolving flesh, 'two cold
liquors by mixture made hot',[20] and Boyle himself showed her how to

weigh air. Pepys was disappointed, 'her dress so antique and her deport-ment so ordinary that I do not like her at all, nor did I hear her say anything that was worth hearing, but she was full of admiration, all admiration'.[21] In April of that year he had seen her at a distance 'with her velvet cap, her hair about her ears, many black patches, because of pimples about her mouth, naked necked, without anything about it, and a black just-au-corps'.[22] It is Pepys, too, who is responsible for the hypothesis that *The Humorous Lovers*, performed at the Duke's Theatre in the spring of 1667, was not, as credited, by the Duke of Newcastle, but his wife. 'Did go by coach to see the silly play of my Lady Newcastle's, called *The Humorous Lovers*; the most silly thing that ever come upon a stage. I was sick to see it, but yet would not but have seen it, that I might better understand her.'[23]

Dramatically her plays are of little interest, though often the philo-sophy behind them is interesting. In *The Wits' Cabal*, printed in the play collection *Kingdom's Intelligence* in 1662, but written before 1660, a group of young girls set up a female academy. The men, who are refused admission, set up a rival academy next door but, as their discus-sions always return to the pros and cons of women it fails, and they resort to blowing trumpets outside the women's lectures to break them up. Margaret Cavendish was incensed by the constant attacks by men upon the shallowness of women, and she frequently hit back. 'In their dressings and fashions they are more fantastical, various and unconstant than women are . . . And do not men run visiting from house to house for no other purpose but to twattle?'[24]

She is one of the first writers against blood sports, and human chauvinism: 'It troubles my conscience to kill a fly, and the groans of a dying beast strike my soul.'[25]

She died in January 1673, and was buried in Westminster Abbey on 17 January. Her husband lived for a further four years.

Her works have been defended by Charles Lamb, George Etherege, Thomas Shadwell, Thomas Hobbes and Katherine Philips, who wrote her this poem shortly before her own death in 1663.[26]

> That nature in your frame has taken care,
> As well your birth as beauty do declare,
> Since we at once discover in your face,
> The lustre of your eyes and of your race:
> And that your shape and fashion does attest,
> So bright a form has yet a brighter guest,
> To future times authentic fame shall bring,
> Historians shall relate and poets sing.
> But since your boundless mind upon my head
> Some rays of splendour is content to shed;
> And least I suffer by the great surprise
> Since you submit to meet me in disguise,
> Can lay aside what dazzles vulgar sight,
> And to Orinda can be Policrite.

You must endure my vows, and find the way
To entertain such rites as I can pay,
For so the power divine new praise acquires,
By scorning nothing that it once inspires.
I have no merits that your smile can win,
Nor offering to appease you when I sin,
Nor can my useless homage hope to raise
When what I cannot serve I strive to praise.
But I can love, and love at such a pitch,
As I dare boast it will ev'n you enrich,
For kindness is a mine, when great and true
Of nobler ore than ever Indians knew,
'Tis all that mortals can on Heav'n bestow,
And all that Heav'n can value here below.

Unfortunately, the importance of the Duchess of Newcastle is a negative one. Virginia Woolf analysed it perfectly in *A Room Of One's Own*: 'What a vision of loneliness and riot the thought of Margaret Cavendish brings to mind! as if some giant cucumber had spread itself over all the roses and carnations in the garden and choked them to death . . . the Duchess became a bogey to frighten clever girls with.'

In the mid-seventeenth century, drama held apparently inexhaustible attractions even for any would-be writer. But by the early eighteenth century, its charms were failing. Despite the success of her fiction, Aphra Behn had stuck with the stage; coming a generation later, Delarivier Manley was readier to turn to prose fiction and journalism. Eliza Haywood (1693?–1756) had been married ten years, since the age of twenty, when she ran away and became an actress. Writing was in her, and so she wrote for the stage, but not for long; after only three moderately successful plays (*The Fair Captive, Frederick*, and *A Wife To Be Let*) written in the 1720s, she turned to fiction, churning out the successful romances that made her queen of the scandal-sheet, as popular as Defoe. Female wits could still make themselves heard, but not best on the stage — nearer Grub Street.

PART TWO

The Plays

A NOTE ON THE TEXTS

The first priority in choosing plays for this collection was to include plays that show these writers at their best *as playwrights*, in writing for the theatre. I have also tried to represent the range of their work as far as a selection can. Aphra Behn's output is large and ranges widely; because her greatest skill was in managing the sweep and overall movement of a play, extracts do her poor service, and in choosing *The Lucky Chance* I have settled on the play that best shows the range she achieves while maintaining a sure-footed intrigue. Her best-known play, *The Rover*, has the charm of youthful freshness, but is available in a paperback reprint; I have therefore preferred this late work. On a par with Susannah Centlivre's *The Wonder!* is her *A Bold Stroke For A Wife*, and here again my choice was determined by the availability of the latter in paperback reprint. The introductory notes indicate what seems to me most valuable in each of the plays.

All have been edited from seventeenth and eighteenth century editions, but I have kept in mind that these were not published for twentieth-century readers. Restoration texts were usually advertised 'as acted', and so sold as souvenirs, generally to people who had seen the production and were familiar with the ways of their theatres. Often these were hasty and unsupervised books, with misplaced stage directions, cast-lists difficult to comprehend without having seen the production, and sometimes even with scenes in jumbled order. To provide texts that could be used as modern theatre-scripts, I have corrected such obvious errors, expanded stage directions and speech-prefixes, and amplified and rearranged the lists of characters in order of dramatic interest rather than — as in Restoration practice — in order of social rank, with segregated lists of characters in descending order from king to commoner (and men above women!)

To establish the texts I have gone to many different editions of both *The Wonder!* and *The Lucky Chance*. There are only two editions of *The Fatal Friendship*. Catherine Trotter was not fond of printers after her *Love at a Loss* was ruined in the printing. This led her to spend many years working on the play in the hope of re-issuing it under a different name. When she started work on editing her collected works I believe she was attempting to produce a text of *The Fatal Friendship* knowing her prospective readers might not remember the original production, and have therefore chosen this later text to include here.

The Royal Mischief and *The Innocent Mistress* are only available in one edition, and both are scattered with serious printing errors which I have attempted to correct here. The only copy of the 1697 edition of *The Female Wits* listed in the Wing Catalogue is well guarded in the Henry E. Huntingdon Library, San Marino, and so I have used the more easily accessible 1704 edition. In this, apart from correcting obvious errors I have also elided the parts of Mr Verbruggen with Mr Johnson, and Mrs Kent with Mrs Cross. All four 'characters' were actual members of the Drury Lane company, were involved in the creation of the joke against Mrs Manley, and obviously nobody wanted to be left out of its execution. Having all four swells the cast but, so far as any subsequent production is concerned, introduces unnecessary bittiness.

I have not followed the Restoration practice of capitalising nouns somewhat arbitrarily. Spelling and punctuation have been modernised where it seemed necessary, but usage modified only in the cases where it would cause real confusion to retain archaism. I have put asides into brackets. I have also included a glossary.

The flattering letters to noblemen which were added to printed plays to help sell books have been omitted. Prologues and epilogues were not always by the playwright, nor always performed, and so all have been omitted. Where these raise matters of particular interest they have been summarised or cited in the accounts of the individual writers.

THE LUCKY CHANCE

O R

AN ALDERMAN'S BARGAIN

BY

APHRA BEHN

first performed Drury Lane Theatre, *c*. April 1686

Although exploiting a craze for jokes about demons and ghosts to spin out the intrigue, *The Lucky Chance* draws most of its impetus from Aphra Behn's understanding of what it's like to be hard up. In earlier Restoration comedy, money had tended to marry money; so while heroines were often also heiresses, their fortunes were just a bonus, gilding for lilies. But by the start of the 1680s, political instability and economic uncertainty were beginning to bite: in a London that could now support only one theatre, penury began to feature more in plays. Otway produced characters on their beam ends, as Otway himself often was; there were comedies debating whether penniless girls might not have a better life as a kept woman or a courtesan than as a wife. In keeping with the new harshness of the times, wit fell from favour and popular taste now preferred overtly brutal farce.

For Aphra Behn, a shortage of funds was nothing new, and this is perhaps why she manages to be funny when other dramatists were becoming hysterical. In *The Lucky Chance*, penury has decided her heroines to marry rich old men. The aim of their boyfriends' intriguing is not simply to recapture them, but to check that their feelings have survived the turns finance has given to their fortunes. It is complicated because the women in turn probe to discover whether men who must test them can actually love them, and because their distaste for their husbands isn't enough to sanction brutality towards them. These feelings provide the undertow.

The more obvious glory of the play is its disgusting old men. Because they were a comic common-place, impotent old lechers were often merely run of the mill creations. Not so with Aphra Behn, who clearly knew enough to endow hers with quite dreadful vitality. Although hilariously gross, particularly when they get together to drink and to gloat, they are easily frightened, pitiful as well as dangerous in their unease. This balance and sanity in their creator may have attracted Congreve: he later borrowed from this play, giving his Fondlewife the same baby-talk that appears whenever lust prompts Sir Feeble Fainwood to regress into nursery-smut.

The play contains extremes; from flop-house squalor and difficulties with the pawn-broker, it reaches poise and elegance in the lyrics for the songs. The ending draws on another sort of sophistication, an understanding that capture and possession aren't enough to make marriages.

In *The Lucky Chance*, Mrs Behn is credited (*Oxford Dictionary of Quotations* and elsewhere) with the first use of the phrase, 'Here today, and gone tomorrow'.

CHARACTERS

BELLMOUR, in love with Leticia, in hiding to avoid arrest for his part in a duel

LETICIA, young and virginal, but about to marry Sir Feeble Fainwood

GAYMAN, a spark of the town, in love with Julia but impoverished and going under the name Wasteall

JULIA, now LADY FULBANK, honest and generous, in love with Gayman, but recently married to the wealthy banker, Sir Cautious Fulbank

SIR FEEBLE FAINWOOD, an old alderman, about to be married to Leticia

SIR CAUTIOUS FULBANK, an old banker, already married to Julia

DIANA, daughter to Sir Feeble Fainwood, virtuous and in love with Bredwell

BREDWELL, brother to Leticia and apprenticed to Sir Cautious Fulbank, in love with Diana

BEARJEST, nephew to Sir Cautious Fulbank, a fop, wooing Diana

CAPTAIN NOISEY, Bearjest's friend and companion

GAMMER GRIME, a blacksmith's wife and Gayman's landlady

PERT, maidservant to Julia

PHILLIS, maidservant to Leticia

SUSAN, maidservant to Sir Feeble Fainwood

RAG, footman to Gayman

RALPH, footman to Sir Feeble

DICK, footman to Sir Cautious

MR CHEEK, a musician

MR GINGLE, a musician

A Parson; a Shepherd; fiddlers; dancers; singers; porters; servants; a postman

The action takes place in London.

ACT I

THE STREET, AT BREAK OF DAY

Enter BELLMOUR, *disguised in a travelling habit*

BELLMOUR   Sure 'tis the day that gleams in yonder east,
The day that all but lovers blest by shade
Pay cheerful homage to:
Lovers, and those pursued like guilty me
By rigid laws, which put no difference
'Twixt fairly killing in my own defence,
And murders bred by drunken arguments,
Whores, or the mean revenges of a coward.
This is Leticia's father's house. . . (*Looking about*)
And that the dear balcony
That has so oft been conscious of our loves;
From whence she's sent me down a thousand sighs,
A thousand looks of love, a thousand vows!
O thou dear witness of those charming hours,
How do I bless thee, how am I pleased to view thee
After a tedious age of six months' banishment.

Enter several musicians

FIDDLER   But hark ye, Mr Gingle, is it proper to play before the
wedding?
GINGLE   Ever while you live, for many a time in playing after the
first night, the bride's sleepy, the bridegroom tired, and both so out
of humour, that perhaps they hate anything that puts 'em in mind
they are married.

They play and sing

> Rise, Cloris, charming maid arise!
> And baffle breaking day,
> Show the adoring world thy eyes
> Are more surprising gay;
> The Gods of love are smiling round,
> And lead the bridegroom on,
> And Hymen has the altar crowned,
> While all thy sighing lovers are undone.
>
> To see thee pass they throng the plain;
> The groves with flowers are strown,
> And every young and envying swain

Wishes the hour his own.
Rise then, and let the God of day,
When thou dost to the lover yield,
Behold more treasure given away
Than he in his vast circle e'er beheld.

Enter PHILLIS *on the balcony; throws them money*

BELLMOUR   Hah, Phillis, Leticia's woman!

GINGLE   Fie, Mrs Phillis, do you take us for fiddlers that play for hire? I came to compliment Mrs Leticia on her wedding morning because she is my scholar.

PHILLIS   She sends it only to drink her health.

GINGLE   Come, lads, let's to the tavern then.

Exeunt musicians

BELLMOUR   Hah! Said he Leticia?
Sure I shall turn to marble at this news,
I harden, and cold damps pass through my senseless pores.
Ha, who's here?

Enter GAYMAN, *wrapped in his cloak*

GAYMAN   'Tis yet too early, but my soul's impatient.
And I must see Leticia. (*Goes to the door*)

BELLMOUR   Death and the devil, the bridegroom!
Stay, Sir, by heaven you pass not this way.

Goes to the door as he is knocking, pushes him away, and draws

GAYMAN   Hah! What art thou that durst forbid me entrance? Stand off.

They fight a little, and closing view each other

BELLMOUR   Gayman!

GAYMAN   My dearest Bellmour!

BELLMOUR   Oh thou false friend, thou treacherous base deceiver!

GAYMAN   Hah, this to me, dear Harry?

BELLMOUR   Whither is honour, truth and friendship fled?

GAYMAN   Why, there ne'er was such a virtue, 'Tis all a poet's dream.

BELLMOUR   I thank you, Sir.

GAYMAN   I'm sorry for't, or that ever I did anything that could deserve it: put up your sword, an honest man would say how he's offended, before he rashly draws.

BELLMOUR   Are you not going to be married, Sir?

GAYMAN   No Sir, not as long as any man in London is so, that has but a handsome wife, Sir.

BELLMOUR   Are not you in love, Sir?

GAYMAN   Most damnably, and would fain lie with the dear jilting gipsy.

BELLMOUR   Hah, who would you lie with, Sir?

GAYMAN   You catechise me roundly, 'tis not fair to name, but I am no starter, Harry, just as you left me, you find me. I am for the faithless Julia still, the old Alderman's wife. 'Twas high time the city should lose their charter, when their wives turn honest. But pray, Sir, answer me a question or two.

BELLMOUR   Answer me first, what make you here this morning?

GAYMAN   Faith, to do you service. Your damned little jade of a mistress has learned of her neighbours the art of swearing and lying in abundance, and is—

BELLMOUR (*Sighing*)   To be married!

GAYMAN   Even so, God save the mark, and she'll be a fair one for many an arrow besides her husband's, though he's an old Finsbury hero this threescore years.

BELLMOUR   Who mean you?

GAYMAN   Why, thy cuckold that shall be, if thou be'st wise.

BELLMOUR   Away! Who is this man? Thou dalliest with me.

GAYMAN   Why, an old knight, and alderman here o' th' city, Sir Feeble Fainwood, a jolly old fellow, whose activity is all got into his tongue, a very excellent teaser, but neither youth nor beauty can grind his dudgeon to an edge.

BELLMOUR   Fie, what stuff's here!

GAYMAN   Very excellent stuff, if you have but the grace to improve it.

BELLMOUR   You banter me, but in plain English tell me, what made you here thus early, entering yon house with such authority?

GAYMAN   Why, your mistress Leticia, your contracted wife, is this morning to be married to old Sir Feeble Fainwood, induced to't I suppose by the great jointure he makes her, and the improbability of your ever gaining your pardon for your high duel. Do I speak English now, Sir?

BELLMOUR   Too well; would I had never heard thee.

GAYMAN   Now I being the confidant in your amours, the Jack-go-between, the civil pimp, or so, you left her in charge with me at your departure.

BELLMOUR   I did so.

GAYMAN   I saw her every day, and every day she paid the tribute of a shower of tears, to the dear lord of all her vows, young Bellmour. Till, faith, at last, for reasons manifold I slacked my daily visits.

BELLMOUR   And left her to temptation, was that well done?

GAYMAN   Now must I afflict you and myself with a long tale of causes why, or be charged with want of friendship.

BELLMOUR   You will do well to clear that point with me.

GAYMAN   I see you're peevish, and you shall be humoured. You
know my Julia played me e'en such another prank as your false one
is going to play you, and married old Sir Cautious Fulbank here
i'th' city; at which you know I stormed, and raved, and swore, as
thou would now, and to as little purpose. There was but one way
left, and that was cuckolding him.

BELLMOUR   Well, that design I left thee hot upon.

GAYMAN   And hotly have pursued it: swore, wept, vowed, wrote,
upbraided, prayed and railed, then treated lavishly, and presented
high, till, between you and I, Harry, I have presented the best part
of eight hundred a year into her husband's hands, in mortgage.

BELLMOUR   This is the course you'd have me steer, I thank you.

GAYMAN   No, no, pox on't, all women are not jilts. Some are honest,
and will give as well as take, or else there would not be so many broke
i'th' city. In fine, Sir, I have been in tribulation, that is to say,
moneyless, for six tedious weeks, without either clothes, or equipage
to appear withal, and so not only my own love affair lay neglected,
but thine too, and I am forced to pretend to my lady that I am
i'th' country with a dying uncle, from whom, if he were indeed dead,
I expect two thousand a year.

BELLMOUR   But what's all this to being here this morning?

GAYMAN   Thus have I lain concealed like a winter fly, hoping for
some blessed sunshine to warm me into life again, and make me
hover my flagging wings, till the news of this marriage (which fills
the town) made me crawl out this silent hour, to upbraid the fickle
maid.

BELLMOUR   Did'st thou? Pursue thy kind design. Get me to see her,
and sure no woman, even possessed with a new passion, grown
confident even to prostitution, but when she sees the man to whom
she's sworn so very very much, will find remorse and shame.

GAYMAN   For your sake, though the day be broke upon us, and I'm
undone, if seen, I'll venture in. . . (*Throws his cloak over*)

Enter SIR FEEBLE FAINWOOD, SIR CAUTIOUS FULBANK,
BEARJEST, *and* NOISEY. *They pass over the stage, and go into the
house*

Hah, see the bridegroom! And with him my destined cuckold, old
Sir Cautious Fulbank. Hah, what ail'st thou, man?

BELLMOUR   The bridegroom! Like Gorgon's head he's turned me
into stone.

GAYMAN   Gorgon's head, a cuckold's head, 'twas made to graft upon.

BELLMOUR   By heaven I'll seize her even at the altar, and bear her
thence in triumph.

GAYMAN   Ay, and be borne to Newgate in triumph, and be hanged in triumph. 'Twill be cold comfort, celebrating your nuptials in the press-yard, and be waked next morning, like Mr Barnardine in the play. Will you please to rise and be hanged a little, Sir?

BELLMOUR   What wouldst thou have me to do?

GAYMAN   As many an honest man has done before thee. . . cuckold him, cuckold him.

BELLMOUR   What, and let him marry her! She that's mine by sacred vow already! By heaven it would be flat adultery in her!

GAYMAN   She'll learn the trick, and practise it the better with thee.

BELLMOUR   O heavens! Leticia marry him and lie with him! Here will I stand and see this shameful woman, sce if she dares pass by me to this wickedness.

GAYMAN   Hark ye, Harry, in earnest have a care of betraying yourself; and do not venture sweet life for a fickle woman, who perhaps hates you.

BELLMOUR   You counsel well, but to see her married! How every thought of that shocks all my resolution! But hang it, I'll be resolute and saucy, despise a woman who can use me ill, and think myself above her.

GAYMAN   Why, now thou art thyself, a man again. But see, they're coming forth, now stand your ground.

Enter SIR FEEBLE, SIR CAUTIOUS, BEARJEST, NOISEY, LETICIA, *sad,* DIANA, PHILLIS. *They pass over the stage*

BELLMOUR   'Tis she! Support me, Charles, or I shall sink to earth. Methought in passing by she cast a scornful glance at me. Such charming pride I've seen upon her eyes, when our love quarrels armed 'em with disdain. I'll after 'em; if I live she shall not 'scape me.

BELLMOUR *offers to go,* GAYMAN *holds him*

GAYMAN   Hold, remember you're proscribed, and die if you are taken.

BELLMOUR   I've done, and I will live, but he shall ne'er enjoy her. Who's yonder? Ralph, my trusty confidant?

Enter RALPH

Now though I perish I must speak to him. Friend, what wedding's this?

RALPH   One that was never made in heaven, Sir; 'tis Alderman Fainwood, and Mrs Leticia Bredwell.

BELLMOUR   Bredwell, I have heard of her, she was mistress—

RALPH   To fine Mr Bellmour, Sir, ay, there was a gentleman. . . But rest his soul, he's hanged, Sir. (*Weeps*)

BELLMOUR   How! Hanged?

RALPH   Hanged, Sir, hanged, at The Hague in Holland.

GAYMAN   I heard some such news, but did not credit it.
BELLMOUR   For what, said they, was he hanged?
RALPH   Why, e'en for high treason, Sir, he killed one of their kings.
GAYMAN   Holland's a commonwealth, and is not ruled by kings.
RALPH   Not by one, Sir, but by many. This was a cheesemonger, they
    fell out over a bottle of brandy, went to snicker snee, Mr Bellmour
    cut his throat, and was hanged for't, that's all, Sir.
BELLMOUR   And did the young lady believe this?
RALPH   Yes, and took on most heavily, the doctors gave her over,
    and there was the devil to do to get her to consent to this marriage.
    But her fortune was small, and the hope of a ladyship, and a gold
    chain at the Spittal sermon, did the business, and so your servant,
    Sir.

Exit RALPH

BELLMOUR   So, here's a hopeful account of my sweet self now.

Enter POSTMAN *with letters*

POSTMAN   Pray, Sir, which is Sir Feeble Fainwood's?
BELLMOUR   What would you with him, friend?
POSTMAN   I have a letter here from The Hague for him.
BELLMOUR   (From The Hague! Now have I a curiosity to see it.) I am
    his servant, give it me. (POSTMAN *gives it him, and exits*) Perhaps
    here may be the second part of my tragedy. I'm full of mischief,
    Charles, and have a mind to see this fellow's secrets. For from this
    hour I'll be his evil genius, haunt him at bed and board, he shall not
    sleep nor eat, disturb him at his prayers, in his embraces, and tease
    him into madness. Help me, invention, malice, love and wit. (*Opening
    the letter*) Ye Gods, and little fiends, instruct my mischief. (*Reads*)

'Dear Brother,
According to your desire I have sent for my son from St Omer's,
whom I have sent to wait on you in England. He is a very good
accountant, and fit for business, and much pleased he shall see that
Uncle to whom he's so obliged, and which is so gratefully acknowledged
by, dear brother,
Your affectionate brother,

Francis Fainwood'

Hum, hark ye, Charles, do you know who I am now?
GAYMAN   Why, I hope a very honest friend of mine, Harry Bellmour.
BELLMOUR   No, Sir, you are mistaken in your man.
GAYMAN   It may be so.
BELLMOUR   I am, d'ye see, Charles, this very individual, numerical
    young Mr . . . what ye call 'um Fainwood, just come from St Omer's
    into England, to my Uncle the Alderman. I am, Charles, this very man.

GAYMAN   I know you are, and will swear't upon occasion.

BELLMOUR   This lucky thought has almost calmed my mind. And if I don't fit you, my dear Uncle, may I never lie with my Aunt.

GAYMAN   Ah, rogue, but prithee what care have you taken about your pardon? 'Twere good you should secure that.

BELLMOUR   There's the devil, Charles, had I but that. . . but that seldom fails, but yet in vain, I being the first transgressor since the Act against duelling. But I am impatient to see this dear delight of my soul, and hearing from none of you this six weeks, came from Brussels in this disguise, for the Hague I have not seen, though hanged there. But come, let's away, and complete me a right St Omer's spark, that I may present myself as soon as they come from church.

SCENE II

INSIDE SIR CAUTIOUS FULBANK'S HOUSE

Enter LADY FULBANK, PERT *and* BREDWELL. BREDWELL *gives her a letter*

LADY FULBANK (*reads*)   'Did my Julia know how I languish in this cruel separation, she would afford me her pity, and write oftener. If only the expectation of two thousand a year kept me from you, ah, Julia, how easily would I abandon that trifle for your more valued sight; but that I know a fortune will render me more agreeable to the charming Julia, I should quit all my interest here, to throw myself at her feet, to make her sensible how I am entirely her adorer, Charles Gayman.' Faith, Charles you lie, you are as welcome to me now, now when I doubt thy fortune is declining, as if the universe were thine.

PERT   That, Madam, is a noble gratitude. For if his fortune be declining, 'tis sacrificed to his passion for your ladyship. 'Tis all laid out on love.

LADY FULBANK   I prize my honour more than life. Yet I had rather have given him all he wished of me, than be guilty of his undoing.

PERT   And I think the sin were less.

LADY FULBANK   I must confess, such jewels, rings and presents as he made me must needs decay his fortune.

BREDWELL   Ay, Madam, his very coach at last was turned into a jewel for your ladyship. Then, Madam, what expenses his despair have run him on. . . as drinking and gaming, to divert the thought of your marrying my old master.

LADY FULBANK   And put in wenching, too.

BREDWELL   No, assure yourself, Madam.

LADY FULBANK (*to* BREDWELL)   Of that I would be better
    satisfied, and you too must assist me, as e'er you hope I should be
    kind to you in gaining you Diana.

BREDWELL   Madam, I'll die to serve you.

PERT   Nor will I be behind in my duty.

LADY FULBANK   Oh, how fatal are forced marriages!
    How many ruins one such match pulls on!
    Had I but kept my sacred vows to Gayman,
    How happy had I been, how prosperous he!
    Whilst now I languish in a loathed embrace,
    Pine out my life with age, consumptions, coughs.
    But dost thou fear that Gayman is declining?

BREDWELL   You are my lady, and the best of mistresses, therefore I
    would not grieve you, for I know you love this best, but most
    unhappy man.

LADY FULBANK   You shall not grieve me, prithee on.

BREDWELL   My master sent me yesterday to Mr Crap his scrivener,
    to send to one Mr Wasteall, to tell him his first mortgage was out,
    which is two hundred pounds a year, and who has since engaged
    five or six hundred more to my master. But if this first be not
    redeemed, he'll take the forfeit on't, as he says a wise man ought.

LADY FULBANK   That is to say, a knave, according to his notion of
    a wise man.

BREDWELL   Mr Crap, being busy with a borrowing Lord, sent me to
    Mr Wasteall, whose lodging is in a nasty place called Alsatia, at a
    black-smith's.

LADY FULBANK   But what's all this to Gayman?

BREDWELL   Madam, this Wasteall was Mr Gayman.

LADY FULBANK   Gayman! Saw'st thou Gayman?

BREDWELL   Madam, Mr Gayman, yesterday.

LADY FULBANK   When came he to town?

BREDWELL   Madam, he has not been out of it.

LADY FULBANK   Not at his Uncle's in Northamptonshire?

BREDWELL   Your ladyship was wont to credit me.

LADY FULBANK   Forgive me, you went to a blacksmith's.

BREDWELL   Yes Madam, and at the door encountered the beastly
    thing he calls a landlady, who looked as if she had been of her own
    husband's making, composed of moulded smith's dust. I asked for
    Mr Wasteall, and she began to open, and did so rail at him, that what
    with her Billingsgate, and her husband's hammers, I was both deaf
    and dumb. At last the hammers ceased, and she grew weary, and
    called down Mr Wasteall. But he not answering I was sent up a ladder

rather than a pair of stairs. At last I scaled the top, and entered the enchanted castle; there did I find him, spite of the noise below, drowning his cares in sleep.

LADY FULBANK   Whom found'st thou? Gayman?

BREDWELL   He, Madam, whom I waked, and seeing me, Heavens what confusion seized him, which nothing but my own surprise could equal. Ashamed, he would have turned away, but when he saw, by my dejected eyes, I knew him, he sighed, and blushed, and heard me tell my business. Then begged I would be secret, for he vowed his whole repose and life depended on my silence. Nor had I told it now, but that your Ladyship may find some speedy means to draw him from this desperate condition.

LADY FULBANK   Heavens, is't possible?

BREDWELL   He's driven to the last degree of poverty. Had you but seen his lodgings, Madam!

LADY FULBANK   What were they?

BREDWELL   'Tis a pretty convenient tub, Madam. He may lie along in't. There's just room for an old joined stool besides the bed, which one cannot call a cabin, about the largeness of a pantry bin, or a usurer's trunk. There had been dornex curtains to't in the days of yore, but they were now annihilated, and nothing left to save his eyes from the light but my landlady's blue apron, tied by the strings before the window, in which stood a broken six-penny looking-glass, that showed as many faces as the scene in Henry the Eighth, which could but just stand upright, and then the comb case filled it.

LADY FULBANK   What a lewd description hast thou made of his chamber.

BREDWELL   Then for his equipage, 'tis banished to one small Monsieur, who, saucy with his master's poverty, is rather a companion than a footman.

LADY FULBANK   But what said he to the forfeiture of his land?

BREDWELL   He sighed and cried, 'Why, farewell dirty acres; It shall not trouble me, since 'twas all for love!'

LADY FULBANK   How much redeems it?

BREDWELL   Madam, five hundred pounds.

LADY FULBANK   Enough, you shall in some disguise convey this money to him, as from an unknown hand, I would not have him think it comes from me, for all the world. That nicety and virtue I protest I am resolved to keep.

PERT   If I were your ladyship, I would make use of Sir Cautious's cash: pay him in his own coin.

BREDWELL   Your Ladyship would make no scruple of it, if you knew how this poor gentleman has been used by my unmerciful master.

LADY FULBANK   I have a key already to his counting house; it being lost, he had another made, and this I found and kept.

BREDWELL   Madam, this is an excellent time for't, my master being gone to give my sister Leticia at church.

LADY FULBANK   'Tis so, and I'll go and commit the theft, whilst you prepare to carry it, and then we'll to dinner with your sister, the bride.

SCENE III

THE HOUSE OF SIR FEEBLE

Enter SIR FEEBLE, LETICIA, SIR CAUTIOUS, BEARJEST, DIANA, *and* NOISEY. SIR FEEBLE *sings and salutes them*

SIR FEEBLE   Welcome! *Joan Sanderson*! Welcome, welcome. (*Kisses the bride*) Ods bobs, and so thou art, sweetheart.

BEARJEST   Methinks my lady bride is very melancholy.

SIR CAUTIOUS   Ay, ay, women that are discreet are always thus upon their wedding day.

SIR FEEBLE   Always by day-light, Sir Cautious. (*Sings*)

> *But when bright Phoebus does retire,*
> *To Thetis' bed to quench his fire,*
> *And do the thing we need not name,*
> *We mortals by his influence do the same.*
> *Then, then the blushing maid lays by*
> *Her simpering, and her modesty;*
> *And round the lover clasps and twines*
> *Like ivy, or the circling vines.*

Here, Ralph, the bottle, rogue, of sack, ye rascal. Hadst thou been a butler worth hanging thou wouldst have met us at the door with it. Ods bobs, sweetheart, thy health.

BEARJEST   Away with it, to the bride's Haunce in Kelder.

SIR FEEBLE   Go to, go to, rogue, go to, that shall be, knave, that shall be the morrow morning. He, ods bobs, we'll do't, sweetheart; here's to't. (*Drinks again*)

LETICIA   I die but to imagine it, would I were dead indeed.

SIR FEEBLE   Hah, hum, how's this? Tears upon the wedding day? Why, why, you baggage you, ye little ting, fool's face, away you rogue, you're naughty, you're naughty. (*Patting and playing, and following her*) Look, look, look now, buss it, buss it, buss it and friends; did'ums, did'ums beat its none silly baby, away you little hussy, away, and pledge me. . .

She drinks a little

SIR CAUTIOUS   A wise discreet lady, I'll warrant her. My lady would
   prodigally have took it off all.
SIR FEEBLE   Dears, its nown dear Fubs, buss again, buss again, away,
   away, away, ods| bobs,| I long for night, look, look Sir Cautious, what
   an eye's there!
SIR CAUTIOUS   Ay, so there is, brother, and a modest eye too.
SIR FEEBLE   Adad, I love her more and more. Ralph, call old Susan
   hither. Come Mr Bearjest, put the glass about. Ods bobs, when I was
   a young fellow I would not let the young wenches look pale and wan,
   but would rouse 'em and touse 'em, and blowze 'em, till I put a
   colour in their cheeks, like an apple John, assacks. Nay, I can make a
   shift still, and pupsey shall not be jealous.

Enter SUSAN. SIR FEEBLE *whispers to her, she goes out*

LETICIA   Indeed not I, Sir, I shall be all obedience.
SIR CAUTIOUS   A most judicious lady, would my Julia had a little
   of her modesty. But my lady's a wit.

Re-enter SUSAN, *with a box*

SIR FEEBLE   Look here my little puskin, here's fine play-things for
   its nown little coxcomb, go, get you gone, get you gone, and off
   with these St Martin's trumpery, these play-house glass baubles, this
   necklace, and these pendants, and all this false ware; ods bobs, I'll
   have no counterfeit gear about thee, not I. See these are right as the
   blushes on thy cheeks, and these as true as my heart, girl. Go, put
   'em on, and be fine. (*Gives them to her*)
LETICIA   Believe me, Sir, I shall not merit this kindness.
SIR FEEBLE   Go to, more of your love, and less of your ceremony,
   give the old fool a hearty buss, and pay him that way. Hark ye, little
   wanton tit, I'll steal up and catch ye and love ye, adod I will. Get ye
   gone, get ye gone.
LETICIA   Heavens, what a nauseous thing is an old man turned lover!

Exeunt LETICIA *and* DIANA

SIR CAUTIOUS   How, steal up, Sir Feeble? I hope not so. I hold it
   most indecent before the lawful hour.
SIR FEEBLE   Lawful hour! Why, I hope all hours are lawful with a
   man's own wife.
SIR CAUTIOUS   But wise men have respect to times and seasons.
SIR FEEBLE   Wise young men, Sir Cautious; but wise old men must
   nick their inclinations, for it is not as 'twas wont to be, for it is not
   as 'twas wont to be. (*Singing and dancing*)

Enter RALPH

RALPH   Sir, here's a young gentleman without would speak with you.
SIR FEEBLE   Hum, I hope it is not that same Bellmour come to forbid the banns; if it be, he comes too late, therefore bring me first my long sword, and then the gentleman.

Exit RALPH

BEARJEST   Pray Sir, use mine, it is a travelled blade I can assure you, Sir.
SIR FEEBLE   I thank you, Sir.

Enter RALPH *and* BELLMOUR *disguised, gives* SIR FEEBLE *a letter. He reads*

How. . . my nephew! Francis Fainwood! (*Embraces him*)
BELLMOUR   (I am glad he has told me my christian name.)
SIR FEEBLE   Sir Cautious, know my nephew, 'tis a young St Omer's scholar, but none of the witnesses.
SIR CAUTIOUS   Marry, Sir, and the wiser he, for they got nothing by't.
BEARJEST   Sir, I love and honour you, because you are a traveller.
SIR FEEBLE   A very proper young fellow, and as like old Frank Fainwood as the devil to the collier. But, Francis, you are come into a very lewd town, Francis, for whoring, and plotting, and roaring, and drinking, but you must go to church, Francis, and avoid ill company, or you may make damnable havoc in my cash, Francis, what! You can keep merchants' books?
BELLMOUR   That's been my study, Sir.
SIR FEEBLE   And you will not be proud, but will be commanded by me, Francis?
BELLMOUR   I desire not to be favoured as a kinsman, Sir, but as your humblest servant.
SIR FEEBLE   Why, thou'rt an honest fellow, Francis, and thou'rt heartily welcome, and I'll make thee fortunate. But come, Sir Cautious, let you and I take a turn i'th' garden, and get a right understanding between your nephew Mr Bearjest, and my daughter Dy.
SIR CAUTIOUS   Prudently thought on, Sir, I'll wait on you.

Exeunt SIR FEEBLE, *and* SIR CAUTIOUS

BEARJEST   You are a traveller, I understand.
BELLMOUR   I have seen a little part of the whole world, Sir.
BEARJEST   So have I, Sir, I thank my stars, and have performed most of my travels on foot, Sir.
BELLMOUR   You did not travel far then, I presume, Sir?

BEARJEST   No, Sir, it was for my diversion indeed, but I assure you, I travelled into Ireland a-foot, Sir.

BELLMOUR   Sure, Sir, you go by shipping into Ireland?

BEARJEST   That's all one, Sir, I was still a-foot, ever walking on the deck.

BELLMOUR   Was that your farthest travel, Sir?

BEARJEST   Farthest, why that's the end of the world, and sure a man can go no farther.

BELLMOUR   Sure, there can be nothing worth a man's curiosity?

BEARJEST   No, Sir, I'll assure you, there are the wonders of the world. Sir, I'll hint you this one. There is a harbour which since the creation was never capable of receiving a lighter, yet by another miracle the King of France was to ride there with a vast fleet of ships, and to land a hundred thousand men.

BELLMOUR   This is a swinging wonder, but are there store of mad-men there, Sir?

BEARJEST   That's another rarity, to see a man run out of his wits.

NOISEY   Marry, Sir, the wiser they, I say.

BEARJEST   Pray Sir, what store of miracles have you at St Omer's?

BELLMOUR   None, Sir, since that of the wonderful Salamanca doctor, who was both here and there at the same instant of time.

BEARJEST   How, Sir? Why, that's impossible.

BELLMOUR   That was the wonder, Sir, because 'twas impossible.

NOISEY   But 'twas a greater, Sir, that 'twas believed.

Enter LADY FULBANK, PERT, SIR CAUTIOUS, *and* SIR FEEBLE

SIR FEEBLE   Enough, enough, Sir Cautious, we apprehend one another. Mr Bearjest, your uncle here and I have struck the bargain, the wench is yours with three thousand pound present, and something more after death, which your uncle likes well.

BEARJEST   Does he so, Sir, I'm beholden to him. Then 'tis not a pin matter whether I like or not, Sir.

SIR FEEBLE   How, Sir, not like my daughter Dy?

BEARJEST   Oh Lord, Sir, die or live, 'tis all one for that, Sir, I'll stand to the bargain my uncle makes.

PERT   Will you so, Sir? You'll have very good luck if you do.

BEARJEST   Prithee, hold thy peace, my lady's woman.

LADY FULBANK   Sir, I beg your pardon for not waiting on you to church, I knew you would be private.

Enter LETICIA, *in fine jewels*

SIR FEEBLE   You honour us too highly now, Madam.

SIR FEEBLE *presents his wife, who salutes her*

LADY FULBANK   Give you joy, my dear Leticia! I find, Sir, you were
  resolved for youth, wit and beauty.
SIR FEEBLE   Ay, ay, Madam, to the comfort of many a hoping
  coxcomb. But Lette, rogue Lette, thou would not make me free o'th'
  city a second time. Would thou entice the rogues with the twire and
  the wanton leer, the amorous simper that cries 'come kiss me', then
  the pretty round lips are pouted out? The rogue, how I long to be at
  'em! Well, she shall never go to church more, that she shall not.
LADY FULBANK   How, Sir, not to church, the chiefest recreation of
  a city lady?
SIR FEEBLE   That's all one, Madam, that tricking and dressing, and
  prinking and patching is not your devotion to heaven, but to the
  young knaves that are licked and combed and are minding you more
  than the parson. Ods bobs, there are more cuckolds destined in the
  church, than are made out of it.
SIR CAUTIOUS   Ha, ha, ha, he tickles ye i'faith, ladies.
BELLMOUR   Not one chance look this way, and yet,
    I can forgive her lovely eyes,
    Because they look not pleased with all this ceremony,
    And yet, methinks, some sympathy in love
    Might this way glance their beams. . . I cannot hold
    . . . Sir, is this fair lady my aunt?
SIR FEEBLE   Oh Francis! Come hither, Francis. Lette, here's a young
  rogue has a mind to kiss thee.

  SIR FEEBLE *puts them together, she starts back*

  Nay, start not, he's my own flesh and blood, my nephew, baby. Look,
  look how the young rogues stare at one another; like will to like, I
  see that.
LETICIA   There's something in his face so like my Bellmour, it calls
  my blushes up, and leaves my heart defenceless.

  Enter RALPH

RALPH   Sir, dinner's on the table.
SIR FEEBLE   Come, come, let's in then, gentlemen and ladies,
    And share today my pleasures and delight,
    But. . .
    Adds bobs, they must be all mine own at night.

ACT II

SCENE I

GAYMAN'S LODGINGS

Enter GAYMAN *in a night-cap, and an old campaign coat tied about him, very melancholy*

GAYMAN   Curse on my birth! Curse on my faithless fortune!
Curse on my stars, and curst be all, but love!
That dear, that charming sin, though 't have pulled
Innumerable mischiefs on my head,
I have not, nor I cannot find repentance for.
No, let me die despised, upbraided, poor:
Let fortune, friends and all abandon me
But let me hold thee, thou soft smiling God,
Close to my heart while life continues there.
Till the last panting of my vital blood,
Nay, the last spark of life and fire be love's!

Enter RAG

How now, Rag, what's o'clock?

RAG   My belly can inform you better than my tongue.

GAYMAN   Why, you gormandizing vermin you, what have you done with the three pence I gave you a fortnight ago?

RAG   Alas, Sir, that's all gone long since.

GAYMAN   You gutling rascal, you are enough to breed a famine in a land. I have known some industrious footmen that have not only gotten their own living, but a pretty livelihood for their masters, too.

RAG   Ay, till they came to the gallows, Sir.

GAYMAN   Very well, Sirrah, they died in an honourable calling, but hark ye, Rag, I have business, very earnest business abroad this evening. Now, were you a rascal of docity, you would invent a way to get home my last suit that was laid in lavender, with the appurtenar thereunto belonging, as periwig, cravat, and so forth.

RAG   Faith, master, I must deal in the black art then, for no human means will do't. And now I talk of the black art, Master, try your power once more with my landlady.

GAYMAN   Oh! name her not, the thought on't turns my stomach, a sight of her is a vomit; but he's a bold hero that dares venture on her for a kiss, and all beyond that sure is hell itself, yet there's my last, last refuge, and I must to this wedding. I know not what, but something whispers me, this night I shall be happy, and without Julia 'tis impossible!

RAG   Julia, who's that? my Lady Fulbank, Sir?

GAYMAN   Peace, Sirrah, and call. . . a. . . no, pox on't, come back. . .
and yet. . . yes. . . call my fulsome landlady.

Exit RAG

Sir Cautious knows me not by name or person. And I will to this
wedding, I'm sure of seeing Julia there, and what may come of that.
But here's old Nasty coming, I smell her up. Hah, my dear landlady.

Enter RAG *and* LANDLADY

Quite out of breath, a chair there for my landlady.

RAG   Here's ne'er a one, Sir.

LANDLADY   More of your money and less of your civility, good
Mr Wasteall.

GAYMAN   Dear landlady. . .

LANDLADY   Dear me no dears, Sir, but let me have my money, eight
weeks' rent last Friday; besides taverns, ale-houses, chandlers,
laundresses' scores, and ready money out of my purse, you know it, Sir.

GAYMAN   Ay, but your husband don't. Speak softly.

LANDLADY   My husband! What, do you think to fright me with my
husband? I'd have you to know I'm an honest woman, and care not
this. . . for my husband. Is this all the thanks I have for my kindness,
for patching, borrowing and shifting for you? 'Twas but last week I
pawned my best petticoat, as I hope to wear it again, it cost me six
and twenty shillings besides making, then this morning my new
Norwich mantua followed, and two postle spoons, I had the whole
dozen when you came first, but they dropped, and dropped, till I had
only Judas left for my husband.

GAYMAN   Hear me, good landlady.

LANDLADY   Then I've passed my word at the George Tavern for forty
shillings for you, ten shillings at my neighbour Squabs for ale, besides
seven shillings to mother Suds for washing, and do you fob me off
with my husband?

GAYMAN   Here, Rag, run and fetch her a pint of sack, there's no other
way of quenching the fire in her flabber chops.

Exit RAG

But my dear landlady, have a little patience.

LANDLADY   Patience! I scorn your words, Sir, is this a place to trust
in? Tell me of patience, that used to have my money beforehand.
Come, come, pay me quickly, or old Gregory Grime's house shall be
too hot to hold you.

GAYMAN   Is't come to this, can I not be heard?

LANDLADY   No, Sir, you had good clothes when you came first, but
they dwindled daily, till they dwindled to this old campaign, with

tanned coloured lining, once red, but now all colours of the rainbow,
a cloak to skulk in a-nights, and a pair of piss-burned shammy breeches.
Nay, your very badge of manhood's gone too.

GAYMAN   How, landlady! Nay then i'faith no wonder if you rail so.

LANDLADY   Your silver sword I mean, transmogrified to this two-
handed basket hilt, this old Sir Guy of Warwick, which will sell for
nothing but old iron. In fine, I'll have my money, Sir, or i'faith
Alsatia shall not shelter you.

Enter RAG

GAYMAN   Well, landlady, if we must part, let's drink at parting. Here,
landlady, here's to the fool that shall love you better than I have done.
(*Sighing, he drinks*)

LANDLADY   Rot your wine, d'ye think to pacify me with wine, Sir?

She refuses to drink. He holds open her jaws and RAG *throws a glass
of wine into her mouth*

What, will you force me? No, give me another glass, I scorn to be so
uncivil to be forced. My service to you, Sir. This shan't do, Sir.

She drinks. He, embracing her, sings

> *Ah Cloris, 'tis in vain you scold.*
> *Whilst your eyes kindle such a fire,*
> *Your railing cannot make me cold,*
> *So fast as they a warmth inspire.*

LANDLADY   Well Sir, you have no reason to complain of my eyes, nor
my tongue neither, if rightly understood. (*Weeps*)

GAYMAN   I know you are the best of landladies, as such I drink your
health. (*He drinks*) But to upbraid a man in tribulation. . . fie, 'tis not
done like a woman of honour, a man that loves you too.

LANDLADY   I am a little hasty sometimes, but you know my good
nature. (*She drinks*)

GAYMAN   I do, and therefore trust my little wants with you. I shall
be rich again, and then my dearest landlady. . .

LANDLADY   Would this wine might ne'er go through me if I would
not go, as they say, through fire and water, by night or by day for
you. (*She drinks*)

GAYMAN   And as this is wine, I do believe thee. (*He drinks*)

LANDLADY   Well, you have no money in your pocket now, I'll
warrant you; here, here's ten shillings for you old Gregory knows not
of.

She opens a great greasy purse

GAYMAN   I cannot in conscience take it, good faith, I cannot. Besides, the next quarrel you'll hit me in the teeth with it.

LANDLADY   Nay, pray no more of that; forget it, forget it. I own I
was to blame. Here Sir, you shall take it.

GAYMAN   Ay, but what should I do with money in these damned
breeches! No, put it up, I can't appear thus. No, I'll stay at home, and
lose my business.

LANDLADY   Why, is there no way to redeem one of your suits?

GAYMAN   None, none, I'll e'en lay me down and die.

LANDLADY   Die, marry, Heaven forbid, I would not for the world.
Let me see, hum, what does it lie for?

GAYMAN   Alas dear landlady, a sum, a sum.

LANDLADY   Well, say no more, I'll lay about me.

GAYMAN   By this kiss but you shall not. . . (Assafetida, by this light.)

LANDLADY   Shall not? That's a good one, i'faith. Shall you rule, or I?

GAYMAN   But should your husband know it?

LANDLADY   Husband, marry come up, husbands know wives' secrets?
No, sure, the world's not so bad yet. Where do your things lie? And
for what?

GAYMAN   Five pounds equips me. Rag can conduct you, but I say
you shall not go. I've sworn. . .

LANDLADY   Meddle with your matters; let me see, the caudle cup
that Molly's grandmother left her will pawn for about that sum. I'll
sneak it out. Well, Sir, you shall have your things presently, trouble
not your head, but expect me.

Exeunt LANDLADY *and* RAG

GAYMAN   Was ever man put to such beastly shifts? S'death how she
stank, my senses are most luxuriously regaled, there's my perpetual
music too. . . (*Knocking of hammers on an anvil*) The ringing of bells
is an ass to't.

Enter RAG

RAG   Sir, there's one in a coach below would speak to you.

GAYMAN   With me, and in a coach! Who can it be?

RAG   The Devil, I think, for he has a strange countenance.

GAYMAN   The Devil! Show yourself a rascal of parts, Sirrah, and wait
on him up with ceremony.

RAG   Who, the Devil, Sir—?

GAYMAN   Ay, the Devil, Sir, if you mean to thrive.

Exit RAG

Who can this be? But see, he comes to inform me. Withdraw.

Enter BREDWELL *dressed like a devil*

BREDWELL   I come to bring you this. . . (*Gives him a letter*)
GAYMAN (*reads*)
   'Receive what love and fortune present you with, be grateful and be
   silent, or 'twill vanish like a dream, and leave you more wretched
   than it found you.

Adieu'

   Hah. . . (*Gives him a bag of money*)
BREDWELL   Nay view it, Sir, 'tis all substantial gold.
GAYMAN   (Now dare not I ask one civil question for fear it vanish
   all.) But I may ask, how 'tis I ought to pay for this great bounty.
BREDWELL   Sir, all the pay is secrecy.
GAYMAN   And is this all that is required, Sir?
BREDWELL   No, you're invited to the shades below.
GAYMAN   Hum, shades below! I am not prepared for such a journey,
   Sir.
BREDWELL   If you have courage, youth or love, you'll follow me:
   (*In feigned heroic tone*)
   When night's black curtain's drawn around the world,
   And mortal's eyes are safely locked in sleep,
   And no bold spy dares view when Gods caress,
   Then I'll conduct thee to the banks of bliss.
   Durst thou not trust me?
GAYMAN   Yes, sure, on such substantial security. (*Hugs the bag*)
BREDWELL   Just when the day is vanished into night,
   And only twinkling stars inform the world,
   Near to the corner of the silent wall,
   In fields of Lincoln's-Inn, thy spirit shall meet thee.
   Farewell.

Exit BREDWELL

GAYMAN   Hum, I am awake, sure, and this is gold I grasp.
   I could not see this devil's cloven foot;
   Nor am I such a coxcomb to believe
   But he was as substantial as his gold.
   Spirits, ghosts, hobgoblins, furies, fiends and devils,
   I've often heard old wives fright fools and children with,
   Which, once arrived to common sense, they laugh at.
   No, I am for things possible and natural:
   Some female devil, old and damned to ugliness,
   And past all hopes of courtship and address,
   Full of another devil called desire,
   Has seen this face, this shape, this youth,
   And thinks it's worth her hire. It must be so.
   I must moil on in the damned dirty road,

And sure, such pay will make the journey easy,
And for the price of the dull, drudging night,
All day I'll purchase new and fresh delight.

Exit GAYMAN

SCENE II

SIR FEEBLE'S HOUSE

Enter LETICIA, *pursued by* PHILLIS

PHILLIS   Why, Madam, do you leave the garden, for this retreat to melancholy?

LETICIA   Because it suits my fortune and my humour; and even thy presence would afflict me now.

PHILLIS   Madam, I was sent after you. My lady Fulbank has challenged Sir Feeble at bowls, and stakes a ring of fifty pound against his new chariot.

LETICIA   Tell him I wish him luck in everything but in his love to me. Go tell him I am viewing of the garden.

Exit PHILLIS

Blessed be this kind retreat, this 'lone occasion
That lends a short cessation to my torments,
And gives me leave to vent my sighs and tears. (*Weeps*)

Enter BELLMOUR *at a distance behind her*

BELLMOUR   And doubly blessed be all the powers of love,
That gave me this dear opportunity.

LETICIA   Where were you, all ye pitying Gods of love,
That once seemed pleased at Bellmour's flame and mine,
And, smiling, joined our hearts, our sacred vows,
And spread your wings, and held your torches high?

BELLMOUR   Oh. . . (*She starts, and pauses*)

LETICIA   Where were you now, when this unequal marriage
Gave me from all my joys, gave me from Bellmour;
Your wings were flaged, your torches bent to earth,
And all your little bonnets veiled your eyes;
You saw not, or were deaf and pitiless.

BELLMOUR   Oh my Leticia!

LETICIA   Hah, 'tis there again; that very voice was Bellmour's.
Where art thou, oh thou lovely charming shade?
For sure, thou canst not take a shape to fright me.
What art thou?. . . speak!

Not looking behind her yet, for fear

BELLMOUR   Thy constant true adorer, who all this fatal day has
     haunted thee to ease his tortured soul. (*Approaching her*)
LETICIA   (*speaking with signs of fear*)
     My heart is well acquainted with that voice,
     But, oh, my eyes dare not encounter thee.
BELLMOUR   Is it because thou'st broken all thy vows?
     Take to thee courage, and behold thy slaughters.
LETICIA   Yes, though the sight would blast me, I would view it.
     (*Turns*) 'Tis he, 'tis very Bellmour! or so like. . .
     I cannot doubt but thou deserv'st this welcome. (*Embraces him*)
BELLMOUR   Oh my Leticia!
LETICIA   I'm sure I grasp not air; thou art no phantom.
     My arms return not empty to my bosom,
     But meet a solid treasure.
BELLMOUR   A treasure thou so easily threw'st away;
     A riddle simple love ne'er understood.
LETICIA   Alas, I heard, my Bellmour, thou wert dead.
BELLMOUR   And was it thus you mourned my funeral?
LETICIA   I will not justify my hated crime.
     But, oh, remember I was poor and helpless,
     And much reduced, and much imposed upon. (BELLMOUR *weeps*)
BELLMOUR   And want compelled thee to this wretched marriage. . .
     did it?
LETICIA   'Tis not a marriage, since my Bellmour lives;
     The consummation were adultery.
     I was thy wife before, would thou deny me?
BELLMOUR   No, by those powers that heard our mutual vows,
     Those vows that tie us faster than dull priests.
LETICIA   But, oh my Bellmour, thy sad circumstances
     Permit thee not to make a public claim.
     Thou art proscribed, and diest if thou art seen.
BELLMOUR   Alas!
LETICIA   Yet I would wander with thee o'er the world,
     And share thy humblest fortune with thy love.
BELLMOUR   Is't possible, Leticia, thou would'st fly
     To foreign shores with me?
LETICIA   Can Bellmour doubt the soul he knows so well?
BELLMOUR   Perhaps in time the King may find my innocence, and
     may extend his mercy. Meantime I'll make provision for our flight.
LETICIA   But how 'twixt this and that can I defend myself from the
     loathèd arms of an impatient dotard, that I may come a spotless maid
     to thee?
BELLMOUR   Thy native modesty and my industry
     Shall well enough secure us.

Feign your nice virgin-cautions all the day;
Then trust at night to my conduct to preserve thee.
And wilt thou yet be mine? Oh, swear anew,
Give me again thy faith, thy vows, thy soul,
For mine's so sick with this day's fatal business,
It needs a cordial of that mighty strength;
Swear, swear, so as if thou break'st
Thou may'st be anything but damned, Leticia.

LETICIA   Thus then, and hear me, Heaven! (*Kneels*)
BELLMOUR   And thus, I'll listen to thee. (*Kneels*)

Enter SIR FEEBLE, LADY FULBANK *and* SIR CAUTIOUS

SIR FEEBLE   Lette, Lette, Lette, where are you, little rogue, Lette?
Hah, hum, what's here. . . ?

BELLMOUR *snatches her to his bosom, as if she fainted*

BELLMOUR   Oh Heavens, she's gone, she's gone!
SIR FEEBLE   Gone, whither is she gone? It seems she had the wit to
take good company with her.

The women go to her, and take her up

BELLMOUR   She's gone to Heaven, Sir, for ought I know.
SIR CAUTIOUS   She was resolved to go in a young fellow's arms, I see.
SIR FEEBLE   Go to, Francis, go to.
LADY FULBANK   Stand back, Sir, she recovers.
BELLMOUR   Alas, I found her dead upon the floor.
I should have left her so if I had known your mind.
SIR FEEBLE   Was it so, was it so? Got so, by no means, Francis?
LETICIA   Pardon him Sir, for surely I had died, but for his timely
coming.
SIR FEEBLE   Alas, poor pupsey, was it sick? Look here, here's a fine
thing to make it well again. Come buss, and it shall have it. Oh, how
I long for night. Ralph, are the fiddlers ready?
RALPH   They are tuning in the hall, Sir.
SIR FEEBLE   That's well, they know my mind. I hate that same twang,
twang, twang, fum, fum, tweedle, tweedle, tweedle, then screw go
the pins, till a man's teeth are on edge, then 'snap' says a small gut, and
there we are at a loss again. I long to be in bed with a hey tredodle,
tredodle, tredodle, with a hey tredool, tredodle, tredo. . . (*Dancing and
playing on his stick like a flute*)
SIR CAUTIOUS   A prudent man would reserve himself. Good-sacks, I
danced so on my wedding-day, that when I came to bed, to my shame
be it spoken, I fell fast asleep, and slept till morning.
LADY FULBANK   Where was your wisdom then, Sir Cautious? But I
know what a wise woman ought to have done.

SIR FEEBLE   Odsbobs, that's wormwood, that's wormwood. I shall
have my young hussy set a-gog too. She'll hear there are better
things in the world than she has at home, and then, odsbobs, and then
they'll ha't, adod they will, Sir Cautious. Ever while you live, keep
a wife ignorant, unless a man be as brisk as his neighbours.

SIR CAUTIOUS   A wise man will keep 'em from bawdy christ'nings
then, and gossipings.

SIR FEEBLE   Christ'nings and gossipings! Why, they are the very
schools that debauch our wives, as dancing-schools do our daughters.

SIR CAUTIOUS   Ay, when the overjoyed good man invites 'em all
against that time twelve-month: 'Oh he's a dear man', cries one; 'I
must marry', cries another; 'here's a man indeed, my husband, God
help him'.

SIR FEEBLE   Then he falls to telling of her grievance, till (half
maudlin) she weeps again. 'Just my condition,' cries a third. So the
frolic goes round, and we poor cuckolds are anatomised, and turned
the right side outwards; adsbobs, we are, Sir Cautious.

SIR CAUTIOUS   Ay, ay, this grievance ought to be redressed, Sir
Feeble. The grave and sober part o'th' nation are hereby ridiculed.
Ay, and cuckolded, too, for ought I know.

LADY FULBANK   Wise men knowing this, should not expose their
infirmities, by marrying us young wenches, who, without instruction,
find how we are imposed upon.

Enter fiddlers, playing, MR BEARJEST *and* DIANA *dancing,*
BREDWELL *and* NOISEY, *etc.*

LADY FULBANK   So, Cousin, I see you have found the way to Mrs.
Dy's heart.

BEARJEST   Who, I, my dear Lady Aunt? I never knew but one way to
a woman's heart, and that road I have not yet travelled. For my uncle,
who is a wise man, says matrimony is a sort of a. . . kind of a, as it
were, d'ye see, of a voyage, which every man of fortune is bound to
make one time or other, and Madam, I am, as it were, a bold
adventurer.

DIANA   And are you sure, Sir, you will venture on me?

BEARJEST   Sure, I thank you for that, as if I could not believe my
uncle, for in this case a young heir has no more to do, but to come
and see, settle, marry, and use you scurvily.

DIANA   How, Sir, scurvily?

BEARJEST   Very scurvily, that is to say, be always fashionably drunk,
despise the tyranny of your bed, and reign absolutely; keep a seraglio
of women, and let my bastard issue inherit; be seen once a quarter, or
so, with you in the park for countenance, where we loll two several
ways in the gilt coach like Fanus, or a spread-eagle.

DIANA   And do you expect I should be honest the while?

BEARJEST   Heaven forbid, not I, I have not met with that wonder in all my travels.

LADY FULBANK   How, Sir, not an honest woman?

BEARJEST   Except my Lady Aunt. Nay, as I am a gentleman and the first of my family, you shall pardon me, here, cuff me soundly. (*Kneels to her*)

Enter GAYMAN, *richly dressed*

GAYMAN   This love's a damned bewitching thing. Now, though I should lose my assignation with my devil, I cannot hold from seeing Julia tonight. Hah! There! And with a fop at her feet. Oh vanity of woman! (*Softly pulls her*)

LADY FULBANK   Oh Sir, you're welcome from Northamptonshire.

GAYMAN   (Hum, surely she knows the cheat.)

LADY FULBANK   You are so gay, you save me, Sir, the labour of asking if your uncle be alive.

GAYMAN   (Pray heaven she have not found my circumstances! But if she have, confidence must assist me.)
And, Madam, you're too gay for me to inquire
Whether you are that Julia which I left you?

LADY FULBANK   Oh doubtless, Sir. . .

GAYMAN   But why the devil do I ask? Yes, you are still the same: one of those hoiting ladies, that love nothing like fool and fiddle, crowds of fops, had rather be publicly though dully flattered than privately adored. You love to pass for the wit of the company, by talking all and loud.

LADY FULBANK   Rail on, till you have made me think my virtue at so low ebb it should submit to you.

GAYMAN   What, I'm not discreet enough.
I'll babble all in my next high debauch;
Boast of your favours, and describe your charms
To every wishing fool.

LADY FULBANK   Or make most filthy verses of me
Under the name of Cloris, you Philander,
Who, in lewd rhymes, confess the dear appointment,
What hour, and where, how silent was the night,
How full of love your eyes, and wishing mine.
Faith, no. If you can afford me a lease of your love
Till the old gentleman my husband depart this wicked world,
I'm for the bargain.

SIR CAUTIOUS   Hum, what's here, a young spark at my wife? (*Goes about them*)

GAYMAN   Unreasonable Julia, is that all
My love, my sufferings, and my vows must hope?
Set me an age, say when you will be kind,

And I will languish out in starving wish;
But thus to gape for legacies of love,
Till youth be past enjoyment,
The devil I will as soon. Farewell. (*Offers to go*)

LADY FULBANK   Stay, I conjure you, stay.

GAYMAN   (And lose my assignation with my devil.)

SIR CAUTIOUS   'Tis so, ay, ay. 'Tis so, and wise men will perceive it.
'Tis here, here in my forehead. It more than buds, it sprouts, it
flourishes.

SIR FEEBLE   So, that young gentleman has nettled him, stung him to
the quick. I hope he'll chain her up, the gad-bee's in his conundrum.
In charity I'll relieve him. Come my Lady Fulbank, the night grows
old upon our hands; to dancing, to jiggiting, come. Shall I lead
your Ladyship?

LADY FULBANK   No, Sir, you see I am better provided. . . (*Takes*
GAYMAN's *hand*)

SIR CAUTIOUS   Ay, no doubt on't, a pox on him for a young
handsome dog. (*They all dance*)

SIR FEEBLE   Very well, very well, now the posset, and then, ods bobs,
and then. . .

DIANA   And then we'll have t'other dance.

SIR FEEBLE   Away girls, away, and steal the bride to bed; they have
a deal to do upon their wedding nights, and what with the tedious
ceremonies of dressing and undressing, the smutty lectures of the
women by way of instruction, and the little stratagems of the young
wenches, ods bobs, a man's cozen'd of half his night. Come gentlemen,
one bottle, and then we'll toss the stocking.

Exeunt all but LADY FULBANK *and* BREDWELL, *who are talking,*
and GAYMAN

LADY FULBANK   But dost thou think he'll come?

BREDWELL   I do believe so, Madam.

LADY FULBANK   Be sure you contrive so he may not know whither,
or to whom he comes.

BREDWELL   I warrant you, Madam, for our parts.

Exit BREDWELL.   GAYMAN *attempts to sneak out*

LADY FULBANK   How now? What? Departing?

GAYMAN   You are going to the bride-chamber.

LADY FULBANK   No matter, you shall stay. . .

GAYMAN   I hate to have you in a crowd.

LADY FULBANK   Can you deny me? Will you not give me one lone
hour i'th' garden?

GAYMAN   Where we shall only tantalise each other with dull kissing,
and part with the same appetite we met? No, Madam. Besides I

have business.

LADY FULBANK   Some assignation, is it so indeed?

GAYMAN   Away! You cannot think me such a traitor. 'Tis most important business.

LADY FULBANK   Oh, 'tis too late for business, let tomorrow serve.

GAYMAN   By no means; the gentleman is to go out of town.

LADY FULBANK   Rise the earlier then. . .

GAYMAN   But, Madam, the gentleman lies dangerously sick, and should he die. . .

LADY FULBANK   'Tis not a dying uncle, I hope, Sir?

GAYMAN   Hum.   .

LADY FULBANK   The gentleman a-dying, and to go out of town tomorrow?

GAYMAN   Ay, he goes in a litter. 'Tis his fancy, Madam. Change of air may recover him.

LADY FULBANK   So may your change of mistress do me, Sir, farewell.

Exit LADY FULBANK

GAYMAN   Stay, Julia. Devil be damned, for you shall tempt no more. I'll love and be undone. But she is gone and if I stay the most that I shall gain is but a reconciling look, or kiss. . . No, my kind goblin, I'll keep my word with thee, as the least evil; A tantalizing woman's worse than devil.

ACT III

SCENE I

SIR FEEBLE'S HOUSE

A song made by MR CHEEK

> *No more, Lucinda, ah! expose no more*
> *To the admiring world those conquering charms:*
> *In vain all day unhappy men adore,*
> *What the kind night gives to my longing arms.*
> *Their vain attempts can ne'er successful prove,*
> *Whilst I so well maintain the fort of love.*
>
> *Yet to the world with so bewitching arts,*
> *Your dazzling beauty you around display,*
> *And triumph in the spoils of broken hearts*
> *That sink beneath your feet, and crowd your way.*
> *Ah! suffer now your cruelty to cease,*
> *And to a fruitless war prefer a peace.*

Enter RALPH *with light,* SIR FEEBLE, *and* BELLMOUR, *sad*

SIR FEEBLE   So, so, they're gone. Come, Francis, you shall have the
honour of undressing me for the encounter; but 'twill be a sweet one,
Francis.

BELLMOUR   (Hell take him, how he teases me!) (*Undressing him all the
while*)

SIR FEEBLE   But is the young rogue laid, Francis, is she stolen to bed?
What tricks the young baggages have to whet a man's appetite!

BELLMOUR   Ay, Sir. (Pox on him, he will raise my anger up to
madness, and I shall kill him to prevent his going to bed to her.)

SIR FEEBLE   A piss of these bandstrings. The more haste, the less
speed.

BELLMOUR   (Be it so in all things, I beseech thee, Venus.)

SIR FEEBLE   Thy aid a little, Francis. (BELLMOUR *pinches him by
the throat*) Oh, oh thou chok'st me! 'Sbobs, what dost mean?

BELLMOUR   You had so hampered 'em, Sir. (The devil's very
mischievous in me.)

SIR FEEBLE   Come, come, quick, good Francis. Adod, I'm as yare as a
hawk at the young wanton. Nimbly, good Francis, untruss, untruss.

BELLMOUR   (Cramps seize ye. What shall I do? The near approach
distracts me.)

SIR FEEBLE   So, so, my breeches, good Francis. But well, Francis, how
dost think I got the young jade, my wife?

BELLMOUR   With five hundred pound a year jointure, Sir.

SIR FEEBLE   No, that would not do, the baggage was damnably in love
with a young fellow they call Bellmour, they say, that's truth on't;
and a pretty estate. But, happening to kill a man, he was forced to fly.

BELLMOUR   That was great pity, Sir.

SIR FEEBLE   Pity! Hang him, rogue, 'sbobs, and all the young fellows
in the town deserve it. We can never keep our wives and daughters
honest for rampant young dogs, and an old fellow cannot put in
amongst 'em , under being undone, with presenting, and the devil and
all. But what dost think I did? Being damnably in love, I feigned a
letter as from the Hague, wherein was a relation of this same Bellmour
being hanged.

BELLMOUR   Is't possible, Sir, you could devise such news?

SIR FEEBLE   Possible, man! I did it, I did it! She swooned at the
news, shut herself up a whole month in her chamber, but I presented
high. She sighed and wept, and swore she'd never marry: still I
presented. She hated, loathed, spat upon me: still, adod, I presented.
Till I presented myself effectually in church to her, for she at last
wisely considered her vows were cancelled since Bellmour was hanged.

BELLMOUR   Sir, this was very cruel, to take away his fame, and then
his mistress.

SIR FEEBLE   Cruel! Thou'rt an ass! We are but even with the brisk
    rogues, for they take away our fame, cuckold us, and take away our
    wives. So, so, my cap, Francis.
BELLMOUR   And do you think this marriage lawful, Sir?
SIR FEEBLE   Lawful! It shall be when I've had livery and seisin of her
    body, and that shall be presently, rogue, quick. Besides, this Bellmour
    dares as well be hanged as come into England.
BELLMOUR   If he gets his pardon, Sir.
SIR FEEBLE   Pardon! No, no, I have took care for that, for I have,
    you must know, got his pardon already.
BELLMOUR   How, Sir! Got his pardon. That's some amends for
    robbing him of his wife.
SIR FEEBLE   Hold, honest Francis. What, dost think 'twas in
    kindness to him? No, you fool, I got his pardon myself, that nobody
    else should have it, so that if he gets anybody to speak to his Majesty
    for it, his Majesty cries he has granted it. But for want of my
    appearance he's defunct, trussed up, hanged, Francis.
BELLMOUR   This is the most excellent revenge I ever heard of.
SIR FEEBLE   Ay, I learnt it of a great politician of our times.
BELLMOUR   But have you got his pardon?
SIR FEEBLE   I've done't, I've done't. Pox on him, it cost me five
    hundred pounds, though. Here 'tis. My solicitor brought it me this
    evening. (*Gives it him*)
BELLMOUR   (This was a lucky hit, and if it 'scape me, let me be
    hanged by a trick indeed.)
SIR FEEBLE   So, put it into my cabinet, safe, Francis, safe.
BELLMOUR   Safe, I'll warrant you, Sir.
SIR FEEBLE   My gown, quick, quick, t'other sleeve, man. So now my
    night-cap. Well, I'll in, throw open my gown to fright away the
    women, and jump into her arms.

Exit SIR FEEBLE

BELLMOUR   He's gone. Quickly, oh love, inspire me!

Enter a FOOTMAN

FOOTMAN   Sir, my master, Sir Cautious Fulbank, left his watch on
    the little parlour table tonight, and bid me call for't.
BELLMOUR   Hah, the bridegroom has it, Sir, who is just gone to bed.
    It shall be sent him in the morning.
FOOTMAN   'Tis very well, Sir, your servant.

Exit FOOTMAN

BELLMOUR   Let me see. Here is the watch, I took it up to keep for
    him. But his sending has inspired me with a sudden stratagem that

will do better than force to secure the poor trembling Leticia, who,
I am sure, is dying with her fears.

Exit BELLMOUR

SCENE II

THE BEDCHAMBER

LETICIA *undressing by the women at the table. Enter* SIR FEEBLE
FAINWOOD

SIR FEEBLE   What's here? What's here? The prating women still. Ods
bobs, what, not in bed yet, for shame of love, Leticia?

LETICIA   For shame of modesty, Sir. You would not have me go to
bed before all this company.

SIR FEEBLE   What, the women! Why, they must see you laid.
'Tis the fashion.

LETICIA   What, with a man? I would not for the world. (Oh Bellmour,
where art thou with all thy promised aid?)

DIANA   Nay, Madam, we should see you laid indeed.

LETICIA   First in my grave, Diana.

SIR FEEBLE   Ods bobs, here's a compact amongst the women — high
treason against the bridegroom — therefore ladies, withdraw, or adod
I'll lock you all in. (*He throws open his gown; they run away, he locks
the door*) So, so, now we're alone, Leticia. Off with this foolish
modesty, and night-gown, and slide into my arms. (*She runs from
him*) H'e' my little puskin. What, fly me, my coy Daphne? (*He
pursues her. Knocking is heard*) Hah, who's that knocks, who's
there?

BELLMOUR   'Tis I, Sir, 'tis I, open the door presently.

SIR FEEBLE   Why, what's the matter, is the house o-fire?

BELLMOUR   Worse Sir, worse.

LETICIA   ('Tis Bellmour's voice!)

SIR FEEBLE *opens the door.* BELLMOUR *enters with the watch in
his hand*

BELLMOUR   Oh Sir, do you know this watch?

SIR FEEBLE   This watch!

BELLMOUR   Ay Sir, this watch?

SIR FEEBLE   This watch! Why prithee, why dost tell me of a watch?
'Tis Sir Cautious Fulbank's watch. What then, what a pox dost
trouble me with watches? (SIR FEEBLE *attempts to eject*
BELLMOUR, *who returns immediately*)

BELLMOUR   'Tis indeed his watch, Sir, and by this token he has sent
for you to come immediately to his house, Sir.

SIR FEEBLE   What a devil. . . art mad, Francis? Or is His Worship mad,
or does he think me mad? Go, prithee tell him I'll come tomorrow.
(SIR FEEBLE *continues his attempt to put him out*)

BELLMOUR   Tomorrow, Sir! Why all our throats may be cut before
we go to him tomorrow.

SIR FEEBLE   What say'st thou, throats cut?

BELLMOUR   Why, the City's up in arms, Sir, and all the aldermen
are met at Guildhall; some damnable plot, Sir.

SIR FEEBLE   Hah, plot, the aldermen met at Guildhall! Hum! Why,
let 'em meet, I'll not lose this night to save the nation.

LETICIA   Would you to bed, Sir, when the weighty affairs of state
require your presence?

SIR FEEBLE   Hum, met at Guildhall. My clothes, my gown again,
Francis, I'll out, out! What, upon my wedding night? No, I'll in.
(SIR FEEBLE, *putting on his gown, pauses, pulls it off again*)

LETICIA   For shame, Sir, shall the reverend council of the city debate
without you?

SIR FEEBLE   Ay, that's true, that's true. Come, truss again, Francis,
truss again. Yet, now I think on't, Francis, prithee run thee to the
hall, and tell 'em 'tis my wedding-night, d'ye see, Francis, and let
somebody give my voice for. . .

BELLMOUR   What, Sir?

SIR FEEBLE   Adod, I cannot tell. Up in arms, say you! Why, let 'em
fight. Dog fight bear, mun, I'll to bed. Go!

LETICIA   And shall his Majesty's service and safety lie unregarded for
a slight woman, Sir?

SIR FEEBLE   Hum, his Majesty! Come, haste, Francis, I'll away. And
call Ralph, and the footmen, and bid 'em arm; each man shoulder
his musket and advance his pike, and bring my artillery impliments
quick, and let's away. Pupsey, I'll bring it a fine thing yet before
morning, it may be. Let's away: I shall grow fond and forget the
business of the nation. Come, follow me, Francis.

Exit SIR FEEBLE. BELLMOUR *runs to* LETICIA

BELLMOUR   Now my Leticia, if thou e'er didst love,
If ever thou design'st to make me blest
Without delay fly this adulterous bed.

SIR FEEBLE   (*within*) Why, Francis, where are you, knave?

BELLMOUR   I must be gone lest he suspect us. I'll lose him and return
to thee immediately. Get thyself ready.

LETICIA   I will not fail, my love.

Exit BELLMOUR

Old man, forgive me, thou the aggressor art,
Who rudely forced the hand without the heart.
She cannot from the paths of honour rove,
Whose guide's religion, and whose end is love.

Exit LETICIA

SCENE III

A WASH-HOUSE, OR OUT-HOUSE

Enter BREDWELL, *disguised like a devil, with a dark lantern, leading* GAYMAN

BREDWELL   Stay here till I give notice of your coming.

Exit BREDWELL, *leaving his dark lantern*

GAYMAN   Kind light, a little of your aid. Now must I be peeping, though my curiosity should lose me all. Hah, zouns, what's here, a hovel or a hog-sty? Hum, see the wickedness of man, that I should find no time to swear in, but just when I'm in the devil's clutches.

Enter PERT, *dressed as an old woman, with a staff*

PERT   Good even to you, fair Sir.
GAYMAN   Ha, defend me! If this be she, I must rival the Devil, that's certain.
PERT   Come, young gentleman, dare not you venture?
GAYMAN   (He must be as hot as Vesuvius that does. I shall never earn my morning's present.)
PERT   What, do you fear a longing woman, Sir?
GAYMAN   (The devil I do, this is a damned preparation to love.)
PERT   Why stand you gazing, Sir? A woman's passion is like the tide, it stays for no man when the hour is come.
GAYMAN   (I'm sorry I have took it at its turning; I'm sure mine's ebbing out as fast.)
PERT   Will you not speak, Sir? Will you not on?
GAYMAN   I would fain ask a civil question or two first.
PERT   You know too much curiosity lost paradise.
GAYMAN   Why, there's it now.
PERT   Fortune and love invite you, if you dare follow me.
GAYMAN   (This is the first thing in petticoats that ever dared me in vain. Were I but sure she were but human now, for sundry considerations she might down, but I will on.)

She goes, he follows

SCENE IV

A CHAMBER IN THE APARTMENT OF LADY FULBANK

Enter PERT, *followed by* GAYMAN *in the dark. Soft music plays.
She leaves him*

GAYMAN   Hah, Music, and excellent!

SINGER

> *Oh! Love, that stronger art than wine,*
> *Pleasing delusion, witchery divine,*
> *Wont to be praised above all wealth,*
> *Disease that has more joys than health:*
> *Though we blaspheme thee in our pain,*
> *And of thy tyranny complain,*
> *We all are bettered by thy reign.*
>
> *What reason never can bestow,*
> *We to this useful passion owe.*
> *Love wakes the dull from sluggish ease,*
> *And learns a clown the art to please:*
> *Humbles the vain, kindles the cold,*
> *Makes misers free, and cowards bold.*
> *'Tis he reforms the sot from drink,*
> *And teaches airy fops to think.*
>
> *When full brute appetite is fed,*
> *And choked the glutton lies, and dead,*
> *Thou new spirits dost dispense,*
> *And find'st the gross delights of sense,*
> *Virtue's unconquerable aid,*
> *That against nature can persuade;*
> *And makes a roving mind retire*
> *Within the bounds of just desire.*
> *Cheerer of age, youth's kind unrest,*
> *And half the Heaven of the blest.*

GAYMAN   Ah, Julia, Julia! If this soft preparation were but to bring
me to thy dear embraces, what different motions would surround my
soul from what perplex it now?

*Enter nymphs and shepherds who dance. Then two dance alone. All
go out but* PERT *and a* SHEPHERD

If these be devils they are obliging ones. I did not care if I ventured
on that last female fiend.

SHEPHERD

> *Cease your wonder, cease your guess,*
> *Whence arrives your happiness.*
> *Cease your wonder, cease your pain,*
> *Human fancy is in vain.*

CHORUS

> *'Tis enough, you once shall find,*
> *Fortune may to worth be kind;*
> *And love can leave off being blind.*

They give him gold

PERT

> *You, before you enter here*
> *On this sacred ring must swear,*

PERT puts the ring on GAYMAN's finger, holds his hand

> *By the figure which is round,*
> *Your passion constant and profound;*
> *By the Adamantine Stone,*
> *To be fixed to one alone:*
> *By the lustre, which is true,*
> *Ne'er to break your sacred vow.*
> *Lastly, by the gold that's tried,*
> *For love all dangers to abide.*

They all dance about him, while PERT and SHEPHERD sing

SHEPHERD

> *Once about him let us move,*
> *To confirm him true to love.*

PERT

> *Twice with mystic turning feet,*
> *Make him silent and discreet.*

SHEPHERD

> *Thrice about him let us tread,*
> *To keep him ever young in bed.*

SHEPHERD

> *Forget Aminta's proud disdain;*
> *Haste here, and sigh no more in vain,*
> *The joy of love without the pain.*

PERT

> *That God repents his former slights,*
> *And fortune thus your faith requites.*

BOTH

> Forget Aminta's proud disdain;
> Then taste, and sigh no more in vain,
> The joy of love without the pain,
> The joy of love without the pain.

Exeunt all dancers. GAYMAN *looks on himself, and feels about him*

GAYMAN   What the Devil can all this mean? If there be a woman in the case, sure I have not lived so bad a life to gain the dull reputation of so modest a coxcomb, but that a female might down with me without all this ceremony? Is it care of her honour? That cannot be; this age affords none so nice. Nor fiend nor goddess can she be, for these I saw were mortal. No, 'tis a woman, I am positive. Not young nor handsome, for then vanity had made her glory to have been seen. No, since 'tis resolved a woman, she must be old and ugly, and will not baulk my fancy with her sight, but baits me more with this essential beauty.
Well, be she young or old, woman or devil,
She pays, and I'll endeavour to be civil.

SCENE V

IN THE SAME HOUSE

After a knocking, enter BREDWELL *in his masking habit, with his vizard in the one hand, and a light in the other, in haste*

BREDWELL   Hah, knocking so late at our gate.

He opens the door. Enter SIR FEEBLE, *dressed, and armed from head to toe, with a broad waist-belt stuck round with pistols, a helmet, scarf, buff-coat and half-pike*

SIR FEEBLE   How now, how now, what's the matter here?
BREDWELL   Matter? (What, is my lady's innocent intrigue found out?) Heavens, Sir, what makes you here in this warlike equipage?
SIR FEEBLE   What makes you in this showing equipage, Sir?
BREDWELL   I have been dancing among some of my friends.
SIR FEEBLE   And I thought to have been fighting with some of my friends. Where's Sir Cautious? Where's Sir Cautious?
BREDWELL   Sir Cautious, Sir? In bed.
SIR FEEBLE   Call him, call him quickly, good Edward.
BREDWELL   (Sure, my lady's frolic is betrayed and he comes to make mischief. However, I'll go and secure Mr Gayman.)

Exit BREDWELL

Enter SIR CAUTIOUS *and* DICK *with light*

DICK   Pray, Sir, go to bed. Here's no thieves. All's still and well.

SIR CAUTIOUS   This last night's misfortune of mine, Dick, has kept
me waking, and methought all night I heard a kind of a silent noise.
I am still afraid of thieves. Mercy upon me to lose five hundred
guineas at one clap, Dick. Hah, bless me! what's yonder? Blow the
great horn, Dick! Thieves! Murder, murder!

SIR FEEBLE   Why, what a pox, are you mad? 'Tis I, 'tis I, man.

SIR CAUTIOUS   I, who am 'I'? Speak — declare -- pronounce.

SIR FEEBLE   Your friend, old Feeble Fainwood.

SIR CAUTIOUS   How, Sir Feeble! (At this late hour, and on his
wedding night.) Why, what's the matter Sir, is it peace or war with
you?

SIR FEEBLE   A mistake, a mistake. Proceed to the business, good
brother, for time is precious.

SIR CAUTIOUS   (Some strange catastrophe has happened between
him and his wife tonight, and makes him disturb me thus.) Come, sit,
good brother, and to the business, as you say.

They sit, one at one end of the table, the other at the other. DICK
*sets down the light and goes out. Both sit gaping and staring and
expecting when either should speak*

SIR FEEBLE   As soon as you please, Sir. (Lord, how wildly he stares!
He's much disturbed in's mind.) Well Sir, let us be brief.

SIR CAUTIOUS   As brief as you please, Sir. Well, brother?

Pausing still

SIR FEEBLE   So, Sir.

SIR CAUTIOUS   (How strangely he stares and gapes — some deep
concern.)

SIR FEEBLE   Hum. . . hum.

SIR CAUTIOUS   I listen to you, advance.

SIR FEEBLE   Sir?

SIR CAUTIOUS   (A very distracted countenance. Pray Heaven he be
not mad, and a young wife is able to make an old fellow mad, that's
the truth on't.)

SIR FEEBLE   (Sure, 'tis something of his lady, he's so loth to bring it
out.) I am sorry you are thus disturbed, Sir.

SIR CAUTIOUS   No disturbance to serve a friend.

SIR FEEBLE   I think I am your friend indeed, Sir Cautious, or I
would not have been here upon my wedding night.

SIR CAUTIOUS   (His wedding night, there lies his grief, poor heart!
Perhaps she has cuckolded him already.) Well, come, brother, say
such things are done.

SIR FEEBLE   Done, hum, come, out with it. Brother, what troubles you tonight?

SIR CAUTIOUS   (Troubles me? Why, knows he I am robbed?)

SIR FEEBLE   I may perhaps restore you to the rest you've lost.

SIR CAUTIOUS   The rest, why, have I lost more since? Why, know you then who did it? Oh, how I'd be revenged upon the rascal!

SIR FEEBLE   ('Tis jealousy, the old worm that bites.) Who is it you suspect?

SIR CAUTIOUS   Alas, I know not whom to suspect, I would I did; but if you could discover him I would so swinge him.

SIR FEEBLE   I know him. What, do you take me for a pimp, Sir? I know him — there's your watch again, Sir. I'm your friend, but no pimp, Sir. (SIR FEEBLE *rises in rage*)

SIR CAUTIOUS   My watch, I thank you, Sir, but why pimp, Sir?

SIR FEEBLE   Oh, a very thriving calling, Sir, and I have a young wife to practise with. I know your rogues.

SIR CAUTIOUS   A young wife! ('Tis so, his gentlewoman has been at hot cockles without her husband, and he's horn-mad upon it. I suspected her be so close in with his nephew, in a fit with a pox.) Come, come, Sir Feeble, 'tis many an honest man's fortune.

SIR FEEBLE   I grant it, Sir, but to the business, Sir, I came for.

SIR CAUTIOUS   With all my soul.

They sit gaping and expecting when either should speak. Enter
BREDWELL *and* GAYMAN *at the door.* BREDWELL *sees them and puts* GAYMAN *back again*

BREDWELL   Hah, Sir Feeble and Sir Cautious there! What shall I do? For this way we must pass, and to carry him back would discover my lady to him, betray all, and spoil the jest. Retire, Sir, your life depends upon your being unseen.

They go out

SIR FEEBLE   Well, Sir, do you not know that I am married, Sir? And this my wedding night?

SIR CAUTIOUS   Very good, Sir.

SIR FEEBLE   And that I long to be in bed?

SIR CAUTIOUS   Very well, Sir.

SIR FEEBLE   Very good, Sir, and very well, Sir. Why then, what the Devil do I make here, Sir? (SIR FEEBLE *again rises in a rage*)

SIR CAUTIOUS   Patience, brother — and forward.

SIR FEEBLE   Forward! Lend me your hand, good brother, let's feel your pulse. How has this night gone with you?

SIR CAUTIOUS   Ha, ha, ha, this is the oddest conundrum. (Sure, he's mad, and yet, now I think on't, I have not slept tonight, nor shall I

ever sleep again till I have found the villain that robbed me.)
(SIR CAUTIOUS *weeps*)

SIR FEEBLE   (So, now he weeps — far gone — this laughing and
weeping is a very bad sign!) Come, let me lead you to your bed.

SIR CAUTIOUS   (Mad, stark mad.) No, now I'm up 'tis no matter,
pray ease your troubled mind. I am your friend — out with it — what,
was it acted, or but designed?

SIR FEEBLE   How, Sir?

SIR CAUTIOUS   Be not ashamed, I'm under the same predicament I
doubt, little better than a. . . but let that pass.

SIR FEEBLE   Have you any proof?

SIR CAUTIOUS   Proof of what, good Sir?

SIR FEEBLE   Of what? Why, that you're a cuckold, Sir, a cuckold if
you'll have it.

SIR CAUTIOUS   Cuckold! Sir, do ye know what ye say?

SIR FEEBLE   What I say?

SIR CAUTIOUS   Ay, what you say! Can you make this out?

SIR FEEBLE   I make it out!

SIR CAUTIOUS   Ay, Sir — if you say it, and cannot make it out,
you're a. . .

SIR FEEBLE   What am I, Sir? What am I?

SIR CAUTIOUS   A cuckold as well as myself, Sir. And I'll sue you for
Scandalum Magnatum. I shall recover swingeing damages with a City
jury.

SIR FEEBLE   I know of no such thing, Sir.

SIR CAUTIOUS   No, Sir?

SIR FEEBLE   No, Sir.

SIR CAUTIOUS   Then what would you be at, Sir?

SIR FEEBLE   I be at, Sir! What would you be at, Sir?

SIR CAUTIOUS   Ha, ha, ha! Why, this is the strangest thing, to see an
old fellow, a magistrate of the City, the first night he's married
forsake his bride and bed and come armed, cap-à-pied, like Gargantua,
to disturb another old fellow, and banter him with a tale of a tub,
and all to be-cuckold him here! In plain English, what's your business?

SIR FEEBLE   Why, what the Devil's your business, and you go to that?

SIR CAUTIOUS   My business, with whom?

SIR FEEBLE   With me, Sir, with me. What a pox do you think I do
here?

SIR CAUTIOUS   'Tis that I would be glad to know, Sir.

Enter DICK

SIR FEEBLE   Here, Dick, remember I've brought back your master's
watch. Next time he sends for me o'er night, I'll come to him in the
morning.

SIR CAUTIOUS   Ha, ha, ha, I send for you? Go home and sleep,

Sir, and ye keep your wife waking to so little purpose, you'll go near to be haunted with a vision of horn.

SIR FEEBLE   Roguery, knavery, to keep me from my wife — look ye, this was the message I received.

He goes to tell him. Enter BREDWELL *in a white sheet like a ghost, speaking to* GAYMAN *who stands within*

BREDWELL   Now, Sir, we are two to two, for this way you must pass to be taken in the lady's lodgings. I'll first adventure out to make you pass the safer (and that he may not, if possible, see Sir Cautious, whom I shall fright into a trance, I am sure. And Sir Feeble, the Devil's in it, if he know him).

GAYMAN   A brave kind fellow this.

BREDWELL, *stalking on as a ghost past the two old men*

SIR CAUTIOUS   Oh, undone, undone. Help, help! I'm dead, I'm dead!

SIR CAUTIOUS *falls down on his face.* SIR FEEBLE *stares and stands still*

BREDWELL   (As I could wish. Come on, thou ghastly thing, and follow me.)

Enter GAYMAN, *like a ghost, with a torch*

SIR CAUTIOUS   Oh, Lord! Oh, Lord!

GAYMAN   Hah! Old Sir Feeble Fainwood! Why, where the Devil am I? 'Tis he, and be it where it will I'll fright the old dotard for cozening my friend of his mistress. (GAYMAN *stalks on*)

SIR FEEBLE (*trembling*)   Oh guard me, guard me, all ye powers!

GAYMAN   Thou call'st in vain, fond wretch, for I am Bellmour,
Whom first thou robbed of fame and life,
And then what dearer was, his wife.

GAYMAN *goes out, shaking his torch at him*

SIR CAUTIOUS   Oh, Lord, Oh, Lord!

Enter LADY FULBANK *in an undress, and* PERT *undressed*

LADY FULBANK   Heavens, what noise is this? So he's got safe out, I see. (*Sees* SIR FEEBLE *armed*) Hah, what thing art thou?

SIR FEEBLE   Stay, Madam, stay — 'tis I, a poor trembling mortal.

LADY FULBANK   Sir Feeble Fainwood! Rise, are you both mad?

SIR CAUTIOUS   No, no, Madam, we have seen the Devil.

SIR FEEBLE   Ay, and he was as tall as the Monument!

SIR CAUTIOUS   With eyes like a beacon, and a mouth, Heaven bless us, like London Bridge at full tide.

SIR FEEBLE   Ay, and roared as loud.
LADY FULBANK   Idle fancies! What makes you from your bed, and
   you, Sir, from your bride?
SIR FEEBLE   Oh, that's the business of another day, a mistake only,
   Madam.
LADY FULBANK   Away, I'm ashamed to see wise men so weak —
   the phantoms of the night, or your own shadows, the whimsies of the
   brain for want of rest, or perhaps Bredwell, your Man, who, being
   wiser than his master, played you this trick to fright you both to bed.
SIR FEEBLE   Hum, adod, and that may be, for the young knave
   when he let me in tonight was dressed up for some waggery.
SIR CAUTIOUS   Ha, ha, ha, 'twas even so, sure enough, brother.
SIR FEEBLE   Ods bobs, but they frighted me at first basely. . . But
   I'll home to Pupsey. There may be roguery as well as here. Madam,
   I ask your pardon, I see we're all mistaken.
LADY FULBANK   Ay, Sir Feeble, go home to your wife.

SCENE VI

DARKNESS. THE STREET

Enter BELLMOUR. *He knocks at the door,* PHILLIS *opens it*

PHILLIS   Oh, are you come, Sir? I'll call my lady down.
BELLMOUR   Oh, haste, the minutes fly — leave all behind, and bring
   Leticia only to my arms.

   A noise of people

   Hah, what noise is that? 'Tis coming this way. I tremble with my
   fears, hah, death and the Devil, 'tis he.

   Enter SIR FEEBLE *and his men, armed. He too goes to the door,
   and knocks*

   Ay, 'tis he, and I'm undone — what shall I do to kill him now?
   Besides, the sin would put me past all hopes of pardoning.
SIR FEEBLE   A damned rogue to deceive me thus.
BELLMOUR   Hah — see, by Heaven, Leticia. Oh, we are ruined!
SIR FEEBLE   Hum, what's here, two women?

   SIR FEEBLE *stands a little off. Enter* LETICIA *and* PHILLIS
   softly, undressed, with a box

LETICIA   Where are you, my best wishes? Lord of my vows, and
   charmer of my soul? Where are you?
BELLMOUR   Oh, Heavens! (*He draws his sword half-way*)

SIR FEEBLE   (Hum, who's here? My gentlewoman — she's monstrous kind of the sudden. But whom is't meant to?)

LETICIA   Give me your hand, my love, my life, my all. Alas! Where are you?

SIR FEEBLE   (Hum, no, no, this is not to me. I am jilted, cozened, cuckolded, and so forth.)

Groping, she takes hold of SIR FEEBLE

LETICIA   Oh, are you here? Indeed you frighted me with your silence — here, take these jewels and let us haste away.

SIR FEEBLE   (Hum, are you thereabouts, mistress? Was I sent away with a sham plot for this? She cannot mean it to me.)

LETICIA   Will you not speak? Will you not answer me? Do you repent already? Before enjoyment are you cold and false?

SIR FEEBLE   (Hum, before enjoyment, that must be me. Before enjoyment.) Ay, ay, 'tis I. (*Merrily*) (I see a little prolonging a woman's joy sets an edge upon her appetite.)

LETICIA   What means my dear? Shall we not haste away?

SIR FEEBLE   (Haste away! There 'tis again. No, 'tis not me she means) What, at your tricks and intrigues already? Yes, yes, I am destined a cuckold!

LETICIA   Say, am I not your wife? Can you deny me?

SIR FEEBLE (*merrily*)   Wife! adod 'tis I she means, 'tis I she means.

LETICIA   Oh, Bellmour, Bellmour!

SIR FEEBLE *starts back from her hands*

SIR FEEBLE   Hum, what's that, Bellmour?

LETICIA   Hah! Sir Feeble! He would not, Sir, have used me thus unkindly.

SIR FEEBLE   Oh, I'm glad 'tis no worse. (Bellmour quoth 'a! I thought the ghost was come again.)

PHILLIS   Why did you not speak, Sir, all this while? My lady weeps with your unkindness.

SIR FEEBLE   I did but hold my peace to hear how prettily she prattled love. But fags, you are naught to think of a young fellow, ads bobs, you are now.

LETICIA   I only say he would not have been so unkind to me.

SIR FEEBLE   But what makes ye out at this hour, and with these jewels?

PHILLIS   Alas, Sir, we thought the City was in arms, and packed up our things to secure 'em, if there had been a necessity for flight. For had they come to plundering once, they would have begun with the rich Aldermen's wives, you know, Sir.

SIR FEEBLE   Ads bobs, and so they would. But there was no arms, nor mutiny. Where's Francis?

BELLMOUR   Here, Sir.

SIR FEEBLE   Here, Sir! Why, what a story you made of a meeting in the hall, and arms, and — a — the Devil of anything was stirring, but a couple of old fools that sat gaping and waiting for one another's business.

BELLMOUR   Such a message was brought me, Sir.

SIR FEEBLE   Brought! Thou'rt an ass, Francis, but no more — come, come, let's to bed.

LETICIA   To bed, Sir! What, by daylight? For that's hasting on. I would not for the world — the night would hide my blushes, but the day. . . would let me see myself in your embraces.

SIR FEEBLE   Embraces, in a fiddlestick. Why, are we not married?

LETICIA   'Tis true, Sir, and time will make me more familiar with you, but yet my virgin modesty forbids it. I'll to Diana's chamber. The night will come again.

SIR FEEBLE   For once you shall prevail, and this damned jaunt has pretty well mortified me. A pox of your mutiny, Francis. Come, I'll conduct thee to Diana and lock thee in, that I may have thee safe, rogue.
We'll give young wenches leave to whine and blush,
And fly those blessings which, ads bobs, they wish.

ACT IV

SCENE I

SIR FEEBLE'S HOUSE

Enter LADY FULBANK, GAYMAN, *sighing and gently pulling her back by the hand.* RALPH *meets them*

LADY FULBANK   How now, Ralph, let your lady know I am come to wait on her.

Exit RALPH

GAYMAN   Oh, why this needless visit? Your husband's safe, at least till evening, safe. Why will you not go back and give me one soft hour, though to torment me?

LADY FULBANK   You are at leisure now, I thank you, Sir. Last night when I, with all love's rhetoric pleaded, and Heaven knows what last night might have produced, you were engaged! False man, I do believe it, and I am satisfied you love me not.

She walks away in scorn

GAYMAN   Not love you!
  Why do I waste my youth in vain pursuit,
  Neglecting interest, and despising power?
  Unheeding and despising other beauties.
  Why at your feet are all my fortunes laid,
  And why does all my fate depend on you?
LADY FULBANK   I'll not consider why you play the fool,
  Present me rings and bracelets, why pursue me,
  Why watch whole nights before my senseless door,
  And take such pains to show yourself a coxcomb.
GAYMAN   Oh! Why all this?
  By all the powers above, by this dear hand,
  And by this ring, which on this hand I place,
  On which I've sworn fidelity to love,
  I never had a wish or soft desire
  To any other woman
  Since Julia swayed the empire of my soul.
LADY FULBANK   (Hah, my own ring I gave him last night.)
  Your jewel, Sir, is rich.
  Why do you part with things of so much value
  So easily, and so frequently?
GAYMAN   To strengthen the weak arguments of love.
LADY FULBANK   And leave yourself undone?
GAYMAN   Impossible, if I am blessed with Julia.
LADY FULBANK   Love's a thin diet, nor will keep out cold.
  You cannot satisfy your dunning tailor
  To cry — I am in love! Though possibly you
  May your seamstress.
GAYMAN   Does ought about me speak such poverty?
LADY FULBANK   I am sorry that it does not, since to maintain this
  gallantry 'tis said you use base means, below a gentleman.
GAYMAN   Who dares but to imagine it is a rascal, a slave, below a
  beating. What means my Julia?
LADY FULBANK   No more dissembling, I know your land is gone.
  I know each circumstance of all your wants. Therefore, as e'er you
  hope that I should love you ever, tell me where 'twas you got this
  jewel, Sir.
GAYMAN   (Hah — I hope 'tis not stolen goods.) Why, on the sudden,
  all this nice examining?
LADY FULBANK   You trifle with me and I'll plead no more.
GAYMAN   Stay — why — I bought it, Madam —
LADY FULBANK   Where had you money, Sir? You see, I am no
  stranger to your poverty.
GAYMAN   This is strange, perhaps it is a secret.
LADY FULBANK   So is my love, which shall be kept from you.

She attempts to go

GAYMAN (*sighing*)   Stay, Julia — your will shall be obeyed.
Though I had rather die than be obedient,
Because I know you'll hate me when 'tis told.
LADY FULBANK   By all my vows, let it be what it will,
It ne'er shall alter me from loving you.
GAYMAN   I have, of late, been tempted, with presents, jewels, and
large sums of gold.
LADY FULBANK   Tempted? By whom?
GAYMAN   The Devil, for ought I know.
LADY FULBANK   Defend me, Heaven! the Devil? I hope you have
not made a contract with him.
GAYMAN   No, though in the shape of a woman it appeared.
LADY FULBANK   Where met you with it?
GAYMAN   By magic art I was conducted — I know not how,
To an enchanted palace in the clouds, where I was so attended —
Young dancing, singing fiends innumerable.
LADY FULBANK   Imagination, all!
GAYMAN   But for the amorous Devil, the old Proserpine —
LADY FULBANK   Ay, she, what said she?
GAYMAN   Not a word. Heaven be praised, she was a silent Devil, but
she was laid in a pavilion all formed of gilded clouds which hung by
geometry, whither I was conveyed after much ceremony, and laid in
a bed with her, where, with much ado and trembling with my fears,
I forced my arms about her.
LADY FULBANK   (And sure that undeceived him.)
GAYMAN   But such a carcass 'twas, deliver me, so shrivelled, lean
and rough, a canvas bag of wooden ladles were a better bedfellow.
LADY FULBANK   (Now, though I know that nothing is more distant
than I from such a monster, yet this angers me.) Death! could you
love me and submit to this?
GAYMAN   'Twas that first drew me in. The tempting hope of means
to conquer you, would put me upon any dangerous enterprise. Were
I the Lord of all the universe, I am so lost in love, for one dear night
to clasp you in my arms I'd lavish all that world, then die with joy.
LADY FULBANK   ('Slife, after all to seem deformed, old, ugly.)

She walks in a fret

GAYMAN   I knew you would be angry when you heard it.

He pursues her in a submissive posture. Enter SIR CAUTIOUS,
BEARJEST, NOISEY *and* BREDWELL

SIR CAUTIOUS   How, what's here? My lady with the spark that
courted her last night? Hum, with her again so soon? Well, this

impudence and importunity undoes more City wives than all their
unmerciful finery.

GAYMAN   But Madam —

LADY FULBANK   Oh, here's my husband, you'd best tell him your
story. (*Angrily*) What makes him here so soon?

SIR CAUTIOUS   (Me his story! I hope he will not tell me he's a mind
to cuckold me.)

GAYMAN   (A Devil on him, what shall I say to him?)

LADY FULBANK   (What, so excellent at intrigues, and so dull at an
excuse?)

GAYMAN   Yes, Madam, I shall tell him —

Enter BELLMOUR

LADY FULBANK   Is my lady at leisure for a visit, Sir?

BELLMOUR   Always, to receive your ladyship.

She goes out

SIR CAUTIOUS   With me, Sir, would you speak?

GAYMAN   With you, Sir, if your name be Fulbank.

SIR CAUTIOUS   Plain Fulbank! Methinks you might have had a
Sir-reverence under your girdle, Sir. I am honoured with another
title, Sir —

SIR CAUTIOUS *goes talking to the rest*

GAYMAN   With many, Sir, that very well becomes you —

GAYMAN *pulls* SIR CAUTIOUS *a little aside*

I've something to deliver to your ear.

SIR CAUTIOUS   (So, I'll be hanged if he do not tell me I'm a cuckold
now. I see it in his eyes.) My ear, Sir! I'd have you to know I scorn
any man's secrets, Sir, for aught I know you may whisper treason
to me, Sir. (Pox on him, how handsome he is, I hate the sight of the
young stallion.)

GAYMAN   I would not be so uncivil, Sir, before all this company.

SIR CAUTIOUS   Uncivil! (Ay, ay, 'tis so, he cannot be content to
cuckold, but he must tell me so, too.)

GAYMAN   But since you will have it, Sir, you are a rascal, a most
notorious villain, Sir, d'ye hear?

SIR CAUTIOUS (*laughing*)   Yes, yes, I do hear — and am glad 'tis no
worse.

GAYMAN   Griping as Hell, and as insatiable, worse than a brokering
Jew, not all the Twelve Tribes harbour such a damned extortioner.

SIR CAUTIOUS   Pray under favour, Sir, who are you?

GAYMAN (*pulling off his hat*)   One whom thou hast undone.

SIR CAUTIOUS (*smiling*)   (Hum — I'm glad of that, however.)

GAYMAN   Racking me up to starving want and misery, then took advantage to ruin me.

SIR CAUTIOUS (*smiling*)   (So, and he'd revenge it on my wife.)

GAYMAN   Do you not know one Wasteall, Sir?

Enter RALPH *with wine, sets it on a table*

SIR CAUTIOUS   Wasteall — ha, ha, ha — if you are any friend to that poor fellow you may return and tell him, Sir, d'ye hear, that the mortgage of two hundred pound a year is this day out, and I'll not bait him an hour, Sir — ha, ha, ha — what, do you think to hector civil magistrates?

GAYMAN   Very well, Sir, and is this your conscience?

SIR CAUTIOUS   Conscience! What do you tell me of conscience? Why, what a noise is here, as if the undoing a young heir were such a wonder! Ods so, I've undone a hundred without half this ado.

GAYMAN   I do believe thee, and am come to tell you I'll be none of that number, for this minute I'll go and redeem it and free myself from the Hell of your indentures.

SIR CAUTIOUS   (How, redeem it! Sure the Devil must help him then.) Stay, Sir, stay. Lord, Sir, what need you put yourself to that trouble? Your land is in safe hands, Sir. Come, come, sit down, and let us take a glass of wine together, Sir.

BELLMOUR   Sir, my service to you.

GAYMAN   Your servant, Sir. (Would I could come to speak to Bellmour which I dare not do in public, lest I betray him. I long to be resolved where 'twas Sir Feeble was last night — if it were he — by which I might find out my invisible mistress.)

NOISEY   Noble Mr Wasteall.

NOISEY salutes him, so does BEARJEST

BELLMOUR   Will you please to sit, Sir?

GAYMAN   I have a little business, Sir, but anon I'll wait on you — your servant, gentlemen — I'll to Crap, the scrivener's.

GAYMAN *goes out*

SIR CAUTIOUS (*to* NOISEY)   Do you know this Wasteall, Sir?

NOISEY   Know him, Sir! Ay, too well.

BEARJEST   The world's well mended with him, Captain, since I lost my money to him and you at the George in Whitefriars.

NOISEY   Ay, poor fellow — he's sometimes up and sometimes down, as the dice favour him.

BEARJEST   Faith and that's pity. But how came he so fine o'th' sudden? 'Twas but last week he borrowed eighteen pence of me on his waistbelt to pay his dinner at an ordinary.

BELLMOUR   Were you so cruel, Sir, to take it?

NOISEY   We are not all one man's children. Faith, Sir, we are here today and gone tomorrow.

SIR CAUTIOUS   I say 'twas done like a wise man, Sir, but under favour, gentlemen, this Wasteall is a rascal.

NOISEY   A very rascal, Sir, and a most dangerous fellow. He cullies in your 'prentices and cashiers to play, which ruins so many o'th' young fry i'th'City.

SIR CAUTIOUS   Hum, does he so, d'ye hear that, Edward?

NOISEY   Then he keeps a private press and prints your Amsterdam and Leyden libels.

SIR CAUTIOUS   Ay, and makes 'em too, I warrant him. A dangerous fellow.

NOISEY   Sometimes he begs as a lame soldier with a wooden leg.

BEARJEST   Sometimes, as a blind man, sells switches in Newmarket Road.

NOISEY   At other times he roams the country like a gypsy; tells fortunes and robs hedges when he's out of linen.

SIR CAUTIOUS   Tells fortunes, too! Nay, I thought he dealt with the Devil. Well, gentlemen, you are all wide o' this matter, for to tell you the truth he deals with the Devil, gentlemen, otherwise he could never have redeemed his land.

BELLMOUR   How, Sir, the Devil!

SIR CAUTIOUS   I say the Devil! Heaven bless every wise man from the Devil.

BEARJEST   The Devil, hah! There's no such animal in nature. I rather think he pads.

NOISEY   Oh Sir, he has not courage for that, but he's an admirable fellow at your lock.

SIR CAUTIOUS   Lock! My study lock was picked! I begin to suspect him.

BEARJEST   I saw him once open a lock with the bone of a breast of mutton, and break an iron bar asunder with the eye of a needle.

SIR CAUTIOUS   Prodigious! Well, I say the Devil still.

Enter SIR FEEBLE

SIR FEEBLE   Who's this talks of the Devil! A pox of the Devil, I say, this last night's Devil has so haunted me.

SIR CAUTIOUS   Why, have you seen it since, brother?

SIR FEEBLE   In imagination, Sir.

BELLMOUR   How, Sir, a Devil?

SIR FEEBLE   Ay, or a ghost.

BELLMOUR   Where, good Sir?

BEARJEST   Ay, where? I'd travel a hundred mile to see a ghost.

BELLMOUR   Sure, Sir, 'twas fancy.

SIR FEEBLE   If 'twere a fancy, 'twas a strong one; and ghosts and
fancy are all one if they can deceive. I tell you, if ever I thought in
my life I thought I saw a ghost, ay, and a damnable impudent ghost
too, he said he was a fellow here they call Bellmour.

BELLMOUR   How, sir!

BEARJEST   Well, I would give the world to see the Devil, provided he
were a civil affable Devil, such a one as Wasteall's acquaintance is.

SIR CAUTIOUS   He can show him too soon, it may be. I'm sure, as
civil as he is, he helps him to steal my gold, I doubt, and to be sure,
gentlemen, you say he's a gamester. I desire when he comes anon,
that you would propose to sport a die or so, and we'll fall to play for
a teaster, or the like, and if he sets any money I shall go near to know
my own gold, by some remarkable pieces amongst it, and if he have
it, I'll hang him, and then his six hundred a year will be my own,
which I have in mortgage.

BEARJEST   Let the Captain and I alone to top upon him. Meantime
Sir, I have brought my music to entertain my mistress with a song.

SIR FEEBLE   Take your own methods, Sir, they are at leisure, while
we go drink their healths within. Adod I long for night. We are not
half in kilter, this damned ghost will not out of my head yet.

Exeunt all but BELLMOUR

BELLMOUR   Hah, a ghost! What can he mean? A ghost, and Bellmour
Sure, my good angel, or my genius, in pity of my love, and of Leticia
But see, Leticia comes, but still attended.

Enter LETICIA, LADY FULBANK, *and* DIANA

BELLMOUR (*aside to her, in passing by*)   (Remember, oh, remember
to be true.)

BELLMOUR *goes out*

LADY FULBANK   I was sick to know with what Christian patience
you bore the martyrdom of this night.

LETICIA   As those condemned bear the last hour of life. A short
reprieve I had, and by a kind mistake, Diana only was my bedfellow.
(*She weeps*)

DIANA   I wish for your repose you ne'er had seen my father. (*She
too weeps*)

LETICIA   And so do I, I fear he has undone me.

DIANA   And me, in breaking of his word with Bredwell.

LADY FULBANK   So, as Trinculo says, would you were both hanged for me, for putting me in mind of my husband, for I have e'en no better luck than either of you. Let our two fates warn your approaching one. I love your Bredwell and must plead for him.

DIANA   I know his virtue justifies my choice, but pride and modesty forbids I should, unloved, pursue him.

LETICIA   Wrong not my brother so, who dies for you.

DIANA   Could he so easily see me given away, without a sigh at parting? For all the day a calm was in his eyes, and unconcerned he looked and talked to me, in dancing never pressed my willing hand, nor with a scornful glance reproached my falsehood.

LETICIA   Believe me, that dissembling was his masterpiece.

DIANA   Why should he fear? Did not my father promise him?

LETICIA   Ay, that was in his wooing time to me, but now 'tis all forgotten.

Music at the door. After which enter BREDWELL *and* BEARJEST

LADY FULBANK   How now, Cousin! Is this high piece of gallantry from you?

BEARJEST   I find my cousin is resolved to conquer. He assails with all his artillery of charms. We'll leave him to his success, Madam.

Exeunt LETICIA *and* LADY FULBANK

Oh Lord, Madam, you oblige. Look, Ned, you had a mind to have a full view of my mistress, Sir, and here she is. (*He stands gazing*) Go, salute her. (Look how he stands now. What a sneaking thing is a fellow who has never travelled and seen the world!) Madam, this is a very honest friend of mine, for all he looks so simply.

DIANA   Come, he speaks for you, Sir.

BEARJEST   He, Madam! Though he be but a banker's 'prentice, Madam, he's as pretty a fellow of his inches as any i'th'City. He has made love in dancing schools, and to ladies of quality in the middle gallery, and shall joke ye, and repartee with any foreman within the Walls. Prithee to her, and commend me. I'll give thee a new point cravat.

DIANA   He looks as if he could not speak to me.

BEARJEST   Not speak to you! Yes, gad Madam, and do anything to you too.

DIANA   Are you his advocate, Sir?

BEARJEST (*scornfully*)   For want of a better.

BEARJEST *stands behind* BREDWELL, *pushing him on*

BREDWELL   An advocate for love I am, and bring you such a message from a heart.

BEARJEST   Meaning mine, dear Madam.

BREDWELL   That when you hear it, you will pity it.

BEARJEST   (Or the Devil's in her.)

DIANA   I have many reasons to believe it is my fortune you pursue,
not person.

BEARJEST   (There is something in that, I must confess.) But say
what you will, Ned.

BREDWELL   May all the mischiefs of despairing love fall on me if
it be.

BEARJEST   That's well enough.

BREDWELL   No, were you born an humble village maid, that fed a
flock upon the neighbouring plain, with all that shining virtue in
your soul, by Heaven I would adore you, love you, wed you, though
the gay world were lost by such a nuptial;

BEARJEST *looks on him.* BREDWELL *recollects himself*

this I would do, were I my friend the squire.

BEARJEST   Ay, if you were me you might do what you pleased,
but I'm of another mind.

DIANA   Should I consent, my father is a man whom interest sways,
not honour, and whatsoever promises he's made you he means to
break 'em all, and I am destined to another.

BEARJEST   How, another? His name, his name, Madam. Here's Ned
and I fear ne'er a single man i'th'nation. What is he, what is he?

DIANA   A fop, a fool, a beaten ass — a blockhead!

BEARJEST   What a damned shame's this, that women should be
sacrificed to fools, and fops must run away with heiresses, whilst
we men of wit and parts dress and dance, and cock and travel for
nothing but to be tame keepers.

DIANA   But I, by Heaven, will never be that victim.
But where my soul is vowed 'tis fixed forever.

BREDWELL   Are you resolved, are you confirmed in this?
O my Diana, speak it o'er again.

BREDWELL *runs to her, and embraces her*

Bless me, and make me happier than a monarch.

BEARJEST   Hold, hold, dear Ned, that's my part. I take it.

BREDWELL   Your pardon, Sir, I had forgot myself.
But time is short, what's to be done in this?

BEARJEST   Done! I'll enter the house with fire and sword, d'ye see;
not that I care this — but I'll not be fobbed off. What do they take
me for? A fool? An ass?

BREDWELL   Madam, dare you run the risk of your father's displeasur
and run away with the man you love?

DIANA   With all my soul.

BEARJEST   That's hearty, and we'll do't, Ned and I here. And I love
an amour with an adventure in't, like Amadis de Gaul. Hark ye, Ned,
get a coach and fix ready tonight when 'tis dark at the back gate.

BREDWELL   And I'll get a parson ready in my lodging, to which I
have a key through the garden by which we may pass unseen.

BEARJEST   Good. Mun, here's company.

Enter GAYMAN *with his hat and money in it,* SIR CAUTIOUS *in
a rage,* SIR FEEBLE, LADY FULBANK, LETICIA, CAPTAIN
NOISEY, *and* BELLMOUR

SIR CAUTIOUS   A hundred pound lost already! Oh coxcomb, old
coxcomb, and a wife coxcomb, to turn prodigal at my years. Why,
I was bewitched!

SIR FEEBLE   'Shaw, 'twas a frolic, Sir, I have lost a hundred pound
as well as you. My lady has lost, and your lady has lost, and the rest —
what, old cows will kick sometimes, what's a hundred pound?

SIR CAUTIOUS   A hundred pound! Why 'tis a sum, Sir, a sum!
Why, what the Devil did I do with a box and dice?

LADY FULBANK   Why, you made a shift to lose, Sir! And where's
the harm of that? We have lost and he has won; anon it may be your
fortune.

SIR CAUTIOUS   Ay, but he could never do it fairly, that's certain.
Three hundred pound! Why, how came you to win so unmercifully,
Sir?

GAYMAN   Oh, the Devil will not lose a gamester of me, you see, Sir.

SIR CAUTIOUS   The Devil! Mark that, gentlemen!

BEARJEST   The rogue has damned luck, sure; he has got a fly.

SIR CAUTIOUS   And can you have the conscience to carry away all
our money, Sir?

GAYMAN   Most assuredly, unless you have the courage to retrieve it.
I'll set it at a throw, or any way. What say you gentlemen?

SIR FEEBLE   Ods bobs, you young fellows are too hard for us every
way, and I'm engaged at an old game with a new gamester here who
will require all an old man's stock.

LADY FULBANK   Come Cousin, will you venture a guinea? Come,
Mr Bredwell.

GAYMAN   Well, if nobody dare venture on me, I'll send away my
cash.

They all go to play at the table, leaving SIR CAUTIOUS, SIR FEEBLE
and GAYMAN

SIR CAUTIOUS   Hum, must it all go? (A rare sum, if a man were but
sure the Devil would stand neuter now.) Sir, I wish I had anything
but ready money to stake: three hundred pound, a fine sum!

GAYMAN   You have moveables Sir, goods, commodities.

SIR CAUTIOUS   That's all one, Sir. That's money's worth, Sir, but if
 I had anything that were worth nothing.
GAYMAN   You would venture it. I thank you Sir. I would your
 lady were worth nothing.
SIR CAUTIOUS   Why so, Sir?
GAYMAN   Then I would set all 'gainst that nothing.
SIR CAUTIOUS   What, set it against my wife?
GAYMAN   Wife, Sir! Ay, your wife.
SIR CAUTIOUS   Hum, my wife against three hundred pounds! What,
 all my wife, Sir!
GAYMAN   All your wife! Why Sir, some part of her would serve my
 turn.
SIR CAUTIOUS   Hum — my wife. (Why, if I should lose, he could
 not have the impudence to take her.)
GAYMAN   Well, I find you are not for the bargain, and so I put up.
SIR CAUTIOUS   Hold, Sir, why so hasty? My wife? No, put up your
 money, Sir. What, lose my wife for three hundred pounds!
GAYMAN   Lose her, Sir! Why, she shall be never the worse for my
 wearing, Sir! (The old covetous rogue is considering on't I think.)
 What say you to a night? I sct it to a night. There's none need know
 it, Sir.
SIR CAUTIOUS   Hum — a night! Three hundred pounds for a night!
 (Why, what a lavish whoremaker's this? We take money to marry
 our wives but very seldom part with 'em, and by the bargain get
 money.) For a night, say you? (Gad, if I should take the rogue at his
 word 'twould be a pure jest.)
SIR FEEBLE   Are you not mad, brother?
SIR CAUTIOUS   No, but I'm wise, and that's as good. Let me
 consider.
SIR FEEBLE   What, whether you shall be a cuckold or not?
SIR CAUTIOUS   Or lose three hundred pounds — consider that. A
 cuckold! Why 'tis a word, an empty sound; 'tis breath, 'tis air, 'tis
 nothing. But three hundred pounds, Lord, what will not three
 hundred pounds do? You may chance to be a cuckold for nothing,
 Sir.
SIR FEEBLE   It may be so, but she shall do't discreetly then.
SIR CAUTIOUS   Under favour, you're an ass, brother. This is the
 discreetest way of doing it, I take it.
SIR FEEBLE   But would a wise man expose his wife?
SIR CAUTIOUS   Why, Cato was a wiser man than I, and he lent his
 wife to a young fellow they called Hortensius, as story says, and can
 a wise man have a better precedent than Cato?
SIR FEEBLE   I say Cato was an ass, Sir, for obliging any young rogue
 of 'em all.
SIR CAUTIOUS   But I am of Cato's mind. Well, a single night, you say.

GAYMAN   A single night: to have, to hold, possess and so forth at
discretion.

SIR CAUTIOUS   A night. I shall have her safe and sound i'th'morning?

SIR FEEBLE   Safe, no doubt on't, but how sound?

GAYMAN   And for non-performance you shall pay me three
hundred pounds. I'll forfeit as much if I tell —

SIR CAUTIOUS   Tell? Why, make your three hundred pounds six
hundred, and let it be put into the *Gazette* if you will, man. But is't
a bargain?

GAYMAN   Done. Sir Feeble shall be witness, and there stands my hat.

*GAYMAN puts down his hat of money and each of them takes a box
and dice, and kneel on the stage. The others come and watch*

SIR CAUTIOUS   He that comes first to one and thirty wins.

They throw and count

LADY FULBANK   What are you playing for?

SIR FEEBLE   Nothing, nothing, but a trial of skill between an old
man and a young — and your Ladyship is to be Judge.

LADY FULBANK   I shall be partial, Sir.

SIR CAUTIOUS   Six and five's eleven. (*Throws, and pulls the hat
towards him*)

GAYMAN   Quatre, trois. Pox of the dice.

SIR CAUTIOUS   Two fives — one and twenty. (*Sets up, pulls the hat
nearer*)

GAYMAN   Now, Luck — doublets of sixes — nineteen.

SIR CAUTIOUS   Five and four — thirty. (*Draws the hat to him*)

SIR FEEBLE   Now if he wins it, I'll swear he has a fly indeed. 'Tis
impossible without doublets of sixes.

GAYMAN   Now Fortune smile, and for the future frown. (*Throws*)

SIR CAUTIOUS   Hum, two sixes. (*He rises and looks dolefully around*)

LADY FULBANK   How now? What's the matter you look so like an
ass, what have you lost?

SIR CAUTIOUS   A bauble, a bauble! 'Tis not for what I've lost, but
because I have not won.

SIR FEEBLE   You look very simple, Sir, what think you of Cato now?

SIR CAUTIOUS   A wise man may have his failings.

LADY FULBANK   What has my husband lost?

SIR CAUTIOUS   Only a small parcel of ware that lay dead upon my
hands, sweetheart.

GAYMAN   But I shall improve 'em, Madam, I'll warrant you.

LADY FULBANK   Well, since 'tis no worse, bring in your fine dancer,
Cousin, you say you brought to entertain your mistress with.

BEARJEST goes out

GAYMAN   Sir, you'll take care to see me paid tonight?

SIR CAUTIOUS   Well, Sir, but my Lady, you must know, Sir, has
the common frailties of her sex, and will refuse what she even longs
for if persuaded by me.

GAYMAN   'Tis not in my bargain to solicit her, Sir. You are to
procure her, or three hundred pounds, Sir, choose you whether.

SIR CAUTIOUS   Procure her! With all my soul, Sir. Alas, you mistake
my honest meaning, I scorn to be so unjust as not to see you abed
together; and then agree as well as you can, I have done my part. In
order to this, Sir, get but yourself conveyed in a chest to my house
with a direction upon it for me, and for the rest —

GAYMAN   I understand you.

SIR FEEBLE   Ralph, get supper ready.

Enter BEARJEST *with dancers. All go out but* SIR CAUTIOUS

SIR CAUTIOUS   Well, I must break my mind, if possible, to my Lady,
but if she should be refractory now, and make me pay three hundred
pounds. . . ? Why, sure, she won't have so little grace. Three hundred
pounds saved is three hundred pounds got, by our account. Could all
Who of this City-Privilege are free,
Hope to be paid for cuckoldom like me,
Th'unthriving merchant, whom grey hair adorns,
Before all ventures would ensure his horns,
For thus, while he but lets spare rooms to hire,
His wife's cracked credit keeps his own entire.

ACT V

SCENE I

SIR CAUTIOUS' HOUSE

Enter BELLMOUR *alone, sad*

BELLMOUR   The night is come for my Leticia.
The longing bridegroom hastens to his bed,
Whilst she, with all the languishment of love
And sad despair, casts her fair eyes on me,
Which silently implore I would deliver her.
But how. Ay, there's the question — hah —
(*Pausing*)
I'll get myself hid in her bedchamber,
And something I will do may serve us yet.
If all my arts should fail I'll have recourse

(*Draws a dagger*)
To this, and bear Leticia off by force.
But see, she comes.

Enter LADY FULBANK, SIR CAUTIOUS, SIR FEEBLE, LETICIA,
BEARJEST, NOISEY, GAYMAN.   *Exit* BELLMOUR

SIR FEEBLE   Lights there, Ralph. And my Lady's coach there.

BEARJEST *goes to* GAYMAN

BEARJEST   Well, Sir, remember you have promised to grant me my
diabolical request, in showing me the Devil.
GAYMAN   I will not fail you, Sir.
LADY FULBANK   Madam, your servant. I hope you'll see no more
ghosts, Sir Feeble.
SIR FEEBLE   No more of that, I beseech you, Madam. Prithee, Sir
Cautious, take away your wife. Madam, your servant.

They all go out after the light

Come, Lette, Lette, hasten, rogue, hasten to thy chamber; away, here
be the young wenches coming.

Puts her out, he goes out

Enter DIANA, *puts on her hood and scarf*

DIANA   So, they are gone to bed. And now for Bredwell.
The coach waits and I'll take this opportunity.
Father, farewell. If you dislike my course,
Blame the old rigid customs of your force.

She goes out

SCENE II

A BEDCHAMBER

Enter SIR FEEBLE, LETICIA *and* PHILLIS

LETICIA   Ah, Phillis! I am fainting with my fears. Hast thou no
comfort for me?

SIR FEEBLE *undresses to his gown*

SIR FEEBLE   Why, what art doing there, fiddle fadling? Adod, you
young wenches are so loth to come to but when your hand's in. You
have no mercy upon us poor husbands.
LETICIA   Why do you talk so, Sir?
SIR FEEBLE   Was it angered at the Fool's prattle? tum-a-me, tum-a-me,

I'll undress it, effags I will, roguey.

LETICIA   You are so wanton, Sir, you make me blush. I will not go
to bed unless you'll promise me.

SIR FEEBLE   No bargaining, my little hussy. What, you'll tie my
hands behind me, will you?

She goes to the table

LETICIA   What shall I do? Assist me, gentle maid, thy eyes methinks
put on a little hope.

PHILLIS   Take courage, Madam, you guess right. Be confident.

SIR FEEBLE   No whispering, gentlewoman, and putting tricks into
her head that shall cheat me of another night. Look on that silly
little round chitty-face, look on those smiling roguish loving eyes
there, look, look how they laugh, twire and tempt. He, rogue, I'll
buss 'em there, and here, and everywhere. Ods bobs, away, this is
fooling and spoiling of a man's stomach, with a bit here and a bit
there. To bed, to bed.

*As she is sitting at her dressing table, he looks over her shoulder, and
sees her face in the glass*

LETICIA   Go you first, Sir, I will but stay to say my prayers (which
are that Heaven would deliver me).

SIR FEEBLE   Say thy prayers! What, art thou mad! Prayers upon
thy wedding night! A short thanksgiving or so, but prayers, quoth
'a. . . 'Sbobs you'll have time enough for that, I doubt.

LETICIA   I am ashamed to undress before you, Sir. Go to bed.

SIR FEEBLE   What, was it ashamed to show its little white foots, and
its little round bubbies? Well, I'll go, I'll go. I cannot think on't, no,
I cannot.

Going towards the bed, BELLMOUR *comes forth from between the
curtains, his coat off, his shirt bloody, a dagger in his hand, and his
disguise off*

BELLMOUR   Stand!

SIR FEEBLE   Ah!

LETICIA
and PHILLIS } (*squeak*)   Oh, Heavens!

LETICIA   Why, is it Bellmour?

BELLMOUR   Go not to bed! I guard this sacred place, and the
adulterer dies that enters here.

SIR FEEBLE   (Oh, why do I shake?) Sure I'm a man, what are thou?

BELLMOUR   I am the wronged, the lost and murdered Bellmour.

SIR FEEBLE   Oh, Lord, it is the same I saw last night — Oh! Hold thy
dread vengeance, pity me, and hear me. Oh! a pardon, a pardon.
(What shall I do? Oh! where shall I hide myself?)

BELLMOUR   I'th'utmost borders of the earth I'll find thee.
  Seas shall not hide thee, nor vast mountains guard thee.
  Even in the depth of Hell I'll find thee out,
  And lash thy filthy and adulterous soul.
SIR FEEBLE   Oh, I am dead, I'm dead! Will no repentance save me?
  'Twas that young Eve that tempted me to sin. Oh!
BELLMOUR   See, fair seducer, what thou'st made me do;
  Look on this bleeding wound, it reached my heart,
  To pluck my dear tormenting image thence,
  When news arrived that thou had'st broke thy vow.
LETICIA   Oh hide that fatal wound, my tender heart faints with a
  sight so horrid! (*She seems to weep*)
SIR FEEBLE   So, she'll clear herself, and leave me in the Devil's
  clutches.
BELLMOUR   You've both offended Heaven, and must repent or die.
SIR FEEBLE   Ah, I do confess I was an old fool, bewitched with
  beauty, besotted with love, and do repent most heartily.
BELLMOUR   No, you had rather yet go on in sin.
  Thou wouldst live on, and be a baffled cuckold.
SIR FEEBLE   Oh, not for the world, Sir! I am convinced and mortified.
BELLMOUR   Maintain her fine, undo thy peace to please her, and still
  be cuckold'on, believe her, trust her and be cuckolded still.
SIR FEEBLE   I see my folly, and my age's dotage, and find the Devil
  was in me. Yet spare my age, ah, spare me to repent.
BELLMOUR   If thou repent'st, renounce her, fly her sight,
  Shun her bewitching charms, as thou would'st Hell,
  Those dark eternal mansions of the dead
  Whither I must descend.
SIR FEEBLE   Oh, would he were gone!
BELLMOUR   Fly, be gone, depart, vanish forever from her to some
  more safe and innocent apartment.
SIR FEEBLE   Oh, that's very hard.

He goes back trembling, BELLMOUR *follows in, with his dagger up,
both go out*

LETICIA   Blest be this kind release, and yet, methinks, it grieves me
  to consider how the poor old man is frighted.

BELLMOUR *re-enters, puts on his coat*

BELLMOUR   He's gone, and locked himself into his chamber, and
  now, my dear Leticia, let us fly.
  Despair till now did my wild heart invade,
  But pitying love has the rough storm allayed.

                                                    Exeunt

SCENE III

SIR CAUTIOUS FULBANK'S GARDEN

Enter two PORTERS *and* RAG, *bearing* GAYMAN *in a chest. They set it down. He comes forth with a dark lantern*

GAYMAN   Set down the chest behind yon hedge of roses, and then put on those shapes I have appointed you, and be sure you well-favouredly bang both Bearjest and Noisey, since they have a mind to see the Devil.

RAG   Oh, Sir, leave 'em to us for that, and if we do not play the Devil with 'em, we deserve they should beat us. But Sir, we are in Sir Cautious' garden, will he not sue us for a trespass?

GAYMAN   I'll bear you out, be ready at my call.

They all go out, leaving GAYMAN

Let me see. I have got no ready stuff to banter with, but no matter, any gibberish will serve the fools. 'Tis now about the hour of ten, but twelve is my appointed lucky minute, when all the blessings that my soul could wish shall be resigned to me.

Enter BREDWELL

Hah! Who's there? Bredwell?

BREDWELL   Oh, are you come, Sir, and can you be so kind to a poor youth, to favour his designs and bless his days?

GAYMAN   Yes, I am ready here with all my Devils, both to secure you your mistress, and to cudgel your Captain and Squire for abusing me behind my back so basely.

BREDWELL   'Twas most unmanly, Sir, and they deserve it. I wonder that they come not.

GAYMAN   How durst you trust her with him?

BREDWELL   Because 'tis dangerous to steal a City heiress. And let the theft be his, so the dear maid be mine. Hark — sure they come.

Enter BEARJEST, *who runs into* BREDWELL

Who's there, Mr Bearjest?

BEARJEST   Who's that, Ned? Well, I have brought my mistress. Hast thou got a parson ready, and a licence?

BREDWELL   Ay, ay, but where's the lady?

BEARJEST   In the coach, with the Captain, at the gate. I came before to see if the coast be clear.

BREDWELL   Ay, Sir, but what shall we do? Here's Mr Gayman come on purpose to show you the Devil as you desired.

BEARJEST   Pshaw! A pox of the Devil, man, I can't attend to speak with him now.

GAYMAN   How, Sir! Do you think my Devil of so little quality to
    suffer an affront unrevenged?
BEARJEST   Sir, I cry his Devilship's pardon, I did not know his
    quality. I protest Sir, I love and honour him, but I am now just
    going to be married, Sir, and when that ceremony's past I'm ready to
    go to the Devil as soon as you please.
GAYMAN   I have told him your desire of seeing him and should you
    baffle him?
BEARJEST   Who I, Sir? Pray let his Worship know I shall be proud of
    the honour of his acquaintance, but, Sir, my mistress and the parson
    wait in Ned's chamber.
GAYMAN   If all the world wait, Sir, the Prince of Hell will stay for
    no man.
BREDWELL   Oh Sir, rather than the Prince of the Infernals shall be
    affronted, I'll conduct the lady up, and entertain her till you come
    Sir.
BEARJEST   Nay, I have a great mind to kiss his paw, Sir, but I could
    wish you'd show him me by daylight, Sir.
GAYMAN   The Prince of Darkness does abhor the light. But, Sir, I
    will for once allow your friend the Captain to keep you company.

Enter NOISEY *and* DIANA

BEARJEST   I'm much obliged to you, Sir. Oh, Captain — (*Talks to
    him*)
BREDWELL   Haste dear, the parson waits,
    To finish what the Powers designed above.
DIANA   Sure, nothing is so bold as maids in love.

                                                    They go out

NOISEY   Pshaw! He, conjure? He can fly as soon.
GAYMAN   Gentlemen, you must be sure to confine yourselves to this
    circle, and have a care you neither swear, nor pray.
BEARJEST   Pray, Sir! I dare say neither of us were ever that way gifted.

A horrid noise, then soft music

GAYMAN   Cease your horror, cease your haste,
    And calmly as I saw you last,
    Appear! Appear!
    By the pearls and diamond rocks,
    By thy heavy money-box,
    By thy shining petticoat,
    That hid thy cloven feet from note,
    By the veil that hid thy face,
    Which else had fright'd human race,

Appear, that I thy love may see,
Appear, kind fiends, appear to me.

Soft music ceases

(A pox of these rascals, why come they not?)

*Four enter from the four corners of the stage. To music that plays
they dance, and in the dance, dance around* BEARJEST *and* NOISEY
and kick, pinch and beat them

BEARJEST   Oh, enough, enough! Good Sir, lay 'em, and I'll pay the mus

GAYMAN   I wonder at it. These spirits are in their nature kind and
peaceable, but you have basely injured somebody; confess and they
will be satisfied.

BEARJEST   Oh good Sir, take you your Cerberuses off. I do confess,
the Captain here and I have violated your fame.

NOISEY   Abused you and traduced you, and thus we beg your pardon.

GAYMAN   Abused me! 'Tis more than I know, gentlemen.

BEARJEST   But it seems your friend the Devil does.

GAYMAN   (By this time Bredwell's married.) Great Pantamogun,
hold, for I am satisfied.

Exeunt DEVILS

And thus undo my charm.

Takes away the circle. BEARJEST *and* NOISEY *run out*

So, the fools are gone. And now to Julia's arms.

SCENE IV

LADY FULBANK'S ANTE-CHAMBER

She is discovered at her glass with SIR CAUTIOUS, *undressed*

LADY FULBANK   But why tonight? Indeed you're wondrous kind,
methinks.

SIR CAUTIOUS   Why, I don't know, a wedding is a sort of an alarm to
love, it calls up every man's courage.

LADY FULBANK   Ay, but will it come when 'tis called?

SIR CAUTIOUS   (I doubt you'll find it, to my grief.) But I think 'tis
all one to thee, thou care'st not for my compliment, no, thou'dst
rather have a young fellow.

LADY FULBANK   I am not used to flatter much. If forty years were
taken from your age 'twould render you something more agreeable to
my bed, I must confess.

SIR CAUTIOUS   Ay, ay, no doubt on't.

LADY FULBANK   Yet you may take my word without an oath; were you as old as Time and I were young and gay as April flowers, which all are fond to gather, my beauties all should wither in the shade, e'er I'd be worn in a dishonest bosom.

SIR CAUTIOUS   Ay, but you're wondrous free methinks, sometimes, which gives shrewd suspicions.

LADY FULBANK   What, because I cannot simper, look demure, and justify my honour when none questions it? Cry 'fie', and 'out upon the naughty women', because they please themselves, and so would I?

SIR CAUTIOUS   How, would what, cuckold me?

LADY FULBANK   Yes, if it pleased me better than virtue, Sir. But I'll not change my freedom and my humour, to purchase the dull fame of being honest.

SIR CAUTIOUS   Ay, but the world, the world.

LADY FULBANK   I value not the censures of the crowd.

SIR CAUTIOUS   But I am old.

LADY FULBANK   That's your fault, not mine.

SIR CAUTIOUS   But being so, if I should be good-natured and give thee leave to love discreetly —

LADY FULBANK   I'd do't without your leave, Sir.

SIR CAUTIOUS   Do't? What, cuckold me!

LADY FULBANK   No, love discreetly, Sir, love as I ought, love honestly.

SIR CAUTIOUS   What, in love with anybody but your own husband?

LADY FULBANK   Yes.

SIR CAUTIOUS   Yes, quoth'a! Is that your loving as you ought?

LADY FULBANK   We cannot help our inclinations, Sir, no more than time or light from coming on. But I can keep my virtue, Sir, entire.

SIR CAUTIOUS   What, I'll warrant, this is your first love, Gayman?

LADY FULBANK   I'll not deny that truth, though even to you.

SIR CAUTIOUS   Why, in consideration of my age, and your youth, I'd bear a conscience provided you do things wisely.

LADY FULBANK   Do what thing, Sir?

SIR CAUTIOUS   You know what I mean. . .

LADY FULBANK   Hah — I hope you would not be a cuckold, Sir.

SIR CAUTIOUS   Why, truly in a civil way, or so.

LADY FULBANK   There is but one way, Sir, to make me hate you, and that would be tame suffering.

SIR CAUTIOUS   (Nay, and she be thereabouts there's no discovering.)

LADY FULBANK   But leave this fond discourse, and, if you must, let us to bed.

SIR CAUTIOUS   Ay, ay, I did but try your virtue, mun, dost think I was in earnest?

Enter SERVANT

SERVANT   Sir, here's a chest directed to your Worship.
SIR CAUTIOUS   (Hum, 'tis Wasteall. Now does my heart fail me.)
   A chest, say you. . . to me. . . so late. I'll warrant it comes from
   Sir Nicholas Smuggle, some prohibited goods that he has stolen the
   custom of and cheated his Majesty. Well, he's an honest man, bring
   it in.

Exit SERVANT

LADY FULBANK   What, into my apartment, Sir, a nasty chest?
SIR CAUTIOUS   By all means, for if the searchers come, they'll never
   be so uncivil to ransack thy lodgings, and we are bound in Christian
   charity to do for one another. Some rich commodities, I am sure, and
   some fine nic-nac will fall to thy share, I'll warrant thee. (Pox on him
   for a young rogue, how punctual he is!)

SERVANTS *re-enter with the chest*

   Go, my dear, go to bed. I'll send Sir Nicholas a receipt for the chest,
   and be with thee presently.

SIR CAUTIOUS, SERVANTS *and* LADY FULBANK *leave*

GAYMAN *peeps out of the chest, and looks round him, wondering*

GAYMAN   Hah, where am I? By Heaven, my last night's vision! 'Tis
   that enchanted room, and yonder's the alcove! Sure 'twas indeed
   some witch, who, knowing of my infidelity, has by enchantment
   brought me hither. 'Tis so, I am betrayed. (*He pauses*) Hah! Or was
   it Julia that last night gave me that lone opportunity? But hark, I
   hear someone coming. (*He shuts himself in*)

Enter SIR CAUTIOUS

SIR CAUTIOUS (*lifting up the chest-lid*)   So, you are come, I see. (*He
   goes and locks the door*)
GAYMAN   (Hah — he here! Nay then, I was deceived, and it was
   Julia that last night gave me the dear assignation.)

SIR CAUTIOUS *peeps into the main bedchamber*

LADY FULBANK (*within*)   Come, Sir Cautious, I shall fall asleep
   and then you'll waken me.
SIR CAUTIOUS   Ay, my dear, I'm coming. She's in bed. I'll go put
   out the candle and then. . .
GAYMAN   Ay, I'll warrant you for my part.
SIR CAUTIOUS   Ay, but you may over-act your part, and spoil all.
   But, Sir, I hope you'll use a Christian conscience in this business.

GAYMAN   Oh doubt not, Sir, but I shall do you reason.

SIR CAUTIOUS   Ay, Sir, but. . .

GAYMAN   Good Sir, no more cautions; you, unlike a fair gamester, will rook me out of half my night. I am impatient.

SIR CAUTIOUS   Good Lord, are you so hasty? If I please, you shan't go at all.

GAYMAN   With all my soul, Sir. Pay me three hundred pounds, Sir.

SIR CAUTIOUS   Lord, Sir, you mistake my candid meaning still. I am content to be a cuckold, Sir, but I would have things done decently, d'ye mind me?

GAYMAN   As decently as a cuckold can be made, Sir. But no more disputes, I pray, Sir.

SIR CAUTIOUS   I'm gone! I'm gone! But hark ye, Sir, you'll rise before day?

> SIR CAUTIOUS *goes out, then returns*

GAYMAN   Yet again!

SIR CAUTIOUS   I vanish, Sir, but hark ye, you'll not speak a word, but let her think 'tis I.

GAYMAN   Begone, I say, Sir.

> SIR CAUTIOUS *runs out*

I am convinced last night I was with Julia.
O sot, insensible and dull!

Enter softly to the main bedchamber SIR CAUTIOUS

SIR CAUTIOUS   So, the candle's out. Give me your hand.

He leads GAYMAN *softly in*

SCENE V

SCENE CHANGES TO THE BEDCHAMBER

LADY FULBANK *supposed in bed.*
Enter SIR CAUTIOUS *and* GAYMAN *by dark*

SIR CAUTIOUS   Where are you, my dear? (*He leads* GAYMAN *to the bed*)

LADY FULBANK   Where should I be? In bed. What, are you by dark?

SIR CAUTIOUS   Ay, the candle went out by chance.

GAYMAN *signs to him to be gone. He makes grimaces as loth to go, and exits*

SCENE VI

SCENE DRAWS OVER, AND REPRESENTS ANOTHER ROOM
IN THE SAME HOUSE

Enter PARSON, DIANA *and* PERT *dressed in* DIANA's *clothes*

DIANA   I'll swear, Mrs Pert, you look very prettily in my clothes,
and since you, Sir, have convinced me that this innocent deceit is not
unlawful, I am glad to be the instrument of advancing Mrs Pert to a
husband she already has so just a claim to.
PARSON   Since she has so firm a contract, I pronounce it a lawful
marriage. But hark, they are coming, sure.
DIANA   Pull your hoods down, and keep your face from the light.

DIANA *runs out*

Enter BEARJEST *and* NOISEY, *disordered*

BEARJEST   Madam, I beg your pardon. I met with a most devilish
adventure. Your pardon too, Mr Doctor, for making you wait. But
the business is this, Sir, I have a great mind to lie with this young
gentlewoman tonight, but she swears if I do the parson of the parish
shall know it.
PARSON   If I do, Sir, I shall keep counsel.
BEARJEST   And that's civil, Sir. Come, lead the way,
With such a guide, the Devil's in't if we can go astray.

SCENE VII

SCENE CHANGES TO THE ANTE-CHAMBER

Enter SIR CAUTIOUS

SIR CAUTIOUS   Now cannot I sleep, but am as restless as a merchant
in stormy weather, that has ventured all his wealth in one bottom.
Woman is a leaky vessel: if she should like the young rogue now, and
they should come to a right understanding, why then I am a Wittal,
that's all, and shall be put in print at Snowhill with my effigies
o'th'top, like the sign of Cuckold's Haven. Hum, they're damnable
silent. Pray Heaven he has not murdered her, and robbed her. Hum,
hark, what's that? A noise! He has broke his covenant with me, and
shall forfeit the money. How loud they are! Ay, ay, the plot's
discovered, what shall I do? Why, the Devil is not in her, sure, to be
refractory now, and peevish. If she be, I must pay my money yet,

and that would be a damned thing. Sure, they're coming out. I'll
retire and hear how 'tis with them.

He retires

Enter LADY FULBANK *undressed,* GAYMAN *half undressed upon his knees following her, holding her gown*

LADY FULBANK   Oh! You unkind! What have you made me do?
Unhand me, false deceiver, let me loose!
SIR CAUTIOUS (*peeping*)   Made her do? So, so, 'tis done. I'm glad
of that.
GAYMAN   Can you be angry, Julia, because I only seized my right of
love.
LADY FULBANK   And must my honour be the price of it? Could
nothing but my fame reward your passion? What, make me a base
prostitute, a foul adult'ress? Oh, be gone, be gone, dear robber of my
quiet.
SIR CAUTIOUS   (Oh fearful!)
GAYMAN   Oh! Calm your rage, and hear me. If you are so,
You are an innocent adult'ress.
It was the feeble husband you enjoyed
In cold imagination, and no more.
Shyly you turned away, faintly resigned.
SIR CAUTIOUS   (Hum, did she so?)
GAYMAN   Till excess of love betrayed the cheat.
SIR CAUTIOUS   (Ay, ay, that was my fear.)
LADY FULBANK   Away, be gone. I'll never see you more.
GAYMAN   You may as well forbid the Sun to shine.
Not see you more! Heavens! I before adored you,
But now I rave! And with my impatient love,
A thousand mad and wild desires are burning!
I have discovered now new worlds of charms,
And can no longer tamely love and suffer.
SIR CAUTIOUS   (So, I have brought an old house upon my head,
Entailed cuckoldom upon myself.)
LADY FULBANK   I'll hear no more. Sir Cautious! Where's my
husband? Why have you left my honour thus unguarded?
SIR CAUTIOUS   (Ay, ay, she's well enough pleased, I fear, for all.)
GAYMAN   Base as he is, 'twas he exposed this treasure, like silly
Indians bartered thee for trifles.
SIR CAUTIOUS   (Oh treacherous villain!)
LADY FULBANK   Hah, my husband do this?
GAYMAN   He, by love, he was the kind procurer,
Contrived the means, and brought me to thy bed.
LADY FULBANK   My husband! My wise husband!

What fondness in my conduct had he seen,
To take so shameful and so base revenge?
GAYMAN   None. 'Twas filthy avarice seduced him to't.
LADY FULBANK   If he could be so barbarous to expose me,
Could you, who loved me, be so cruel too?
GAYMAN   What, to possess thee when the bliss was offered?
Possess thee too without a crime to thee?
Charge not my soul with so remiss a flame,
So dull a sense of virtue to refuse it.
LADY FULBANK   I am convinced the fault was all my husband's.
(*Kneels*) And here I vow, by all things just and sacred,
To separate forever from his bed.
SIR CAUTIOUS   (Oh, I am not able to endure it.)
Hold, oh hold, my dear.

He kneels as she rises

LADY FULBANK   Stand off! I do abhor thee.
SIR CAUTIOUS   With all my soul, but do not make rash vows, they
break my very heart. Regard my reputation.
LADY FULBANK   Which you have had such care of, Sir, already.
Rise, 'tis in vain you kneel.
SIR CAUTIOUS   No, I'll never rise again. Alas! Madam, I was merely
drawn in. I only thought to sport a die or so, I had only an innocent
design to have discovered whether this gentleman had stolen my gold,
that so I might have hanged him.
GAYMAN   A very innocent design, indeed!
SIR CAUTIOUS   Ay, Sir, that's all, as I'm an honest man.
LADY FULBANK   I've sworn, nor are the stars more fixed than I.

Enter SERVANT

SERVANT   How! my Lady, and his Worship up? Madam, a gentleman
and a lady below in a coach knocked me up, and say they must speak
with your Ladyship.
LADY FULBANK   This is strange! Bring them up.

Exit SERVANT

Who can it be, at this odd time of neither night nor day?

Enter LETICIA, BELLMOUR *and* PHILLIS

LETICIA   Madam, your virtue, charity and friendship to me, has made
me trespass on you for my life's security, and beg you will protect
me, and my husband.

She points at BELLMOUR

SIR CAUTIOUS   So, here's another sad catastrophe!

LADY FULBANK   Hah, does Bellmour live? Is't possible? Believe me,
    Sir, you ever had my wishes, and shall not fail of my protection now.
BELLMOUR   I humbly thank your Ladyship.
GAYMAN   I'm glad thou hast her, Harry, but doubt thou durst not
    own her. Nay, durst not own thyself.
BELLMOUR   Yes, friend, I have my pardon.
    But, hark, I think we are pursued already;
    But now I fear no force.

A noise of somebody coming in

LADY FULBANK   However, step into my bedchamber.

            Exeunt LETICIA, GAYMAN, BELLMOUR *and* PHILLIS

Enter SIR FEEBLE *in an antic manner*

SIR FEEBLE   Hell shall not hold thee, nor vast mountains cover thee,
    but I will find thee out and lash thy filthy and adulterous carcass.

Coming up in a menacing manner to SIR CAUTIOUS

SIR CAUTIOUS   How, lash my filthy carcass? I defy thee, Satan.
SIR FEEBLE   'Twas thus he said.
SIR CAUTIOUS   Let who will say it, he lies in's throat.
SIR FEEBLE   How, the ghostly, hush, have a care, for 'twas the
    ghost of Bellmour. Oh, hide that bleeding wound, it chills my soul!

Runs to LADY FULBANK

LADY FULBANK   What bleeding wound? Heavens, are you frantic,
    Sir?
SIR FEEBLE   No. But for want of rest, I shall e'er morning. She's
    gone, she's gone, she's gone. (*He weeps*)
SIR CAUTIOUS   Ay, ay, she's gone, she's gone, indeed. (*He weeps
    too*)
SIR FEEBLE   But her let go, so I may never see that dreaded vision. . .
    Hark ye, Sir, a word in your ear: have a care of marrying a young\wife.
SIR CAUTIOUS (*weeping*)   Ay, but I have married one already.
SIR FEEBLE   Hast thou? Divorce her, fly her, quick. Depart, be
    gone, she'll cuckold thee, and still she'll cuckold thee.
SIR CAUTIOUS   Ay, brother, but whose fault was that? Why, are
    not you married?
SIR FEEBLE   Mum! No words on't, unless you'll have the ghost
    about your ears. Part with your wife, I say, or else the Devil will
    part ye.
LADY FULBANK   Pray go to bed, Sir.
SIR FEEBLE   Yes, for I shall sleep now I shall lie alone. (*Weeps*)
    Ah, fool, old, dull, besotted fool, to think she'd love me. 'Twas

by base means I gained her; cozened an honest gentleman of fame
and life.

LADY FULBANK   You did so, Sir, but 'tis not past redress, you may
make that honest gentleman amends.

SIR FEEBLE   Oh would I could, so I gave half my estate.

LADY FULBANK   That penitence atones with him and Heaven.
Come forth, Leticia, and your injured ghost.

Re-enter LETICIA, GAYMAN, BELLMOUR *and* PHILLIS

SIR FEEBLE   Hah, ghost! Another sight would make me mad indeed.

BELLMOUR   Behold me, Sir, I have no terror now.

SIR FEEBLE   Hah, who's that, Francis! My nephew Francis?

BELLMOUR   Bellmour, or Francis, choose you which you like, and I
am either.

SIR FEEBLE   Hah, Bellmour! And no ghost?

BELLMOUR   Bellmour, and not your nephew, Sir.

SIR FEEBLE   But art alive? Ods bobs, I'm glad on't, Sirrah. But are
you the real Bellmour?

BELLMOUR   As sure as I'm no ghost.

GAYMAN   We all can witness for him, Sir.

SIR FEEBLE   Where be the minstrels? We'll have a dance, adod we
will. Ah! Art thou there, thou cozening little chits-face? A vengeance
on thee, thou madest me an old, doting, loving coxcomb, but I forgive
thee, and give thee all thy jewels, and you your pardon, Sir, so you'll
give me mine, for I find you young knaves will be too hard for us.

BELLMOUR   You are so generous, Sir, that 'tis almost with grief I
receive the blessing of Leticia.

SIR FEEBLE   No, no, thou deservest her, she would have made an
old, fond blockhead of me, and one way or other you would have
had her, ods bobs, you would.

Enter BEARJEST, DIANA, PERT, BREDWELL *and* NOISEY

BEARJEST   Justice, Sir, justice! I have been cheated, abused,
assassinated and ravished!

SIR CAUTIOUS   How, my nephew ravished?

PERT   No, Sir, I am his wife.

SIR CAUTIOUS   Hum! My heir marry a chambermaid!

BEARJEST   Sir, you must know I stole away Mrs Dy, and brought her
to Ned's chamber here to marry her.

SIR FEEBLE   My daughter Dy stolen!

BEARJEST   But I being to go to the Devil a little, Sir, whip, what
does he, but marries her himself, Sir, and fobbed me off here with my
lady's cast petticoat.

NOISEY   Sir, she's a gentlewoman, and my sister, Sir.

PERT   Madam, 'twas a pious fraud, if it were one, for I was contracted
to him before. See, here it is.

Gives it 'em

ALL   A plain case, a plain case.

SIR FEEBLE   Hark ye, Sir, have you had the impudence to marry my daughter, Sir?

To BREDWELL, *who, with* DIANA, *kneels*

BREDWELL   Yes, Sir, and humbly ask your pardon, and your blessing.

SIR FEEBLE   You will ha't, whether I will or not, rise, you are still too hard for us. Come, Sir, forgive your nephew.

SIR CAUTIOUS   Well, Sir, I will, but all this while you little think the tribulation I am in; my Lady has forsworn my bed.

SIR FEEBLE   Indeed, Sir, the wiser she.

SIR CAUTIOUS   For only performing my promise to this gentleman.

SIR FEEBLE   Ay, you showed her the difference, Sir, you're a wise man. Come, dry your eyes, and rest yourself contented. We are a couple of old coxcombs. D'ye hear, Sir, coxcombs.

SIR CAUTIOUS   I grant it, Sir, and if I die, Sir, I bequeath my Lady to you, with my whole estate. My nephew has too much already for a fool. (*To* GAYMAN)

GAYMAN   I thank you, Sir. Do you consent, my Julia?

LADY FULBANK   No, Sir, you do not like me: 'a canvas bag of wooden ladles were a better bedfellow'.

GAYMAN   Cruel tormentor! Oh, I could kill myself with shame and anger!

LADY FULBANK   Come hither, Bredwell. Witness for my honour, that I had no design upon his person but that of trying his constancy.

BREDWELL   Believe me, Sir, 'tis true I feigned a danger near just as you got to bed, and I was the kind Devil, Sir, that brought the gold to you.

BEARJEST   And you were one of the Devils that beat me and the Captain here, Sir?

GAYMAN   No, truly, Sir, those were some I hired to beat you for abusing me today.

NOISEY   To make you amends, Sir, I bring you the certain news of the death of Sir Thomas Gayman, your uncle, who has left you two thousand pounds a year.

GAYMAN   I thank you, Sir. I heard the news before.

SIR CAUTIOUS   How's this, Mr Gayman, my Lady's first lover?
I find, Sir Feeble, we were a couple of old fools indeed, to think at our age to cozen two lusty young fellows of their mistresses. 'Tis no wonder that both the men and the women have been too hard for us; we are not fit matches for either, that's the truth on't.
That warrior needs must to his rival yield,
Who comes with blunted weapons to the field.

THE FATAL FRIENDSHIP

BY

CATHERINE TROTTER

first performed Lincoln's Inn Fields Theatre, *c*. May 1698

The Fatal Friendship is a tragedy of situation rather than of character. The source of its situation is Catherine Trotter's admiration of Thomas Otway's two most successful tragedies. From *The Orphan* (1680) she took the unconsummated bigamy, but made one of her men choose the predicament into which Otway had propelled his heroine. And, although the friendship of her title has exact and obvious parallel in Otway's *Venice Preserved* (1682), she also took the insensitive father who afflicts its heroine, and gave him as an extra nuisance to her Gramont. However, where Otway's heroines were pitiable victims, there only to wail, the women in *The Fatal Friendship* are as active as anyone in bringing about calamity.

Contemporary tragedies of situation had been fundamentally static plays, in which pressure shifted, first on to one victim, then on to another, so that each could take turns in venting as much painful emotion in as highly-coloured language as possible, verging towards, and sometimes touching on, madness. But, like the language of her play, Catherine Trotter's characters are notable for their restraint. Because they are all so devoted to secrecy, reluctant to tell all at once, and conceal the most crucial points for as long as they can bear, their fates are always pending, the outcome hangs in the balance, and there is suspense to the last.

Some of her most charged scenes result from these uncertainties. In the two interviews between Felicia and Lamira, for instance, each at some point takes the upper hand. It is never clear which is torturer, which victim, and the roles switch, and switch over again. The secrets and the lies are, predictably, exposed, but the timing is not predictable, and on it the effect depends. Once all the possible catastrophes are irrevocably complete, Gramont hears the King has changed heart, and he reproaches himself for failing to await 'providence'. The obvious reaction is to wonder why providence (or the King) dallied so long, though, of course, swifter action, sparing suffering, would mean no play. The theological gesture here has no connection with the excitements of the drama preceding it, but the discrepancy already suggests that when Catherine Trotter turned all her attention to theology, drama would no longer concern her.

CHARACTERS

COUNT ROQUELAURE, rich and in love with Felicia

GRAMONT, his son, secretly married to Felicia for two years; recently returned from the war against Spain

CASTALIO, Gramont's close friend and fellow officer in the French army; a Neapolitan, in love with Lamira

FELICIA, secretly married to Gramont; has borne him a son

BELLGARD, Felicia's brother

LAMIRA, a young widow, related to Bellgard and Felicia; secretly in love with Gramont

BERNARDO, a Neapolitan officer in the French army under Castalio

MARIAN, Lamira's maidservant

A Soldier; servants; attendants

The action takes place in France, after a war against Spain.

ACT I

SCENE I

Enter BELLGARD *and* FELICIA

BELLGARD   Felicia, you are young and full of hopes,
Unknowing how the world will disappoint 'em,
But I have seen such strange unlook'd for chances,
Such fatal blasts to blooming expectations,
As teaches me judiciously to fear,
And cautiously advise. Can I remember
Our noble family in dazzling splendours,
As rich as ancient, made the mark of envy,
Now, by an enemy's successful faction
Maliciously unjust, without regard,
Reduc'd so low, that I (the only left,
To keep our name from falling with our fortune)
Have but sufficient means, with thrifty care,
Just to preserve you, and your infant sisters,
From asking help at charitable hands.
Can I consider this,
And not use all a brother's interest in you
To move you to embrace a happy offer,
To place you sure in that exalted rank,
Which both by birth and merit is your due?

FELICIA   You have so dear an interest in my heart,
That tho' you had not all authority,
Yet ever where I could control myself,
You still should govern me. But Oh my brother,
There is a strong reluctance in my soul,
Which to myself denies me my consent,
For this unequal match.

BELLGARD   'Tis true the Count Roquelaure has not the charms of
      youth,
But then consider, he's without their faults.
I've weighed it for you with a brother's love,
And find the youthful balance far the lighter.
Marriage requires a steady, ripen'd virtue,
Judgement to choose, solidity to fix,
Prudence to govern, all by experience perfected.

FELICIA   'Tis not the Count's grave years makes me abhor the match,
But some more secret cause, yet to myself unknown.

BELLGARD   Sister, I fear you know the cause too well;
He's father to Gramont. Ha! that conscious blush

Confesses I have guessed it,
A shameful witness of your childish passion.
Is it not time to throw away the toy
You cried for when a girl?

FELICIA   Forgive me an involuntary fault.
Love took possession of my infant heart,
Grew up with me, a dear, familiar guest,
And now refuses to remove his seat.

BELLGARD   Reason must dispossess him.

FELICIA   Could reason tell me, I had placed my love
On a vile object, half the work were done.
But you have owned he merits all your friendship.
Nay, 'twas your fondness for him first raised mine,
And all that can be offered now against him
Amounts to this: that he's a younger brother,
Whose fortune is injurious to his worth.

BELLGARD   Could yours repair the wrong his fortune does him,
I could with joy bestow you to your wishes,
But am too fond, too tender of you both,
To give consent, that you should starve together.
For shame, Felicia, let not passion sway you
Thus to your ruin.
I have till now giv'n way to all your folly,
In hopes that time and absence would destroy it,
Nor ever pressed you to a second choice,
These full two years since first I knew your loves,
And made Gramont forbear to visit you,
But must no longer thus indulge your weakness.

FELICIA   If for two years I have forborne to see him,
Is not that sacrifice sufficient from a sister?
Must I be made the next to one I hate?
You cannot be so cruel; do but defer it,
Who knows the turns of fortune?
You have seen, you say, a fatal one in ours.
Why may not those, who now are at the lowest,
By some more happy chance be raised as high?

BELLGARD   There's not a ground to hope for young Gramont.
He meant to raise his fortune as a soldier,
And might have reached the noblest height in war,
Had not that fatal quarrel, in which he killed
The general's only son, soon stopped his progress,
In whose revengeful father he will find
An enemy, as powerful at court,
As in the army.

FELICIA   'Twas well he 'scaped with life.

BELLGARD   For the security of the survivor,
   They would not fight in France,
   And yet the general at his return,
   By arbitrary law, condemned, and would have shot him,
   Had not his noble friend, the brave Castalio,
   Charged on his guard, freed him, and kept the sight,
   Till he escaped in safety.
FELICIA   (For which may he, or never need, or always find a friend.)
BELLGARD   You see the desperate state of his affairs,
   Therefore be wise, and tempt not your ill fate.
   Either resolve to marry Count Roquelaure,
   Or share a beggar's fortune with his son.
FELICIA   Why would you force me to a wretched choice?
   You have been hitherto a parent to me.
   How am I grown so burdensome a charge
   That you would cast me from you, tho' to ruin?
BELLGARD   I would prevent your ruin and my own,
   And if you'd have me still a parent to you,
   I shall expect th'obedience of a daughter,
   Or else by heav'n, I'll turn you to your lover.

Exit BELLGARD

FELICIA   Then I must perish with him. Alas! my brother,
   Thou little think'st to what thou dost persuade me.
   My husband's father? Oh my barbarous stars!
   For sure love could not shoot so cross a dart.
   What's to be done? Should I confess our marriage?
   Oh no, his fiery temper could not brook it!
   And how would my Gramont's harsh father use him?

Enter GRAMONT

   Oh! He is sent by heav'n to my relief!
   My dear Gramont!
GRAMONT   My dearest wife, what sadness hangs upon thee?
   Am I not welcome to those weeping eyes?
FELICIA   More than the light; but they have cause to weep
   For you, and me, and for our helpless infant.
   My brother has been pleading for your father;
   Threatens, if I refuse to marry him,
   To throw me, as a stranger, from his care.
GRAMONT   My poor Felicia, what thou bearest for me.
   How shall I recompense thy suffering virtue?
   Oh, what a line of woes I fixed thee to,
   When Hymen drew the knot!
FELICIA   Do you repent that knot?

GRAMONT   By Heav'n, my love, I cannot.
FELICIA   Then I am happy.
GRAMONT   Nothing is so, that's placed within my fate:
    A wretch but born to scatter miseries
    On all, whom love brings near enough to reach 'em.
FELICIA   Have you received no news yet of our child?
GRAMONT   None for this full three weeks, which much concerns me,
    But I have sent a messenger express
    To learn its health, who will return this day.
FELICIA   Heav'n guard the tender babe.
GRAMONT   Oh! my heart bleeds for that dear part of me.
    Now I am lost to all my hopes of fortune,
    Precariously depending on my father,
    How may it be exposed to wants, and cares!
    Farewell, my dear, I must not stay with thee,
    Tomorrow we will give some hours to love.
    Where shall I see you?
FELICIA   Here, if you please; my brother will be early out.
GRAMONT   I will not fail.
FELICIA   Let it be early then, you bring me joy,
    And I have need of it.
GRAMONT   Impatient wishes,
    Eager as in our first soft stealths of love,
    Will keep me waking till the longed for hour.
FELICIA   But how, my dearest, durst you venture now?
GRAMONT   I met your brother going to Lamira's,
    And took advantage just to steal a look,
    And beg the dear appointment for tomorrow.
    He expects me there, where he imagines I design
    To make addresses, being a young, rich widow.
    But thou art all the treasure I can covet.
FELICIA   My life, you'll not forget, tomorrow early.
GRAMONT   Can I forget my only happiness?

Exeunt, separately

SCENE II

LAMIRA'S HOUSE

Enter BELLGARD *and* LAMIRA

LAMIRA   You've counselled like that friend I ever thought you.
    A friend both to my honour and my interest.
BELLGARD   Not my own honour can be dearer to me.

With pain I see your hours of rest disturbed
By jealous spies, or crowds of hoping lovers,
Regardless of your fame, for their own interest.
LAMIRA   Oh, how much happier, and to be envied,
Is she, whose humble fortune enough supplying
Nature's wants,
Has not exposed her to the treacherous arts,
And false pretences of designing men!
BELLGARD   The hard condition, by which you possess
So large a fortune, gives you equal means
To free yourself from those designing lovers.
LAMIRA   For which I have intended to declare
The secret of my husband's jealous bounty.
BELLGARD   You've prudently resolved. But why, Lamira,
Are you regardless of Castalio's vows?
He loves and seeks you for yourself alone,
Nay, when I told him you refused all offers,
Forfeiting, if you wed, your best possessions,
With eager words, and eyes that sparkled joy,
Pressing me in his arms, he said, 'Oh friend,
How much more dear to me would such a sacrifice
Make the adored Lamira! Could I hope
She would for me abandon all her glittering fortune,
To reward my love with noble treasure,
How would I then improve your King's regard for me,
How welcome all his bounty, and his honours,
To doubly recompense what she can lose,
And make her great beyond my own ambition.'
LAMIRA   'Twas generously spoke,
Deserving all esteem, and gratitude.
That, as a debt his merit claims, I pay.
But 'twere to tempt ill fate, to strip myself
Of what I now possess secure from hazard,
To run th'uncertain fortunes of a stranger,
Depending on the breath of a King's favour,
Which should he lose, he'll ne'er return to Naples.
BELLGARD   You've urged as an objection that which most
Should recommend him: where can he be a stranger?
What monarch would not cherish such a subject?
What nation not be proud t'adopt a son so worthy?
He, that to the last of a large fortune
Supplied the public wants, whilst there was hopes
To free his country from th'invading Spaniard,
Then, courted by the conqueror, disdains
All obligations from his country's tyrant,

But banishing himself seeks nobler refuge
In a foreign court.
Still let me speak him, for he's brave in all.
With what a modest greatness he refused
All honours which our king pressed his accepting,
But what were in the army,
Seeming to scorn the lazy gifts of favour,
As if all glories were below his virtue,
But what in arms he forced from unbribed fame.

LAMIRA   We have cause to bless the choice, for he is said
To have done important service in the war.

BELLGARD   The Court have styled him France's better genius,
The soldiers idolise him; and as admired
He's loved by all, unless the general,
Who looks with envy on his rising fortune.

LAMIRA   A dangerous enemy.

BELLGARD   He has indeed, with all a soldier's heart,
The closer malice of a subtle statesman.
And the contempt of his authority
Castalio showed in forcing from the guards
His friend Gramont, by him unjustly sentenced,
I fear, may rouse his hatred to revenge.

LAMIRA   It was a godlike action; his friendship
For Gramont shows he not only knows himself
To merit, but values it in others.

BELLGARD   The choice his heart here makes is the best proof of that,
But let what you admire give softer thoughts,
And whisper to your heart, if for Gramont
He could do thus, what would not love inspire!

LAMIRA   I prize it to its height; but when you'd plead
Castalio's cause with me, name not Gramont.

BELLGARD   Not name him! Why is that an obstacle?

LAMIRA   No matter, nothing; 'twas a half-formed thought,
I know not what it meant, you may speak of him.

BELLGARD   Let me by any argument prevail
At least to know if he has leave to hope?

LAMIRA   Then think not that I wrong Castalio's worth,
When I declare, he has not, cannot have
An interest in my heart. I value him,
But 'twere unjust to give him hopes of more.
Love is not in our power.

BELLGARD   Madam, I've done. Though grieved at my success,
Since 'tis in vain, I'll touch this theme no more.
You've reason now, delivered from the tyrant
Your parents forced upon your tender years,

To let your heart direct your second choice.

LAMIRA   Oh! I fear the heedless partial guide
Would blindly lead me on some fatal ruin.

BELLGARD   Unjustly you distrust it. Tell me whither,
Where would it direct you,
And I may better judge how faithfully.

LAMIRA   Perhaps I have not ventured to consult it,
'Tis safest not to ask, or hear advice,
When 'tis as pleasing as 'tis dangerous.

BELLGARD   True, if we can avoid it,
But inclination's an officious counsellor,
That waits not to be asked, and will be heard.
Tell me, Lamira, what has yours been saying?

LAMIRA   Nothing.

BELLGARD   Is this your friendship? (for I would not plead
Our kindred blood, but a more near alliance)
Is this your boasted truth, and trust in me?

LAMIRA   I would not hide from you,
But what I would conceal from my own heart.
Let me, Bellgard, yet, oh, I fear, I fear,
It speaks too much, and loud, not to be heard,
And plain enough for you to understand.

BELLGARD   If I have leave to guess, I think I could.
May I interpret what your eyes have spoke,
And some late words confirm?

LAMIRA   Oh, my shame! In such a fruitful harvest
Of voluntary growth, untoiled for hearts,
T'ave cast my own upon a barren soil,
That yields me no return.

BELLGARD   You know not that; Gramont may love in secret,
Not daring to reveal it, or hope success,
Where he beholds the noblest offers scorned,
Sees mighty fortunes every day rejected.
Do not his late assiduous visits speak
All that a fortune low as his should dare?

LAMIRA   Suppose it did. What though our hearts were one,
If we must live at an eternal distance?

BELLGARD   What hinders you to be forever joined?

LAMIRA   Are not the obstacles invincible?

BELLGARD   Is any such to love?

LAMIRA   My husband's will.
And yet I could submit to his severity,
Throw all my titles and my treasure from me,
And think Gramont too full a recompense.
But then to see him miserably poor,

Wretched for me, my love could never bear it.
BELLGARD   Generous and tender, all, I see, that's left
For friendship now to undertake, or hope,
Is not to cure, but satisfy her love.
There may be found a way both to secure
Your happiness and fortune.
LAMIRA   How, whilst my husband's sister lives?
You know
I forfeit all to her upon a second marriage.
BELLGARD   But if you keep it secret, who shall claim the forfeit?
LAMIRA   How carefully contrive my happiness!
But alas! vainly my busy, pleased imagination
Has leaped at once o'er all difficulties,
When yet the first and greatest is unpassed.
He does not, and perhaps will never love me.
BELLGARD   Not love you! Those eyes, that with their native fires
Scorched so many, now love has added his.
What heart so frozen not to feel their heat!
Gramont, I think, will presently be here,
For so he promised. Will you for a while
Leave us together, and permit me to sound his thoughts?
LAMIRA   What, court him for me!
BELLGARD   You have not used to doubt
The safety of your honour in my hands.

Enter MARIAN

MARIAN   Here's a gentleman without to wait upon your ladyship.
LAMIRA   Admit him. If 'tis Gramont,
I am too much disordered yet to see him,
Make my excuse, and, my best friend, remember,
I trust you with the nicest dearest parts of me,
My love and honour.

Exit LAMIRA

BELLGARD   Both shall be my care.
Her satisfaction chiefly I regard,
But since she's resolute against Castalio,
This new design, which way so e'er I view it,
Gives me a pleasing prospect. Gramont I love,
And for his interest wish it, next for Felicia's.
Her little rest of hopes, eluded thus,
May turn her thoughts on search of certainties,
And make Roquelaure appear a happy refuge.

Enter GRAMONT

GRAMONT   Alone, Bellgard? Where's the fair Lamira?

BELLGARD   Some small affairs detain her for the present,
  She'll not be long.

GRAMONT   'Tis pity we should bear the weight of business.
  Her youth and charms would fit more soft employments.

BELLGARD   That youth and charms will well reward the man,
  Who frees her from that weight. What think you of it?
  Could you not bear the toil, for such a prize?

GRAMONT   Nothing would seem a toil, or difficult,
  To one, that could have hopes of gaining it.

BELLGARD   Pr'ythee, attempt it.

GRAMONT   What vanity can make me hope success,
  When those, who much excel me every way,
  In merit as in fortune, yet are slighted?
  I could have no pretence for such presumption.

BELLGARD   Your noble birth forbids that imputation,
  And the alliance of so great a family,
  As yours, may well be coveted.
  Lamira values you, and such esteem,
  When love and youth like yours together plead,
  Is quickly raised to passion and desire.

GRAMONT   If so, why are those more deserving lovers
  Who have, with youth, charms that I want, refused?

BELLGARD   You know my interest in her. Perhaps the friendship
  I've expressed for you may've turned the balance,
  Where merit was but equal. Howe'er it be,
  Not one of those, who long have languished for her,
  Does she receive with half that complaisance,
  Or speak of in such terms of admiration,
  As I have heard her, when your name was mentioned.

GRAMONT   She fears to give encouragement to her adorers.
  Should I commence the lover, like them I should be used.

BELLGARD   Is it a prize of such low consequence,
  Not worth the hazarding of a refusal?
  Unless your faith already is bestowed,
  Let me engage you to it, on our friendship.

GRAMONT   (My faith! I must not leave him that suspicion.)
  There needs not, sure, so dear a conjuration
  To make me aim at what all France contests for:
  An ample fortune, with so bright a beauty.

Enter LAMIRA

LAMIRA   My blushes own me guilty of a rudeness,
  Tho', Sir, I hope my cousin has excused me.

BELLGARD   I'll leave you now to make your own apology.

Exit BELLGARD

GRAMONT   We have been lamenting, Madam, that so long
　　You have condemned yourself to bear alone
　　The painful load of business.
LAMIRA   I had rather much sustain that load for ever
　　Than, seeking ease, only to change my burden
　　For a much worse and heavier.
GRAMONT   Among the many would be proud to bear it,
　　Can you not find out one, on whom to throw it
　　Upon easier terms? Or may I ask,
　　Why you, who can dispose of thousand hearts,
　　Let all alike be wretched?
LAMIRA   Had high ambition been my darling passion,
　　I had been tempted to exalt my fate,
　　But my own honours bound my largest wishes,
　　And fortune has not been a niggard to me.
　　Therefore, all pleas but merit unconsidered,
　　My heart bestows me freely on the man
　　Whom it shall speak most worthy.
GRAMONT   What vain presumer dare pretend, or think
　　To merit such a wonder? This resolution known,
　　What forward lover would not cease his suit,
　　In just despair of ever gaining it?
LAMIRA   Either you flatter me, or are too modest.
　　Whither was I going? I have observed
　　The most deserving ever most distrustful
　　Of their own worth; which if it be fault,
　　It is the only I've remarked in you.
　　But all that diffidence and modesty,
　　Speak louder for you than the boasts of others.
GRAMONT   Then it must speak, for you have silenced me.
　　Henceforward I shall only dare to wish,
　　That you were less divine, or I more worthy.
LAMIRA   You're worthy all that you can dare to ask.
GRAMONT   I ne'er shall dare to ask a prize too noble
　　For any mortal aim.

Exit GRAMONT, *bowing*

LAMIRA   So cold!
　　Or is it the character of awful love?
　　If so, my words were kind, and plain enough
　　To chase away his fears.
　　'Tis now too late that humble way to move;
　　Respect is rudeness, when we offer love.

Exit LAMIRA

ACT II

SCENE I

COUNT ROQUELAURE'S HOUSE

Enter BELLGARD, *and a* SERVANT *of the Count*

SERVANT   Be pleased to stay here, Sir,
  My lord will wait upon you instantly.
BELLGARD   You have told him I am here?
SERVANT   I did, and hear him coming.

Exit SERVANT

Enter ROQUELAURE

COUNT   You're welcome, my Bellgard, the only man,
  That can give comfort to my tortured heart.
BELLGARD   None can be prouder, or more joy'd to serve you.
COUNT   I'm just returned from visiting your sister,
  Whom I have seen in such a graceful sorrow,
  As heightened all her charms, and my desire
  More than it moved my pity.
BELLGARD   And how, my lord,
  Has she received the honour you design her?
COUNT   With such aversion as she'd meet her fate.
  At first I found her in a solemn sadness,
  Her eyes all languishing, fixed on the ground.
  But, roused at my approach, the flowing blood
  Flushed to her cheeks, yet soon again forsook 'em.
  Thus, pale and trembling we met, alike disordered,
  Though with such different passions; hate in her
  Produced the same effect as love in me.
BELLGARD   Hate, my lord?
  Can you suspect her of so great injustice?
COUNT   What else can make her so inexorable?
  Upon her knees she fell, and grasping mine,
  She, weeping, begged me to desist my suit,
  With such engaging action, and words so moving,
  As whilst they made me wish I could obey her,
  Deprived me of the power.
BELLGARD   Stubborn girl!
COUNT   Finding me more inflamed and still persisting,
  She said I might expose her to your anger,
  And all the ruin you had lately threatened,
  But there was such an obstacle in nature,
  As never would permit her to be mine.

BELLGARD   So positive, my lord? I'll make her find
    There's not an obstacle but I can vanquish.
COUNT   I fear her early kindness for my son,
    Which we too long neglected.
    Tho' they seem parted now, their rooted loves
    May join, and still produce fresh springing hopes.
BELLGARD   Then we must strive to blast 'em. I could wish
    Gramont were married to yours and his own liking.
    What think you of Lamira for a daughter?
COUNT   So well, I must not think of it.
BELLGARD   My lord, I've a relation's interest in her,
    And more, that of a friend; on which relying,
    I have proposed it to her, and may tell you,
    She much esteems your son, and would be proud
    Of your alliance, which, if desired by you,
    I know she'll not refuse.
COUNT   'Tis generously offered, and here he comes

    Enter GRAMONT

    To join with me in thanks. Your looks are sad,
    My son, is there a cause?
GRAMONT   There is, my lord, if I have any sense
    Of honour, gratitude, or friendship. Castalio
    Is this day brought here a prisoner, to the castle,
    Where he is kept in chains, as he were guilty
    Of some flagitious action.
COUNT   For what is he so used?
GRAMONT   For me; you know, my Lord,
    He saved my life with hazard of his own,
    For which the general committed him,
    And representing, to the absent King
    The case, as he thought fit, next had him fined
    Three thousand crowns, and keeps him thus secured,
    Till 'tis discharged.
BELLGARD   Some such mean vengeance,
    I apprehended from his barbarous nature.
GRAMONT   Castalio, of a generous soul,
    Knowing no use of wealth but to bestow
    On other wants, scarce mindful of his own,
    I know must needs be unprepared for this.
    Tho' his great services and merit plead,
    Malice in power will be heard against 'em,
    And his reward be there to starve neglected.
COUNT   Honour forbid!
GRAMONT   Honour, justice, gratitude, and friendship,

All forbid! Yet I, th' unhappy cause,
Look on, and suffer it, unable to assist him.
COUNT   He must, he shall be aided, and by you,
For whom he suffers all.
GRAMONT   Oh, my honoured father, more than father now,
'Tis more than life you've given, like that, un-asked,
Restored a friend to me, preserved my honour.
How shall I pay my thanks!
COUNT   To save you that, be all the act your own.
GRAMONT   Would Heav'n but give the power!
COUNT   Give it yourself, and lose no time in wishing.
A friend and father point you out the way:
You know Lamira.
GRAMONT   Ha! What of her, my lord?
COUNT   She may be yours.
GRAMONT   Mine, my lord?
BELLGARD   One thing 'tis fit you know e'er you determine.
Her deceased husband, by nature jealous and severe,
Left the considerablest part of her estate,
Conditional, that she remain unmarried.
The terms, to one so young, unreasonable
And unjust. Therefore I think 'em not in honour
Obligatory; only to keep the marriage secret,
Whilst her sister lives, to whom she forfeits,
If so you can approve it.
GRAMONT   Far be it from me t'expose Lamira
To such a hazard of her ruin.
'Twill be impossible to keep it secret.
BELLGARD   Her long refusal of the greatest matches
Has raised in many different conjectures,
All which to end, she'll suddenly declare
The true conditions of her husband's will.
That will prevent all pryings or suspicions
Of her marriage.
COUNT   Especially to him. A younger brother
Will ne'er be thought an object for her choice,
And prudence must direct the management
Of future accidents that may occur.
BELLGARD   My lord, I'll leave you to consult together.

Exit BELLGARD

COUNT   You seem not much to relish this proposal.
Could you expect a match so advantageous?
GRAMONT   Marriage, my lord, I hold a sacred bond,
Which should be made for nobler ends than interest;

  Hearts should first be joined.

COUNT And who deserves your heart more than Lamira?

GRAMONT It is not merit only gives us love,
  Else every heart would take the same impression.
  But each, we see, receives a different image,
  As it were fitted for that stamp alone.
  Hers is perhaps of too refin'd a nature
  To strike this grosser mould. I cannot mend it,
  And hope you will not press a monstrous union
  Of things by nature not agreeing.

COUNT By Heav'n, a mere rebellious spirit moves thee
  To this refusal. Had it not been offered,
  Thy own desires would have prevented us.

GRAMONT Can I so far forget my filial duty?
  My lord, I honour you, and your commands,
  Equal almost to Heaven's, but you have told me
  A state so lasting should be well considered
  E'er resolved on, and that marriage-bonds
  Were of too pond'rous weight for youth to bear.

COUNT Are you still a boy? I have considered for you.
  Your part is to obey.

GRAMONT I have yet too large a stock of coming years,
  To be laid out upon one hasty purchase.

COUNT Go, satisfy your friend thus, tell him the last
  Of that fine fancied stock shall be laid out
  For his relief.

GRAMONT Oh Castalio!

COUNT You love him well indeed, ingrateful wretch!
  Insensible of every benefit!
  What an indulgent father have I been!
  When thy extravagance had left thee friendless,
  Pursued by many, by the rest abandoned,
  I took thee to my bosom, sheltered thee
  Ev'n from royal anger, used all my interest
  With vast expense to gain thy pardon,
  And this day resolved to pay th' exacted sum,
  For which 'twas granted. But, ungracious boy,
  I'll not so dearly buy thy liberty,
  Till thou can'st find a better way to use it,
  Than disobeying me.

GRAMONT I know I don't deserve it. Give me up
  To death, to banishment, or slavery,
  I'll own your justice. But let not poor Castalio
  Suffer for my fault.
  His freedom will not cost you half so dear,

Nor he be so ingrateful.
COUNT   Impudent request! What friendship do I owe him,
For sending me such a rebellious son?
You may go to him,
And rot for me together in a dungeon.
Hence from my house, and till thou art obedient,
By Heav'n, if thou wert starving at my gates,
I'd send thee no relief. The first I do,
May it become to both eternal ruin.
Now, foolish boy, go seek a better fortune.

Exit COUNT ROQUELAURE

GRAMONT   Cast from the field, the Court, and my own father,
Where should I fly? To poor Felicia's arms,
She's kind, and will be fond to share my misery.
Alas! too soon she must, thus she'll be used,
For so her brother threatened. Cruel thought!
Must I behold that tender part of me,
Exposed to all th'extremities of want,
My helpless infant asking food in vain?
Oh fate! Oh Heaven! you cannot mean it.
They're innocent: how, how have we deserved your anger?
If there be a guilt, it must be mine.
Why then, ye powers,
Must she be involved in my unhappiness?
Oh! you are just, and cannot suffer it.
Thus prostrate I implore, Oh spare her, Heav'n.
Wreak, wreak on me your vengeance; but she is part of me,
And so must share it.
Oh! let me fly from thought, or from the world,
E'er this impetuous ruin overwhelm
My sinking reason. Oh! I shall grow mad!

Exit GRAMONT

SCENE II

A PRISON

CASTALIO   No, proud, insulting Spain! not ev'n thus
Can I repent my leaving conquered Naples.
Thy pageant freedom, and precarious honours
Were heavier baser slavery than these chains,
And I am less ashamed of them, tho' here

Perhaps the object of Lamira's scorn.
Ha! What of that? By Heav'n, I cannot form
One thought for glory, since I knew that woman,
But still 'tis mixed with love, with passion fanned,
And makes the best and bravest of my actions
But glittering frailties. She is strangely charming.
Well, is it not enough to think her so?
Or say I wish her mine?
But why thus fix my soul upon a woman?
Why these tumultuous ravings, hopes and fears?

Enter GRAMONT

(Gramont! I blush, as if I thought he saw my heart,
Ashamed to own myself for what I am.
Stifling my passion may extinguish it.
No more of this.) My friend, this welcome sight
Makes all my wrongs and pains insensible:
That thou art free, and safe, is to Castalio
Ease and liberty.
GRAMONT   Dearer than either, how do I enjoy 'em,
Whilst purchased at the sad expense of yours.
How can I look upon a friend thus ruined,
By saving me at his extremest peril,
Whilst I but mourn for him, with aidless pity!
CASTALIO   No, my Gramont,
'Tis not for freeing thee, that I am thus.
Occasions had been found, tho' this not given,
T'exert the general's malice. But do not grieve.
His triumph is but short. I shall be free.
GRAMONT   You hide a truth you fear t'afflict me with.
I know that public spirit which, at Naples,
Made you, in favour of the common interest,
Neglect your own, has moved you here; as noble,
Your frequent bounties to the murmuring soldiers
Must have disabled you for the discharge
Of such a sum.
CASTALIO   I could no less than give to your King's service
What he so frankly had bestowed on me,
And being just upon the point of battle,
'Twas then the only way to quell the mutiny.
But can I doubt to find him grateful now,
Whose generosity, when undeserved,
I have so far experienced?
I every hour expect Bernardo's coming,
And doubt not but he brings me liberty.

That faithful follower of my fortunes, hearing
The general had left the camp and ordered
My removal hither, hast'ned to Court,
That he might there in person answer ought
Alleged against me. In confidence, the King,
When well informed of the injustice done me,
Will soon command my freedom.

GRAMONT   You'll find you have a subtle enemy,
Tho' in his hate bare-faced, close in revenge,
Which having failed, when against me directed,
I fear will now be bent with surer aim,
And fall with double force on you.

CASTALIO   He should indeed have made my ruin sure,
Or not have dared so much.

GRAMONT   What can his motive be of sending you from th'army?

CASTALIO   He durst not in his absence trust me to
The soldiers' love, which he had found, when present,
Scarce his authority could balance. That chiefly,
But in part he serves his malice. Pleased,
Whilst he can, to make me bear the hardships
And inconvenience of a common prison,
He has intended me the vilest usage,
Allotting me a dark and noisome dungeon,
Tho' I'm by stealth allowed the freedom of this air.

Enter BERNARDO

Bernardo returned already? What news from Court?

BERNARDO   That you have been too honest.

CASTALIO   I shan't repent it.

BERNARDO   By Heav'n, I'd rather seen you led in triumph
A slave to Spain. They might have showed you
As an enemy, but had not called you traitor.

CASTALIO   Ha! But thou talk'st with rage. Speak to my understanding.

BERNARDO   My lord, your pardon, 'tis my hearty love
Makes me forget all method and respect.
I've been at Court, where sure no honest man
Can keep his temper.

CASTALIO   Why, what reception found you there?

BERNARDO   Such as they'd give a man the plague had seized.
All shunned me as I passed, and those in office,
When I desired admittance to the presence,
Would not know me.

CASTALIO   Denied to see the King?

BERNARDO   I would not be denied.

CASTALIO.   Be brief to your success with him.

BERNARDO   He asked me coldly if I came to speak
 In your defence. I said I hoped 'twas needless
 To defend an act, which all brave men,
 And friends to justice, must admire.
CASTALIO   What did the King return?
BERNARDO   He owned Gramont had been unjustly sentenced,
 And therefore had his pardon.
 But 'twas of ill example to oppose
 In such a hostile way a general's orders,
 And might encourage others, if your fine
 Should be remitted. I urged your services,
 And lastly, that you had not asked for favour,
 But that to keep his soldiers in their duty,
 Who mutinied for pay, you had stripped yourself
 Of what might now discharge you. He said, you'd been
 Too zealous in his service; so abruptly left me.
CASTALIO   By Heav'n, I think he's in the right, if zeal
 Be thus rewarded.
BERNARDO   My lord, the King's abused.
 The treacherous general has found a spring
 That will supply his malice: whilst you have any virtues,
 He makes 'em all appear as arts put on
 T'ingratiate with the soldiers, on design
 To serve the Spanish interest.
CASTALIO   How, taxed with treason! the basest too,
 Made blacker by th'ingratitude! He dares not say it,
 Nor would the King believe it.
BERNARDO   Somewhat that way his last words seem t'import.
 But what I further learned was from an officer
 That honours you, and whom the general trusts.
 A correspondence held with Spain is talked of,
 With hints of proofs to be produced against you.
CASTALIO   Impossible! my words, my heart and actions
 Have been open. There's such unartful plainness
 In my nature, as cannot be suspected.
GRAMONT   There's no security against such malice,
 As makes your highest virtues seem your crimes,
 And princes, ever in jealousy of power,
 Give easy credit to reports of danger.
BERNARDO   Doubtless he will not fail of evidence
 To back his accusation. In short, my lord.
 Unless you know or find some speedy way
 To free yourself and face your base detractors,
 I would not answer for your life.
GRAMONT   Oh fate!

All this t'oppress a wretch already loaded!
Ruin on ruin heaped!
Is't not enough to have determined mine,
But I must put all that surround me down
To crush me in my fall, and with my own,
Bring all the weight of their destruction on me?
It is not to be borne. What, to be made
Ill fate's curst instrument, distributer
Of direst miseries, and bane of virtue!
I am all this, I, I, Castalio, am
The baleful planet, whose malignant influence
Ruins your fortunes, blasts your spreading glories,
And all your kinder stars had purposed you, defeats.

CASTALIO   You share too much my wrongs, but have not caused 'em.
Let your resentment strike where justice bids,
I must not see you rashly lose your passion
Against a man I love, my only friend.

GRAMONT   Alas! you do not know with how much reason
My passion spoke, nor what a wretch I am,
Abandoned by my father, banished his house,
And with his curse, if ever I return.

CASTALIO   For ever?

GRAMONT   It must be ever, the only terms
Of my admittance ne'er can be performed.

CASTALIO   'Tis cruel, what cause can you have given him to proceed
To such extremities?

GRAMONT   You know the dearest secret of my life,
My long concealed, and unsuspected marriage.

CASTALIO   'Tis then discovered?

GRAMONT   Not that, nor dare I own it.
My father loves Felicia, not knowing her
My wife, and has commanded me t'accept
Another, whom fortune, birth, and nature
Have left without objection, which my refusing
Has thus irreconcilably incensed him.

CASTALIO   Your case indeed is hard.

GRAMONT   Yet there is worse behind.
I've not disclosed the wound that grieves me most,
Not spoke how you're involved in my undoing.
My father was disposed in gratitude,
For a son's life and liberty received,
To have performed the terms of gaining yours,
But thus offended at my disobedience,
Your saving me appears an injury.
His hate extends to you, and now he's fixed

Not to relieve, tho' he should see you perish.
Heav'ns! should the fate of such a man,
By which the world's might rather be determined,
Itself be influenced by any other's?
But why must I be made his destiny?
Yes, yes, trace back through all the windings of your fortune,
And you will find, that I alone have been
Your evil genius; that you have cause to curse
Your fatal friendship, the unlucky hour
You saved my life, or that which gave me birth.
Oh, that it ne'er had been! I want the patience
To support this load of wretched life,
That growing heavier as it wastes, leaves not
A hope of ease. Tell me, Castalio, friend,
Through all this gloom of endless miseries,
Is there a dawn of any comfort left me?

CASTALIO   Nor endless, my Gramont, nor comfortless.
No man can be to that degree unhappy,
That has on any terms his fortune in his power,
For his rejecting that, when virtue bids,
Shews there's a good in her that would not fix,
Unless it could reward his choice.

Enter a SOLDIER

SOLDIER   My lord, I beg you'll retire to your chamber.
The governor will be returned this minute,
And must not know you have had this liberty.

CASTALIO   I thank thee, honest soldier. Farewell, my friend,
Remember death's the worst we have to fear,
And that, whilst we unmoved preserve our virtue,
Rather to be desired.

CASTALIO *goes within.* GRAMONT *advances.*
The scene changes to the outside of the castle

GRAMONT   To be desired, indeed, since virtue here
Is ever thus oppressed, without relief,
But in its future prospect.

Enter a SERVANT

SERVANT   Sir, I am sent with an unwelcome message
From my lord, your father. The time you took
For payment of your fine being now expired,
'Tis rigorously demanded, and by my lord refused.
He says he would advise you so to act
That it may be discharged; if not, you must

Deliver up your person, for he vows
He never will assist you.
GRAMONT   Tell him, I will obey him. This alone were light,
But added to the rest completes the weight.

Enter another SERVANT

What news hast thou? How does my little son?
Thy looks forbode me ill. If my child is dead,
Smile when thou tell'st me, for he is happy.
SERVANT   Sir, he lives, but in a wretched state,
The place you sent him to being near the sea,
His nurse walked often with him on the shore,
But most unhappily, some weeks ago,
Was by our famous pirate seen, and seized,
And with her infant charge carried on board.
GRAMONT   Oh, fatal accident, a strange one, too!
What can the villain gain by such a prize?
Methinks it should be more a burden to him,
Than advantage.
SERVANT   They say he does it, Sir,
In hopes of a considerable ransom,
If his young captives prove of quality,
But if he finds they will not be redeemed,
He throws 'em to the mercy of the waves.
GRAMONT   Ha! what pains the fates are at to make a villain of me!
Must it be so? Shall I give up my honour
To save myself, and all I love from ruin?
No, that's in my own power, the rest in fate's,
And, spite of fate, I'll keep my honesty:
Tho' my best friend must be for me undone,
In fame, in fortune, and perhaps his life,
A sacrifice to treacherous revenge;
My infant by inhuman pirates murdered,
The dearest fruit of my Felicia's love;
My wife too, Oh my wife, she'll be thrown out
To wander through the world, poor, and distressed,
To curse her fatal love, to curse her husband,
The wretched source of bitterest miseries,
Who sees her starving, and can give no succour.
I cannot bear the thought, it shall not be;
I'd pluck those eyes out, rather than behold it.
So dear I hold her, I could cut off these limbs
To let her piece-meal feed upon my flesh.
I must, I must prevent at any rate
This dismal scene of misery and ruin,

Turn villain, any thing, when she's at stake,
My child too, and my best friend. I could, by Heav'n,
Suffer a thousand racking deaths for each,
And should I sacrifice 'em all, to keep
A little peace of mind, the pride of never straying?
Walk on by rules, and calmly let 'em perish,
Rather than tread one step beyond to save 'em?
Forbid it nature! No, I'll leap o'er all.
Castalio, my suffering babe and loved Felicia,
See how dear you're to me, how strong my love,
When it can turn the scale against my virtue.
Nay, now 'tis plain; not I, but fate resolves it,

Enter BELLGARD

He's surely sent just at this very point
To keep me warm, and firm for villainy.
Welcome, Bellgard. Where's Lamira? Where my father?
Tell him I will be his, and hers, and yours,
Mould me as you please, but take me quickly,
For now I grow impatient. When shall it be done?
BELLGARD   Gramont, I love you, and am much rejoiced
To see you fond of your own happiness,
But yet must wonder at this new impatience.
GRAMONT   I dare not trust delays, they're dangerous,
May hinder or reveal the fatal secret
That you know would ruin us.
But let us not confide in our best friends,
Or near relations. Shall we swear to it?
You'll not discover it where you most could trust:
Your sister, or if any one is dearer.
BELLGARD   On my honour, but there needs no oath.
My friendship to you both will tie me stricter.
I was just going to my lord, your father,
Shall I tell him? But we'll go together,
Since you are for dispatch, he best can forward it.
GRAMONT   I'll wait on you, 'tis done, I'm entered now,
And to plunge through, must leave all thought behind me.
No happiness I for myself expect,
But would preserve my friends from ruin.
Let me without a partner be unfortunate,
'Tis all the privilege I beg from fate.

Exeunt

ACT III

SCENE I

LAMIRA'S HOUSE

Enter COUNT ROQUELAURE *and* LAMIRA

LAMIRA   'Tis I, my lord, am honoured in your choice,
To make me sharer of your noble blood.
COUNT   We shall esteem our house with greater cause,
When it can boast of such an ornament.
But as the happiness is most my son's,
He best can pay you our acknowledgements,
For what he wanted confidence to ask.
LAMIRA   He seems to want no virtue for perfection,
But a just sense of his exalted worth.
He comes, and now that fortune joins with it,

Enter GRAMONT *and* BELLGARD

My heart grows bold, and tells me he has charms
Which it must love, and will not be controlled.
COUNT   Bellgard, your fair relation has consented
To all our wishes, tho' beyond our hopes.
BELLGARD   She has obliged us all, but you, Gramont,
Will have the greatest sense, as well as share
Of the good fortune.
GRAMONT   'Tis so above what I can say, or think,
I could not hope, nor ought to have aimed at it.
COUNT   You must not wonder, Madam, if my son
Is eager to secure a happiness,
Which want of merit makes him fear to lose.
He pressed me ere I came, if I prevailed
To beg you'd not delay to crown his wishes.
LAMIRA   So small a prize would not be worth the price
Of a long expectation.
GRAMONT   It might reward an age of expectation.
COUNT   But happiness can never come too soon.
May not th' account of his begin tomorrow?
LAMIRA   Nay, now you are too hasty.
COUNT   Bellgard, you'll join in intercession with us.
BELLGARD   If but to avoid suspicion, it were best
To use dispatch.
GRAMONT   (Oh Felicia?)
COUNT   (Ha! Methought he named Felicia!)
We must not let him cool, since all's agreed.

What hinders that it be tonight?
LAMIRA   Tonight?
GRAMONT   Why not tonight? (It cannot be too soon,
  Since it must be.)
LAMIRA   (Why must our sex seem shy of what they wish?)
BELLGARD   Dare you trust your chaplain with the secret?
LAMIRA   I know none fitter.
BELLGARD   Then all is ready for the ceremony.
  Come, Lamira, you should be above
  This little affectation, this maiden coyness.
  Away with it, you must not now deny,
  There's no pretence for it.
LAMIRA   You have an absolute command of me,
  But methinks this is too sudden.
COUNT   Oh, the more unexpected, the more pleasing.
BELLGARD   I had designed before an entertainment
  Of music here tonight, most fortunately
  On this occasion.
  'Twere best to have it in this antechamber,
  Whilst we within conclude the happy union.
  Come, Gramont, you'll lead your bride.
COUNT   Haste, you lose time, the night is almost spent.
LAMIRA   How pleased we are with importunity,
  That makes our own desires seem condescension?
  Who pleads a cause like this, can never fail,
  If not their arguments, love will prevail.

A musical interlude. Afterwards GRAMONT *is found sitting alone*

GRAMONT   It must not be. 'Twere base to wrong her so.
  Ha, base? Why, what's the part I have already acted?
  Am I not now initiated villain?
  Have I the smallest claim to honour left?
  Or can it be possessed by halves? No,
  Indivisible, it, like the soul,
  Must animate entire, in every part,
  But one base act completes that character,
  Stamps villain on the whole. Be then a villain.
  — Ha! Felicia, my love! How could I think it?
  How once imagine it were possible
  For one possessing all thy Heav'n of beauties
  To take another to his loathing arms!
  No, in this shipwreck of my honour, virtue,
  I'll save the treasure of my faith to thee.

'Tis all I have left of good, my darling store,
And I will hug myself, and pride in that.

Enter LAMIRA

LAMIRA   Is it not time, Gramont, to think of rest?
The morning breaks upon your night's devotions.
GRAMONT   Perhaps I have some cares, that keep me waking,
With which I would not load your peaceful breast.
LAMIRA   Oh, can you think that I behold you thus
And keep my peace? Thus giv'n up to sadness,
And for untimely thought, neglecting me?
What is it? Speak your griefs, what cause so pressing
To allow no respite upon a time like this,
Which for the wretched'st pair that fate e'er joined,
Us'd to put on at least a form of joy?
GRAMONT   Mine is indeed a most uncommon cause,
But do not seek to know it.
LAMIRA   No, I need not;
Now it speaks itself, you do not love me,
That, that alone could keep you from me thus.
GRAMONT   Suppose th'idea of a suffering friend,
For me this instant bearing cruel hardships,
Had checked me from indulgent thoughts of ease,
Would that excuse me to you?
How, clasped in those soft arms, could I be called
The friend, the other half of poor Castalio,
Whose fainting limbs rude circling irons load?
LAMIRA   I know your friend's misfortune, and his worth,
I know you owe him much,
And will not tax you of too nice a gratitude.
Be such a lover as you are a friend.
This cause of sadness shall be soon removed.
Three thousand crowns will give Castalio freedom,
Which shall be sent him instantly. Within there,
Marian. (*She talks aside with* MARIAN)
GRAMONT   Down, down, proud swelling heart, why shouldst thou
mount
Above my grovelling fate?
Thou can'st not raise it to thy height, yield then,
Be vile as that.
LAMIRA (*to* MARIAN)   Bid him haste, and say Gramont has sent him.
Let him not mention me.

Exit MARIAN

Still are you sad?

GRAMONT   I'm but correcting a proud rebel here,
    That would not be obliged. I shall have peace,
    When I have taught it to be as ungrateful,
    As I must be.
LAMIRA   To whom?
GRAMONT   Madam, to you.
LAMIRA   Why to me? Why must you be ungrateful?
    Can you not love me?
GRAMONT   You know not what a bankrupt you have trusted,
    So poor, so ruined, that for all he owes you,
    The kindest, best return that he can make,
    Is thus to shun your bed.
LAMIRA   Am I then your aversion?
GRAMONT   Believe me, 'tis the highest mark of value,
    That neither your resentment can provoke,
    Nor all your beauties tempt me to abuse you.
LAMIRA   Abuse? Is that a husband's language?
    How?
    What mean you? Speak the cause of this behaviour.
GRAMONT   It is not to be told; let it suffice
    That as the present circumstances are,
    If I should take a husband's privilege,
    The consequence would be to you most fatal.
    Ask not the cause, I cannot tell you more.
LAMIRA   Say, only say, it is not want of love,
    And I will seek no further.
GRAMONT   Were all the fire of every heart you have inflamed,
    Raging at once in mine, this were the greatest proof
    That I could give you, of true affection.
LAMIRA   Oh, could I be convinced of that, Gramont,
    I should not envy the most happy bride.
    I have no thought, no wish beyond your love;
    Make me secure of that, and I am blest.
    Why art thou thus unmoved, thou cruel savage?
    Hast thou no sensibility, no fire in thy soul?
    Or have not I the art to blow the flame?
    Instruct me then, if 'tis not yet too late,
    If 'tis not kindled at another's charms.
    That was an injurious thought, chide it away,
    Tell me you could not be so false, so base.
    You do not answer!
    Nay, then I fear I am abused indeed.
    Speak quickly, swear I am not, the very fear's
    Distracting, not to be borne, swear you are thus by nature,
    Thus cold, insensible to all the sex

As you are now to me, swear that,
And I'll complain no more of your indifference,
But with submissive duty, tenderest care,
And most unwearied love, still strive to move
Thy cold, obdurate heart. Is there a hope to gain it?

GRAMONT   Madam, you set it at too high a rate,
It is not worth your least concern or thought.

LAMIRA   Why, why inhuman dost thou answer thus,
Regardless of the doubts that rack my soul?
Oh speak, reply to them, e'er they distract me.
'Tis enough, enough. Thy silence speaks
The dumb confession of a guilty mind.
Ay, there it is, thou false, perfidious man!
'Tis to a rival I am sacrificed.
But think'st thou I will tamely bear my wrongs,
And let her triumph in 'em? Dare not to see her,
For, if thou dost, I'll find the strumpet out.
Confusion! Slighted, for another, too!
Oh, how I'll be revenged! I'll know this sorceress,
Make her most infamous,
I'll be your plague, anticipate your hell!

GRAMONT   Why all this for a bare imagination?

LAMIRA   Is it no more? Then you may join with me
To curse this creature of my fancy.
Let all united mischiefs light upon her,
Diseases make her loathsome to your arms,
Deformity, a horror to your eyes,
May pinching wants bring her to beggary,
And infamy divert all pity from her.

GRAMONT   Oh, hold! You stab my soul. If you must curse,
On me let all your imprecations fall,
For I alone am guilty.

LAMIRA   Why thus concerned for one that has no being,
But in a bare imagination? Dissembling,
Vilest wretch! Thou thing below my anger!
There have been glorious villains that may look
With scorn on thee, disdaining thy low ends;
A paltry bait of fortune, poor spirited,
Mean traitor, what indigent abandoned creature
Is this, that hopes to vaunt it in my spoils,
Yet must be purchased at no less a rate
Than such an insolent disdain of me?
What are your terms? What she? And what her charms?
Let's know the state and reason of this preference —
Stubborn and dumb! Am I not worth an answer?

GRAMONT   What, Madam, can I answer to your rage?
LAMIRA   My wrongs, thy own upbraiding guilt thou can'st not answer.
    I do not rage, nor is there any rage
    For injuries like this.
    All that has had the name of passion, fury,
    Ev'n to madness, here is higher reason.
    So basely us'd! A rival's property!
    Unvalued, thus despised for her, tormenting!
    What easy fool did'st think thou hast secured?
    Mistaken man! Thou hast roused a woman's rage,
    In spite of all thy hard'ned villainy,
    Thou shalt repent thou didst provoke me thus.
    I'll haunt your steps, and interrupt your joys,
    Fright you with curses from your minion's arms,
    Pursue you with reproaches, blast her fame.
    I'll be the constant bane of all your pleasures,
    A jarring, clamorous, very wife to thee,
    To her a greater plague than thou to me.

                                                    Exit LAMIRA

GRAMONT   Let my Felicia 'scape her jealous fury,
    And with whatever force her vengeance strike.
    It is not worth my fear. She must be yet
    Too much transported with her rage t'observe me.
    I'll take the occasion, and somewhere near Bellgard's
    Remain unseen, till I may have admittance
    To my love.
    Her nature's calm, by no rough passions tossed,
    A harbour from this tempest, upon her gentle bosom
    All the disorders of my soul will cease,
    Or I despair ever to find my peace.

                                                         Exit

SCENE II

BELLGARD'S HOUSE

FELICIA   'Tis yet too soon t'expect him; the sprightly day
    Cannot move swift enough for love's impatience.
    Doubtless my kind Gramont is wishing too
    For the blest minute, waiting, as he's wont,
    Like a fond lover, ready to seize the first
    That gives us liberty. Oh, that dear man!

Who, that were so beloved, would grudge to bear
More than I suffer for him? That kind, that faithful
Partner of my griefs.

Enter BELLGARD

BELLGARD   So early up, sister?
FELICIA   I was not much disposed for sleep this morning.
BELLGARD   Perhaps my coming home so late disturbed you.
FELICIA   'Twas late indeed.
BELLGARD   Th'occasion may excuse it.
FELICIA   Am I to know th'occasion?
BELLGARD   Only a friend's marriage. ('Twill be fit
    To let Felicia know Gramont is married,
    But not to whom; whilst that is unsuspected,
    The secret's safe.)
FELICIA   May I ask what friend? Or is't a secret, brother?
BELLGARD   'Tis indeed a secret, sister, but you
    Should know it, if I were sure 'twould not disturb you.
FELICIA   That I dare promise you.
    It is not in the power of any one,
    To raise the least concern in me that way.
BELLGARD   Then I may safely tell you, but with charge
    Not to reveal it, Gramont last night was married.
FELICIA   Gramont! You jest with me.
BELLGARD   On my faith, I'm serious.
FELICIA   (What can he mean?) To whom, brother?
BELLGARD   For that you must excuse me, I've given my honour
    Not to disclose it to my dearest friend.
FELICIA   Unless you tell me that, I shall believe
    You said it but to try me.
BELLGARD   Were it not a secret of importance,
    Or if my own, I would not hide it from you,
    None but his father and myself were trusted,
    My faith, my honour, friendship, are engaged.
FELICIA   (With what concern he speaks! And yet it cannot be.)
BELLGARD   I conjure you, sister, not to mention this.
FELICIA   Why such a secret? But you're not in earnest.
BELLGARD   Why should you doubt, when I affirm it thus
    Not from report, but my own certain knowledge?
    Myself was present at the nuptial tie,
    A witness of their vows.
FELICIA   If there is faith in man, this can't be truth.
    I fancy, brother, this is but designed
    To try how I could bear it.

BELLGARD   Those are woman's arts, I understand 'em not.
   Heav'n knows no greater truth than what I've told you.

FELICIA   Swear, by that Heav'n, you're sure Gramont is married,
   And I will doubt no longer.

BELLGARD   Am I not worth your credit? Why all this doubting?
   By every name that's good, Gramont is married.
   I saw him married.

FELICIA   Wretched woman!

BELLGARD   How, Felicia!

FELICIA   Oh, I must not think it,
   He can't be guilty of so base an action.

BELLGARD   What foolish passion's this?

FELICIA   And yet my brother swears it, swears he saw it.
   Oh Gramont! Is all my love and faith rewarded thus?

BELLGARD   For shame at least conceal your folly,
   This fondness for a man, who cares not for you,
   Perhaps scarce thinks of you.

FELICIA   Oh, to be so abused!

BELLGARD   What said you? So abused?

FELICIA   He has wronged me basely.

BELLGARD   Ha! Hast thou not wronged thyself, giv'n up
   Thy honour to him?

FELICIA   Oh, forgive me, brother. . .

BELLGARD   Dar'st thou own thy infamy, yet hope to be forgiv'n?

FELICIA   I am married.

BELLGARD   No, strumpet, he but served his lust with thee,
   And now has paid thee as thou dost deserve,
   Too wise to marry where he found not virtue.

FELICIA   Can you suspect me of a thing so vile!
   No, by all goodness, I am not dishonest,
   But by all lawful bonds his real wife.

BELLGARD   Oh, curse! What do I hear? What have I done?
   Base dog, so to betray, abuse my friendship,
   Whither does all this lead? Where can it end?
   'Tis misery, dishonour without end,
   And I the instrument of all this ruin.
   Villain, perfidious villain! Ay, trait'ress, weep,
   Weep for thy shame, thy sin, thy disobedience,
   Rebellious girl, pollution of my blood!

FELICIA   Oh, I deserve all this, that could deceive
   And disobey the best of brothers.

BELLGARD   You've met a just return of your ingratitude
   To all my love and tender care of you.

FELICIA   I have indeed. I have no husband now,
   And where, alas, where will my little son

Now find a father?

BELLGARD   A son! Is then this cursed,
Unhappy marriage of so long a date?

FELICIA   Two years I've been his wife, and brought in secret
A wretched infant to partake our sorrows,
And now they are completed. Oh, my brother,
Tread me to the earth,
Double your anger on me, 'tis but just,
That I may fall a load of miseries,
And never, never rise.

BELLGARD   Alas, she moves my soul. . . pr'ythee no more,
Thy fault was great, but now thy punishment
Has so exceeded it, I must forgive thee.
Rise, Felicia, I am still a brother.
Wipe off these tears, thou shalt have justice done thee,
Trust me, thou shalt.

FELICIA   Oh, you are too good. But, my dear brother,
For whom am I so treacherously abandoned?

BELLGARD   Oh, that gives double edge to my resentment!
The other innocent, and more abused,
Shares in our blood as well as injuries.
What? Did the villain think our family
Were woman all, whom he might poorly wrong,
Safe from th'avenging hand of manly justice?

FELICIA   Is she a relation? What, Lamira?
Now I reflect on it, he spoke last night
Of some addresses there.

BELLGARD   Sister, be satisfied, my honour is
Too nearly touched to let you be abused.
With that compose yourself. But, poor Lamira!
Who can bear this fatal story to her?
I, who have been th'unlucky instrument,
Dare not speak it, till with the villain's blood
I've washed off the dishonour.

Exit BELLGARD

FELICIA   Is this the joy, the longed for morning promised!
Are all those tender, charming ecstasies
And soft embraces, which my love expected,
Now giv'n to another! Oh, 'tis death!
This very minute she holds him in her arms,
Thinks him all hers; he lies transported, too,
With perjured breath gives all my vows away.
Can I endure it? Oh Gramont!
He must be mine. I'll pierce his faithless heart

With my upbraidings. Oh, she shall not have him,
I'll tear him from her, I will, I will,
She shall not, must not have him. Ha!

As she is going out, LAMIRA *meets her*

LAMIRA   Why start you? Is there ought in me to fright?
FELICIA   Lamira here!
LAMIRA   Is that so strange? I come to seek your brother.
    The hour's indeed unusual; but my business
    Will well excuse to him this early visit.
FELICIA   Early indeed for lovers so newly joined to part.
LAMIRA   (Ha, does she know it?) What lovers do you speak of?
FELICIA   Too well you know. Would I had died ere known it.
    Why must I live to speak his infamy?
    Faithless and perjured, he is still Gramont,
    Once so beloved, so kind, and seeming true.
LAMIRA   (Is't then Felicia? She, whom nature meant
    A friend, my rival, cause of all my unhappiness?
    But how am I betrayed to her!
    How this curst secret known!)
    If once so kind, who tells you he is false?
FELICIA   Heav'n would not leave such baseness undetected,
    The sacred vows he made last night to you,
    Were mine before,
    And, oh, how oft in ecstasies of love repeated!
    How, pressing me in his fond arms, he has sworn
    They never should embrace another!
LAMIRA   (Too faithful villain!)
    What of this? Suppose he liked you once,
    Does that oblige him not to mend his choice?
    Is he to blame if you want charms to fix him?
FELICIA   Madam, I'll not dispute with you my charms,
    But urge my right in him. That plea's sufficient,
    Whate'er I am, to make your loves a crime.
LAMIRA   Because he swore to you, think you, that men
    Remember oaths in their loose pleasures made?
    What can you hope for from so vain a plea?
    'Tis wise in one, who sees herself abandoned,
    To mourn in silence; pursuits, reproaches, or complaints,
    May lose her fame, but ne'er retrieve the lover.
    Had you beheld last night what wonderous love he showed,
    You'd be convinced his heart's too deeply fixed
    E'er to be moved, and cease your vain lamenting.
FELICIA   Such wonderous love! Oh, I know too well
    How many tender ways he has to charm,

And make himself believed.
But could he be all that for any other,
So soft, so nice, so passionately fond,
So much transported, as I've seen the charmer?

LAMIRA   Poor credulous creature! When he seemed so fond,
You should have been less kind to have secured him,
Or made him more than swear.

FELICIA   What means all this?
You speak, as if you thought me not his wife.

LAMIRA   His wife?

FELICIA   Why with that scorn? His wife, his lawful wife,
As firmly as the holy priest could make me.

LAMIRA   Felicia, 'tis too much. If he is false,
He has gone too far to leave you that pretence,
Nor will it be believed.

FELICIA   I have sufficient witness, and every legal proof
Of what I say. But let himself appear,
Let him look on me, and try, if he has courage
To disown his first, his only wife.

LAMIRA   Then what am I?
If this is truth, is it your part to rail?
Am not I most abused, dishonoured, ruined?
But it cannot be. What, by a priest?
Legally married, said you?

FELICIA   Heav'n witness, that I am.
But yesterday I saw him too,
All love, all tenderness, and full of me.
Sure some curst arts must have been practised on him,
Some philtre he has drunk, no other way
You could have charmed him from me.

LAMIRA   Are there such arts?
Indeed the mighty fondness you so boast of,
May make it out of doubt.

FELICIA   Alas, my arts
Have been of little force, for I have lost him.
Oh, have I lost for ever all the joys
I found in him; the solid happiness
Of minds united; must we ne'er again
With equal wishes, equal transports, meet?

LAMIRA   Never, never, I henceforth forbid it.

FELICIA   What right can you pretend to of forbidding?

LAMIRA   The right, which one that's injured has to vengeance.
Th'ungrateful traitor that abused my love,
Shall give, nor know no joy in any others.
Think you, I'd patiently behold the villain

Possessing, and possessed, by a loved rival?
FELICIA   Madam, I think you neither have the right,
    Nor power to hinder it, if we agree.
LAMIRA   You dare not. My wrongs shall rise and check the very wish,
    Strike him with shame, and you with jealousy
    That shall prevent, or poison all your joys.
    But if thou art so poorly spirited,
    T'accept and yield t'adulterated love,
    I'll disappoint your wishes when they're highest.
    Fired with full hope, and nearer expectation,
    When all thy eager senses are at once
    Crowding to feast on his delusive charms,
    Ere thou can'st taste, I'll stab him in thy arms.

Exit LAMIRA

FELICIA   Alas, we ne'er can meet in joy again.
    Nay, now perhaps he means no more to see me.
    I would but once, but live to see him once,
    Take my last leave of him, and then the world,
    For when I'm his no more, I would be nothing.

Exit FELICIA

ACT IV

SCENE I

FELICIA *alone.* GRAMONT *enters to her*

GRAMONT   I waited long, my love, to find you free,
    And had almost despaired of seeing you.
FELICIA   A sight you could have been most willingly
    Dispensed from.
GRAMONT   Why dost thou say so? 'Tis unkind, thou know'st
    I ever thought the hours I passed with thee,
    The happiest of my life.
FELICIA   Perhaps you did,
    Perhaps you loved me once.
GRAMONT   And do not still?
FELICIA   Oh Gramont, would you had never said you loved,
    Or I had ne'er believed you.
GRAMONT   Not love? If I have any good in me,
    'Tis the sincere affection which I bear thee.

What means my dear?

FELICIA   Have I not been a fond, a faithful wife?

GRAMONT   Not malice can deny it.

FELICIA   Why am I then forsaken for another?

GRAMONT   Forsaken?

FELICIA   You, who a thousand times
Have sworn our marriage was the weakest bond
That held you to me; you, to break them all!

GRAMONT   Ha!

FELICIA   Or tho' you had not loved me, could you do
So base a thing?

GRAMONT   Oh, don't upbraid me; that thou know'st my shame,
Is punishment enough.

FELICIA   Could you be false to me, that doted on you?
Ungrateful man! (How can I live without him!)

GRAMONT   Thou break'st my heart.

FELICIA   You've broke my heart, and may I not complain?
Unkind Gramont!

GRAMONT   Oh, turn thy eyes away,
For their reproaches sting me to the quick.

FELICIA   Nay, then I'll fix 'em till your heart relent
With pity, for the miseries you've caused.
Look on me, look upon your wretched wife!

GRAMONT   A wretch like me should be excluded ever
From the blessed vision! I dare not look on thee.

FELICIA   Then tell me, if I e'er deserved your love,
What have I done to lose it?

GRAMONT   Lose it! If I had not loved thee tenderly,
I had not been a villain.

FELICIA   For love of me?

GRAMONT   For thee! T'avert the miseries,
Which threat'ned thee, and our unhappy infant,
I sacrificed my honour.

FELICIA   What miseries would not I share with you,
Rather than share yourself with any other!
I would have starved first, or have begged your food,
To have kept you mine. But now you are Lamira's.

GRAMONT   I am unworthy to be thine, Felicia.
All I can ask thee now is to forgive me.

FELICIA   Alas, what's my forgiveness! My brother and Lamira
Will pursue you. She does not love like me.

GRAMONT   No matter, their resentment I can bear,
But not Felicia's. See, thy wretched husband
Kneels at thy feet, to beg compassion of thee,
Entreats thee, when he falls beneath his griefs,

Or by thy brother's vengeance, to bestow
Some pity on him. Think, remember still
'Twas love of thee made him unworthy of thee. . .
But if she can forgive, she must be good,
And then must hate me too, despise, condemn me.
Oh, curse!
Let me grow here, become one piece with earth,
Lost to myself, all eyes, and all remembrance.

FELICIA   Oh, I can't bear to see you thus, oh, rise!
What would you have me to do for you?

GRAMONT   For me! Use me like what I am, a dog,
Fit to be spurned, kicked from you like a cur.

FELICIA   Don't distract yourself.

GRAMONT   What, outlive my honesty, and not be mad!
Lose thy esteem, lose my Felicia's heart,
Deserve to lose 'em too, and not be mad!

FELICIA   Oh Gramont!
If you had loved but half so faithfully
As your Felicia does, she had not lost you.

GRAMONT   Thou didst; but now you cannot, must not love me.

FELICIA   Oh! I never knew till now how much I love you!
Be what you will, or use me how you will,
You've fixed yourself so firmly to my heart,
I can't divide it from you.
'Tis full, 'tis breaking now with fears for you.

GRAMONT   Thou dear example of fidelity, (*rising*)
What dost thou fear? Come to my arms, and tell me.

FELICIA   Oh, fly to mine, and then I can fear nothing,
I'll hold thee here, and fate shall never reach thee.

GRAMONT   Not if thou lov'st me. Oh, I see thou dost,
And circled thus, I'm happy once again.

FELICIA   How have you swore no other e'er should thus embrace you!

GRAMONT   I swear again, none ever did, or shall.

FELICIA   Tell me not that. Last night. . . think on last night.

GRAMONT   Base as I was last night, I could not break that vow.

FELICIA   Oh Gramont! do not deceive me more;
Lamira boasts the wondrous love you showed.

GRAMONT   To her? If it were love not once to touch her,
Or ev'n approach her bed. By Heav'n I did it not.

FELICIA   I will believe you.

GRAMONT   Thou may'st, my love. I think thou dost forgive me, too.
Oh, let me keep thee then for ever thus!
For whilst I am possessed of so much goodness,
I shall believe I'm honest. Am I not, Felicia?
No, thou know'st I am not.

Why dost thou touch me then? Fly, fly away,
Or thou art lost, not innocence can save thee.
FELICIA   Alas, what mean you?
GRAMONT   'Tis dangerous to be near me.
If fate should now be hurling vengeance on me,
Might it not strike thee too?
FELICIA   Heav'n avert it ever! I would fain
Hope all may yet be well.
GRAMONT   Well! Can'st thou redeem my honour, clear my fame?
I shall be pointed at, a noted villain,
Where can I fly from the reproaching sight
Of all that once esteemed me? Or how endure it,
When the very thought strikes such confusion?
Better I might have borne the worst of miseries,
That threatened me; which not the meanest wretch,
That begs, or toils for bread, but can support,
And does not truck his honesty for fortune,
Thou, coward, durst not. Now how wilt thou bear
The infamy thy baseness loads thee with?
FELICIA   Alas, 'tis I have caused your infamy,
My inconsiderate passion has exposed you.
What madness moved me to reveal the fatal secret!
Was that a remedy! What could I intend,
What consequence expect, but your destruction!
Oh! I can ne'er enough revenge it on myself,
Nor you enough reproach me!
GRAMONT   Thou'rt not to blame.
FELICIA   Indeed I am, it was my duty, as your wife,
Whate'er I suffered, not to have accused you,
And as I loved, I should have had no thought
Of my own misery whilst you were happy.
GRAMONT   How can'st thou speak so kindly to a man
That has undone thee! Thou dost not, sure, look forward
On thy ruin, or thou could'st ne'er forgive me.
Nay, by Heav'ns it stains thy virtue, as I am now,
To use me with such tenderness.
FELICIA   Would you not have me love you?
GRAMONT   It is not for thy honour to show affection
For one thou must despise. I will not let thee
Wrong thyself so much, but leave thee to reflect,
And thou wilt meet me next, as I deserve,
With coldness, anger, and disdain.
FELICIA   Impossible. . . you are not going thus!
GRAMONT   I should, and thou should'st not retain me.
FELICIA   I would retain thee ever.

GRAMONT   Oh Felicia!...
    Yet I will go... look not so killing soft,
    Think on thy honour, think I am a villain,
    Learn to despise me, struggle with thy heart,
    Strive thy ill-placed affection to remove,
    As I now tear myself from all I love.

Exit GRAMONT

FELICIA   Is it a fault to love him? If it be,
    In punishing impute his crime to me.
    I'll pay for both a double penalty,
    However cruel Heaven intends his share,
    Beyond what life, all, all that love can bear.

Exit FELICIA

SCENE II

LAMIRA'S HOUSE

Enter LAMIRA *and* MARIAN

LAMIRA   When will these struggling passions cease to rage,
    Anger and love, pity and jealousy?
    Whilst each are striving to possess me wholly,
    They rend my soul among 'em.
MARIAN   Neither must now have any share in it.
    Since, Madam, you're resolved to leave the world,
    Heav'n claims your heart entire.
LAMIRA   Yes, Marian, I have vowed myself to Heav'n,
    The safe retreat from fears and vain desires.
    But something must be done to satisfy
    The discontent of my disordered thoughts,
    That no unruly one may there disturb me.
MARIAN   The place will be your sanctuary from 'em,
    A holy cloister's gates shut with the world
    All human passions and reflections out.
LAMIRA   What? Can I there
    Think tamely on my injuries,
    And be pleased the villain 'scaped unpunished?
MARIAN   Do you imagine, Madam, then Bellgard
    Will not revenge you?
LAMIRA   Ha! Bellgard!
    Good Heaven forbid. His way would be too fatal,
    Not clear my spotted honour,

But stain it worse with blood. A wicked justice
To punish his by a more horrid crime.
I dread to think it! Bellgard is violent,
And may do sudden mischief, if not hindered.

MARIAN   Felicia may perhaps have power to calm
Her brother's fierce resentments, she's mild enough
Soon to forgive and plead for him that wronged her.

LAMIRA   Felicia plead! Felicia save his life,
And he be her reward, blest in each other!
Oh, what a torturing thought! Can I endure it?
Nor love, nor honour can.

MARIAN   You're neither pleased, that he should die, nor live.
What way would you dispose him?

LAMIRA   Rather to death, than her. But there is yet
Something I would be at, I know not how,
Scarce what. Ha, is it Gramont!

Enter GRAMONT

Com'st thou t'insult o'er one whom thou hast ruined?
Or think'st thou yet thy baseness undiscovered?

GRAMONT   Not to conceal, but to confess my crime,
Not to insult, but to implore forgiveness,
I thus approach you.

LAMIRA   How dar'st thou hope I can forgive such wrongs?

GRAMONT   Unless your goodness, Madam, I must own
My hope has no foundation.
I've nought to plead but what must more incense you.
If I say Castalio's suffering moved me,
Should I, to serve a friend, abuse your love?
Or if I urge Felicia's dearer interest,
Th'excuse can but inflame your hatred to me.

LAMIRA   Is it then so? Let me hear thee speak
Thyself a villain. Is she your wife?

GRAMONT   To her misfortune, and my shame, she is.
Fool! not to think her happiness enough.
Whilst she was mine, how could I fear to want it?

LAMIRA   Tortures and death! What brutal insolence!
Gramont, it seems you came not to incite
My pity, but my vengeance.

GRAMONT   Neither, Madam,
I am too guilty to deserve your pity,
And need not urge revenge, since you can have
No greater than I mean to give you soon.
I only beg your anger mayn't survive me,
Or curse pursue me farther than the grave.

LAMIRA   Is it to hinder that you take such pains
       To let me know to whom I owe my ruin,
       That I may turn my curses on Felicia?
GRAMONT   Heav'n forbid! She's innocent, and wronged
       As much as you.
LAMIRA   What are her wrongs? How offered to be named with mine?
       No, traitor, thou may'st know mine are unequalled,
       When even thy baseness could not make 'em greater.
GRAMONT   Madam, I think I had the power to wrong you more,
       Which my not using may, I hope, in part
       Atone for what I did.
LAMIRA   I know 'twas not respect for me, nor honour
       Stopped thee in thy course of mischief.
       Thy inclination lagged ere it was complete,
       Or thy firm villainy would ne'er have failed thee.
GRAMONT   Can there be such stupidity in nature,
       To be insensible to so much beauty?
LAMIRA   Ay, now thou hast it. Fawn and flatter well,
       Daub o'er my injuries with soothing words,
       And make me take 'em all for obligations.
       Say how you love; say with how much regret
       You sacrificed your wishes. Is it not thus?
       Have not my charms done wondrous execution?
GRAMONT   Had not Felicia first. . .
LAMIRA   No more; thou wilt not suffer me one moment
       To forget that hated name. Left, thou
       Should'st be, alone the object of my rage.
       But fear not, she shall share it.
GRAMONT   Oh, rather double it on me.
LAMIRA   Fond, doting fool!
       Thou dost but show me, in thy care for her,
       The near and surest way to thy destruction.
       And I will strike where I may wound thee deepest,
       Add all the fury of a slighted rival
       To the calm justice of revenge on thee.
GRAMONT   Madam, I find whatever I can say,
       But more foments your anger, therefore leave you.
       I go to satisfy your just resentment,
       But if my death's too little to appease it,
       Rather than punish others for my crime,
       Still hate me, let your rage, without control,
       Load me with curses, till they sink my soul.

                                          Exit GRAMONT

LAMIRA   Perdition seize it, despair
　　　And all the racks I feel, revenge me on thee!
　　　No fears, no tenderness but for Felicia?
　　　Is this the way t'appease my just resentment,
　　　To tell me, 'twas for love of her he wronged me?
　　　There's then no other way to punish him,
　　　But by the loss of her. They must be parted. . .

Enter CASTALIO

　　　Did I not order none should be admitted?
MARIAN   I did not hear you, Madam.
LAMIRA   No matter, you might have thought it was not proper.
CASTALIO   With all the awe of one that fears t'offend,
　　　And knows not whether he offends or not,
　　　I pay this duty. Impatient, and yet more
　　　In dread to know my fate
　　　From her that's mistress of it.
LAMIRA   Unseasonable importunity!
　　　My lord, I cannot think this meant to me,
　　　I have no power, alas, not of my own,
　　　Much less another's fate.
CASTALIO   Your fate is Heaven's care, and, oh, that mine
　　　Were yours as much as it is in your power.
LAMIRA   You know not what you wish, but let it end.
　　　'Tis a discourse I'm not disposed to hear,
　　　And if, my lord, you value my repose,
　　　You'll not pursue it further.
CASTALIO   Then I am doomed, doomed to despair for ever,
　　　Since but to hear of love from me offends you.
LAMIRA   From you, or any other, I hate the name,
　　　And fly from all that wear a form of kindness,
　　　For 'tis in that alone men can deceive.
CASTALIO   'Tis oft indeed put on for a disguise,
　　　Yet must be worn by those who would be known
　　　For what they really are.
LAMIRA   There's no reality, no truth in man;
　　　But where it most appears, and seems least feigned,
　　　'Tis there the master-piece of villain lies.
CASTALIO   You speak as if some one, whom you had trusted,
　　　Had deceived you.
LAMIRA   Yes, I have been deceived.
CASTALIO   Who durst attempt it?
LAMIRA   One in whom you and all mankind have been
　　　Deceived. Oh traitor! Who could have suspected
　　　That modest show of honesty and honour?

Exquisite, finished, Oh ungrateful villain!

CASTALIO   The thought disorders you. It must be sure
Somewhat of weight that can transport you thus.

LAMIRA   I had forgot myself. . .
'Tis true, I have some cause to be disturbed.
But pardon me, that I so ill acquit myself
Of the respect I owe you thus to expose it.

CASTALIO   Madam, I'll take my leave, if I constrain you,
But wish you could esteem me worth your trust,
As one, by whom all your concerns are held
More than in equal balance with his own.

LAMIRA   What use of friendship, trust, or to complain
Of injuries for which there's no redress?

CASTALIO   There's then revenge.

LAMIRA   But that you cannot give.

CASTALIO   I think I shall not boast to say, there's no one
In your cause shall dare beyond me.
Speak who the traitor is, that has abused you,
And if, to do you justice,
There be an obstacle or danger I refuse
T'encounter, let me be branded for a coward.

LAMIRA   There is an obstacle has greater force
Than any danger can: 'Tis one you love,
Whom if I named, you would not credit me,
One you esteem your friend, your nearest friend.

CASTALIO   My friend! Who durst usurp that sacred name,
And injure me, where I'm most sensible?
This gives me double right to seek revenge.
You must not, will not now conceal him from me.

LAMIRA   Ere long the public rumour will inform you.
This cursed adventure will be blazed among 'em.
I shall be made the common theme and mirth;
My honour lie at every whisper's mercy
That's pleased to pass his censure on my conduct.

CASTALIO   Permit me then to ask it from yourself,
That if I hear rash tongues too bold with it,
I may with more assurance vindicate you.

LAMIRA   'Tis the most strange unhappy story, so full
Of baseness, height'ned with all the aggravations
Of vilest treachery and ingratitude,
For he had such endearing obligations,
I hazarded my ruin, all for him,
O'er-ruled by a destructive passion, nay, 'twas madness,
The blot of life, and stain of all my glory.

CASTALIO   Was he beloved, and yet could injure you?

How? In what nature? 'Twas impossible
For one so blest, not to return affection.
LAMIRA   Would that were all his crime, but he has basely
Deceived, abused, wronged me in such a nature,
I cannot speak it. . . Conscious of my folly,
For I have been as weak, as he perfidious,
Press me no further to declare my shame.
CASTALIO   Then name the traitor to me, and I will tear
The secret from his heart; with life extort it.
LAMIRA   A villain's life's too mean a sacrifice.
No, let me think. . . Somewhat I had designed
Of lasting torment suited to his crime. . .
That first I'll try, but if without success,
May use your friendship,
Till when, I beg you'll inquire no further.
CASTALIO   Madam, I must obey, and will no longer
Trouble you in this disorder; but when you are pleased
To let me know the man you have been deceived in,
You shall have proof
My soul disdains all friendship with a traitor.

Exit CASTALIO

LAMIRA   Yes, thou shalt live to see thyself abandoned,
And taste with me the pangs of hopeless love.
That one, who could be guilty of this baseness,
Should know to love with such fidelity!
Oh, what a happiness to possess that heart,
So fond, so true! Could it have first been mine!
What full delights has not Felicia known?
Eternal woes succeed 'em. Be they remembered
But to increase the curse of deprivation.
The stings of shame and causeless jealousy
Sharpen the pains of everlasting absence
That I decree 'em. Bellgard must be advised with
And won, if I have any power with him,
To set his rage the bounds I have given mine.
I'd not be cruel, nor too tamely bear,
Both the extremes are shunned in this design,
And therefore 'tis but just to hope success.
What can revenge, honour, and love, have less?

Exit LAMIRA

ACT V

SCENE I

FELICIA   Distracted with some dismal apprehension,
In vain I seek, for ease, to change the prospect.
Whatever way I turn my roving thoughts,
'Tis still but a new scene of misery.
Were my Gramont safe from my brother's rage,
And the world's censure, 'twere yet impossible
Ever to reconcile him to himself.

Enter BELLGARD *and* LAMIRA

LAMIRA   Whate'er can satisfy my injured honour,
May well, Bellgard, be thought for yours sufficient.
BELLGARD   I don't dispute it, Madam.
LAMIRA   Nor do you grant it.
BELLGARD   Honour gives different laws to different sexes,
Mine says this sword alone can do me justice.

BELLGARD *stands apart*

FELICIA   What can this unexpected visit mean?
LAMIRA   You seem to take me for an enemy.
Perhaps you look on me with rival eyes,
But I am come in friendship.
FELICIA   'Tis what, indeed, I did not hope, and scarce dare credit.
LAMIRA   You're innocent to me, as I to you;
Tho' both each other's chief unhappiness.
But there's another guilty cause of that,
Him only we should hate, let us be friends.
Disgusted with the world, I have resolved,
The short remainder of this wretched life,
To be a strict recluse by holy vows,
And leave to you, Felicia, the possession
Of all that fortune I am mistress of.
FELICIA   This is amazing, Madam! How have I
Deserved from you such kindness?
LAMIRA   Your merit is unquestioned, and to me
You are a near relation.
My gift is only charged with one condition,
The same I have imposed upon myself,
That you shall never see Gramont again,
In which I have consulted both our honours.
FELICIA   It were not much, indeed, for you to see him.
But what in you is virtue, would in me,

Who am his wife, be impious.
LAMIRA   Not since he first has broke his faith with you:
By that you are absolved.
FELICIA   The marriage vows are not conditional,
The tie's as strong, my duty still the same,
Howe'er he fail in his.
LAMIRA   It can't oblige you to depend on one
Who wants assistance to support himself.
FELICIA   Yes, Madam, I must share my husband's fate,
However wretched.
When he's deprived of every other comfort,
In that extremity he'll need me most.
BELLGARD   And think'st thou he shall keep thee? Be advised,
Felicia, you may lose him on worse terms.
FELICIA   To me all terms in losing him are equal.
LAMIRA   She dotes upon him.
BELLGARD   Infamously dotes.
I tell thee, by my honour, thou shalt lose
Both him, and me, wander where'er thou can'st,
I will not know thee in the last distress.
And for thy villain husband —
FELICIA   Let him but wander with me, I ask no more,
And we will take our weary steps somewhere remote,
Where we can ne'er be more a burden to you,
Nor shall you ever hear that there is such
A wretched pair in being.
BELLGARD   Do not hope it, for by my life I swear,
If thou dar'st now refuse to abandon him,
Where'er you think to fly from my resentment,
There's not a place so distant can contain you,
But I'll pursue you to, and tear thee from him.
FELICIA   Do you grudge us ev'n misery together?
LAMIRA   Together! 'Tis a word, tho' joined with death,
I cannot hear thee name. Madam, accept
My offered friendship, or you shall find
I can resent the slight, and, if provoked,
Am not a despicable enemy.
FELICIA   Your hate can execute no worse
Than what in friendship's name you have proposed,
For 'tis the utmost fate can do against me.
BELLGARD   Shameless creature! to confess this fondness
For a man thou know'st to be a villain.
FELICIA   Alas! what fondness? Have I asked ought for him,
But what the worst of enemies in malice
Would condemn him to?

        To taste the bitterness of poverty,
        Roving like vagabonds about the world,
        For ever banished from our country, friends,
        And all we hold most dear.
LAMIRA   But one another, there you expect to find
        An ample recompense for all you lose,
        And be instead of all the world to him.
        Is that a state for such a criminal?
        What satisfaction to my injured love?
        No, he shall share the torments he has caused,
        Languish in fruitless wishes, curst with despair,
        Eternally deprived of all he loves.
        Oh, I have felt, and know 'tis death, 'tis Hell.
        That, that's a vengeance for me to take,
        Tho' much too gentle for the traitor's crime.
FELICIA   How has he merited such cruelty?
        Had he last night, when all was in his power,
        Taken advantage of consenting love
        On your unguarded honour, this resentment
        Would well become you then, and were but just.
        You know how far he was from such a thought.
LAMIRA   Then he boasts, and makes a merit of it
        To my rival.
FELICIA   I thought it one to you.
        It seems you do not.
LAMIRA   No, since 'twas meant a sacrifice to thee,
        Even honour is my scorn, when I must owe it
        To that blind dotage which I see thee proud of.
        But though thou triumph'st now, know, rival, know,
        That stupid constancy in ill-placed love,
        Ere long, to both the greatest curse shall prove.
BELLGARD   I'll attend you, Madam, to the Count Roquelaure's.
        Now hear, inglorious girl, mark my last words.
        Thy obstinacy but confirms my hate,
        Undoes thyself, and wings thy husband's fate.
FELICIA   Oh, do not go thus cruelly resolved!
        Stay, brother, on my bended knees I beg you.
        Cannot these trembling hands a while retain you?
        Give but some days to a poor sister's tears,
        But till the fierceness of your rage abate,
        Till you can calmly weigh the wrong he has done,
        With all the miseries that led him to it.
        Oh, think what would become of you yourself,
        If Heaven were thus severe for every fault committed,
        And, as you hope for mercy from above,

Now show it to a brother's first offence.
BELLGARD   To one that Heaven detests! No, may I ne'er
Find mercy there, if ever I forgive him.

Exeunt BELLGARD *with* LAMIRA

FELICIA   He's bent on death, and nothing can avert it.
I've done, and here will lie to wait the wound
That through Gramont's will shortly pierce this heart.
I shall behold him soon, stabbed, mangled, murdered.
Oh barbarous brother! Oh Gramont! He's lost!
I shall ne'er see him more, but cold and ghastly,
Breathing his last, and weltering in his blood.
Then there's an end of all my miseries,
For that I can't outlive. Oh, must I live to see it!

FELICIA *weeps. Enter* GRAMONT

GRAMONT   Upon the floor! Oh, most afflicting sight!
Thither the weight of woes I've heaped upon thee
Has pressed thee down. This is a scene of sadness
More expressive than the most moving words.
Why art thou thus, Felicia? Thou should'st not so
Indulge thy griefs. Be calm, and well consider
As now thy circumstances are, what way
May best be thought to make thee least unhappy.
FELICIA   There's not a medium.
I can have no misfortunes, if I've you,
Nor ever think of happiness without you.
GRAMONT   Alas, Felicia!
FELICIA   You pity me, as if
You knew how cruelly I have been used,
How deaf my brother is to all my prayers.
GRAMONT   Do not offend him. There is hope, my love,
When I am gone, he'll still be careful of thee.
FELICIA   Gone! Then you can think of going from me?
Of leaving your Felicia?
GRAMONT   In life I ne'er can leave thee,
And there's not a pain in death but that.
FELICIA   You speak, methinks, as one resolved on death.
Must you conspire too with those that hate me?
GRAMONT   Thou'st cause to wish I had died before thou knew'st me.
FELICIA   I could not then have felt the loss,
But now the very fear is unsupportable,
'Twas that had filled my bursting heart o'erwhelmed,
And laid me on the earth, as now you found me.
And 'tis the only blow of fate I have not strength to bear.

GRAMONT   How can I hear thee speak so tenderly,
 And think I have undone thee! Oh Felicia!
 Thy love gives double weight to my afflictions.
 What is there should induce me then to live?
FELICIA   If you have any love for me, the thought
 How miserable I shall be without you.
GRAMONT   I know too well thy tenderness of nature,
 Know I am too much loved. But thou may'st learn
 By thy unhappy husband, there's not a state
 So miserable, but may with greater ease
 Be suffered than dishonour. Would'st thou not blush
 To live with one distrusted, shunned and looked on
 As a knave by all mankind? Can I,
 Or would'st thou have me bear it?
FELICIA   I could for you.
 The world's opinion would not weigh with me
 Against your least disturbance.
GRAMONT   Why will you plead so earnestly a cause,
 In which if you believed you could prevail,
 You would yourself despise me?
FELICIA   There was a time,
 When I might be assured I would prevail;
 When the least show of discontent from me
 Had power to shake your firmest resolution,
 But then you loved me.
GRAMONT   Do I not love you?
FELICIA   You see me drowned in tears, o'erwhelmed in grief,
 Hear me implore, and bear it all unmoved!
GRAMONT   Unmoved! You know not what a war you've raised
  within me:
 There's not a word you speak, but would o'ercome me.
 But when I think thou'lt share in my disgrace,
 For that I know thy love would make thee do —
FELICIA   No, no, Gramont, were your concern for me,
 'Twould most be shown where I am most concerned.
 But there you are insensible, or think not,
 Or care not what I shall suffer.
GRAMONT   Oh! 'tis a thought divides me from myself,
 Staggers my resolution, makes me wish
 The greatest, that thou could'st hate thy husband.
 Every, every way, I must undo thee:
 'Tis only left me now to choose the noblest,
 And that should be endured with least affliction.
FELICIA   You've found the way indeed to shorten mine.
 Already your unkindness breaks my heart!

GRAMONT   Thou art unkind to use such wounding words,
  That know'st my heart too tender to endure it.
  What would'st thou have me do?
FELICIA   Oh, what indeed? For what should I entreat,
  Now all that soft, that dear affection's lost,
  That once could have denied Felicia nothing?
  What have I more to lose?
GRAMONT   I can deny thee nothing. Where wilt thou lead me?
  Every tear thou shed'st draws with it my heart's blood.
  Rather than see thee thus, I'd bear with life,
  With infamy. Must I, Felicia? Shall I?
FELICIA   Nothing for me. I am not worthy your care,
  And death will quickly free me from my woes.
GRAMONT   Thou art my only care. Take, take me to thy bosom,
  There hide me from my shame, and from myself,
  Do with me what thou wilt, but let me never think —
FELICIA   Would you forsake these arms,
  That tremble with delight whilst they embrace thee?
GRAMONT   Talk on, and let me gaze on thee forever,
  Till I forget there's ought on earth besides,
  And thou art goodness all, all joy and blessings.
FELICIA   Would you forget there's ought on earth but me?
  Then sure you could for me forsake the rest.
  Could you forever leave the busy world,
  To seek with me some unknown, distant refuge,
  Whither the ills we fear can ne'er pursue us?
GRAMONT   Alas! Thou talk'st but as thy love would have it,
  Thou know'st too well it is not in my power.
FELICIA   Had I not thought it was, I should not have proposed it.
GRAMONT   Could I provide thee even but the bare
  Necessities of nature, what's beyond
  I know thy generous kindness well could spare.
  But can I take thee hence, to see thee perish
  Under the extremities of griping wants
  Thou hast not felt, and can'st not apprehend?
  The smallest of those hardships, to which thou would'st expose
  Thy tender body, does far surpass thy strength.
FELICIA   Love will supply my strength, and as I can,
  I'll labour for our food, or beg an alms,
  And we shall find some friendly barn to shelter us
  At night, whil'st we repose our weary limbs.
  But could you, my Gramont, endure your share?
  And if the product of our toils falls short,
  Take cheerfully the scraps of charity?
  Sometimes perhaps your sleep may be disturbed

By a poor hungry infant's cries. Could you,
With patience, bear it? Could you in such a state
Find any joy in me? Would you not leave me,
Leave me, and my poor condition? My love,
Why this? The tears are starting at your eyes!

GRAMONT   Is this thy fate at last? And must I see thee
Suffer all the miseries, which, when
I did but fear for thee, o'ercame my virtue!
'Twas this idea, and have I brought 'em on thee!
Made thy ruin more inevitable!
Give me patience, Heav'n, that I should force thee
To this wretched state!

FELICIA   'Tis my choice,
I have preferred it to a splendid fortune,
Which now is offered me.

GRAMONT   What fortune? Or how offered?

FELICIA   Lamira's. She leaves the world, and would have bribed me
With her trifling gift to part with you.

GRAMONT   Did you refuse it?

FELICIA   Could I do otherwise?

GRAMONT   'Twas reproaching me. Did you not then think?
(By Heav'n I know you did) with scorn you thought
This was the bait, this bait, which I despise,
'Twas that seduced my husband.

FELICIA   Not from your faith to me, that you preserved,
Though, by provoking her, you hazarded
The loss e'en of the bait that tempted you.
Have I done more for you?

GRAMONT   Yet there's a cause,
That will induce you to accept the offer,
Your son, Felicia, he must perish else.

FELICIA   He must submit to share his wretched parents' fate.

GRAMONT   His fate is yet more cruel! I durst not tell thee,
Loth to increase the sorrows that too deeply pierced thee,
But since 'tis in thy power to redeem him.

FELICIA   Redeem him!

GRAMONT   From pirates' hands. But yesterday
The fatal news was brought me.

FELICIA   Oh, 'tis too much!

GRAMONT   Weep not, but think how thou may'st ransom him.

FELICIA   Alas! Have I the means?

GRAMONT   Thou may'st. But I, I always am an obstacle,
Where any good's proposed. Turn, turn, Felicia,
All thy tenderness upon that dear
Innocent part of me, thou dost misplace it here.

FELICIA   At any other rate I would preserve him,
   But in exchange for you he's only dear to me
   As he is yours.
GRAMONT   Then as he is mine, I beg thee to relieve him.
FELICIA   Oh, 'tis the strongest trial! But to part with you,
   That, that's the hard condition! Impossible!
   Is there no other hope? No way to free him?
   Somewhat I must endeavour, perhaps your father
   May compassionate his innocence,
   Though his unhappy parents have offended.
GRAMONT   Try, my Felicia, if there's any mixture
   Of the least tenderness in his hard nature,
   Thou hast power to extract it.
FELICIA   Ere this he knows our marriage.
   Thither Lamira going hence intended.
GRAMONT   Then haste, my love, before th'impression ta'en
   From her resentment strike too deep for thee t'efface.
FELICIA   I will. But dare I leave you? Will you promise,
   Till my return, to shun my brother's sight?
GRAMONT   What need of promises? Thou know'st thy power.
FELICIA   May I rely upon your love?
GRAMONT   Thou would'st, if thou could'st know with what
     reluctance
   I now part with thee, scarce could it be
   More sensible, if we were ne'er to meet again.
FELICIA   Perhaps we never may.
GRAMONT   Why said'st thou that?
   Thy sad forboding words struck to my heart,
   As if fate had pronounced 'em.
FELICIA   Then I fear,
   Fate has indeed pronounced 'em.
GRAMONT   We'll disappoint it,
   Cling to each other thus, and never part.
FELICIA   We shall not at this rate. Unless you throw me
   From your arms, I have not power to leave 'em.
GRAMONT   No, thou shalt not.
FELICIA   Is then your son forgot?
GRAMONT   Alas! My child! It will be so, 'tis vain
   To strive, for destiny's irrevocable.
FELICIA   And we must part.
GRAMONT   But must I lose thee, too?
FELICIA   If destiny will have it.
GRAMONT   Thou'rt gone!
FELICIA   Oh my Gramont!
GRAMONT   Farewell.

FELICIA   I fear forever.

GRAMONT   Forever! Never see thee! O Felicia!

Enter CASTALIO

Castalio! The man I would most shun.
How shall I look on him, or how receive him!
CASTALIO   This is beyond my hope. I came to ask
Where I might find my friend, and I have met thee.
Let me embrace thee, give thee thy Castalio,
Thine, my Gramont, for 'tis from thee I hold
My freedom, life and honour, I've nothing that's my own,
Nothing of worth, but what I owe to thee.
GRAMONT   My lord, you owe me nothing.
CASTALIO   Is this the way to greet my clasping arms?
You answer too with an unusual strangeness,
And wrong me with a title less than friend,
The only one I glory in.
GRAMONT   Yet 'tis the only one dishonours you.
CASTALIO   To be called your friend?
GRAMONT   When you know me, you will disdain the name.
CASTALIO   'Tis therefore I am fond of it, because I know you.
GRAMONT   For what I seemed, but till this day I never
Rightly knew myself.
CASTALIO   I know you better than you do yourself.
GRAMONT   Do you know me for a vile, a coward wretch,
That dares not look ill fortune in the face,
And only sides with honour till interest clashes with it?
CASTALIO   You give me the reverse of what you are.
GRAMONT   I said you did not know me.
CASTALIO   Not in that character.
I know you firm to honour, have seen you dare
The worst of fortune's malice. Is it not for honour
You have now incurred a father's anger,
And exposed yourself to all the ruin
That must follow it?
GRAMONT   Perhaps that was my mind of yesterday,
I may have changed it since. Rely on no man,
He that this hour is honest, the next may be a villain.
CASTALIO   I think you're changed indeed, your words are wild,
Your looks disordered, Heav'n preserve your reason!
GRAMONT   Heav'n rather take it from me! 'Tis the best wish
For me, unless I could recall the past.
There's nothing now in future fate but madness

    Can give me any ease.
CASTALIO   It grieves my soul to hear you! Have better hopes,
    I may have power to serve you. Why thus reserved?
    We've used with friendship to beguile our griefs,
    Whilst we discharged 'em on each other's breast.
GRAMONT   Let me forget I ever had your friendship,
    'Tis now the greatest torment of my thoughts,
    When you no more can cheer or pity me,
    Can be that friend no more.
CASTALIO   Not less a friend for being more unhappy,
    I'm still the same to you.
GRAMONT   Oh, Oh, Castalio! Were I still the same!
    But now —
CASTALIO   What now?
GRAMONT   Spare me this, Heav'n! Drive me where I may ne'er
    Behold this man, and let me be exposed
    The public scorn, marked out for infamy,
    And hooted by the gaping multitude.
    Not all the ignominy th'united world
    Could heap on me would half so much confound me
    As but to look on him, and think what once
    I was in his esteem, and, oh, what now I am!
CASTALIO   Am I so dreadful! Trust me I'll use you gentler
    Than you would yourself. What is't you labour with?
    Shall I assist you in the pang of birth?
    Somewhat you've done amiss, which you repent of.
    Let me be judge, for you are too severe.
    I know you ever would condemn yourself
    With strictest rigour for the smallest frailties.
GRAMONT   Is't me you speak of?
CASTALIO   I've chid you oft, and yet I loved you for it.
GRAMONT   And would you then have thought I could commit
    The basest, meanest, the most treacherous action?
CASTALIO   Impossible.
GRAMONT   I thought so, too. It seems we were mistaken.
CASTALIO   What have you done? I have a friend's concern,
    And ought to know it.
GRAMONT   Indeed I don't deserve your least concern.
    But for your peace of mind inquire no further,
    Believe I am unworthy of your friendship,
    And think of me no more. But if you hear my name
    Avoid the story that must follow it,
    For you would hate yourself if you should know
    How ill you had placed your kindness.
CASTALIO   You make me still

More eager to inquire. By our past friendship
I conjure you tell me. Your heart seems bursting
With the fatal secret, and yet you will not vent it.

GRAMONT   Can you not guess?

CASTALIO   I cannot, nor let me longer
Importune to learn it from yourself.

GRAMONT   Have you not some remembrance what yesterday
I said my father had proposed?

CASTALIO   Which you refused?

GRAMONT   Perhaps I did not.

CASTALIO   Did not what?
I mean what was not in your power t'accept.

GRAMONT   What's that?

CASTALIO   The marriage.

GRAMONT   Why not in my power?

CASTALIO   Because it would have been the highest baseness.

GRAMONT   Are base things never done?

CASTALIO   You could not do it.

GRAMONT   Oh friend!

CASTALIO   I'll not believe it.

GRAMONT   You think too well of me.

CASTALIO   I'm sorry for't.

GRAMONT   Now then you know me rightly.

CASTALIO   Could you. . .

GRAMONT   Urge not my crime against me; it needs not.
Your awful virtue checks, and strikes me deeper
Than your reproaches can.

CASTALIO   I've thought too far, it can't be yet completed,
You've only giv'n hopes you would comply,
Perhaps a promise.

GRAMONT   'Tis done. Less had not gained my end,
Which partly is accomplished. You are free,
I had no other means of serving you.

CASTALIO   And did you think I prized my honour less
Than liberty, that I would have it purchased
On dishonest terms? You know Castalio
As little, as I have hitherto known you.

GRAMONT   In what I did I gratified myself,
Nor aimed I at acknowledgements from you.

CASTALIO   You might have made your own advantage, then.
But what had I to do with your mean tricks?
Was't not enough I suffered in my friendship
But you must undermine my honour, too,
And draw me for the prize of villainy?
I'll not endure it.

GRAMONT   All the dishonour's mine.

CASTALIO   Can I share the profit, and not the infamy?
  Who is there seeing me enjoy this freedom
  That will not think I'm pleased, nay, was accomplice
  In the guilt that wrought it? The air I breathe,
  The every step I tread reproaches me
  The terms on which 'twas gained, 'twas basely done.

GRAMONT   There's not a term that's vile enough for me,
  But 'twas a villainy too much my own
  To reach your fame. How could you be accomplice?
  Nor is it known what means was used to free you.
  It can't reflect on you.

CASTALIO   It shall not.
  I disdain t'accept inglorious liberty.
  Take back the shameful ransom, I'll to prison,
  And resume my chains, bestow the purchase
  Of your treachery on knaves, I'll none of it.

GRAMONT   Stay, stay, my lord, there's yet a surer way
  To clear your fame, the blood of him that stained it.
  Take, take my life, 'tis a just sacrifice,
  You owe it to yourself, to honour,
  And the name of friend so long abused.

CASTALIO   Is this the man
  I called my friend, and was I thus deceived?
  I find indeed Lamira well observed,
  There's the least truth where most it does appear.
  Ha! that thought has roused one that alarms my heart,
  She said 'twas one esteemed my friend that wronged her.
  Is't possible that he, the man, whom I
  Preferred to all the world should be ordained
  The ruin of the only thing besides
  That could be dear to me?

GRAMONT   What said you? Do you love her?

CASTALIO   Whom, what her? 'Tis not Lamira thou'st abused.

GRAMONT   Nothing but this could aggravate my crime,
  Or my remorse. And was it wanting, Heaven,
  Must every blow, which I or fate strikes for me,
  Fall heavier still on him? Why, why is this?

CASTALIO   That I alone may have the right of vengeance,
  Which now my injuries are ripe for. Traitor,
  Defend thy life.

GRAMONT   A traitor's is not worth defending.
  Freely I resign it, 'tis a burden
  Which I would bless the hand that frees me from.

CASTALIO   Coward! Thou would'st preserve it, thou know'st I scorn

To take it thus unguarded.

GRAMONT   You ought to take it as a criminal's,
   Nor dare I lift my hand against a man
   Whom I have so much wronged, as if I meant
   To justify my baseness.

CASTALIO   'Tis all the satisfaction thou can'st make,
   And I demand it of thee.

GRAMONT   My life I offer,
   I open to your point, and stand your justice.

CASTALIO   Is't thus you should maintain a lady's favours?
   Not with this coldness you received her kindness,
   Whilst in her arms you revelled. Death and Hell!
   That such a villain should, though but one moment,
   Be possessed of all that bliss! Oh, 'tis a heaven to think,
   And 'twas all his, all the transporting beauties
   In his power. Cursed, torturing thought!

GRAMONT   You causelessly torment yourself. I've not possessed.

CASTALIO   How's that? You said you had married her.

GRAMONT   'Tis true, last night.

CASTALIO   And not possess? Come, doubly damn thyself,
   Forswear the wickedness thou hast committed,
   Swear thou hast not enjoyed her.

GRAMONT   I swear by all things sacred.

CASTALIO   Thou art perjured.

GRAMONT   May then the perjury be ne'er forgiv'n,
   If I have falsely sworn.

CASTALIO   What could prevent it?
   'Tis unusual to leave a bride
   Upon the wedding night. Where were you then?
   For I must know the truth.

GRAMONT   With her.

CASTALIO   Do you trifle with me?

GRAMONT   No. What I have sworn is truth.

CASTALIO   Could she be so reserved not to consent,
   When it might bear the colour of a duty?
   Impossible!

GRAMONT   I did not ask.

CASTALIO   That's more impossible.
  Do not abuse me
  With a soothing tale.
  I am too much concerned to be imposed on,
  And, be assured, will clear to the least doubt.
  Answer me then, what hindered you to ask?

GRAMONT   My guilt already hung too heavy on me.

CASTALIO   But how? On what pretence? How would she bear the
   slight?

Once more I say, I will not be deceived,
Therefore 'twere vain t'attempt it.
But now I will be calm, and, as a friend,
Conjure you tell me punctually what passed.

GRAMONT   I made some weak excuses, which, at first,
She seemed to take, till having further proved
With little arts the temper of my heart,
She imputed it to indifference to her.
Then grew suspicious of some prepossession,
To which she thought herself a sacrifice.
Some words that slipped from me confirmed her in it,
And worked her to a rage, in which she left me.

CASTALIO   And did you calmly, firmly, stand all this?
Th'insinuations of her softer passion,
Her pangs in jealousy, and her resentment?
What man could have the force?

GRAMONT   'Twas your good genius, doubtless, gave it me,
I have nothing of my own but weakness, baseness.

CASTALIO   This were enough to cancel yet a greater,
To see her in the height of all her charms,
Loosened to love and languishing desire,
And not be tempted. By Heaven, I think had I
Myself been lost, not all my honour could
Have guarded me against so strong a trial.
Instead of the reproaches I designed,
I must confess an awful admiration,
Amazed and conscious of superior virtue.

GRAMONT   What virtue was't in me? I looked not on her
With a lover's eyes. Oh, that I had known you did,
But I was never worthy of your trust!

CASTALIO   Fearful of my success, I would have hid
My weakness from myself. Yet in the hopes
Bellgard might influence her, to him alone
I ventured to disclose it.

GRAMONT   To Bellgard!

CASTALIO   He promised to assist me with his interest.

GRAMONT   To assist you!

CASTALIO   You know his power with her.

GRAMONT   Too well I know it, 'twas he proposed, nay, urged
This fatal marriage, which but for him
Would never have been thought on.

CASTALIO   Is't possible?

GRAMONT   Most true.

Enter BELLGARD

CASTALIO   Perfidious! Bellgard, you have betrayed me basely.

BELLGARD   Betrayed you?
CASTALIO   Basely I said, and thus maintain it. Draw.
BELLGARD   I scorn a baseness. You tax me most unjustly.
CASTALIO   Then right yourself.
BELLGARD   My sword would be employed
    Much better to my choice, against that villain.
CASTALIO   If villain be the mark, mine is as well directed.
BELLGARD   Ha!
CASTALIO   Were you not instrumental in his marriage?
    You pressed it on, nay, were the first proposer.
BELLGARD   I was, but knew I then —
CASTALIO   You knew enough
    To make it a base injury to me.
    If you dare vindicate the treachery,
    Guard well your life, for that must answer it.
BELLGARD   What I have done, will bear a calmer test,
    I would be justified, for yet I'm tame.
CASTALIO   Say rather, thou'rt a coward.
BELLGARD   Provoke me not.
    Or to your cost you'll find I am no coward.
CASTALIO   I've found you to my cost a viler thing,
    Dissembling, false, and faithless to your trust.
BELLGARD   As free from either as yourself, Castalio.
CASTALIO   He that dares say it lies.
BELLGARD   Nay then —

    BELLGARD *draws. They fight.* GRAMONT *interposes*

GRAMONT   Bellgard!
    Castalio! What means this rashness? Am not I
    The cause of your debate, the fittest object
    Of your rage? On me your points should turn,
    Or hear at least what each has to allege.
    My lord, I beg you, hold.
CASTALIO   You have your wish.

    GRAMONT *accidentally wounds* CASTALIO

GRAMONT   By all my crimes, this cursed hand has struck him.
CASTALIO   Methinks I feel 'tis too the hand of fate,
    It seems to have reached at life.
GRAMONT   Heaven forbid!
    But is it to be doubted? Did I e'er
    Endeavour the prevention of an ill,
    But I became the cause, and made it surer?
BELLGARD   A curse attends the best designs of wicked men,
    And did'st thou hope to prosper?

GRAMONT   Castalio! I have killed him. My blood is chilled
   With horror of the deed.
   Now is it time
   To sink me to th'abyss? Or have I yet
   More mischiefs to perform?
BELLGARD   No, 'tis thy last,
   But I must clear myself to you, Castalio,
   Then for revenge. Be witness for me, Heaven,
   That I not only did acquit myself
   With honour of the trust reposed in me,
   But with the zeal of a most hearty friend,
   Nor ceased I, till Lamira had declared
   She never could return your love, and owned
   Her folly there.
CASTALIO   Gramont has every way been my destruction.
GRAMONT   What a heart-breaking sound! Was it for this
   You saved my life? Is this the best return
   A friend could make? Happy for both you had
   Been less a friend, then you had lived to bless
   Mankind, and I had died without their curse,
   And all this weight of guilt upon my head.
   But blood atones for blood, it shall be so.
   Oh, 'tis too sure! Life staggers in his eyes!
   Yet, yet support it, one moment to behold
   A justice done you.
BELLGARD   'Tis well thought on, haste then to give it him.

   BELLGARD *offers to fight*

GRAMONT   No more of that, you said I had done already
   My last mischief, now for the first good action
   Of my life, this to Castalio's wrongs.

   GRAMONT *stabs himself just as* COUNT ROQUELAURE,
   LAMIRA *and* FELICIA *enter*

CASTALIO   'Tis too much.
FELICIA   Oh Heaven!
LAMIRA   Desperate remorse!
COUNT   Oh my son!
FELICIA   Now you are satisfied, now you have killed him,
   Inhuman brother, tigers, murderers, devils!
GRAMONT   Oh my dear, thy grief's the sharpest wound.
FELICIA   Is this the promise you in parting made me?
GRAMONT   Look there, and tell thyself if I could keep it.
FELICIA   Castalio dying?
GRAMONT   Murdered by this hand.

CASTALIO   An accidental blow.
COUNT   Unhappy son of a more wretched father.
GRAMONT   My lord, a dying son dares ask forgiveness. . . .

Enter BERNARDO

    Bernardo! Thou art come to imp my ascending prayers
    With juster imprecations. Behold what I have done.
BERNARDO   Oh, my dear lord.
CASTALIO   If thou has loved me, express it not in grieving,
    But in endeavouring to defend my fame
    Against the malice of my enemies.
BERNARDO   It needs not. The general's treachery is detected
    By those he had suborned, and he disgraced.
    A messenger is from the King arrived,
    Inviting both Gramont and you to Court
    With high expectations of his royal favour,
    And offers of what satisfaction you demand
    For all your injuries.
CASTALIO   Bear him my dying thanks. Now I am ready.
    'Tis enough my honour will survive me,
    And I was born to die.

    CASTALIO *dies*

GRAMONT   Oh, what a wretch was I, that could not wait
    Heaven's time, the providence that never fails
    Those who dare to trust it. Durst I have been honest,
    One day had changed the scene, and made me happy.
    But, oh, your son, Felicia.
COUNT   I'll take him to my care.
    I've been to blame in using thee so harshly,
    But all that's thine shall find my kindness doubled,
    Felicia's now my daughter, as thy wife,
    She shall be dearest to me.
GRAMONT   Then all my cares are ended. Be happy, my Felicia,
    If thou would'st have thy husband's spirit rest.

    GRAMONT *dies*

COUNT   He's gone forever.
FELICIA   Oh! Oh!
COUNT   'Tis Heaven's will, my child.

    FELICIA *swoons upon the body*

    Some help, she swoons.

    Attendants come about her

LAMIRA   How tenderly she loved him. Poor Felicia.

COUNT   Pity from one who needs it more herself!
　　What reparation can be made, Lamira?

LAMIRA   The world can make me none. There's nothing here
　　But a vicissitude of miseries.
　　If there is any joy that's permanent,
　　It must be in that calm, that heavenly state
　　To which my future days are dedicated.

BELLGARD   'Tis the best asylum for human frailty,
　　Of which Gramont is a most strange example.
　　He was by nature honest, just, and brave,
　　In many trials showed a steady virtue,
　　Yet by one sharp assault at last was vanquished.
　　None know their strength; let the most resolute
　　Learn from this story to distrust themselves,
　　Nor think by fear the victory is less sure,
　　Our greatest danger's when we're most secure.

THE ROYAL MISCHIEF

BY

MARY DELARIVIER MANLEY

first performed Lincoln's Inn Fields Theatre, *c*. April 1696

In *The Royal Mischief* Mrs Manley uses a medium now unfamiliar except in opera-houses: heroic tragedy. Though once hugely popular, with exotic sets and lavish spectacle adding to its appeal, most heroic drama now seems merely wooden and too overblown, impossibly crammed with tirades in which virtuous characters try to excel each other in goodness; its relation to Restoration comedy is, suggests Anne Barton, 'much as a photographic negative stands to its developed print'. But, by near-elimination of the heroic code, with its abstract demands and its absolute virtues, Mrs Manley made herself a broader and more accommodating canvas. More than once her characters remark how unattractive and inhuman they find virtue and perfection – fittingly, being themselves animated by desires, and addicted to varied imperfections.

What the form usefully provided was its highly inflated idiom, whose very emptiness splendidly catches those unrealities spawned by life in a hot-house. Here, the point of the clichés is that they are poor clichés. Dictates as to how women and wives should behave appear in several scenes of fairly seedy bullying, not merely as lies, but as weapons *men* wield to goad and manipulate each other. When over-self-righteous characters condemn Homais, they lapse into remote neo-Platonic jargon so vapid that the audience is left to reflect only on the impulses behind their disapproval. Bombast gets punctured regularly, often amusingly: after one of her husband's particularly tedious monologues, Homais remarks, 'My Lord, you moralise too far.' Even Bassima – most-nearly heroic and certainly least likable of the characters – turns out to be less worried about ideals of conduct than about what other people (especially her father) will say about her. And when Selima tells her husband off (he's been caught chasing a princess), she claims she's less enraged by his infidelity than the clumsiness with which he tries to cover it, an insult to her intelligence: 'Thou wrong'st my wit.'

Homais, the central character, is a sympathetically studied *femme fatale*. Had the play held to the black-and-white morality of earlier heroic drama, she would be a cartoon villainess, along the lines of Settle's *Empress of Morocco* (who boasted in couplets, back in 1673, 'Let single murders common hands suffice,/I scorn to kill less than whole families'). But it was in recoil from captivity imposed during her pregnancy that Mrs Manley had become a writer. Like her creator,

Homais endures confinement from her husband, and it is this that sparks the action of the play. Not merely sensual and frustrated, beautiful and ruthless, Homais gains a third dimension in her devastating candour, and this makes for some remarkably outspoken scenes. (Elizabeth Barry, who had an unrivalled reputation in smouldering tragic parts, and also for lewdness in her private life, at first turned the part of Homais down, upset by its 'warmth'.) Homais' is a passionate intelligence. She appears at her most devastating when an ex-lover tries to blackmail her back to bed, first by describing their first orgasm, and then by suggesting she enjoy him by imagining him to be her present lover. What rebuffs him is her clear account of just what feelings do remain once passion ends.

At the end Homais is killed. But, then, so is almost everyone else. As she dies she imagines an after-life where she can enjoy such alarming vitality that it seems her death results more from sheer excess of energy than from any stab of moral retribution.

CHARACTERS

THE PRINCE OF LIBARDIAN, known as 'The Protector' of his state; elderly, impotent, and married to

HOMAIS, who is young and beautiful, and who has been confined in the Castle of Phasia, watched over by a bishop while her husband went to war. She has fallen in love with

LEVAN DADIAN, the Prince of Colchis, her husband's nephew and ward, who has never met Homais, and has recently married (for political reasons)

BASSIMA, daughter of the ruler of Abca, recently conquered in war. She was captured by

OSMAN   Chief Visier to the Prince of Libardian, and now married to his Prince's sister. Osman had previously loved Homais, but took the coyness with which she met his advances as a refusal. He now loves Princess Bassima, and has revealed this to

ISMAEL, an officer in the army who is Osman's younger brother. After Osman felt himself rebuffed by Homais, Ismael continued to woo where his brother had been discouraged, and was Homais' first lover, until her husband sent him away to war. He is ambitious, and plans to reveal his brother's infatuation to

SELIMA, wife to Osman, and sister of the Prince of Libardian

ACMAT, a eunuch, is Homais' trusted friend

Officers; ladies; eunuchs; slaves; guards and four mutes

The action takes place in the Castle of Phasia in Libardian, and in the Prince of Colchis' camp, nearby.

ACT I

A ROYAL APARTMENT IN THE CASTLE OF PHASIA

Enter HOMAIS *and* ACMAT

HOMAIS   'Tis finished, and a work speaks loud as fame,
    Where crowns and sceptres truckle to his virtue,
    My conquering cousin has the war o'ercome,
    And now slowly returns, with honour pressed,
    As thick'ning laurels, sprung to stop his passage,
    Will turn a necessary march to one
    Long solemn triumph.
ACMAT   He brings the Princess with him, and sure
    Such beauty should be tasted leisurely,
    Lest the rich cordial prove too strong for life
    And ruin that which 'twas designed to bless.
HOMAIS   Name her not, she's a disease to all my hopes,
    Like early blasts upon too forward blossoms,
    Reduces all into their former nothing.
ACMAT   Might I but hope my long tried service
    And secrecy, the rarity of courts,
    Which still ,where you're concerned, bids me be dumb,
    Forget I've life, and ranks me with the dead,
    Could this and more deserve your royal ear,
    I would be bold to ask the cause of your
    Disorder.
HOMAIS   Why thou, my Acmat, who hast known my weaknesses,
    And marked the various changes of my temper,
    Should'st know my griefs can have no other rise
    But love's almighty passion.
ACMAT   My sense had touched the mark,
    If that my memory in all its search
    Could but have fixed your new disquiets on
    A person fit to fill your royal breast.
    Osman the new-made Visier you detest,
    His cousin Ismael you have enjoyed,
    And sure such fires did never wait possession,
    Since that, none has approached your royal sight
    Fit to give love or to create desire,
    Or if there had I soon had marked the man,
    For love like yours in absence may be hid,
    In presence never!

HOMAIS   Right thou hast guessed,
   And yet the wound is love. But such a love,
   So hopeless, so fantastic, all my stock
   Of youth and charms cannot forbid despair.
ACMAT   Impossible. You know not half your power.
   Those eyes did never vainly shoot a dart,
   Such are their fires, so sparkling, so attractive,
   So passionately soft and tender,
   So full of that desire they give, as though
   The glorious heaven stood ready for possession.
   You never look but to command our love,
   And give your lover hope. . .
   Then how should you despair?
HOMAIS   Had they inimitable lustre,
   Were all my charms unequalled, like that bright
   Light above, superior and alone, yet
   To the man, who never either saw, nor
   Heard their power, my sunshine would be lost.
ACMAT   Is there on Earth a wretch so much unblest.
   Our Eastern World is full of Homais' beauty,
   And I am bold to think you have not loved beyond.
   No second Alexander fills the globe,
   No glorious busy hero, to enslave
   Your heart at distance, and with unseen fame,
   Make conquest easy. Name but the happy man,
   And I'll secure him yours.
HOMAIS   Dull, dull, eunuch,
   What lethargy has stole thy reason from thee,
   Cold through thy veins, and mingled with thy blood?
   How far would'st thou extend thy busy search,
   Hunt round the globe for airy heroes,
   When the reality's at home. The Prince
   . . . The inimitable Prince of Colchis.
   Thou start'st. . .
   Despair surround me, if thy coward blood
   Has not forsook thy ghastly face
   The gorgon name has turned him to a statue.
ACMAT   My fears are yours, nor can I choose but fear,
   When that must bring despair which causes love.
   Your eyes in all their glorious course (and sure
   They are omnipotent) could not have shone
   Upon a soil so barren; no kindly hopes,
   No prospect of return, no flatt'ring gleams
   Of sunshine through the show'rs to make us
   Hope a calm. First, here, your husband's nephew's

Just married to a young and beauteous Princess.
Time has scarce lent a hand to pluck the fruit,
Or say 'twere gathered, yet the flavour lasts.
Then, he's a Prince so much renowned for virtue,
So true a copy of the long-past heroes,
As will serve for an original to ages yet to come.
But, oh, that which concludes his character,
Destroys us more, abundant gratitude,
And love to the Protector. . .
'Tis to your Lord he owes his conquered fields,
Who gave his laurels growth, mixed with his own,
To make one lasting shade, which all your rays
Can never penetrate.

*She seems disordered during this speech, and at length sinks down
in a chair*

HOMAIS   A heavy doom,
  Too strong for life to bear.
ACMAT   How lawless is a woman's love,
  The swelling current will admit no bounds,
  For if not gratified they die. . .
  Help there, the Princess swoons.

Her maids appear

HOMAIS   Bid 'em be gone,
  Alas, it is not in their pow'r to help.
  This raging fire blazes to such a height,
  That till 'tis quenched, life cannot come in doubt.
  I find, I feel, the burning at my heart,
  Which now (when thou had'st thought my reason lost)
  Shifted the scene, and brought my anguish back.
ACMAT   In all the course of love's tyrannic power
  I have not heard a passion like to yours,
  Unsought, unseen, to throw your heart away.
  A gem of that inestimable price,
  Should be the blest reward of long paid service,
  And a flame, lasting and clear, as those bright eyes
  That lighted it.
HOMAIS   Thy vulgar soul moves in the common road,
  Mine loathes the beaten path and starts aside
  To seek new regions out, disgusted with the old,
  And now the rich discovery is made,
  I'll push the bold adventure on,
  And either die or conquer. .

ACMAT   Change but the climate and the crown is yours,
   Survey the globe, choose where your eyes would reign,
   Or were it possible to mount the skies,
   And wander through the starry courts above,
   Not one bright dazzling God but would forgo
   His heav'n for yours, and dote on the exchange,
   Such magic's in your looks, none but
   The Prince of Colchis can resist them.

HOMAIS   How dares my slave speak these uneasy truths?
   Thy barren soul ne'er knew the growth of love,
   And wert not called to threaten but advise.
   No more expostulate a growing flame,
   More than ambition bold, than anger fierce,
   Nor can but with possession be abased.
   My life, my soul, my all is fixed upon enjoyment,
   Resistance but augments desire.
   If thou would'st live, threaten no more despair.
   I've named the goal, lend me thy aid to reach it.

ACMAT   If I have been displeasing to your ear,
   Let my mistaken zeal meet your forgiveness,
   For I have err'd to think of a defence
   When you prepare to arm. Such courage and
   Such beauty must make the universal
   World your slaves, nor will I more exempt the
   Prince, could you but triumph there, the rest were
   Easy conquest.

HOMAIS   Dost thou remember in my virgin bloom,
   When time had scarce lent colour to my beauty,
   The Visier Osman made an interest here,
   My native modesty taught long denials,
   (For 'tis but by degrees our sex grow bold,
   Start at the name they after grow familiar with)
   Piqued with delays, he urged his suit no more,
   Nor took advantage of consenting love,
   But left the bargain dead upon my hands,
   For which, if ever I forgive the baulk,
   May lasting disappointments hunt me out,
   Watch all my steps and double as I turn,
   Dash the full bowl when lifted to my lips,
   And all the senses eager for the tastes.

ACMAT   'Twas then young Ismael returned from travail,
   High in his youth and with success made bold
   He stormed your heart and took it by assault,
   Made himself master of your richest treasure,
   For which the Visier dragged him from your arms,

       Sent him to wars to disappoint you more,
       And would have crossed your marriage with my lord.
HOMAIS   But all those pangs which then thou saw'st me
       Suffer from Osman's scorn, and Ismael's loss,
       Were minutes to the mighty ages now,
       For had this happened to an untried courage,
       The weighty hand had sunk the novice down,
       Unable to support the pond'rous blow.
ACMAT   Yet e'er the sun has gilded the meridian,
       You may have hopes to see your lover here,
       For so the trumpet from my lord reports,
       Last night they passed the River Phasis,
       And pitched their camp along its swelling side.
       The Protector will undoubtedly be fond
       To entertain his niece and nephew here,
       And do them honour in his own dominions.
       Now, e'er the Princess treads her Colchian grounds,
       Prepare your charms, and let us see
       What wounds your eyes can make.
HOMAIS   They blaze with more than comet fires,
       The great and sure portents of following fate,
       For Bassima or I must make the Prodigy.
       Trumpets, hark, they come. . . support
       Me, Acmat, or I shall sink with transport.
       Ay, now the fatal trial's near: death or
       A heart more worth than thousand lives.
       Again they sound. Feel but my throbbing heart
       How swift it plays, were it as loud 'twould pay
       The music back, and speak both gratitude
       And love in strains unheard before.

    Enter a SLAVE

SLAVE   Madam, the Prince has entered.
HOMAIS   What Prince?
SLAVE   The Prince, my lord.
HOMAIS   Haste, and say I wait him here.
       What an unwholesome air that breath has cast,
       'T has damped my fires and almost put out life.
       My senses turn, and my chilled blood, that ran
       In streams before, falls drop by drop as frost
       Had numbed the passage.
ACMAT   Compose yourself, and meet my lord with smiles,
       His jealous age suspicious of a slight,
       Expects more welcome than a youthful lover.
       Wear close your thoughts, untold, they are your own,

Nature has been so bounteous to our kind,
Unless we lend the clue they cannot reach our hearts.
HOMAIS   'Tis most unlucky thus to be deceived
Upon the first expectance. Oh, thou eternal
Searcher of our hearts, that can'st in thy large
Book read our unhappy destinies long
Ages off, if I am doomed a martyr
To my love, shorten my pains, and let my
Death be instant.
ACMAT   Your music flourishes.
My lord is in the lodgings, I hear him come.
Shift, swift, your look, or you destroy us all.

Enter the PRINCE OF LIBARDIAN *and* ATTENDANTS

PRINCE OF LIBARDIAN   O my fair Princess, the joys of long past
    life
Are crowded in this moment, and a new
Glittering store revealed to make me further
Dote upon your treasure.
HOMAIS   My lord, you're welcome. . .
PRINCE OF LIBARDIAN   So cold, 'my lord, you're welcome'. . .
Death meet my wishes, if this minute, when
I hugged the dear enchantress to my bosom,
That swelled to meet the load, her snowy arms
Kept not a most ingrateful distance,
Nor circled me. The least familiar welcome!
And when I thought to mingle kisses with her,
She met my burning lips with her cold cheeks,
Covered all o'er with a thick, damp sweat,
Which nothing could supply but strong aversion.
HOMAIS   Yet e'er, my lord, you quarrel with my welcome,
Allow me leave to say it was unkind
To give the style and dignity of regent
The empty name of honour without power,
Whilst yon proud pampered prelate bore the sway,
Denied me leave to pass the castle-gates,
And suffered none to have access, but just
My women, and my slaves. Hence 'twas I found
My servants were his creatures, my guards
My gaolers, and himself the master spy.
PRINCE OF LIBARDIAN   Oh, can you blame me to preserve a good
On which the safety of my life depends?
Who but a fool would leave his wealth at large
To the uncertain chance of robbers' hands,
When by securing it 'tis sure his own?

   I am that wretch undone the moment when
   I lose your treasure.
HOMAIS 'Tis the prerogative of age to talk.
   They dream broad 'wake, and then speak as they dream.
PRINCE OF LIBARDIAN Unequal nature, why hast thou bestowed
   A larger privilege of mind than body?
   For whilst we find and feel our passions strong,
   We vainly hope the consequence as young.
   By love made bold we hunt the beauteous chase,
   Nor heed our lag of body in the race,
   Till taught too late in such ingrateful arms,
   'Tis youth to youth can only furnish charms.
   Oh, could I hide me ever from your eyes,
   You should no more my love or age despise.
HOMAIS My lord, you moralise too far. Forgive
   My sex's frailty. I'm a woman, made
   Passionate by want of liberty.
   I'll learn to wear my fetters lighter,
   And if you please, will suit my welcome to it.
PRINCE OF LIBARDIAN Wert thou but truly kind,
   What worlds of bliss could'st thou not give!
   Thy eye, thy lips, thy thousand beauties
   Were too divine a feast for mortal taste.
   Oh, let me be but well dissembled with,
   And I will lie for ever in thy arms,
   Nor never wake to find the fond illusion,
   But think it all substantial shining treasure.
HOMAIS Well, now we are friends. . .
   Let me, like other warriors' wives,
   First give a kiss, and then, my dear, what news?
   How went the battle, how the peace, who wears
   The thickest laurel, and whose name sounds
   Sweetest in the mouth of fame?
PRINCE OF LIBARDIAN Our conquering cousin,
   Young Levan Dadian, has out-stripped my age,
   Foiled all my glories by his rising splendour,
   For when the battle hung in long suspense,
   And the nice goddess would be wooed by neither,
   (Though each contending for the lover's prize
   Did things beyond a lover's height)
   Till the young fiery Abcan Prince,
   With a fresh body of selected horse,
   Broke in upon my rear, my slaughtered men
   Supplied the luxury of death with a
   Full feast, who did but taste before.

Then young Levan flew to prevent the
Inevitable stroke, which the up-lifted
Hand of fate stood ready to discharge.
By heaven, it gave at once both spite and joy,
To see this infant eagle, hatched underneath
The cover of my wings, now imp my flight,
And far out-soar my height.

HOMAIS   But where's this young triumpher? Should we not
Meet him now, with low paeans, and strow his
Passage with unfading laurels? Do not
All kneel to Heaven for benefits; why not
To heroes too, when they perform the work
As well? I am indebted for a husband's life,
And loathe the stain of vulgar souls' ingratitude.
Lead me to pay the tribute of my thanks,
For I, my lord, am burdened with the weight.

PRINCE OF LIBARDIAN   Incumbent duty has discharged your debt.
For, when the fatal circumstance proclaimed
The field our own, I ran to give him joy.
He swore by all those hovering ghosts just
Then departed, that 'twas more satisfaction
To preserve my life, than find himself
A conqueror.

HOMAIS   But pray, my lord, what of the Visier Osman?
Has he deserved your mighty trust and favour?
He could not, sure, forsake in that extremity
A prince who did him honour?

PRINCE OF LIBARDIAN   Why do you envy me, inhuman princess,
That moment's peace our reconcilement brought?
Or is't impossible my joys should know the
Date of one small hour? But, to retort that
Poison to your heart with which you have
Infected mine, know that your minion's lost
For ever to your charms.

HOMAIS   Not dead, my lord?

PRINCE OF LIBARDIAN   Then you avow him such! (See if the blood
Has not forsook her cheeks, and left her
Beauties pale. I'll try if jealousy, my
Cursed tormentor, can have power to send the roses back.)
Your lover dotes to death upon the Princess.
I'm sorry, for my sister's sake, but Bassima's
Bright virtue leaves no suspicion of a stain.
Like a divinity, she teaches fear
And reverence to all who worship her.

HOMAIS   May we not see this goddess? Will she not

Deign, with the divinity you mention,
To grace our little Court? Or must I pay
My adorations at her own?
PRINCE OF LIBARDIAN   No, Homais, 'tis too dangerous a world
For ladies of your temper. I have declined
Seeing my nephew here, lest the Court tide
Of liberty should drown your fame, for in
The fatal wreck, my life could never 'scape
The tempest.
HOMAIS   Then I'm, it seems, confined, till age, or grief,
Presents me death. The works will not be long
A-doing. What signifies the crown upon my head,
When none can see how well the circle fits,
How rich and sparkling are the diamonds,
The pearls how Orient, and how well such
Glory suits the wearer's face?

Enter SELIMA *with her attendants*

SELIMA   My only brother, welcome to my heart,
I had much sooner run to give you joy,
And tell you mine, but that I know, when
Lovers meet, all other visitants are
But intruders.
PRINCE OF LIBARDIAN   My dearest Selima,
I designed this favour in your lodgings,
But greeting you is everywhere a pleasure.
SELIMA   I am going on a visit to the camp,
(The Visier sends he cannot leave the Prince)
And hope, at my return, better to speak
The transport of my joy for your arrival.
PRINCE OF LIBARDIAN   I'll wait you to your chariot.

Exit PRINCE *leading* SELIMA

HOMAIS   Dull princess.
Thou art a tool I must employ to make
The work I labour with complete. Acmat,
Dost thou not think my projects all aground
And my spent vessel ready to be wrecked?
But yet I'll not despair. Revenge does
Aid my love, and from within I feel
Undoubted omens of success.
In this extremity all aids I'll try,
For he must either love, or I must die.

They leave the stage

ACT II

SCENE I

A PAVILION ROYAL

Enter OSMAN *and* ISMAEL

OSMAN   What boots it thus to drag a wretched being,
    A lifeless lump, without one ray of hope?
    By Heav'n, I'll lay me down, and breathe my soul
    In sighs, at my too cruel sovereign's feet,
    There grasp with my cold hands her flying
    Beauties, till I have urged her glorious eyes
    To shed some pitying tears.
ISMAEL   Rouse up your self, and bear you like a man,
    The lord of womankind, born to command
    That sex which we entreat. But when we whine
    At your romantic rate we move not love,
    But scorn. They like the forward and the bold,
    For virtue in such souls is like their form,
    Only exterior beauty, worn to deceive
    The credulous world and buy opinions
    From the common rout.
    But when they meet a lover to their wish
    They gladly throw the borrowed veil aside,
    And naked in his arms disclose the cheat.
OSMAN   You speak of common women, are those fit
    To meet comparison with our blest princess,
    Of whom 'tis blasphemy to think her mortal
    To any but our lord the Prince?
ISMAEL   Fine stuff.
    What, do you dote upon a new-found species?
    I thought you loved her as she was a woman,
    As nature bids us love, not with platonic
    Nonsense. When you have reckoned all her
    Beauties up, the sex is loveliest in her.
    Bate that circumstance, and a fair picture
    Does the work as well. If she be a woman,
    Resolve to win her, and the work is done.
    Is she, d'y'think, the only frozen of
    Her sex, whom the hot sun of love can't melt?
OSMAN   Thou art a libertine, and think'st all humankind
    As eager for enjoyments as thyself.
ISMAEL   I think you should, with such a prize in view,
    Or else forgo your title of a man,

Strip off those borrowed ornaments, and take
An eunuch's garb and rank. By love, the
Universal world's great lord, were I as her,
I would not give one smile to so much weakness.

OSMAN   She has commanded on the forfeit of my life
Not to presume to name my love again.

ISMAEL   She doubts the consequence.
Her sex's frailty can't resist the
Battery. The next attempt lays all her
Beauties prostrate. O Visier, had I but
The prospect of thy joys, tomorrow's sun
Should never touch the West till I had
Bathed, nay, wantoned, in that sea of pleasure.

OSMAN   Alas, I dare not raise my thoughts that way,
For, as I told you, when I urged my love,
She chid me into everlasting silence,
And on those hard conditions, gave her hand,
In token of forgiveness.

ISMAEL   Her blessed hand.
By Heaven, it was too mightily earnest,
Her heart was long since yours, and the bright
Body next will follow. Oh, I could crush
Thee now with envy at thy joys, for though
I wish thee happy, I shall die to know
Thou art so. Not that I love her more than
As she is a woman, the brightest of her kind,
Next the Libardian princess, whose charms
I never yet saw equalled.

OSMAN   Why, Ismael,
Because ye have enjoyed, do you praise a lady
Guilty of all those passions which a woman's
Breast can breed? Her virtues, senses, fame, are
All made slaves to luxury, lewd in her
Nature, guilty from her cradle, void of
Religion and morality, she knows no
Tie of conscience nor affection rather
Than lose what her vile sense calls pleasure.
Murder and incest would be easy crimes
Had she but power to act, as sure she
Has the will. The earth would groan to bear her.

ISMAEL   I praised her not
For anything but beauty, and what eye
So ever sees, it must allow her that.

OSMAN   I grant her form is excellent, but sure,
My Princess does as much deserve our wonder.

    Hast thou forgot the time when thou did'st play
    The orator on her perfections, and
    I could scarce be heard but as an echo?

ISMAEL   I am not at such odds with my remembrance
    To need so strict a reconcilement.

OSMAN   Give me leave, 'tis the fond lovers' pleasure
    Still to be speaking of the thing they love.
    I'll pass the circumstance of war, and lead
    You to that scene where first we saw the Princess.
    Retired, according to the Abcan mode,
    To pass in tents the raging summer's heat,
    Far, as she thought, from the rude noise of war,
    Surrounded with a train of sixty ladies,
    All bright as stars, fit nymphs for such a goddess,
    Herself, more than Diana, fair, than Venus, lovely,
    Dressed with such negligence as left her swelling
    Snowy breasts and her white arms all naked
    To the gazer's view. How often have I blessed
    That friendly planet, by whose officious heat
    Those dazzling beauties were revealed!

ISMAEL   You dote and yet want courage for the joy,
    Our sex can never bear themselves too bold,
    Provided still we lay the stress on love,
    For when we warmest urge our fierce desire,
    The self-conceited she mistakes the cause,
    Nor nicely weighs the influence of temper,
    But thinks them all strong arguments of passion
    Which nothing but her beauty could inspire.

OSMAN   I cannot think she loves me.

ISMAEL   Yet, when we first surprised her in the forest,
    Our warlike party struck such terror to
    Her train, that not one guard, nor slave, but fled
    As fast as their wild fear could carry 'em.
    She stood alone unmoved, and to my sense,
    Her darting looks spoke much more love than fear,
    For at her feet, when you had laid your sword,
    She bade you take it up, and said she did
    Not fear that hand would ever ill employ it.

OSMAN   That minute looked my liberty away,
    For when my gracious conqueress saw herself
    My prisoner, she blushed, confessed her quality,
    And said her father would not let her long
    Be such. I told her I was more her slave,
    And in that newness of my love, spoke things
    Which even thy boldness did condemn.

At last I tore myself from this enchantress,
Nor took advantage of the chance of war,
But left her free, and at her own dispose,
Which when she saw, she bowed, and smiling said
She never should forget her conqueror.

ISMAEL   'Twas well our party knew her not,
The gallantry had cost you else your head.

OSMAN   After victory, the peace soon followed,
And I was sent by proxy to espouse her.
Since that I have not dared to speak of love,
Nor interrupt the joys our sovereign gives,
With my too melancholy fate.

ISMAEL   Do you not see, she's sullen at her fortune,
And smiles not on the Prince but with constraint?
Her eyes have lost that shining power,
With which they darted on us in the forest.
She now appears musing, reserved and sad.
To me 'tis plain that he has not her heart.
Press her again, and if she not avow
It's yours, discard me from your friendship.

OSMAN   I will, for though she banish me forever,
I cannot be more wretched than I am.
But, oh, I must not think on her high joys,
Lest I grow giddy with the distant prospect,
And lag beneath, when love calls on to climb.

Enter a SLAVE

SLAVE   The Princess Selima alighted at your tent.
OSMAN   Tell her I wait upon her instantly.

Exit SLAVE

How shall I look upon that injured princess,
When cold civility is all my treat,
Undone by want, and yet have too much love.
But since no ill is such to us till known,
I'll keep the wounding secret from her ear,
And be unhappy to myself alone.

Exit OSMAN

ISMAEL   This Visier stands between me and the seals.
His death procured, the ministry were mine.
No way so likely to remove him thence,
As his mad, doting passion for the Princess,
Which for that reason I encourage him in.
To the Protector I have told the secret,

Whose jealousy will never let it rest
Till he has lodged it in bright Homais' breast,
From whence her sure revenge will strike much fires
As well continued may the hero send
To seek in unknown worlds his sorrow's end.

Enter ACMAT

ACMAT   My lord, you're welcome from the wars in peace.
ISMAEL   Thou blessed contriver of my highest joys,
   How fares my ever charming Princess?
ACMAT   Oh, much more beautiful than ever. This
   Year has brought a wonderful addition.
   Each day discloses something new. Though to
   Have seen the perfect charmer, one would have
   Thought long since 'twas an accomplished work, and
   Nature could not add another beauty.
ISMAEL   May I not visit her tonight?
ACMAT   Where is the Prince of Colchis?
ISMAEL   At dinner with the Princess.
ACMAT   Are we private?
ISMAEL   We are.
   Speak what thou hast to say, and do not fear.
ACMAT   My lord, where gratitude and interest join,
   There we may hope to find fidelity.
   'Tis on this rock my Princess builds her hopes.
   If they succeed the Visier's seat is yours.
   But I have news will strike your heart with wonder.
   She loves your Prince, and much I fear will die
   If not beloved again.
ISMAEL   Impossible.
   He knows her not, nor has she ever seen him.
ACMAT   Love enters at the ears as well as eyes.
   His fame has touched her mind, his form her heart,
   For though you had forsook her arms for glory,
   And left the beauteous circle unemployed,
   The little god gave new desires, as loth
   To lose so bright a vot'ry, and caused her
   Languish for a prince unknown. My lord, to
   Help the fatal mischief on, made her the
   Present of his nephew's picture,
   By which she so indulged her fond desire,
   That soon her reason fled, and left her heart
   A prey to passion, nor could her stars resist it.
ISMAEL   Levan indeed by nature is so warm,
   So true a lover of the charming sex,

That 'tis the only hint of human
Frailty in him, nor can his temper catch
A blaze from any other fire, though to his
Wife, whom policy made such, he seems
To wear the effects of duty more than love.

ACMAT   Therefore this picture can create anew.
Her eyes have more than magic art to light 'em,
Could he but see 'em once, the work were done.
Move him to view this wonder of her sex,
And raise his pity for her hard confinement.
And, if you find it proper, move the love
Which Osman bears his Princess to Selima.
I have dispatched a letter, the style and
Character to her unknown, which brings the
Fatal news, by which we have a perfect
Spy upon them both. Her jealousy will
Never let it rest till she has explored the
Secret to our wish.

ISMAEL   I'll prove the chance, when dinner's done
He comes this way to lead the Princess
To her private lodgings, and there he leaves her
To an hour's repose. But, say I bring him
Forth to view the castle, the old Protector
Will engross the visit, and Homais but
Be satisfied in part.

ACMAT   We have drenched him
With an opiate draught, whose powerful
Charms he'll not be able to throw off till
He has paid the tribute of eight hours' sleep.
If our propitious stars but join, there may
Be wonders wrought ere then, to make you great
And Homais happy.

ISMAEL   To compass both I'll
Run the hazard of Levan's displeasure,
And rather crush my fortune than her hopes.

A flourish of music, then enter LEVAN *leading* BASSIMA.
The ladies following, they pass across the stage

ISMAEL   Soft rest wait on Your Majesty. Acmat
Withdraw, the Prince will instantly return.
Occasion speaks, and we must haste to answer.
The glowing metal's ready on the anvil,
And fate calls on to strike.

ACMAT *withdraws*

LEVAN   I have a new-born dullness hangs upon me,
   A mighty heaviness, unknown till now.
   I fear my fate is busy for some change,
   And this the sure forerunner of the tempest.

ISMAEL   Suppose you try the Princess' arms?
   Those mighty joys which she can give
   Would steal this heavy dullness from your heart,
   And send it to your eyes in golden slumbers.

LEVAN   I would have stayed. She seemed averse.
   And I love nothing by constraint.

ISMAEL   How, refuse your company! By Heaven,
   I do not like the news. A wife should wake
   Herself to watch her husband's slumbers.

LEVAN   Is there such complaisance in marriage?

ISMAEL   In love I'm sure there is, and unless you
   Will exclude that passion from it,
   This and much more attends the union.

LEVAN   My lord, you are experienced in the art,
   Describe me such a woman whose cold
   Civility makes all her liking.

ISMAEL   In those who truly love they meet its joys
   With as much eagerness as we can give 'em.
   Their glowing lips, their sparkling, dying eyes
   Speak rapture all, they grasp us close, and give
   Their souls in kisses. Words are too gross to
   Mingle with such pleasures. The sacred
   Mystery transcends our sense, and better
   Suits our wonder than description.

LEVAN   This is not what I asked.

ISMAEL   This is the general character. Nature
   Has lent that common softness to the sex.
   They're lovers all, or else they are not woman,
   Though I must own a husband may not
   Always be the object of desire.

LEVAN   What does the woman then?

ISMAEL   She who likes her lover more
   Loathes the enclosure of her husband's arms,
   Coldly receives his kisses and his vows,
   And answers all his eager joys with sighs.
   But they are sighs of sorrow, not of love,
   And when he urges her unkindness to her,
   She lays it on the coldness of her temper,
   Though to her lover she's as hot as flames.
   The silly husband must believe her ice,
   Which nothing natural has power to thaw

But love, being the original of all.
Nothing that's made by love can live without it.
LEVAN   By Hell, thou hast described the Princess
   As right as if with me thou had'st shared her arms.
ISMAEL   Sacred sir, I must not mean her majesty.
LEVAN   I wish I could not mean her neither.
   O, Ismael, thou hast raised a Hell of doubts,
   Deep, horrid deep, ne'er to be fathomed more.
   But by thyself prove that she loves another,
   (For 'tis most certain she is cold to me
   As marble tombs, or snow on tallest hills)
   And I'll renounce at once her love and bed,
   Forsake the ungrateful partner of my throne,
   And give her beauties up to strictest justice.
   As for her minion, who so e'er he be,
   That durst presume to mingle with my joys,
   And taste uncalled the royal feast of kings,
   Though but in thought he had offended, yet
   His guardian angel should not save his head:
   The minute that I know the wretch, he dies.
ISMAEL   Tomorrow's sun shall bring your further news.
   Till then conceal your doubts, and this discovery,
   And if I mark you not the traitor plain,
   May all your indignation fall on me.
   And let me meet that death which he deserves.
LEVAN   Be sure thou dost it, for royal anger
   Should not be unjustly raised; the fatal
   Blaze burns all it lightens on, and if not
   Kindled right, proves worse than lenity.
   I'll hug no more the enchantress in my arms,
   Nor give her cause to laugh at my indulgence,
   Till I have proved her virtue clear. If not,
   We part forever.
ISMAEL   Suspend these troubled thoughts,
   Unbend your cares, and give your eyes the leave
   To view the only miracle of beauty.
   Your uncle's wife has sure engrossed the style.
   But I'd forget, an eunuch waits without,
   Sent by her orders. Will you please to
   Admit him?
LEVAN   From Homais! Let him enter.

            ISMAEL *goes out, and returns with* ACMAT

ACMAT   Long live the glorious Prince of Colchis,
   (For thus by me my royal mistress speaks)

May all his undertakings meet success,
Great as his merits, equal to her wishes.
May Fortune in his cause change her inconstancy,
And lose for him the name of fickle goddess.
She would have come herself to bind this prayer
Had not her inclinations been debarred.
But though she never be so blessed to meet your eyes,
Though everlasting distance prove her lot,
Dividing what her strong desire has joined,
She begs you keep this little picture for her sake.

LEVAN   My lord, has not the painter flattered her?

ISMAEL   Sir, I think he scarce can do her justice,
She has charms which art can never copy.

LEVAN   Then she is sure above all mortal frame,
Her eyes have rays, her face a glory through
The whole, that strikes full at my heart.
(*He kisses the picture*)
Now when I put the colours to my lips,
My heart flew at the touch, eager to meet
Her beauties. I'll gaze no more, there's magic
In the circle.

ACMAT   Sure there's a sympathy between you, for
Thus she bears her when she sees your picture,
Which drawn at length, almost as graceful as
The original, is the chief ornament
Of her apartment, answering
Exactly to her waking curtains.
How often have I seen this lovely Venus,
Naked, extended in the gaudy bed,
Her snowy breast all panting with desire,
With gazing, melting eyes, survey your form,
And wish in vain 't had life to fill her arms.

ISMAEL   The god of love forbids you to deceive her.
Such cruelties can never suit the brave.
Courage and clemency are equal virtues.
A hero should extend to all his mercy,
But mostly, sure, to those who love and
Languish for him.

LEVAN   I'll hear no more. Y'are charmers all,
And I am to myself the worst deceiver.

ACMAT   Then shall I tell the wretched lady
You have refused her love, nor dare I urge it more?

LEVAN   Alas! I die for that as much as she,
But our hard fate has parted us forever.

ACMAT   Is this then what your majesty returns?

LEVAN   Tell her her charms have wondrous power,
   And were we both at liberty to choose,
   This night should see her mine, but there's a
   Noble lord, the partner of her bed,
   Whom I can never wrong.
ACMAT   Nor could you, though he found you there, 'tis none
   To take what cannot fit another's use.
   What boots the empty name without possession?
   The love of nature has divorced him from her,
   Her beauty lies neglected at his side,
   Nor is he other than a proxy sent,
   Sent to espouse, but never taste.
   The virgin fruit as yet remains untouched,
   And if not plucked by you, must fall ungathered.
ISMAEL   Are you a man, and can resist this offer?
   Refuse her love, and kill her with disdain?
   At least, in gratitude, you should provide
   To make the charmer easy in her chains.
   'Tis pity that a light which might have cheered
   All eyes, should be itself condemned to darkness.
   Come, Sir, the castle is in view;
   Or will you stay and dally with a wife
   That loathes your arms, and sports in another's.
LEVAN   That thought is death, and every place where she
   Has been is Hell to my sick thoughts.
   Lead to the castle, there my fortune calls me.
   Be't good or ill, I'll now obey the summons.
   Eunuch, be gone and tell her I am coming.
   But bid the Princess veil her charms
   In pity to my fate, lest if they shine
   Too bright they dazzle my weak sight forever.

Exit ACMAT

ISMAEL   'Twere not amiss, for fear this visit to
   Observing eyes should seem particular,
   To give your orders that the Princess, when
   She wakes, attended by the Visier, may
   Meet us at the castle.
LEVAN   Then see it done.
   And yet, methinks, I would avoid her sight
   Till the great trial of her virtue's past.
   Oh, how unconstantly our fortune turns.
   One hour in joy, the next with sorrow mourns.

They all leave

ACT III

SCENE I

A ROOM IN THE CASTLE OF PHASIA

Enter HOMAIS, *alone*

HOMAIS   He sleeps as sound as if he never were
    To wake again. Now could one ask him what
    Avails his prisons, spies, and jealousies?
    Would he not say a woman's wit
    Had made them fruitless all?
    Strict silence fills the lodgings, the music's placed,
    The banquet's ready, and I more so than all.
    Will he not come? 'Tis a long parley.
    Methinks on such a summons he should grow
    Fond of a surrender. But hence, begone
    These melancholy doubts that load my thoughts,
    And turn them into fears. The phantoms
    Cannot stand the day-break of my eyes,
    (*Looks in her glass*)
    Ay, see, they fly before this lovely face.
    My hopes glow in my cheeks and speak my joy,
    My eyes take fire at their own lustre, and
    All my charms receive addition from themselves,
    Pleased at their own perfection.

Enter ACMAT

ACMAT   The prince is coming, he follows hard
    Upon the scent, and soon the royal hunter
    Will press on to find your charms at bay.
    He seems disgusted at the Princess.
    You have a nobler game to play.
    Let him not find you vicious, and his throne
    And bed are surely yours forever.
HOMAIS   What? To conceal desire when every
    Atom of me trembles with it! I'll strip
    My passion naked of such guile, lay it
    Undressed and panting at his feet, then try
    If all his temper can resist it. (*Music flourish*)
    But hark! The sign the Prince is coming.
    My love distracts me. Where shall I run
    That I may gather strength to stem this tide
    Of joy? Should he now take my senses in
    Their hurry, the rage my passion gives would

Make my fate more sudden than severest
Disappointments. Coward heart, dar'st thou not
Stand the enjoyment of thy own desires?
Must I then grant thee time to reason with?
Thy weakness be gone, and see thou do not
Trifle moments more rich than all the
Blooming years thou hast pass'd.

She goes in. Song and music

> *Unguarded lies the wishing maid,*
> *Distrusting not to be betrayed,*
> *Ready to fall, with all her charms,*
> *A shining treasure to your arms.*
>
> *Who hears this story must believe,*
> *No swain can truer joy receive.*
> *Since to take love and give it too*
> *Is all that love for hearts can do.*

Enter LEVAN *and* ISMAEL

LEVAN   Since I have entered this enchanted palace,
And trod the ground where Homais dwells,
Methinks I walk in clouds, and breath the air of love.
There's not a strain the music gave
But melted part of my resolves.
Where's the Protector? My sinking virtue
Needs a prop. It staggers far, and much I
Doubt will ever re-collect again.
ISMAEL   No matter. Let the painted idol fall.
A tomb so rich as Homais' arms
Would make one fond of fate. Look back to ages
Past, and say 'What hero thought not love his
Richest purchase? That gave their sword the
Keenest edge, and sent them round the Universe
To hunt applause from the fair mouth of some
Exalted charmer.'
LEVAN   You speak of lawful loves. Were mine but such
I'd gladly lose the rank of kings, yet find
More joys than ever circled in a monarch's crown.
But incest shocks my nature, blisters my
Tongue, and carries venom in it. Avaunt,
Be gone, and do not crowd my thoughts, I'd tear
My reason from its centre ere that should
Make it giddy, divorce my body from
Its life rather than wallow in mud.

And yet the gathering cloud looks monstrous black;
    Should it once burst, 'twould surely scatter fate.
ISMAEL   For shame, belie not thus our sex's courage!
    Forgive me, Sir, I'm zealous for your joys.
    I'll fetch the Princess' eyes, and try if they'll
    Not make you blush your cowardice away.

    ISMAEL *leads* HOMAIS *in*

LEVAN   By Heav'n, a greater miracle than Heav'n can show.
    Not the bright empress of the sky
    Can boast such majesty. No artist could
    Define such beauty. See how the dazzling
    Form gives on; she cuts the yielding air, and
    Fills the space with glory. Respect should carry
    Me to her, but admiration here has
    Fixed my feet, unable to remove.
HOMAIS   Where shall I turn my guilty eyes?
    Oh, I could call on mountains now to sink my shame,
    Or hide me in the clefts of untried rocks,
    Where roaring billows should outbeat remembrance.
    Love, which gave courage till the trial came,
    That led me on to this extravagance,
    Proves much more coward than the heart he fills,
    And like false friends in this extremity,
    Thrusts me all naked on to meet a foe
    Whose sight I have not courage to abide.

    She leans on ISMAEL, *and holds her handkerchief to her face*

LEVAN   Permit me take this envious cloud away
    That I may gaze on all the wonders there.
    Oh, do not close those beauteous eyes, unless
    Indeed you think there's nothing here deserves
    Their shining.
HOMAIS   The light in yours eclipses mine.
    See how they wink and cannot bear your lustre.
    Oh, could I blush my shame away, then I
    Would say your charms outgo my wishes
    And I'm undone by too much excellence.
LEVAN   As strangers a salute is due. Were the
    Protector here, he'd not refuse it. (*They kiss*)
    'Tis ecstasy and more. What have I done?
    Her heart beats at her lips, and mine flies up
    To meet it. See the roses fade, her swimming
    Eyes give lessening light, and now they dart no more.

She faints! By heav'n, I've caught the poison
Too, and grow unable to support her.

She sinks down in a chair, he falls at her feet

ACMAT   (He's caught, as surely as we live.
Her eyes have truer magic than a philtre.
We'll not intrude into a monarch's secrets.
The god of love himself is painted blind,
To teach all other eyes they should be veiled
Upon his sacred mysteries.)

He shuts the scene, screens and curtains are drawn to conceal the couple

ISMAEL   Whilst we approached the castle gates
He showed such fits and starts of noble temper,
So much his virtue strove to mount desire,
That had I not been there, the holy part
Had surely conquered.

Music is heard

ACMAT   The music speaks the Princess' approach.
ISMAEL   Let us withdraw, and leave her to her fate.
The Visier, taught by me, will on the first
Fair minute tempt her ruin. Pity indeed
Such innocence should fall, but interest
Is a state much unacquainted with remorse.

They leave

Enter SELIMA, *alone*

SELIMA   I have gained this place before them.
Now, if the fatal letter be not a liar, the
Guilty pair will take advantage of our
Absence, and here employ swift time to the
Worst mischief. But should I find it once,
For on surmise I never will condemn him,
My lord and I must part for evermore.
They come. Here I'll abscond me for the time.
In love all stratagems are lawful
That serves to show if what we love deserves it.

She absconds, concealing herself from the PRINCESS BASSIMA
and OSMAN *who enter in conversation*

OSMAN   Yet, e'er your majesty removes,
Be pleased to hear your wretched lover speak.

Oh, do not turn that gracious form away.
There is no spark of ill attends my flame;
Refined by you, it lives without desire.
Permission to explore my wants, and tell
My ungiving goddess I adore her,
Cruel, discourteous though she be, is the
Extent of my petition.

BASSIMA   Do you not know that I am fond of glory,
Am born a noble, virtuous princess,
Just married to a royal husband,
Whose love and yours admit of no compare?
His, like a lawful household flame, designed
For use, not mischief, gives moderate
Warmth and wholesome heat, yours scorns the narrow
Bounds, and soars aloft: where'er it touches
It consumes, with sure destruction seizes
All the fabric, lays waste the noble pile,
And of a goodly building makes an heap of ashes.

OSMAN   No, let the urn be only filled with mine,
To those incendiary eyes I'll offer
Up their longed-for sacrifice.
No more will I offend your happy lord,
Your royal birth, nor idol honour.
The count's too large for my low state
To reckon with.
This hour I take me from your eyes,
Ne'er to see 'em more.
Nor will I ask the tribute of your tears,
Though so severe a fate might well deserve it.
So true a love, so innocent a flame,
A heart which, scorned by you,
Disdains its native seat,
Loathes the anxiety it finds within,
And tempts me beyond life, to seek a better,
Where no remembrance of your scorn intrudes.
For when the sickening soul once takes her flight,
Once rests her wings on that eternal night,
She bids an everlasting long adieu
To all the world, and all she valued, too.

BASSIMA   First, stay, and hear a wretch, more such than you.
Methinks thus taught I grow in love with fate,
And long to share in yours. But I should speak
No more, since speaking is a crime. Go then,
And leave me here to weep a loss, that
Will be truly mine.

OSMAN   Rich tears! What power lies in those falling drops.
       They rivet me more fast than a thousand chains,
       And makes that fate, which now appeared so fair,
       Compared with that rich life, which you can give,
       Horrid, deformed and shocking,
       Such as my happier state would most avoid,
       Fit only to deceive despairing mortals,
       Whose bitter cups are brim full, running o'er
       From pain, and thought of pain.
BASSIMA   'Tis I then that should seek that land of ease,
       For I am all which you have named,
       Wretched, forlorn, and desperate. Oh, thou
       Eternal power that first made fate,
       If I have sinned, 'twas by your own decree.
       Why send you passion of desire and joy,
       And then command us those passions to destroy,
       When long foreseeing that we can't do so,
       Dooms us rewards of everlasting woe?
       Where's then the kindness to their likeness shown,
       Cast in a form they vainly call their own?
       Fond ignorance, for they are all divine,
       Exempt from what unhappy mortals fear,
       Nor can their beings fail, like those who wander here.
       Hence, then, thou false received belief, be gone,
       And let us see we're like ourselves alone.
OSMAN   Who gives my princess grief?
BASSIMA   You, only you.
       The Earth's united hatred could not harm
       Me equal to your kindness. It strikes at
       Innocence and fame, and lays my virtue
       Level with the vilest,
       Makes marriage an uneasy bondage,
       And the embraces of my lord a loathsome
       Penance. What would you more? The time is come
       That I must speak to make my ruin certain.
       Like some prophetic priestess, full of the
       God that rends her, must breathe the baleful
       Oracle or burst. My crowding stars just
       Now appear to fight, and dart upon me
       With malignant influence. Nor can my
       Reason stop the dictates of my heart,
       They echo from my mouth in sounds of love,
       But such a love as never woman knew.
       'Twas surely given by fate, I would have said
       From Heaven, but that inspires but good,

And this is surely none.

OSMAN   The good is all to come. The ill is past.
Believe me, Madam, I who feel the change,
The happy turn, your kind complaint has brought,
Though I, before, thought life a worthless rag,
A garment of too vile a price to wear,
Would not now change it for a monarch's state,

BASSIMA   You draw too nigh,
For fenced about with chastity and glory,
Which like a magic circle shall enfold me,
You must not hope to pass the sacred round,
Lest sure destruction prove our lot forever.

OSMAN   One splendid day o'er-rates a scanty age;
Who would not be ten thousand years a wretch
To be one hour a god? So great a blessing
As your love was never meant a curse;
Or if it were, who would not be forever
Cursed, to be but once so blessed.

BASSIMA   You like a lover entertain your fancy,
But I have still the fatal land in view,
Where death of honour waits on that of life.
Now let us part, lest we should meet on that.
See, at your feet I beg for life and fame.
Nay, do not interrupt me, I'll not rise.
Could I have found relief from Heaven, or hence,
(*Pointing to her breast*) I had not kneeled to you.
My inauspicious fate comes fast upon me.
You, only you, can stop its headlong course.
I charge you then, by honour, glory, fame,
By love, the mighty god that now torments me,
You yield me not, a sinful slave, to death,
Torn in my conscience, mangled in my virtue,
But fly from hence, never to see me more.
Or should you stay, dare not to meet my eyes
With yours, those tell-tales of your passion,
Lest I break rudely from my husband's arms,
And fly to death in yours.

OSMAN   Can that be death to you which gives me life?
Now whilst I raise your beauties from the ground,
I feel such joys as life knew not before.
Oh, how can I, in one short moment,
Lavish the treasure of my life away?
At least allow me time for my undoing,
For death or life were a more equal choice.
Permit me to attend you to the Prince,

    And in your evening walk I'll wait you
    With my last resolves.
BASSIMA   See they agree with mine,
    And then in spite of love, or stars, or fate,
    We will be guiltless, though unfortunate.

They leave

SELIMA *comes forward*

SELIMA   Ah, siren! How she sings my lord to ruin.
    Ah, Visier! Am I thus repaid? I made
    Thy fortune, but I could not make thee love.
    But, oh, my wrongs should not admit reflection,
    Revenge and jealousy are entered here,
    They spread their sails, and must my fortunes steer.

Exit SELIMA

Curtains are drawn to discover LEVAN *and* HOMAIS, *with* ISMAEL *and* ACMAT *in waiting*

LEVAN   Where has this moment's transport led me?
    To joys untold, unproved, unthought, till now.
    Thou, goddess, who hast taught me best to love,
    Receive my thanks for thy enlightening power,
    Nor is there any due to my past virtue.
    What praise to stand when no temptation's near?
    No sooner had this sun shone with full force,
    But that it burst the brittle toy to pieces.
    Honour and justice are low sounds, can scarce
    Be heard when love is named.
    Where's the Protector? I'll wait him on my knees,
    And since he has not enjoyed urge him by all
    The love he bears me, by that he swore my
    Dying father when to his care he gave
    The royal trust to bless my youth
    With what can never fit his age.
ISMAEL   His grant will in conjunction meet your
    Other stars, for e'er swift time has slipped o'er
    Many hours, you shall have proof so plain
    Of Bassima's injustice that you shall think
    It none to part with her forever,
    And with this brighter constellation fill her room.
ACMAT   The Princess waits you at the banquet.
    When she returns, my royal mistress,
    If she pleases, must attend her, and ere

    Next rising Phoebus walks his cirque,
    Your joys shall be as lawful as they're great.
HOMAIS   Impossible, for I've embraced a god.
    No mortal sense can guess his excellence,
    Where the divine impress has been
    A pleasing trickling cools through all my veins
    And tempers into love, what else would be
    Distraction.

A dance performed by indians

LEVAN   I minded not the sports, you only fill
    My sight. How could I choose but dote
    Where gratitude and merit meet to grace
    Each other? One draws my heart, the other
    Charms my reason.
HOMAIS   Show to the banquet.
LEVAN   In vain I go.
    Love has reduced my senses all to one,
    And I can feast on nothing else but you.

They all leave

ACT IV

SCENE I

THE CURTAIN FLIES UP TO THE SOUND OF FLUTES AND
HAUTBOYS, AND DISCOVERS THE RIVER PHASIS, SEVERAL
LITTLE GILDED BOATS, WITH MUSIC IN THEM, A WALK OF
TREES THE LENGTH OF THE HOUSE, LIGHTS FIXED IN
CRYSTAL CANDLESTICKS TO THE BRANCHES, SEVERAL
PERSONS IN THE WALK, AS IN ATTENTION

HOMAIS *and* ISMAEL *come forward to the front. The camp is
supposed to be near the scene*

Song, set by Mr Finger, and sung by Mrs Hudson

> *The sweets of peace succeeds our toils of war,*
> *Unfading beauty gilds our hemisphere,*
> *Rewards with her the conqueror's toils,*
> *No joy so great as are her smiles,*
> *No dart so keen as from her eyes are cast,*
> *No breath so sweet as what with her is lost.*
> *Then all to beauty bend their lowly knee,*
> *And worship as the reigning deity.*

> *The soldier filled with scars boasts not a part*
> *So penetrable as the warrior's heart.*
> *Ungentle to his friends, rough to his foes,*
> *Beauty can all his storms compose.*
> *Nor all the honours of the dusky field,*
> *Compared with her, can one rich moment yield.*
> *Then to all beauty, &c.*

GRAND CHORUS

> *Then crown her, crown her, crown her straight,*
> *Crown this goddess of our fate;*
> *Adore, adore, adoring lie,*
> *She'll raise your souls to ecstasy.*
> *Come all to beauty bend their lowly knee,*
> *And worship as the reigning deity.*

ISMAEL   Well did I prophesy, my conquering goddess,
When first you made me slave to all your charms,
Joined ecstasy to transport, and left me
Panting with your beauties, that they were called
To better fortune than my arms. Not that
My Prince can more adore than I, but
He wears crowns to make his love more shining.
Oh, I shall turn my dazzled sight away,
When I behold him feasting on your charms,
And burn with envy more than he for love.

HOMAIS   Late, when he urged me on the unwelcome theme,
If I was un-enjoyed by the Protector,
I swore such things as set his doubts aside.
Then seeking for what sweets my lips could give,
My eager arms, unknowing, pressed him close,
Forgetful of feigned virtue, or ambition.
This raised his longings to their utmost height,
That — answering all my burning looks with his,
And intermingling fervent sighs and kisses —
Not vast imagination can define
(Though boundless as luxurious woman's wishes)
Those joys which die upon my breath unutterable.

ISMAEL   But must your first adorer have no favours?
Will he not be allowed sometimes a taste,
Some small remains of former heavenly bounty?
Methinks you should not, sure, so far forget
Those moments, sacred to our love and me,
When close you grasped me — at your new found joys
An unbeliever till you proved the wonder,
And felt the mighty ecstasy approach —

Then swore, whatever royal lover should
Succeed, you never would forget the first
Discoverer.

HOMAIS   Nor do I, Ismael, for I'll serve your fortunes,
But for my heart, the Prince is there already,
Now in my arms should I receive another,
The load would be unpleasing.

ISMAEL   I'll give you leave to fancy I am him,
For while I press you close, and feel your charms,
No circumstance can make the joy uneasy.

HOMAIS   Oh, did you know the difference
Between a new-born passion, and a former!
Nothing remains but memory and wonder,
Not the least warmth of kind desire or joy.
Nay, scarce can we believe, or make that faith
A miracle, how we could dote, as they reproach we did,
How love so much, that which at present seems unlovely.

ISMAEL   When time has worn the gaudy gilding off,
The sacred varnish that your liking gives,
He will then seem forlorn and stale as me,
An object less for love than wonder.

HOMAIS   Impossible! He's here for evermore,
Fixed in my heart immovable, immortally,
The lord of all its changes and desires.
Nor can revolving time present my eyes
An excellence, to tempt their faith from him,
The greatest excellence.

ISMAEL   Madam, you speak as eager lovers use,
Show me but one who, tho' inconstant as
The rising winds or flowing seas, still
Swears not fealty to the reigning object,
Nay, fancies he shall surely keep it, too,
Tho' he has broke ten thousand vows before,
Took new desires, new faith for every fair,
And loathed as much as ever he had liked.
'Tis one great point of love, first to impose
Upon our own belief, so self-deceived
Are better fitted to deceive another.

Enter ACMAT

HOMAIS   Waive we this argument till time decide it.
'Tis most remote and cross to our affairs,
That should not dally now, but execute;
For e'er your stars begin to disappear,
There must be mischief wrought of such a hue,

As, tho' black in itself, will brighten me.

ACMAT   The means is here, wisely you have conceived.
(*Shows her a vial*)
Whilst Bassima has life, your throne will be
Unsettled, for tho' the Prince may wish her death,
Her royal birth will scarce permit it on
Suspicion, and he would cover all his
Walks with justice, but say that he should doom
Her after, this makes but surer work.

HOMAIS   'Till ten is all the time we can call ours,
And there's but scanty sand 'till that arrives.
The opium's force will be expired by then,
When he awakes he will be seized with rage
And jealousy, to find me absent. Nay,
In the camp, too. What will he say? Late tho'
It be, he'll venture here, and much I fear,
Will seize his right, to the confusion of
My hopes forever.

ACMAT   Nor has the Princess Selima, as yet,
The engine on which all our mischief turns,
Found a propitious hour to tell her wrongs,
Tho' now as I departed your lover stopped,
And asked for Princess Homais. Uneasily
He cast his eyes in search of yours, and seems
Unentertained 'till he can meet them.
Soon as your charms appear, they'll make their way,
And draw him farther from the clinging crowd.
Then let your sister lay that stamp, as sends
Your enemies to rest, and makes you rise a queen.

HOMAIS   This asks more time than fate will now allow.
Draw near, my lord, I would not speak too loud,
The walks of kings are full of ears and eyes.
The Princess falls my victim to ambition,
The Visier to revenge and disappointment,
And both are shuffled hence to make your part
Of greatness. I would not shine without you,
Could the old Prince but keep 'em company,
Whilst Acmat holds the Princess' cup.
How easy 'twere to hush a sleeping man,
And send him to his bed of rest forever.

ACMAT   None but yourself could have so well contrived.
It saves a tedious, sure expostulation
Between Levan and him. To you the shame
And dread of the reproach has played his part too long,
'Twere time he left the stage to other actors.

ISMAEL   Madam, I understand you well, but swear
    First, if I do this (for much it shocks my soul
    To be myself the ruffian) swear,
    Charmer, swear by those bright eyes that light me
    To my ruin, thou can'st damn the race of
    Mankind with a look, and make 'em start to
    Crimes they most detested, swear by this kiss,
    Which steals my virtue from me, and turns thy
    Lover to a murderous villain,
    To bless my longing arms with their first joys,
    And let me find reward and Heaven in yours.
HOMAIS   I swear, my love, by this repeated kiss.
    But lose no time, an old man has
    Not blood to spare, besides 'twould make a noise.
    His breath but stopped will do the work, and pass
    As a lethargic fit to them who knew
    His sleep, but not the cause.
ISMAEL   I'll use the Prince's name for my admittance.
    When next you see me, know the task is done.
    Your eyes shall guide the way to him,
    Light in the dark, and steel my fainting arm.
    But go, my charmer, find your monarch out,
    And set your sister's task, whilst I prepare for mine.

Exit ISMAEL

HOMAIS   He's in the walk, and see, he draws this way,
    My sister with him, too! Nay, then the ice
    Is broke, and I must venture over.

Enter LEVAN *and* SELIMA *in conversation, attended by a full court*

LEVAN   Said you, so kind to him, so cold to me,
    Her marriage an uneasy bondage,
    And my embrace a loathsome penance.
    This hour I cut the Gordian Knot asunder,
    Nor in my arms will more enfold the sorceress.
    Oh, woman fair only to outward show,
    Well have the pens of men and angels
    Been employed to paint your snares!
    Well have the saints and fathers taught us to
    Beware those shining evils, and, as we
    Love our souls, avoid their faithless charms.
HOMAIS   You should not, sure, for one, condemn us all!
    For there are women who have truth and constancy
    As bright and lasting as the noblest male,
    And 'tis a miracle to my belief

How Princess Bassima could break them both to you.

SELIMA   Ay, Madam, there my wonder meets with yours.
　　How she could wrong a Prince of so much worth —
　　Were she not hotter than the flames of hell,
　　Or the infernal shees that yell below,
　　His youth and vigour might have quenched her fever.

HOMAIS   But are you sure 'tis true? Methinks I would
　　Not willingly believe our rank held one so bad.

SELIMA   These ears and eyes beheld and heard them both,
　　How after she had vomited her black
　　And infamous assurances of hatred
　　To her lord, he took the adult'ress in his arms —
　　The serpent, who, unhissing, sought to sting him —
　　And having praised and kissed her close, begged that
　　This evening walk might fix their last resolves.

LEVAN   And so it shall, but blood must be the cement.
　　I'll hear no more, reserve it for her judges,
　　And plead thou then that they might find her guilty.
　　My rage is mounted to that height already,
　　That should I hear it once again repeated,
　　Without their aid, I should condemn and execute.
　　(To one of the courtiers) My lord,
　　Assemble straight the council, and say I
　　Will be instantly among them.
　　Let the ambassador from Abca sit
　　Upon the bench in Osman's room, he represents
　　Her father's person, and shall not say she
　　Fell without his hearing.

HOMAIS   I've heard indeed,
　　The amorous Visier, ere the battle past,
　　Surprised the Princess and her Court within
　　A forest, ere yet the chance of war was cast,
　　Or fate determined, which to make the vanquished
　　All know the value of a prize like that,
　　The only daughter of our monarch foe,
　　He weighed it, too, but with the lover's reason,
　　Which will have all things sacrificed to love,
　　And therefore only made her heart his prize.
　　In gallantry he left her person free,
　　And promised soon to visit her in Abca,
　　There to receive reward for this important service.

LEVAN   That article alone will cost his head.
　　A royal prisoner should not be released
　　But by a nation's voice. They are both doomed,
　　And if there be but justice in our land,

He shall not live to see tomorrow's sun.

SELIMA   His head, alas, said you his head, my lord?
No, let the cursed adult'ress fall,
The gaudy bait that tempted his weak faith,
Proud to be made the royal eagle's prey,
But do not take his life, let him be banished
From all eyes but mine;
My arms shall be the chains to hold him close,
That he may never trouble you no more.

LEVAN   All that my honour will permit I'll do,
Till then, prepare to meet the council.
Come, beauteous Homais, this hour is due to
Justice, all the rest of life to love.

HOMAIS, LEVAN and his ATTENDANTS *depart;* SELIMA *remains alone*

SELIMA   As her intents were ill, so be her fate,
I must not pity one that ruins me.
But, see, my traitor husband coming here!
This then's the meeting place, she'll not be
Absent long. Oh, for the bolts from Jupiter's
High hand, that I might strike their infamy,
And sink the siren with unerring thunder!

Enter the Visier, OSMAN

OSMAN   The Princess Homais's settled in our Court.
If not by love undone, I am by spite.
Than woman's malice nothing is so sure.
If we with disappointment\meet their charms,
Once treat their proffered love with cheapness,
Or throw the melting snowball from our hands,
Till kindly warmth has turned it to a thaw,
Their indignation falls like hail around us,
Nor never cease the storm till death ensue.
This at another time would meet my care,
When passion reigned less mistress of my reason.
Of honour, and of all, now careless grown,
Wounded by love, no other power I own.
Thus blindly to my own destruction run,
Knowing those ills which yet I cannot shun,
For with love's power my wretched state's undone.

SELIMA   Ah, traitor, thou art blind indeed not to
Avoid the person thou, like me, hast injured.

OSMAN   My dearest Selima, I saw you not.

SELIMA   Trust me, I credit you in this.
But where's the Princess, traitor?

OSMAN   What Princess, Madam?

SELIMA   Oh! Proper stuff to cheat a woman's ear,
But not a wronged one, steeled like me
To both your ruins.

OSMAN   These are riddles. What, because you
Heard me argue with myself concerning
Princess Homais, your jealousy's revived.
I tell you now, as I have often said,
That of all womankind, she is the last
And worst in my esteem.

SELIMA   Oh, I see well the dark confusion of thy soul,
How the blood flushes to your guilty face,
Then sinks again, and leaves pale fear behind.
Dost thou not curse a wife's prerogative,
The hard confinement which that tie imposes,
Where law and conscience speaks against desire?
Had I not evidence too strong to be disproved,
Yourself would witness most against you.

OSMAN   If I betray surprise, 'tis that an absence
Long as mine should not have cured suspicion,
When — by our nuptial vow, I swear — I have
Declined her sight, because I would your jealousy.

SELIMA   In this thou wrong'st my wit as well as love.
Oh, for the power of Heaven to search thy heart,
Each guilty corner of that faithless breast.
I would in sight of all expose thy fraud,
Fix my avenging hand upon thy baseness,
And make thee stand their object, as thou'rt mine.

OSMAN   One of your woman's fits, I'll leave you to them.
When you're in better temper I am for you;
Till then reason is lost, as well as innocence.

SELIMA   Take thy way, mine leads t' th' death of Bassima.
I go to plead my wrongs, and her adultery,
Where, if the council find you not, doom both
To suffer largely as your sins. Yet Heaven's
High hand will surely search and punish.

OSMAN   I thought I heard you name Her Majesty.

SELIMA   Yes, traitor, know I saw and heard thee all,
When at the castle thou did'st break my heart
In seeking hers, died for her guilty love
Whilst I am lost for thine.

OSMAN   Then you have heard a most unhappy pair,
Much innocent, and much unfortunate,
And well can tell yourself there's nothing passed
That wrongs all those embraces due to you.

SELIMA   Traitor, the treason's levelled at my heart.
  Would'st take me in thy arms, and wish it her,
  Kiss me, in thought how much her kiss exceeds,
  Absent to love, though present to your sight.
  Oh, the bare name racked me to that degree
  That I will fly to make her judges strike.
OSMAN   Stir not, I charge you, from this fatal place,
  For she is innocent as angels are,
  Free from the stain or wish of evil.

Kneels on her robe

I, only I, am criminal.
  Would'st thou have vengeance, wreak it on thy lord,
  But spare, oh spare her inoffending charms,
  And take thy husband's life.
SELIMA   O Heaven, she comes! See, gods, the guilty fair
  Come to the adult'rous meeting with my lord.
  My aching senses would not bear the sight.
  Loose me, I will be gone, unless like lightning
  I could blast ye both, turn all her beauties
  To that monstrous hue as should
  Bespeak her fiend in form as well as mind.

SELIMA *exits, as* PRINCESS BASSIMA *enters with her* ATTENDANTS

BASSIMA   'Tis an unusual gallantry, my lord,
  To find a husband at his lady's feet.
  I fain would count it as a lucky omen.
  Would you but aid as I design, we need
  Not fear no ill. Leave this unhappy land,
  And make the Abcan court your own,
  My father shall receive you next his heart,
  And what his kingdom can command shall be
  At your dispose.
OSMAN   O fate, now are thy ministers at work,
  That scatter death and mischief round the globe.
  Ah, Princess, guiltless as thou art charming,
  These are not times for virtue to succeed.
  See how my eyes rain tears to speak your wrongs.
  My wife, enraged with jealousy, desires your death,
  And now is parted to declare in council,
  With unthought aggravations, all the
  Story of our wretched loves.
BASSIMA   My destiny was striving hard for light,
  And now it breaks up on us.
OSMAN   But, Madam, there remains one means of safety.

Whilst yet the council are in close debate,
We'll get the start of time, and fly to Abca.
My horses, fleet as wind, will reach that Court
Before tomorrow's setting sun.

BASSIMA   What, me, my lord?
Can you believe so poorly of me
To think that I would sell my fame for life,
And fly with him whom they declare my lover?
No, were ten thousand deaths now armed against me,
Contending which should first present me fate,
I would sustain them all, or more, as far
As life and my capacity extended,
Rather than seek this guilty means of safety.

OSMAN   Then fly without me. I'll procure a servant,
Diligent and faithful, to attend you.
Take any means so you preserve your life,
Though I no more should prove so blessed to see you.
I'll to the port direct my utmost speed.
Levan fears and obeys the Ottoman
Authority: if I engage the Sultan
On our side, you need not doubt the arbitration . . .

BASSIMA   Still would they say we were combined together,
And, though at present parted, mean to meet again.
No, though unhappy, I will trust my fate,
She strikes but once, though she be ne'er so sure,
Death is the end ordained for mortal life,
And if it meets us half upon the road
It saves the labour of the rest.

Enter to them THE PRINCE OF LIBARDIAN

PRINCE OF LIBARDIAN   Innocent and wretched lovers, I have
Much to say and narrow time to speak.
Now in the walk, thus muffled as you see,
Unknown, I have attended Homais' steps.
My leisure shall explain the rest, for now
She prides it as she goes, and fancies all
Our heads beneath. Your Majesty must take
My castle as your refuge. A chariot
Waits not far, but whilst the weighty matter
On the bench has drawn the crowd to leave the
Walk thus empty, aid me, my lord, to seize
My wife by force. When she is taken from
My nephew's eyes, he may to yours do justice.

OSMAN   Ten thousand blessings load your age for this.
I wait Your Highness.

THE PRINCE *leaves with* OSMAN

BASSIMA   Life, what art thou, that we are fond to keep
    Thee? The wretched, who do daily worse than die,
    Yet would live worse so they might still preserve thee.
    What we shall be, when dead, kills us whilst living.
    O unseen destiny, whate'er thou art,
    Reveal thyself, and kill us not with doubts.
    (*Shrieks off-stage*)
    Hark, they have got the Princess. Must I go?
    How the world will condemn thee for this flight,
    And yet I take it with my husband's uncle,
    One deeply wronged like me; the cause is common.
    Now should I fall till time has cleared my virtue,
    My fame must perish with me. The standard
    Which the world condemns or clears us by
    Is not our innocence, but our success.

Enter THE PRINCE OF LIBARDIAN

PRINCE OF LIBARDIAN   Madam, the trait'ress is secured.
    Thus far justice has met success,
    The omen's good, be the event the same,
    And we will right my honour and your fame.

They all leave

ACT V

SCENE I

THE ROYAL APARTMENT IN THE CASTLE OF PHASIA.

HOMAIS *is discovered bound. Enter* FOUR MUTES, *three with bow strings, the other with a bowl of poison. They rank themselves in dumb show on one side of the stage*

Enter THE PRINCE OF LIBARDIAN

PRINCE OF LIBARDIAN   Our castle is surrounded by Levan.
    Eager and swift, as lovers to their joys,
    He flies to his and my undoing.
    Yet ere we meet as foes,
    And bring our quarrel to the fatal field,
    The wretch that made us such shall taste my justice.
    See where she lies! Oh, pity, nature, thou

So much should'st err; so far bestow thy utmost
Cost upon the case, and leave the building empty,
The lovely frame exhausted all thy store,
And beggared thee so far, thou could'st not look
Within to aid her wants. Hence monstrous forms
And unimagined ills inhabit there,
But death shall fright them thence.
I will not stay to argue with my wrongs,
For fear her eyes steal my complaints away.
Be dumb her charms, let me be deaf and blind,
Till fate has played the mighty part in hand.

HOMAIS   You need not bring your sight to urge my faults,
They stand full blown to my repenting eyes.
Sure there are hours of ill that wait us all,
And fate has made us subject to their call,
Though some are blacker stained than others are,
There's none can say their lives were ever fair.
Then on our guardian gods be all the fault,
Not having watched our frailty as they ought,
Back to themselves, I do retort the blame,
Who carelessly resign our trusted fame.

PRINCE OF LIBARDIAN   It is not wise to wrangle thus with whom
You are to meet so soon.
Behold the fatal choice. Would'st thou be hours
In dying, here is a draught will give thee
Time to ask Heaven pardon for thy sins.
Or if that thou hast fallen beyond its mercy,
And think'st within thyself 'tis vain to ask it,
Then here's the bow string will be sudden with you,
Despatch the doubtful journey thou must take,
And send thee to thy home with smaller cost.
They're cordials all, which but a friend like me
Could minister to one so foul, so sick
To death, as thou. Which shall the garland wear
For having made the odious Homais fair?

HOMAIS   They are indeed rich cordials all which, if
Not urged by you, had met my wishes.
Swelled with the fatal draught, I should have burst
These bonds, that now confine me close, and at
Your feet, in floods of tears, and oft repeated
Wishes for forgiveness have left my dying breath.
Now I shall part displeased to think that love,
Which oft you swore proof against any change,
Could not survive one fault.

PRINCE OF LIBARDIAN   Oh, women! Exquisite in all that's ill!
    Were they so swift to shun as to excuse
    Their faults, how perfect would they be!
    None that had sinned as high as thou
    Could once have thought my justice too severe.
    But not to leave you matter for dislike,
    Your form I love, though I abhor your faults.
    Did I once listen to what passion speaks,
    Those lovely eyes would soon persuade my heart,
    With all your guilt, to dote upon their shrine.
    Therefore, no more to dally with a flame
    That may confound my honour and my reason,
    I will unloose your bonds
    And leave you to yourself to choose your fate.

Unbinds her and is going

HOMAIS   Oh, do not stir unless you would forestall
    The use of these, and make despair my doom.
    Thus on my knees, in thanks for my deliverance,
    I'll clasp your flying feet, nor loose my hold,
    Till you've vouchsafed an answer to my prayer.
PRINCE OF LIBARDIAN   We minutely expect a sharp assault.
    Here my revenge performed, I shall have time
    To argue with Levan of his injustice,
    Force him recall that sentence on his wife,
    Who by his fawning council stands convicted
    Of adultery, banished forever all
    Her husband's territories, her eyes put out —
    Those lights, which dazzled all the gazing crowd —
    Her hands, her nose, her lips, to be cut off.
    Then thus exposed, thus branded, thus abused,
    Sent back with ignominy to her father.
    The Visier, too, crammed in a roaring cannon,
    Discharged in air, to expiate the crime
    Of high-placed love. My sister widowed, and
    Myself undone are ills your eyes have caused.
    You bow-string mutes approach,
    And since she would not, I'll determine for her.
    Do your office.
HOMAIS   Hold, hold, my lord. Ah, wretch, thou art undone!
    Slaves, stay till I require your speed. See, see,
    He will not have you be so sudden.
    Give me but leave to speak this once,
    This only now, and I am dumb forever.
PRINCE OF LIBARDIAN   What can'st thou urge of weight to
    recompense

This respite which I borrow of revenge?
HOMAIS   Nothing, nothing, I but move your pity.
   Oh, think, I charge you, by your own blessed soul,
   If thus you sink me now amidst my sins,
   What will become of mine?
   Eternity, that never-ending time,
   The present and the future all in one,
   That worse than deadliest foes could ever think us.
   'Tis but the uncharitable voice of Hell
   That wishes pain and misery forever.
   To give my body, which you once thought beauteous,
   An endless prey to those affrighting fiends —
   This was your love, and this your kind revenge!
PRINCE OF LIBARDIAN   Oh, I've a sea of tenderness within me,
   And thou hast moved my tears by such a spring
   That now they flow to drown revenge forever.
HOMAIS   My dearest lord, 'tis more than safety to
   Believe that yet you love me, to see those
   Falling tears, to hear those rising sighs,
   And know my soul is precious in your eyes.
   Oh, let me live to make amends for this,
   Or else in Hell the thoughts of my ingratitude
   Will be my strongest circumstance of woe.
PRINCE OF LIBARDIAN   O Homais, say that I should spare thy life
   And thou should'st fall again, what Hell were then
   Sufficient for revenge?
HOMAIS   None. None.
   Kill in my sins, and may I burn forever.
PRINCE OF LIBARDIAN   'Tis grief for thy immortal part that holds
   My hands, and now I look again upon thee —
   That beauteous frame, had it a soul to suit
   Such glory, when fading here might rise, an
   Ornament to all those shining courts above.

   Trumpets are heard as if to an assault

   Hark! the assault begins.
   Remember, Homais, that thou bear'st thee well,
   Or else thy life's my certain forfeit.
   Wait on the Princess, bring her comfort in
   Her sorrows, and say I will expose my life to serve her.

He leads HOMAIS *off-stage, and then returns; signs away the mutes
and exits. A long alarm, repeated shouts off-stage of 'Long live
the* PRINCESS HOMAIS', *'Long live* LEVAN, *The Prince of Colchis'.
Then re-enter* HOMAIS *with* ACMAT, *and* OFFICERS, GUARDS
and SOLDIERS

HOMAIS   Thanks, worthy soldiers, such are noble sounds,
That save at once our lives and fame from ruin.
My lord, by those designs which Acmat has
Delivered, conspired the fall of both.
Now in a civil war he fain would steep you,
Defends the adulterous Princess and her minion
Against her godlike lord, and my protector.
'Tis to your timely aid all owe our safeties,
And therefore, that Levan (who by your means
Is entering here) may praise your diligence,
Haste and secure the Visier from escaping.

OFFICER   Now when the gates were opened to the Prince,
And Acmat had proclaimed your interest here,
Osman retreated from the walls in haste,
Loudly exclaimed against your sacred name,
And with his sword dividing all our ranks,
Opened himself a passage to the palace
And took the way to Princess Bassima's
Apartment.

HOMAIS   The villain helps to show himself.
Secure the avenues, let none escape,
Till the victorious Prince arrives.
As for that saucy peremptory priest,
Who sent my lord on errand to the camp,
Secure him close, nor let him eat nor sleep
Till death shall close his eyes. He who durst wake
His Prince, when I ordained him rest, whilst he
Himself has life, shall never rest.

OFFICER   Your orders shall be straight obeyed.

HOMAIS   You're worth our royal care, and soon shall find
The effects of all my promises to all.
Till then my thanks and praises shall attend you.

ALL   Long live the Princess Homais!

HOMAIS   Now to your several posts, and guard the palace,
My own particular guard attend without.
After a moment's conference with Acmat
I do myself intend to meet the conqueror.

OFFICER   Prosperity attend Your Highness.

All exit except HOMAIS *and* ACMAT

ACMAT   I had forgot the most important news,
Relying on a better star to govern here,
Soon as the Princess was arrived, thirsty
With flight and sorrow, I administered,
According to our yesternight's resolves,

In her sherbet, the cure of all her ills.
HOMAIS   Done like a Princess' minister. Now, when
    I visited, I found her fainting, the
    Poison and her fears begin to operate,
    Nor can she long remain to cross our hopes.
ACMAT   That done, I made my interest with the
    Officer whose turn it was to guard the gate
    To admit the Prince, and set your title up.
    Nor had my lord escaped, if in that minute,
    Though ignorant of what I purposed to him,
    With a small train he had not parted hence,
    Leaving the Visier to command the castle.
    Himself, as they report, designs for Ablas,
    And in the head of their united force,
    Will soon return to try his fate by battle.
HOMAIS   Therefore, therefore, whilst he's alive, how dare
    I think of any crown but his? He who
    Has sworn my death will surely act it.
    Do thou make haste to Ismael,
    'Tis but a moment since they are departed,
    His youth will soon o'ertake their speed.
    Tell him my prayers and vengeance shall go with him,
    And charge him strike to save a thousand lives,
    To rid my heart of its worst passion, fear,
    That nothing may remain but transport here.

They all leave

The scene changes to reveal the PRINCESS BASSIMA *fainting upon a couch. The Visier* OSMAN *enters to her*

OSMAN   Ah, Madam, we are lost, betrayed to ruin!
    The shameless Homais has undone us all.
    The soldiers have revolted to her side,
    The Prince, her lord, departed from the castle,
    Levan, victorious now, is entering here.
BASSIMA   Then death's the cure of all,
    And I am hastening to him.
    Since last we met I'm grown familiar with him,
    And we have now contracted such a friendship
    That I am certain nothing can disjoin us.
OSMAN   Therefore, my Princess, since your fate and mine
    Are both so near, and there remains no means
    To save you, let us employ the time
    In kind revenge, and Heavenly joys.
    Oh, do not banish me from Earth unblessed!

Send not your true adorer hence
Unrecompensed for all his constant love.
BASSIMA   There's none but you could make me hear these words,
But by the eminent disorder here
I now conjure you, Osman, not to name
A thought that may offend my glory.
Fain I would part at peace with all,
And something more, with you. But this is not the way.
OSMAN   Oh, do not argue thus, my fair, with him
Who has not time to loose the doors I've fastened
All behind. They've five to force, before they
Can disturb us, an age if well employed.
I count such vast delight in your embrace,
That should my life exceed that charming point,
The ecstasy would blunt the sharpest sword,
For I could feel no other death but joy.
BASSIMA   O honour, glory, guard me!
OSMAN   They're all but empty, notionary sounds.
The world already does conclude me happy,
Will you be more unkind than they?
You, who of all the world alone can make me blessed.
Alas! we have not time to lose.
Already they would force the door that leads
To this apartment. Your joys, midst all this
Noise and horror, would prevent another thought.
Show now that you have truly liked, and in
This latest hour of life do not oppose
A barren shadow to my love, unknown
To any but ourselves.
BASSIMA   Destroy me not, my lord, by these requests,
For I forbid not only hopes, but wishes.
That faithfulness I owe my royal lord,
That veneration all must pay to virtue,
And a fair conscience, peace, are more
Than force sufficient to repel your suit.
Then regulate your flame by mine, and well
Consider that a transitory moment
Ought to hold little weight, compared to
Everlasting life.
OSMAN   Inhuman Princess!
BASSIMA   You ought not think me so. Had I been such,
Now in my husband's arms I'd flourish fair,
Not in a narrow corner of the world,
Hunted, detested by my greatest friends,
And yet so far in love with misery

To court my dying, since 'tis by your love.
Oh, you know little not to know 'tis much
For souls so truly wed to virtue
To balance with themselves as I have done,
Which is the dearest to me, you or glory.

OSMAN   Did you but love like me, you would by all
Those joys prevent the vulgar road of death,
Or, which is worse, that which will follow your denial.

BASSIMA   I have a war within, which death
Only can conquer. None but myself can tell
The racking pains I bear. You see me dying
Either by treason, or that time allotted
To me. Cease then this most extravagant request.
Resign, like me, your wishes and
Desires. Scarce can we hear the words we speak
For the rude noise and fury of our foes.

A noise at the door

Hark, how they strive to bring us threatened fate!
Ah, Heavens, is this a time to deal for guilt,
When others would repent them of their sins?
We who have lived till now so void of crimes,
Let us not think it proper to begin 'em.

OSMAN   Heavens! Is it possible you should permit
This unexampled virtue thus to fall?
Have you not left one means to save her,
She who deserves a thousand altars
To her name? Earth is indeed too vile to bear her,
Above she'll shine, as in her proper sphere.
Forgive me, charming excellence. I, who
Durst think you had a mortal part, with rude
Unhallowed fires approached such sanctity,
Now full of wonder am convinced your charms
Are much too pure for ought but His Omnipotence
That framed them.

The door is forced open. LEVAN *and* HOMAIS *enter with* OFFICERS,
GUARDS *and* SOLDIERS

LEVAN   Seize the villain.
I will remit of her inhuman sentence,
Eternal banishment be all her doom.
Grant her repentance, Heaven, for her dark sin to me.

To one of the Court, who goes out

My lord, give present orders to the soldiers
That they respect as mine my uncle's person,
My quarrel never did extend to him.
When he returns my arms are open to him,
For I've a weighty favour to request.

BASSIMA   By our unhappy hymen, I conjure you
Spare Osman's life, for all his crime was mine.

OSMAN   Believe her not, such white could know no stain,
And 'tis my curse that I must speak her innocent,
Even whilst confessing love was on her lips,
Her cold, her candid virtue damped the sound,
That but the echo only was enjoyed.

HOMAIS   D'ye stand unmoved before a rival's boasting?
Go, bear him to immediate execution,
And in that way the council has decreed.

LEVAN   You've roused me up to noble justice,
Be sudden as revenge and hate could wish.

OSMAN   Farewell, sweet saint, till we shall meet above.
Now soldiers, to that fate which none can shun.

OSMAN *is taken and carried off*

BASSIMA   Yet call your faithful Visier back.
Oh, send, and stop his way to execution,
Pity a most unhappy bride, who ere
She saw your eyes, received a wound from his.
Love has, like fate, its 'pointed hour,
And irresistible their force,
But, made a wretched victim to the state,
With all this languishment about me,
My royal father gave me to your arms.
I strove to vanquish this uneasy passion,
Knew all your godlike virtues, and adored them,
But yet unaided, could not do you justice.
To Osman I revealed the unhappy flame,
Conjured him, as my only cure, to take
My father's Court for ours, his wife o'erheard
The fatal dialogue, and now for that he dies.

A gun is shot off

The horrid cannon is discharged. I need no more.
Ah, Heaven receive thee to its joys.

Swoons in the LADIES' *arms*

LEVAN   When beauty pleads, what rage can keeps its height?
And I am framed by nature full of pity,

But rivalled love there's none should calmly bear.

Enter an OFFICER

OFFICER   Your orders, Sir, are punctually obeyed.
    The Visier went undaunted to his fate,
    Nor at the horrid manner was concerned,
    But cried, 'twas glorious all he underwent
    For Bassima. Then as the orders ran,
    Alive we crammed him in the fatal cannon,
    Which in a moment was discharged in air,
    His carcass shattering in a thousand pieces.
    Now dread and horror fell on all the crowd
    At so unheard and unimagined death.
BASSIMA   The veil of death spreads o'er my darkened sight.
    'Twas kind whoever dealt this mischief to me,
    They're much too exquisite for nature's pangs.
    Can you forgive the errors of my fate?
    I summon all my latent strength thus low
    To ask it of you. Farewell, my lord, and, oh, believe
    Glory was still my darling virtue,
    Nor did a love, strong as my amorous
    Stars could give, once tempt me to forsake it.
    For you, who were too much divine for me,
    I beg from Heaven a long and glorious reign.
    My stars shone sullenly upon my birth,
    Let 'em not quench my fame and life together.

    BASSIMA *dies*

LEVAN   How calm she went. Should she be innocent,
    Eternal grief and horror would surround me.
    Nor could the globe afford my fellow wretch.
    O Heavens, what state is mine, that I must hope
    My wife was false?
HOMAIS   Drown all these melancholy thoughts in joy,
    Fortune has made our victory complete.
    The storm that threatened black is now o'erblown,
    And the bright shining sun of love appears,
    Unintermixed with any ill presage.
LEVAN   By Heaven, my Homais, I adore thee strangely.
    My soul takes fire at every glance of thine.
    So dear thou art to every corner of me,
    So true a mistress of my thoughts and person,
    That I will gaze my miseries away,
    And in thy arms remember nought but thee.

As LEVAN *is embracing her,* THE PRINCE OF LIBARDIAN *enters with his sword drawn, runs at her, and kills her*

HOMAIS   Ah, traitor, Hellhound, thou hast done thy worst.
PRINCE OF LIBARDIAN   Thus I've discharged the debt I owed.
    Stretch Acmat's tortures to their utmost length.
    Her minion, Ismael, whom she sent to take my life
    Is by my subjects packed to Hell before her.
    Room, ye infernal powers, for three more vile
    Than ever flamed below!
HOMAIS   Thou dotard, impotent in all but mischief,
    How could'st thou hope, at such an age, to keep
    A handsome wife? Thy own, thy devil will
    Tell thee 'tis impossible.
    Thus I dash thee with my gore,
    And may it scatter unthought plagues around thee,
    Curses more numerous than the ocean's sand,
    Much more inveterate than woman's malice,
    And but with never-ending time expiring.
PRINCE OF LIBARDIAN   Rail on, thou can'st deceive no more.
HOMAIS   O thou too faintly lover! can'st thou hear him?
    That coward Ismael, too, who reaped my foremost joys,
    What an effeminate troupe have I to deal with.
    I'll meet and sink him in the hottest lake,
    Nay, plunge to keep him down. Oh, I shall reign
    A welcome ghost, the fiends will hug my royal mischief.
    Grim Osman and his Princess grace my train,
    One sent by poison, t'other by new fires.
    But thou, my darling evil,
    When fate had nothing else to do but join us,
    When expectation beat the loudest march,
    And full-blown joys within an instant of us,
    'Tis more than life can bear to be defeated.
    Be thou a shade and let us mingle then,
    There feast at large what we but tasted here.
    Thus with my utmost force I'll bear thee with me,
    Thus strangle thy loved neck, thus die together,
    But, oh, a curse on fate and my expiring strength.

She reaches to strangle LEVAN, *but, in the effort, dies*

PRINCE OF LIBARDIAN   O nephew, how wert thou misled,
    Thy noblest nature turned to vilest uses,
    Made Homais' tool to hew ambition,
    Murder, incest, for her? I dare not tell
    Thee yet, how much to blame thou art.

Enter an OFFICER

OFFICER   My lord, the Princess Selima, distracted
    With her griefs, ranges the fatal plain,
    Gathering the smoking relics of her lord,
    Which singe her as she grasps them. Now on the
    Horrid pile herself had heaped. I left her
    Stretched along, bestowing burning kisses
    And embraces on every fatal piece.

PRINCE OF LIBARDIAN   Remove her, for your life, with gentlest
    force,
    And then, with care, convey her to my tent.
    I'm lost amidst this round of fate — what crimes
    Were ours, that you should thus severely blast
    The royal fame?

LEVAN   And here stand I, the cursed cause of all,
    As unconcerned as though the beauteous pair
    That fell by me were still alive.
    But mighty grief has stopped the passage up,
    Extremest detestation of myself
    Has left me means to speak no other way but thus.

    LEVAN *falls upon his sword*

PRINCE OF LIBARDIAN   Add not new crimes to the unhappy count,
    Deluded Prince, this was no way to expiate
    For thy faults. Live to convince the world
    By a more just and glorious reign
    That they were fate's, not yours.

LEVAN   'Tis past. Behold the murderer of Bassima,
    Who took his uncle's wife, and hugged the incest,
    And would you wish me life? I, wretch, who gave
    Her up, a prey to her avenger, proved
    In effect the inhuman butcherer
    Of nature's fairest work.

PRINCE OF LIBARDIAN   Her two extremes,
    So foul and yet so fair, she cannot paint again.
    Oh, in a cause so bad, to lose thee
    Thus, after all my ardent longings,
    And mighty strivings to advance your glory,
    Unwreathed this brow to place on yours the laurel,
    Showed you to conquered nations, as my boasting
    Proved to be made your glory's foil.
    My dearness to thee more urges tears of grief
    Than anger from me.

LEVAN   By all your mighty wrongs and my undoing

By death's inevitable pangs that now assail me,
I thought her unenjoyed,
And Bassima that monster she was made.
O injured saint, dart from thy Heaven upon me,
And grant that pardon which thou asked of me,
To you my sins can never think forgiveness,
Nor, after incest, could I live to wear it.
Beauty, death's keenest dart,
More fruitful far than any other fate,
By whose enchantments all my glories fade
And innocence, unwary, is betrayed.

LEVAN *dies*

PRINCE OF LIBARDIAN   Oh, horror, horror, horror!
What mischief two fair guilty eyes have wrought.
Let lovers all look here, and shun the dotage.
To Heaven my dismal thoughts shall straight be turned,
And all these sad disasters truly mourned.

They all leave

THE INNOCENT MISTRESS

BY

MARY PIX

first performed Lincoln's Inn Fields Theatre, *c*. June 1697

What gives *The Innocent Mistress* a contemporary ring is Mary Pix's seemingly casual ease in catching the reflexes of a sophisticated world. People speculate whether the couple next door actually are married, and then forget them. Someone remarks how little money there is around and how much high living, too. An overweight teenager gets cross when told to take up slimming, and tipples the family liquor on the sly. Less formal than earlier comedy, this world has a more relaxed, shifting substance and its own kind of alertness.

There's not much time for posturing. When lofty rhetoric gets carried along by its own windiness, it's soon punctured. Lovers woo self-mockingly, seeing the theatrical aspect that is inescapably in their talk, enjoying it, too. Less lovable people already know they may be jeered at, alert to how they must seem. Servants don't merely serve, but stage-manage, too, and the most telling argument against promiscuity is that it involves so much extra work for the servants.

There seems to be continual need to generate crisis — emergencies occur. That may be what has taught everyone to be so alert. Once dealt with, danger looks hilarious enough, but it bites at the time. Mrs Pix manages to make whatever is happening matter enough for us not to be amused when true feeling is threatened.

It's an enjoyable world to inhabit once (like Mrs Beauclair) you have a sure sense of what you want and a relish for theatricality in seeking it. Always ready to turn to disguise to test her lover, she expects him to fail, and is always amused by his obliging readiness to let her down. Indeed, when he appears true, she can't resist mocking, herself as much as him: it doesn't do to believe that kind of satisfaction is *too* real.

Because she gains such credibility for people so alert to theatricality, Mrs Pix makes her outrageously tight plotting work, with just the right degree of control and speed. She also manages emotion, though never so much as to sink the play into the bathos that fills her tragedies. The whole point is getting away with as much as possible, as successfully as circumstances permit.

It seems surprising that the play's printers should have got the order of such well-ordered scenes in a muddle, except that each one is so vivid (and, almost always, hilarious) as to be self-sustaining.

The original (and only) edition is not only flawed in its order, but also littered with mistakes in characters, names, settings and division of scenes. I have attempted to correct all its errors in the following text.

CHARACTERS

MRS BEAUCLAIR, an independent woman, niece and friend to Sir
    Charles Beauclair, and attracted to his friend Sir Francis Wildlove

SIR CHARLES BEAUCLAIR, a younger brother who has been
    married off while young to a rich ill-favoured widow and has
    afterwards come into his own estate. Now in love with Bellinda

LADY BEAUCLAIR, wife to Sir Charles, an ill-bred woman who has,
    by her previous husband

PEGGY, her daughter, equally ill-bred

BELLINDA, in fact MARIANNE, daughter to Lord Belmour, living in
    town under an assumed name since cast off by her family. Now in
    love with Sir Charles, and friend to his niece, Mrs Beauclair

SQUIRE BARNABY CHEATALL, a very foolish fellow, brother to the
    ill-bred Lady Beauclair

ARABELLA, a young lady left ˙n the guardianship of Cheatall's late
    father

BEAUMONT, an honest country gentleman, in love with Arabella, and
    friend to

SIR FRANCIS WILDLOVE, man-about-town and very gallant

MR FLYWIFE, alias ALLEN, a merchant, recently returned from the
    Indies

MRS FLYWIFE, kept by Flywife and going by his name

JENNY, maid to Mrs Flywife

SPENDALL, a sharper, a hanger-on to Sir Charles

LYEWELL, a rake, companion to Spendall

EUGENIA, maidservant to Lady Beauclair

JAMES, manservant to Sir Charles

GENTIL, manservant to Cheatall

SEARCHWELL, manservant to Sir Francis

DRESSWELL, maidservant to Mrs Beauclair

BETTY, maidservant to Bellinda

WILL, boy to Mrs Beauclair

Drawers and servants; a boy; a woman

The action takes place in London.

ACT I

SIR FRANCIS WILDLOVE *in his chamber dressing*

SIR FRANCIS   Searchwell!

SEARCHWELL   Sir.

SIR FRANCIS   Get me some small beer, and dash a little langoone in it, else 'twill go down my burning stomach ten degrees colder than ice. I should have met my old friend and collegian, Beaumont, who came to town last night, but wine and women drove it clear out of my head.

SEARCHWELL   Sir, he's here.

Enter BEAUMONT

SIR FRANCIS   Welcome, dear friend. I pr'ythee pardon my omission, faith 'twas business that could not be left to other hands.

BEAUMONT   Women, I suppose, and that excuse I know a man of your kidney thinks almighty.

SIR FRANCIS   Even so. Well, by my life, I am heartily glad to see you. Why, thou hast been an age confined to barren fields and senseless groves, or conversation stupid and dull as they. How can'st thou waste thy youth, happy youth, the very quintessence of life, from London, this dear epitome of pleasure?

BEAUMONT   Because excess of drinking cloys my stomach, and impudence in women absolutely turns it. Then I hate the vanity of dress, and fluttering, where eternal noise and nonsense reigns. This considered, what should I do here?

SIR FRANCIS   Not much, in troth.

BEAUMONT   But you, my friend, run the career your appetite directs, taste all those pleasures I despise. You can tell me what humour's most in fashion, what ruling whim, and how the ladies are.

SIR FRANCIS   Why, faith, there's no great alteration. The money is indeed very much scarcer, yet, what perhaps you'll think a wonder, dressing and debauchery increases. As for the damosels, three sorts make a bushel, and will be uppermost. First, there's your common jilts will oblige everybody.

BEAUMONT   These are monsters, sure.

SIR FRANCIS   You may call 'em what you please, but they are very plentiful, I promise you. The next is your kept mistress, she's a degree modester, if not kind to each, appears in her dress like quality, whilst her ogling eyes, and too frequent debauches discovers her the younger sister only to the first.

BEAUMONT   This I should hate for ingratitude.

SIR FRANCIS   The third is not a whore, but a brisk, airy, noisy
coquette, that lives upon treating. One spark has her to the play,
another to the park, a third to Windsor, a fourth to some other
place of diversion. She has not the heart to grant 'em all favours, for
that's their design at the bottom of the treats, and they have not
the heart to marry her, for that's her design, too, poor creature. So
perhaps a year, or it may be two, the gaudy butterfly flutters round
the kingdom, then if a foolish cit does not take compassion, sneaks
into a corner, dies an old maid, despised and forgotten. The men that
fit those ladies are your rake, your cully, and your beau.

BEAUMONT   I hope Sir Francis Wildlove has more honour than to
find a mistress among such creatures.

SIR FRANCIS   Gad, honest, honourable Ned, I must own I have a
fling at all. Sometimes I think it worth my while to make a keeper
jealous; frequently treat the coquette, till either she grows upon me,
or I grow weary of her. Then 'tis but saying a rude thing, she quarrels,
I fly to the next bottle, and there forever drown her remembrance.

BEAUMONT   'Tis pity that the most noblest seeds of nature are most
prone to vice.

SIR FRANCIS   Such another grave speech would give me a fit of the
colic.

BEAUMONT   Well, I find 'tis in vain to tell you my story, without I
have a desire to be swingingly laughed at.

SIR FRANCIS   Nay, nay, why so? I'd sacrifice my life to serve my
friend.

BEAUMONT   To confess the truth, I'm in love.

SIR FRANCIS   Is that such a wonder? Why, I have been so a thousand
times, old boy.

BEAUMONT   Ay, but desperately, virtuously.

SIR FRANCIS   There the case differs. I doubt, friend, you have
applied yourself to the wrong man.

BEAUMONT   Are you not acquainted with Sir Charles Beauclair?

SIR FRANCIS   Yes, intimately.

BEAUMONT   Then, in short, his lady and a booby brother of hers
have got my mistress in their power. She was the daughter of an
eminent merchant, one Sir George Venturewell, who, dying, left her
to the care of my lady Beauclair's father. He proved, like most
guardians, a great knave, forged a will which gave my Arabella nothing,
unless she married this two-legged thing, his son. Some of her friends
contested with 'em, but the lawyer's roguery, through the guardian's
wealth, prevailed, and she is again in their possession. The old fellow
is dead, but the sister and brother pretend to manage her.

SIR FRANCIS   Your case is desperate. I fear Sir Charles can do you
but little service in't.

BEAUMONT   Why, he lives with his wife. . .

SIR FRANCIS   Yes, modestly. He knows nothing of her concerns, and desires she should know nothing of his. Did you never hear of her character?

BEAUMONT   No.

SIR FRANCIS   She is certainly the most disagreeable of the whole sex; has neither sense, beauty or good manners. Then her humour is so implacable she hunted her first husband into the Indies, where he died, Heaven knows when or how.

BEAUMONT   What the devil made Sir Charles marry her?

SIR FRANCIS   Even that tempting devil, interest. She was vastly rich, he a younger brother. Since the estate and title of his family is fallen to him, and I dare swear he'd willingly give a leg or an arm to be freed from the intolerable plague of a wife whom no mortal can please.

Enter a SERVANT

SERVANT   Sir Charles Beauclair is coming to wait upon your honour.

SIR FRANCIS   I am glad on't. I fancy there's a sympathy in your humours that will soon excite a friendship, for he, notwithstanding the provocation of an ugly scolding wife at home, and the temptation of a good estate, and a handsome fellow into the bargain, instead of making his life easy with jolly bonarobas, dotes on a platonic mistress, who never allows him greater favours than to read plays to her, kiss her hand, and fetch heart-breaking sighs at her feet. With her she has obliged his charming niece to be, almost always. Faith, nothing but the horrible fear of matrimony before my eyes keeps me from loving Mrs Beauclair. She is pretty, without affectation, has but just pride enough to become her, and gravity enough to secure her from scandal. To all this add twelve thousand pounds in ready money.

Enter SIR CHARLES BEAUCLAIR *and* MR SPENDALL

SIR CHARLES   And is not that last the most prevailing argument, ha, Frank?

SIR FRANCIS   No, Sir Charles, chains of gold won't tempt my freedom from me. But here's a gentleman, fixed in the dull matrimonial road, uneasy if he meets with interruption, though it throws him on the flowery fields of liberty, he's my particular friend, and labours under the pangs of disappointed love. 'Tis in your power to assist him in his delivery. I know you are compassionate in these cases.

SIR CHARLES   You may promise for me to the utmost, I am ready.

BEAUMONT   Fame reports you a true English gentleman.

SIR CHARLES   You may command me, Sir.

SPENDALL   (Dear Sir Charles, lend me one guinea more, the estate's entailed, my father will die, and I shall get an heiress.)

SIR CHARLES   Here, take it, and leave lying.
SPENDALL   I'll be with you again at dinner.
SIR CHARLES   I don't question it.

Exit SPENDALL

SIR FRANCIS   Searchwell, has there been no letters for me this morning?
SEARCHWELL   No, sir.
SIR FRANCIS   Stay you at home, and if there comes one, find me out with it.
SEARCHWELL   I will, sir.
SIR FRANCIS   Come, Sir Charles, shall we to the chocolate house, there you shall hear Mr Beaumont's story.
SIR CHARLES   With all my heart. Hark you, Sir Francis, I have an entertainment of excellent music promised me this afternoon. You know I cannot have it at home, so I have borrowed some apartments of obliging Mrs Bantum, the Indian woman, and will try to prevail with the ladies to come.
SIR FRANCIS   Dear Sir Charles, introduce me.
SIR CHARLES   You'll think your hours thrown away in the company of civil women.
SIR FRANCIS   Faith, I scarce dare trust your niece's eyes, they gain too much upon my heart. I am always forced, after I have seen her, to have recourse to the glass, to secure myself from romantic constancy.
BEAUMONT   Now you talk of romantics, in troth, I think I'm a perfect knight errant, for besides my own lady I'm in quest of another fair fugitive, by the desire of her father. Have you not heard of the death of my Lord Belmour's heir, and absence of his only daughter, Marianne?
SIR FRANCIS   Yes, yes.
BEAUMONT   The old lord has given me her picture, with an earnest petition that I would endeavour to find her. He pressed me so I could not refuse it, though I have small probability on my side.
SIR FRANCIS   She's now a prodigious heiress. What could be the meaning of running from all her friends?
BEAUMONT   Too studious for her sex, she fell upon the seducers of the women: plays and romances. From thence she formed herself a hero, a cavalier, that could love and talk like them; whilst her father, without consulting her, provided a husband, rich, but wanting all such accomplishments. This man she called monster, and finding the marriage unavoidable, took her jewels, and what money was in her power, and in the stage-coach fled to this populous wilderness, if that can be proper, for here we are in crowds concealed as well as in a desert.

SIR FRANCIS   'Twas strange.
SIR CHARLES   I pity her, for I hate an innocent inclination crossed.

Enter a SERVANT

SERVANT   Sir, your coach is ready.
SIR FRANCIS   *Allons*, gentlemen.

Exeunt

SCENE II

BELLINDA'S APARTMENT

BELLINDA *enters with a book*

BELLINDA   In vain I fly to books, the tuneful numbers give me not
a moment's ease. In vain I've strove to walk in virtue's high, unerring
paths. Blind, rash, inconsiderate love has pushed me from the
blissful state, and fixed me struggling 'midst ten thousand dangers.
Here, sweet bard, thou suits me well,
'My anxious hours roll heavily away,
Deprived of sleep by night or peace by day.'

Enter MRS BEAUCLAIR

MRS BEAUCLAIR   Poor, disconsolate damosel, come leave this soft
melancholy poetry, it nurses your disease.
BELLINDA   You, indeed, like a bright ray of comfort, shoot through
my endless night. Where's my dear destruction?
MRS BEAUCLAIR   Mr Spendall said he would be here at noon.
BELLINDA   He's ever here, I feel him busy at my heart, and when
the wished minute of his approach comes on, every artery catches
the convulsive joy. Dost not thou think me mad?
MRS BEAUCLAIR   A little crazed or so, my dear.
BELLINDA   Bedlam, o'er this, had been my proper mansion if your
sweet company had not composed my jarring thoughts, and given the
warring torments intervals of rest.
MRS BEAUCLAIR   I must confess, though I am wild to the very verge
that innocence allows, yet, when my uncle, that dear good man, told
me if e'er I meant to oblige him I must be a companion, friend, and
lover of his mistress, the proposition startled me. But then I did not
think there had been such a mistress as my Bellinda, nor platonic
love in real practice.
BELLINDA   True, my dear friend, our love is to the modern age
unpractised and unknown, yet so strict and so severe are rigid honour's

laws, that though not grossly, yet we still offend. Had not Fate fixed a bar unpassable between us, how should I have blessed the accident that brought us first acquainted?

MRS BEAUCLAIR   You never told me the story.

BELLINDA   In short, 'twas thus: Coming from the play, masked, with a young lady, a fluttering fellow seized me, and, in spite of my entreaties, grew rudely troublesome. I was never used to such behaviour, and it thoroughly frighted me. Sir Charles, being near, saw my unfeigned concern, and generously made the brute desist, then led me safely to a coach. Observing where I bid the coachman drive, he came to wait upon me. My fair friend again was with me, and 'twas by her persuasions that I saw him. We found his conversation nicely civil and full of innocent delight. I blushed, and fondly thought this man my amorous stars, in kindness, destined for my happiness, but oh! . . .

MRS BEAUCLAIR   But oh, he was married, and that spoiled all.

BELLINDA   Therein I only can accuse him of deceit. He kept his marriage a fatal secret till I had lost the power to banish him.

MRS BEAUCLAIR   I pr'ythee, dear Bellinda, where wert thou bred? I am sure this lewd town never gave you such nice notions of honour.

BELLINDA   My friendship bars you of nothing but inquiring who I am.

MRS BEAUCLAIR   'Tis true. I beg your pardon and am silent.

BELLINDA   Only this I'll tell you, Madam, and as a warning, never resolve, although you think it fully in your power to keep your resolution. Mark it in me, I that thought to have stood the fairest pattern of my sex, and would have blotted all the annals of guilty love, yet now am lost, fonder of my Beauclair than of family or fame, yet know him married, and divine and human laws against me.

MRS BEAUCLAIR   For human laws, I know not what to say; but, sure, Heaven had no concern, 'twas a detested match. Ruling friends and cursed avarice joined this unthinking youth to the worst of women. But no more of this. How d'ye like your new lodgings? The house is very large, have you no good neighbours?

BELLINDA   You know 'tis not my way to be acquainted. My impertinent maid sometimes teases me with a relation of a merchant and pretty lady who came from the Indies and lodge here.

MRS BEAUCLAIR   What are they, Mrs Betty?

BETTY   Nay, my lady will ne'er hear me out, but I am sure they are worth anybody's observation. He looks like a surly, old, rich cuff, and she like an intriguing, beautiful jilt, as fine as a queen covered with jewels.

BELLINDA   Ha' done with your description, I am sick of 'em both.

MRS BEAUCLAIR   Lord, you are so peevish. Pray, give me leave to ask Mrs Betty a few more questions about 'em. What's his name?

BETTY   An odd one, Madam, they call him Mr Flywife.

MRS BEAUCLAIR   An odd one indeed, and contradicting his actions
when such a fine dame belongs to him.

BELLINDA   Thou art a little gossip to trouble thy head with other
people's affairs. I heard news of you, Madam, the other day, they
say you are in love, for all your seeming indifference.

MRS BEAUCLAIR   Yes, in troth, I am a little that way inclined.
But my spark is indeed too far from your Cassandra rules, his
mistresses are neither angels nor goddesses. Truly, Sir Francis
Wildlove is too mad even for me, though the devil's in it, I can't
forbear thinking of the rambler.

BELLINDA   Your virtue and beauty may reclaim him.

MRS BEAUCLAIR   It may be so, but I doubt he don't like reforming
so well as to try it.

Enter SIR CHARLES

Ha, see who appears, comely as rising day, amidst ten thousand
eminently known. Bellinda, this heroic is designed for you, though
somewhat barren in invention, I was forced to borrow it.

BELLINDA   Cheerful, and thy mind at ease, happy girl.

SIR CHARLES (*taking* BELLINDA's *hand*)   My blessing.

BELLINDA   My fate, which I should, but cannot, curse.

SIR CHARLES   Cousin, I am glad to find you here. You shall help
persuade Bellinda to go abroad. I have promised to bring you both to
Mrs Bantum's. I have provided a trifle of a dinner, and excellent
music for digestion. There's only a country gentleman and Sir
Francis. I know you love Sir Francis, Niece.

MRS BEAUCLAIR   You may be mistaken, Sir. Grant I did, would
you have me meet him? Dear Uncle, don't make me so ridiculous.

SIR CHARLES   I thought, Niece, you durst have trusted me with
your conduct. My friends are no brainless beaux, no lady libellers
that extend innocent favours, and bespatter the reputations they
cannot ruin.

MRS BEAUCLAIR   Then you think your friend, Sir Francis, a very
modest man?

SIR CHARLES   No, my dear, but your mildest men, if they have
sense, as I am sure he has, know how to treat women of honour.

MRS BEAUCLAIR   Nay, I am soon convinced. What say you, Madam?

BELLINDA   I will go, for perhaps, Sir Charles, you think I've only
invented fears of being known, but you'll surely find, if any accident
discovers me, I shall be seen by you no more.

SIR CHARLES   See thee no more! Yes, I would see thee, though
barred by foreign or domestic foes, set on thy side father or husband,
on mine wife and children, I'd rush through all nature's ties to gaze
on thee, to satisfy the longings of my soul, and please my fond,

desiring eyes.

BELLINDA   Chide him, Beauclair, let him not talk thus.

MRS BEAUCLAIR   Before he came you were at it. What can I say to two mad folks?

Enter SPENDALL

SPENDALL   Your servant, ladies. Sir Charles, is it not dinnertime? I'm as hungry as a—

MRS BEAUCLAIR   Horse. I know the old expression. Were I my uncle, I'd as soon build a hospital for the lazy as undertake to satisfy thy voracious appetite.

SIR CHARLES   How hast thou of late disobliged my niece that she is so severe upon me?

SPENDALL   Only told her ladyship a truth she could not bear.

MRS BEAUCLAIR   A truth from thee? I rather think I could not hear it.

SPENDALL   I said, a she-wit was as great a wonder as a blazing star and, as certainly, foretold the world's turning upside-down. Yet, spite of that, the lady will write.

MRS BEAUCLAIR   Brute! What did I ever write, unless it was thy character, and that was so adroit, you had like to hang yourself?

SIR CHARLES   For my sake, Cousin, forbear.

MRS BEAUCLAIR   Let him take pet and not come to dinner today, if he thinks fit, 'tis not I that care.

SPENDALL   No, I will come.

MRS BEAUCLAIR   That I would have sworn.

SPENDALL   To give occasion that you may draw this shining weapon wit. It will dazzle the assembly, if it pierces only me, no matter.

MRS BEAUCLAIR   Stuff, pshaw! Will you come, Madam, and put on your things?

Exeunt LADIES

SIR CHARLES   Dear Spendall, I must beg of you to step to our house. I made my wife a kind of promise to dine with her today.

SPENDALL   What shall I say?

SIR CHARLES   Say I'm gone to Court. She loves the thoughts of being great, though most unfit for it.

SPENDALL   But you know you promised to carry her daughter, Miss Peggy, with you next time you went thither.

SIR CHARLES   True. Say I'm gone to the Tower.

BELLINDA (*within*)   Are you ready?

SIR CHARLES   I am called. Say anything the devil puts into your head.

Exit SIR CHARLES

SPENDALL   Yes, I shall say what the devil puts into my head, but
    not what you expect. Am I not then ungrateful? Has he not for
    several months fed, clothed and supported me? But what for, to be
    a mere letter-carrier, an honourable pimp for platonic love? He shall
    find I can employ my parts better. He trusts me for his pleasure, and
    I'll betray him for mine.

Enter LYEWELL

    Ha. Lyewell! Why come you hither?
LYEWELL   Phough, I saw Sir Charles and the ladies go out. Besides,
    I want money. I did not serve you so when I was in my Lord
    Worthy's family.
SPENDALL   Pr'ythee, don't be so surly. Here's a crown for thee, but I
    expect some service for't. Is there ever a strumpet in your catalogue
    so well bred as to write?
LYEWELL   All the whores in town can scrawl, if that will do.
SPENDALL   Let one of 'em send immediately a nameless letter to
    my Lady Beauclair, and inform her that Sir Charles will be today at
    Mrs Bantum's with a whore between three and four, that hour lest
    she comes too soon and disturb our dinner. Well, the heiress is
    coming, I shall make thee amends.
LYEWELL   Ay, when you marry Mrs Beauclair.
SPENDALL   Hang her. I hinted love but once, and she has abused me
    ever since. I have no luck with the wits. Now I have better chase in
    view: a wealthy fool, a fool, the prerequisite of a sharper. Come with
    me, and I'll instruct you further.

Exeunt

SCENE III

Enter MRS FLYWIFE *and* JENNY

MRS FLYWIFE   Oh, how happy am I to breathe again my native
    London air! I vow the smoke of this dear town delights me more
    than all the Indian groves. Happy, too, in meeting with one like
    thee. Thou understand'st intrigues, art cunning, subtle as all our
    sex ought to be who deal with those deluders, men.
JENNY   Then your Ladyship liked not the Indies?
MRS FLYWIFE   How was't possible I should? Our beaux were the
    refuse of Newgate, and our merchants the offspring of foolish,
    plodding cits.
JENNY   Why went you, Madam?
MRS FLYWIFE   So great is my opinion of your faith, I dare trust you

with all my past love. My parents bred me at a boarding school, and died when I was about fourteen, leaving me nothing for my portion but pride and a few tawdry clothes. I was a forward girl, and, bartering what I had not the wit to prize, a never-to-be-recovered fame was soon maintained in finery, idleness, and darling pleasure. But the deceitful town grew weary of me sooner than I expected, and sick of that, seeing other new faces preferred before me, so picking up some monies, and a handsome garb, I ventured to Jamaica.

JENNY   Madam, I hear my master unlock his study.

MRS FLYWIFE   Oh heavens! This foolish story put Sir Francis Wildlove's letter quite out of my mind. Have you writ as I directed?

JENNY   Yes, Madam.

MRS FLYWIFE   Give me the letter and be gone. I would not have him think us great.

Exit JENNY

Enter MR FLYWIFE. *As* MRS FLYWIFE *goes to put up the letter hastily, she drops it*

Come, fubby, will you go into the dining-room? The chocolate is ready.

MR FLYWIFE   And you, methinks, are ready too, Madam. Beyond sea 'twas a courted favour, dressed seldom and careless, but since arrived at this damned town no cost, nor pains is spared. Curse upon my doting folly, that listened to thy prayers, and spite of my oath and strong aversion brought you back to the high road of hell.

MRS FLYWIFE   Is then my tried constancy suspected? Did I for this deny the richest planters of the place, who courted me in an honest, lawful way, and would have parted with their wealth, dearer to their souls, to have called me wife, whilst I, slighting all their offers, gave up my unsullied bloom to you, only on your protested love. Leaving Jamaica, fled with you to a remoter world, because you said your circumstances was such, that if you lived with me, your English friends must believe you dead.

MR FLYWIFE   Well, and what was my return to all this boasted kindness? You may remember, Madam, your cargo was sunk so low 'twould scarce afford at the next ship's approach another London topping, when I, without a hated look, for life poured on ye more riches than all your husband-pretenders joined together could aim at, gave you such a separate fortune, that, indeed, I was forced to obey your desires in coming into England, lest you should do't without my leave.

MRS FLYWIFE   Well, well, thou art a good boy. Pr'ythee no more wrangling, fubby. I vow and swear tomorrow I'll be as great a slattern as ever was if that will please you, so I will.

MR FLYWIFE   Ay, and want to go out today, for all the gazing fops
to admire, though I have told you I can't appear till I have inquired
into my affairs; then tomorrow, if you stay at home with me,
sackcloth will serve turn.

MRS FLYWIFE   Lord, you are so froppish. If I was your wife, sure,
fubby, you would not be so jealous.

MR FLYWIFE   My wife, quotha! No, no, I was once bewitched, but I
found such a plague that . . . no more wives, I say.

MRS FLYWIFE   Well, I'll be anything to please fubby. Will you go
in? Our breakfast will be cold.

Exit MRS FLYWIFE

MR FLYWIFE (*taking up the letter*)   I'll follow you. Ha! What's here?
A sonnet, I'll warrant. Her gaping abroad has brought this. A letter
of her own, only the hand is scrawled to disguise it. 'If I were
convinced your passion was real, perhaps you might have no cause
to complain.' Fine, advancing devil. 'Be constant and discreet, you'll
find none of our sex ungrateful.' By thy burning lust, that's a damned
lie, for thou art thyself a most ungrateful jilt. I'll catch her now, ere
the devil can be at her elbow to invent a lie, and if one wheedling
tongue does not destroy all my senses, she shall feel my rage.

Enter SERVANT

SERVANT   Sir, the captain comes to bring you news your ship is safe
in the river.

MR FLYWIFE   Be damned. There let it sink.

SERVANT   Shall I tell him so, Sir?

MR FLYWIFE   Jackanapes, I'll come to him.

Exit SERVANT

Is it impossible in nature to be happy with or without a woman? If
they are virtuous they are peevish, ill-natured, proud and coy,
If fair and complacent, they please as well,
For then, by Heav'n, they are false as Hell.

ACT II

SCENE I

Enter MRS FLYWIFE *and* JENNY

MRS FLYWIFE   Ha, ha, ha! I can't forbear laughing at your great concern.

JENNY   Oh, Madam, if you did but see what a passion my master was in you would not be so merry. He was like to beat the sea-captain, though he brought him the good news of his ship's arrival.

MRS FLYWIFE   Phough, mind what I say, and fear not. I warrant you shall have the letter again, and liberty to find Sir Francis Wildlove with it.

JENNY   Madam, he comes.

MRS FLYWIFE   Well, well, be sure you do it handsomely. (*Sings*)

Never, never let her be your wife

.That was loud that he might think me merry. Speak, hussy.

Enter FLYWIFE

JENNY (*crying*)   Pray, Madam, search again. I have been a month of writing on't, and took it out of a book, too. The man has sent me forty before I could make shift to answer one till now. Oh! Oh!

MRS FLYWIFE   Pr'ythee don't tease me. I dropped it. 'Tis gone. I'll write another for you, since you say the man is for a husband and can so well maintain you. Be quiet!

MR FLYWIFE   (What's this? Faith not improbable! 'Tis not my damosel's hand, now I have considered on't again.)

JENNY   I had rather lost my best petticoat by half.

MRS FLYWIFE   Cease your noise, or leave the room.

MR FLYWIFE   What's the matter? (Having no occasion for a quarrel will be money in my pocket, I am sure.)

MRS FLYWIFE   Why, fubby, this foolish wench, it seems, has a country lover, and begged of me to direct a letter to him, which in troth I have lost, so she howls, that's all, fubby.

MR FLYWIFE   And I have found it. Come, Jenny, to make amends for your sorrow, I'll write the superscription. Whither is it to go?

JENNY   (Madam, Madam?)

MRS FLYWIFE   Oh, I think I remember. To Geoffrey Scatterlove at the Bull Inn in Cambridge. So seal it and carry it, for these silly girls never think it safe unless they give it into the Post House themselves. But make haste.

JENNY (*kissing the letter*)   Have I got thee again, my dear sweet letter?

MRS FLYWIFE   A very raw, foolish girl this, my dear.

MR FLYWIFE   Faith, puggy, there had like to have been a quarrel. I
    was almost afraid that letter was a piece of gallantry of yours.
MRS FLYWIFE   Ay, ay, you are always suspecting me, when Heaven
    knows I am such a poor, constant fool, I never so much as dream of
    any man but my own dear fubby. (*He clutches her*) Fubby, let I go.
MR FLYWIFE   No, no, I'll run away, I won't hear you, I won't hear
    you.

Exit MR FLYWIF

MRS FLYWIFE   Then I'll follow and I am sure prevail. Oh, had my
    sex but half my cunning, the deceivers would find themselves
    deceived. From my gallants I never found, but gave 'em killing
    charms.
    Fools! When we love, our liberties we lose,
    But when beloved, with ease we pick and choose.

Exit MRS FLYWIFE

SCENE II

Enter LADY BEAUCLAIR *and* CHEATALL

LADY BEAUCLAIR   Brother, I say you're a fool.
CHEATALL   Fool in your face! I'm no more a fool than yourself.
    What would you have a man do? Must I ravish her? Don't I know
    accessories have been hanged? And here you'd have me principal!
    What, I understand law, I won't hang for your pleasure.
LADY BEAUCLAIR   Yes, you understand law. D'ye understand
    parting with a good estate, which you must do if you haven't this
    Arabella? Don't tell me of ne. . . ne. . . necessaries, I say you shall
    marry her.
CHEATALL   Ay, but the craft will be in catching, as the saying is.
    Why, I went but e'en now to take her by the lily-white hand, as the
    poet has it, and she threw a whole dish of scalding hot tea full in
    my face, dish and all. Cousin Peggy saw her. She called her all the
    names in christendom. She'll tell ye the same.
LADY BEAUCLAIR   Ah, poor Peggy! Ay, she don't love to see you
    abused. Were that minx like Peggy you were but too happy. Well,
    when will you give Peggy that diamond necklace? The sparks are
    almost mad for her, and she has Lord knows how many sweethearts.
    There's Squire what d'ye call him?
CHEATALL   (So, now she's got upon her daughter's sweethearts,
    she'll ne'er ha' done.)
LADY BEAUCLAIR   There's Sir John Empty and Mr Flutter, and

Captain Noisy say the finest things to her, but the wench is so coy, and my rogue of a husband will let none of 'em come home to her, but calls 'em fops and boars, and the Lord knows what.

CHEATALL   O Lord, boars! Beaux you mean. O Lord! Boars!

LADY BEAUCLAIR   Well, she has of all sorts. And if there be twenty women in company all the rout is made about her, and the girl doth so blush, I vow and swear it makes her look woundy handsome.

CHEATALL   Ay, you called me fool, but I'll be hanged if ye don't make a fool of her, mark the end on't. Marry her to some honest tradesman, that's fittest for her.

LADY BEAUCLAIR   Pray, don't trouble your musty pate about her. No, she scorns a citizen, she would not have my Lord Mayor's son. She's a girl of discretion. I was married young, too, and I looked after all my first husband's affairs.

CHEATALL   (True! Till he went the Lord knows whither to be quiet.)

LADY BEAUCLAIR   Indeed this young fellow is not worthy the name of a husband. I have a good mind to let the world know what a deceitful piece 'tis.

Enter PEGGY, *eating plum cake*

PEGGY   Mother! Mother!

LADY BEAUCLAIR   What's the matter, child?

PEGGY   Here's Mrs Arabella does nothing but jeer and abuse me. She says eating between meals will spoil my shape, and I snatched a book out of her hand, and she said a primer was fitter for me.

LADY BEAUCLAIR   I'll never endure this. How dare she affront my daughter!

CHEATALL   So, I am like to have a fine life, nothing but scolding and noise. For my part, I'd rather not marry at all. If she is thus randy beforehand, what will she be afterwards? In a short time I shall be made ballads on, and my picture set before 'em just like the summons to Horn Fair.

LADY BEAUCLAIR   Yes, yes, you shall marry her, and we'll tame her, too, I'll warrant you.

PEGGY   Here she comes, here she comes, as mad as a turkey cock.

Enter ARABELLA

ARABELLA   Why am I used thus? Your servants are forbid to call me either coach or chair. Are you my gaoler? You, oaf, I speak to.

CHEATALL   Mistress, 'twould be better for you if you had other words in your mouth, I'll tell you that.

PEGGY   You shan't gallop your. . .

LADY BEAUCLAIR   Hold, Peggy, let me speak. What's the reason, Mrs Arabella, you take this privilege here? You know your fortune is at our dispose, so shall your person be, else you must expect nothing.

ARABELLA   Had I but heard your characters, I'd sooner have been exposed a beggar in this inhospitable world, than e'er set my feet within your doors.

LADY BEAUCLAIR   I'd have you to know our correctors are honest correctors. I wished yours proved so.

CHEATALL   Don't provoke me, I say, don't.

ARABELLA   Why? You won't beat me. I hear there is a sensible man amongst ye. I'll appeal to him, if you'd let me see him.

LADY BEAUCLAIR   That's my husband you mean. No, you shan't see him, not such as you are, if I can help it.

PEGGY   What! Would you see my father-in-law to tell lies and stories to him? No, no, don't mistake yourself.

ARABELLA   Away, you smell of Aqua Mirabilis.

LADY BEAUCLAIR   Oh, impudence! She smell of strong waters! She hates it. Come hither, Peggy. Let me smell. Thy breath used to be as sweet as any cow's.

PEGGY   (What shall I do? I've been at my mother's bottle.) I won't come to satisfy her nor you neither. What ails ye, d'ye know?

ARABELLA   No, I don't, Miss. Well, since I must have neither attendance nor conveniency, I'll go afoot. (ARABELLA *attempts to leave*)

CHEATALL   Hold ye, hold ye. You are not gone yet, as the saying is. (*He takes her by the arm*)

ARABELLA   Was ever usage like this?

LADY BEAUCLAIR   Your usage has been but too good, let me tell you that. I'll show you such usage as you deserve. (*She calls off-stage*) Hug — Uggun — what a devil is your name? I hate a wench with a hard name.

Enter EUGENIA

Here, lock up Mrs Flippant in the dark room.

PEGGY (*jumping about*)   Ay, lock her up, lock her up I say.

CHEATALL (*grinning in her face*)   Yet, Mrs Bella, be ruled by me. Give me one sweet look, and let me take a honey kiss, and you shan't be locked up. No, you shan't be locked up, but go abroad with me, and have your belly full of cakes and custards. Shall I? Shall I?

ARABELLA   There's the kiss. And for a look I wish my eyes were basilisks (*Strikes him*)

PEGGY   O Lord, Mother, how she swears!

CHEATALL   Oh, my chops, my chops! Lock her up! Hang her, she's a fury.

LADY BEAUCLAIR   Abominable! Come hither! Hath she hurt ye?

ARABELLA   (O Eugenia, last night, when you heard my story, you, in gentle pity, wept. Assist me now, or I'm lost.)

EUGENIA   (Have patience, Madam, and believe me yours.)

LADY BEAUCLAIR (*to her brother*)   I say, keep the key yourself, I don't like her greatness with the maid.

CHEATALL   'Tis locking up, I fear 'tis against the law, Sister.

LADY BEAUCLAIR   Phough! I fear nothing. Are you not a squire, and rich? You're above the law.

CHEATALL   Ay, but knights ha' been hanged. I dread hanging. I tremble always when I think on't.

LADY BEAUCLAIR   Hanged! There's no danger of being hanged. What, ha' ye no courage?

CHEATALL   Yes, I have courage, and that she shall find. My injuries, as I have read it, steel my eyes. Mrs Arabella, I could swear the peace against you, and have you before a justice, but I will spare you the shame, and punish you myself. Come along.

ARABELLA   Resistance is in vain, but I will be revenged, or kill myself.

CHEATALL   Ay, ay, kill yourself, and then I shall have your estate, without being troubled with your person. I'll humble you.

ARABELLA   And Heaven punish thee.

CHEATALL   Don't trouble your musty pate about Heaven, as my sister says, but come along.

PEGGY   Away with her! Away with her!

ARABELLA   I take Heaven and Earth to witness, I believe you design to murder me.

CHEATALL   There's no such design. Besides, your witnesses are not valid. I never heard their evidence go in any trial in all my life.

LADY BEAUCLAIR   No, it is not to murder ye, but make ye better. No more words, but let it be done.

They go out, leaving LADY BEAUCLAIR *and* PEGGY

PEGGY   I'm glad she's to be locked up, for had any gentleman come to see me, she's so pert her tongue would ha' been running.

Enter CHEATALL, *with a key,* GENTIL *and* EUGENIA

CHEATALL   Here I have her double locked i'faith, neither window nor mousehole in the room. Gentil, fetch my cloak. I'll to my lawyer, Mr Cobblecase, for my mind misgives me plaguily.

GENTIL   Shall I wait on you, Sir?

CHEATALL   No, no, stay at home, and if anyone asks for Mrs Arabella, say she does not lodge here.

GENTIL   Yes.

CHEATALL   B'w'y'sister.

LADY BEAUCLAIR   Your journey is needless, but you may go if you will, and, d'ye hear, ask Mr Cobblecase to come and dine here. He's a bachelor. You should always be thinking of Peggy.

CHEATALL   Well, well.

Exit

PEGGY   O mother, yonder's Mr Spendall a-coming. He's grown very fine of late.

LADY BEAUCLAIR   Ay, if he would leave your vather's company, and make out what he says about his entailed estate, the man is not to be despised.

Enter SPENDALL

SPENDALL   My lady Beauclair, your most humble. Dear, pretty creature, yours. (*Kisses* PEGGY)

LADY BEAUCLAIR   Lord, Mr Spendall, what d'ye do? Well, I wonder Peg endures it. I'll vow and swear, Mr Spendall, knights presume no farther than to kiss the tip of my daughter's little finger, and you make nothing of her lips.

SPENDALL   How! Make nothing of 'em! Pardon me, Madam, I put 'em to the use nature designed. They are as sweet as. . . and as soft as. . . gad, I must taste 'em again to raise my fancy.

PEGGY   Be quiet. Let me alone, Mr Spendall.

SPENDALL (*singing*)

>   *Oh, give your sweet temptations o'er,*
>   *I'll taste those dangerous lips no more.*

LADY BEAUCLAIR   You're a strange man. But come, sing us a song of your own. Husband says you can make verses.

PEGGY   But let it be as like that as you can, for methinks that is very pretty.

SPENDALL   (Does the fool think I shall make it extempore?) However, I have one pretty near it, as it happens. I'll rather expose myself than not endeavour to divert you, Madam.

Sings whilst the mother and daughter imitate his gestures

>   *At dead of night, when wrapped in sleep,*
>   *The peaceful cottage lay.*
>   *Pastora left her folded sheep,*
>   *Her garland, crook and needless scrip,*
>   *Love led the nymph astray.*

>   *Loose and undressed she takes her flight*
>   *To a near myrtle-shade.*
>   *The conscious moon gave splendid light,*
>   *To bless the ravished lover's sight,*
>   *And gain the loving maid.*

His eager arms the nymph embrace,
And, to assuage the pain,
His restless passion he obeys.
At such an hour, in such a place,
What lover could complain?

In vain she called the conscious moon.
The moon no succour gave.
The cruel stars, unmoved, looked on
And seemed to wink at what was done,
Nor would her humour save.

Vanquished at last by powerful love,
The nymph expiring lay,
No more she sighed, no more she strove,
Since no kind stars were found above,
She blushed, and died away.

Yet blessed the grove, her happy flight,
And youth that did betray,
And panting, dying with delight,
She blessed the kind transporting night,
And cursed approaching day.

LADY BEAUCLAIR   Thank ye, 'tis very fine, I'll vow and swear.

PEGGY   So 'tis indeed, Mother.

LADY BEAUCLAIR   Now, to leave fooling, where's my husband?

SPENDALL   I know not. I haven't seen him these two days. Here my father writes to me, if I will take up, that's the old man's expression, and find a virtuous woman with a fortune, he will give me three thousand pounds down, and settle eight hundred a year, and, faith, I am trying to obey the rich cuff, and wean myself from my old friends and the dear bottle.

LADY BEAUCLAIR   Ay, you do very well, Mr Spendall. I should be overjoyed to see you take up, and perhaps a fortune may be found. I'll say no more, but a thorough reformation will produce strange matters, matters a little thought of. But I'll say no more.

SPENDALL   Your Ladyship must not say a word of this to Sir Charles, for then he'll forbid me the sight of this dear creature, whose charms alone have power to work the mentioned reformation.

LADY BEAUCLAIR   No, no, fear not that, I haven't so many friends to go the ready way to lose 'em.

PEGGY   For my part, I don't love vather so well to tell him anything of us.

Enter a BOY *with a letter*

BOY   Madam, here's a penny post letter to your ladyship.

LADY BEAUCLAIR   To me!

PEGGY   I warrant 'tis to me, from some spark.

Exit BOY

LADY BEAUCLAIR   Stand away, hussy, 'tis directed to my. . . my Lady Beauclair. What's this? (*Stammering*) Mrs Bantum's, the Indian House? Read it, Mr Spendall. Some mischief, I believe.

SPENDALL   'Though unknown, I cannot forbear injustice to your Ladyship's merit. Informing you, that Sir Charles, at four o'clock, will be with a mistress at Mrs Bantum's. Use your discretion, but assure yourself it is a truth.'

LADY BEAUCLAIR   Oh, the villain, the rogue! The confounded whore! I'll tear his and her eyes out. Always at home he's sick or his head aches, and he must lie alone. Ah, Mr Spendall, if I should tell you the naked truth you'd say he was a villain, too. I've often told him his own with tears, and the brazen faced villain has forswore it. My husband with a whore! I have no patience. I'll go there immediatel and stay till he comes.

PEGGY   Ay, do, Mother, and I'll go with you, and help to pull their eyes out.

SPENDALL   Are you both mad? Why, all there love Sir Charles to that degree they'd watch, and turn him back. You'd never conceal your passion. Your only way is to come after the hour, and then you'll certainly surprise 'em.

LADY BEAUCLAIR   That's true. Well, good Mr Spendall, stay and comfort me. I fear I shall have my fits, and then no two men can hold me.

SPENDALL   I would with all my heart, and esteem myself happy to serve you. But my father has sent me twenty guineas for a token, and if I don't go this minute the man will be gone out of town, and carry 'em back with him.

LADY BEAUCLAIR   Nay, that is not to be neglected. Come, child, we'll go to my cousin Prattle's and tell her this news. My husband with a whore! I cannot bear it.

SPENDALL   I must seize a kiss, else I shall faint before I see you again.

PEGGY   Pish, pish, I think the man's distracted.

LADY BEAUCLAIR   Is this a time? And my husband with a whore! I wish my nails were twice as long for her sake. Ah child, thy vather was anotherguess man than this, though he had faults too. Come away. Your servant, Mr Spendall.

PEGGY   Your servant, Sir.

LADY BEAUCLAIR   My husband with a whore!

Exeunt LADY BEAUCLAIR *and* PEGGY

SPENDALL   Ladies, your most obedient slave. Thus far affairs go on
as I could wish. Now, if my lady does but abuse Bellinda till it
come to parting between Sir Charles and she, then my miss, being
out of his tuition, I fear not her falling into mine. She's damned
silly. I am forced to let all courtship lie in kissing, for she understands
a compliment no more than algebra. Well, her wealth makes it up.
Now for dinner.

Exit

SCENE III

ST JAMES'S PARK

Enter SIR CHARLES BEAUCLAIR, BELLINDA *and* MRS
BEAUCLAIR

MRS BEAUCLAIR   This walk i'the park has done me good.
BELLINDA   'Twas very refreshing.
MRS BEAUCLAIR   Is not this better now, dear Bellinda, than reading
and sighing away every beauteous morning?
BELLINDA   Yes, if at each gazer the conscious blushes would forbear
to rise. If I could look upon this object of my love and virtue and
not shrink back, it were true happiness.
SIR CHARLES   My lovely charmer, let me call this day mine and
oblige you to be cheerful.
MRS BEAUCLAIR   I warrant ye, by and by we'll be as merry as
the. . . you know the title that sticks a hand, Uncle. Ha, yonder's
Sir Francis Wildlove, for heaven's sake step behind the trees whilst I
clap on my mask and stroll towards Rosamund's pond, and he, no
doubt, pursues.
BELLINDA   You will not, sure.
MRS BEAUCLAIR   Indeed, my dear gravity, I will. That is, with
your leave, Sir.
SIR CHARLES   Well, thou art a mad girl but I dare trust thee. Come
this way, Madam.

Exeunt SIR CHARLES *and* BELLINDA

MRS BEAUCLAIR *crosses the stage.* SIR FRANCIS WILDLOVE,
following at a distance, speaks

SIR FRANCIS   What's there? A woman well shaped, well dressed,
masked and alone! How many temptations has the devil tacked
together for a poor frail mortal that scarce needed half a one! The
handkerchief dropped, a fair invitation. A deuce take her agility.

She has been too nimble for me, however. I'll venture. Madam, by your remaining when the whole army of beauties are retired, I should guess you pickeer for a particular prize.

MRS BEAUCLAIR   Then I suppose you have vanity enough to think your well-rigged pinnace worth securing.

SIR FRANCIS   Faith, child, I hope you would not find the freight disagreeable.

MRS BEAUCLAIR   Now I could not have thought such a hopeful, proper gentleman would have been straggling in the park this hour. What, no lady of quality nor miss that appears like one to lead out today? No assignation? Or is it the plague upon your fine clothes, credit out, and pocket empty?

SIR FRANCIS   Shall I tell you the truth?

MRS BEAUCLAIR   Yes, if you can find in your heart.

SIR FRANCIS   Why then, faith, I have an appointment; and that with ladies, nay, and music. Yet if you'll be kind, my dear chicken, they shall wait for me in vain. (*Coming nearer her*) By Heaven, a charming side-face.

MRS BEAUCLAIR   Stand off, or I vanish. But tell me what makes you so indifferent to your first engagement? The women are old, I suppose.

SIR FRANCIS   Alas, very buds, my dear.

MRS BEAUCLAIR   Ugly, then.

SIR FRANCIS   Beautiful as angels.

MRS BEAUCLAIR   What can be the matter?

SIR FRANCIS   Don't you guess? Why, they are virtuosos. I have a mistress there. Confound me if I am not damnably in love with her, and yet could never get myself in a vein serious enough to say one, dull, foolish, modest thing to her.

MRS BEAUCLAIR   Poor gentleman! Suppose you practised before you went and fancied me the lady.

SIR FRANCIS   A match.

MRS BEAUCLAIR   With arms across.

SIR FRANCIS   And the looks of an ass, I begin: Ah Madam! How was that sigh?

MRS BEAUCLAIR   Pretty well.

SIR FRANCIS   Behold the humblest of your slaves. See the martyr of your frowns. Those arms must heal the wounds your eyes have made or else I die. They must, they must. (*Rushing upon her*)

MRS BEAUCLAIR (*unmasking*)   Hold! Hold! Sir Charles, Sir Charles, here I shall be ravished in the open park!

SIR FRANCIS   O heavens! Mrs Beauclair!

Enter SIR CHARLES *and* BELLINDA

SIR CHARLES   Why, how now, Frank, in raptures before the face of the world and the sun!

SIR FRANCIS   Pshaw, I do confess I am caught.

BELLINDA   If you had come to any harm, Madam, you might have thanked yourself.

MRS BEAUCLAIR   (No great harm neither to have a hearty hug from the man one loves.)

SIR FRANCIS   Madam, I humbly ask your pardon.

MRS BEAUCLAIR   It is easily granted. 'Twas a frolic of my own beginning.

SIR FRANCIS   This generosity wholly subdues my wandering heart.

MRS BEAUCLAIR   Have a care of getting into the dull, foolish, modest road, Sir Francis.

SIR FRANCIS   No more of that, dear Madam.

SIR CHARLES   Come, I believe dinner stays. Where's your friend Mr Beaumont?

SIR FRANCIS   He'll be there before us.

SIR CHARLES   Let's to our chairs, I dare say the ladies are tired.

BELLINDA   Truly, I am.

Enter JENNY, *and pulls* SIR FRANCIS *by the sleeve. He steps aside with her*

JENNY   Sir, the lady that came lately from the Indies, whom you have seen at the play, sends you this. The oddness of the superscription she'll explain to you.

SIR FRANCIS   Oh, the charming angel! Dear girl, accept my acknowledgement and step behind those trees whilst I lead my mother and my aunt into their chairs. I'll be with you in a moment.

MRS BEAUCLAIR   (Oh, the wretched libertine! But to take notice on't would show too much concern.)

SIR CHARLES   Sir Francis, where are you?

SIR FRANCIS   Here, at your elbow, Sir Charles. Madam, may I presume to lead you to your chair?

MRS BEAUCLAIR   Yes, Sir, though I believe, as your affairs stand, you could 'bate the ceremony.

SIR FRANCIS   The greatest affairs in Christendom should not hinder me from waiting on your ladyship.

They go off, leaving JENNY

JENNY   No, faith, they are not of the shape of motherly and elderly aunts. I'll not stay here, but watch where they go, and tell my lady what a rambler she has chose.

Exit

SCENE IV

A HOUSE

MRS FLYWIFE   So, with much coaxing I have got my jealous fellow
to let me go out this afternoon on the pretence of buying things and
seeing an old aunt. If this wench would come and tell me where the
mad spark will be, I'll venture to give him the meeting.

Enter JENNY

Have you found him?
JENNY   Yes, Madam, but I perceive he's a sad, wild man. He was
engaged with two masks, and would feign have slammed me off 'twas
his mother, but I saw by their mien and dress they were young.
MRS FLYWIFE   What said he to you?
JENNY   Seemed much pleased, but shy. Bid me stay, and promised to
return presently. I thought I should do your ladyship more service
in seeing where they went, so I dogged them to Mrs Bantum's, our
neighbour, and housed them all there.
MRS FLYWIFE   Very good, and by and by I'll to Locket's and send
for him. I fancy I know the gentleman's humours so well that he'll
certainly forsake old acquaintance for those of a newer date, though
he ventures changing for the worse. He seemed eager and pleased,
fierce and fond, and swore my charms were unequalled. His swearing
indeed signifies but little, the banquet o'er,
Yet sure he'll meet when Love and I invite,
For Love's his god, and leads him to delight.

ACT III

SCENE I

Enter EUGENIA *followed by* GENTIL

GENTIL   Whither so fast, Mrs Eugenia?
EUGENIA   Stop me not. I am upon an act of charity, trying to free
the amoured lady. I have been picking up all the rusty keys in the
house in hopes to accomplish it.
GENTIL   Why, you'll lose your place.
EUGENIA   Hang my place. There's not one in the family understands
a grain of civility except Sir Charles. And if he speaks to me my lady
pulls my headclothes off. Come, I know you don't love that lubberly
coxcomb your master. E'en join with me. Assist in Arabella's liberty,
and recover her fortune, and I dare engage she'll make ours. Besides,

to tell you the truth, I have received ten guineas today from one
Mr Beaumont to endeavour her freedom.

GENTIL   That's a most prevailing argument, I confess. What I do is
for your sake, Mrs Eugenia.

EUGENIA   In hopes to go snacks with the gold, ha, Gentil! Well, well,
stay here, I'll return immediately.

Exit and re-enter with ARABELLA

'Tis done, 'tis done. Is this a bird to be concealed in such a dark and
dismal cage?

ARABELLA   Well, thou art a rare girl. Oh, if thou could'st but conjure
now and get the writings for my estate for me, five hundred pounds
should be thy own next moment, wench.

GENTIL   Say you so, Madam? Gad, I'll turn devil, but it shall be done.

EUGENIA   Why, what would that signify to you, fool?

GENTIL   Well, mind the lady's business and let me alone to take
care of yours.

EUGENIA   First let us take care of the squire. Gad, if I don't manage
that booby I'll give you leave to cut my apron and make a slobbering
bib of it.

GENTIL   Well, what's your contrivance?

EUGENIA   Why, I'll go in again, pour down a bottle of red ink I know
of, make all fast, and swear he has murdered ye. A cross old woman
lately, to whom he would give nothing, told him she read it in his
phiz that he would come to be hanged, which the superstitious fool
has ever since been afraid of. Very indifferent circumstances will
confirm that fear and bring him to a compliance.

ARABELLA   My better angel! It has a lucky face, it looks like thee.
But how must I be disposed of?

EUGENIA   If you please to go to Mrs Beauclair's, Sir Charles' niece,
she's a woman cheerful, witty and good, and will assist you in
everything.

ARABELLA   I've heard so well of her I dare venture to be obliged to
her. Come, let's make haste.

EUGENIA   Gentil, get the back door open and let none of the
servants see us go out. I am sure we shall be lucky, because my
termagant lady won't be at home today to disturb us.

ARABELLA   Come then, I long to quit the house I have been so
ill-used in.

Exeunt

SCENE II

MRS BANTUM'S

Enter SIR FRANCIS WILDLOVE

SIR FRANCIS   A deuce of all ill-luck, I have lost my little ambassadress from my dear Indian queen. 'Twas a charmer. How can an old curmudgeon have the impudence to hope he should keep such a lovely creature to himself? For a husband or cully I find by her discourse she has, and by the description she hates him, which is a good step for me.

Enter SEARCHWELL

SEARCHWELL   Sir, all the company is coming into this room to hear the music.

SIR FRANCIS   Gad so, are they? Then I must wait upon Mrs Beauclair down. Sirrah, you are a purblind dog not to find the pretty letter-carrier.

SEARCHWELL   I think I saw a woman as soon as another, else I'm sure I were not fit for your honour's service. I swear she was not in the park. I searched it three times over as carefully as I had been to look for a needle in a bottle of hay and hanged if I did not find it.

SIR FRANCIS   What a comparison the puppy has! D'ye hear, if you do not find her out I shall discard you for an insignificant blockhead, for I am damnably and desperately in love with her mistress.

Exit SIR FRANCIS

SEARCHWELL   Ah lard, ah lard, desperately and damnably in love with her, and never saw her but twice at a play, and then she was in a mask. Well, my master would be the best of men if 'twere not for these whores. I am harassed off my legs after 'em. The pox, the plague, that belongs to 'em. Consume 'em all, I say.

Exit

Enter SIR CHARLES BEAUCLAIR, SIR FRANCIS WILDLOVE, BEAUMONT, SPENDALL, BELLINDA *and* MRS BEAUCLAIR

SIR CHARLES   Ladies, how d'ye like your small regalio?

MRS BEAUCLAIR   Extremely. For ought I know, Sir Charles, you may repeat showing me the way to gad abroad.

BELLINDA   What opinion, Madam, do you think this gentleman will have of us, for I presume the young ladies in the country are not so free of their company?

MRS BEAUCLAIR   No, poor gentlewomen. They are condemned to the government of some toothless aunt or grannum, visit but once a

year, and that in the summer season when the heat covers the ruddy
lassies with sweat and dust. The winter they divert themselves with
blind-man's bluff among the serving men, where too often, one
sprucer than the rest whispers love to Miss Jenny and seduces even
the eldest daughter.

BEAUMONT   Though some have been guilty of those weaknesses
you must not accuse all.

MRS BEAUCLAIR   All who are confined there, never suffered to see
the world. For granting one more thinking than the rest, who has
power and obeys her father in suffering the addresses of the next
adjacent squire, she either dies of a consumption, pining after
pleasures more refined, or else, o'ercome with vapours, runs
melancholy mad.

BEAUMONT (*to* BELLINDA)   Madam, you sighed at this pretty
description.

BELLINDA   Did I?

BEAUMONT   (Both her deportment and face confirm my suspicions.)

SIR CHARLES   You are thoughtful, Frank.

MRS BEAUCLAIR   Would you have him brisker, Uncle? 'Tis but my
clapping on a mask and 'tis done. Sir Francis, do I wrong you? Have
I not seen you at a play slighting all the bare-faced beauties, hunting
a trollop in a mask with pains and pleasure? Nay, more, for her
gaping, nonsensical banters, neglecting immortal Dryden's eloquence,
or Congreve's unequalled wit.

SIR FRANCIS   I own sometimes I divert myself with the little gypsies.

MRS BEAUCLAIR   Ay, and disturb the audience.

SIR FRANCIS   I' faith, Madam, I must speak freely. Though you are
a woman of quality, and my friend's niece, you talk so prettily 'tis
pity you should not do it often in a mask. But then again, you are
so pretty 'tis pity you should ever wear one.

MRS BEAUCLAIR   I did not design by railing to beg a compliment.
Sir Charles, where's the music?

A song by Mrs P ———, sung by Mr Hodgson

> *When I languished*
> *And wished you would something bestow,*
> *You bade me to give it a name.*
> *But, by heaven, I know it as little as you,*
> *Though my ignorance passes for shame.*
> *You take for devotion each passionate glance*
> *And think the dull fool is sincere,*
> *But never believe that I speak in romance*
> *On purpose to tickle your ear.*
> *To please me then more think still I am true,*
> *And hug each apocryphal text;*

> *Though I practise a thousand false doctrines on you*
> *I shall still have enough for the next.*

A dance. Then a dialogue between two platonic lovers: the words by
Mr Motteux, and set by Mr Eccles

HE	*How long must I the hours employ*
	To see, belovèd, yet ne'er enjoy?
	Though to curb loose desires I try
	Sure I may wish at least to die?
	Die then, poor Strephon, wretched swain,
	Nor only live to love in vain.
SHE	*Live, hopeless lover, while I grieve*
	Much for thy fate, but more for mine,
	For mine, my dear, condemned to live,
	To love, be loved, but ne'er be thine.
HE	*Oh, see me, love me, grieve me still,*
	Till love's excess or sorrows' kill,
	'Tis not myself I love, but thee.
	Then I must die to set thee free.
SHE	*No, live and love, though hope is dead,*
	For 'tis a virtue so to love.
	The gold's refined, the dross is fled,
	The martyrs thus in flames improve.
BOTH	*Then let us love on, and never complain*
	But fan the kind fire, and bless the dear pain.
	For why to despair should true lovers be driven
	Since love has his martyrs, he must have his Heaven.

SPENDALL   (My Lady Beauclair will be here straight, I'll e'en march off.) (*Is going*)

SIR CHARLES   What, desert us, Jack? Though the ladies won't drink, you may.

SPENDALL   I beg your pardon, Sir Charles. I have made an assignation with some women of quality of my acquaintance.

MRS BEAUCLAIR   Women of quality! What, your laundress' daughter, or some pert, fleering, tawdry thing of a shop, vain, and proud to lose what she understands not, her reputation? She also brags she's coming to quality when she meets you.

SPENDALL   I shall not expose their names to convince your ladyship of their rank.

BELLINDA   Oh, by no means debar the gentleman of his quality.

SIR FRANCIS   You see the ladies are willing to dismiss you, Jack.

SPENDALL   I'm their very humble servant.

Exit

Immediately after enter LADY BEAUCLAIR, *pushing away a*
SERVANT MAID, *and* PEGGY

LADY BEAUCLAIR   Ye lie, ye damned quean, he is here, ha, and his
minion with him. Let me come at her! (*Leaps and catches hold of*
BELLINDA)

SIR CHARLES   Hell and furies! My wife! Madam, why all this rage?
Don't you see my niece? The other is a friend of hers, a woman of
honour.

LADY BEAUCLAIR   Your niece is a pimp, and she's a whore! I'll
mark her, Sirrah. Villain! Oh, oh, my fits! My fits! (*She falls into a*
chair)

SIR CHARLES   Fly, my Bellinda, from her brutal rage, whilst I,
wedlock's slave, stay and appease this hateful storm.

BELLINDA   'Tis but what I ought to have expected. 'Tis just I should
be punished to prevent my being guilty.

SIR FRANCIS   Dear Beaumont, carry this injured lady off, whilst we
bear the brunt.

MRS BEAUCLAIR   Go to my lodgings, child.

BELLINDA   Anywhere, to death or hell, if there can be a greater
hell than what this bosom feels.

PEGGY   O Lo! O Lo! I believe my mother's dead.

SIR CHARLES   You know the contrary. These fits are a new trick
nature has furnished the sex with. Heretofore tears and smiles were
the highest part their dissimulation could attain.

Exeunt BEAUMONT *and* BELLINDA.

All this while LADY BEAUCLAIR *has been faintly striving, as in a*
fit, and now shrieks out

LADY BEAUCLAIR   Oh! Oh!

MRS BEAUCLAIR   Give her some water.

SIR CHARLES   Give her some wine, else you'll disoblige her more, to
my knowledge, than the fits.

PEGGY   (And well thought on! I'll steal behind and drink a glass of
wine, my stomach's cold.)

She goes to the side-table, whilst they are about the chair, and drinks
two or three glasses of wine

LADY BEAUCLAIR (*starting up*)   No, villain, devil, I'll drink none of
your wine. It may be poisoned.

SIR CHARLES   Oh, you had not lost all your senses? You could hear,
I find.

LADY BEAUCLAIR   Rogue, and I'll make thee feel. I'll tear thy
linen, hair, thy cursed eyes.

SIR CHARLES   Hold, Madam, as I'm a gentleman, use me like one.

MRS BEAUCLAIR   Sir Francis, here's an excellent argument on your side, here's matrimony in its true colours.

SIR FRANCIS   No, Madam, her carriage is not a satire on the whole sex. It but sets off better wives.

LADY BEAUCLAIR   Yes, you were a gentleman, and that was all, when I married ye; the poor, third brother of a knight. 'Twas I brought your estate. If since by your friend's death one has fell, must I be abused, Sirrah?

SIR CHARLES   Madam, you have not been abused. You know that I was in my nonage married, saw not with my own eyes, nor chose for my unhappy self. Ere I lived with ye I possessed an estate nobler, a larger far than yours, which you have still commanded. Nay, I have often urged ye to diversions in hopes it would have altered that unquiet mind, but all in vain.

LADY BEAUCLAIR   Divartions! What divartions? Yes, you had me to the playhouse, and the first thing I saw was an ugly, black devil kill his wife for nothing, then your Metridate, King o' the Potecaries, your Timon the Atheist, the Man in the Moon, and all the rest. Nonsense! Stuff! I hate 'em!

SIR CHARLES   I need say no more. Now, Madam, you have shown yourself.

LADY BEAUCLAIR   Shown, what have I shown? Send for your girl flirt to show. I have nothing but a vartuous face.

MRS BEAUCLAIR   All virtue does not lie in chastity, though that's a great one.

LADY BEAUCLAIR   Well, Cousin, I'm sorry to see you take such courses. I would not have my Peg like you for the 'varsal world. Peg! What a colour this child has got! Fretting for me, I'm afraid, has put her into a fever.

SIR FRANCIS   Come, Madam, let's compose these differences. Your anger is groundless, upon my word. Not well, pretty miss? Will you drink a glass of wine?

PEGGY (*hiccups*)   No, I thank you, I cannot abide it.

LADY BEAUCLAIR   Poor girl! She never drinks anything strong except when she's very sick indeed.

SIR CHARLES   And she's very often sick, poor creature. About some five or six times a day. Madam, shall I wait on you home? I think we may quit this place with shame enough.

PEGGY (*to her mother*)   (Don't be friends, for Mr Spendall sent me word he'd meet us in the park, and if Vather goes with us how shall that be?)

LADY BEAUCLAIR   (I don't intend it.) No, hypocrite, you shan't stir a step with me. If thou dost, I'll make a bigger noise below, and raise the house about thy ears. Come, Peg.

Exeunt LADY BEAUCLAIR *and* PEGGY

MRS BEAUCLAIR   My aunt's noise is her guard. None dare approach her.

SIR CHARLES   Her going out can't be more ridiculous than her coming in.

MRS BEAUCLAIR   Sir Charles, let not your noble courage be cast down.

SIR CHARLES   Outrageous clamours are no news to me, but I dread how my Bellinda may resent it.

SIR FRANCIS   I wonder, Sir Charles, you have patience to live with this violent woman.

SIR CHARLES   'Tis for my fair one's sake, who, nicely jealous the world say she had occasioned our parting, has sworn never to see me more if I attempt it.

Enter SEARCHWELL

SEARCHWELL (*to* SIR FRANCIS)   (Sir, sir, the lady you are so damnably in love with sends word if you'll disengage yourself from your company, she'll be at Locket's in half an hour.)

MRS BEAUCLAIR   Is it so, i'faith?

SIR FRANCIS (*to* SEARCHWELL)   (Coxcomb! What need you ha' spoke so loud?) Tell him I'll not fail to wait on him. Well, Sir Charles, you'll to Bellinda?

SIR CHARLES   No, I'll first go home, and try to stop the further fury of my wife.

SIR FRANCIS   Madam, I had hopes you would have done me the honour to let me wait on you this afternoon, but it has happened so unluckily that an old uncle of mine, to whom I am much obliged. . .

MRS BEAUCLAIR   Oh, I am your uncle's servant. Sir, there needs no excuse, your company being at this time a favour I neither expect nor desire.

SIR CHARLES   Will you go in a chair, niece, or in my coach?

MRS BEAUCLAIR   A chair, if you please, Sir.

SIR FRANCIS   To that give us both leave to wait on you.

MRS BEAUCLAIR   Pray give me leave to speak a word to my boy first. Will!

WILL   Madam?

MRS BEAUCLAIR   Run to my woman and bid her come to her aunt's immediately, and bring me the suit Sir Charles made for the last ball and left at my lodgings. Make haste. Fly.

WILL   I will, madam.

Exit

MRS BEAUCLAIR   Hang it, 'tis but one ridiculous thing, I'm resolved to do it. I'll find these pleasures out that charm this reprobate. Money will make all the drawers mine.

SIR CHARLES   I'm ready to go.

SIR FRANCIS   Madam, be pleased to accept my hand.

Exeunt

SCENE III

MRS BEAUCLAIR'S LODGINGS

Enter BEAUMONT, *leading* BELLINDA

BEAUMONT   Now, Madam, you're safe in the lodgings of your friend, forget the rudeness past.

BELLINDA   Forget it! Impossible. Her words, like poisonous shafts, have pierced my soul, and will forever dwell upon my memory with endless painful racks. Yet look not on me as that vile creature she has represented, but believe me, Sir, I engaged my heart too far before I knew Sir Charles married. When I found my love unjust, how exquisite the torment proved, chilled with watchings, sighs and tears, yet, spite of my distractions, spite of the rising damps and falling dews, 'twas grown too great to be extinguished, 'till this last storm has torn it by the roots to spring no more.

BEAUMONT   (Her every word and looks confirms my thoughts.) Madam, this I dare presume to say, both from his character and my small acquaintance: Sir Charles Beauclair has moral virtues to our late English heroes unpractised and unknown. Yet, if I might advise, you should never see him more, or only to take an everlasting leave.

BELLINDA   Your freedom, I confess, is strange, and your advice is what I had resolved on before.

BEAUMONT   (None but the lovely Marianne could with such becoming majesty have checked a stranger's boldness.) View well these lines, and then confess if they do to the resemblance bear of a soft, charming face you have often, by reflection, seen. (*He gives her a picture*)

BELLINDA   Ha! My own picture, one of the effects of my dear mother's fondness, which she, dying, left in my father's hands. He named me, too, then let everlasting darkness shroud me, let me no more behold the sun or humankind, forget the world as I would be of that forgotten.

BEAUMONT   Turn, Madam, and look upon me as your friend. If you would still remain unknown, my breast shall keep this discovery silent and safe as secrets buried with the dead. Your father gave me that picture, with desires so tender for your return that, I confess, the moved me. I undertook the inquiry, though scarce could hope to

have succeeded. Since your absence your brother's dead, so that
your father, hopeless and childless, mourns, and says your sight
would revive him more than when he first blessed Heaven for your
happy birth and mother's safety.

BELLINDA   My brother dead! Loved youth, I grieve thy untimely
fate, but thou art gone to rest and peace, whilst I am left upon the
rack. Sir, I read in all your words a piercing truth, and an unbiased
honour. They have set my errors full before me. My fled duty returns
as swift as I will do to this wronged parent, hang on his agèd knees,
nor rise 'till I have found forgiveness and my blessing there.

BEAUMONT   Though much I wish your honour and your fame
secure, yet to part such lovers, whom this lewd age will scarce
believe there ever were, grates on my very nature.

BELLINDA   Oh, let me not look back that way, but generously
assist me on, till that dear man, who, witness my disgraces, I value
more than all earth's richest treasures. Tell him, lest he should take
it ill of you, that I have confessed my birth, and have resolved to fly
from him and all the world, and in my father's house remain, as in
a cloister.

BEAUMONT   How will he brook the message?

BELLINDA   Oh, tell him, Sir, that the pangs of parting will scarce
excel those my struggling virtue gave at every guilty meeting, for
there was guilt. Tell him I have sworn to die if he pursues. I blush to
impose all this on you, but if a lover, sure you'll forgive my follies.

BEAUMONT   I'll tell him all. But I must send him, too, a parting
kiss, at least, which must be allowed to such unequalled love.

BELLINDA   Not till all is fixed for my remove, then I once more will
see him. Though my heart strings crack, I'll conquer all these
criminal fires. I have the goal in view. Bright honour leads me on.
The path is glorious, but, oh, 'tis painful, too. Let me retire and tear
him from my doting thoughts, or in the bitter conflict lose the use
of thought.

Exit

BEAUMONT   How strong are the efforts of honour where a good
education grounds the mind in virtue. This unexpected hurry has for
some moments banished my dear Arabella from my thoughts. Oh,
here comes my implement.

Enter SEARCHWELL

Well, how goes affairs?

SEARCHWELL   Rarely, sir. The chambermaid swallowed the guineas
as glibly as a lawyer a double fee from his client's antagonist. She's
bringing the young lady hither. Eugenia talks of a contrivance that
you should instantly appear like a tarpaulin, pretend to be related

to the lady, and fright the Squire into a compliance.

BEAUMONT   Anything to serve my Arabella. We'll meet 'em, and receive their instructions.

Exeunt

SCENE IV

SIR CHARLES BEAUCLAIR'S HOUSE

Enter SIR CHARLES

SIR CHARLES   Sure the world's all running mad, or else resolved to make me so. At home I cannot meet with a sensible answer; but, oh, what touches nearest, the dear, the cruel, the charming maid, Bellinda, will not see me. How shall I appease the offended fair? My wife, too, not returned. Where will this end? Gentil! Eugenia! James!

WITHIN   Sir.

SIR CHARLES   Sir? Where, ye everlasting dormice? Will none come near me?

Exit SIR CHARLES

Enter CHEATALL *and* GENTIL

CHEATALL   Gadzooks! This Counsellor Cobblecase has talked law and drank claret with me 'till my brains are turned topsy-turvy. Gad, I would not have my lady-sister see me now for a king's ransom. Though, udsbores, I know not why she should, because she's a little older, set her eternal clack a-running upon all my actions.

GENTIL   Sir, my lady and miss are both abroad.

CHEATALL   That's well. Why, Gentil, here Cobblecase advises me not to lock up the young woman, but to use her kindly, and, gadzooks, I'm in a plaguey loving humour. I'll try her good nature once again. Hold. Yonder comes Sir Charles. My sister will never forgive me if I let him see her. He's a well-spoken man, if I durst trust him he should solicit for me, but then he's so woundy handsome, and so amorous I doubt he'd speak one word for me, and two for himself, as the saying is.

Enter SIR CHARLES *talking to* EUGENIA

SIR CHARLES   You say you will not injure the Squire?

EUGENIA   No, not in the least. She hath sworn never to marry him, and the law will, in time, recover her right. Only this way is sooner and cheaper.

SIR CHARLES   The lady's free, and I'll neither oppose nor assist it further. Ha, there he stands. How is't, brother?

CHEATALL   Very well, I thank you, Sir Charles.

SIR CHARLES   Your servant.

CHEATALL   Brother, you never care for my company. You take me for a numb-skull, a half-witted fellow, and, udsbores, would you but ha' me to the tavern, you should find I could drink my glass, break my jest, kiss my mistress with the best of ye. Flesh! Try old Barnaby Cheatall at your next jovial meeting.

SIR CHARLES   You're merry, Sir, but I'm in haste.

Exit

CHEATALL   Udsbores! Women and wine, both unwholesome, punish ye. There's a taste of my wit in my cursing, as the whole cargo o' the bullies lies in swearing. There 'tis again, i' faith. Am not I damnable ingenious, Gentil? Live and learn, Sirrah, and be hanged, and forget all, as the saying is. What a dickens ails me? Hanging never comes in my mouth but a qualm comes o'er my stomach. That cursed, old woman! Did'st observe how she looked like the witch before the last new ballad?

GENTIL   She had, indeed, a very prophetic face.

One knocks. GENTIL opens the door. BEAUMONT enters dressed like a seaman

GENTIL   Who would you speak with, Sir?

BEAUMONT   With Mrs Arabella Venturewell.

GENTIL   She's not here.

BEAUMONT   Now, by the cannon's fire, 'tis false. I have come ten thousand leagues to see her, and will not be so answered.

CHEATALL   (A terrible fellow! Gadzooks!) Pray, Sir, what's your business with her?

BEAUMONT   She's my sister. That's sufficient for your impertinence.

CHEATALL   You, the lawful begotten son of Sir George Venturewell? Begging your pardon, I believe you are mistaken, friend, in your father, as many a man may be, for Sir George had never any but this daughter.

BEAUMONT   No, I'm not his lawful begotten son, not the weak offspring of. . .

CHEATALL   O Lard! What pains he takes to tell me he's the son of a whore.

BEAUMONT   Born in India, bred a buccaneer, sword and fire have been my play-fellows and ravishing my pleasure. In far distant worlds I have scattered my rough image and, as my sword has cut off their dull breed, so my vigorous youth has left a race of future heroes.

CHEATALL   A very terrible fellow, as I hope for mercy.

BEAUMONT   Rich with the spoils of long successful war I have visited

this climate in search of Arabella, whom I have often heard my
father mention with much tenderness. I am directed hither, therefore
do not raise my fury with delays for, cause or no cause, if I am
angry, blood must appease it.

CHEATALL   O Lard! O Lard! What shall I do? He'll fright me into a
Kentish ague. I must speak him fair. Good Sir, all your desires shall
be fulfilled. Have but a minute's patience. Come along, Gentil, come
along and help me entreat her to speak him fair or I'm a lost man.
I'll wait upon ye in a twinkling, Sir.

Exit with GENTIL

BEAUMONT   It works as I could wish. It goes against me to terrify
this fool so much, but he deserves it.

Re-enter CHEATALL *and* GENTIL

CHEATALL   (O, Gentil, what shall I say?)

GENTIL   (The lord knows. I don't.)

BEAUMONT   Well, Sir, where's my sister?

CHEATALL   Alas, I think she's vanished.

BEAUMONT   How? D'ye trifle with my anger; bring me stories fit
for a baby? Blood and thunder! If I unsheath my sword it finds a
scabbard in your guts! Confess, or by the cannon's fire. . .

CHEATALL   I do confess that thinking of your coming, and knowing
her too a little wild, lest she should have been out of the way, I locked
her up. But what is now become of her, by the cannon's fire, the
dreadfullest oath I ever heard, I cannot tell.

BEAUMONT   (I shall never hold laughing.)

Enter EUGENIA

EUGENIA   Oh, my conscience! My tortured conscience! I cannot
keep it!

BEAUMONT   What's the matter?

EUGENIA   Oh! I went into her room, where the lady was locked up,
and there's at least a pail full of blood. All the water in the sea will
never wash the stains out. I believe Squire Barnaby and Gentil have
killed her, cut her to pieces and carried her away under their cloaks.

CHEATALL   O impudence! O Lard! O Lard! Sir, I ha'n't the heart to
kill a chicken! I always swoon at the sight of my own blood. Speak,
Gentil, why, thou hast never a cloak. That's a strong proof, Sir.
Gentil has ne'er a cloak.

EUGENIA   Why then it went all under yours. Besides, Gentil has
a large pair of trousers, that I'll swear, for you made him bring my
lady home half a venison pasty in 'em. (*Shrieks out*) Ah! Look o'
their shoes, they have paddled in it.

BEAUMONT   Ay, 'tis so. And so I'll be revenged, cut thee small as the first atoms that huddled up thy senseless carcass, nor will I be troubled to bear thee hence, but stamp thy vile clay to its kindred dust, and leave thee here for rubbish.

CHEATALL   Oh, Sir, upon my knees I beg you'd hear me.

EUGENIA   Hold, Sir, don't kill the miscreant. That will bring yourself into trouble. Our law will hang him, I warrant ye. What made him order her, being here, to be denied?

CHEATALL   Ay, good Sir, let me be hanged! That's my destiny. I see there's no avoiding it. Gentil, beg I may be hanged.

GENTIL. Pray, Sir, let my master be hanged.

BEAUMONT   Well, I'll try your law. If that fails, this, I'm sure, never will (*Pulls out his sword*). How must we proceed, Madam?

EUGENIA   I'll go with ye for a man with the staff of authority. He shall order him. The very stones in the street would turn constables to seize such a monster. Kill a pretty lady and cut her to pieces! Oh, horrid!

CHEATALL   (You are a lying whore, if I durst tell you so.)

BEAUMONT   You, fellow! Come hither.

CHEATALL   Run, Gentil, run. Proffer him all I'm worth.

BEAUMONT (*to* GENTIL)   (When we are gone, carry him to my lodgings. I have told my landlady the story, and she's provided for him.)

GENTIL   It shall be done. Is there no mercy?

CHEATALL   Ah, Lord, no mercy.

BEAUMONT   Well, we'll be with you immediately. Come, Madam.

EUGENIA   Ay, ay, repent and pray, do, Squire, do.

Exeunt EUGENIA *and* BEAUMONT

CHEATALL   O Gentil! That ever I was born! That ever I was born! What did he say to thee, Gentil?

GENTIL   He would have had me turn evidence against your worship, and confess, but I'll be hanged first.

CHEATALL   I'd confess, if I thought 'twould do me any good.

GENTIL   What? Confess you murdered her?

CHEATALL   Ay, anything, anything, anything! Oh, Gentil, it must be this witch. She has carried her away and spilt the blood that her prophecy might come to pass.

GENTIL   Not unlikely. Sir, I have thought of a thing.

CHEATALL   What is't, dear Gentil?

GENTIL   Suppose you and I run away before the constable come? I know a friend will conceal you, and then we may hope to make it up, or hear of her. I can't think she's murdered.

CHEATALL   Nor I neither, except the Devil has done't. But let's away, good Gentil, methinks I hear this magistrate's paw, this

constable just behind me, his voice hoarse with watching, and
swallowing claret bribes. Oh, Gentil, if I should fall into his grip!

GENTIL   Therefore let's hasten to avoid it. Ah, Sir, this is no time
for jesting.

CHEATALL   Too true, Gentil, but wit will o'erflow! I fear I shall
quibble in my prayers, and die with a jest in my mouth. Come, come!
Hanged! Oh Lard, any of the family of the Cheatalls hanged! Oh
Lard, and I the only branch on't. Oh, Gentil, 'tis unsupportable.

GENTIL   Away, away, Sir.

CHEATALL   Oh, that ever I should live to see myself hanged!

Exeunt

ACT IV

SCENE I

A ROOM IN LOCKET'S. A TABLE WITH A FLASK UPON IT

Enter SIR FRANCIS WILDLOVE *and* MRS FLYWIFE

MRS FLYWIFE   Well, this is a strange, mad thing, but my old, cross
fellow will never let me take a mouthful of air. I am sure you will
have an ill opinion of me.

SIR FRANCIS   A kind one, you mean, Madam. I think you generous,
lovely, and all my heart desires.

MRS FLYWIFE   My maid is gone the Lord knows where for fruit. I
swear I tremble coming into a tavern alone.

SIR FRANCIS   A glass of wine will recall the fled red roses, but here's
the nectar thirsty love requires.

Kisses her. MRS BEAUCLAIR *bounces in in men's clothes*

MRS BEAUCLAIR   Oh, pardon and protect me! I'm pursued by
hell-hounds, bailiffs, and, if taken, inevitably ruined.

SIR FRANCIS   The devil take thee and the bailiffs together for an
interrupting young dog!

MRS BEAUCLAIR   You look with a face cruel as they, but, sure, in
those fair eyes I read some pity.

MRS FLYWIFE   (A very handsome fellow.) How came you in trouble,
Sir?

MRS BEAUCLAIR   Alas, Madam, I was put to an attorney, but longing
to turn beau have half ruined my master, wholly lost my friends,
and now am followed by the several actions of my tailor, seamstress,
perruke-maker, hosier and a long etcetera, besides the swingeing'st
debt, my perfumer. Essence and sweet powder has completed my ruin.

SIR FRANCIS   'Tis monstrous to cheat honest tradesmen in dressing up a fop, therefore, unwelcome intruder, I desire you would seek your protection elsewhere.

MRS FLYWIFE   Nay, now you are too severe. The young gentleman in liberty may mend his fortunes, and live to pay his debts. He has a promising face.

SIR FRANCIS   Your pity, Madam, but hastens absence.

MRS BEAUCLAIR   (Will this fellow I thought I had so well instructed never come?)

Enter DRAWER

DRAWER   Sir Francis, a man out of breath says he must speak with you on what concerns your friend's life.

SIR FRANCIS   The devil's in the dice today. Where is he? What's the matter?

Exit with DRAWER

MRS BEAUCLAIR   (Now impudence and eloquence assist me.) What have I done? In seeking to preserve my liberty I have forever lost it. My unexperienced youth ne'er viewed such charms before, and, without compassion, this bondage may be worse than what I avoided.

MRS FLYWIFE (*laughing*)   Meaning me, Sir?

MRS BEAUCLAIR   Nay, I'm a fool, for, bankrupt in wealth, how can I hope to thrive in love, since scarce any of your fair sex, though merit was thrown into the scales, value a man on whom fortune frowns?

MRS FLYWIFE   (I think it is the prettiest youth I ever saw. I have wealth enough to supply his wants. What should then debar me?)

MRS BEAUCLAIR   (So, she eyes me kindly, I'm sure.)

MRS FLYWIFE   Your looks, sweet youth, plead powerful as your language, and to let you see I value not riches, the want of which makes you miserable, accept this ring. 'Twill stop a creditor's mouth, and pay two or three ordinaries at 'The Blue Posts'.

MRS BEAUCLAIR   Oh, wondrous beauty! Thus encouraged, shall I beg another favour: that you would fly from hence before that angry man returns, lest I fall a sacrifice to his jealousy, and see those charming eyes no more.

MRS FLYWIFE   If my maid would come. Ha, here she is!

Enter JENNY

Sure, you have flown.

JENNY   I beg your pardon, Madam, I ne'er went. Sir Francis' gentleman and I were solacing ourselves below, and sent a porter for the fruit, 'till, hearing Sir Francis was gone in a great hurry, he ran after his master, and I came up to see what was the matter.

MRS BEAUCLAIR   (A hopeful mistress and maid! Deliver me from these Town-ladies.) (*Makes to leave*)

MRS FLYWIFE   Ungrateful man, on any pretence to leave me!

MRS BEAUCLAIR   Ungrateful! Monstrous! Had a thousand friends been dying they ought all to have expired ere you have suffered a moment's neglect.

MRS FLYWIFE   This flattery's too gross, young courtier, you must treat me with truth.

MRS BEAUCLAIR   All is truth. My heart, my life is yours.

JENNY   (Another spark! Sure, the Devil's in my mistress.)

MRS FLYWIFE   Well, Sir. I'll consent to your desires, and we'll go from hence at the door towards the park; there's no danger.

MRS BEAUCLAIR   If you are kind, I fear none, Madam.

MRS FLYWIFE   Let me find you what you seem and you shall brave the world and scorn your debts. Jenny, get me a chair, and show this gentleman the house where we lodge. Then come in, let him ask for you; if you can prevent your master's seeing him, do, if not, say it is one you waited upon in his infancy. The disparity of years between you considered, that may pass.

JENNY   (Humph, I shall never like him for this affront.) Yes, Madam, it shall be done.

MRS BEAUCLAIR   Your hand, dear, obliging creature. I hear a noise.

MRS FLYWIFE   Quick, this way. Run you before and pay one of the drawers for this flask of champagne.

Exeunt

Enter SIR FRANCIS, SEARCHWELL *and a* DRAWER

SIR FRANCIS   Ha! Gone! So I thought. Eternal dog, you have been helping in this contrivance. Did you take me for a cully, spawn of Hell? Have I known this damned town so long at last to be catched with such a gross banter? Speak, Sirrah. Who was that imposter that told me my friend Mr Beaumont was taken up for a Jacobite, and the mob was pulling him to pieces?

DRAWER   As I ever hope to outlive your anger and taste again your noble bounty, I knew nothing of him.

SIR FRANCIS   Shut the door, you careless blockhead whom I charged to watch and let nobody come up to me. Now, Sirrah, confess, or I'll make that rogue help me kick thee into a mummy, for though my sword's drawn I scorn to hurt thee that way.

DRAWER   If I should confess you'll kill me, Sir.

SIR FRANCIS   No.

DRAWER   Truly then, Sir, the young spark gave me a guinea to show him the room where your honour was. But for that the fellow seemed so much concerned, I wish I may be hanged if I knew of him any

thing at all, Sir, anything at all, Sir. Good your honour break my
head, and forgive me.

SIR FRANCIS   I will not touch thee. Could I expect more from thy
sordid soul? Gold corrupts mankind. Begone.

Exit DRAWER

This unaccountable jilt has so abused me I could find in my heart
to forsake the gang and lay a penitential dunce at the feet of virtue,
fair Mrs Beauclair.

SEARCHWELL   Pray Heaven, keep you in that good mind.

SIR FRANCIS   Good lack, canting sot, I suppose you was shut up
with a whore, rascal, whilst you ought to have been pimping for me.

SEARCHWELL   Trim tram, Sir.

SIR FRANCIS   How, impudence!

SEARCHWELL   I meant the rhyme should be 'Like mistress, like
maid', for indeed I was employed with my lady's waiting gentlewoman.

SIR FRANCIS   Was ye so, rascal? Could I but find the young stripling
'twould be some satisfaction. Hang't, if I am baulked both in love and
revenge, the cross adventures shall be drowned in brisk champagne.
'Tis the dear glass which eases every smart,
And presently does cure the aching heart.

Exit

SCENE II

OUTSIDE MRS BEAUCLAIR'S LODGINGS

Enter MRS BEAUCLAIR *meeting* DRESSWELL

MRS BEAUCLAIR   O, Dresswell! I'm glad I've met with thee.

DRESSWELL   Lord, Madam, I have been in a sad fright for ye, and
hunted up and down this hour.

MRS BEAUCLAIR   All's well. Let's in there. I'll tell you my
adventures.

DRESSWELL   Then I hope your frolic has been to your ladyship's
satisfaction.

MRS BEAUCLAIR   Yes, yes. I got Sir Francis' mistress from him, and,
faith, I was pursuing my conquest and venturing to her lodging when,
coming to the house, it proved that where Bellinda lodged, and the
lady I suppose, the merchant's wife. I feared I should meet with my
uncle there, and fairly gave the maid the drop. Come, I long to
change my clothes. I'm quite tired with wearing the breeches.

Exeunt

Enter SIR FRANCIS WILDLOVE *and* SEARCHWELL

SIR FRANCIS   Ha! Is not that the young devil that abused me? He
  has entered the house, and I'll be with him presently. Walk
  hereabouts 'till I come out.

Exit

SCENE III

INSIDE THE HOUSE

Enter MRS BEAUCLAIR *and* DRESSWELL

MRS BEAUCLAIR   Are my things ready, and a good fire in the room?
DRESSWELL   Madam, they are.
MRS BEAUCLAIR   Peep out, and see who knocks.
DRESSWELL   Madam, 'tis Sir Francis Wildlove, and he seems in a fury.
MRS BEAUCLAIR   Let him in. I'll do well enough with him. Now
  get you gone and fear nothing.

Exit DRESSWELL

Enter SIR FRANCIS WILDLOVE

SIR FRANCIS   So, Sir, I suppose you think matters have gone
  swingingly on your side, and have laughed immoderately at the
  reflection how those green years have made a fool of me, but chance
  has thrown me on thee once again. And now for those feasts of
  joy. . . an after-reckoning must be paid, young gentleman. (*Draws*)
  You understand my meaning.
MRS BEAUCLAIR   Yes, and will answer it. But hear me first. 'Tis
  to provoke you I speak. Know then your mistress was my easy
  conquest. I scarce had time to say one soft thing before she cried
  'Let's fly, sweet youth, ere that rough man returns, and in thy arms
  forget him'.
SIR FRANCIS   She's a jilt, and for a well-dressed fop would quit a
  man that saved her life.
MRS BEAUCLAIR   Then this ring was presented. I suppose you may
  ha' seen it adorn thy fair hand, and, with ten thousand kisses, 'twas
  whispered, 'you shall not want for gold'.
SIR FRANCIS   Though I value her no more than I do thee, yet I will
  have thy life for harbouring so damned a thought that I was fitter
  for your sport. Come on.
MRS BEAUCLAIR   Hold, hold, Sir Francis. I'll not pretend to take
  your sword, though I could your mistress from ye. See my credentials
  for my cowardice.

She puts up her sword

SIR FRANCIS   Mrs Beauclair! What a blind puppy am I? Twice in one day, that's hard, i'faith.

MRS BEAUCLAIR   Pray return your lady back her favour. (*Gives him the ring*)

SIR FRANCIS   Madam. . .

MRS BEAUCLAIR   Nay, look not concerned. Upon my word, I'll never interrupt you more. Hug in your bosom the plastered mischiefs, their blotted souls and spotted reputations no varnish can cover o'er. Pursue, o'ertake, possess the unenvied 'mongst the painted tribe, most worthily bestow your heart.

SIR FRANCIS   Think ye so meanly of me? My heart bestowed amongst your sex's shame. No, Madam, glorious virtue alone can reach that. My loving is a diversion I can soon shake off.

MRS BEAUCLAIR   That's hard to believe. But I must beg your pardon, I'm in haste to unrig.

SIR FRANCIS   Hear me a moment. You have seen my frailties; if, like Heaven, you can forgive, a truer penitent or a more constant votary no cruel virgin ever found.

MRS BEAUCLAIR   Have a care of the dull road. Sir Francis, farewell.

Exit

SIR FRANCIS   Go thy ways for a pretty, witty, agreeable creature. But if I should seduce her into matrimony I fear the common fate will attend her beauty, quickly tarnish and good humour vanish.

Exit SIR FRANCIS

SCENE IV

THE STREET

Enter SPENDALL *and* LYEWELL

SPENDALL   Ha, Lyewell! I am the happiest man alive, almost out of fortune's power.

LYEWELL   What is't transports you so? Some whim? Some chymical delusion that will fail in the projection and vanish into air?

SPENDALL   Hear me, and then, with admiration, be dumb. Nor dare to contradict my wit or plots again. In short, my Lady Beauclair and Miss are in open rebellion by my persuasion, and to complete my good fortune I have borrowed ten guineas of Sir Charles, with the help of which I'll be married to his daughter-in-law within these two hours.

LYEWELL   Ha! I begin to think the devil has left playing at legerdemain with thee, and, having secured thee, resolves to bestow some of this world's wealth upon thee.

SPENDALL   Can'st not thou procure a Templar's chamber for an hour or two, and appear with the gravity of a long robe?

LYEWELL   With ease. I know a young spark that has fine lodgings there, but by his father is kept at short allowance. A treat, or a very small sum will engage that and all his habiliments.

SPENDALL   Can'st thou not put on the grave look of a starched counsellor?

LYEWELL   Hum! Fum! I'll speak with you immediately. . . You see, friend, I'm busy. . . How was that?

SPENDALL   Pretty well. Come, about it presently, and I'll bring the ladies to you, as my father's chief lawyer. Be sure you tell 'em you have the settlement of his estate upon me in your hands, and seem very desirous I should do well.

LYEWELL   I warrant ye, and shan't we have lusty treats, old boy?

SPENDALL   I thought your conscience had scrupled the proceedings.

LYEWELL   Oh pox, my conscience ne'er troubles me but when affairs go ill.

SPENDALL   Well, make haste, and doubt not feasting. I must to my charge, lest they cool. Fools are seldom long resolved, and I know a finer fellow would get both mother's and daughter's heart. They're now in a friendly, growing warmth, and the old one's imagination tickled as much with thoughts of darling Peggy's marriage as ever 'twas with her own. Farewell! Be sure you observe your directions.

LYEWELL   It shall be done, dear, lucky devil. Hum, hum, I shall be perfect in a grave cough, and a hum of business by that time you come to my chamber.

SPENDALL   Hold! For I had forgot. . . Whereabouts is this chamber, for I guess your Worship's name is not so famous to direct.

LYEWELL   Come, as we go along I'll tell you.

Exeunt

Enter ARABELLA *meeting* EUGENIA

ARABELLA   So, my dear deliverer, how have you succeeded?

EUGENIA   O, Madam, the poor Squire's frighted out of the little wit he had. One scene more and the day's our own.

ARABELLA   What's become of Mr Beaumont?

EUGENIA   He's about some earnest business of Sir Charles Beauclair's. I know not what 'tis, but there's a heavy clutter amongst 'em.

ARABELLA   Well, you brought me to the lady's lodgings, but I believe that's the only place she is not to be found at, for I have waited in vain, with much impatience, to see her.

EUGENIA   Her footman's below, and says she'll be here immediately.

ARABELLA   Pr'ythee let's into the chamber first, and you shall give
an account of the Squire's fright.

EUGENIA   I'll follow you, Madam.

Exeunt

SCENE V

A CHAMBER IN THE TEMPLE

Enter LYEWELL *in a gown*

LYEWELL   So, I'm equipped. The young lawyer snapped at the
guineas and has furnished me throughout, nay, left his boy to boot.
Gad, I believe he'll be famous in his generation, he encourages
mischief so readily. Pox! Would they would come. I'm weary of Cook
upon Lutleton.

Enter BOY

BOY   Sir, Sir, a gentleman and two ladies are coming up.

LYEWELL   'Tis they. You know your cue.

Enter SPENDALL, LADY BEAUCLAIR *and* PEGGY

SPENDALL   Young man, is Counsellor Smart within?

BOY   Sir, he's dispatching some half a score clients, but he'll do that
with a wet finger, and wait on you immediately.

SPENDALL   A witty whoreson. What, a wet finger to lick up the gold,
ha! Well, tell him I'm here.

BOY   Yes, Sir.

Exit

PEGGY   Fine chambers, Mother, and a fine place, I'll swear. Vather
would ne'er let me walk here. Zed 'twasn't fit for young ladies. I'll
vow, I like it woundily.

LADY BEAUCLAIR   Here were counsellors not unfit for you. But
husband was never free you should be seen.

SPENDALL   Now I'm by promise the happy man. My charming dear,
let me beg you'd entertain no other thoughts. Where's this lawyer?
A moment's delay seems an age.

Exit SPENDALL

LADY BEAUCLAIR   Well, daughter, feel how my heart beats. I'm
almost afraid to venture on him for thee.

PEGGY   Don't tell me of your fears. Now you've put a husband in my head I will be married, so I will.

LADY BEAUCLAIR   Ah! Send thee good luck! I shall fall in a fit, I
believe, whilst thou art marrying.

PEGGY   I fear not marrying, not I.

Enter SPENDALL *and* LYEWELL

LYEWELL   Well, Sir, I understand the business. Your father
considering your extravagance, has done more than I thought fit to
tell ye, but after such a proposal you may hear it all. What! This is
the pretty creature, I suppose, you are about marrying.

PEGGY   Yes, Sir.

LADY BEAUCLAIR   Lord, Peggy, you're too forward! I wonder on
ye now. Sir, she is my daughter, and she'll be worth eight thousand
pounds, and a better penny. I would not have her cast away, Sir.

LYEWELL   To be thrown into a young gentleman's arms with a great
estate will be a good cast, I take it, Madam.

LADY BEAUCLAIR   If I were satisfied in that!

LYEWELL   Look ye, Madam, I am a man of business, and many words
are but superfluous. Hum! Hogh! D'ye see, here's the settlement of
his father's estate. Eight hundred pounds a year, and some thousands
in money; a well-made fellow into the bargain. Let me tell ye, Madam,
such offers don't stick o' hand nowadays. You may read the writings
if you please. If you dislike 'em. . . look ye, I have a match in my
eye for the gentleman beyond your daughter's, though I must own
this young lady is much handsomer.

PEGGY (*to her mother*)   (D'ye hear what he says now? You'll never
leave your impartinence, as Vather calls it, pray be quiet. I'm
satisfied, so I am.)

LYEWELL   Will you read 'em, Madam?

LADY BEAUCLAIR (*reads*)   'Noverint etcetera. . .' No, Sir, I don't
understand law. But you look like a good, honest man, Sir, and I
dare take your word. I wish you had seen my daughter sooner.

SPENDALL   (Well said, mother-in-law, that is to be in love with every
new face. I must secure the young one, lest she's of the same mind.)

LADY BEAUCLAIR   I'd willingly have him keep his coach and six.
I think the young woman's face will bear it, and their estates, I hope.

LYEWELL   No doubt on't, Madam. A handsome wife, and a coach and
six, how it attracts all eyes: the envy or the wonder of the park.

SPENDALL   Well, you may do what you please, but the dear one and
I are agreed we'll to church without ye if ye dispute it any longer.

PEGGY   Ay, and so we will, I vow and swear, Mr Spendall.

LADY BEAUCLAIR   For shame, what d'ye talk on? Why, 'tis past the
cannic hour.

SPENDALL   Madam, all people of quality marry at night.

LYEWELL   That they may be sure to go to bed before they repent. A day's consideration might take off their appetite.
LADY BEAUCLAIR   Nay, if people of quality do it, I'm for ye.
PEGGY   And so I am, I vow and swear.
LYEWELL   First, ladies, be pleased to visit my withdrawing room. I have sweetmeats and trinkets there fit for the fair sex, which secures me female visitants.
SPENDALL   Agreed, we'll plunder 'em.
LYEWELL   Then we will seek to join this am'rous pair,
And drown in pleasure thoughts of future care.

Exeunt

SCENE VI

Enter FLYWIFE, *pulling in* MRS FLYWIFE

MR FLYWIFE   Come, pr'ythee, Puggy, do.
MRS FLYWIFE   I'm not in humour.
MR FLYWIFE   What, don't you love me none, Fubby?
MRS FLYWIFE   I hate mankind. Would they were in one consuming blaze, though I were in the midst of 'em.

She flies from him and exit

MR FLYWIFE   Hum, a consuming blaze. What's the matter now? This is some damned intrigue has gone cross. I heard her bid Jenny come into this room, and she'd be with her. That's a quean, I dare swear, at the bottom. I'll creep behind the hangings and hear their discourse.

Enter MRS FLYWIFE *and* JENNY

MRS FLYWIFE   To be tricked thus by a boy, a booby. Sure, this will humble the damned opinion I have of my own wit and make me confess to myself at least I am a fool.
JENNY   Ay, your ladyship was pleased to say I might pass for his nurse. Indeed I believe he has had as good instructors, for I find he's old enough to be too cunning for his benefactress.
MRS FLYWIFE   What did he say when you parted?
JENNY   Madam, I have told you several times. I no sooner showed him the house but he leaped back and seemed surprised. Then, recovering himself, he said he would follow me in. I, according to your directions, watched carefully, but no pretty master came. Nothing vexes me so much as that the little, dissembling sharper should get the ring.
MRS FLYWIFE   Pish! I don't value the trifle three farthings. What's my doting keeper good for, unless it be to give me more? But to lose

the tempting youth!

JENNY   Pray, add Sir Francis Wildlove's loss to it.

MRS FLYWIFE   Peace, fool. I'm thinking why the house should startle him. Ha! Is not here a fine woman lodges, much retired, that seems of quality?

JENNY   Yes, Madam, I never saw her but once. She's a perfect charmer.

MRS FLYWIFE   It must be so. This is some purdue devil of hers that durst not venture in for fear his constancy should be suspected. Pray, watch who comes to her, dog 'em, do something for my ease.

JENNY   Madam, I will.

MRS FLYWIFE   Get me a hackney coach. I'll range the town over, but I'll find Sir Francis Wildlove.

JENNY   My master will be mad.

MRS FLYWIFE   Then he may be sober again, better he mad than I. If he be angry, 'tis but dissembling a little nauseous fondness and all's well again.

They go out

MR FLYWIFE *emerges from the curtain*

MR FLYWIFE   Is it so, thou worst offspring of thy grannum, Eve? But I'll stifle my rage, lest without further proof she wheedles me into a reconciliation; take another coach and follow her, catch her among her comrades without the possibility of an excuse, cut her windpipe and send her to Hell without the possibility of a reprieve. Damn her, damn her!

Exit

SCENE VII

BELLINDA'S APARTMENT

Enter BELLINDA

BELLINDA   The little hurry of my quick remove has took up all my thoughts, and I have not considered what I am about. See him no more, him whom I could not live a day, an hour without! No more behold his eyeballs tremble with respectful passion! Hear no more the soft falling accents of his charming tongue! View him dying at my feet no more! O virtue! Take me to thee, chase from my struggling soul all this fond tenderness, secure me now, and I'm thy votary forever.

Enter BEAUMONT

BEAUMONT   Madam, neglecting even my love, I come to wait on
    your commands.

BELLINDA   Such thanks as an indiscreet and wretched woman can
    return are yours. What said Sir Charles?

BEAUMONT   He received the message as wretches that are afraid to
    die hear the condemning voice, or as the brave the loss of victory,
    or the ambitious that of crowns. He begs that he may haste to plead
    his cause, and seems to live alone upon the hopes his love and
    innocence may alter your resolves.

BELLINDA   Oh, stop him, Sir, some moments longer 'till I am ready
    to be gone. He has a friend too powerful within, and I must fly or I
    shall never overcome.

BEAUMONT   I'll prevent his coming 'till you send. Your servant,
    Madam.

                                                              Exit

BELLINDA   Honour and love. Oh, the torture to think they are
    domestic foes that must destroy the heart that harbours 'em. Had
    my glass but been my idol, my mind loose, unconstant, wavering, like
    my sex, then I might have 'scaped these pangs. Love, as passing
    meteors, with several fires just warms their breasts and vanishes,
    leaving no killing pain behind. 'Tis only foolish. I have made a god
    of my desire greater than ever the poets feigned. My eyes received
    no pleasure but what his sight gave me. No music charmed my ears
    but his dear voice. Racks, gibbets and dungeons, can they equal
    losing all my soul admires? Why named I them? Can there be
    greater racks
    Than what despairing, parting lovers find,
    To part, when both are true, both would be kind?

ACT V

SCENE I

BELLINDA'S LODGINGS

Enter BELLINDA

BELLINDA   He comes! Keep back, full eyes, the springing tears, and
    thou, poor trembling heart, now be manned with all thy strongest
    stoutest resolutions! There will be need.

Enter SIR CHARLES

SIR CHARLES   Ah! Whither shall I throw me? What shall I say?
    Marianne hangs like icicles upon my tongue, but Bellinda flows.

O, Bellinda, I charge thee by that dear name hear and pity me.

BELLINDA (*coldly*) What would you say?

SIR CHARLES   Why, nothing. I do not know that voice. It has stopped the rising words, and I must only answer with my sighs.

BELLINDA   Sir Charles, we have both been punished with unwarrantable love.

SIR CHARLES   Punished! Have we been punished? Now, by all my woes to come, by all my transports past, all thought of my Belinda, there's not a pang, a groan, but brought its pleasure with it. Oh, 'tis happier far to sigh for thee than to have enjoyed another.

BELLINDA   You interrupt me when I just begin. Grant it true, we might have lived till weary grown of one another, till you, perhaps, might coldly say 'I had a mistress. . . ' Now to part, when at the mention of each other's names our hearts will rise, our eyes run o'er, 'tis better much than living to indifference, which time and age would certainly have brought.

SIR CHARLES   Oh, never, never! Though the bauble, gaudy beauty, die, yet sense and humour still remain. On that I should have doted.

BELLINDA   You cannot guess your future by your present thoughts, or, if you could, I am not to be moved forsaking thee, and when I have said that, I need not add all the pleasures. . . In remote and unfrequented shades I'll pass my solitary hours, and like a recluse waste the remainder of my wretched days.

SIR CHARLES   And am I the cause of this melancholy penance? Must my unhappy love rob the world of its fairest ornament? No, Madam, stay, and enjoin me what you please. Condemn my tongue to everlasting silence, let me now and then but gaze, and tell with my eyes what's acting in my heart, or, if you retire, permit me to follow, under the pretence of hunting, the air. . . a thousand things I can invent, create new friendship, caress the whole country o'er to have an opportunity of seeing you, though at a hateful distance, and surrounded by severest friends.

BELLINDA   Ha! Is this the awful love I thought possessed ye? How fatally was I mistaken! What, pursue me to my father's house, fix on my name a lasting blot, a deathless infamy, pollute my native air with unhallowed love, where all my ancestors have, for ages, flourished and left an honest fragrancy behind? Mark me, Sir, you know I do not use to break my word. If, by letters, messages, or the least appearance, though cautiously as treasons plotted against the state, you approach me, I'll fly the kingdom, or, if that is too little, the world.

SIR CHARLES   No, 'tis I have been mistaken. Now, by all the racks, I feel not worth a sigh, a parting drop. No regard of tenderness, no beam of pity from those dear eyes, nor sidelong glance to view my sad distraction! Methinks you have already left me, and I am got

amongst my fellow madmen, tearing my hair, chained to the ground,
foaming and digging up the earth, yet in every smallest interval
of sense calling on Bellinda.

BELLINDA   A noble birth, a censorious world, a mourning father all
plead against thee. Oh, talk no more, lest you force my hand to
some desperate act. And yet, your words pierce my bosom with
greater pain than pointed steel.

SIR CHARLES   I see you are resolved on my undoing; fixed, like my
relentless fate. Therefore I'll not urge another syllable, but quietly,
as dying men when hope's all passed quit life and their dearest
friends forever, ever leave thee.

BELLINDA   That sad, silent look discovers such inward worlds of woe
it strikes me through, staggers my best resolves, removes the props
I have been raising for my sinking fame, and, blind with passion, I
could reel into thy arms. Tell me, on what are thy thoughts employed?

SIR CHARLES   On the curse of life, imposed on us without our
choice, and almost always attended with tormenting plagues.

BELLINDA   Yet we may meet again in peace and joy, when this
gigantic honour appears no bugbear, and our desires lawfully be
crowned. It is a guilty thought, nor shall I ever dare to form it a wish.

SIR CHARLES   But dost thou think we may? (*Embracing her*) What!
Uncontrolled clasp thee thus! O ecstasy, with wild fury run o'er
each trembling beauteous limb, and grasp thee as drowning men the
dear bark from whence they were thrown!

BELLINDA   Away, away! What are we doing? Divide him, heaven,
from my fond, guilty eyes. Set seas and earth and worlds of fire
between us, for virtue, fate and honour, with an united cry, have
doomed that we must meet no more.

Exit

SIR CHARLES   To raging seas, sieges and fields of battle will I fly,
pleasures and pastimes to the woes I feel. O, Bellinda!

Exit

SCENE II

Enter GENTIL

GENTIL   I could laugh my heart sore to see what a condition the fool,
my master's in. Every knocking at the door is as good as a dose of
rhubarb, and every noise makes him leap like a vaulter. Ha! He's
coming, the poor baby dares not be alone.

Enter CHEATALL, *peeping*

CHEATALL   Gentil! Is the coast clear?

GENTIL   Yes, Sir.

CHEATALL   O, Gentil!

GENTIL   What's the matter? You look worse frighted than you were.

CHEATALL   Ay, and well I may. You leave me alone and I shall grow distracted. I have. . . I have seen a ghost.

GENTIL   A ghost! What, Mrs Arabella's ghost?

CHEATALL   Nay, I did not stay to examine that, for, as soon as ever I perceived the glimpse on't, I shut up my eyes, and felt my way out of the chamber.

GENTIL   Where was this ghost, Sir?

CHEATALL   Oh! Behind the bed, behind the bed, Gentil.

GENTIL   Lord, Sir, 'twas nothing but the cloak. I hung it there.

CHEATALL   Was it not? O' my conscience, I thought it had been a giant of a ghost. Hark, hark! What's that?

A cry without, seeming at a distance

BOY (*without*)   A full and true relation of a horrid and bloody murder, committed on the body of Mrs Arabella Venturewell, a young lady, by one Squire Barnaby Cheatall and his man Gentil. Showing how they locked her up in the dark, then cut her to pieces and carried the pieces away under their cloaks and threw them into Chelsea Reach where, at low water, they were found.

CHEATALL   O Lard! O Lard! The pieces found, Gentil!

GENTIL   So it seems, Sir.

BOY (*without*)   A full and true relation of a [etc.]

CHEATALL   Nay, now we shall be hanged for certain. Not the least hopes. Oh! Oh! Oh! (*Crying*)

GENTIL   Come, Sir, have a little courage.

CHEATALL   To confess the truth to thee, I never had any courage in my life, and this would make the stoutest man tremble. Oh!

GENTIL   I am thinking, Sir, why, we was not at Chelsea Reach that day.

CHEATALL   No, no, but maybe they'll swear we was.

GENTIL   My lady and Miss hated her. Sure they ha'n't been so barbarous.

CHEATALL   Like enough. Pin-up petticoats are as convenient as cloaks. Besides, my sister is a fury. I've heard her threaten pulling folks apieces a hundred times, and now she has done't. We'll e'en peach.

GENTIL   What, your own sister!

CHEATALL   Ay, my own mother to save myself. I say we'll peach.

GENTIL   That's not so good, for if they prove themselves innocent

'twill fall upon us again. Hark ye, Sir, there's only Eugenia can
witness against us. Suppose we tried to stifle her evidence with a
swingeing bribe. I never knew a chambermaid refuse greasing in the
fist upon any account.

CHEATALL   My dear Gentil, if she inclines, my offers shall be so large
that for the rest of her life she shall have nothing to do but study
to make her hands white that she may burn all her frippery, and be
able to spark it with quality.

GENTIL   Sir, I'll send her propositions.

CHEATALL (*half draws his sword*)   Do, but if the stubborn jade won't
comply, appoint a private meeting, and stop her mouth with this. . .
Ugh. . . you understand me.

GENTIL   Yes, Sir. (I find his conscience would swallow a real murder.)
Sir, if you please, we'll go in and write what you design to offer her.

CHEATALL   Let us. If you meet her, Gentil, and she's surly,
remember. . . ugh. . . ugh. . . (*Half draws his sword*)

Exeunt

SCENE III

Enter SIR FRANCIS WILDLOVE, *and to him* SEARCHWELL

SEARCHWELL   Sir Charles sends you word he is busy ordering his
affairs, designing with all speed to travel, and says he shall never see
you more, only to take his leave.

SIR FRANCIS   Hey day! O' my conscience this charming little
Beauclair has me under a spell, and I shall meet with nothing but
disappointments till I submit to her.

SEARCHWELL   Ay, Sir, you would soon find the true pleasures of
virtuous love, and a satisfaction in denying your appetite.

SIR FRANCIS   Preaching fool, hold your peace.

Enter a SERVANT

SERVANT   Sir, a gentlewoman below desires to speak with you.

SEARCHWELL   (So, there's no great danger my master should reform
when the devil is always at hand with a temptation in a petticoat.)

SIR FRANCIS   Searchwell, wait on the lady up.

SEARCHWELL   Ah, Lord!

SIR FRANCIS   Sirrah, I shall break your head if you don't leave this
canting trade.

SEARCHWELL   I am gone, Sir.

Exit and re-enters with DRESSWELL

DRESSWELL   (This is a mad message my lady has sent me with to her
    lover. I'm afraid he'll kick me for my news. Hang't he's a gentleman,
    and I'll venture.)
SIR FRANCIS   Ha! Pretty Mrs Dresswell, this is a favour I never
    received from you before. Must I own the blessing only to your
    good-will, or is my happiness greater? Did your lady send?
DRESSWELL   I came from my lady, Sir, but what happiness you'll
    find I know not. Methinks she has done a strange, mad thing.
SIR FRANCIS   What's the matter?
DRESSWELL   She's married, Sir.
SIR FRANCIS   The devil she is.
DRESSWELL   Even so. She said those that she fancied cared not for
    her. Therefore she resolved to bestow herself and fortunes on a
    secret lover, whom indeed her ladyship owns she never valued; a
    gentleman you know, Sir, the worthy Mr Spendall.
SIR FRANCIS (*walks about enraged*)   Damnation! That rake, bully,
    sharper! Damn it, damn it!
DRESSWELL   Here's a note where they are. She desires to see you.
SIR FRANCIS   Tell her I esteem her so much I'll cut the rascal's
    throat she has thought fit to call husband. I'll do it, Madam, though
    I'm hanged at the door. 'Tis the only way I can express my love to
    her now.
DRESSWELL   (Would I were well gone.) I'll tell her, Sir.

Exit

SIR FRANCIS   Married, and to Spendall! Oh, I could despise her. Ha,
    I find 'tis worse with me than I thought. What makes this gnaw my
    heart so else? My fellow libertines will laugh to see me play the fool
    and kill myself. Oh, I could tear in piecemeal the villain that betrayed
    her to endless ruin.

Enter a SERVANT

SERVANT   Sir, there's another lady out of a coach coming upstairs.
SIR FRANCIS   Blockhead, tell her I desire she would break her neck
    down again, and oblige me in riding post to the devil. My coach there!

Throws the fellow down and exit

SERVANT   Oh, my nose, my nose! Why, what's the matter now? I
    thought I should have had a reward for my news. And so I have, I
    think. Oh, my nose!

Enter MRS FLYWIFE

MRS FLYWIFE   Where's Sir Francis? Did you tell him I was coming
    up?

SERVANT   Yes, and he says you may go to the devil. He has spoiled
the ornament of my face, and flung into his coach stark mad.

MRS FLYWIFE   Much of passion shows much of love. My coach shall
follow his. I'll not leave him so.

Exeunt

SCENE IV

Enter MRS BEAUCLAIR, DRESSWELL *and a* WOMAN

MRS BEAUCLAIR   I must confess I am fool enough to be pleased
with Sir Francis' concern. But, oh, my uncle's troubles draw a veil
upon my rising joys, and damp all mirth. Poor Bellinda. She sent a note
to tell me her disorder was such she could not see me. With much ado
I have persuaded Sir Charles to come hither for half an hour and look
into this unlucky piece of matrimony.

DRESSWELL   Madam, they are coming.

MRS BEAUCLAIR   In, in then.

Exeunt

Enter LADY BEAUCLAIR, SPENDALL, PEGGY *and* LYEWELL

LYEWELL   Here, give me a glass of wine. Mrs bride's long life and
lasting happiness.

PEGGY   Thank ye, Sir. Give me a glass, you.

SPENDALL   To me, my love?

PEGGY   Yes.

SPENDALL (*drinks*)   Yours forever.

LADY BEAUCLAIR   Lard, child, you drink too much wine.

PEGGY   Pray, be quiet. I'll drink what I please. I am married now.
Why, sure, I shall have none of your tutoring, i' cod. I'll long for
everything I see, shan't I, you?

SPENDALL   Ay, and have it too, my dear.

PEGGY   I' cod, I'll long for green peas at Christmas, so I will.

LADY BEAUCLAIR   My heart aches. This great concern has made
me sick. Give me a glass.

PEGGY   I am mother's own daughter, feth, I dare confess it now. I
always used to be sick for a glass of wine, ho, ho!

LADY BEAUCLAIR   Sure, the wench is mad.

One knocks

SPENDALL   Ha, dear ladies, go in. 'Tis somebody from Sir Charles,
I believe, I would willingly speak with 'em first.

PEGGY   Ay, ay, let's go in. There's more wine within.
LADY BEAUCLAIR   Be sure you make your estate out plain.
SPENDALL   Yes, yes. (Hark ye, Lyewell, carry 'em out of earshot,
    lest it should prove a dunner.)
LYEWELL   (I warrant.) Come, ladies, we'll in and take a bumper.
PEGGY   O La', you make me so blush. . .

Knocks again

SPENDALL   Boy, open the door.

Exeunt

Enter SIR FRANCIS

SIR FRANCIS   What, grown so great already that I must wait half
    an hour for admittance?
SPENDALL   (He is come from Sir Charles, I'll speak him fair.) Sir
    Francis Wildlove, your very humble servant. I beg ten thousand
    pardons.
SIR FRANCIS   Keep your fawning, and bestow it on fools, 'tis lost
    on me, and will be most grossly answered. I tell ye, you are a rascal.
SPENDALL   Poverty makes many a man so, Sir.
SIR FRANCIS   A presuming rascal! Do I not know thee for the dreg
    of humankind, and shall thy detested arms receive her virgin beauties?
    Life of goodness, soul of honour, wit and sweetness, the only woman
    upon earth I could have loved.
SPENDALL   Sure, you design to banter me! Soul of wit and sweetness!
    The Devil might have had her sweetness for me. 'Twas her money I
    married, faith, Sir Francis, I always took her for a fool.
SIR FRANCIS   Prophaner! This last action only calls her judgement
    in question. Thy death is justice, first to deceive and then abuse her.
    Draw.
SPENDALL   I will draw, though, Gad, I would have sworn never to
    have fought on this occasion.

Enter MRS BEAUCLAIR *and* DRESSWELL, *laughing*

MRS BEAUCLAIR   Ha, ha, ha!
DRESSWELL   Ha, ha, ha!
SIR FRANCIS   Nay, Madam, I'll not disturb your mirth, but be so
    calm to wish it may continue.

Puts up his sword

SPENDALL   What's the meaning of all this? How came Mrs Beauclair
    here?
SIR FRANCIS   Are you not married to this lady?
SPENDALL   No such honour was ever designed for me. Lard, Sir, I

am married to Miss Peggy, Lady Beauclair's daughter. My fool's within. Now I hope I may call her so.

MRS BEAUCLAIR   I doubt, Sir Francis, you counterplotted me, know the truth, and only acted this concern.

SIR FRANCIS   No, by Heaven, nor perfectly my own heart, till this severe trial searched it. Did I dissemble, Madam, your sense would soon discover it. But, by my soul, I love you truly, and if you dare venture on me my future life shall show you how much I honour you.

MRS BEAUCLAIR   Can you then leave all the pretty city wives, which a man of your parts and quality in a quarter of an hour's siege could overcome? In fine, all the charming variety of what was pretty or agreeable in the whole sex, and be confined? Oh, that's a hard word to me.

SIR FRANCIS   With more delight than those surfeiting joys that always left a sting behind 'em afforded.

MRS BEAUCLAIR   Well, Sir, if you can give me your heart, I can allow you great liberties. But when we have played the fool and married, don't you, when you have been pleased abroad, come home surly. Let your looks be kind, your conversation easy, and, though I should know you have been with a mistress, I'd meet you with a smile.

SIR FRANCIS   When I forsake such charms for senseless, mercenary creatures you shall correct me with the greatest punishment on earth, a frown.

MRS BEAUCLAIR   You'll fall into the romantic style, Sir Francis. Mr Spendall, shan't we see your bride?

SPENDALL   Yes, Madam, and I hope your ladyship will prove my friend to Sir Charles.

MRS BEAUCLAIR   Ay, ay, we'll all speak for ye. Had she missed ye there was no great likelihood, as the case was, she would have done better.

SIR FRANCIS   Where is the pretty Miss? Pray conduct us to her.

MRS BEAUCLAIR   Sir Charles will be here presently. I long to hear my aunt set out the greatness of the match.

SPENDALL   This way, Sir.

Exeunt

Enter BEAUMONT, ARABELLA *and* EUGENIA

ARABELLA   Is this the house, Eugenia?

EUGENIA   Yes, Madam.

ARABELLA   Well, thou art a lucky girl to recover my writings with such speed.

EUGENIA   Madam, the Squire would have parted with a limb if I had required it.

BEAUMONT   Madam, it was your promise, whenever you possessed
   your fortune, though I'm sure I never insisted on't, you would be
   mine.
ARABELLA   I have no occasion to break my word, Mr Beaumont.
BEAUMONT   Then I am happy.
ARABELLA   Mrs Eugenia, will you inquire where these bride-folks
   are?
EUGENIA   See, Madam, they are coming.

   Enter LADY BEAUCLAIR, MRS BEAUCLAIR, PEGGY, SIR
   FRANCIS WILDLOVE, SPENDALL *and* LYEWELL

ARABELLA   Will the Squire be here?
EUGENIA   Yes, Madam, I told him of his cousin's marriage, and he
   seems pleased his sister has been tricked.
PEGGY   Lard, you, what d'ye bring one to these folks for? They'll
   do nothing but jeer us.
SPENDALL   Oh, my dear, carry yourself civilly, and everybody will
   love ye.
MRS BEAUCLAIR   Sir Charles will be here presently to wish you
   joy, Madam.
LADY BEAUCLAIR   So, then we shall have noise enough. But I'll be
   as loud as he, I'll warrant him.
MRS BEAUCLAIR   And louder, too, or I'm mistaken.

   Enter SIR CHARLES BEAUCLAIR

SIR CHARLES   Niece, why have you dragged me to this unwilling
   penance? If the girl is ruined what is't to me? My thoughts are full
   of something else.
MRS BEAUCLAIR   My uncle, my father and my friend, yet these
   names do not express half my tenderness. The best of guardians and
   of men, pray change your thoughts of travel. I'll study ten thousand
   things for your diversion.
SIR CHARLES   Not angel's eloquence should alter me. I'll act the
   uneasy part no longer. That woman, the bar to all my happiness, by
   heaven, she's not my wife. 'Tis true. The ceremony of the church
   has passed between us, but she knows I went no further.
MRS BEAUCLAIR   Stay then, and live asunder.
SIR CHARLES   No. So, Madam, you've married your daughter.
LADY BEAUCLAIR   Yes. What then? He has a good estate, when his
   father dies, beside the present settlement, and ready money.
SIR CHARLES   Poor, deluded woman! He has no estate, nor relation
   worth owning. Mr Spendall, generous charity induced me to relieve
   your wants. You have betrayed this young woman, but use her well.
   I have not much to say. I suppose they were both so willing a very
   little pains effected the matter.

LADY BEAUCLAIR   How, rascal? Devil! Have ye married my
    daughter, and have ye nothing, Sirrah?
SPENDALL   Ask Mrs Peggy that.
PEGGY   You make one laugh, I vow and swear.
LADY BEAUCLAIR   Beast! I don't mean so. . . but have ye no
    estate, Sirrah?
SPENDALL   No, faith, Madam, not I. My wife has enough for us
    both, and what matters.
LADY BEAUCLAIR   O, dog! Come away, Peggy, we'll go to Doctors'
    Commons and thou shalt be divorced.
PEGGY   I won't be divorced. I've got a husband and I don't care, I'll
    stay with him.
SPENDALL   That's kindly said, and I engage you shan't repent it.
LADY BEAUCLAIR   Why, Counsellor Smart, why, Counsellor Smart,
    did not ye tell me. . .
SIR FRANCIS   Hey day, Counsellor Smart! Why, this is a fellow many
    degrees worse than your new son-in-law. Hark ye, friend, leave this
    counterfeiting trade or you'll lose your ears. Reform, as your friend
    has done, and marry.
LYEWELL   Hang him, rogue. He's smock-faced, and handsome; I
    shall do no good with the women.
SPENDALL   (Go, be gone, devil, don't disgrace me. I'll meet you at
    the old place.)
MRS BEAUCLAIR   Look what a puff the old lady's in. Aunt, you
    always said you'd match your daughter yourself. You did not desire
    a cunninger head than your own.
LADY BEAUCLAIR   Well, Mrs Flippant, I hope your mad tricks will
    bring you a bastard home at last, and that will be worse.
SIR CHARLES   Nay, Madam, spare my niece. She was ever most
    peaceful to you till you abused her beyond all bearing.
SIR FRANCIS   Mind not a mad woman.

Enter CHEATALL

CHEATALL   Your servant, gentiles! Oh La, Sister, I hear strange news
    Cousin Peggy's married to a sharper, a rake, a cully, they say! I told
    you so, I told you so! Gadzooks! You would not be warned.
LADY BEAUCLAIR   Well, booby, what's that to you, blunderhead?
    (*She strikes him*)
CHEATALL   Pox take your nasty fist! You love fighting, plaguily.
LADY BEAUCLAIR   Well, 'twas passion, you may excuse it when you
    consider my affectations. To make ye amends I'll come and live
    with you, and take care of your estate, and Mrs Arabella's.
CHEATALL   No, no, don't mistake yourself, I'll be a stingy cur no
    longer, but drink my bottle freely, nor sneak out o' the company
    without paying my club, for fear of having my pocket examined by

you. Oh Lard! The ghost! The ghost!

SPENDALL   What, is the man mad?

MRS BEAUCLAIR   You don't understand the whim.

ARABELLA   Come gi' me thy hand, old boy, we'll be friends. I am
no ghost, I assure ye.

CHEATALL   And. . . is not that the hectoring spark your brother, with
his monstrous whiskers pared?

BEAUMONT   Not her brother, Sir, but one who hopes to pretend to
the lady by another title.

CHEATALL   Oh, I find how matters ha' been carried. Much good may
d'ye with her. Gadzooks, she wasn't fit for me. I'm a fool, you know,
Sister.

ARABELLA   You must grant me one request.

CHEATALL   What's that?

ARABELLA   To forgive Gentil. He's going to be married to Eugenia,
but shall have no joys without your pardon.

CHEATALL   Ay, ay, I forgive him, and leave his wife to punish
him. She has a fruitful imagination, let him take care it does not
one day fall upon his own head. Gentil, I am friends, and will give
thee something towards housekeeping.

GENTIL   I thank you, Sir.

EUGENIA   I'm sure it went to my very heart to fright your worship
so.

CHEATALL   You are a wheedling baggage. But 'tis all well. I am well
contented.

Enter MRS FLYWIFE *in a fright*

MRS FLYWIFE   Oh, save me! Save me! I'm pursued by a bloody-minded
monster.

SIR FRANCIS   What's the matter? Is it your husband, Madam?

MRS FLYWIFE   'Tis my tyrant, the devil 'tis.

Enter FLYWIFE, *his hanger drawn*

CHEATALL   Nay, hold ye, mistress, don't ye run behind me, udsbores,
so I may have the sword in my guts by mistake.

BEAUMONT   We'll all protect the lady.

MR FLYWIFE   Protect! Damnation! Do but hear how vile a thing it is!

CHEATALL   Hear! What do I hear, and see? Why, sure this is our
brother, Allen, my sister's first husband, we thought dead in the Indies.

SIR CHARLES   What's that? Speak again, but speak aloud, lest I
should only catch the sound of happiness, and be deceived.

MR FLYWIFE   Has my damned jilt brought me to a greater plague,
my wife? But I'll own to it to punish her. Though I suffer an
abominable torment till next fair wind. The sea's my element, once
there, I'm free. Well, I confess I have found a wife here. Why stare

you so? I am not the first has thought the sight unpleasing.

SIR CHARLES   No, no, talk on. All are hushed, as if a midnight silence reigned.

LADY BEAUCLAIR   Who's this? Are you my first husband Allen? And did you pretend you was dead rather than come home to me, Sirrah?

MR FLYWIFE   Here's a fine greeting.

MRS FLYWIFE   How! Your husband? He's mine, before Heaven! Mr Flywife, won't you own me, Fubby?

MR FLYWIFE   In troth, I think there's scarce a pin to choose. But you have disobliged me last, therefore *avant,* strumpet. Come hither, thou natural, noisy spouse.

MRS FLYWIFE   That shape and face preferred to me?

LADY BEAUCLAIR   I'll be revenged of her, I'm resolved. (*She flies on* MRS FLYWIFE)

MRS BEAUCLAIR   I'm all amazement, Sir Francis. Save the lady, because she was my friend. Return her ring, that may help console her.

SIR FRANCIS (*parting 'em*)   Hold! Ladies, ladies! March off. Here's the bountiful present. Come, come, I doubt not but you've a private pocket.

MRS FLYWIFE   The devil take you all.

Exit

MRS BEAUCLAIR   What miracle is this? Madam, leave your passion and explain it.

PEGGY   Is my own vather come again? Oh la!

SPENDALL   Your own vather come again! Oh la! Then I fear your portion is not at your own dispose, Miss.

PEGGY   Good lord! Does that disturb ye?

MR FLYWIFE   Gentlemen, and now your wonder is a little over, pray let me ask why all this company, and why that gentleman, whom I know not, appears transported.

SIR CHARLES   I'll tell you, Sir. 'Twas my hard fate to marry your lady before your death was well confirmed. That kept it some time private, when, before we came together a quarrel from her uneasy temper arose, and I swore never to bed her. Yet, for our friends' and conveniency's sake, we seemed to live like man and wife. Speak, Madam, is not this true?

LADY BEAUCLAIR   Yes, yes, 'tis true, the more shame for ye.

SIR CHARLES   Here, Sir, receive her, and with her a new date of happiness.

MR FLYWIFE   I guess my future happiness by the past. But since it must be so. . .

SIR CHARLES   Dear niece, go to my house and deliver up whatever is that lady's.

MRS BEAUCLAIR   You'll send to Bellinda?

SIR CHARLES   Myself, myself shall be the messenger.
In my eager mind I'm already there.
Methinks the earth's enchanted and I tread on air.

Exit

MRS BEAUCLAIR   So there's one pleased, I'm sure.

CHEATALL   Well, Brother, you're welcome home, as I may say. Why,
here's Cousin Peggy grown up and married since you went.

MR FLYWIFE   What! Is that bud come to the blossom of matrimony?
All by the mother's contrivance, a wise business, I believe. Sir, I shall
make bold to examine into your estate before I give my daughter any.

SPENDALL   Say ye so? And if you give your daughter none I shall
prove a second Mr Flywife.

PEGGY   What's that, Bold-face?

SPENDALL   Nothing, child.

LADY BEAUCLAIR   Ay, that's a hopeful match. I could find in my
heart to lock myself up and never see your ugly faces again.

Exit

MRS BEAUCLAIR   Let's follow and appease her.

ARABELLA   And, as we go, you shall tell me what makes Sir Charles
thus overjoyed.

MRS BEAUCLAIR   I will, and when we have done what he desired
we'll go all to Bellinda's. There we shall find my uncle.

SIR FRANCIS   Come, Beaumont, let's see the end of this surprising
accident.

MR FLYWIFE   How like a dog a man looks once escaped!
Forced back into the matrimonial noose,
'Tis a damned joy to find the wife I'd lose.

SCENE V

BELLINDA'S APARTMENT. ON A TABLE LIES HER HOOD AND
SCARF

BELLINDA   Sure some unseen power holds me a moment longer. Ah!
'Tis no power but foolish love that shows the path which carries me
from Beauclair, leading to death or, what's worse, despair.

Enter BETTY

BETTY   Madam, the coach is ready.

BELLINDA   I'm coming. Be sure you let none have admittance.
BETTY   I will not, Madam.

Enter SIR CHARLES

BETTY   O, Sir! My lady charged you should not enter.
SIR CHARLES   Away, you trifler. Where's my Bellinda?
BELLINDA   This is unmanly, not to conquer your desires, nor obey
my positive commands!
SIR CHARLES   Oh, stay and hear me. Let me hang upon your knees,
for I am out of breath, clasp and prattle o'er thee, like a glad mother
when she hugs her first-born blessing after the pangs of birth. Mine,
like hers, is folly all, but full of fondness.
BELLINDA   Oh!
SIR CHARLES   Sigh not, my fair. By Heaven I am free from any
chains but thine, free as thy own soul's from vice.
BELLINDA   How! What mean ye? Oh, rise, and stop my growing
fears. Where's your wife? Is she well?
SIR CHARLES   Think not so basely of me. She's well, and in her
husband's arms. Oh, my Bellinda! In her husband's arms! Her first
and only husband, Allen, is returned.
BELLINDA   Forgetting all colder nicer forms, in thy faithful bosom
let me receive such news.
SIR CHARLES   My life!
BELLINDA   My soul!
SIR CHARLES   Ha! The transporting joy has caught her rosy breath,
and those bright eyes are in their snowy lids retired. Oh, this is more,
much more than ten thousand words could have expressed. Wake,
my Bellinda, 'tis thy Beauclair calls.
BELLINDA   Do not view my blushing face. I fear I have offended
that virgin modesty by me still practised and adored. Now we must
stand on forms, till time and decency shall crown our wishes.
SIR CHARLES   My goddess, conqueress, by thee forever I am directed.
BELLINDA   I know thy honest heart so well I do not scruple the
truth of what you have said.
SIR CHARLES   You need not, dearest. See, all our friends come to
confirm it.

Enter SIR FRANCIS WILDLOVE, BEAUMONT, CHEATALL,
MRS BEAUCLAIR *and* ARABELLA

MRS BEAUCLAIR   Joy to my dear Bellinda.
ARABELLA   Permit a stranger to rejoice at the reward of virtue and
constant love.
BELLINDA   Pardon my answers, ladies, when I confess I scarce know
where I am.

SIR CHARLES   Now I can mind the affairs of my friend. Sir Francis,
   I observe you very assiduous to my niece. Has she received you for
   her servant? And are you resolved on the truest happiness, constancy?
SIR FRANCIS   Yes, faith, Sir Charles, I am the lady's dog on a string,
   and have violent pantings towards the delicious charmer. I hope she
   won't long defer my desires. But let that black gentleman I've so
   long dreaded do his worst, he shan't spoil my stomach.
MRS BEAUCLAIR   Ah! Those pantings, Sir Francis, I doubt they
   have moved your stomach so often till they've quite took it away.
SIR FRANCIS   A little forbearance, and such a tempting meal. . .
SIR CHARLES (*to* BEAUMONT)   You, Sir, too are blest. I read it in
   your eyes, and see the lady with ye.
BEAUMONT   I fear no danger now but dying of the pleasing fever
   called rapture.
CHEATALL   To any man's thinking these now are going to Heaven,
   ding, dong. But hear me, ladies, 'faith all young, handsome fellows talk
   just so before matrimony. Seven years hence let me hear of pantings,
   heavings and raptures. No, gadzooks, scarce risings then. I shall live a
   jolly bachelor, and laugh at your indifference. Gadzooks, I shall. . .
MRS BEAUCLAIR   Well said, Squire. We would bring him along,
   Sir Charles. I think him very good humoured to this lady, and believe
   his sister only made him otherwise.
SIR CHARLES   I read in every face a pleasing joy. But you must give
   me leave to think that mine exceeds, raised to unexpected worlds of
   bliss when sunk in sorrows and despair.
   Kind fate, beyond my hopes the weight removed,
   And gave me all, in giving her I loved.

                                                                              Exeunt

THE WONDER!
A WOMAN KEEPS A SECRET

BY

SUSANNAH CENTLIVRE

first performed Drury Lane Theatre, April 1714

The Wonder! begins ominously: morals are commended and nobility extolled. This seems to promise one of those eighteenth-century plays peopled by virtuous beings who entertain only by patiently suffering through a series of misunderstandings that are finally unravelled so rewards can be shared out. Fortunately, the play quickly changes course. Rakish talk is heard. The servants behave as if they were wits in a Restoration comedy, amusingly enough for the author to have to keep reminding us these *are* servants. And when misunderstanding envelops the main characters, they prove capable of accusation and counter-accusation, with a readiness which suggests they shared their schooling with their staff. By the end, when misunderstandings have been cleared up and hard hearts softened, the moral old men turn nasty and begin to squabble over money, leaving the lovers to dance with over-hastily married servants.

The play has, then, one foot in each century, and what Susannah Centlivre has managed in it is brilliant compromise, finding a way to please the new and more po-faced audience with a distressing degree of vitality. In her last plays, annoyance was to overwhelm such canny diplomacy, in the form of bungled structure and open indecency, marks that she was fed up with making concessions. Here, she's being clever and manages bawdy talk (in the discussion of balls) so that you can still be amused even if you have to pretend not to understand it.

It's revealing that, of all the plays in this volume, *The Wonder!* held the stage longest; it was successful for over a century after it appeared, and became a particular favourite of the eighteenth-century actor-manager, David Garrick: compromise and adaptation for the mealy-mouthed were in demand. But although Susannah Centlivre managed it once as well as this, there was no longer a stage where wit could thrive, female or any other kind.

CHARACTERS

DON LOPEZ, a Grandee of Portugal, father to

ISABELLA, who has been promised in marriage by her father to an unseen old man, Don Guzman, and is locked in the house awaiting his arrival

DON FELIX, brother to Isabella, wanted by the authorities for wounding a rival, Don Antonio, in a duel. In love with

VIOLANTE, who, though in love with Don Felix, is booked into a convent by her father

DON PEDRO

FREDERICK, friend to Felix. A merchant

COLONEL BRITON, visiting Portugal on his way home to England after serving in recently settled wars with Spain

GIBBY, his Scottish footman

VASQUEZ, servant to Frederick

FLORA, maid to Violante, in love with

LISSARDO, Don Felix's footman, who also spends time with

INIS, Isabella's maid

English soldier; *Alguazil;* attendants, servants

The action takes place in Lisbon.

ACT I

Enter DON LOPEZ *meeting* FREDERICK

FREDERICK   My lord, Don Lopez.

DON LOPEZ   How d'ye, Frederick?

FREDERICK   At your lordship's service. I am glad to see you look
so well, my lord. I hope Antonio's out of danger?

DON LOPEZ   Quite contrary; his fever increases, they tell me, and the
surgeons are of opinion his wound is mortal.

FREDERICK   Your son, Don Felix, is safe, I hope.

DON LOPEZ   I hope so, too; but they offer large rewards to apprehend
him.

FREDERICK   When heard your lordship from him?

DON LOPEZ   Not since he went. I forbade him writing till the public
news gave him an account of Antonio's health. Letters might be
intercepted, and the place of his abode discovered.

FREDERICK   Your caution was good, my lord. Tho' I am impatient to
hear from Felix, yet his safety is my chief concern. Fortune has
maliciously struck a bar between us in the affairs of life, but she has
done me the honour to unite our souls.

DON LOPEZ   I am not ignorant of the friendship between my son and
you. I have heard him commend your morals, and lament your want
of noble birth.

FREDERICK   That's nature's fault, my lord. It is some comfort not
to owe one's misfortunes to one's self, yet it is impossible not to
regret the want of noble birth.

DON LOPEZ   'Tis a pity indeed such excellent parts as you are master
of, should be eclipsed by mean extraction.

FREDERICK   Such commendation would make me vain, my lord,
did you not cast in the alloy of my extraction.

DON LOPEZ   There's no condition of life without its cares, and it is
the perfection of a man to wear 'em as easy as he can. This unfortunate
duel of my son's does not pass without impression, but since it is past
prevention, all my concern is now how he may escape the punishment.
If Antonio dies, Felix shall for England. You have been there. What
sort of people are the English?

FREDERICK   My lord, the English are by nature what the ancient
Romans were by discipline, courageous, bold, hardy, and in love
with liberty. Liberty is the idol of the English, under whose banner
all the nation lists: give but the word for liberty, and straight more

armed legions would appear than France and Philip keep in constant
pay.

DON LOPEZ   I like their principles. Who does not wish for freedom
in all degrees of life? Though common prudence sometimes makes us
act against it, as I am now obliged to do, for I intend to marry my
daughter to Don Guzman, whom I expect from Holland every day,
whither he went to take possession of a large estate left him by his
uncle.

FREDERICK   You will not surely sacrifice the lovely Isabella to age,
avarice, and a fool! Pardon the expression, my lord, but my concern
for your beauteous daughter transports me beyond that good manners
which I ought to pay your lordship's presence.

DON LOPEZ   I can't deny the justness of the character, Frederick.
But you are not insensible what I have suffered by these wars; and
he has two things which render him very agreeable to me for a son-in-
law, he is rich and well-born. As for his being a fool, I don't conceive
how that can be any blot in a husband who is already possessed of a
good estate. A poor fool indeed is a very scandalous thing, and so
are your poor wits, in my opinion, who have nothing to be vain of
but the inside of their skulls. Now for Don Guzman, I know I can
rule him as I think fit. This is acting the politic part, Frederick,
without which it is impossible to keep up the port of this life.

FREDERICK   But have you no consideration for your daughter's
welfare, my lord?

DON LOPEZ   Is a husband of twenty thousand crowns a year no
consideration? Now I think it a very good consideration.

FREDERICK   One way, my lord. But what will the world say of such
a match?

DON LOPEZ   Sir, I value not the world a button.

FREDERICK   I cannot think your daughter can have any inclination for
such a husband.

DON LOPEZ   There, I believe, you are pretty much in the right, though
it is a secret which I never had the curiosity to inquire into, nor I
believe ever shall. Inclination quoth-a! Parents would have a fine time
if they consulted their children's inclinations! I'll venture you a wager
that in all the garrison towns in Spain and Portugal during the late
war, there was not three women who had not had an inclination for
every officer in the whole army. Does it therefore follow that their
fathers ought to pimp for them? No, no, Sir, it is not a father's
business to follow his children's inclinations till he makes himself a
beggar.

FREDERICK   But this is of another nature, my lord.

DON LOPEZ   Look ye, Sir, I resolve she shall marry Don Guzman the
moment he arrives. Though I could not govern my son, I will my
daughter, I assure you.

FREDERICK   This match, my lord, is more preposterous than that
which you proposed to your son, from whence arose this fatal
quarrel. Don Antonio's sister, Elvira, wanted beauty only, but Guzman
everything but —
DON LOPEZ   Money, and that will purchase everything; and so adieu.

Exit

FREDERICK   Monstrous! These are the resolutions which destroy the
comforts of matrimony. He is rich and well-born! Powerful arguments
indeed! Could I but add them to the friendship of Don Felix, what
might I not hope? But a merchant and a grandee of Spain are
inconsistent names. Lissardo! From whence come you?

Enter LISSARDO *in a riding-habit*

LISSARDO   That letter will inform you, Sir.
FREDERICK   I hope your master's safe?
LISSARDO   I left him so. I have another to deliver which requires
haste. Your most humble servant, Sir. (*Bowing*)
FREDERICK   To Violante, I suppose?
LISSARDO   The same.

Exit

FREDERICK (*reads*)   'Dear Frederick, the two chief blessings of this
life are a friend and a mistress; to be debarred the sight of those, is
not to live. I hear nothing of Antonio's death, and therefore resolve
to venture to thy house this evening, impatient to see Violante, and
embrace my friend. Yours, Felix.' Pray Heaven he comes undiscovered.
Ha! Colonel Briton!

Enter COLONEL BRITON *in a riding-habit*

COLONEL   Frederick, I rejoice to see thee.
FREDERICK   What brought you to Lisbon, Colonel?
COLONEL   *La fortune de la guerre,* as the French say. I have
commanded these three last years in Spain, but my country has
thought fit to strike up a peace, and gives us good protestants leave
to hope for a Christian burial; so I resolved to take Lisbon in my way
home.
FREDERICK   If you are not provided of a lodging, Colonel, I shall
take it as a particular favour. What have we here?
COLONEL   My footman. This is our country dress, you must know,
which for the honour of Scotland I make all my servants wear.

Enter GIBBY *in a highland dress*

GIBBY   What mun I de with the horses, and like, yer honour? They will tack cald gin they stand in the causeway.

FREDERICK   Oh, I'll take care of them. What hoa! Vasquez!

Enter VASQUEZ

Put those horses which that honest fellow will show you into my
stable, do you hear, and feed them well.

VASQUEZ   Yes, Sir. Sir, by my master's orders, I am, Sir, your most
obsequious humble servant. Be pleased to lead the way.

GIBBY   'Sbleed! Gang your gate, Sir, and I sall follow ye. Ise tee
hungry to feed on compliments.

Exit GIBBY *with* VASQUEZ

FREDERICK   Ha! ha! a comical fellow. Well, how do you like our
country, Colonel?

COLONEL   Why, faith, Frederick, a man might pass his time agreeably
enough within-side of a nunnery. But to behold such troops of soft,
plump, tender, melting, wishing, nay, willing girls, too, through a
damned grate, gives us Britons strong temptations to plunder. Ah,
Frederick! your priests are wicked rogues; they immure beauty for
their own proper use, and show it only to the laity to create desires
and inflame account, that they may purchase pardons at a dearer
rate.

FREDERICK   I own wenching is something more difficult here than
in England, where women's liberties are subservient to their inclination
and husbands seem of no effect but to take care of the children which
their wives provide.

COLONEL   And does restraint get the better of inclination with your
women here? No, I'll be sworn, not even in four-score. Don't I know
the constitution of the Spanish ladies?

FREDERICK   And of all the ladies where you come, Colonel; you
were ever a man of gallantry.

COLONEL   Ah, Frederick! the kirk half starves us Scotsmen. We are
kept so sharp at home, that we feed like cannibals abroad. Hark ye:
hast thou never a pretty acquaintance now that thou would'st consign
over to a friend for half an hour, ha?

FREDERICK   Faith, Colonel, I am the worst pimp in Christendom,
you had better trust to your own luck! The women will soon find
you out, I warrant you.

COLONEL   Ay, but it is dangerous foraging in an enemy's country,
and since I have some hopes of seeing my own again, I had rather
purchase my pleasure than run the hazard of a stiletto in my guts.
'Egad, I think I must e'en marry, and sacrifice my body for the good
of my soul. Wilt thou recommend me to a wife then, one that is
willing to exchange her *moidores* for English liberty? Ha, friend?

FREDERICK   She must be very handsome, I suppose?
COLONEL   The handsomer the better, but be sure she has a nose.
FREDERICK   Ay, ay, and some gold.
COLONEL   Oh, very much gold; I shall never be able to swallow the matrimonial pill if it be not well gilded.
FREDERICK   Puh! beauty will make it slide down nimbly.
COLONEL   At first perhaps it may; but the second or third dose will choke me. I confess, Frederick, women are the prettiest playthings in nature, but gold, substantial gold, gives 'em the air, the mien, the shape, the grace, and beauty of a goddess.
FREDERICK   And has not gold the same divinity in their eyes, Colonel?
COLONEL   Too often. Money is the very god of marriage. The poets dress him in a saffron robe, by which they figure out the golden deity, and his lighted torch blazons those mighty charms which encourage us to list under his banner.
None marry now for love, no, that's a jest:
The self-same bargain serves for wife and beast.
FREDERICK   You are always gay, Colonel. Come, shall we take a refreshing glass at my house, and consider what has been said?
COLONEL   I have two or three compliments to discharge for some friends, and then I shall wait on you with pleasure. Where do you live?
FREDERICK   At yon corner house with the green rails.
COLONEL   In the close of the evening I will endeavour to kiss your hand. Adieu.

Exit

FREDERICK   I shall expect you with impatience.

Exit

SCENE II

A ROOM IN DON LOPEZ'S HOUSE

Enter ISABELLA *and* INIS, *her maid*

INIS   For goodness' sake, Madam, where are you going in this pet?
ISABELLA   Anywhere to avoid matrimony. The thought of a husband is as terrible to me as the sight of a hobgoblin.
INIS   Ay, of an old husband. But if you may choose for yourself, I fancy matrimony would be no such frightful thing to you.
ISABELLA   You are pretty much in the right, Inis. But to be forced into the arms of an idiot, a sneaking, snivelling, drivelling, avaricious

fool, who has neither person to please the eye, nor generosity to supply those defects! Ah, Inis! what pleasant lives women lead in England, where duty wears no fetter but inclination! The custom of our country enslaves us from our very cradles, first to our parents, next to our husbands, and when Heaven is so kind to rid us of both these, our brothers still usurp authority, and expect a blind obedience from us; so that maids, wives or widows, we are little better than slaves to the tyrant, man. Therefore, to avoid their power, I resolve to cast myself into a monastery.

INIS   That is, you'll cut your own throat to avoid another's doing it for you. Ah, Madam! those eyes tell me you have no nun's flesh about you. A monastery quoth-a! where you'll wish yourself into the greensickness in a month.

ISABELLA   What care I? There will be no man to plague me.

INIS   No, nor, what's much worse, to please you neither. Odslife, Madam, you are the first woman that ever despaired in a Christian country. Were I in your place. . .

ISABELLA   Why, what would your wisdom do if you were?

INIS   I'd embark with the first fair wind with all my jewels, and seek my fortune on t'other side of the water. No shore can treat you worse than your own. There's ne'er a father in Christendom should make me marry any man against my will.

ISABELLA   I am too great a coward to follow your advice. I must contrive some way to avoid Don Guzman, and yet stay in my own country.

Enter DON LOPEZ

DON LOPEZ   (Must you so, Mistress? But I shall take care to prevent you.) Isabella, whither are you going, my child?

ISABELLA   Ha, my father! To church, Sir.

INIS   (The old rogue has certainly overheard her.)

DON LOPEZ   Your devotion must needs be very strong, or your memory very weak, my dear. Why, vespers are over for this night. Come, come, you shall have a better errand to church than to say your prayers there. Don Guzman is arrived in the river, and I expect him ashore tomorrow.

ISABELLA   Ha! tomorrow!

DON LOPEZ   He writes me word that his estate in Holland is worth twelve thousand crowns a year, which, together with what he had before, will make thee the happiest wife in Lisbon.

ISABELLA   And the most unhappy woman in the world. Oh, Sir, if I have any power in your heart, if the tenderness of a father be not quite extinct, hear me with patience.

DON LOPEZ   No objection against the marriage, and I will hear whatsoever thou hast to say.

ISABELLA   That's torturing me on the rack, and forbidding me to groan. Upon my knees I claim the privilege of flesh and blood. (*Kneels*)

DON LOPEZ   I grant it. Thou shalt have an armful of flesh and blood tomorrow. Flesh and blood quoth-a! Heaven forbid I should deny thee flesh and blood, my girl.

INIS   (Here's an old dog for you.)

ISABELLA   Do not mistake, Sir. The fatal stroke which separates soul and body is not more terrible to the thoughts of sinners, than the name of Guzman to my ears.

DON LOPEZ   Puh, puh! you lie, you lie.

ISABELLA   My frighted heart beats hard against my breast, as if it sought a passage to your feet to beg you'd change your purpose.

DON LOPEZ   A very pretty speech, this. If it were turned into blank verse, it would serve for a tragedy. Why, thou hast more wit than I thought thou had'st, child. I fancy this was all extempore. I don't believe thou did'st ever think one word on't before.

INIS   Yes, but she has, my lord. For I have heard her say the same things a thousand times.

DON LOPEZ   How, how? What, do you top your second-hand jests upon your father, hussy, who knows better what's good for you than you do yourself? Remember 'tis your duty to obey.

ISABELLA (*rising*)   I never disobeyed before, and I wish I had not reason now. But nature hath got the better of my duty, and makes me loathe the harsh commands you lay.

DON LOPEZ   Ha, ha! Very fine! Ha, ha!

ISABELLA   Death itself would be more welcome.

DON LOPEZ   Are you sure of that?

ISABELLA   I am your daughter, my lord, and can boast as strong a resolution as yourself. I'll die before I'll marry Guzman.

DON LOPEZ   Say you so? I'll try that presently. (*Draws*) Here, let me see with what dexterity you can breathe a vein now. (*Offers her his sword*) The point is pretty sharp. 'Twill do your business, I warrant you.

INIS   Bless me, Sir! What, do you mean to put a sword into the hands of a desperate woman?

DON LOPEZ   Desperate! Ha, ha, ha! You see how desperate she is. What, art thou frighted, little Bell? Ha!

ISABELLA   I confess I am startled at your morals, Sir.

DON LOPEZ   Ay, ay, child, thou had'st better take the man. He'll hurt thee the least of the two.

ISABELLA   I shall take neither, Sir. Death hast many doors, and when I can live no longer with pleasure, I shall find one to let him in at without your aid.

DON LOPEZ   Say'st thou so, my dear Bell? Ods, I'm afraid thou art a little lunatic, Bell. I must take care of thee, child.

Takes hold of her, and pulls out of his pocket a key

I shall make bold to secure thee, my dear. I'll see if locks and bars
can keep thee till Guzman come. Go, get into your chamber.
There I'll your boasted resolution try,
And see who'll get the better, you or I.

Pushes her in, and locks the door

ACT II

SCENE I

A ROOM IN DON PEDRO'S HOUSE

Enter VIOLANTE *reading a letter, and* FLORA, *following*

FLORA   What, must that letter be read again?

VIOLANTE   Yes, and again, and again, and again, a thousand times
again. A letter from a faithful lover can ne'er be read too often, it
speaks such soft, such tender things. (*Kisses it*)

FLORA   But always the same language.

VIOLANTE   It does not charm the less for that.

FLORA   In my opinion, nothing charms that does not change, and
any composition of the four and twenty letters, after the first assay,
from the same hand, must be dull, except a bank-note or a bill of
exchange.

VIOLANTE   Thy taste is my aversion. . . (*reads*) 'My all that's charming
since life's not life exiled from thee, this night shall bring me to thy
arms. Frederick and thee are all I trust. These six weeks' absence
has been in love's account six hundred years. When it is dark, expect
the wonted signal at thy window. Till then, adieu. Thine, more
than his own, Felix.'

FLORA   Who would not have said as much to a lady of her beauty,
and twenty thousand pounds? Were I a man, methinks I could have
said a hundred finer things.

VIOLANTE   What would you have said?

FLORA   I would have compared your eyes to the stars, your teeth to
ivory, your lips to coral, your neck to alabaster, your shape to. . .

VIOLANTE   No more of your bombast. Truth is the best eloquence in
a lover. What proof remains ungiven of his love? When his father
threatened to disinherit him for refusing Don Antonio's sister, from
whence sprung this unhappy quarrel, did it shake his love for me?

And now, though strict inquiry runs through every place, with large
rewards to apprehend him, does he not venture all for me?

FLORA   But you know, Madam, your father Don Pedro designs you
for a nun. To be sure, you look very like a nun! And says your
grandfather left you your fortune upon that condition.

VIOLANTE   Not without my approbation, girl, when I come to one
and twenty, I am informed. But, however, I shall run the risk of that.
Go, call in Lissardo.

FLORA   Yes, Madam. Now for a thousand verbal questions.

Exit and re-enter with LISSARDO

VIOLANTE   Well, and how do you do, Lissardo?

LISSARDO   Ah, very weary, Madam. (Faith thou look'st wondrous
pretty, Flora.)

VIOLANTE   How came you?

LISSARDO   *En chevalier,* Madam, upon a hackney jade, which they
told me formerly belonged to an English colonel. But I should have
rather thought she had been bred a good Roman Catholic all her
lifetime, for she down'd on her knees to every stick and stone we
came along by. (My chops water for a kiss, they do, Flora.)

FLORA   (You'd make one believe you are wondrous fond now.)

VIOLANTE   Where did you leave your master?

LISSARDO   (Ods, if I had you alone, housewife, I'd show you how
fond I could be.)

VIOLANTE   Where did you leave your master?

LISSARDO   At a little farmhouse, Madam, about five miles off. He'll
be at Don Frederick's in the evening. (Od, I will so revenge myself
of those lips of thine.)

VIOLANTE   Is he in health?

FLORA   (Oh, you counterfeit wondrous well.)

LISSARDO   (No, everybody knows I counterfeit very ill.)

VIOLANTE   How say you? Is Felix ill? What's his distemper? Ha!

LISSARDO   (A piss on't! I hate to be interrupted.) Love, Madam, love.
In short, Madam, I believe he has thought of nothing but your ladyship
ever since he left Lisbon. I am sure he could not, if I may judge of
his heart by my own. (*Looking lovingly upon* FLORA)

VIOLANTE   How came you so well-acquainted with your master's
thoughts, Lissardo?

LISSARDO   By an infallible rule, Madam; words are the pictures of
the mind, you know. Now, to prove he thinks of nothing but you, he
talks of nothing but you. For example, Madam, coming from shooting
t'other day with a brace of partridges, 'Lissardo,' said he, 'go bid the
cook roast me these Violantes'. (I flew into the kitchen full of
thoughts of thee, cried, 'Here, cook, roast me these Floras'.)

FLORA   (Ha, ha, excellent! You mimic your master then, it seems?)

LISSARDO   (I can do everything as well as my master, you little rogue.) Another time, Madam, the priest came to make him a visit, he called out hastily, 'Lissardo,' said he, 'bring a Violante for my father to sit down on'. Then, he often mistook my name, Madam, and called me Violante. In short, I heard it so often that it became as familiar to me as my prayers.

VIOLANTE   You live very merrily then, it seems.

LISSARDO   Oh! Exceeding merry, Madam. (*Kisses* FLORA's *hand*)

VIOLANTE   Ha! Exceeding merry! Had you treats and balls?

LISSARDO   Oh! Yes, yes, Madam, several.

FLORA   (You are mad, Lissardo, you don't mind what my lady says to you.)

VIOLANTE   Ha! Balls. Is he so merry in my absence? And did your master dance, Lissardo?

LISSARDO   Dance, Madam! Where, Madam?

VIOLANTE   Why, at those balls you speak of.

LISSARDO   Balls! What balls, Madam?

VIOLANTE   Why, sure you are in love, Lissardo. Did not you say, but now, you had balls where you had been?

LISSARDO   Balls, Madam! Odslife, I ask your pardon, Madam! I, I, I had mislaid some wash-balls of my masters t'other day, and because I could not think where I had laid them, just when he asked for them, he fairly broke my head, Madam, and now, it seems, I can think of nothing else. Alas! He dance, Madam! No, no, poor gentleman! He is as melancholy as an unbraced drum.

VIOLANTE   Poor Felix! There, wear that ring for your master's sake, and let him know I shall be ready to receive him.

Exit VIOLANTE

LISSARDO   I shall, Madam. (*Puts on the ring*) Methinks a diamond ring is a vast addition to the little finger of a gentleman. (*Admiring his hand*)

FLORA   (That ring must be mine.) Well, Lissardo, what haste you make to pay off arrears now? (Look how the fellow stands!)

LISSARDO   'Egad, methinks I have a very pretty hand, and very white, and the shape! Faith, I never minded it so much before. In my opinion it is a very fine shaped hand, and becomes a diamond ring as well as the first grandee's in Portugal.

FLORA   (The man's transported!) Is this your love, is this your impatience?

LISSARDO (*takes snuff*)   Now, in my mind, I take snuff with a very jantee air. Well, I am persuaded I want nothing but a coach and a title to make me a very fine gentleman. (*Struts about*)

FLORA   Sweet Mr Lissardo! (*Curtseying*) If I may presume to speak
   to you without affronting your little finger. . .
LISSARDO   Odso, Madam, I ask your pardon, is it to me, or to the
   ring, you direct your discourse, Madam?
FLORA   Madam! Good lack! How much a diamond ring improves one!
LISSARDO   Why, though I say it, I can carry myself as well as anybody.
   But what wert thou going to say, child?
FLORA   Why, I was going to say that I fancy you had best let me keep
   that ring. It will be a very pretty wedding ring, Lissardo, would it not?
LISSARDO   Humph! Ah! But. . . but. . . but I believe I shan't marry
   yet awhile.
FLORA   You shan't, you say. Very well! I suppose you design that
   ring for Inis.
LISSARDO   No, no, I never bribe an old acquaintance. Perhaps I might
   let it sparkle in the eyes of a stranger a little till we come to a right
   understanding. But then, like all other mortal things, it would return
   from whence it came.
FLORA   Insolent! Is that your manner of dealing?
LISSARDO   With all but thee. Kiss me, you little rogue, you. (*Hugging
   her*)
FLORA   Little rogue! Pr'ythee, fellow, don't be so familiar. (*Pushing
   him away*) If I mayn't keep your ring, I can keep my kisses.
LISSARDO   You can, you say! Spoke with the air of a chambermaid.
FLORA   Replied with the spirit of a serving-man.
LISSARDO   Pr'ythee, Flora, don't let you and I fall out. I am in a
   merry humour, and shall certainly fall in somewhere.
FLORA   What care I where you fall in?

Enter VIOLANTE

VIOLANTE   Why do you keep Lissardo so long, Flora, when you
   don't know how soon my father may awake? His afternoon naps
   are never long.
FLORA   (Had Don Felix been with her she would not have thought
   the time long. These ladies consider nobody's wants but their own.)
VIOLANTE   Go, go, let him out, and bring a candle.
FLORA   Yes, Madam.
LISSARDO   I fly, Madam.

Exeunt LISSARDO *and* FLORA

VIOLANTE   The day draws in, and night, the lover's friend, advances.
   Night, more welcome than the sun to me, because it brings my love.
FLORA (*shrieks within*)   Ah, thieves, thieves! Murder, murder!
VIOLANTE (*shrieks*)   Ah! Defend me, Heaven! What do I hear? Felix
   is certainly pursued, and will be taken.

Enter FLORA *running*

How now? Why dost stare so? Answer me quickly. What's the matter?

FLORA   O, Madam! As I was letting out Lissardo, a gentleman rushed between him and I, struck down my candle, and is bringing a dead person in his arms into our house.

VIOLANTE   Ha! A dead person! Heav'n grant it does not prove my Felix.

FLORA   Here they are, Madam.

VIOLANTE   I'll retire till you discover the meaning of the accident.

Exit VIOLANTE

Enter COLONEL *with* ISABELLA *in his arms, sets her down in a chair, and addresses himself to* FLORA

COLONEL   Madam, the necessity this lady was under of being conveyed into some house with speed and secrecy, will, I hope, excuse any indecency I might be guilty of in pressing so rudely into this. I am an entire stranger to her name and circumstances (would I were so to her beauty, too). I commit her, Madam, to your care, and fly to make her retreat secure if the street be clear. Permit me to return, and learn from her own mouth if I can be further serviceable. Pray, Madam, how is the lady of this house called?

FLORA   Violante, Signior. (He is handsome, and promises well.)

COLONEL   Are you she, Madam?

FLORA   Only her woman, Signior.

COLONEL   Your humble servant, Mistress. Pray be careful of the lady.

Gives her two moidores and exits

FLORA   Two *moidores*! Well, he is a generous fellow. This is the only way to make one careful. I find all countries understand the constitution of a chambermaid.

Enter VIOLANTE

VIOLANTE   Was you distracted, Flora, to tell my name to a man you never saw! Unthinking wench! Who knows what this may turn to? What, is the lady dead? Ah! Defend me Heaven! 'Tis Isabella, sister to my Felix. What has befallen her? Pray Heaven he's safe. Run and fetch some cold water. Stay, stay, Flora. Isabella, friend, speak to me. Oh! Speak to me, or I shall die with apprehension.

FLORA   See, she revives.

ISABELLA   Ha! Where am I?

VIOLANTE   With one as sensible of thy pain as thou thyself can'st be.

ISABELLA   Violante! What kind star preserved and lodged me here?

FLORA   It was a terrestrial star called a man, Madam. Pray Jupiter
  he proves a lucky one.
ISABELLA   Oh! I remember now. Forgive me, dear Violante! My
  thoughts ran so much upon the danger I escaped, I forgot.
VIOLANTE   May I not know your story?
ISABELLA   Thou art no stranger to one part of it. I have often told
  thee that my father designed to sacrifice me to Don Guzman, who,
  it seems, is just returned from Holland, and expected ashore
  tomorrow, the day that he has set to celebrate our nuptials. Upon
  my refusing to obey him, he locked me into my chamber, vowing to
  keep me there till he arrived, and force me to consent. I know my
  father to be positive, never to be won from his design. And having
  no hope left me to escape the marriage, I leapt from the window into
  the street.
VIOLANTE   You have not hurt yourself, I hope?
ISABELLA   No. A gentleman passing by accident caught me in his
  arms. At first, my fright made me apprehend it was my father, till
  he assured me to the contrary.
FLORA   He is a very fine gentleman, I promise you, Madam, and a
  well-bred man I warrant him. I think I never saw a grandee put his
  hand into his pocket with a better air in my whole lifetime. Then he
  opened his purse with such a grace, that nothing but his manner of
  presenting me with the gold could equal.
VIOLANTE   There is but one common road to the heart of a servant,
  and 'tis impossible for a generous person to mistake it. Go, leave us,
  Flora.

                                        Exit FLORA

But how came you hither, Isabella?
ISABELLA   I know not. I desired the stranger to convey me to the
  next monastery, but ere I reached the door, I saw, or fancied I saw,
  Lissardo, my brother's man, and the thought that his master might
  not be far off flung me into a swoon, which is all that I can remember.
  Ha! What's here?

Takes up a letter

'For Colonel Briton. To be left at the post-house in Lisbon.' This
  must be dropped by the stranger who brought me hither.
VIOLANTE   You are fallen into the hands of a soldier. Take care he
  does not lay thee under contribution, girl.
ISABELLA   I find he is a gentleman, and if he is but unmarried, I
  could be content to follow him all the world over. But I shall never
  see him more, I fear. (*Sighs and pauses*)
VIOLANTE   What makes you sigh, Isabella?
ISABELLA   The fear of falling into my father's clutches again.

VIOLANTE   Can I be serviceable to you?

ISABELLA   Yes, if you conceal me two or three days.

VIOLANTE   You command my house and secrecy.

ISABELLA   I thank you, Violante. I wish you would oblige me with Mrs Flora a while.

VIOLANTE   I'll send her to you. I must watch if Dad be still asleep, or here will be no room for Felix.

Exit

ISABELLA   Well, I don't know what ails me. Methinks I wish I could find this stranger out.

Enter FLORA

FLORA   Does your ladyship want me, Madam?

ISABELLA   Ay, Mrs Flora. I resolve to make you my confidante.

FLORA   I shall endeavour to discharge my duty, Madam.

ISABELLA   I doubt it not, and desire you to accept this as a token of gratitude.

FLORA   O, dear Signora! I should have been your humble servant without a fee.

ISABELLA   I believe it. But to the purpose. Do you think, if you saw the gentleman who brought me hither, you should know him again?

FLORA   From a thousand, Madam. I have an excellent memory where a handsome man is concerned. When he went away, he said he would return again immediately. I admire he comes not.

ISABELLA   Here, did you say? You rejoice me. Though I'll not see him if he comes. Could not you contrive to give him a letter?

FLORA   With the air of a duenna.

ISABELLA   Not in this house. You must veil and follow him. He must not know it comes from me.

FLORA   What, do you take me for a novice in love-affairs? Though I have not practised the art since I have been in Donna Violante's service, yet I have not lost the theory of a chambermaid. Do you write the letter, and leave the rest to me. Here, here, here's pen, ink and paper.

ISABELLA   I'll do it in a minute. (*Sits down to write*)

FLORA   So! This is a business after my own heart. Love always takes care to reward his labourers, and Great Britain seems to be his favourite country. Oh! I long to see the other two *moidores* with a British air. Methinks there's a grace peculiar to that nation in making a present.

ISABELLA   So, I have done. Now, if he does but find this house again!

FLORA   If he should not, I warrant I'll find him, if he's in Lisbon, for

I have a strong possession that he has two *moidores* as good as ever was told.

Puts the letter into her bosom. Enter VIOLANTE

VIOLANTE   Flora, watch my papa. He's fast asleep in his study. If you find him stir give me notice.

COLONEL *taps at window*

Hark, I hear Felix at the window. Admit him instantly, and then to your post.

Exit FLORA

ISABELLA   What say you, Violante? Is my brother come?
VIOLANTE   It is his signal at the window.
ISABELLA (*kneels*)   O, Violante! I conjure you by all the love thou bear'st to Felix, by thy own generous nature, nay, more, by that unspotted virtue thou art mistress of, do not discover to my brother ·I am here.
VIOLANTE   Contrary to your desire be assured I never shall. But where's the danger?
ISABELLA   Art thou born in Lisbon, and ask that question? He'll think his honour blemished by my disobedience, and would restore me to my father, or kill me. Therefore, dear, dear girl. . .
VIOLANTE   Depend upon my friendship. Nothing shall draw the secret from these lips, not even Felix, though at the hazard of his love. I hear him coming. Retire into that closet.
ISABELLA   Remember, Violante, upon thy promise my very life depends.

Exit ISABELLA

VIOLANTE   When I betray thee, may I share thy fate.

Enter DON FELIX

My Felix, my everlasting love! (*Runs into his arms*)
DON FELIX   My life! My soul! My Violante!
VIOLANTE   What hazards dost thou run for me? Oh, how shall I requite thee?
DON FELIX   If during this tedious painful exile thy thoughts have never wandered from thy Felix, thou hast made me more than satisfaction.
VIOLANTE   Can there be room within this heart for any but thyself? No. If the god of love were lost to all the rest of humankind, thy image would secure him in thy breast. I am all truth, all love, all faith, and know no jealous fears.

DON FELIX   My heart's the proper sphere where love resides. Could
he quit that he would be nowhere found. And, yet, Violante, I'm in
doubt.

VIOLANTE   Did I ever give thee cause to doubt, my Felix?

DON FELIX   True love has many fears, and fear as many eyes as fame,
yet, sure, I think they see no fault in thee.

COLONEL *taps again*

What's that?

Taps again

VIOLANTE   What! I heard nothing.

Again

DON FELIX   Ha! What means this signal at your window?

VIOLANTE   Somewhat, perhaps, in passing by, might accidentally
hit it. It can be nothing else.

COLONEL (*within*)   Hist, hist, Donna Violante! Donna Violante!

DON FELIX   They use your name by accident, too, do they, Madam?

Enter FLORA

FLORA   (There is a gentleman at the window, Madam, which I fancy
to be him who brought Isabella hither. Shall I admit him?)

VIOLANTE   (Admit distraction rather! Thou art the cause of this,
unthinking wretch.)

DON FELIX   What, has Mrs Scout brought you fresh intelligence?
Death! I'll know the bottom of this immediately. (*Offers to go*)

FLORA   Scout! I scorn your words, Signior.

VIOLANTE   Nay, nay, nay, you must not leave me. (*Runs and catches
hold of him*)

DON FELIX   Oh! 'Tis not fair not to answer the gentleman, Madam.
It is none of his fault that his visit proves unseasonable. Pray, let
me go. My presence is but a restraint upon you.

Struggles to get from her. The COLONEL *taps again*

VIOLANTE   (Was ever accident so mischievous!)

FLORA   (It must be the Colonel. Now to deliver my letter to him.)

Exit FLORA. *The* COLONEL *taps louder*

DON FELIX   Hark! He grows impatient at your delay. Why do you
hold the man whose absence would oblige you? Pray, let me go,
Madam. Consider the gentleman wants you at the window. Confusion!

Struggles still

VIOLANTE   It is not me he wants.

DON FELIX   Death! Not you! Is there another of your name in the house? But come on, convince me of the truth of what you say. Open the window. If his business does not lie with you, your conversation may be heard. This, and only this, can take off my suspicion. What, do you pause? Oh, guilt, guilt! Have I caught you? Nay, then I'll leap the balcony. If I remember, this way leads to it.

Breaks from her, and goes to the door where ISABELLA *is*

VIOLANTE   O, Heaven! What shall I do now. Hold, hold, hold, hold! Not for the world. . . you enter there. (Which way shall I preserve his sister from his knowledge?)

DON FELIX   What, have I touched you? Do you fear your lover's life?

VIOLANTE   I fear for none but you. For goodness' sake do not speak so loud, my Felix. If my father hear you, I am lost forever. That door opens into his apartment. What shall I do if he enters? (There he finds his sister. If he goes out, he'll quarrel with the stranger.) Felix, Felix! Nay, do not struggle to be gone, my Felix. (If I open the window he may discover the whole intrigue, and yet, and yet of all evils we ought to choose the least.) Your curiosity shall be satisfied.

Goes to the window and throws up the sash

Whoe'er you are, that with such insolence dare use my name, and give the neighbourhood pretence to reflect upon my conduct, I charge you instantly to be gone, or expect the treatment you deserve.

COLONEL   I ask pardon, Madam, and will obey. But when I left this house tonight. . .

DON FELIX   Good!

VIOLANTE   (It is most certainly the stranger. What will be the event of this, Heaven knows.) You are mistaken in the house, I suppose, Sir.

DON FELIX   No, no, he's not mistaken. Pray, Madam, let the gentleman go on.

VIOLANTE   (Wretched misfortune!) Pray, be gone, Sir, I know of no business you have here.

COLONEL   I wish I did not know it neither. But this house contains my soul. Then, can you blame my body for hovering about it?

DON FELIX   Excellent!

VIOLANTE   (Distraction! He will infallibly discover Isabella.) I tell you again you are mistaken. However, for your own satisfaction, call tomorrow.

DON FELIX   Matchless impudence! An assignation before my face! No, he shall not live to meet your wishes.

Takes out a pistol and goes towards the window. She catches hold of him

VIOLANTE   Ah! (*Shrieks*) Hold, I conjure you.

COLONEL   Tomorrow's an age, Madam! May I not be admitted tonight?

VIOLANTE   If you be a gentleman, I command your absence. (Unfortunate! what will my stars do with me!)

COLONEL   I have done. Only this — be careful of my life, for it is in your keeping.

Exit COLONEL *from window*

DON FELIX   Pray, observe the gentleman's request, Madam. (*Walking off from her*)

VIOLANTE   (I am all confusion)

DON FELIX   You are all truth, all love, all faith! Oh, thou all woman! How I have been deceived. 'Sdeath! Could you not have imposed upon me for this one night? Could neither my faithful love, nor the hazard that I have run to see you, make me worthy to be cheated on? Oh, thou. . .

VIOLANTE   Can I bear this from you! (*Weeps*)

DON FELIX   'When I left this house tonight.' Tonight! The devil! Return so soon!

VIOLANTE   (O, Isabella! What hast thou involved me in!)

DON FELIX   'This house contains my soul.'

VIOLANTE   (Yet I resolve to keep the secret.)

DON FELIX   'Be careful of my life, for it is in your keeping.' Damnation! How ugly she appears! (*Looking at her*)

VIOLANTE   Do not look so sternly on me, but believe me, Felix, I have not injured you, nor am I false.

DON FELIX   Not false! Not injured me! O, Violante, lost and abandoned to thy vice! Not false! Oh, monstrous!

VIOLANTE   Indeed I am not. There is a cause which I must not reveal. Oh, think how far honour can oblige your sex; then allow a woman may be bound by the same rule to keep a secret.

DON FELIX   Honour! What hast thou to do with honour, thou that can'st admit plurality of lovers! A secret! Ha, ha, ha! His affairs are wondrous safe who trusts his secret to a woman's keeping. But you need give yourself no trouble about clearing this point, Madam, for you are become so indifferent to me, that your truth and falsehood are the same.

VIOLANTE   My love! (*Offers to take his hand*)

DON FELIX   My torment! (*Turns from her*)

Enter FLORA

FLORA   (So I have delivered my letter to the Colonel, and received my fee.) Madam, your father bade me see what noise that was. For goodness' sake, Sir, why do you speak so loud?

DON FELIX   I understand my cue, Mistress. My absence is necessary. I'll oblige you. (*Going; she takes hold of him*)

VIOLANTE   Oh, let me undeceive you first!

DON FELIX   Impossible!

VIOLANTE   'Tis very possible, if I durst.

DON FELIX   Durst! Ha, ha, ha! Durst, quoth-a!

VIOLANTE   But another time I'll tell thee all.

DON FELIX   Nay, now or never. . .

VIOLANTE   Now it cannot be.

DON FELIX   Then it shall never be. Thou most ungrateful of thy sex, farewell.

FELIX *breaks from her and exits*

VIOLANTE   Oh, exquisite trial of my friendship! Yet, not even this shall draw the secret from me.
That I'll preserve, let fortune frown or smile,
And trust to love my love to reconcile.

Exit

ACT III

SCENE I

A CHAMBER IN DON LOPEZ'S HOUSE

Enter DON LOPEZ

DON LOPEZ   Was ever man thus plagued? Odsheart, I could swallow my dagger for madness. I know not what to think. Sure Frederick had no hand in her escape. She must get out of the window and she could not do that without a ladder, and who could bring it to her but him? Ay, it must be so. The dislike she showed to Don Guzman in our discourse today confirms my suspicion, and I will charge him home with it. Sure, children were given me for a curse! Why, what innumerable misfortunes attend us parents! When we have employed our whole care to educate and bring our children up to years of maturity, just when we expect to reap the fruits of our labour, a man shall, in the tinkling of a bell, see one hanged and the other whored. This graceless baggage! But I'll to Frederick immediately. I'll take the *alguazil* with me and search his house, and if I find her, I'll use her. . . by St Anthony, I don't know how I'll use her.

Exit DON LOPEZ

SCENE II

THE STREET

Enter COLONEL *with* ISABELLA's *letter in his hand.* GIBBY *following*

COLONEL   Well, though I could not see my fair incognito, fortune, to make me amends, has flung another intrigue in my way. Oh! how I love these pretty, kind, coming females that won't give a man the trouble of racking his invention to deceive them. O, Portugal! Thou dear garden of pleasure, where love drops down his mellow fruit, and every bough bends to our hands, and seems to cry, 'Come, pull and eat.' How deliciously a man lives here, without fear of the stool of repentance! This letter I received from a lady in a veil, some duenna, some necessary implement of Cupid. I suppose this style is frank and easy, I hope like her that writ it. 'Sir, I have seen your person, and like it,' very concise, 'and if you'll meet me at four o'clock in the morning, upon the Terriero de Passa, half an hour's conversation will let me into your mind.' Ha, ha, ha! A philosophical wench! This is the first time I ever knew a woman had any business with the mind of a man. 'If your intellects answer your outward appearance, the adventure may not displease you. I expect you'll not attempt to see my face, nor offer anything unbecoming the gentleman I take you for.' Humph, the gentleman she takes me for! I hope she takes me to be flesh and blood, and then I'm sure I shall do nothing unbecoming a gentleman. Well, if I must not see her face, it shall go hard if I don't know where she lives. Gibby!

GIBBY   Here, an lik yer honour.

COLONEL   Follow me at a good distance, do you hear, Gibby.

GIBBY   In troth dee I, weel eneugh, Sir.

COLONEL   I am to meet a lady upon the Terriero de Passa.

GIBBY   The deel an mine eyn gin I ken her, Sir.

COLONEL   But you will when you come there, Sirrah.

GIBBY   Like eneugh, Sir. I have as sharp an eyn tull a bonny lass as ere a lad in awe Scotland. And what mun I dee wi' her, Sir?

COLONEL   Why, if she and I part, you must watch her home, and bring me word where she lives.

GIBBY   In troth sal I, Sir, gin the deel tak her not.

COLONEL   Come along then, it is pretty near the time. I like a woman that rises early to pursue her inclination.

Thus we improve the pleasures of the day,
While tasteless mortals sleep their time away.

Exeunt COLONEL *and* GIBBY

SCENE III

FREDERICK'S HOUSE

Enter INIS *and* LISSARDO

LISSARDO   Your lady run away, and you know not whither, say you?
INIS   She never greatly cared for me after finding you and I together.
   But you are very grave methinks, Lissardo.
LISSARDO (*looking on the ring*)   Not at all. I have some thoughts
   indeed of altering my course of living. There is a critical minute
   in every man's life, which, if he can but lay hold of, he may make his
   fortune.
INIS   (Ha! What do I see? A diamond ring! Where the deuce had he
   that ring?) You have got a very pretty ring there, Lissardo.
LISSARDO   Ay, the trifle is pretty enough, but the lady who gave it
   to me is a bonaroba in beauty, I assure you. (*Cocks his hat and struts*)
INIS   I can't bear this. The lady! What lady, pray?
LISSARDO   Oh fie! There's a question to ask a gentleman.
INIS   A gentleman! Why, the fellow's spoiled! Is this your love for me?
   Ungrateful man! You'll break my heart, so you will. (*Bursts into tears*)
LISSARDO   Poor tender-hearted fool!
INIS   If I knew who gave you that ring, I'd tear her eyes out, so I
   would. (*Sobs*)
LISSARDO   So, now the jade wants a little coaxing. Why, what dost
   weep for now, my dear? Ha!
INIS   I suppose Flora gave you that ring. But I'll. . .
LISSARDO   No, the devil take me if she did. You make me swear
   now. (So, they are all for the ring, but I shall bob them.) I did but
   joke. The ring is none of mine, it is my master's. I am to give it to
   be new set, that's all. Therefore, pr'ythee, dry thy eyes, and kiss me.
   Come.

Enter FLORA

INIS   And do you really speak truth now?
LISSARDO   Why do you doubt it?
FLORA   (So, so, very well! I thought there was an intrigue between
   him and Inis, for all he has forsworn it so often.)
INIS   Nor ha'n't you seen Flora since you came to town?
FLORA   (Ha! How dare she name my name?)
LISSARDO   No, by this kiss I ha'n't. (*Kisses her*)
FLORA   (Here's a dissembling varlet!)
INIS   Nor don't you love her at all?
LISSARDO   Love the devil! Why, did I not always tell thee she was
   my aversion?
FLORA   Did you so, villain? (*Strikes him a box on the ear*)

LISSARDO   (Zounds, she here! I have made a fine spot of work on't.)

INIS   What's that for? Ha! (*Brushes up to her*)

FLORA   I shall tell you by and by, Mrs Frippery, if you don't get about your business.

INIS   Who do you call Frippery, Mrs Trollop? Pray, get about your business, if you go to that. I hope you pretend to no right and title here.

LISSARDO   (What the devil! Do they take me for an acre of land, that they quarrel about right and title to me?)

FLORA   Pray, what right have you, Mistress, to ask that question?

INIS   No matter for that. I can show a better title to him than you, I believe.

FLORA   What, has he given thee nine months' earnest for a living title? Ha! ha!

INIS   Don't fling your flaunting jests to me, Mrs Boldface, for I won't take 'em, I assure you.

LISSARDO   So! Now I'm as great as the famed Alexander. But, my dear Statira and Roxana, don't exert yourselves so much about me. Now, I fancy if you would agree lovingly together, I might, in a modest way, satisfy both your demands upon me.

FLORA   You satisfy! No, Sirrah, I am not to be satisfied so soon as you think, perhaps.

INIS   No, nor I neither. What! Do you make no difference between us?

FLORA   You pitiful fellow you! What! You fancy, I warrant, I gave myself the trouble of dogging you out of love to your filthy person. But you are mistaken, Sirrah. It was to detect your treachery. How often have you sworn to me that you hated Inis, and only carried fair for the good cheer she gave you, but that you could never like a woman with crooked legs, you said?

INIS   How, how, Sirrah, crooked legs! Ods, I could find in my heart. . . (*Snatching up her petticoat a little*)

LISSARDO   Here's a lying young jade now! Pr'ythee, my dear, moderate thy passion. (*Coaxing*)

INIS   I'd have you to know, Sirrah, my legs were never. . . Your master I hope, understands legs better than you do, Sirrah.

LISSARDO   My master! So, so. (*Shaking his head and winking*)

FLORA   (I am glad I have done some mischief, however.)

LISSARDO (*to* INIS)   Art thou really so foolish to mind what an enraged woman says? Don't you see she does it on purpose to part you and I? (*Runs to* FLORA) Could not you find the joke without putting yourself in a passion, you silly girl, you! Why, I saw you follow us, plain enough, mun, and said all this that you might not go back with only your labour for your pains. But you are a revengeful young slut though, I tell you that. But come, kiss and be friends.

FLORA   Don't think to coax me. Hang your kisses.

DON FELIX (*within*)   Lissardo!

LISSARDO   Odsheart! Here's my master. The devil take both these jades for me. What shall I do with them?

INIS   (Ha! 'Tis Don Felix's voice. I would not have him find me here with his footman for the world.)

DON FELIX (*within*)   Why, Lissardo, Lissardo!

LISSARDO   Coming, Sir. What a pox will you do?

FLORA   Bless me, which way shall I get out?

LISSARDO   Nay, nay, you must e'en set your quarrel aside and be content to be mewed up in this clothes-press together, or stay where you are and face it out. There is no help for it.

FLORA   Put me anywhere rather than that. Come, come, let me in.

He opens the press and she goes in

INIS   I'll see her hanged before I'll go into the place where she is. I'll trust fortune with my deliverance. Here used to be a pair of backstairs. I'll try to find them out.

Exit INIS

Exit DON FELIX *and* FREDERICK

DON FELIX   Was you asleep, Sirrah, that you did not hear me call?

LISSARDO   I hear you, and answered you I was coming, Sir.

DON FELIX   Go, get the horses ready. I'll leave Lisbon tonight, never to see it more.

LISSARDO   Hey day! What's the matter now?

Exit LISSARDO

FREDERICK   Pray, tell me, Don Felix, what has ruffled your temper thus?

DON FELIX   A woman. O, friend! Who can name woman, and forget inconstancy?

FREDERICK   This from a person of mean education were excusable. Such low suspicions have their source from vulgar conversation. Men of your politer taste never rashly censure. Come, this is some groundless jealousy. Love raises many fears.

DON FELIX   No, no. My ears conveyed the truth into my heart, and reason justifies my anger. O, my friend! Violante's false, and I have nothing left but thee in Lisbon which can make me wish ever to see it more, except revenge upon my rival, of whom I'm ignorant. Oh, that some miracle would reveal him to me, that I might, through his heart, punish her infidelity!

Enter LISSARDO

LISSARDO   O, Sir! Here's your father, Don Lopez, coming up.

DON FELIX   Does he know that I am here?

LISSARDO   I can't tell, Sir. He asked for Don Frederick.

FREDERICK   Did he see you?

LISSARDO   I believe not, Sir. For as soon as I saw him I ran back to give my master notice.

DON FELIX   Keep out of his sight, then, and, dear Frederick, permit me to retire into the next room, for I know the old gentleman will be very much displeased at my return without his leave.

Exit DON FELIX

FREDERICK   Quick, quick, be gone! He is here.

Enter DON LOPEZ, *speaking as he enters*

DON LOPEZ   Alguazil, wait you without, till I call for you. Frederick, an affair brings me here, which requires privacy, so that if you have anybody within earshot, pray order them to retire.

FREDERICK   We are private, my lord, speak freely.

DON LOPEZ   Why, then, Sir, I must tell you that you had better have pitched upon any man in Portugal to have injured than myself.

DON FELIX (*peeping*)   What means my father?

FREDERICK   I understand you not, my lord.

DON LOPEZ   Though I am old, I have a son — Alas! why name I him? He knows not the dishonour of my house.

DON FELIX   I am confounded! The dishonour of his house!

FREDERICK   Explain yourself, my lord. I am not conscious of any dishonourable action to any man, much less to your lordship.

DON LOPEZ   'Tis false. You have debauched my daughter.

DON FELIX   Debauched my sister! Impossible! He could not, durst not be that villain.

FREDERICK   My lord, I scorn so foul a charge.

DON LOPEZ   You have debauched her duty, at least, therefore instantly restore her to me, or, by St Anthony, I'll make you.

FREDERICK   Restore her, my lord! Where shall I find her?

DON LOPEZ   I have those that will swear she is here in your house.

DON FELIX   Ha! In this house!

FREDERICK   You are misinformed, my lord! Upon my reputation, I have not seen Donna Isabella since the absence of Don Felix.

DON LOPEZ   Then pray, Sir, if I am not too inquisitive, what motive had you for those objections you made against her marriage with Don Guzman yesterday?

FREDERICK   The disagreeableness of such a match, I feared would give your daughter cause to curse her duty if she complied with your demands. That was all, my lord.

DON LOPEZ   And so you helped her through the window, to make her disobey.

DON FELIX   Ha, my sister gone! Oh, scandal to our blood!

FREDERICK   This is insulting me, my lord, when I assure you I have neither seen nor know anything of your daughter. If she is gone, the contrivance was her own, and you may thank your rigour for it.

DON LOPEZ   Very well, sir. However, my rigour shall make bold to search your house. Here, call in the *alguazil*.

FLORA (*peeping*)   The *alguazil*! What in the name of wonder will become of me?

FREDERICK   The *alguazil*! My lord, you'll repent this.

Enter ALGUAZIL *and* ATTENDANTS

DON LOPEZ   No, Sir, 'tis you that will repent it. I charge you in the King's name to assist me in finding my daughter. Be sure you leave no part of the house unsearched. Come, follow me.

DON LOPEZ *gets towards the door where* FELIX *is.* FREDERICK *draws and plants himself before the door*

FREDERICK   Sir, I must first know by what authority you pretend to search my house, before you enter here.

ALGUAZIL   How, Sir! Dare you presume to draw your sword upon the representative of Majesty? I am, Sir, I am His Majesty's Alguazil, and the very quintessence of authority. Therefore put up your sword or I shall order you to be knocked down, for know, Sir, the breath of an *alguazil* is as dangerous as the breath of a demi-culverin.

DON LOPEZ   She is certainly in that room, by his guarding the door. If he disputes your authority, knock him down, I say.

FREDERICK   I shall show you some sport first. The woman you look for is not here. But there is something in this room which I'll preserve from your sight at the hazard of my life.

DON LOPEZ   Enter, I say. Nothing but my daughter can be there. Force his sword from him.

DON FELIX *comes out and joins* FREDERICK

DON FELIX   Villains, stand off! Assassinate a man in his own house!

DON LOPEZ   Oh, oh, oh, *misericordia*! What do I see? My son!

ALGUAZIL   Ha, his son! Here's five hundred pounds good, my brethren, if Antonio dies. And that's in the surgeon's power, and he's in love with my daughter, you know, so seize him. Don Felix, I command you to surrender yourself into the hands of justice, in order to raise me and my posterity. And in consideration you lose your head to gain me five hundred pounds, I'll have your generosity recorded on your tombstone, at my own proper cost and charge. I hate to be ungrateful.

DON LOPEZ   Hold, hold! Oh, that ever I was born!
FREDERICK   Did I not tell you you would repent, my lord? What
hoa! Within there!

Enter SERVANTS

Arm yourselves, and let not a man in nor out but Felix.
DON FELIX   Generous Frederick!
FREDERICK   Look ye, Alguazil, when you would betray my friend for
filthy lucre, I shall no more regard you as an officer of justice, but
as a thief and robber thus resist you.
DON FELIX   Come on, Sir, we'll show you play for the five hundred
pounds.
ALGUAZIL   Fall on, seize the money, right or wrong, ye rogues.

They fight

DON LOPEZ   Hold, hold. Alguazil, I'll give you the five hundred
pounds that is my bond to pay upon Antonio's death, and twenty
pistoles however things go, for you and these honest fellows to drink
my health.
ALGUAZIL   Say you so, my lord? Why, look ye, my lord, I bear the
young gentleman no ill will, my lord. If I get but the five hundred
pounds, my lord, why, look ye, my lord, 'tis the same thing to me,
whether your son be hanged or not, my lord.
DON FELIX   Scoundrels!
DON LOPEZ   Ay, well, thou art a good-natured fellow, that's the
truth on't. Come then, we'll to the tavern, and sign and seal this
minute. O Felix! Why would'st thou serve me thus? But I cannot
upbraid thee now, nor have I time to talk. Be careful of thyself, or
thou wilt break my heart.

Exeunt DON LOPEZ, ALGUAZIL *and* ATTENDANTS

DON FELIX   Now, Frederick, though I ought to thank you for your
care of me, yet till I am satisfied as to my father's accusation, for
I overheard it all, I can't return the acknowledgements I owe you.
Know you ought relating to my sister?
FREDERICK   I hope my faith and truth are known to you, and here,
by both I swear I am ignorant of everything relating to your father's
charge.
DON FELIX   Enough, I do believe thee. O, Fortune! Where will thy
malice end?

Enter VASQUEZ

VASQUEZ   Sir, I bring you joyful news.
DON FELIX   What's the matter?

VASQUEZ   I am told that Don Antonio is out of danger, and now in
the palace.

DON FELIX   I wish it be true; then I am at liberty to watch my rival,
and pursue my sister. Pr'ythee, Frederick, inform thyself of the
truth of this report.

FREDERICK   I will this minute. Do you hear, let nobody into Don
Felix till my return.

Exit FREDERICK

VASQUEZ   I'll observe, Sir.

Exit VASQUEZ

FLORA (*peeping*)   They have almost frightened me out of my wits,
I'm sure. Now Felix is alone, I have a good mind to pretend I came
with a message from my lady; but how then shall I say I came into
the cupboard?

VASQUEZ *appears, seeming to oppose the entrance of somebody*

VASQUEZ   I tell you, Madam, Don Felix is not here.

VIOLANTE (*within*)   I tell you, Sir, he is here, and I will see him.

DON FELIX   What noise is that?

VIOLANTE (*breaking in*)   You are as difficult of access, Sir, as a first
minister of state.

FLORA   My stars, my lady here! (*She shuts the press close*)

DON FELIX   If your visit was designed to Frederick, Madam, he is
abroad.

VIOLANTE   No, Sir, the visit is to you.

DON FELIX   You are very punctual in your ceremonies, Madam.

VIOLANTE   Though I did not come to return your visit, but to take
that which your civility ought to have brought me.

DON FELIX   If my eyes, my ears, and my understanding lied, then I
am in your debt; else not, Madam.

VIOLANTE   I will not charge them with a term so gross to say they
lied, but call it a mistake, nay, call it anything to excuse my Felix.
Could I, think ye, could I put off my pride so far, poorly to
dissemble a passion which I did not feel, or seek a reconciliation with
what I did not love? Do but consider, if I had entertained another,
should not I rather embrace this quarrel, pleased with the occasion
that rid me of your visits, and gave me freedom to enjoy the choice
which you think I have made? Have I any interest in thee but my love?
Or am I bound by ought but inclination to submit and follow thee? No
law, whilst single, binds us to obey; but your sex are, by nature and
education, obliged to pay a deference to all womankind.

DON FELIX   These are fruitless arguments. 'Tis most certain thou

wert dearer to these eyes than all that Heaven e'er gave to charm
the sense of man; but I would rather tear them out than suffer them
to delude my reason and enslave my peace.

VIOLANTE   Can you love without esteem? And where is the esteem for
her you still suspect? O, Felix, there is a delicacy in love, which equals
even a religious faith! True love never doubts the object it adores, and
sceptics there will disbelieve their sight.

DON FELIX   Your notions are too refined for mine, Madam.

Enter VASQUEZ

DON FELIX   How now, Sirrah, what do you want?

VASQUEZ   Only my master's cloak out of this press, Sir, that's all.

DON FELIX   Make haste, then.

VASQUEZ *opens the press, sees* FLORA, *and roars out*

VASQUEZ   Oh, the devil, the devil!   (*Exit*)

FLORA   Discovered! Nay, then legs befriend me.   (*Runs out*)

VIOLANTE   Ha! A woman concealed! Very well, Felix.

DON FELIX   A woman in the press?

Enter LISSARDO

How the devil came a woman there, Sirrah?

LISSARDO   What shall I say now?

VIOLANTE   Now, Lissardo, show your wit to bring your master off.

LISSARDO   Off, Madam! Nay, nay, nay, there, there needs no great
wit to, to, to bring him off, Madam; for she did, and she did not come,
as, as, as, a, a, man may say, directly to, to, to, to speak with my
master, Madam.

VIOLANTE   I see by your stammering, Lissardo, that your invention
is at a very low ebb.

DON FELIX   'Sdeath! Rascal, speak without hesitation, and the truth
too, or I shall stick my spado in your guts.

VIOLANTE   No, no, your master mistakes; he would not have you
speak the truth.

DON FELIX   Madam, my sincerity wants no excuse.

LISSARDO   (I am so confounded between one and the other, that
I can't think of a lie.)

DON FELIX   Sirrah, fetch me this woman back instantly. I'll know
what business she has here.

VIOLANTE   Not a step; your master shall not be put to the blush.
Come, a truce, Felix. Do you ask me no more questions about the
window, and I'll forgive this.

DON FELIX   I scorn forgiveness where I own no crime. But your soul,
conscious of its guilt, would fain lay hold of this occasion to blend

your treason with my innocence.

VIOLANTE   Insolent! Nay, if, instead of owning your fault, you
endeavour to insult my patience, I must tell you, Sir, you don't
behave yourself like that man of honour you would be taken for.
You ground your quarrel with me upon your own inconstancy; 'tis
plain you are false yourself, and would make me the aggressor. It was
not for nothing the fellow opposed my entrance. This last usage has
given me back my liberty, and now my father's will shall be obeyed
without the least reluctance. And so your servant.

Exit

DON FELIX   O, stubborn, stubborn heart, what wilt thou do? Her
father's will shall be obeyed! Ha! That carries her to a cloister, and
cuts off all my hopes at once. By Heaven, she shall not, must not leave
me. No, she is not false, at least my love now represents her true,
because I fear to lose her. Ha! Villain, art thou here?

He turns upon LISSARDO

Tell me this moment who this woman was, and for what intent she
was here concealed, or. . .

LISSARDO   Ah, good Sir! Forgive me, and I'll tell you the whole
truth. (LISSARDO *falls on his knees*)

DON FELIX   Out with it then.

LISSARDO   It, it, it was Flora, Sir, Donna Violante's woman. You
must know, Sir, we have had a sneaking kindness for one another a
great while. She was not willing you should know it, so when she
heard your voice, she ran into the clothes-press. I would have told you
this at first, but I was afraid of her lady's knowing it. This is the truth,
as I hope for a whole skin, Sir.

DON FELIX   If it be not, I'll not leave you a whole bone in it, Sirrah.
Fly, and observe if Violante goes directly home.

LISSARDO   Yes, Sir, yes.

DON FELIX   Fly, you dog, fly.

Exit LISSARDO

I must convince her of my faith. Oh, how irresolute is a lover's heart!
My resentments cooled when hers grew high, nor can I struggle longer
with my fate; I cannot quit her, no, I cannot, so absolute a conquest
has she gained. How absolute a woman's power!
In vain we strive their tyranny to quit,
In vain we struggle, for we must submit.

SCENE IV

THE TERRIERO DE PASSA

Enter COLONEL *and* ISABELLA, *veiled.* GIBBY *at a distance*

COLONEL   Then you say it is impossible for me to wait on you home, Madam?

ISABELLA   I say it is inconsistent with my circumstances, Colonel, and that way impossible for me to admit of it.

COLONEL   Consent to go with me, then. I lodge at one Don Frederick's, a merchant, just by here. He is a very honest fellow, and I dare confide in his secrecy.

ISABELLA   (Ha! Does he lodge there? Pray Heaven I am not discovered

COLONEL   What say you, my charmer? Shall we breakfast together? I have some of the best tea in the universe.

ISABELLA   Puh! tea! Is that the best treat you can give a lady at your lodgings, Colonel?

COLONEL   Well hinted. No, no, no, I have other things at thy service, child.

ISABELLA   What are those things, pray?

COLONEL   My heart, soul and body into the bargain.

ISABELLA   Has the last no encumbrance upon it? Can you make a clear title, Colonel?

COLONEL   All freehold, child, and I'll afford thee a very good bargain. (*He embraces her*)

GIBBY   O' my saul, they mak muckle words about it. Ise sae weary with standing. Ise e'en tak a sleep. (*Lies down*)

ISABELLA   If I take a lease it must be for life, Colonel.

COLONEL   Thou shalt have me as long or as little time as thou wilt, my dear. Come, let's to my lodgings, and we'll sign and seal this minute.

ISABELLA   Oh, not so fast, Colonel. There are many things to be adjusted before the lawyer and the parson come.

COLONEL   The lawyer and parson! No, no, you little rogue, we can finish our affairs without the help of the law, or the gospel.

ISABELLA   Indeed but we can't, Colonel.

COLONEL   Indeed! Why, hast thou then trepanned me out of my warm bed this morning for nothing? Why, this is showing a man half famished a well-furnished larder, then clapping a padlock on the door till you starve him quite.

ISABELLA   If you can find in your heart to say grace, Colonel, you shall keep the key.

COLONEL   I love to see my meat before I give thanks, Madam. Therefore uncover thy face, child, and I'll tell thee more of my mind. If I like you. . .

ISABELLA   I dare not risk my reputation upon your ifs, Colonel, and
so adieu.
COLONEL   Nay, nay, nay we must not part.
ISABELLA   As you ever hope to see me more, suspend your curiosity
now. One step farther loses me forever. Show yourself a man of
honour, and you shall find me a woman of honour.
COLONEL   Well, for once I'll trust to a blind bargain, Madam.

He kisses her hand. She leaves

But I shall be too cunning for your ladyship, if Gibby observes my
orders. Methinks these intrigues which relate to the mind are very
insipid. The conversation of bodies is much more diverting. Ha! What
do I see? My rascal asleep! Sirrah, did not I charge you to watch the
lady? And is it thus you observe my orders, ye dog?

COLONEL *kicks* GIBBY *all the while, and he shrugs, and rubs his
eyes and yawns*

GIBBY   That's true, an' like yer honour; but I thought that when
yence ye had her in yer ane hands, ye might a' ordered her yer sel
weel eneugh without me, en ye ken, an' like yer honour.
COLONEL   Sirrah, hold your impertinent tongue, and make haste
after her. If you don't bring me some account of her, never dare
to see my face again.

Exit

GIBBY   Ay, this is bony wark indeed! To run three hundred mile to
this wicked town, and before I can weel fill my weam to be sent a
whore-hunting after this black she-devil. What gate sal I gang to
speer for this wutch now? Ah, for a ruling elder, or the kirk's
treasurer, or his mon, I'd gar my master mak twa o' this. But I am
sure there's na sic honest people here, or there wud na be sa mickle
sculdudrie.

Enter an English soldier passing along

Geud mon, did you see a woman, a lady, ony gate hereawa e'en
now?
ENGLISHMAN   Yes, a great many. What kind of a woman is it you
inquire after?
GIBBY   Geud troth, she's na kenspeckle, she's aw in a cloud.
ENGLISHMAN   What! 'Tis some Highland monster which you brought
over with you, I suppose. I see no such, not I. Kenspeckle, quoth-a!
GIBBY   Huly, huly, mon. The deel pike out yer een, and then ye'll
see the better, ye Portgise tike.
ENGLISHMAN   What says the fellow?

GIBBY   Say! I say I'm a bater fellow than e'er stude upon yer shanks,
and gin I hear mair o' yer din, deel o' my saul, Sir, but Ise crack yer
croon.

ENGLISHMAN   Get you gone, you Scotch rascal, and thank your
heathen dialect, which I don't understand, that you ha'n't your
bones broke.

GIBBY   Ay! An ye dinna understand a Scotsman's tongue, Ise see
gin ye can understand a Scotsman's gripe. Wha's the bater mon now,
Sir?

Lays hold of him, strikes up his heels, and gets astride of him.
VIOLANTE *crosses the stage.* GIBBY *jumps up from the man, and
brushes up to* VIOLANTE

GIBBY   I vow, Madam, but I am glad that ye and I are forgather'd.

VIOLANTE   What would the fellow have?

GIBBY   Nothing. Away, Madam. Wo worthy yer heart, what a muckle
deal o' mischief had you like to bring upon poor Gibby!

VIOLANTE   The man's drunk.

GIBBY   In troth am I not. And gin I had na found ye, Madam, the
Laird knows when I should; for my maister bad me ne'er gang hame
without tidings o' ye, Madam.

VIOLANTE   Sirrah! Get about your business, or I'll have your bones
drubbed.

GIBBY   Geud faith, my maister has e'en done that t'yer honds, Madam.

VIOLANTE   Who is your master, Sir?

GIBBY   Mony a ane speers the gate they ken right weel. It is no sa lang
sen ye parted wi' him. I wish he ken ye half as weel as ye ken him.

VIOLANTE   Pugh! The creature's mad, or mistakes me for someone
else. And I should be as mad as he to talk to him any longer.

VIOLANTE *enters* DON PEDRO's *house. Enter* LISSARDO *at the
upper end of the stage*

LISSARDO   So she's gone home, I see. What did that Scots fellow
want with her? I'll try to find it out. Perhaps I may discover something
that may make my master friends with me again.

GIBBY   Are ye gone, Madam? A deel scope in yer company, for I'm
as weese as I was. But I'll bide and see wha's house it is, gin I can
meet with ony civil body to speer at. Weel, of aw men in the warld, I
think our Scotsmen the greatest feuls, to leave their weel-favoured
honest women at hame to rin walloping after a pack of gycarlings
here, that shame to show their faces, and peur men, like me, are
forced to be their pimps. A pimp! Godswarbit! Gibby's ne'er be a
pimp, and yet, in troth, it's a thriving trade. I remember a countryman
o' my ane, that by ganging o' sic like errants as I am now, came to
get preferment. My lad, wot ye wha lives here?

LISSARDO   Don Pedro de Mendosa.

GIBBY   And did you see a lady gang in but now?

LISSARDO   Yes, I did.

GIBBY   And d'ye ken her tee?

LISSARDO   It was Donna Violante, his daughter. (What the devil makes him so inquisitive? Here is something in it, that is certain.) 'Tis a cold morning, Brother, what think you of a dram?

GIBBY   In troth, very weel, Sir.

LISSARDO   You seem an honest fellow. Pr'ythee, let's drink to our better acquaintance.

GIBBY   Wi'aw my heart, Sir. Gang your gate to the next house, and Ise follow ye.

LISSARDO   Come along then.

Exit

GIBBY   Don Pedro de Mendosa! Donna Violante, his daughter! That's as reight as my leg now. Ise need na mare. I'll tak a drink, and then to my maister.

Ise bring him news will mak his heart full blee;

Gin he rewards it not, deel pimp for me.

Exit

ACT IV

SCENE I

VIOLANTE'S LODGINGS

Enter ISABELLA *in a gay temper, and* VIOLANTE *out of humour*

ISABELLA   My dear! I have been seeking you this half hour, to tell you the most lucky adventure.

VIOLANTE   And you have pitched upon the most unlucky hour for it that you could possibly have found in the whole four and twenty.

ISABELLA   Hang unlucky hours! I won't think of them. I hope all my misfortunes are past.

VIOLANTE   And mine all to come.

ISABELLA   I have seen the man I like.

VIOLANTE   And I have seen the man who I could wish to hate.

ISABELLA   And you must assist me in discovering whether he can like me or not.

VIOLANTE   You have assisted me in such a discovery already, I thank ye.

ISABELLA   What say you, my dear?

VIOLANTE   I say I am very unlucky at discoveries, Isabella. I have too
lately made one pernicious to my ease: your brother is false.

ISABELLA   Impossible!

VIOLANTE   Most true.

ISABELLA   Some villain has traduced him to you.

VIOLANTE   No, Isabella. I love too well to trust the eyes of others.
I never credit the ill-judging world, or form suspicions upon vulgar
censures. No, I had ocular proof of his ingratitude.

ISABELLA   Then I am most unhappy. My brother was the only
pledge of faith betwixt us. If he has forfeited your favour, I have no
title to your friendship.

VIOLANTE   You wrong my friendship, Isabella. Your own merit
entitles you to everything within my power.

ISABELLA   Generous maid! But may I not know what grounds you
have to think my brother false?

VIOLANTE   Another time. But tell me, Isabella, how can I serve you?

ISABELLA   Thus then — The gentleman that brought me hither I have
seen and talked with upon the Terriero de Passa this morning, and
I find him a man of sense, generosity and good humour. In short he
is everything that I would like for a husband, and I have dispatched
Mrs Flora to bring him hither. I hope you'll forgive the liberty I
have taken.

VIOLANTE   Hither! To what purpose?

ISABELLA   To the great universal purpose, matrimony.

VIOLANTE   Matrimony! Why, do you design to ask him?

ISABELLA   No, Violante, you must do that for me.

VIOLANTE   I thank you for the favour you design me, but desire to
be excused. I manage my own affairs too ill to be trusted with those
of other people. Besides, if my father should find a stranger here, it
might make him hurry me into a monastery immediately. I can't
for my life admire your conduct, to encourage a person altogether
unknown to you. 'Twas very imprudent to meet him this morning,
but much more so to send for him hither knowing what inconveniency
you have already drawn upon me.

ISABELLA   I am not insensible how far my misfortunes have
embarrassed you, and, if you please, sacrifice my quiet to your own.

VIOLANTE   Unkindly urged! Have I not preferred your happiness to
everything that's dear to me?

ISABELLA   I know thou hast. Then do not deny me this last request
when a few hours perhaps may render my condition able to clear
thy fame, and bring my brother to thy feet for pardon.

VIOLANTE   I wish you don't repent of this intrigue. I suppose he
knows you are the same woman that he brought in here tonight.

ISABELLA   Not a syllable of that. I met him veiled, and to prevent
him knowing the house I ordered Mrs Flora to bring him by the back

door into the garden.

VIOLANTE   The very way which Felix comes. If they should meet there would be fine work. Indeed my dear, I can't approve of your design.

Enter FLORA

FLORA   Madam, the Colonel waits your pleasure.

VIOLANTE   How durst you go upon such a message, Mistress, without acquainting me?

ISABELLA   'Tis too late to dispute that now, dear Violante. I acknowledge the rashness of the action. But consider the necessity of my deliverance.

VIOLANTE   That is indeed a weighty consideration. Well, what am I to do?

ISABELLA   In the next room I'll give you instructions. In the meantime, Mrs Flora, show the Colonel into this.

Exit FLORA *one way and* ISABELLA *and* VIOLANTE *another*

Re-enter FLORA *with the* COLONEL

FLORA   The lady will wait on you presently, Sir.

Exit

COLONEL   Very well. This is a very fruitful soil. I have not been here quite four and twenty hours, and I have three intrigues upon my hands already. But I hate the chase without partaking the game.

Enter VIOLANTE *veiled*

(Ha! A fine-sized woman. Pray Heaven she proves handsome.) I am come to obey your ladyship's commands.

VIOLANTE   Are you sure of that, Colonel?

COLONEL   If you be not very unreasonable indeed, Madam. A man is but a man. (*Takes her hand and kisses it*)

VIOLANTE   Nay, nay, we have no time for compliments, Colonel.

COLONEL   I understand you, Madam. *Montre moi votre chambre.* (*He takes her in his arms*)

VIOLANTE   Nay, nay, hold, Colonel. My bedchamber is not to be entered without a certain purchase.

COLONEL   Purchase! Humph! (This is some kept mistress, I suppose, who industriously lets out her leisure hours.) Look ye, Madam, you must consider we soldiers are not over-stocked with money. But we make ample satisfaction in love. We have a world of courage upon our hands now, you know. Then pr'ythee use a conscience and I'll try if my pocket can come up to your price. (*Puts his hand into his pocket*)

VIOLANTE   Nay, don't give yourself the trouble of drawing your purse, Colonel, my design is levelled at your person, if that be at your own disposal.

COLONEL   Ay, that it is, faith, Madam, and I'll settle it as firmly upon thee.

VIOLANTE   As law can do it.

COLONEL   Hang law in love affairs. Thou shalt have right and title to it out of pure inclination. A matrimonial hint again! (Gad, I fancy the women have a project on foot to transplant the union into Portugal.)

VIOLANTE   Then you have an aversion to matrimony, Colonel. Did you ever see a woman, in all your travels, that you could like for a wife?

COLONEL   A very odd question. Do you really expect that I should speak truth now?

VIOLANTE   I do, if you expect to be dealt with, Colonel.

COLONEL   Why then. . . yes.

VIOLANTE   Is she in your own country, or this?

COLONEL   This is a very pretty kind of a catechism. But I don't conceive which way it turns to edification. In this town, I believe, Madam.

VIOLANTE   Her name is. . .

COLONEL   Ay, how is she called, Madam?

VIOLANTE   Nay, I ask you that, Colonel.

COLONEL   Oh, oh, why, she is called. . . Pray, Madam, how is it you spell your name?

VIOLANTE   O, Colonel, I am not the happy woman, nor do I wish it.

COLONEL   No, I am sorry for that. (What the devil does she mean by all these questions?)

VIOLANTE   Come, Colonel, for once be sincere. Perhaps you may not repent it.

COLONEL   Faith, Madam, I have an inclination to sincerity, but I'm afraid you'll call my manners in question. (This is like to be but a silly adventure, here's so much sincerity required.)

VIOLANTE   Not at all. I prefer truth before compliment in this affair.

COLONEL   Why then, to be plain with you, Madam, a lady last night wounded my heart by a fall from a window, whose person I could be contented to take, as my father took my mother, till death us doth part. But whom she is, or how distinguished, whether maid, wife or widow, I can't inform you. Perhaps you are she.

VIOLANTE   Not to keep you in suspense, I am not she, but I can give you an account of her. That lady is a maid of condition, has ten thousand pounds, and if you are a single man her person and fortune are at your service.

COLONEL   I accept the offer with the highest transports. But say, my charming angel, art thou not she? (*He offers to embrace her*) (This is a lucky adventure.)

VIOLANTE   Once again, Colonel, I tell you I am not she. But at six this evening you shall find her on the Terriero de Passa, with a white handkerchief in her hand. Get a priest ready, and you know the rest.

COLONEL   I shall infallibly observe your directions, Madam.

Enter FLORA *hastily, and whispers to* VIOLANTE *who starts and seems surprised*

VIOLANTE   Ha, Felix crossing the garden, say you, what shall I do now?

COLONEL   You seem surprised, Madam.

VIOLANTE   O, Colonel, my father is coming hither, and if he finds you here, I am ruined.

COLONEL   Odslife, Madam, thrust me anywhere. Can't I get out this way?

VIOLANTE   No, no, no, he comes that way. How shall I prevent their meeting? Here, here, step into my bedchamber and be still, as you value her you love. Don't stir till you've notice, as ever you hope to have her in your arms.

COLONEL   On that condition I'll not breathe.

Exit COLONEL

Enter DON FELIX

DON FELIX   I wonder where my dog of a servant is all this while. But she is at home I find. How coldly she regards me. You look, Violante, as if the sight of me were troublesome.

VIOLANTE   Can I do otherwise, when you have the assurance to approach me, after what I saw today.

DON FELIX   Assurance, rather call it good nature, after what I heard last night. But such regard to honour have I in my love to you, I cannot bear to be suspected, nor suffer you to entertain false notions of my truth without endeavouring to convince you of my innocence; so much good nature have I more than you, Violante. Pray, give me leave to ask your woman one question. My man assures me she was the person you saw at my lodgings.

FLORA   I confess it, Madam, and ask your pardon.

VIOLANTE   Impudent baggage, not to undeceive me sooner. What business could you have there?

DON FELIX   Lissardo and she, it seems, imitate you and I.

FLORA   I love to follow the example of my betters, Madam.

DON FELIX   I hope I am justified.

VIOLANTE   Since we are to part, Felix, there needs no justification.

DON FELIX   Methinks you talk of parting as a thing indifferent to you. Can you forget how you have loved?

VIOLANTE   I wish I could forget my own passion. I should with less concern remember yours. But for Mrs Flora. . .

DON FELIX   You must forgive her. Must, did I say? I fear I have no power to impose, though the injury was done to me.

VIOLANTE   'Tis harder to pardon an injury done to what we love than to ourselves. But at your request, Felix, I do forgive her. Go watch my father, Flora, lest he should awake and surprise us.

FLORA   Yes, Madam.

Exit

DON FELIX   Dost thou then love me, Violante?

VIOLANTE   What need of repetition from my tongue, when every look confesses what you ask?

DON FELIX   Oh! Let no man judge of love but those who feel it. What wondrous magic lies in one kind look. One tender word destroys a lover's rage, and melts his fiercest passion into soft complaint. Oh, the window, Violante, would'st thou but clear that one suspicion!

VIOLANTE   Pr'ythee, no more of that, my Felix, a little time shall bring thee perfect satisfaction.

DON FELIX   Well, Violante, on that condition you think no more of a monastery. I'll wait with patience for this mighty secret.

VIOLANTE   Ah, Felix, love generally gets the better of religion in us women. Resolutions made in heat of passion ever dissolve upon reconciliation.

Enter FLORA *hastily*

FLORA   O, Madam, Madam, Madam! My lord your father has been in the garden, and locked the back door, and comes muttering to himself this way.

VIOLANTE   Then we are caught. Now, Felix, we are undone.

DON FELIX   Heavens forbid, this is most unlucky. Let me step into your bedchamber, he won't look under the bed. There I may conceal myself.

He runs to the door and pushes it open a little

VIOLANTE   (My stars! If he goes in there he'll find the Colonel.) No, no, Felix, that's no safe place, my father often goes thither, and should you cough or sneeze we are lost.

DON FELIX   (Either my eyes deceived me, or I saw a man within. I'll watch him close. She shall deal with the devil if she conveys him out without my knowledge.) What shall I do then?

VIOLANTE   Bless me, how I tremble!

FLORA   O, invention! invention! I have it, Madam. Here, here, here, Sir, off with your sword, and I'll fetch you a disguise.

She runs in and fetches out a riding-hood

DON FELIX   Ay, ay, anything to avoid Don Pedro.
VIOLANTE   Oh, quick, quick, quick! I shall die with apprehension.

FLORA *puts the riding-hood on* DON FELIX

FLORA   Be sure you don't speak a word.
DON FELIX   Not for the Indies. (But I shall observe you closer than
you imagine.)
DON PEDRO (*within*)   Violante, where are you, child? (*He enters*)
Why, how came the garden door open? Ha! How now. Who have we
here?
VIOLANTE   (Humph! He'll certainly discover him.)
FLORA   'Tis my mother, and please you, Sir.

She and DON FELIX *both curtsey*

DON PEDRO   Your mother! By St Anthony she's a strapper. Why,
you are a dwarf to her. How many children have you, good woman?
VIOLANTE   (Oh! If he speaks we are lost.)
FLORA   Oh! Dear Signior, she can't hear you. She has been deaf these
twenty years.
DON PEDRO   Alas, poor woman. Why, you muffle her up as if she
were blind, too.
DON FELIX   (Would I were fairly off.)
DON PEDRO   Turn up her hood.
VIOLANTE   (Undone forever. St Anthony forbid.) Oh Sir, she has
the dreadfullest unlucky eyes. Pray, don't look upon them. I made
her keep her hood shut on purpose. Oh, oh, oh!
DON PEDRO   Eyes! Why, what's the matter with her eyes?
FLORA   My poor mother, Sir, is much afflicted with the colic, and
about two months ago she had it grievously in her stomach, and was
over-persuaded to take a dram of filthy English Geneva, which
immediately flew up into her head, and caused such a deflixion in
her eyes, that she could never since bear the daylight.
DON PEDRO   Say you so. Poor woman! Well, make her sit down,
Violante, and give her a glass of wine.
VIOLANTE   Let her daughter give her a glass below, Sir. For my part
she has frighted me so, I shan't be myself these two hours. I am sure
her eyes are evil eyes.
DON FELIX   (Well hinted.)
DON PEDRO   Well, well, do so. Evil eyes, there is no evil eyes, child.

Exeunt DON FELIX *and* FLORA

VIOLANTE   (I am glad he's gone.)
DON PEDRO   Hast thou heard the news, Violante?

370   THE FEMALE WITS

VIOLANTE   What news, Sir?

DON PEDRO   Why, Vasquez tells me that Don Lopez's daughter
Isabella is run away from her father. That lord has very ill fortune
with his children. Well I'm glad my daughter has no inclination to
mankind, that my house is plagued with no suitors.

VIOLANTE   This is the first word I ever heard of it. I pity her frailty.

DON PEDRO   Well said, Violante. Next week I intend thy happiness
shall begin.

VIOLANTE   (I don't intend to stay so long, I thank you, Papa.)

DON PEDRO   My lady abbess writes word she longs to see thee, and
has provided everything in order for thy reception. Thou wilt lead a
happy life, my girl. Fifty times before that of matrimony, where an
extravagant coxcomb might make a beggar of thee, or an ill-natured
surly dog break thy heart.

FLORA   (Break her heart! She had as good have her bones broke as
to be a nun. I am sure I had rather of the two.) You are wondrous
kind, Sir, but if I had such a father I know what I would do.

DON PEDRO   Why, what would you do, minx, ha?

FLORA   I would tell him I had as good right and title to the laws of
nature and the end of creation as he had.

DON PEDRO   You would, Mistress. Who the devil doubts it? A good
assurance is a chambermaid's coat of arms, and lying and contriving
the supporters. Your inclinations are on the tip-toe, it seems. If I
were your father, housewife, I'd have a penance enjoined you so
strict that you should not be able to turn in your bed for a month.
You are enough to spoil your lady, housewife, if she had not
abundance of devotion.

VIOLANTE   Fie, Flora, are you not ashamed to talk thus to my father?
You said yesterday you would be glad to go with me into the
monastery.

DON PEDRO   She go with thee? No, no, she's enough to debauch the
whole convent. Well, child, remember what I said to thee next week.

VIOLANTE   (Ay, and what, am I to do this too?) I am all obedience,
Sir. I care not how soon I change my condition.

FLORA   (But little does he think what change she means.)

DON PEDRO   Well said, Violante. (I am glad to find her so willing to
leave the world, but it is wholly owing to my prudent management.
Did she know that she might command her fortune when she came
at age or upon the day of marriage, perhaps she'd change her note.
But I have always told her that her grandfather left it with this
proviso: that she turned nun. Now a small part of this twenty
thousand pounds provides for her in the nunnery, and the rest is my
own. There is nothing to be got in this life without policy). Well,
child, I am going into the country for a few days to settle some
affairs with thy uncle, and then. . . come help me on with my cloak,
child.

VIOLANTE   Yes, Sir.

Exeunt VIOLANTE *with* DON PEDRO

FLORA   So now for the Colonel. (*Goes to the chamber door*) Hist,
hist, Colonel.
COLONEL (*peeping*)   Is the coast clear?
FLORA   Yes, if you can climb, for you must get over the wash-house,
and jump from the garden wall into the street.
COLONEL   Nay, nay, I don't value my neck if my incognita answers
but thy lady's promise.

Exeunt COLONEL *and* FLORA

Re-enter DON PEDRO *and* VIOLANTE

DON PEDRO   Goodbye, Violante. Take care of thyself, child.
VIOLANTE   I wish you a good journey, Sir.

Exit DON PEDRO

Now to set my prisoner at liberty. . .

Enter DON FELIX *behind* VIOLANTE

DON FELIX   (I have lain perdue under the stairs till I watched the
old man out.)
VIOLANTE   So, Sir, you may appear. (*Goes to the door*)
DON FELIX   May he so, Madam? I had cause for my suspicion, I find,
treacherous woman.
VIOLANTE   Nay, then all's discovered.
DON FELIX (*draws*)   Villain, whoe'er thou art, come out I charge
thee, and take the reward for thy adulterous errand.
VIOLANTE   (What shall I say? Nothing but the secret I have sworn to
keep can reconcile this quarrel.)
DON FELIX   A coward! Nay, then I'll fetch you out. Think not to
hide thyself. No, by St Anthony, an altar should not protect thee,
even there I'd reach thy heart, tho' all the saints were armed in thy
defence.

Exit

VIOLANTE   Defend me, Heaven! What shall I do? I must discover
Isabella, or here will be murder.

Enter FLORA

FLORA   I have helped the Colonel off clear, Madam.
VIOLANTE   Say'st thou so, my girl? Then I am armed.

Re-enter DON FELIX

DON FELIX   Where has the devil in compliance to your sex conveyed him from my just resentments?

VIOLANTE   Him? Who do you mean, my dear inquisitive spark? Ha, ha, ha, will you never leave these jealous whims?

DON FELIX   Will you never cease to impose upon me?

VIOLANTE   You impose upon yourself, my dear. Do you think I did not see you? Yes, I did, and resolved to put this trick upon you. I knew you'd take the hint, and soon relapse into your wonted error. How easily your jealousy is fired! I shall have a blessed life with you.

DON FELIX   Was there nothing in it then, but only to try me?

VIOLANTE   Won't you believe your eyes?

DON FELIX   No, because I find they have deceived me. Well, I am convinced that faith is as necessary in love as in religion, for the moment a man lets a woman know her conquest, he resigns his senses, and sees nothing but what she'd have him.

VIOLANTE   And as soon as that man finds his love returned, she becomes as errant a slave as if she had already said after the priest.

DON FELIX   The priest, Violante, would dissipate those fears which cause these quarrels. When wilt thou make me happy?

VIOLANTE   Tomorrow I will tell thee. My father is gone for two or three days to my uncle's, we have time enough to finish our affairs. But pr'ythee leave me now, for I expect some ladies to visit me.

DON FELIX   If you command it. Fly swift, ye hours, and bring tomorrow on. You desire I would leave you, Violante?

VIOLANTE   I do at present.

FELIX   So much you reign the sovereign of my soul,
That I obey without the least control.

Exit DON FELIX

Enter ISABELLA

ISABELLA   I am glad my brother and you are reconciled, my dear, and the Colonel escaped without his knowledge. I was frighted out of my wits when I heard him return. I know not how to express my thanks, woman, for what you suffered for my sake, my grateful acknowledgements shall ever wait you, and to the world proclaim the faith, truth and honour of a woman.

VIOLANTE   Pr'ythee don't compliment thy friend, Isabella. You heard the Colonel, I suppose?

ISABELLA   Every syllable, and am pleased to find I do not love in vain.

VIOLANTE   Thou hast caught his heart, it seems, and an hour hence may secure his person. Thou hast made hasty work on't, girl.

ISABELLA   From hence I draw my happiness. We shall have no accounts to make up after consummation.

She, who for years protracts her lover's pain,
And makes him wish, and wait, and sigh in vain,
To be his wife, when late she give consent,
Finds half his passion was in courtship spent;
Whilst they who boldly all delays remove,
Find every hour a fresh supply of love.

ACT V

SCENE I

FREDERICK'S HOUSE

Enter DON FELIX *and* FREDERICK

DON FELIX   This hour has been propitious. I am reconciled to
Violante. And you assure me Antonio is out of danger.

FREDERICK   Your satisfaction is doubly mine.

Enter LISSARDO

DON FELIX   What haste you made, Sirrah, to bring me word if
Violante went home.

LISSARDO   I can give you very good reasons for my stay, Sir. Yes,
Sir, she went home.

FREDERICK   Oh, your master knows that, for he has been there
himself, Lissardo.

LISSARDO   Sir, may I beg the favour of your ear?

DON FELIX   What have you to say?

LISSARDO *whispers.* DON FELIX *seems uneasy*

FREDERICK   (Ha! Felix changes colour at Lissardo's news. What
can it be?)

DON FELIX   A Scots footman that belongs to Colonel Briton, an
acquaintance of Frederick, say you? (The devil! If she be false, by
Heaven I'll trace her.) Pr'ythee, Frederick, do you know one Colonel
Briton, a Scotsman?

FREDERICK   Yes, why do you ask me?

DON FELIX   Nay, no great matter. But my man tells me that he has
had some little difference with a servant of his, that's all.

FREDERICK   He's a good, harmless, innocent fellow. I am sorry for
it. The Colonel lodges in my house. I knew him formerly in England,
and met him here by accident, last night, and gave him an invitation
home. He is a gentleman of good estate besides his commission, of
excellent principle and strict honour, I assure you.

DON FELIX   Is he a man of intrigue?

FREDERICK   Like other men, I suppose. Here he comes.

Enter COLONEL

Colonel, I began to think I had lost you.

COLONEL   And not without some reasons, if you knew all.

DON FELIX   There's no danger of a fine gentleman's being lost in this
town, Sir.

COLONEL   That compliment don't belong to me, Sir, but I assure you
I have been very near being run away with.

FREDERICK   Who attempted it?

COLONEL   Faith, I know her not, only that she is a charming woman;
I mean, as much as I saw of her.

DON FELIX   My heart swirls with apprehension. Some accidental
re-encounter.

FREDERICK   A tavern, I suppose, adjusted the matter.

COLONEL   A tavern! No, no, Sir, she is above that rank, I assure you.
This nymph sleeps in a velvet bed, and lodgings every way agreeable.

DON FELIX   Ha! a velvet bed! I thought you said but now, Sir, you
knew her not.

COLONEL   No more I don't, Sir.

DON FELIX   How came you then so well acquainted with her bed?

FREDERICK   Ay, ay, come, come, unfold.

COLONEL   Why then you must know, gentlemen, that I was conveyed
to her lodgings by one of Cupid's emissaries, called a chambermaid,
in a chair, through fifty blind alleys, who, by the help of a key, let
me into a garden.

DON FELIX   (S'death, a garden, this must be Violante's garden!)

COLONEL   From thence conducted me into a spacious room, then
dropped me a curtsey, told me her lady would wait on me presently,
so, without unveiling, Modesty withdrew.

DON FELIX   (Damn her modesty, this was Flora!)

FREDERICK   Well, how then, Colonel?

COLONEL   Then, Sir, immediately from another door issued forth
a lady, armed at both eyes, from whence such showers of darts fell
round me, that, had I not been covered with the shield of another
beauty, I had infallibly fallen a martyr to her charms for you must
know I just saw her eyes. Eyes, did I say? No, no, hold, I saw but one
eye, though I suppose it had a fellow equally as killing.

DON FELIX   But how came you to see her bed, Sir? (S'death, this
expectation gives a thousand racks.)

COLONEL   Why, upon her maid giving notice her father was coming,
she thrust me into the bedchamber.

DON FELIX   On her father's coming?

COLONEL   Ay, so she said, but putting my ear to the keyhole of the door, I found it was another lover.

DON FELIX   (Confound the jilt. 'Twas she without dispute.)

FREDERICK   Ah, poor Colonel! Ha, ha, ha.

COLONEL   I discovered they had had a quarrel, but whether they were reconciled or not, I can't tell, for the second alarm brought the father in good earnest, and had like to have made the gentleman and I acquainted, but she found some other stratagem to convey him out.

DON FELIX   (Contagion seize her, and make her body ugly as her soul! There's nothing left to doubt of now. 'Tis plain 'twas she. Sure he knows me, and takes this method to insult me. S'death, I cannot bear it.)

FREDERICK   So, when she had dispatched her old lover, she paid you a visit in her bedchamber, ha, Colonel?

COLONEL   No, pox take the impertinent puppy, he spoiled my diversion, I saw her no more.

DON FELIX   (Very fine! Give me patience, Heaven, or I shall burst with rage.)

FREDERICK   That was hard.

COLONEL   Nay, what was worse, the nymph that introduced me conveyed me out again over the top of a high wall, where I ran the danger of having my neck broke, for the father, it seems, had locked the door by which I entered.

DON FELIX   (That way I missed him. Damn her invention.) Pray, Colonel, was this the same lady you met upon the Terriero de Passa this morning?

COLONEL   Faith, I can't tell, Sir, I had a design to know who that lady was, but my dog of a footman, whom I had ordered to watch her home, fell fast asleep. I gave him a good beating for his neglect, and I have never seen the rascal since.

FREDERICK   Here he comes.

Enter GIBBY

COLONEL   Where have you been, Sirrah?

GIBBY   Troth Ise been seeking yee an like yer honour these twa hoors an meer. I bring yee glad teedings, Sir.

COLONEL   What, have you found the lady?

GIBBY   Geud faite ha I, Sir, an shee's called Donna Violante, and her parent, Don Pedro de Mendosa, an gin yee wull gang wa mi, an't like ye'r honour, Ise mak you ken the huse right weel.

DON FELIX   (O torture! torture!)

COLONEL   (Ha, Violante! That's the lady's name of the house where my incognita is, sure it could not be her, at least it was not the same house, I'm confident.)

FREDERICK   Violante. 'Tis false. I would not have you credit him,
  Colonel.

GIBBY   The deel burst my bladder, sir, gin I lee.

DON FELIX   Sirrah, I say you do lie, and I'll make you eat it, you
  dog. (DON FELIX kicks GIBBY) And if your master will justify
  you.

COLONEL   Not I, faith, Sir, I answer for nobody's lies but my own.
  If you please, kick him again.

GIBBY   But gin he dus Ise ne take it, Sir, gin he was a thousand
  Spaniards. (Walks about in a passion)

COLONEL   I owed you a beating, Sirrah, and I'm obliged to this
  gentleman for taking the trouble off my hands, therefore say no
  more, d'ye hear, Sir?

GIBBY   Troth de I, Sir, and seel tee.

FREDERICK   This must be a mistake, Colonel, for I know Violante
  perfectly well, and I'm certain she would not meet you upon the
  Terriero de Passa.

COLONEL   Don't be too positive, Frederick, now I have some reasons
  to believe it was that very lady.

DON FELIX   You'd very much oblige me, Sir, if you'd let me know
  these reasons.

COLONEL   Sir.

DON FELIX   Sir, I say I have a right to inquire into these reasons you
  speak of.

COLONEL   Ha, ha, really, Sir, I cannot conceive how you or any
  man can have a right to inquire into my thoughts.

DON FELIX   Sir, I have a right to everything that relates to Violante,
  and he that traduces her fame and refuses to give his reasons for't is a
  villain. (Draws)

COLONEL   (What the devil have I been doing? Now blisters on my
  tongue by dozens!)

FREDERICK   Pr'ythee, Felix, don't quarrel till you know for what.
  This is all a mistake, I'm positive.

COLONEL   Look ye, Sir, that I dare draw my sword. I think we'll
  admit of no dispute, but though fighting's my trade, I'm not in love
  with it, and I think it more honourable to decline this business than
  pursue it. This may be a mistake, however I'll give you my honour
  never to have any affair directly or indirectly with Violante, provided
  she is your Violante, but if there should happen to be another of her
  name I hope you would not engross all the Violantes in the kingdom.

DON FELIX   Your vanity has given me sufficient reasons to believe
  I'm not mistaken. I am not to be imposed upon, Sir.

COLONEL   Nor I bullied, Sir.

DON FELIX   Bullied! 'sdeath! Such another word and I'll nail thee to
  the floor.

COLONEL   Are you sure of that, Spaniard. (*Draws*)
GIBBY (*draws*)   Say ne meer, mon, aw my sol here's twa to twa,
    donna fear, Sir, Gibby stonds by ye for the honour a Scotland.
    (*Vapours about*)
FREDERICK   (*Interposes*) By St Anthony, you shan't fight on bare
    suspicion. Be certain of the injury and then. . .
DON FELIX   That I will this moment, and then, Sir, I hope you are
    to be found.
COLONEL   Whenever you please, Sir.

Exit DON FELIX

GIBBY   S'bleed, Sir, there neer was Scotsman yet that shamed to
    show his face. (*Strutting about*)
FREDERICK   So quarrels spring up like mushrooms in a minute.
    Violante and he was but just reconciled, and you have furnished him
    with fresh matter for falling out again, and I am certain, Colonel,
    Gibby is in the wrong.
GIBBY   Gin I be, Sir, the mon that tald me leed, and gin he dud, the
    deel be my landlard, hell my winter's quarters, and a rope my winding
    sheet, gin I dee no lik him as lang as I can hold a stick in my hond, now
    see yee.
COLONEL   I am sorry for what I have said, for the lady's sake, but
    who could divine that she was his mistress? Pr'ythee who is this warm
    spark?
FREDERICK   He is the son of one of our grandees, named Don Lopez
    de Pemental, a very honest gentleman, but something passionate in
    what relates to his love — he is an only son, which perhaps may be
    one reason for indulging his passion.
COLONEL   When parents have but one child, they either make a
    madman, or a fool of him.
FREDERICK   He is not the only child, he has a sister; but I think, thro'
    the severity of his father, who would have married her against her
    inclination, she has made her escape and notwithstanding he has
    offered five hundred pounds he can get no tidings of her.
COLONEL   Ha! How long has she been missing?
FREDERICK   Nay, but since last night, it seems.
COLONEL   Last night! The very time! How went she?
FREDERICK   Nobody can tell, they conjecture thro' the window.
COLONEL   I'm transported! This must be the lady I caught; what
    sort of a woman is she?
FREDERICK   Middle-sized, a lovely brown, a fine, pouting lip, eyes
    that roll and languish, and seem to speak the exquisite pleasure that
    her arms could give!
COLONEL   Oh! I'm fired with his description, 'tis the very she.
    What is her name?

FREDERICK   Isabella. You are transported, Colonel?

COLONEL   I have a natural tendency in me to the flesh, thou know'st, and who can hear of charms so exquisite, and yet remain unmoved? (Oh, how I long for the appointed hour! I'll to the Terriero de Passa, and wait my happiness; if she fails to meet me, I'll once more attempt to find her at Violante's in spite of her brother's jealousy.) Dear Frederick, I beg your pardon, but I had forgot I was to meet a gentleman upon business at five, I'll endeavour to dispatch him and wait on you again as soon as possible.

FREDERICK   Your humble servant, Colonel.

Exit

COLONEL   Gibby, I have no business with you at present.

Exit

GIBBY   That's weel, naw will I gang and seek this loon, and gar him gang with me to Don Pedro's huse, gin he'll no gang of himsel, Ise gar him gang by the lug, Sir; Godswarbit Gibby hates a lear.

Exit

SCENE II

VIOLANTE'S LODGINGS

Enter VIOLANTE *and* ISABELLA

ISABELLA   The hour draws on, Violante, and now my heart begins to fail me, but I resolve to venture for all that.

VIOLANTE   What, does your courage sink, Isabella?

ISABELLA   Only the force of resolution a little retreated, but I'll rally it again for all that.

Enter FLORA

FLORA   Don Felix is coming up, Madam.

ISABELLA   My brother! Which way shall I get out? Dispatch him as soon as you can, dear Violante. (*Exit into the closet*)

VIOLANTE   I will.

Enter DON FELIX *in a surly posture*

VIOLANTE   Felix, what brings you so soon; did not I say tomorrow?

DON FELIX   (My passion chokes me, I cannot speak. Oh, I shall burst!) (*Throws himself into a chair*)

VIOLANTE   Bless me! are you not well, my Felix?

DON FELIX   Yes. No. I don't know what I am.

VIOLANTE   Hey day! What's the matter now? Another jealous whim!

DON FELIX   (With what an air she carries it. I sweat at her impudence.)

VIOLANTE   If I were in your place, Felix, I'd choose to stay at home, when these fits of spleen were upon me, and not trouble such persons as are not obliged to bear with them.

Here DON FELIX *affects to be careless of her*

DON FELIX   I am very sensible, Madam, of what you mean: I disturb you no doubt, but were I in a better humour, I should not incommode you less. I am but too well convinced that you could easily dispense with my visit.

VIOLANTE   When you behave yourself as you ought to do, no company so welcome, but when you reserve me for your ill-nature I waive your merit, and consider what's due to myself, and I must be free to tell you, Felix, that these humours of yours will abate, if not absolutely destroy, the very principles of love.

DON FELIX (*rising*)   And I must be so free to tell you, Madam, that since you have made such ill returns to the respect that I have paid you, all you do shall be indifferent to me for the future, and you shall find me abandon your empire with so little difficulty, that I'll convince the world your chains are not so hard to break as your vanity would tempt you to believe. I cannot brook the provocation you give.

VIOLANTE   This is not to be borne. Insolent! You abandon! You! Whom I have so often forbade ever to see me more! Have you not fallen at my feet? Implored my favour and forgiveness? Did you not trembling wait, and wish, and sigh, and swear yourself into my heart? Ingrateful man! If my chains are so easily broke as you pretend, then you are the silliest coxcomb living you did not break 'em long ago; and I must think him capable of brooking anything on whom such usage could make no impression.

ISABELLA (*peeping*)   A deuce take your quarrels, she'll never think on me.

DON FELIX   I always believed, Madam, my weakness was the greatest addition to your power; you would be less imperious had my inclination been less forward to oblige you. You have indeed forbade me your sight, but your vanity even then assured you I would return, and I was fool enough to feed your pride. Your eyes, with all their boasted charms, have acquired the greatest glory in conquering me, and the brightest passage of your life is wounding this heart with such arms as pierce but few persons of my rank. (*He walks about in a great pet*)

VIOLANTE   Matchless arrogance! True, Sir, I should have kept measures better with you if the conquest had been worth preserving, but we easily hazard what gives us no pain to lose. As for my eyes, you are mistaken if you think they have vanquished none but you. There are men above your boasted rank who have confessed their power, when their misfortune in pleasing you made them obtain such a disgraceful victory.

DON FELIX   Yes, Madam, I am no stranger to your victories.

VIOLANTE   And what you call the brightest passage of my life is not the least glorious part of yours.

DON FELIX   Ha, ha, don't put yourself into a passion, Madam, for I assure you, after this day, I shall give you no trouble. You may meet your sparks on the Terriero de Passa at four in the morning without the least regard of mine, for when I quit your chamber the world shan't bring me back.

VIOLANTE   I am so well pleased with your resolution I don't care how soon you take your leave. But what you mean by the Terriero de Passa I can't guess.

DON FELIX   No, no, no, not you! You was not upon the Terriero de Passa at four this morning?

VIOLANTE   No, I was not. But if I was, I hope I may walk where I please, and at what hour I please, without asking you leave.

DON FELIX   Oh, doubtless, Madam! And you might meet Colonel Briton there, and afterwards send your emissary to fetch him to your house, and upon your father's coming in thrust him into your bedchamber, without asking my leave! 'Tis no business of mine if you are exposed among all the footmen in town. Nay, if they ballad you, and cry you about at a halfpenny-a-piece they may, without my leave.

VIOLANTE   Audacious! Don't provoke me, don't. My reputation is not to be sported with at this rate. No, Sir, it is not. (*Bursts into tears*) Inhuman Felix! (Oh, Isabella, what a train of ills hast thou brought on me?)

DON FELIX   (Ha! I cannot bear to see her weep. A woman's tears are far more fatal than our swords.) O, Violante, s'death! what a dog am I? Now have I no power to stir; dost not thou know such a person as Colonel Briton? Pr'ythee tell me, did'st not thou meet him at four this morning upon the Terriero de Passa?

VIOLANTE   Were it not to clear my fame, I would not answer thee, thou black ingrate! But I cannot bear to be reproached with what I even blush to think of, much less to act. By Heaven, I have not seen the Terriero de Passa this day.

DON FELIX   Did not a Scots footman attack you in the street, neither, Violante?

VIOLANTE   Yes, but he mistook me for another, or he was drunk, I know not which.

DON FELIX   And do not you know this Scots Colonel?

VIOLANTE   Pray, ask me no more questions; this night shall clear my
reputation, and leave you without excuse for your base suspicions.
More than this I shall not satisfy you, therefore pray leave me.

DON FELIX   Did'st thou ever love me, Violante?

VIOLANTE   I'll answer nothing. You was in haste to be gone just
now. I should be very well pleased to be alone, Sir. (*She sits down,
and turns aside*)

DON FELIX   I shall not long interrupt your contemplation. (Stubborn
to the last!)

VIOLANTE   (Did ever woman involve herself as I have done?)

DON FELIX   (Now would I give one of my eyes to be friends with
her, for something whispers to my soul she is not guilty.)

*He pauses, then pulls a chair and sits by her at a little distance,
looking at her some time without speaking. Then draws a little
nearer to her*

Give me your hand at parting, however, Violante, won't you?
(*Here he lays his hand upon her knee several times*) Won't you, won't
you, won't you?

VIOLANTE (*half regarding him*) Won't I do what?

DON FELIX   You know what I would have, Violante. O, my heart!

VIOLANTE (*smiling*)   I thought my chains were easily broke. (*Lays her
hand into his*)

DON FELIX (*draws his chair close to her, and kisses her hand in a
rapture*) Too well thou knowest thy strength! O my charming angel,
my heart is all thy own! Forgive my hasty passion, 'tis the transport
of a love sincere.

DON PEDRO (*within*)   Bid Sancho get a new wheel to my chariot
presently.

VIOLANTE   Bless me! My father returned! What shall we do now,
Felix? We are ruined past redemption.

DON FELIX   No, no, no, my love! I can leap from thy closet
window. (*He runs to the door where* ISABELLA *is, who claps to the
door, and bolts it from inside*)

ISABELLA (*peeping*)   Say you so? But I shall prevent you.

DON FELIX   Confusion! Somebody bolts the door within side. I'll
see who you have concealed here, if I die for't. O Violante! hast
thou again sacrificed me to my rival? (*Draws*)

VIOLANTE   By Heaven, thou hast no rival in my heart, let that
suffice. Nay, sure, you will not let my father find you here.
Distraction!

DON FELIX   Indeed, but I shall, except you command this door to be
opened, and that way conceal me from his sight. (*He struggles with
her to come to the door*)

VIOLANTE   Hear me, Felix, though I were sure the refusing what

you ask would separate us for ever, by all that's powerful, you shall
not enter here. Either you do love me, or you do not. Convince me
by your obedience.

DON FELIX   That's not the matter in debate. I will know who is in
this closet, let the consequence be what it will. Nay, nay, nay, you
strive in vain; I will go in.

VIOLANTE   You shall not go in. . .

Enter DON PEDRO

DON PEDRO   Hey day! What's here to do? I will go in, and you
shan't go in, and, I will go in! Why, who are you, Sir?

DON FELIX   (S'death! What shall I say now!)

DON PEDRO   Felix? Pray, what's your business in my house? Ha, Sir?

VIOLANTE   Oh, Sir, what miracle returned you home so soon? Some
angel 'twas that brought my father back to succour the distressed.
This ruffian here, I cannot call him gentleman, has committed such
an uncommon rudeness as the most profligate wretch would be
ashamed to own.

DON FELIX   (Ha, what the devil does she mean?)

VIOLANTE   As I was at my devotion in my closet I heard a loud
knocking at our door, mixed with a woman's voice, which seemed
to imply she was in danger.

DON FELIX   (I am confounded!)

VIOLANTE   I flew to the door with utmost speed, where a lady,
veiled, rushed in upon me, who, falling on her knees, begged my
protection from a gentleman, who, she said, pursued her. I took
compassion on her tears, and locked her into this closet. But in the
surprise, having left open the door, this very person whom you see,
with his sword drawn, ran in, protesting if I refused to give her up
to his revenge, he'd force the door.

DON FELIX   (What in the name of goodness does she mean to do,
hang me?)

VIOLANTE   I strove with him till I was out of breath, and had you not
come as you did, he must have entered, but he's in drink, I suppose,
or he could not have been guilty of such an indecorum. (*Glaring at*
FELIX)

DON PEDRO   I'm amazed!

DON FELIX   (The devil never failed a woman at a pinch! What a tale
has she formed in a minute. In drink, quotha; a good hint. I'll lay
hold on't, to bring myself off.)

DON PEDRO   Fie, Don Felix! No sooner rid of one broil, but you are
commencing another. To assault a lady with a naked sword derogates
much from the character of a gentleman, I assure you.

DON FELIX (*counterfeits drunkenness*)   Who, I, assault a lady? Upon

honour, the lady assaulted me, Sir, and would have seized this
body politic upon the King's highway! Let her come out and deny
it if she can. Pray, Sir, command the door to be opened and let her
prove me a liar if she knows how! I have been drinking right French
claret, but I love my own country for all that.

DON PEDRO   Ay, ay, who doubts it, Sir? Open the door, Violante,
and let the lady come out. Come, I warrant thee, he shan't hurt her.

DON FELIX   Ay, now which way will she come off?

VIOLANTE (*unlocks the door*)   Come forth, Madam, none shall dare
to touch your veil. I'll convey you out with safety, or lose my life.
(I hope she understands me.)

Enter ISABELLA *veiled, and crosses the stage*

ISABELLA   (Excellent girl!)

Exit

DON FELIX   The devil! A woman! I'll see if she be really so. (*Offers
to follow her*)

DON PEDRO (*draws*)   Not a step, Sir, till the lady be past your
recovery. I never suffer the laws of hospitality to be violated in my
house, Sir. I'll keep Don Felix here till you see her safe out, Violante.

VIOLANTE (*to* FELIX)   Get clear of my father, and follow me to the
Terriero de Passa, where all mistakes shall be rectified.

Exit

DON PEDRO   Come, Sir, you and I will take a pipe and a bottle
together.

DON FELIX   Damn your pipe, Sir. I won't smoke, I hate tobacco,
nor I, I, I, I won't drink, Sir. No, nor I won't stay, neither, and
how will you help yourself?

DON PEDRO   As to smoking, or drinking, you have your liberty, but
you shall stay, Sir. (*Gets between him and the door*)

DON FELIX   Shall I so, Sir, but I tell you, old gentleman, I am in haste
to be married, and so God be with you. (*Strikes up his heels and exit*)

DON PEDRO   Go to the devil! In haste to get married, quotha; thou
art in a fine condition to get married, truly!

Enter a SERVANT

SERVANT   Here's Don Lopez de Pemental to wait on you, Signior.

DON PEDRO   What the devil does he want? Bring him up, he's in
pursuit of his son, I suppose.

Enter DON LOPEZ

DON LOPEZ   I am glad to find you at home, Don Pedro. I was told you was seen upon the road to ———— this afternoon.

DON PEDRO   That might be, my lord; but I had the misfortune to break the wheel of my chariot, which obliged me to return. What is your pleasure with me, my lord?

DON LOPEZ   I am informed that my daughter is in your house, Don Pedro.

DON PEDRO   That's more than I know, my lord, but here was your son just now as drunk as an emperor.

DON LOPEZ   My son, drunk! I never saw him drunk in my life. Where is he, pray, Sir?

DON PEDRO   Gone to be married.

DON LOPEZ   Married! To whom? I don't know that he courted anybody.

DON PEDRO   Nay, I know nothing of that. Within there!

Enter SERVANT

Bid my daughter come hither, she'll tell you another story, my lord.

SERVANT   She's gone out in a chair, Sir.

DON PEDRO   Out in a chair! What do you mean, Sir?

SERVANT   As I say, Sir, and Donna Isabella went in another just before her, and Don Felix followed in another. I overheard them all bid the chairs go to Terriero de Passa.

DON PEDRO   Ha! What business has my daughter there? I am confounded, and know not what to think. Within there!

Exit

DON LOPEZ   My heart misgives me plaguily. Call me an *alguazil*. I'll pursue them straight.

SCENE III

THE STREET BEFORE DON PEDRO'S HOUSE

Enter LISSARDO

LISSARDO   I wish I could see Flora; methinks I have an hankering kindness after the slut. We must be reconciled.

Enter GIBBY

GIBBY   Aw my sol, Sir, but Ise blithe to find yee here now.

LISSARDO   Ha! Brother! Give me thy hand, boy.

GIBBY   Not se fast, se ye me, brether me ne brethers. I scorn a lyar as muckle as a theife, se ye now, and yee must gang intul this house with me, and justifie to Donna Violante's face that she was the lady that gang'd in here this morn, se yee me, or the deel ha sol, Sir, but ye and I shall be twa folks.

LISSARDO   Justify it to Donna Violante's face, quotha; for what? Sure you don't know what you say.

GIBBY   Troth de I, Sir, as weel as ye dee; therefore come along and mak no meer words about it. (*Knocks hastily at the door*)

LISSARDO   Why, what the devil do you mean? Don't you consider you are in Portugal? Is the fellow mad?

GIBBY   Fallow? Ise none of your fallow, Sir, and gin this place were hell, id gar ye dee me justice. (LISSARDO *going*) Nay, the deel a feet ye gang. (*Lays hold of him, and knocks again*)

Enter DON PEDRO

DON PEDRO   How now! what makes you knock so loud?

GIBBY   Gin this be Don Pedro's house, Sir, I would speak with Donna Violante, his daughter.

LISSARDO   (Ha! Don Pedro himself! I wish I were fairly off.)

DON PEDRO   Ha! What is it you want with my daughter, pray?

GIBBY   An she be your doughter, and lik yer honour, command her to come out, and answer for herself now, and either justify or disprove what this child told me this morn.

LISSARDO   (So, here will be a fine piece of work.)

DON PEDRO   Why, what did he tell you, ha?

GIBBY   Be me sol, Sir, Ise tell you aw the truth; my master got a pratty lady upon the how de yee call't, Passa, here at five this morn, and he gar me watch her heam, and in troth I lodg'd her here, and meeting this ill-favoured theife, se ye me, I spierd wha she was, and he told me her name was Donna Violante, Don Pedro de Mendosa's daughter.

DON PEDRO   Ha! my daughter with a man abroad at five in the morning! Death, hell, and furies! By St Anthony I'm undone! (*Stamps*)

GIBBY   Wunds, Sir, ye put yer saint intul bony company.

DON PEDRO   Who is your master, you dog you? Adsheart, I shall be tricked of my daughter, and my money, too, that's worst of all.

GIBBY   Ye dog you! S'blead, Sir, don't call names, I won't tell you wa my master is, se ye me now.

DON PEDRO   And who are you, rascal, that knows my daughter so well? Ha! (*Holds up his cane*)

LISSARDO   (What shall I say to make him give this Scots dog a good beating?) I know your daughter, Signior? Not I, I never saw your daughter in all my life.

GIBBY (*knocks him down with his fist*)   Deel ha my sol, Sar, gin ye get no your carich for that lye now.

DON PEDRO   What hoa! Where are all my servants?

Enter SERVANTS *on one side;* COLONEL, DON FELIX, ISABELLA, *and* VIOLANTE *on the other side*

Raise the house in pursuit of my daughter.

SERVANT   Here she comes, Signior.

COLONEL   Hey day! What is here to do?

GIBBY   This is the loon lik tik, and lik yer honour, that sent me heam with a lye this morn.

COLONEL   Come, 'tis all well, Gibby. Let him rise.

DON PEDRO   I am thunderstruck, and have not power to speak one word.

DON FELIX   This is a day of jubilee, Lissardo. No quarrelling with him this day.

LISSARDO   A pox take his fists! Egad, these Britons are but a word and a blow.

Enter DON LOPEZ

DON LOPEZ   So, have I found you, daughter. Then you have not hanged yourself yet, I see.

COLONEL   But she is married, my lord.

DON LOPEZ   Married! Zounds, to whom?

COLONEL   Even to your humble servant, my lord. If you please to give us your blessing. (*Kneels*)

DON LOPEZ   Why, hark ye, Mistress, are you really married?

ISABELLA   Really so, my lord.

DON LOPEZ   And who are you, Sir?

COLONEL   An honest North Briton by birth, and a colonel by commission, my lord.

DON LOPEZ   A heretic! The devil! (*Holds up his hands*)

DON PEDRO   She has played you a slippery trick indeed, my lord. (*to* VIOLANTE) Well, my girl, thou hast been to see thy friend married. Next week thou shalt have a better husband, my dear.

DON FELIX   Next week is a little too soon, Sir. I hope to live longer than that.

DON PEDRO   What do you mean, Sir? You have not made a rib of my daughter too, have you?

VIOLANTE   Indeed but he has, Sir. I know not how, but he took me in an unguarded minute when my thoughts were not over strong for a nunnery, Father.

DON LOPEZ   Your daughter has played you a slippery trick, too, Signior.

DON PEDRO   But your son shall be never the better for't, my lord: her twenty thousand pounds was left on certain conditions, and I'll not part with a shilling.

DON LOPEZ   But we have a certain thing called law shall make you do justice, Sir.

DON PEDRO   Well, we'll try that, my lord. Much good may it do you
with your daughter-in-law.

Exit

DON LOPEZ   I wish you much joy of your rib.

Exit

Enter FREDERICK

DON FELIX   Frederick, welcome! I sent for thee to be witness of my
good fortune, and make one in a country dance.

FREDERICK   Your messenger has told me all, and I sincerely share in
all your happiness.

COLONEL   To the right about, Frederick, with thy friend joy.

FREDERICK   I do with all my soul. And Madam, I congratulate your
deliverance. Your suspicions are cleared now, I hope, Felix?

DON FELIX   They are, and I heartily ask the Colonel pardon, and wish
him happy with my sister, for love has taught me to know that every
man's happiness consists in choosing for himself.

LISSARDO (*to* FLORA)   After that rule I fix here.

FLORA   That's your mistake. I prefer my lady's service and turn you
over to her that pleaded right and title to you today.

LISSARDO   Choose, proud fool. I shan't ask you twice.

GIBBY   What say you now, lass? Will ye ge yer maiden-head to poor
Gibby? What say you, will ye dance the Reel of Bogye with me?

INIS   That I may not leave my lady I take you at your word and,
tho' our wooing has been short, I'll by her example love you dearly.

Music plays

DON FELIX   Hark! I hear the music. Somebody has done us the favour
to send for them. Call them in.

A country dance

GIBBY   Waunds, this is bonny music. How caw ye that thing that ye
pinch by the craig and tickle the weam, ont make it cry Grum, Grum.

FREDERICK   Oh! that's a guitar, Gibby.

DON FELIX   Now, my Violante, I shall proclaim thy virtues to the
world.
No more let us thy sex's conduct blame,
Since thou'rt a proof to their eternal fame,
That man has no advantage but the name.

APPENDICES

Or I could write like the two female things,
With muse pen-feathered, giltless yet of wings;
And yet it strives to fly, and thinks it sings,
Just like the dames themselves who slant in town
And flutter loosely, but to tumble down.
The last that writ. . .
Told a high princess she from men had torn
Those bays which they had long engrossed and worn.
But when she offers at our sex thus fair,
With four fine copies of her play. . . Oh rare,
If she feels manhood shoot, 'tis I know where.
Let them scrawl on, and loll, and wish at ease
(A feather oft does woman's fancy please),
'Till by their muse, more jilt than they, accurst,
We know, if possible, which writes the worst.

'Animadversions on Mr Congreve's Late Answer'
Anonymous, (1698)

THE FEMALE WITS

OR

THE TRIUMVIRATE OF POETS AT REHEARSAL

ANONYMOUS

first performed Drury Lane Theatre, *c.* 1697

When Mary Delarivier Manley's *The Royal Mischief* was performed by the Actors' Company at Lincoln's Inn Fields in the spring of 1696, the two women whom some people would have liked to think Mrs Manley's rivals sprang into verse with eulogistic tributes.

Mary Pix wrote:

> As when some mighty hero first appears,
> And in each act excels his wanting years,
> All eyes are fixed on him, each busy tongue
> Is employed in the triumphant song.
> Even pale envy hangs her dusky wings,
> Or joins with brighter fame and hoarsely sings,
> So you, the unequalled wonder of the age,
> Pride of our sex, and glory of the stage,
> Have charmed our hearts with your immortal lays,
> And tuned us all with everlasting praise.
> You snatch laurels with undisputed right,
> And conquer when you but begin to fight.
> Your infant strokes have such Herculean force,
> Your self must strive to keep the rapid course,
> Like Sappho, charming, like Aphra, eloquent,
> Like chaste Orinda, sweetly innocent. . .

and Catherine Trotter:

> Th' attempt was brave, how happy your success,
> The men with shame, our sex with pride, confess,
> For us you've vanquished, though the toil was yours,
> You were our champion, and the glory ours.
> Well you've maintained our equal right in fame,
> To which vain man had quite engrossed the claim.
> I knew my force too weak, and but assayed
> The borders of their empire to invade,
> I incite a greater genius to my aid.
> The war begun, you generously pursued,
> With double arms you every way subdued,
> Our title cleared, nor can a doubt remain,
> Unless in which you'll greater conquest gain,
> The comic, or the loftier tragic strain.
> The men, o'ercome, will quit the field
> Where they have lost their hearts, the laurel yield.

The one thing that had not been expected was this mutual support among the women playwrights. What had been expected was a cat-fight. In his preface to *All For Love* (1677) John Dryden had written of his two historical heroines, Cleopatra and Octavia: 'And it is not unlikely, that two exasperated rivals should use such satire as I have put into their mouths; for, after all . . . they were both women.' In the same frame of mind, when they did not get a squabble in reality, an anonymous group made one up and presented it as *The Female Wits*, included here to show what these women were up against.

CHARACTERS

MARSILIA, a poetess that admires her own works, and a great lover of
flattery [Mary Delarivier Manley]

PATIENCE, her maid

MRS WELLFED, one that represents a fat, female author. A good,
sociable, well-matured companion that will not suffer martyrdom
rather than take off three bumpers in a hand [Mary Pix]

CALISTA, a lady that pretends to the learned languages, and assumes
to herself the name of critic [Catherine Trotter]

MR AWDWELL, a gentleman of sense and education, in love with
Marsilia

MR PRAISEALL, a conceited, cowardly coxcomb. A pretender likewise
to Marsilia's affections

LORD WHIFFLE, an empty piece of noise that always shows himself at
rehearsals and in public places

MRS CROSS, actress who plays
    ISABELLA, wife to Fastin and in love with Amorous

MR JOHNSON, actor who plays
    LORD WHIMSICAL, husband to Lady Loveall

MR PINKETHMAN, actor who plays
    AMOROUS, steward to Lord Whimsical, and in love with Isabella

MRS LUCAS, actress who plays
    BETTY USEFUL, a necessary convenience of maid to Lady Loveall

MR POWELL, actor who plays
    FASTIN, son to Lord Whimsical, husband to Isabella, and in love with
    his father's wife

MRS KNIGHT, actress who plays
    LADY LOVEALL, wife to Lord Whimsical, and in love with Fastin

Actor playing servant; actors as dancers

Little boy; two men; two scene-men

*In this play, there are many surreptitious entrances and exits – as indeed
there are in real-life rehearsals. In order to keep the feel of this, I have
left many characters' entrances and exits unmarked.*

ACT I

A DRESSING-ROOM, TABLE AND TOILET FURNISHED

Enter MARSILIA *in a nightgown, followed by* PATIENCE

MARSILIA   Why, thou thoughtless, inconsiderable animal! Thou drivelling, dreaming lump! Is it not past nine o'clock? Must not I be at the rehearsal by ten, Brainless? And here's a toilet scarce half furnished!

PATIENCE   I am about it, Madam.

MARSILIA   Yes, like a snail! 'Mount, my aspiring spirit! Mount! Hit yon azure roof, and justle Gods!' (*Repeats*)

PATIENCE   Madam, your things are ready.

MARSILIA   Abominable! Intolerable! Past enduring! (*Stamps*) Speak to me whilst I am repeating! Interrupting wretch! What, a thought more worth than worlds of thee! What a thought I have lost! Ay, ay, 'tis gone beyond the clouds. (*Cries*) Whither now, Mischievous? Do I use to dress without attendance? So, finely prepared, Mrs Negligence! I never wear any patches!

PATIENCE   Madam?

MARSILIA   I ask you if ever you saw me wear any patches? Whose cook-maid wert thou, pr'ythee? The barbarous noise of thy heels is enough to put the melody of the Muses out of one's head. Almond milk for my hands! Sour! By Heaven this monster designs to poison me.

PATIENCE   Indeed, Madam, 'tis but just made. I would not offer such an affront to those charming hands for the world.

MARSILIA   Commended by thee! I shall grow sick of 'em. Well, but Patty, are not you vain enough to hope from the fragments of my discourse you may pick up a play? Come, be diligent, it might pass amongst a crowd, and do as well as some of its predecessors.

PATIENCE   (Nothing but flattery brings my Lady into a good humour.) With your Ladyship's directions I might aim at something.

MARSILIA   My necklace.

PATIENCE   Here's a neck! Such a shape! Such a skin! (*Tying it on*) Oh! if I were a man, I should run mad!

MARSILIA   (Humph! The girl has more sense that I imagined. She finds out those perfections all the *beau monde* have admired). Well, Patty, after my third day I'll give you this gown and petticoat.

PATIENCE   Your Ladyship will make one of velvet, I suppose.

MARSILIA   I guess I may. See who knocks.

                                    PATIENCE *goes out and returns*

PATIENCE   Madam, 'tis Mrs Wellfed.

MARSILIA   That ill-bred, ill-shaped creature! Let her come up. She's
foolish and open-hearted. I shall pick something out of her that may
do her mischief, or serve me to laugh at.

PATIENCE   Madam, you invited her to the rehearsal this morning.

MARSILIA   What if I did? She might have attended me at the playhouse
Go, fetch her up.

Enter MRS WELLFED *and* PATIENCE

WELLFED   Good morrow, Madam.

MARSILIA   Your servant, dear Mrs Wellfed, I have been longing for
you this half hour.

WELLFED   'Tis near ten.

MARSILIA   Ay, my impertinence is such a trifle. But Madam, are we
not to expect some more of your works?

WELLFED   Yes; I am playing the fool again. The story is —

MARSILIA   Nay, for a story, Madam, you must give me leave to say,
there's none like mine. The turns are so surprising, the love so
passionate, the lines so strong, 'Gad, I'm afraid there's not a female
actress in England can reach 'em.

WELLFED   My language!

MARSILIA   Now you talk of language, what do you think a lord said
to me t'other day? That he had heard I was a traveller, and he believed
my voyage had been to the poet's Elysium, for mortal fires could
never inspire such words! Was not this fine?

WELLFED   Extravagantly fine! But, as I was saying —

MARSILIA   Mark but these two lines.

WELLFED   Madam, I have heard 'em already. You know you repeated
every word of your play last night.

MARSILIA   I hope, Mrs Wellfed, the lines will bear the being heard
twice and twice, else 'twould be bad for the sparks who are never
absent from the playhouse, and must hear 'em seventeen or eighteen
nights together.

WELLFED   How, Madam! That's three or four more than *The Old
Batchelor* held out.

MARSILIA   Madam, I dare affirm there's not two such lines in the
play you named. Madam, I'm sorry I am forced to tell you, interruptio
is the rudest thing in the world.

WELLFED   I am dumb. Pray, proceed.

MARSILIA   Pray, observe.
   'My scorching raptures make a boy of Jove;
   That ramping God shall learn of me to love.
   My scorching. . . '

WELLFED   Won't the ladies think some of those expressions indecent?

MARSILIA   Interrupting again, by Heav'n! Sure, Madam, I understand the ladies better than you. To my knowledge they love words that have warmth, and fire, etcetera, in 'em. Here, Patty, give me a glass of sherry, my spirits are gone. No manchet sot! Ah! the glass not clean! She takes this opportunity because she knows I never fret before company. I! do I use to drink a thimbleful at a time? (*Throws it in her face*) Take that to wash your face.

PATIENCE   (These are poetical ladies with a pox to 'em.)

MARSILIA   My service to you, Madam, I think you drink in a morning.

WELLFED   Yes, else I had never come to this bigness, Madam. To the increasing that inexhausted spring of poetry that it may swell, o'erflow, and bless the barren land.

MARSILIA   Incomparable, I protest!

PATIENCE   Madam Calista to wait upon your ladyship.

MARSILIA   Do you know her, child?

WELLFED   No.

MARSILIA   Oh! 'Tis the vainest, proudest, senseless thing. She pretends to Grammar, writes in Mood and Figure, does everything methodically. Poor creature! She shows me her works first. I always commend 'em, with a design she should expose 'em, and the Town be so kind to laugh her out of her follies.

WELLFED   That's hard in a friend.

MARSILIA   But 'tis very usual. Dunce! Why do you let her stay so long?

Exit PATIENCE

Re-enter with CALISTA

MARSILIA   My best Calista! The charming'st nymph of all Apollo's train, let me embrace thee!

WELLFED   (So, I suppose my reception was preceded like this.)

MARSILIA   Pray, know this lady, she is a sister of ours.

CALISTA   (She's big enough to be the mother of the Muses.) Madam, your servant.

WELLFED   Madam, yours. (*Salute*)

MARSILIA   Now here's the Female Triumvirate. Methinks 'twould be but civil of the men to lay down their pens for one year and let us divert the Town. But if we should, they'd certainly be ashamed ever to take 'em up again.

CALISTA   From yours we expect wonders.

MARSILIA   Has any celebrated poet of the age been lately to look over any of your scenes, Madam?

CALISTA   Yes, yes, one that you know, and who makes that his pretence for daily visits.

MARSILIA   But I had rather see one dear player than all the poets in the kingdom.

CALISTA   Good Gad! That you should be in love with an old man!

MARSILIA   He is so with me. And you'll grant 'tis a harder task to
rekindle dying coals than set tinder on a blaze.

WELLFED   I guess the spark. But why then is your play at this house?

MARSILIA   I thought you had known 'thad been an opera, and such
an opera! But I won't talk on't till you see it. Mrs Wellfed, is not your
lodgings often filled with the cabals of poets and judges?

WELLFED   Faith, Madam, I'll not tell a lie for the matter, they never
do me the honour.

MARSILIA (*to* CALISTA)   I thought so when I asked her.

WELLFED   My brats are forced to appear of my own raising.

MARSILIA   Nay, Mrs Wellfed, they don't come to others to assist, but
admire.

PATIENCE   Madam, Mr Awdwell and and Mr Praiseall are below.

MARSILIA   Dear ladies, step in with me, whilst I put on my mantua.
Bring 'em up, and then come to me. What does that Awdwell here
again today? Did not I do him the honour to go abroad with him
yesterday? Sure that's enough for his trifle of a scarf. Come, ladies.
'That ramping god shall learn of me to love.'

Exeunt

Enter MR AWDWELL *and* MR PRAISEALL

AWDWELL   So, Mr Praiseall, you are come, I suppose, to pay your
tribute of encomiums to the fair lady and her works.

PRAISEALL   The lady sometimes does me the honour to communicate.
My poor abilities are at her service, though I own myself weak.

AWDWELL   Then you are not fit for the lady's service, to my
knowledge.

PRAISEALL   Why, Sir? I was long an Oxonian, till a good estate and
the practice of the law tempted me from my studies.

AWDWELL   Sir, I'll tell you my opinion of the University students.
They are commonly as dull as they are dirty, and their conversation
is as wretched as their feeding, yet every man thinks his parts
unquestionable if he has been at Oxford. Now, all the observation I
have made of Oxford is it's a good place to improve beggars, and to
spoil gentlemen, to make young master vain, and think nobody has
wit but himself.

PRAISEALL   While the lady has more complaisant sentiments, yours
shan't disturb me, Sir, I assure you.

AWDWELL   (What is't bewitches me to Marsilia! I know her a coquet,
I know her vain and ungrateful, yet wise as Almanzor, knowing all
this, I still love on!)

PRAISEALL   (I wish Marsilia would come! That fellow looks as if he
had a mind to quarrel. I hate the sight of a bent brow in a morning, I

am always unlucky the whole day after.)

AWDWELL   Oh, one thing more of your darling Oxford. You know if
you get learning it robs a man of his noblest part, courage. This your
mighty bard, by experience, owns: the learned are cowards by
profession. Do you feel any of your martial heat returns?

PRAISEALL   (Ay, he will quarrel, I find.) Sir, I was never taught to
practise feats of arms in a lady's ante-chamber.

AWDWELL   (The fool's afraid. Yet shall I have the pleasure to see
Marsilia prefer this fop to me before my face?)

Enter MARSILIA, CALISTA, *and* MRS WELLFED

MARSILIA   I must beg your learned ladyship's pardon, Aristotle never
said such a word, upon my credit. Patty, what an air these pinners
have: pull 'em more behind. Oh my stars, she has pulled my head-
clothes off!

CALISTA   I cannot but remind you, Madam, you are mistaken, for I
read Aristotle in his own language. The translation may alter the
expression.

AWDWELL   (Oh, that I could but conjure up the old philosopher to
hear these women pull him in pieces!)

MARSILIA   Nay, Madam, if you are resolved to have the last word, I
ha'done, for I am no lover of words upon my credit.

PRAISEALL   (I am glad to hear her say sh'as done, for I dare not
interrupt her.) Madam, your ladyship's most humble.

MARSILIA   (Humph! That might ha' been said to me more properly.)

PRAISEALL   Mrs Wellfed, tho' last, not least.

WELLFED   That's right, Mr Praiseall.

PRAISEALL   In love, I meant, Mrs Wellfed.

WELLFED   Pr'ythee, add 'Good Tribonius', don't steal by halves,
Mr Praiseall.

PRAISEALL   Lord, you are so quick!

MARSILIA   Well, you are come to go with us to the rehearsal.

PRAISEALL   'Tis a pleasing duty, Madam, to wait on your ladyship.
But then to hear the wondrous product of your brain is such a
happiness, I only want some of Marsilia's eloquence to express it.

AWDWELL   (How this flattery transports her; swells her pride almost
to bursting!)

MARSILIA   I do avow, Mr Praiseall, you are the most complaisant
man of the age.

AWDWELL   Are you yet at leisure, Madam, to tell me how you do?

MARSILIA   You see my engagements, and have chosen a very busy
time to ask such an insignificant question.

AWDWELL   What, it wants a courtly phrase?

MARSILIA   Must I meet with nothing but interruption? Mr Praiseall!

PRAISEALL   Madam?

MARSILIA   I think I have not seen you these two days.

PRAISEALL   So long I've lived in Greenland, seen no sun, nor felt no warmth.

MARSILIA   Heav'ns, Mr Praiseall, why don't you write? Words like those ought to be preserved in characters indelible, not lost in air.

AWDWELL   'Tis pity your ladyship does not carry a commonplace book.

MARSILIA   For yourself 'twould be more useful. But, as I was going to tell you, Mr Praiseall, since I saw you I have laid a design to alter *Catiline's Conspiracy*.

PRAISEALL   An undertaking fit for so great a hand.

MARSILIA   Nay, I intend to make use only of the first speech.

AWDWELL   That will be an alteration indeed!

MARSILIA   Your opinion was not asked. Nor would I meddle with that, but to let the world, that is so partial to those old fellows, see the difference of a modern genius. You know that speech, Mr Praiseall, and the ladies too, I presume?

CALISTA   I know it so well as to have turned it into Latin.

PRAISEALL   That was extraordinary. But let me tell you, Madam Calista, 'tis a harder task to mend it in English.

MARSILIA   True, true, Mr Praiseall, that all the universe must own. Patty, give me another glass of sherry, that I may speak loud and clear. Mr Praiseall, my service to you.

PRAISEALL   I kiss your unequalled hand.

WELLFED   (This drinking is the best part of the entertainment in my opinion.)

MARSILIA   Now, Mr Praiseall.

PRAISEALL   I am all ear.

MARSILIA   I would you were, I was just beginning to speak.

PRAISEALL   Mum, I ha' done a fault.

AWDWELL   (Sure this scene will chase her from my soul.)

MARSILIA   'Thy head! Thy head! Proud city!' I'll say no more of his, I don't love to repeat other people's works. Now my own: 'Thy solid stones, and thy cemented walls, this arm shall scatter into atoms, then on thy ruins will I mount! Mount, my aspiring spirit, mount! Hit yon azure roof, and justle gods.' My fan, my fan, Patty.

                                                    Exit PATIENCE

All clap

PRAISEALL   Ah! Poor Ben! Poor Ben! You know, Madam, there was a famous poet picked many a hole in his coat in several prefaces. He found fault, but never mended the matter. Your ladyship has laid his honour in the dust. Poor Ben! 'Tis well thou art dead, this news had broke thy heart.

MARSILIA   Then in the *Conspiracy,* I make Fulvia a woman of the nicest honour. And such scenes!

WELLFED   Madam, you forget the rehearsal.

MARSILIA   O Gods, that I could live in a cave! Echoes would repeat, but not interrupt me. Madam, if you are beholden to those creatures, I am not, let 'em wait, let 'em wait, or live without me if they can.

Enter PATIENCE

PATIENCE   Madam, your chair-men are come.

MARSILIA   Let them wait, they are paid for't.

PATIENCE   (Not yet, to my knowledge, whatever they be after the third day. There's a long bill, I'm sure.)

MARSILIA   How do you think to go, Mrs Wellfed? Shall Pat call you another chair?

WELLFED   I have no inclination to break poor men's backs! I thank you, Madam, I'll go a-foot.

CALISTA   A-foot!

WELLFED   Ay, a-foot, 'tis not far, 'twill make me leaner. Your servant, ladies.

Exit

MARSILIA   Your servant.

PRAISEALL   A bouncing dame! But she has done some things well enough.

MARSILIA   Fie, Mr Praiseall! That you should wrong your judgement thus! Don't do it because you think her my friend. I profess I can't forbear saying her heroics want beautiful uniformity as much as her person, and her comedies are as void of jests as her conversation.

PRAISEALL   I submit to your ladyship.

AWDWELL   Madam, shall I crave leave to speak a few words with you before you go?

MARSILIA   I must gratify you, though 'tis to my prejudice. My dear Calista, be pleased to take my chair to the playhouse and I'll follow you presently.

CALISTA   I will. But make haste.

MARSILIA   Fear not. Yours waits below, I suppose, Sir.

PRAISEALL   Yes, Madam.

MARSILIA   Pray, take care of the lady 'till I come.

PRAISEALL   Most willingly.

Exeunt PRAISEALL *and* CALISTA

MARSILIA   What a ridiculous conceited thing it is! A witty woman conceited looks like a handsome woman set out with frippery.

AWDWELL   Railing should be my part. But, Marsilia, I'll give it a genteeler name, and call it complaining.

MARSILIA   Pshaw! You are always a-complaining, I think. Don't put
me out of humour now I am just going to the rehearsal.

AWDWELL   Why are you so ungrateful? Is it from your lands watered
by Helicon, or my honest dirty acres your maintenance proceeds? Yet
I must stand like a foot-boy, unregarded, whilst a noisy fool takes
up your eyes, your ears, your every sense.

MARSILIA   Now, Mr Awdwell, I'll tell you a strange thing. The
difference between you and I shall create a peace, as thus: you have
a mind to quarrel, I have not, so that there must be a peace, or only
war on your side. Then again, you have a mind to stay here, I have a
mind to go, which will be a truce at least. (*She starts to leave*)

AWDWELL   Hold, Madam, do not tease me thus. Though you know
my follies and your power, yet the ill-used slave may break his chain.

MARSILIA   What would the man have? If you'll be good-humoured,
and go to the playhouse, do. If not, stay here. Ask my maid questions,
increase your jealousy, be dogged and be damned.

AWDWELL   Obliging? If I should go I know my fate. 'Twould be like
standing on the rack.

MARSILIA   While my play's rehearsing! That's an affront I shall never
forgive whilst I breathe.

AWDWELL   Though I thought not of your play.

MARSILIA   That's worse.

AWDWELL   Your carriage, your cruel carriage, was the thing I meant.
If there should be a man of quality, as you call 'em, I must not dare
to own I know you.

MARSILIA   And well remembered. My lord Duke promised he'd be
there. O Heavens! I would not stay another moment, no, not to
finish a speech in *Catiline*. What a monster was I to forget it! Oh Jehu!
My lord Duke, and Sir Thomas! Pat, another chair, Sir Thomas and
my lord Duke both stay.

Exit running

AWDWELL   Follow, follow. Fool, be gorged and glutted with abuses,
then throw up them and love together.

Exit

SCENE II

THE PLAYHOUSE

Enter MR JOHNSON, MR PINKETHMAN, MRS LUCAS, *and*
MRS CROSS

CROSS   Good morrow, Mrs Lucas. Why, what's the whim that we must
be all dressed at rehearsal as if we played?

LUCAS   'Tis by the desire of Madam Maggot, the poetess, I suppose.

CROSS   She is a little whimsical, I think, indeed, for this is the most
incomprehensible part I ever had in my life. And when I complain,
all the answer I get is, ' 'tis new, and 'tis odd', and nothing but new
things, and odd things will do. Where's Mr Powell, that we may try
a little before she comes?

JOHNSON   At the tavern, Madam.

CROSS   At the tavern in a morning?

JOHNSON   Why, how long have you been a member of this congregation,
pretty miss, and not know honest George regards neither times nor
seasons in drinking?

Enter MRS WELLFED

CROSS   Oh! Here comes Mrs Wellfed. Your servant, Madam.

WELLFED   Your servant, gentlemen and ladies.

LUCAS   Sit down, Mrs Wellfed, you are out of breath.

WELLFED   Walking a-pace, and this ugly cough. (*Coughs*) Well, the
lady's a-coming, and a couple of beaux, but I perceive you need not
care who comes, you are all dressed.

CROSS   So it seems. I think they talk she expects a duke.

WELLFED   Here's two of the company.

Enter MR PRAISEALL *and* CALISTA

PRAISEALL   Dear Mrs Cross, your beauty's slave.

CROSS   Upon condition, 'tis then, if I have no beauty, you are no
slave, and the matter is just as 'twas.

PRAISEALL   Sharp, sharp! Charming Isabella, let me kiss the strap of
your shoe, or the tongue of your buckle.

CROSS   (Now have I such a mind to kick him i' the chops.) Oh fie,
Sir, what d'ye mean?

CALISTA   So, now he's got among the players, I may hang myself
for a spark.

PINKETHMAN   Pr'ythee, Johnson, who is that?

JOHNSON   He belongs to one of the Inns of Chancery.

PINKETHMAN   A lawyer?

JOHNSON   I can't say that of the man neither, though he sweats hard
in term time, and always is as much at Westminster as he that has
most to do.

PINKETHMAN   Does he practise?

JOHNSON   Walking there, much.

PINKETHMAN   But I mean the laws?

JOHNSON   How to avoid its penalty only. The men are quite tired
with him, so you shall generally see him dagling after the women. He
makes a shift to saunter away his hours till the play begins. After, you
shall be sure to behold his ill-favoured phiz peeping out behind the
scenes at both houses.

PINKETHMAN   What, at one time?

JOHNSON   No, faith, 'tis his moving from one house to t'other takes
up his time, which is the commodity sticks of his hands, for he has
neither sense nor patience to hear a play out.

PINKETHMAN   I have enough of him, I thank you, Sir.

CALISTA (to WELLFED)   How d'ye, Madam?

WELLFED   At your service, Madam.

CALISTA   Marsilia committed me to the care of Mr Praiseall, but more
powerful charms have robbed me of my gallant.

WELLFED   I thank heaven I'm big enough to take care of myself. Indee
to neglect a young, pretty lady, expose her unmasked amongst a
company of wild players, is very dangerous.

CALISTA   (Unmasked! Humph! I'll be even with you for that.) Madam
I have read all your excellent works, and I dare say, by the regular
correction, you are a Latinist, tho' Marsilia laughed at it.

WELLFED   Marsilia shows her folly in laughing at what she don't
understand. Faith, Madam, I must own my ignorance, I can go no
further than the eight parts of speech.

CALISTA   Then I cannot but take the freedom to say you, or whoever
writes, imposes upon the Town.

WELLFED   'Tis no imposition, Madam, when everybody's inclination's
free to like or dislike a thing.

CALISTA   Your pardon, Madam.

PRAISEALL   How's this? Whilst I am making love I shall have my two
heroines wage war. Ladies, what's your dispute?

WELLFED   Not worth appealing to a judge, in my opinion.

CALISTA   I'll maintain it with my life. Learning is absolutely necessary
to all who pretend to poetry.

WELLFED   We'll adjourn the argument, Marsilia shall hear the cause.

PRAISEALL   Ay, if you can persuade her to hold her tongue so long.

WELLFED   I wish I could engage you two in a Latin dispute, Mr
Praiseall, and you should tell how often the lady breaks Pris—
Pris— What's his name? His head, you know.

PRAISEALL   Priscian, you mean. Hush! Hush!

WELLFED   He cares not for entering the lists neither. Come, Mr
Praiseall, I'll put you upon a more pleasing task. Try to prevail with
that fair lady to give us her new dialogue.

PRAISEALL   What, my angel?
WELLFED   Mrs Cross, I mean.
PRAISEALL   There is no other she, Madam.
CROSS   Sir!
PRAISEALL   Will you be so good to charm our ears, and feast our
eyes? Let us see and hear you in perfection.
CROSS   This compliment is a note above *ela*. If Marsilia should catch
me anticipating her song she'd chide sadly.
WELLFED   Oh, we'll watch. I'll call Mr Leveridge.

Song by MRS CROSS

PRAISEALL   Thank you ten thousand times, my dear.
CALISTA   I'm almost weary of this illiterate company.
WELLFED   Now, Mr Praiseall, get but Mrs Lucas' new dance, by that
time, sure, the lady will come.
PRAISEALL   I'll warrant ye my little Lucas. (*Sings*)

> *With a trip and a gim*
> *And a whey and a jerk*
> *At parting.*

Where art thou, my little girl?
LITTLE BOY   She is but drinking a dish of coffee, and will come
presently.
PRAISEALL   Pshaw! Coffee! What does she drink coffee for? She's
lean enough without drinking coffee.
PINKETHMAN   Ay, but 'tis good to dry up humours.
PRAISEALL   That's well, i'faith! Players dry up their humours! Why,
what are they good for then? Let her exert her humours in dancing,
that will do her most good, and become her best. Oh, here she comes!
You little rogue, what do you drink coffee for?
LUCAS   For the same reason you drink claret, because I love it.
PRAISEALL   Ha, pert! Come, your last dance, I will not be denied.
LUCAS   I don't intend you shall. I love to dance, as well as you do to
see me.
PRAISEALL   Say'st thou so? Come on then, and when thou hast done
I'll treat you all in the Green Room with chocolate. Chocolate,
hussy, that's better by half than coffee.
ALL   Agreed.

A dance by MRS LUCAS

PRAISEALL   Tightly done, i'faith, little girl.

Enter MRS KNIGHT

CROSS   Good morrow, Mrs Knight. Pray, dear Mrs Knight, tell me your opinion of this play. You read much, and are a judge.

KNIGHT   Oh, your servant, Madam! Why truly, my understanding is
so very small I can't find the lady's meaning out.

CROSS   Why, the masters admire it.

KNIGHT   So much the worse. What they censure most times prospers,
and, commonly, what they admire miscarries. Pshaw! They know
nothing. They have power, and are positive, but have no more a right
notion of things, Mrs Cross, than you can have of the pleasures of
wedlock, that are unmarried.

CROSS   I submit to better judgement in that, Madam. I am sure the
authoress is very proud and impertinent, as indeed most authors are.
She's a favourite, and has put 'em to a world of expense in clothes.
A play well-dressed, you know, is half in half, as a greater writer says.
The *Morocco* dresses, when new formerly for *Sebastian,* they say
enlivened the play as much as the Pudding and Dumpling song did
Merlin.

KNIGHT   This play must be dressed if there's any credit remains, tho'
they are so cursedly in debt already.

CROSS   It wants it, Madam, it wants it.

WELLFED   Well, ladies, after this play's over, I hope you'll think of
mine. I have two excellent parts for ye.

BOTH   We are at your service.

WELLFED   Mr Pinkethman! Mr Pinkethman! What, d'ye run away from
a body?

PINKETHMAN   Who I? I beg your pardon, Madam.

WELLFED   Well, Mr Pinkethman, you shall see what I have done for
you in my next.

PINKETHMAN   Thank ye, Madam, I'll do my best for you, too.

WELLFED   Mr Johnson!

PINKETHMAN   So, now she's going her rounds.

WELLFED   Mr Johnson! Deuce on him, he's gone! Well, I shall see him
by and by.

Enter MR PRAISEALL

PRAISEALL   Ladies, the chocolate is ready, and longs to be conducted
by white hands to your rosy lips!

WELLFED   Rarely expressed! Come, ladies.

All but MRS KNIGHT *and* MRS WELLFED *go out*

KNIGHT   I believe our people would dance after any Tom Dingle for
a penn'orth of sugar plums.

WELLFED   Come, Mrs Knight, let you and I have a bottle of sherry.

KNIGHT   No, I thank you, I never drink wine in a morning.

WELLFED   Then you'll never write plays, I promise you.

KNIGHT   I don't desire it.

WELLFED   If you please, Madam, to pass the time away, I'll repeat one of my best scenes.

KNIGHT   (Oh Heavens! No rest!) Madam, I doubt the company will take it amiss. I am your very humble servant.

Exit hastily

WELLFED   What! Fled so hastily! I find poets need be a little conceited, for they meet with many a baulk. However, scribbling brings this satisfaction, that like our children, we are generally pleased with it ourselves.
So the fond mother's rapt with her prattling boys,
Whilst the free stranger flies th'ungrateful noise.

Exit

ACT II

SCENE I

Enter CALISTA *and* MRS WELLFED

CALISTA   I think Marsilia is very tedious.

WELLFED   I think so, too. 'Tis well 'tis Marsilia, else the players would never have the patience.

CALISTA   Why, do they love her?

WELLFED   No, but they fear her, that's all one. Oh! Yonder's Mr Powell, I want to speak with him.

CALISTA   So do I.

Enter MR POWELL

WELLFED   Your servant, Mr Powell.

CALISTA   Sir, I am your humble servant.

POWELL   (Ounds! What, am I fell into the hands of two female poets? There's nothing under the sun, but two bailiffs, I'd have gone so far to have avoided.)

CALISTA   I believe, Mr Powell, I shall trouble you quickly.

POWELL   When you please, Madam.

CALISTA   Pray, Mr Powell, don't speak so carelessly. I hope you will find the characters to your satisfaction. I make you equally in love with two very fine ladies.

POWELL   Oh, never stint me, Madam, let it be two dozen, I beseech you.

CALISTA   The thought's new, I'm sure.

POWELL   The practice is old, I am sure.

WELLFED   Now, Mr Powell, hear mine. I make two very fine ladies in love with you, is not that better? Ha!

CALISTA   Why, so are my ladies.

WELLFED   Nay, if you go to that, Madam, I defy any ladies, in the pale, or out of the pale, to love beyond my ladies. I'll stand up for the violence of my passion, whilst I have a bit of flesh left on my back, Mr Powell!

CALISTA   Lord, Madam, you won't give one leave to speak!

POWELL   (O Gad! I am deaf, I am deaf, or else would I were.)

WELLFED   Well, Mr Powell, when shall mine be done?

CALISTA   Sure, I have Mr Powell's promise.

WELLFED   That I am glad on. Then I believe mine will come first.

CALISTA   D'ye hear that, Mr Powell! Come, pray, name a time.

WELLFED   Then I'll have time set, too.

POWELL   O Heav'ns! Let me go! Yours shall be done today and yours tomorrow. Farewell for a couple of teasers! Oh the devil!

Flinging from them. MARSILIA, *entering, meets him*

MARSILIA   What, in a heat, and a passion, and all that, Mr Powell? Lord! I'll tell you, Mr Powell, I have been in a heat, and a fret, and all that, Mr Powell! I met two or three idle people of quality, who, thinking I had no more to do than themselves, stopped my chair, and teased me with a thousand foolish questions.

POWELL   Ay, Madam, I ha' been plagued with questions, too.

MARSILIA   There's nothing gives me greater fatigue than anyone that talks much. Oh! 'Tis the superlative plague of the universe. Ump! This foolish patch won't stick. O Lord! Don't go, Mr Powell, I have a world of things to say to you. (*Patching at her glass*)

POWELL   The more's my sorrow.

Enter MR PRAISEALL *and* MRS KNIGHT

MARSILIA   How do you like my play, Mr Powell?

POWELL   Extraordinary, Madam, 'tis like your ladyship, a miracle.

CALISTA   How civilly he treats her.

WELLFED   He treats her with what ought to be despised, flattery.

MARSILIA   What was that you said? Some fine thing, I dare swear? Well, I beg your pardon a thousand times, my head was got to *Catiline.* Oh, Mr Powell, you shall be Catiline, not Ben Jonson's fool, but my Catiline, Mr Powell.

POWELL   I'd be a dog to serve your ladyship, as a learned author has it.

MARSILIA   O my Jehu! What, nobody come?

KNIGHT   Nobody, Madam! Why, here's all the players.

MARSILIA   Granted, Mrs Knight, and I have great value for all the
players, and yourself in particular, but give me leave to say, Mrs
Knight, when I appear, I expect all that have any concerns in the
playhouse should give their attendance, knights, squires or however
dignified or distinguished.

KNIGHT   I beg your pardon, Madam, if we poor folks without titles
could have served you, we are ready.

MARSILIA   Mr Powell! Mr Powell! Pray, stand by my elbow. Lord, I
don't use to ask a man twice to stand by me.

POWELL   Madam, I am here.

PRAISEALL   (Ha! A rising favourite that may eclipse my glory.)
Madam, I have been taking true pains to keep your Princes and
Princesses together here.

MARSILIA   Pray, don't interrupt me, Mr Praiseall, at this time.
Mr Powell, I suppose you observe, throughout my play I make the
heroes and heroines in love with those they should not be?

POWELL   Yes, Madam.

MARSILIA   For look ye, if every woman had loved her own husband,
there had been no business for a play.

POWELL   But, Madam, won't the critics say the guilt of their passion
takes off the pity?

MARSILIA   O, Mr Powell, trouble not yourself about the critics, I am
provided for them. My prologue cools their courage I warrant 'em.
Ha'n't you heard the humour?

POWELL   No, Madam.

MARSILIA   I have two of your stoutest men enter with long truncheons.

POWELL   Truncheons! Why truncheons?

MARSILIA   Because a truncheon's like a quarter staff, has a mischievous
look with it, and a critic is cursedly afraid of anything that looks
terrible.

PRAISEALL   Why, Madam, there are abundance of critics, and witty
men that are soldiers.

MARSILIA   Not one, upon my word, they are more gentlemen than
to pretend to either. A witty man and a soldier! You may as well
say a modest man and a courtier. Wit is always in the civil power,
take my word for it. Courage and honesty work hard for their bread.
Wit and flattery feeds on fools, and if they are counted wise, who
keeps out of harm's way, there's scarce a fool now in the kingdom.

PRAISEALL   Why, Madam, I have always took care to keep myself
out of harm's way. Not that it is my pretence to wit, for I dare look
thunder in the face, and if you think no wit has courage, what made
you send for me?

POWELL   (Here's good sport towards.)

MARSILIA   Because I have occasion for nothing but wit. I sent for
you to vouch for mine, and not fight for your own. Mr Powell, let

us mind our cause.

PRAISEALL   Damme, I dare fight!

MARSILIA   Not with me, I hope. This is all interruption by Heav'n!

PRAISEALL   'Tis well there's not a man asserts your cause. (*Walks about*)

MARSILIA   How, sir! Not a man assert my cause?

PRAISEALL   No. If there were, this instant you should behold him weltering at your feet.

POWELL   Sir!

PRAISEALL   Hold, honest George! I'll not do the town such an injury to whip thee thro' the guts.

MARSILIA   Barbarous, not to endure the jest the whole audience must hear with patience.

Enter MR AWDWELL

AWDWELL   What's here, quarrelling? Come on. I thank Heaven I never was more inclined to bloodshed in my life.

PRAISEALL   This is my evil genius. I said I should have no luck today. Mr Awdwell, your very humble servant. Did you hear a noise as you came in? 'Twas I made the noise, Mr Awdwell, I'll tell you how 'twas.

AWDWELL   Do, for I am resolved to justify the lady.

PRAISEALL   Then you must know, I was trying to act one of Marsilia's heroes, a horrible, blustering fellow! That made me so loud, Sir. Now, says Mr Powell, you do it awkwardly. Whip, says I, in answer like a choleric fool, and out comes poker. Whether George was out so soon I can't say.

POWELL   How, Sir! My sword in the scabbard, and yours drawn!

PRAISEALL   Nay, nay, maybe it was, George. But now we are as good friends as ever. Witness this hearty hug! (*To* MARSILIA) Madam, I invented this story to prevent your rehearsals being interrupted.

MARSILIA   I thank you, Sir, your cowardice has kept quietness.

PRAISEALL   Your servant, Madam, I shall find a time.

AWDWELL   So shall I!

PRAISEALL   'Tis hard tho' one can't speak a word to a lady without being overheard.

MARSILIA   Come, Mr Awdwell, sit down, I am obliged to you for what you have done. But this fellow may make a party for me at the coffee house, therefore, pr'ythee let him alone. Tho' I believe my play won't want it. Now, clear the stage. Prompter, give me the book! Oh, Mr Powell, you must stay, I shall want your advice. I'll tell ye time enough for your entrance.

POWELL   Madam, give me leave to take a glass of sack. I am qualmish.

MARSILIA   O, fie, Mr Powell, we'll have sack here. D'ye see, ladies, you have teased Mr Powell sick. Well, impertinence in a woman is the devil!

WELLFED   Shall we stay to be affronted?

CALISTA   Pr'ythee, let's stay and laugh at her 'opera', as she calls it, for I hear 'tis a very foolish one.

MARSILIA   Come, Prologue-speakers! Prologue-speakers! Where are you? I shall want sack myself, by and by, I believe.

Enter two men with whiskers, large truncheons, dressed strangely

MARSILIA   Lord, Mr Powell, these men are not half tall enough, nor half big enough! What shall I do for a bigger sort of men?

POWELL   Faith, Madam, I can't tell. They say the race diminishes every day.

MARSILIA   Ay, so they do with a witness, Mr Powell. Oh, these puny fellows will spoil the design of my prologue! Hark ye! Mr Powell, you know the huge, tall monster that comes in one play, which was taken originally from Bartholomew Fair? Against this is spoke publicly. Could we not contrive to dress up two such things? 'Twould set the upper gallery a-clapping like mad. And let me tell you, Mr Powell, ·that's a clapping not to be despised.

POWELL   We'll see what may be done. But, Madam, you had as good hear these speak it now.

MARSILIA   Well, sheep-biters, begin!

FIRST MAN   'Well, brother monster, what do you do here?'

MARSILIA   Ah! And t'other looks no more like a monster than I do. Speak it fuller in the mouth, dunce. 'Well, brother monster, what do you do here?'

FIRST MAN   'Well, brother monster, what do you do here?'

SECOND MAN   'I have come to put the critics in a mortal fear.'

MARSILIA   O Heavens! You should have everything that is terrible in that line! You should speak it like a ghost, like a giant, like a mandrake, and you speak it like a mouse.

POWELL   Madam, if you won't let 'em proceed we shan't do the first act this morning.

MARSILIA   I have no patience! I wish you would be a monster, Mr Powell, for once, but then I could not match you neither.

POWELL   I thank you, Madam. Come, these will mend with practice.

MARSILIA   Come, begin then, and go through with it roundly.

FIRST MAN   'Well, brother monster, what do you do here?'

SECOND MAN   'I come to put the critics in a mortal fear.'

FIRST MAN   'I'm also sent upon the same design.'

SECOND MAN   'Then let's our heavy truncheons shake and join.'

MARSILIA   Ah! The devil take thee for a squeaking treble! D'ye mention shaking your truncheons, and not so much as stir 'em, Block! By my hopes of *Catiline* you shall never speak it. Give me the papers, quickly. (*Throws their truncheons down*)

FIRST MAN   Here's mine.

SECOND MAN   And mine, and I'm glad on it.

MARSILIA   Out of my sight, begone I say! (*Pushes them off*) Lord!
Lord! I shan't recover my humour again this half hour!

POWELL   Why do you vex yourself so much, Madam?

AWDWELL   Poetry ought to be for the use of the mind, and for the
diversion of the writer, as well as the spectator, but to you, sure,
Madam, it proves only a fatigue and a toil.

MARSILIA   Pray, Mr Awdwell, don't come here to make your
remarks. What, I shan't have the privilege to begin a passion for you!
Shall I? How dare you contradict me?

PRAISEALL   But you shall be in a passion, if you have a mind to it,
by the club of Hercules. Ah, Madam, if we had but Hercules, Hercules
and his club would have done rarely. Dear Madam, let 'em have clubs
next time. Do, Madam. Let 'em have clubs. Let it be my thought.

MARSILIA   What, for you to brag on't all the Town over! No, they
shan't have clubs. Though I like clubs better myself, too.

PRAISEALL   I ha' done, I ha' done.

MARSILIA   O Heavens! Now I have lost Mr Powell, with your
nonsensical clubs. Would there was a lusty one about your empty
pate.

PRAISEALL   I ha' done. I ha' done, Madam.

MARSILIA   Mr Powell! Mr Powell!

SCENE-MAN   He's gone out of the house, Madam.

MARSILIA   O the devil! Sure I shall go distracted! Where's this book?
Come, we'll begin the play. Call my lady Loveall, and Betty Useful,
her maid. Pray, keep a clear stage. Now look you, Mr Praiseall, 'thas
been the received opinion and practice in all your late operas to take
care of the songish part, as I may call it, after a great man, and for
the play, it might be *The History of Tom Thumb*. No matter how, I
have done just the contrary, took care of the language and plot, and
for the music, they that don't like it may go and whistle.

AWDWELL   Why would you choose to call it an opera, then?

MARSILIA   Lord, Mr Awdwell, I shan't have time to answer every
impertinent question.

PRAISEALL   No, Sir! We haven't the time. It was the lady's will, and
that's almighty reason.

AWDWELL   (I shall have an opportunity to kick that fellow.)

MARSILIA   I wonder my lord Duke's not come, nor Sir Thomas?
Bless me! What a disorder my dress is in. Oh! These people will give
me the spleen intolerably! Do they design ever to enter or no? My
spirits are quite gone! They may do e'en what they will.

WELLFED   They are entering, Madam.

MARSILIA   Mrs Wellfed, you know where to get good wine, pray,
speak for some, then, perhaps, we shall keep Mr Powell.

WELLFED   I'll take care of it, I warrant you.
MARSILIA   I knew 'twas a pleasing errand.

Enter MRS KNIGHT *as* LADY LOVEALL *and* MRS LUCAS *as*
BETTY USEFUL

MARSILIA   Come, child, speak handsomely, this part will do you a
kindness.
BETTY   'Why do those eyes, love's tapers, that on whomsoever they
are fixed kindle straight desire, now seem to nod and wink and hardly
glimmer in their sockets?'
MARSILIA   Mr Praiseall, is not that simile well carried on?
PRAISEALL   To an extremity of thought, Madam. (But I think 'tis
stole.)
LOVEALL   'Art thou the key to all my secrets, privy to every rambling
wish, and can'st not guess my sorrows?'
BETTY   'No! For what lover have ye missed, honest Betty Useful has
been the contriver, guide and close concealer of your pleasures.
Amorous, the steward, you know is yours, the butler too bows beneath
your conquering charms, and you have vowed your wishes in your
own family should be confined. Who then of worth remains?'
LOVEALL   'O Betty! Betty!'
MARSILIA   Good Mrs Knight, speak that as passionately as you can,
because you are going to swoon, you know, and I hate women should
go into a swoon, as some of our authors make 'em, without so much
as altering their face or voice.
LOVEALL   Madam, I never knew 'Betty' sound well in heroic.
MARSILIA   Why, no, Mrs Knight, therefore in that lies the art, for
you make it sound well. I think I may say, without a blush, I am
the first that made heroic natural.
LOVEALL   I'll do my best. 'O Betty! Betty! Fear and love, like
meeting tides, o'erwhelm me. The rolling waves beat sinking nature
down, and ebbing life retires!' (*Swoons*)
MARSILIA   What d'ye think of that, Mr Praiseall? There's a clap, for
a guinea. Gad, if there is not, I shall scarce forbear telling the audience
they are uncivil.
PRAISEALL   Nor, Gad, I shall scarce forbear fighting 'em one by one.
But hush! Now let's hear what Betty says.
BETTY   'O, my poor lady! Look up, fair saint! Oh, close not those
bright eyes! If 'tis in Betty's power they shall still be feasted with the
object of their wishes.'
PRAISEALL   Well said, honest Betty.
MARSILIA   Nay, she is so throughout the play, to the very last, I
assure you.
LOVEALL   'Yes, he shall be mine! Let law and rules confine the
creeping stoic, the cold lifeless hermit, or the dissembling brethren

of broad hats and narrow bands, I am a libertine, and being so, I love my husband's son, and will enjoy him.'

MARSILIA   There's a rant for you! O Lord! Mr Praiseall, look how Mrs Betty's surprised. Well, she does a silent surprise the best i'th'world. I must kiss her. I cannot help it, 'tis incomparable! Now speak, Mrs Betty, now speak.

BETTY   'My master's son, just married to a celebrated beauty, with which he comes slowly on, and beneath this courteous roof rests this night his wearied head.'

LOVEALL   'Let me have music then to melt him down. He comes and meets this face to charm him. 'Tis done! 'Tis done! By Heaven, I cannot bear the reflected glories of those eyes, all other beauties fly before me.'

BETTY   'But Isabella is—'

MARSILIA   Now Betty's doubting. Dear Mrs Knight, in this speech stamp as Queen Statira does, that always gets a clap. And when you have ended, run off, thus, as fast as you can drive. Oh Gad! Deuce take your confounded stumbling stage. (*Stumbles*)

PRAISEALL   O Madam!

MARSILIA   Hush! Hush! 'Tis nothing! Come, Madam.

LOVEALL   'No more, he is mine, I have him fast. Oh! The ecstasy!'

MARSILIA   Now stamp and hug yourself, Mrs Knight, 'Oh the strong ecstasy'.

LOVEALL   'Mine! Forever mine!'

Exit

BETTY   'But you must ask me leave first. Yes, I will assist her, for she is nobly generous, and pays for pleasure as dear as a chambermaid's avarice requires! Then, my old master. Why, I fear him not. He is an old bookworm, never out of his study, and whilst he finds out a way to the moon, my lady and I'll tread another beaten road much pleasanter. My next task must be to tempt Fastin with my lady's beauty. This Isabella. . .'

Enter MR PINKETHMAN *as* AMOROUS, *the steward*

AMOROUS   'Did I not hear the name of Isabella? Isabella, charming as Venus rising from the sea, or Diana descending on Latmus top, too like Diana much I fear. O Isabella! Where art thou? I lose my way in tears, and cannot find my feet.'

Exit

MARSILIA   D'ye mark! This was Mr Amorous, the steward, and he was transported, he never saw Betty. Look, Betty's surprised again.

PRAISEALL   'Tis amazingly fine!

BETTY   'What's this I have heard? It makes for us. Mischief and
   scandal are a feast for them who have passed the line of shame.
   Amorous has a wife, and Isabella's Fastin's. Work on together, work,
   work, on together, work.'
MARSILIA   Now make haste off, Mrs Betty, as if you were so full of
   thought you did not know what you did. Gentleman and ladies,
   how d'ye like the first scene?

Exit BETTY

PRAISEALL   If your ladyship swore, you might justly use Ben
   Jonson's expression: 'By Gad 'tis good!'
MARSILIA   What say you, Calista?
CALISTA   'Tis beyond imitation. (I never heard such stuff in my life.)
MARSILIA   Did you observe Betty said her master was finding out a
   new way to the moon?
PRAISEALL   Yes, marry, did I, and I was thinking to ask if I might
   not go with him, for I have a great mind to see the moon world.
MARSILIA   And you shall see it all, and how they live in't, before the
   play's done. Here they have talked of the *Emperor of the Moon,* and
   The World in the Moon, but discovered nothing of the matter. Now,
   again, I go just contrary, for I say nothing, and show all.
PRAISEALL   And that's kindly done to surprise us with such a sight.
MARSILIA   Observe, and you'll be satisfied. Call Fastin and Isabella,
   attended, that is to say call Mr Powell, and Mistress Cross, and the
   mob, for their attendants look much like the mob. Mr Praiseall, do
   you know where the scene of this play lies?
PRAISEALL   Gad forgive me for a sot. Faith I ha'n't minded it.
MARSILIA   Why, to tell you the truth, 'tis not yet resolved, but it
   must be in some warm climate, where the sun has power, and where
   there's orange groves, for Isabella, you'll find, loves walking in
   orange groves.
PRAISEALL   Suppose you lay it in Holland. I think we have most of
   our oranges and lemons from thence.
AWDWELL   Well said, geographer.
MARSILIA   No, no, it must be somewhere in Italy. Peace! They are
   coming.

Enter MR POWELL *as* FASTIN *and* MRS CROSS *as* ISABELLA
attended

Attendants, don't tread upon their backs, keep at an awful distance
there. So, upon my train! Ah, thou blockheads, thou art as fit for
a throne as a stage!
FASTIN   Shall I speak, Madam?
MARSILIA   Ay, dear Mr Powell, soon as you please.

FASTIN   'Welcome, dear Isabella, to this peaceful seat. Of all my
father's mansions, this is his choice. This, surrounded by these
melancholic groves, it suits his philosophic temper best. Yet fame
reports he has so long given his studies truce as to wed a young and
beauteous bride.'

PRAISEALL   Why, Madam, had my lady Loveall never seen this spark?

MARSILIA   No, no, but she had heard of him, and that's all one. Don't
ask a question just when people are a-speaking, good Mr Praiseall.

PRAISEALL   I beg your pardon.

MARSILIA   Pish! Come, Mrs Cross.

ISABELLA   'Close by there is an orange grove, dark as my thoughts,
yet in that darkness lovely. There, my lord, with your leave, I'd walk.'

FASTIN   'Your pleasure shall be mine.'

MARSILIA   Lead her to the side scene, Mr Powell. Now come back
again.

FASTIN   'To desire and love to walk alone shows her thoughts
entertain and please her more than I, that's not so well.'

MARSILIA   Mark! He is beginning to be jealous. Now comes Betty,
and I dare be bold to say here's a scene excels Iago and the Moor.

PRAISEALL   Come, dear Mrs Betty Useful! Oh, she's my heart's
delight!

Enter BETTY USEFUL

FASTIN   'What fair nymph is this?'

BETTY   'From the bright partner of your father's bed, too sweet a
blossom, alas, to hang on such a withered tree, whose sapless trunk
affords no nourishment to keep her fresh and fair! From her I come
to you and charming Isabella. But where is that lady? Can you be
separate? Can anything divide her from your fond eyes?'

MARSILIA   Now she begins.

FASTIN   'By her own desire she chooses solitudes and private walks,
flies these faithful arms, or if she meets 'em, cold and clammy as the
damp of death, her lips still join my longings.'

BETTY   'Cold sweats, privacies and lonely hours? All signs of strong
aversion. Oh, had your fate but thrown you on my lady, her very
eyes had raised your passion up to madness.'

FASTIN   'Thou hast already kindled madness here. Jealousy, that
unextinguished fire that with the smallest fuel burns, is blazing round
my heart. Oh! Courteous maid, go on! Inform me if my love is false.'

BETTY   'As yet, I cannot. The office is ungrateful, but for your sake
I'll undertake it.'

FASTIN   'Do, and command me ever.'

BETTY   'The fair Clemene— '

FASTIN   'My mother do you mean?'

BETTY   'Call her not so, unless you break her heart. A thousand tender

names all day and night she gives you. But you can never 'scape her
lips. Her curtains by me drawn wide, discover your goodly figure.
Each morn the idols brought, eagerly she prints the dead colours,
throws her tawny arms abroad, and vainly hopes kisses so divine
would inspire the painted nothing, and mould into man.'

MARSILIA   Is not this moving, Mr Praiseall?

PRAISEALL   Ay, and melting too; i' gad, would I was the picture
for her sake.

FASTIN   'What's this I hear?'

PRAISEALL   Nay, no harm, Sir.

MARSILIA   Fie! Mr Praiseall! Let your ill-timed jests alone.

PRAISEALL   I ha' done, I ha' done.

MARSILIA   Mr Powell, be pleased to go on.

FASTIN   'What's this I hear?'

BETTY   'Her own picture, which sure she sees by sympathy, you'll
entertain by me, she prays you to accept.' (*Gives the picture*)

MARSILIA   Now, dear Mr Powell, let me have the pleasure to hear
you rave. O! Mr Praiseall, this speech! I die upon this speech!

PRAISEALL   Would we could hear it, Madam, I am preparing to clap.

FASTIN   'What's this thou hast given me? There's more than
necromantic charms in every bewitching line. My trembling nerves are
in their infancy. I am as cold as ice!'

MARSILIA   Ay, ay. Love comes just like an ague fit.

FASTIN   'What alteration here? Now I am all on fire! Alcides' shirt
sticks close. Fire, incestuous fire. I blaze! I burn! I roast! I fry! Fire!
Fire!'

Exit

BETTY   'And my lady will bring water, water, ha, ha, ha!'

MARSILIA   Laughing heartily, Mrs Betty, go off laughing.

BETTY   'Ha, ha, ha!'

Exit

MARSILIA   So, Mr Praiseall, here's a difficult matter brought about
with much ease.

PRAISEALL   Yes, faith, Madam, so there is. The young gentleman
made no great scruple to fall in love with his mother-in-law.

MARSILIA   O fie, Mr Praiseall, 'twas the strugglings of his virtue put
him in such a passion.

PRAISEALL   Ah! Madam! When once virtue comes to struggle, either
in male or female, it commonly yields.

MARSILIA   You are waggish. Now for my dance. Mrs — Mrs Cross,
Mrs Cross, come, you little cherubim, your dance.

A dance

AWDWELL   Pray, Madam, who is this dance to entertain?

MARSILIA   What, do you sit an hour to study a cross-question? Why, to satisfy you, Sir. You are to suppose Fastin, in passing towards his mother's lodgings, may, out of some gallery, see it. Now you are answered.

AWDWELL   I am.

PRAISEALL   Ay, and sufficiently, too. A gallery, balcony, twenty peepholes. . . .

Enter MRS CROSS

CROSS   Madam, I could wish you would not be disobliged if I gave up this part. I shall get myself, nor you, no credit by it.

MARSILIA   How, Mrs Cross, 'disobliged'! Assure yourself, I shall resent it ill to the last degree. What, throw up my heroine! My Isabella! Was there ever a character more chaste, more noble, or more pitiful?

CROSS   Yes, very chaste, when I am in love with my father-in-law's steward, I know not why, nor wherefore.

MARSILIA   Mrs Cross, I maintain, no woman in the playhouse, nor out of the playhouse, can be chaster than I make Isabella. But trouble your head no further, I'll do the part myself.

CROSS   With all my heart.

MARSILIA   And let me tell you, Mistress Cross, I shall command whatever is in the wardrobe, I assure you!

CROSS   Any of my gowns are at your service, if they'll fit you, Madam.

MARSILIA   Nay, they shall be. Perhaps, without boasting, I command them that command you.

CROSS   Perhaps 'tis not worth boasting on. There's your part.

Exit

MARSILIA   A little, inconsiderable creature! Well, she shall see how much better 'twill be done, and for mere madness hang herself in her own garters. Mrs Wellfed, I'll wear a white feather, that, I believe, will become me best. Patty! Is Patty there?

PATIENCE   Yes, Madam.

MARSILIA   Patty, run to the Exchange, bring me a dozen yards of scarlet ribbon, d'ye hear, Patty, some shining patches, some pulvil and essence. My lord Duke shall help me to jewels. Throw up her part! I'll fit her. Let her see how the Town will receive her after I have trod the stage.

AWDWELL   Why, Madam, you are not in earnest!

MARSILIA   By my hopes of *Catiline,* I am.

AWDWELL   For Heaven's sake, don't make yourself so irrecoverably ridiculous.

PRAISEALL   Do, Madam, I say. Gad, I'll make such a party! Gad, I'll do nothing but clap from the time I come into the house 'till I go out. Ouns, I'll be hanged if it don't bring a swingeing audience on the third day.

AWDWELL   To dance naked on the third day would bring a bigger audience. Why don't you persuade the lady to do that? (*Speaking loud to* MARSILIA) Do, Marsilia, be ruled by your vanity, and that good friend Mr Praiseall, but rest assured, after such a weakness, I will never see your face again.

MARSILIA   (Ha! I must not lose him.) Why, Mr Awdwell, would you have such a hopeful play lost? Can you be so unreasonable to desire it? And that part ruins all.

AWDWELL   Give me the part, and I'll try to persuade Mrs Cross.

MARSILIA   Do, that's a good boy. And I won't disoblige him this two days.

AWDWELL   Is't possible! Will you dine at your own lodgings today? I'll give order for some dishes of meat there?

MARSILIA   Yes, yes.

AWDWELL   Don't serve me now as you did when I provided a handsome dinner for you at my own house, and you whisked to Chelsea in a coach, with the Lord knows who.

MARSILIA   No, I scorn it.

Exit MR AWDWELL

PRAISEALL   You was talking of wine. There is some within, pray you take a recruit before you proceed.

MARSILIA   A good motion. Wait upon these two ladies in, and I'll follow. I must practise a little, least Mrs Cross should prove stubborn, and then not my father's ghost should hinder me.

CALISTA   We'll begin your health.

Exeunt, leaving MARSILIA

MARSILIA   Do. 'Whom shall I curse? My birth, my fate, or stars? All are my foes! All bent to ruin innocence!'

Enter PATIENCE *with patches, powder, looking-glass, etc.*

PATIENCE   O Madam!

MARSILIA   How now, Impertinence! Was not you told of interrupting once today? Look how she stands now! How long must I expect what you have to say?

PATIENCE   My Lord Whiffle is come to wait on your ladyship, and sends to know whether you are at leisure.

MARSILIA   Ay, he understands breeding and decorum. Is my dress in great disorder?

PATIENCE   You look all charming, Madam.

MARSILIA   Hold the glass. Give me some patches. My box is done. I
am much obliged to his lordship for this honour. Some powder. (*Pulls
the box out of her pocket*) Put my gown to rights, and shake my tail.
The unmannerly blockheads have made a road over it, and left the
vile impression of their nauseous feet. Well, how do I look now, Patty?
PATIENCE   Like one of the Graces dressed for a ball at the Court of
Orleans.
MARSILIA   Ha, ha, ha, well said, Patty. Now for my dear, dear Lord
Whiffle.

Enter AWDWELL

AWDWELL   How!
MARSILIA   And how, too! Why, look ye, Mr Awdwell, my lord is
come to pay his respects to me, and I will pay my respects again to
my lord, in spite of your tyrannical pretentions. And so, your humble
servant.

Exit with PATIENCE

AWDWELL   Who would a kind and certain mistress choose,
Let him, like me, take one that loves a muse.

Exit

ACT III

SCENE I

Enter LORD WHIFFLE, MARSILIA, AWDWELL, PRAISEALL,
WELLFED *and* CALISTA

WELLFED   For my part I am quite tired, and have a great mind to
steal home to dinner. Will you please to go with me, Madam?
CALISTA   With all my heart. Marsilia's so taken up with my lord
they'll never miss us.
WELLFED   Come, then.

Exeunt CALISTA *and* WELLFED

MARSILIA *and* WHIFFLE *talk, both looking in a great glass*

MARSILIA   Thus I have told your lordship the first part, which is past.
WHIFFLE   I conceive you, Madam, I have the whole story in a corner
of my head entire, where no other thought shall presume to interpose.
Confound me, if my damned barber has not made me look like a
mountebank. This wig shall never endure, that's certain.

MARSILIA   Now I must beg your lordship to suppose Fastin, having seen his mother-in-law, is wholly captivated with her charms, and Betty and she have both forsworn the consummation of her marriage with Fastin's father. So he takes her to an adjacent castle of his, she having cast the old philosopher in a deep sleep. I'm forced to tell your lordship this because the play does not mention it.

AWDWELL   I am afraid your ladyship will be wanted, like the chorus of old, to enlighten the understanding of the audience.

MARSILIA   Mere malice, spite, and burning malice, by the gods!

WHIFFLE   Very good, my coat is as full of wrinkles as an old woman's face, by jove.

PRAISEALL   Madam, ha'n't they took Betty with 'em to his castle?

MARSILIA   Yes, yes, but, Mr Praiseall, you must keep your distance a little now, and not interrupt me when I am talking to my lord.

PRAISEALL   I am as dumb as a fish.

MARSILIA   Now, if your lordship pleases to sit down, you will see my opera begin, for though some of the play is over, there has been no scene opera-ish yet.

AWDWELL   Opera-ish! That's a word of your own, I suppose, Madam?

PRAISEALL   Ne'er the worse for that, I hope, Sir. Why mayn't the ladies make a word as well as the men?

WHIFFLE   The lady shall make what words she pleases, and I will justify her in't.

AWDWELL   And I will laugh at her for it.

MARSILIA   Well, Mr Awdwell, these affronts are not so soon forgot as given.

AWDWELL   Use your pleasure, Madam, the fool's almost weary.

MARSILIA   He nettles me, but I think I have him in my power. Is your lordship ready to observe?

WHIFFLE   Madam, I am all attention.

MARSILIA   Come. The night scene there. A dark grove made glorious by a thousand burning lights. By Heavens, my words run of themselves into heroic! Now let 'em enter.

Enter FASTIN *and* LADY LOVEALL

FASTIN   'Could age expect to hold thee! O thou heavenly charmer! Was there such an impudence in impotence! If that old dotard has lived past his reason he must be taught it. Yes, it shall dazzle in his eyes.'

AWDWELL   A very dutiful son, this.

MARSILIA   Sir, I desire your absence if you won't let the players go on. His father has done a very foolish thing, and must be called to account for it.

WHIFFLE   Right, Madam, all old men do foolish things when they marry young wives, and ought to meet with exemplary punishments.

MARSILIA   Ay, your lordship understands the justice of the thing.
Mrs Knight, if you please.

LOVEALL   'Whilst my ears devour your protested love, my heart
dances to the music of your vows. But is there no falsehood in a
form so lovely? If there is, these eyes that let the object in, must
weep forever!'

FASTIN   'By honour and by glory, I love thee more than mortal can
express or bear.'

MARSILIA   Now, Mr Powell, my rhyme with a boon grace.

FASTIN   'My scorching rapture makes a boy of Jove;
That ramping god shall learn of me to love.'

MARSILIA   How does your lordship like these lines?

WHIFFLE   Madam, they exceed any of our modern flights as far as a
description of Homer's does Mr Settle's 'Poet in Ordinary' for my
Lord Mayor's Show.

PRAISEALL   After what my lord has said I dare not speak, but I am
all admiration.

MARSILIA (*to* MRS KNIGHT)   Madam, I beg your pardon for this
interruption. My friends here will treat me with flattery.

LOVEALL (*to* FASTIN)   (And you will be so vain to believe it none.)
'Nor Isabella shall not— '

FASTIN   'Be named only for punishment. Her adultery with Amorous
is plain, therefore he shall be disgraced, and die.'

AWDWELL   Who has told him this?

MARSILIA   Why, Betty has told him, tho' Isabella was innocent as to
the matter of fact. Indeed fate over-ruled her inclination. I will not
answer you another question, I protest. Find it out as the rest of the
world does.

FASTIN (*to* ATTENDANTS)   'Guard the orange grove. There let
Isabella remain a prisoner, whilst I entertain the fair Clemene with a
song and dances here.'

Italian song by MR PATE

MARSILIA   This song's my own, and I think soft and moving.

WHIFFLE   My slackened fibres! My soul's dissolved.

MARSILIA   Now the grotesque entertainment. I have mine performed
by women, because it should differ from t'other house. If it has done
'em an injury I am sorry, but it could not be hoped the play must not
be absolutely without ornament. Pray, take care, gentlewomen, as
we poets are fain to do, that we may excel the men, who first led the
way.

Dance. After the dance, a drum beats. Enter BETTY

PRAISEALL   O, Mrs Betty!

MARSILIA   Hold your peace, Mrs Betty's in haste.

BETTY   'Fly, Sir, fly. Old Whimsical is waked by another wretch, a
    fornicator, who has lived past the pleasure of the sin. These withered
    cuffs come on, followed by a monstrous rabble, to seize the lady.'
LOVEALL   'Alas, I fear.'
FASTIN   'Talk not of fear, my love, while I am by. Thou art as safe
    as if ten thousand legions were thy guard. First to the castle I will
    take my way, and leave thee there secure. In the meantime my men
    fall on upon his mobbish soldiers, but spare the stubborn old man,
    because he is my father.'

Exeunt

MARSILIA   Now there's his duty, there's his duty! D'ye hear that,
    Mr Quarrelsome!
AWDWELL   Wondrous duty! Sets the rabble about his father's ears,
    and bids 'em not hurt him.
MARSILIA   Now, my lord and gentlemen and ladies. . . Where are the
    ladies?
PRAISEALL   I have missed 'em a great while, Madam. But I would not
    interrupt you to tell you of it.
MARSILIA   Ill-bred things! Who do they expect should have patience
    with their dull stuff? But, as I was saying, I must beg you once again
    to suppose old Lord Whimsical Loveall is attacking his son's castle,
    and beaten back. Now they are behind the scenes. Sound a storm
    again, three times. Now we'll suppose 'em repulsed. And from the
    castle let the trumpets and violins join in a tune of victory. So, there's
    a battle well over.
WHIFFLE   With a very little trouble. But, Madam, had not the storming
    the castle been as good a scene as the taking of Jerusalem?
MARSILIA   Granted, my lord. But I have a castle taken upon the stage,
    and twice, you know, had been repetition.
PRAISEALL   True. Your ladyship was never in the wrong in your life,
    unless it was when you said I had no courage.
MARSILIA   Change the scene to the orange grove.

Enter ISABELLA

Your servant, Mrs Cross, I am glad to see you again.
ISABELLA   Truly the gentleman would not be denied. Tho' really,
    Madam, 'twas only fear I should not serve you in't made me backward.
MARSILIA   All's well, and I'm pleased. Will you give yourself the
    trouble to enter again, because that will make you look more alone.
ISABELLA   Yes, Madam.

Goes out and re-enters

'Methought I heard the sound of war pierce the hollow groves. Else 'twas my melancholy fancy chimed to my sick brain. Yet it cannot be delusion, for I am a prisoner. A surly fellow, who looked as if pity was his foe, told me I here must wait my lord's commands. O, Fastin! If thou art cruel or unkind thou art justly so, for I came to thy arms without a heart, without love's flames, or desire to kindle 'em. Oh, why was Amorous sent to my father's castle to begin the parley? 'Tis true he's in the vale of years. Yet, oh, such charms remain! He found the way to my unguarded heart. Nor need he storm, I could not the least opposition make. He straight was Lord of all within. Yet, chaste as fires which consume in urns, and vainly warm the dead, so useless is my flame!'

MARSILIA   My lord! Would your lordship imagine Mrs Cross should dislike the part, when I defy all the virgins in Europe to make so cold a simile as that?

WHIFFLE   Thou'st turned me into marble. I am a statue upon the tomb where the urn's enclosed.

PRAISEALL   My teeth chatter in my head.

AWDWELL   (Oh, for a couple of good cudgels to warm the coxcombs!)

MARSILIA   Well, dear Isabella, proceed.

ISABELLA   'Thou, Mother Earth, bear thy wretched daughter, open thy all-receiving womb, and take thy groaning burden in!'

MARSILIA   Now you'll see this act very full of business. Come, Lord Whimsical and Amorous, hastily.

Enter MR JOHNSON *as* WHIMSICAL *and* AMOROUS

WHIMSICAL   'Raise thee from earth, thou most unhappy wife of my most wicked son! Fly, whilst faithful Amorous and I protect thee from what his savage rage has doomed.'

ISABELLA   'What has he doomed? Alas, I dare not fly with you and Amorous.'

AMOROUS   'Then leave me here to death. Follow your father, and shun approaching danger.'

ISABELLA   'What death? What danger? Make me understand you.'

MARSILIA   Ay, poor lady, she's unwilling Amorous should die, too.

WHIMSICAL   'Your husband loudly proclaims you an adulteress, and means to make war on that fair work of heaven, your face, and noseless send you back to your own father.'

AMOROUS   'Oh, horrid! Hasten, Madam, from the brutal tyrant.'

ISABELLA   'I must consult my immortal honour. That's a beauty to me more valued than nature's out-works, a face. Let me consider. 'Tis my husband's father. To retire till I am justified cannot be a crime. Sir, I am resolved to go.
My innocence is white as alpine snow,
By these tears, which never cease to flow.'

MARSILIA   Your pardon, Mrs. . . , give me leave to instruct you in a
    moving cry. Oh, there's a great deal of art in crying. Hold your
    handkerchief thus. Let it meet your eyes, thus. Your head declined,
    thus. Now, in a perfect whine, crying out these words, 'By these
    tears, which never cease to flow.' Is not that right, my lord?
WHIFFLE   O Gad! Feelingly passionate, Madam. Were your ladyship
    to do it the whole house would catch the infection, and, as in France,
    they are all in a tune, they'd here be all in tears.
AWDWELL   Now I fancy 'twould have just the contrary effect on me.
MARSILIA   O Jehu, how I am tortured with your nonsense! Proceed,
    for Heaven's sake. Let my ears be diverted with my own words, for
    yours grate 'em beyond enduring.
ISABELLA   Must I repeat this stuff again?
MARSILIA   Stuff! My spirit rises at her. But 'tis in vain to resent it.
    The truth on't is, poets are so increased, players value 'em no more
    than. . .
AWDWELL   Spiteful devils.
MARSILIA   Ballad singers. Well, Mrs Cross, I'll not trouble you again.
    Amorous shall suppose you are going. Come, Mr Pinkethman.
AMOROUS   'Then, with this flaming sword I'll clear the way,
    And hunt for danger in the face of day.'
MARSILIA   Well, Mr Pinkethman, I think you are obliged to me for
    choosing you for a hero. Pray do it well, that the Town may see I
    was not mistaken in my judgement. Fetch large strides. Walk thus.
    Your arms strutting, your voice big, and your eyes terrible.
    'Then with this flaming sword I'll clear the way.'
AMOROUS   'Then thus I'll clear your way,
    And hunt for danger in the face of day.' (*Draws*)
ISABELLA   'Alas, does any oppose us?'
WHIMSICAL   'Only some straggling fellows, which Amorous will
    scour, and in the corner of the grove the chariot waits.'

                                          Exeunt

MARSILIA   Now will your lordship please to conceive these three are
    got into my Lord Whimsical's castle? Whither Fastin, mad with
    jealousy and love, pursues. Now your lordship shall see the storming
    of a fort, not like your *Jerusalem,* but the modern way. My men shall
    go all up thro' a trap-door, and ever now and then one drop polt down
    dead.

Talking eagerly she throws my lord's snuff box down

WHIFFLE   Like my snuff box, Madam. 'Ouns, my snuff cost two
guineas.
MARSILIA   I beg your lordship's pardon.

PRAISEALL   Two guineas! It shan't be all lost then. (*Picks up the snuff*)

MARSILIA   Are you ready? (*Goes into the scenes*)

(WITHIN) Yes, yes, Madam.

A castle storming

MARSILIA   My lord, my lord, this will make you amends for·your snuff! Drums beat. Mount, ye lumpish dogs! What are you afraid of? You know the stones are only wool. Faster, with more spirit! Brutes. O Jehu! I am sorry I had not this castle taken by women, then it had been done like my grotesque dance there. Mount, mount, rascals! (*Bustling among 'em, she loses her head-cloths*) Patty, Patty, my head, my head! The brutes will trample it to pieces. Now, Mr Powell, enter like a lion.

Enter FASTIN, *followers*, LOVEALL, BETTY, *etc.*

FASTIN   'By Heaven, I'll tear her from her lover's arms, my father only spare.'

LOVEALL   'Spare him not. Hear my charge.
Aim every arrow at his destined head.
There is no peace 'till that curst villain's dead.'

MARSILIA   Look, look, my lord, where Mr Powell's got.

LOVEALL   'Oh, the rash young man. Save him, Gods!'

BETTY   'Protect him, Venus!'

PRAISEALL   How heartily Betty prays, and to her own deity, I dare swear.

FASTIN   'They fly! They fly! Sound trumpets! Sound! Let Clemene's music join. Confine my father to yon distant tower. I'll not see him 'till I have punished the adult'ress. Set wide the gates, and let Clemene know she's mistress here.'

LOVEALL   'Where is he? Let me fly and bind his wounds up with my hair, lull him upon my own bosom, and sing him into softest ease.
To feast and revels dedicate the day.
Let the old miser's stores be all exposed and made the soldiers' prey!
D'ye hear, let the butler die, lest he tell tales.'

BETTY   'Madam, he shall, then. Nobody will dare contradict us in the cellar neither.'

Exeunt

PRAISEALL   Well said, Mrs Betty. She loves a cup. I like her the better for it.

AWDWELL   A hopeful wife, this! Does she go on thus triumphant?

MARSILIA   I have sworn to answer you no more questions.

WHIFFLE   Indeed, Madam, you have made her very wicked.

MARSILIA   The woman is a little mischievous. But your lordship shall
see I'll bring her to condign punishment. My lord, I will be bold to
say here is a scene coming wherein there is the greatest distress that
ever was seen in a play. 'Tis poor Amorous and Isabella. Mr Praiseall,
do you remember that old Whimsical was all along a philosopher?
Come, let down the chariot.

PRAISEALL   Lord, Madam, do you think I don't! Why, was not he
and I a-going to the moon together?

MARSILIA   Right! You must keep a steady and a solid thought to
find the depths of this play out. Now, my lord, be pleased once
again to conceive these poor lovers hunted above the castle, at last
taking sanctuary in a high pair of leads, which adjoins to the old
man's study. Conceive also their enemies at their heels. How then can
these lost creatures 'scape?

AWDWELL   Maybe they both leapt over the leads and broke their
necks.

WHIFFLE   That's one way. But pray let's hear the lady's.

MARSILIA   You must know, my lord, at first I designed this for
tragedy, and they were both taken. She was poisoned, and died, like
an innocent lamb, as she was indeed. I was studying a death for him.
Once I thought boys should shoot him to death with pot-guns, for
your lordship may be pleased to understand Amorous had been a
soldier, tho' now he was a steward of the family, and that would
have been disgrace enough, you know. But at length I resolved to ram
him into a great gun, and scatter him o'er the sturdy plain. This, I say,
was my first resolve. But I considered 'twould break the lady's heart.
So there is nothing in their parts tragical, but as your lordship shall
see, miraculously I turned it into an opera.

WHIFFLE   Your ladyship's wit is almighty, and produces nothing but
wonders.

PRAISEALL   The devil take his lordship, he is always beforehand with
me, and goes so confounded high there's no coming after him.

MARSILIA   Your lordship shall see what, I think, their operas have not
yet had.

*The leads of a castle. The sun seen a little beyond. A chariot stands
upon the leads. Enter* ISABELLA, *followed by* AMOROUS

ISABELLA   'Now death's in view, methinks I fear the monster. Is
there no god that pities innocence? O, thou all-seeing sun, contract
thy glorious beams, hide me, in darkness hide me!'

AWDWELL   I am sorry to find your heroine shrink.

MARSILIA   Oh, 'tis more natural for a woman than bold, as an
imprisoned cat, to fly death i'th'face, as 'twas. Humph! Was it you I
took pains to convince? Pray, no more interruption of this scene.

AMOROUS   'Ten massive doors, all barred with wondrous strength,
impede their passage. Rest then, thou milk-white, hunted hind,
forget the near approach of fear, and hear the story of my love.'

AWDWELL   Hey, boy, little Amorous! He'll lose no opportunity.

PRAISEALL   He is not like to have many. He was a fool if he did not
improve 'em.

ISABELLA   'We soon shall mount yon blissful seats! Let us be robed
with innocence, lest we want admittance there.'

AMOROUS   'All dreams! Mere dreams! Bred from the fumes of
crabbed education, and must we for this lose true substantial pleasure?
By Heaven, 'twould be a noble justice to defeat their malice. They
hung us for imaginary crimes, and we must die like fools for doing
nothing.'

PRAISEALL   Well urged, Amorous.

WHIFFLE   Bold, I vow.

MARSILIA   A lover should be so, my lord.

AMOROUS   'But give me up the Heaven my ravenous love requires.
Let me fill my senses with thy sweetness, then let 'em pour upon
me. I could laugh at all their idle tortures, every pleased limb should
dance upon the wheel.'

MARSILIA   Dance upon the wheel! That's a new thought, I am sure,
my lord.

WHIFFLE   Your tract is all new, and must be uncommon, because
others can never find it.

PRAISEALL   (A pox on him! He has outdone me again.)

MARSILIA   I am your lordship's very humble servant. My lord, how
Amorous gazes on her!

WHIFFLE   Piercing eyes, I confess.

PRAISEALL   An irresistible leer. (I got in a word!)

ISABELLA   'Take off your eyes. Mine should be fixed above, but love
draws 'em downwards, and almost pulls my heart along.'

AMOROUS   'Give me your heart! O arms! Oh, give me all! See, at
your feet the wretched Amorous falls! Be not more cruel than our
foes. Behold me on the torture! Fastin cannot punish me with half the
racks denying beauty lays on longing love.'

ISABELLA   'I recover strength. Rise and begone. Alas, thou can'st
not go. Then at an awful distance, cold as ice, not dare to let thy hot
breath again offend my chaste ears! If thou hast, a dagger rams thy
passion down thy throat.'

MARSILIA   Won't this be a surprise, my lord, to see her have such
an icy fit?

WHIFFLE   When I thought she was just going to melt.

AMOROUS   'See, you are obeyed. Shivering, your erst-while raging
lover stands. Your words and looks, like frost on flowers, have
nipped my hopes and fierce desires!'

PRAISEALL   Alas, poor Amorous!

A noise without

MARSILIA   Do you hear, my lord? Does not your heart ache for the poor lovers?

WHIFFLE   I am ready to swoon, Madam.

PRAISEALL   Would I had some cordial-water.

AWDWELL   Art thou, Marsilia, wilt thou confess it, so weak to believe these coxcombs?

MARSILIA   I always choose to believe what pleases me best. If a schoolboy had been told so often of a fault as you have been of interruption he had certainly left it. Make a noise again without.

ISABELLA   'Alas, my fears return. What shall I do? I dare not die.'

AMOROUS   'Oh, let not monstrous fear deform the beauties of thy soul, but brave thy fate.'

MARSILIA   Louder. 'But brave thy fate.' Strain your voice. I tell you Mr Pinkethman, this speaking loud gets the clap.

AMOROUS   (Pox of this heroic, I shall tear my lungs.) 'But brave thy fate.'

MARSILIA   Ay, that goes to one's very heart.

AWDWELL   And rends one's head.

ISABELLA   'I cannot, I dare not. Oh, they come! Where shall I hide me?'

She gets into the chariot

AMOROUS   'For Heaven's sake, Madam, come from hence. This will expose us to all their scorn.'

He goes in after her

MARSILIA   Now, now, up with it. Here, my lord, here's the wonder. This very chariot Whimsical had been making fifty years, contrived beyond all human art for the sun to draw up to the moon, at this very critical minute the matter's affected. Is not your lordship surprised?

WHIFFLE   I know not where I am!

PRAISEALL   Oh, this is a plain case! So while the old cuckold was watching his chariot, his wife had opportunity to make him one.

MARSILIA   Right, right, Mr Praiseall. Now Amorous finds it move.

AMOROUS   'Ha! The chariot moves. A miracle is known in our preservation.'

ISABELLA   'Oh! I die with fear!'

MARSILIA   Now she falls in a swoon, and never wakes 'till they come into another world.

PRAISEALL   Egad, 'tis well I am not in the chariot with her.

MARSILIA   You may open the door. They are out of sight.

Enter FASTIN, LADY LOVEALL, *and* BETTY

FASTIN   'Where is the Hellish pair? Let my eyes be fastened on 'em, that I may look 'em dead.'

MARSILIA   Look dreadfully, sweet Mr Powell, look dreadfully.

AWDWELL   Hark'ee, Madam, only one thing, did you never hear an old proverb: 'He that has a house of glass should never throw stones at his neighbours'? I think this young gentleman is guilty of much the same fault.

MARSILIA   Lord! Lord! I told you once before, he did not know his father was married to her, he took her for a pure virgin. Come, Mr Powell, go on.

FASTIN   'Where are you hid? In what lustful corner?'

LOVEALL   'Alas, I fear they have escaped, and I have such a detestation for ill women 'twould grieve me much to have 'em go unpunished.'

BETTY   'I am sure they took the stairs that led this way, and must be here. Let me ferret 'em.'

PRAISEALL   God-a-mercy, Betty! Let Betty alone.

BETTY   'A-dad, I can't set eyes on 'em, high nor low.'

PRAISEALL   No, they are too high for thee, indeed, little Betty.

MARSILIA   Pray, Mr Praiseall, be quiet. Here's a great scene coming.

PRAISEALL   I am silent as the grave.

FASTIN   'In vain they think to 'scape my rage by thus evading it, for if the earth holds 'em, they shall be found.'

BETTY   'Why, where's my master's conjuring chariot, I wonder, that he always told us would carry him to Heaven, when we little thought on't? It used to stand here.'

LOVEALL   'It did so.'

BETTY   'Perhaps they are gone to Elysium in it.'

LOVEALL   'No, fool, Elysium has no room for lawless lovers.'

BETTY   '(Then you must never come there, I'm sure.)'

MARSILIA   That's the first ill word Betty has given her mistress, and that was to herself, too.

FASTIN   'Let my chariots be prepared. We'll leave this hated place, and in my castle unlade our cares. Love shall crown our hours, and wine and music rob 'em of 'em with delight.'

LOVEALL   'Whilst I weave flowery chaplets for your hair,
Revels and masques to please your sight prepare,
Feed on your presence, on your absence grieve,
Love you alone, for you alone I'll live.'

MARSILIA   Now quick, quick, get behind her, Mr, lest she should resist. The rest disarm Mr Powell.

Enter LORD WHIMSICAL *and others*

WHIMSICAL   'Not fit to live, nor die! But death thou best deservest.'
  (*Stabs her*)
LOVEALL   'Oh, thou impotence, only strong in mischief. That feeble,
  aged arm has reached my youthful heart.'
FASTIN   'Slaves, unhand me! Oh! Clemene! Oh!
LOVEALL   'Let me come at the dotard, let me cover the blood-thirsty
  man with livid gore.'
MARSILIA   D'ye hear, property man? Be sure some red ink is
  handsomely conveyed to Mrs Knight.
FASTIN   'Move, dogs. Bear me to her, that I may press her close, and
  keep in life.'
MARSILIA   Strive and struggle now, Mr Powell. Lord, you scarce
  stir. Hold me, hold me, some of you. Observe: 'that I may press her
  close, and keep in life', ye see, my breath's almost gone. Oh, if we
  poets did but act, as well as write, the plays would never miscarry.
FASTIN   Why, there's enough of you, both males and females.
  Entertain the Town when you will. I'll resign the stage, with all my
  heart.
MARSILIA   And, by my hopes of *Catiline,* I'll propose it. But now,
  pray, go on.
FASTIN   'I say, loose your plebeian goals, and let me reach my love.'
MARSILIA   Well, that's your own, but 'twill do. You may speak it,
  Mr Powell.
WHIMSICAL   'What, the sorceress! Thy father's wife, rash boy!'
FASTIN   'Ha, ha, ha, ha! Your wife! I have heard indeed of old men
  that wanted virgins when vital warmth was gone.'
WHIMSICAL   'To that title does Clemene's impudence pretend. Speak,
  lewd adult'ress.'
LOVEALL   'Yes, I will speak, and own it all. Why should I mince the
  matter, now I've lost my hopes of him? For the old skeleton, sign
  alone, and shadow of a man, I might have yet been pure. But whilst
  gay youths adorned thy family, Clemene would not sigh in vain.'
FASTIN   'What's this I hear?'
BETTY   'My lady dying! I am not yet prepared to bear her company.
  I'll e'en shift for one. I would not willingly leave this wicked world
  before I have tasted a little more on't.'
PRAISEALL   True, Mrs Betty. Slip beside me, and thou art gone.
MARSILIA   See, my lord, they are all struck in a maze.

                                                    Exit BETTY

WHIFFLE   'Tis very amazing!
WHIMSICAL   'Why, Fastin, stare you thus? Is her wickedness such
  news? Go, bear her off, and let her die alone.'
LOVEALL   'Do, convey me hence, for not the gaping pipes of burning
  sulphur, nor grinning hideous fiends can jerk my soul like that old

husband. Fogh! How he stinks! Set him afire with all his chymistry about him. See how he'll blaze on his own spirits.'

FASTIN   'Rage not. It wastes thy precious life.'

AWDWELL   Then he loves her still?

MARSILIA   Yes. What, you think him hot and cold in a quarter of an hour?

LOVEALL   'Fastin, farewell. O, thou only youth whom I can truly say I loved, for thee I'd run this mad risk again, for thee I die. Away, away! And let me do the work of children in the dark.'

Exit LADY LOVEALL, *led off*

WHIMSICAL   'Where's my chariot? My chariot of the sun, slaves! Who has removed it? If it jogged but a hair awry it may set me backwards ten tedious years. But it is gone! Where can it be?'

Runs up and down to look for it

FASTIN   'Defeated love! Approaching shame! Remorse and deathless infamy! They crowd one breast too much. Here's to give 'em vent.' (*Stabs himself*)

WHIMSICAL   'Oh! 'Tis gone! 'Tis gone! My chariot! Oh, my chariot!'

FASTIN   'See, Clemene, see, thy adorer comes! Guiltily fond, and pressing after thee.' (*Dies*)

WHIMSICAL   'Have you all looked below? Is there no news of this inestimable chariot?'

SERVANT   'No, my lord. And here your son is dead.'

WHIMSICAL   'Why dost thou tell me of my son, the blind work of chance, the sport of darkness, which produced a monster? I've lost an engine, the laboured care of half a hundred years. It is gone! I shall go mad.'

MARSILIA   Good Mr What-d'-call-'um, this last speech to the highest pitch of raving.

WHIMSICAL   'Ha! The sun has got it. I see the glorious tract. But I will mount and yet recover it. The covetous planet shall not dare to keep it for the use of his paramour. Bear me, ye winds, upon your blustering wings, for I am light as air, and mad as rolling tempests.'

Exit

MARSILIA   Is not this passion well expressed?

AWDWELL   'Tis indeed all mad stuff.

MARSILIA   Your word neither mends nor mars it, that's one comfort. Mr Powell, will you walk off, or be carried off?

POWELL   I'll make use of my legs, if you please, Madam. Your most humble servant.

MARSILIA   Mr Powell, yours. I give you ten thousand thanks for your

trouble. I hope, Mr Powell, you are convinced this play won't fail.
POWELL   Oh lord, Madam, impossible!

Exit

MARSILIA   Well, sure, by this play the Town will perceive what a
    woman can do. I must own, my lord, it stomachs me sometimes to
    hear young fops cry 'There's nothing like Mr Such-a-one's plays, and
    Mr Such-a-one's plays.'
WHIFFLE   But, Madam, I fear our excellent entertainment's over. I
    think all your actors are killed.
MARSILIA   True, my lord, they are most of 'em dispatched. But now,
    my lord, comes one of my surprises. I make an end of my play in
    The World in the Moon.
WHIFFLE   In The World in the Moon!
PRAISEALL   Prodigious!
MARSILIA   Scene-men! Where the devil are these blockheads?
    Scene-men!
(WITHIN)   Here, here.
MARSILIA   Come, one of your finest scenes, and the very best that
    ye know must be when the Emperor and Empress appear.
SCENE-MEN   How d'ye like this, Madam?
MARSILIA   Ay, ay, that will do.
WHIFFLE   'Tis everything the stage can afford in perfection.
PRAISEALL   And which no stage in the world can equal.
MARSILIA   O fie! Mr Praiseall, you often go to Lincoln's Inn Fields.
PRAISEALL   I have said it, let t'other house take it how they will.
WHIFFLE   What, are these men, or monsters?
MARSILIA   My lord, this is very true. I'll believe the historian for he
    was there, my lord. The World in the Moon is as fine a place as this
    he represents. But the inhabitants are a little shallow, and go, as you
    see, upon all fours. Now I design Amorous and Isabella shall bring
    in such a reformation. Then all the heroes of the moon-world shall
    fall in love with Isabella, as, you know, in *Aureng-Zebe* they are all
    in love with Indamora. Oh, that's sweet, a pretty name, but a deuce
    on't, my brother Bay's has scarce left a pretty name for his successors.
PRAISEALL   Dear Madam, are these crawling things to speak, or no?
MARSILIA   Patience is a great virtue, Mr Praiseall.
AWDWELL   (And your spectators must exercise it, o' my conscience.)
MARSILIA   Pray now, my lord, be pleased to suppose this is the
    Emperor's wedding day. Music and dance.

Dance upon all fours. Song

    What's the whispering for?
ONE OF THEM   Why, Madam, to tell you the truth, in short, we are

not able to continue in this posture any longer, without we break our backs. So we have unanimously resolved to stand upright.

All the men and women stand upright

PRAISEALL   Hey! Here's another surprise!

MARSILIA   O! The Devil! You have spoilt my plot! You have ruined my play, ye blockheads! Ye villains, I'll kill you all, burn the book, and hang myself!

Throws down the book and stamps upon it. WHIFFLE *takes it up*

WHIFFLE   Hold, Madam! Don't let passion provoke you, like the knight of old, to destroy what after-ages cannot equal.

MARSILIA   Why, my lord, Amorous and Isabella was to come in and there would have been such a scene! Asses! Idiots! Jolts! But they shall never speak a line of mine, if it would save 'em from inevitable ruin. I'll carry it to t'other house this very moment.

AWDWELL   Won't ye go home to dinner first?

MARSILIA   Dinner be damned! I'll never eat more. See too if any of their impudent people come to beg my pardon, or appease me, well. . . I will go, that's resolved.

PRAISEALL   Madam, consider, could they not stoop again when Isabella's come in. I'll try how 'tis. (*Stoops*) 'Ouns, 'tis devilish painful.

MARSILIA   Don't tell me 'tis painful. If they'll do nothing for their livings let 'em starve and be hanged. My chair there.

WHIFFLE   Madam, my coach is at your service, it waits without.

MARSILIA   (To be in my lord's coach is some consolation.) My lord, I desire to go directly into Lincoln's Inn Fields.

WHIFFLE   Where you please, Madam.

MARSILIA   I'll never set my foot again upon this confounded stage. My opera shall be first, and my *Catiline* next, which, I'd have these to know, shall absolutely break 'em. They may shut up their doors, stroll or starve or do whatever the devil puts in their hands, no more of Marsilia's works, I assure 'em. Come, my lord.

AWDWELL   You won't go, Madam?

MARSILIA   By my soul, I will. Your damned ill-humour began my misfortunes. Farewell, Momus. Farewell, idiots. Hoarse be your voices, rotten your lungs, want of wit and humour continue upon your damned poets, and poverty consume you all!

Exit

PRAISEALL   What, ne'er a word to me! Or did she put me among the idiots? Sir, the lady's gone.

AWDWELL   And you may go after. There's something to help you forward. (*Kicks him*)

PRAISEALL   I intend, Sir, I intend it.

Exit

Enter MR POWELL, MRS KNIGHT, MRS CROSS *etc., laughing*

AWDWELL   So, what's the news now?

POWELL   Oh, my sides! My sides! The wrathful lady has run over a chair, shattered the glasses to pieces. The chair-men, to save it, fell pell-mell in with her. She has lost part of her tail, broke her fan, tore her ruffles, and pulled off half my lord Whiffle's wig, with trying to rise by it. So they are, with a chagrin air, and tattered dress, gone into the coach. Mr Praiseall thrust in after 'em, with the bundle of fragments his care had picked up from under the fellow's feet. Come, to make some atonement, entertain this gentleman with the dance you are practising for the next new play.

A dance

AWDWELL   Mr Powell, if you'll do me the favour to dine with me, I'll prevent the dinner I bespoke going to Marsilia's lodgings, and we'll eat it here.

POWELL   With all my heart. I am at your service.

AWDWELL   Thus warned,
I'll leave the scribbler to her fops, and fate;
I find she's neither worth my love or hate.

CHRONOLOGY

ABBREVIATIONS: BS — Bridges St Theatre; DG — Dorset Garden Theatre; DL — Drury Lane Theatre; LIF — Lincoln's Inn Fields Theatre; Q — Queen's Theatre, Haymarket.

DATE	THE COUNTRY	THE THEATRE	THE FEMALE WITS
			?1625 Birth of Cavendish
			1631 Jan Birth of Philips
			?1632 Birth of Wharton
			?1640 Birth of Behn
1660	May Accession of Charles II	Thomas Killigrew granted patent for King's Co. at Gibbon's tennis court, Vere St, and Davenant granted patent for Duke's Co. at Salisbury Court	
1661		June Lisle's tennis court in Lincoln's Inn Fields opened as theatre for Duke's Co.	
1662	Charter granted to Royal Society		Feb Cavendish's *Kingdom's Intelligencer* (14 plays) published

1663	May King's Co. move to new theatre in Bridges St, Drury Lane Aug Lord Chamberlain orders arrest of all acting without authority		May Possible London production of Philips' *Pompey*
1664	Dryden/Howard's *Indian Queen* at BS	June Death of Philips	
1665	June Lord Chamberlain's decree closes all theatres until winter of 1666		
1666	Fire of London	Pix born	
1667	Dutch in the Medway Treaty of Breda		
1668	On death of Davenant, actors Thomas Betterton and Henry Harris manage Duke's Co. Dryden becomes Poet Laureate	Feb Philips' *Horace* at Court Cavendish's *Plays* (5) published	
1669		Jan Philips' *Horace* at BS *c.* Aug Boothby's *Marcelia* at BS ? Centlivre born	
1670	Congreve born	*c.* Dec Behn's *Forced Marriage* at LIF	

Additional events:
2nd Dutch War — Plague in London (1665)

DATE	THE COUNTRY	THE THEATRE	THE FEMALE WITS
1671		Buckingham's *Rehearsal* at BS, Nov Duke's Co. move from LIF to new Dorset Garden Theatre	? Polwhele's *Frolic* c. May Behn's *Amorous Prince* at LIF
1672	3rd Dutch War	Jan BS demolished by fire, King's Co. move into LIF Dryden's *Marriage à La Mode* at LIF	?Manley born
1673	Test Act against Catholics		Jan Death of Cavendish Feb Behn's *Dutch Lover* at DG
1674	Peace with Dutch	Mar King's Co. move to Wren's new theatre in Drury Lane	
1675		Dryden's *Aureng-Zebe* at DL, Wycherley's *Country Wife* at DL	
1676		William Smith replaces Harris as co-manager of Duke's Co. Sept Lord Chamberlain replaces Killigrew as manager of King's Co. with actors Charles Hart, Michael Mohun, Edward Kynaston and William Cartwright Etherege's *Man of Mode* at DG	c. Sept Behn's *Abdelazer* at DG c. Sept Behn's *Town Fop* at DG

Year			
1677	Nov Marriage of William of Orange to Princess Mary	Dryden's *All for Love* at DL Lee's *Rival Queens* at DL Feb Charles Hart takes full authority for King's Co. Conflicts within the co. continue over next few years	Mar Behn's *Rover* at DG May La Roche-Guilhen's *Rare En Tout* at Court
1678	Popish Plot		Jan Behn's *Sir Patient Fancy* at DG
1679	First Whig Parliament May First Exclusion Bill July Parliament dissolved Aug Charles II dangerously ill Sept James, Duke of York and Monmouth exiled		c. Mar Behn's *Feigned Courtesans* at DG Aug Trotter born c. Sept Behn's *Young King* at DG
1680		Charles Killigrew becomes manager of King's Co. Otway's *Orphan* at DG	
1681	King dissolves Parliament at Oxford		c. April Behn's *Rover* (2nd Part) at DG c. Nov Behn's *False Count* at DG c. Dec Behn's *Roundheads* at DG
1682		May Smith and Betterton take over King's Co. and United Co. is formed. Only one theatre now active in London Otway's *Venice Preserv'd* at DG	c. Mar Behn's *City Heiress* at DG Mar Behn's 'Like Father Like Son' at DG Aug Behn's pro. and epi. to *Romulus and Hersilia*

DATE	THE COUNTRY	THE THEATRE	THE FEMALE WITS
1683	Rye House Plot	Death of Thomas Killigrew	
1684			
1685	Feb Death of Charles II Accession of James II Duke of Monmouth's rebellion	Official mourning closes theatres 5 Feb–27 April Death of Otway	
1686	Pro-Catholic laws introduced		Feb Wharton's *Love's Martyr* registered April Behn's *Lucky Chance* at DL
1687			*c.* Mar Behn's *Emperor of the Moon* at DG
1688	Birth of Prince to James Glorious Revolution Nov William III lands at Torbay and becomes King when James flees country		April Death of Behn
1689	Toleration Act	Shadwell made Poet Laureate	
1690	Battle of the Boyne		*c.* Nov Behn's *Widow Ranter* at DL
1691		United Co. direct energies more into operatic spectacles than drama. Death of Etherege	

Year		
1692	Death of Lee	
	Death of Shadwell	
1693	Autumn Alexander Davenant, proprietor of United Co., absconds, Sir Thomas Skipwith and Christopher Rich acquire greater financial control	
	Congreve's *Old Batchelor* at DL	
1694	Death of Queen Mary	Dec Death of Queen Mary closes theatres
	Bank of England founded	
1695	Actors Thomas Betterton, Elizabeth Barry and Anne Bracegirdle rebel against Skipwith and Rich, and set up their own co. at LIF when theatres re-open in April	*c.* Sept 'Ariadne's' *She Ventures and He Wins* at LIF
	Congreve's *Love for Love* at LIF	*c.* Dec Trotter's *Agnes de Castro* at DL
	Southerne's *Oroonoko* at DL	
1696	Jan All plays to be licensed, by order of Parliament	*c.* Feb Behn's *Younger Brother* at DL
	Vanbrugh's *The Relapse* at DL	*c.* Mar Manley's *Lost Lover* at DL
		c. April Manley's *Royal Mischief* at LIF
		May Pix's *Ibrahim 13th* at DL
		Sept Pix's *Spanish Wives* at DL

DATE	THE COUNTRY	THE THEATRE	THE FEMALE WITS
1697		June Obscenities and other scandalous matters to be deleted by Master of Revels Vanbrugh's *The Provoked Wife* at LIF. ? *The Female Wits* at DL	*c.* June at LIF Pix's *Innocent Mistress* *c.* Aug at LIF A Young Lady's *Unnatural Mother* *c.* Nov at LIF Pix's *Deceiver Deceived*
1698		Collier's *Short View* published	*c.* May at LIF Trotter's *Fatal Friendship* *c.* June at LIF Pix's *Queen Catherine*
1699			
1700		Death of Dryden DL adapted by Rich to increase audience capacity. Actors forced ten feet back into the proscenium arch Congreve's *Way of the World* at LIF	*c.* May at LIF Pix's *False Friend* at LIF Mar Pix's *Beau Defeated* at LIF Sept at DL Centlivre's *Perjured Husband* Nov at DL Trotter's *Love at a Loss*
1701	Act of Settlement Death of James II		Feb at DL Trotter's *Unhappy Penitent* *c.* Mar at LIF Pix's *Czar of Muscovy* Mar at LIF Pix's *Double Distress* at LIF *c.* Oct at LIF Wiseman's *Antiochus*

1702	Mar Death of William III Accession of Queen Anne July Tories in Mar Daily Courant, first English daily newspaper, published by Elizabeth Mallet	Mar Theatres closed for mourning, 8–23 April	June at LIF Centlivre's Beau's Duel Dec at LIF Centlivre's Stolen Heiress
1703		June Vanbrugh buys land in Haymarket for new theatre	June at DL Centlivre's Love's Contrivance Nov Pix's Different Widows at LIF
1704	Aug Battle of Blenheim	Jan Lord Chamberlain's order: all plays to be performed, old or new, songs, prologues and epilogues to be licensed. Restrictions on wearing of masks by women in theatres	
1705	Oct Whigs in	April Queen's Theatre, Haymarket opens. Actors' Co. leave LIF and join Vanbrugh's Co. July Actors' Co. return to LIF until autumn when Q acoustics are improved	Feb Centlivre's Gamester at LIF May Pix's Conquest of Spain at Q Nov at DL Centlivre's Basset Table

DATE	THE COUNTRY	THE THEATRE	THE FEMALE WITS
1706	Battle of Ramillies Conquest of the Netherlands	Owen Swiny takes over management of Q, some of Rich's DL Co. permitted to act with Queen's Co. as Rich turns more towards singing, dancing and exotic entertainments Farquhar's *The Recruiting Officer* at DL	Feb *Trotter's Revolution of Sweden* at Q June Pix's *Adventures in Madrid* at Q Nov Centlivre's *Platonic Lady* at Q Dec Manley's *Almyna* at Q
1707	Union with Scotland	Farquhar's *Beaux' Stratagem* at LIF	
1708		LIF advertised to let as tennis court Jan London companies unite at DL. Q specialises in Italian opera	
1709	*Tatler* first published	DG demolished. Autumn Betterton's Co. returns to Q, rival co. under Aaron Hill at DL	*c.* May Death of Pix May Centlivre's *Busy Body* at DL Dec Centlivre's *Man's Bewitched* at Q
1710	Sept Tories in	Nov Licence issued to Swiny, Wilks, Cibber and Dogget at DL, now sole drama co. in London	Mar Centlivre's *Bickerstaff's Burying* at DL Dec Centlivre's *Mar-plot at* DL
1711	*Spectator* first published		Death of Mme La Roche-Guilhen

Year		
1712		Jan Centlivre's *Perplexed Lovers* at DL
1713	Addison's *Cato* at DL	
1714	Aug Death of Queen Anne Accession of George I Dec Monopoly on drama broken by opening of new LIF theatre under John Rich	April Centlivre's *Wonder!* at DL
1715	Jacobite Rebellion	Centlivre's *Gotham Election* published
1716		May Davys' *Northern Heiress* at LIF Dec Centlivre's *Cruel Gift* at DL
1717	LIF managed by Theosophilus Keene and Christopher Bullock Birth of David Garrick	May Manley's *Lucius* at DL
1718		Feb Centlivre's *Bold Stroke for a Wife* at LIF
1719		May Aubert's *Harlequin Hydaspes* at LIF

DATE	THE COUNTRY	THE THEATRE	THE FEMALE WITS
1720		Dec New Theatre in Haymarket opens, used principally by foreign companies	
			1722 Oct Centlivre's *Artifice* at DL
			1723 Dec Death of Centlivre
			1724 Mar Centlivre's *Wife Well Managed* at Q
			July Death of Manley
			1749 May Death of Trotter

NOTES

BACKGROUND

1. Thomas Shadwell, *The Virtuoso* (1677), act I; scene V.
2. *A Room of One's Own* (1928) chapter 3.
3. Hugh Hunt, 'Restoration Acting', in *Restoration Theatre*, ed. John Russell Brown and Bernard Harris (1965).
4. *A Short View of the Prophaneness and Immorality of the English Stage* (1698)
5. 'Whenever she acted any of these. . . parts, she forced tears from the eyes of her auditory', John Downes, *Roscius Anglicanus* (1708); 'Mrs Barry made this complaint in so pathetic a manner as drew tears from the greatest part of the audience', Thomas Betterton, *History of the English Stage* (1741), etc.
6. The Theatre Royal, Bridges Street, had a total area of 6,496 square feet; *the stage* of the current Theatre Royal, Drury Lane, has an area of 6,400 square feet.
7. During a performance of Joe Orton's *Entertaining Mr Sloane*.

KATHERINE PHILIPS

1. John Aubrey, *Brief Lives, c.* 1670—93, ed. Oliver Lawson Dick (1950).
2. Jeremy Taylor, *Works,* ed. Reginald Heber (1828).
3. Ibid.
4. *Letters from Orinda to Poliarchus* (2nd ed., 1729).
5. 'To Mrs M.A.'
6. *Letters.*
7. Ibid.
8. Ibid.
9. Ibid.
10. Ibid.
11. Ibid.
12. Ibid.
13. Ibid.
14. Ibid.
15. Ibid.
16. Ibid.
17. Ibid.
18. Ibid.
19. Ibid.
20. Entry for 1662—3 season in *The London Stage*, ed. William Van Lennep, Part I (1965).
21. *Letters.*
22. Ibid.

23. *Biographia Dramatica* (1812). Initially written by David Erskine Baker in 1764, it was continued by Isaac Reed and Stephen Jones up to 1812.
24. Introduction to *Works of Katherine Philips* (1710).
25. B.M. Add. MSS 36916, folio 62.
26. Pepys, *Diary*, 19 January 1669.
27. Preface to *Pompey*.
28. *Letters.*
29. *Works of Katherine Philips.*
30. Aubrey, *Brief Lives.*

APHRA BEHN
 1. George Woodcock, *The Incomparable Aphra* (1948).
 2. Aphra Behn, *Oroonoko* (1688).
 3. Ibid.
 4. Williamson's State Papers, PRO.SP.29/167, no. 160 (16 August 1666-N.S.).
 5. Ibid., PRO.SP.29/169, no. 118 (31 August 1666-N.S.).
 6. Ibid., PRO.SP.29/169, no. 38 (27 August 1666-N.S.).
 7. Ibid., PRO.SP.29/170, no. 75 (5 September 1666-N.S.).
 8. John Evelyn, *Diary,* 5 September 1666.
 9. Annexed to S.P. Dom. Car. II. 251, no. 91.
10. Downes, *Roscius Anglicanus.*
11. *Works of Aphra Behn.* ed. Montague Summers. (1915).
12. Gerard Langbaine. *An Account of the Lives and Characters of the English Dramatic Poets* (1691).
13. Thomas Shadwell, *The Tory Poets — A Satire* (1682).
14. Lord Chamberlain's Warrant, 12 August 1682.
15. Epilogue to *Romulus and Hersilia.*
16. John Genest, *Some Account of the English Stage* (10 vols, 1832).
17. Anthony Aston, *A Brief Supplement* (1748).
18. Bulstrode Whitelock, *Commonplace Book.*
19. Published as 'Song to Mr J.H.' in *Muses' Mercury* (1707).
20. *Love Letters to a Gentleman,* Letter II.
21. Ibid., Letter III.
22. Ibid., Letter IV.
23. Ibid., Letter VI.
24. Ibid., Letter VII.
25. Anon., published *c.* 1687.
26. 5 vols, (1778—93).
27. J. Doran, *Annals of the English Stage,* ed. R. W. Lowe (1888).
28. *English Women of Letters* (1862).
29. *Lives of the English Dramatic Poets.*
30. Langbaine/Gildon, *Lives and Characters* 1699.
31. *A Room of One's Own.*

CATHERINE TROTTER
1. Thomas Birch, *The Life of Mrs Catherine Cockburn* (appended to his edition of her *Works*) (2 vols, 1751).
2. Ibid.
3. Ibid.
4. Edmund Gosse, *Catherine Trotter, Precursor of the Blue Stockings* (1916).
5. Langbaine/Gildon, *Lives and Characters*.
6. Gosse, *Catherine Trotter*.
7. *William Congreve: Letters and Documents*. ed. John C. Hodge. (1964).
8. Birch, *Catherine Cockburn*.
9. Langbaine/Gildon, *Lives and Characters*.
10. Birch, *Catherine Cockburn*.
11. Ibid.
12. Ibid.
13. Ibid.
14. Genest, *Some Account of the English Stage*.
15. Quoted in Gosse, *Catherine Trotter*.
16. Paul Hazard, *The European Mind 1680–1715* (1964).
17. Birch, *Catherine Cockburn*.
18. Ibid.
19. Congreve, *Letters*.
20. Birch, *Catherine Cockburn*.
21. Ibid.
22. Ibid.
23. Ibid.
24. Ibid.
25. Ibid.
26. Ibid.
27. Ibid.
28. Gosse, *Catherine Trotter*.
29. Birch, *Catherine Cockburn*.

MARY DELARIVIER MANLEY
1. *The Adventures of Rivella* (1714).
2. Sloane MS. f. 117. 1708.
3. *Adventures of Rivella*.
4. Edmund Curll (ed.) Introduction to *Memoirs of the Life of Mrs Manley*, a re-issue of *Rivella* (1725).
   Adventures of Rivella.
6. Ibid.
7. Ibid.
8. Ibid.
9. *Secret Memoirs and Manners of Several Persons of Quality, of both sexes. From the New Atalantis, an Island in the Mediterranean, written originally in Italian* (1709).

10. Ibid.
11. Ibid.
12. Ibid.
13. Ibid.
14. Ibid.
15. *Adventures of Rivella.*
16. Ibid.
17. Ibid.
18. Ibid.
19. Ibid.
20. Preface to *The Lost Lover* (1696).
21. Giles Jacob, *Poetical Register* (1719).
22. 'To the Reader' – *The Royal Mischief.*
23. Ibid.
24. Ibid.
25. Ibid.
26. *Adventures of Rivella.*
27. Ibid.
28. Ibid.
29. Ibid.
30. *Memoirs of Europe.*
31. *Adventures of Rivella.*
32. (*London Stage* entry for 16.12.1706). Seat prices were raised 'by reason of the extraordinary charges for habits' and the play was performed the immediate week before Christmas, and this is seen as the reason for the play not achieving the success all expected.
33. *New Atalantis.*
34. Narcissus Luttrell, *A Brief Historical Relation of State Affairs* (1857).
35. Ibid.
36. *Adventures of Rivella.*
37. *Letters and Works of Lady Mary Wortley Montagu*, ed. W. Moy Thomas. (1893).
38. Jonathan Swift, *Journal to Stella*, 14.4.1711.
39. Ibid. 14.4.1711.
40. Ibid. 28.1.1712.
41. Edmund Curll, *Impartial History of John Barber* (1741).
42. Ibid.
43. *Notes and Queries; Article by Augustus de Morgan* (1856).
44. *Adventures of Rivella.*

MARY PIX
 1. Anon. *A Comparison Between the Two Stages* (1702).
 2. According to *Les Régistres de L'Académie Française* (1672–1793), the bienniel 'Prix de Poésie' was awarded in August 1697 to Mlle Bernard, in 1699 it was shared by M. L'Abbé Mongin and M. de

Clerville, and in 1701 it was again won by a woman, Mme Durand.

3. *Animadversions on Mr Congreve's Late Answer* (1698).
4. Dedication to *The Deceiver Deceived.*
5. Prologue to *Queen Catherine.*
6. Genest, *Some Account of the English Stage.*
7. Downes, *Roscius Anglicanus.*
8. Langbaine/Gildon, *Lives and Characters.*
9. Joseph Trapp, *The Players Turned Academics* (1703).
10. *The Post Boy,* 26—8 May 1709.

SUSANNAH CENTLIVRE

1. *Notes and Queries* (September 1953).
2. Jacob, *Poetical Register.*
3. In *The Political State of Great Britain,* vol. 26 (1723).
4. Jacob, *Poetical Register.*
5. Mottley, *Compleat List of English Dramatic Poets* (1747).
6. Ibid.
7. Ibid.
8. Act III, scene ii.
9. Preface to *The Platonic Lady.*
10. 16 June 1703.
11. Preface to *The Platonic Lady.*
12. Dedication to *The Basset Table.*
13. *Apology for the Life of Colley Cibber* (1740).
14. Mottley, *Compleat List.*
15. Dedication to *The Platonic Lady.*
16. Drury Lane, 12 May 1709.
17. Mottley, *Compleat List.*
18. No. 19, 24 May 1709.
19. Mottley, *Compleat List.*
20. Ibid.
21. 12—14 December 1709.
22. *Mar-plot,* December 1710 entry in *The London Stage.*
23. Preface to *The Perplexed Lovers.*
24. Ibid.
25. Ibid.
26. *The Examiner,* 16 September 1816.
27. Dedication to *The Gotham Election.*
28. Ibid.
29. Ibid.
30. 1717.
31. *Oxford English Dictionary,* 3rd ed 1933.
32. *Daily Journal,* 7 November 1722.
33. Mottley, *Compleat List.*
34. W.R. Chetwood, *The British Theatre* (1750).
35. Trapp, *Players Turned Academics.*

THE OTHER WOMEN PLAYWRIGHTS

1. Gerard Langbaine.
2. John Verney to Edward Verney, quoted in 29 May 1677 entry in *The London Stage.*
3. Presumably the Duchess of Portsmouth, Louise de Quérouaille, Charles II's principal mistress.
4. *The True News; or: Mercurius Anglicus,* 4–7 February 1680.
5. Dedication to 'Love's Martyr'.
6. Add. MS. 28693.
7. Preface to *She Ventures and He Wins.*
8. Act I, scene i.
9. Preface to *The Northern Heiress.*
10. *The Northern Heiress,* act I.
11. Ibid.
12. Preface to *The Self Rival.*
13. Langbaine, *An Account of the Lives and Characters of the English Dramatic Poets.* 1691.
14. *Some Account of the English Stage.*
15. Preface to *Plays Never Before Printed* (1668).
16. *Sociable Letters,* no. CL.
17. Christopher Hatton, *Correspondence,* 7 August 1665 (vol. 1).
18. *A True Relation* (1814).
19. Letter quoted in Introduction to Everyman edition of *Life of. . . William Cavendish.*
20. Pepys, *Diary,* 30 May 1667.
21. Ibid. 30 May 1667.
22. Ibid. 26 April 1667.
23. Ibid. 30 March 1667.
24. *Nature's Pictures* (1656).
25. *True Relation.*
26. *To My Lady Margaret Cavendish, Choosing the Name Policrite.*

GLOSSARY TO THE PLAYS

adamantine stone — unbreakable stone

Alamanzor — the romantic lead in Dryden's *Conquest of Granada*

Alexander — Alexander the Great had two wives, Roxana and Statira, the main characters in Lee's *Rival Queens*

alguazil — Spanish arresting officer

allay — to put down or calm, or to mix with something inferior

allons — let us go

Alsatia — sanctuary district of Whitefriars. Refuge for people wishing to avoid bailiffs and creditors

anotherguess — of a different kind

antic — as if mad

apocryphal — spurious

Apple John — a kind of apple said to keep two years and to be in perfection when shrivelled and withered

Aqua Mirabilis — a preparation distilled from cloves, nutmeg, ginger, and spirit of wine

assafetida — ill-smelling medicinal gum resin

assiduous — constant

Aureng-Zebe — Dryden's play, in which a mother falls in love with her step-son

avant — move on

bandstrings — strings for fastening collar

Mrs Bantum's — Bantum's coffee house near Guildhall

bark — small sailing ship

Mr Barnadine — dissolute prisoner in Shakespeare's *Measure for Measure*

basilisks — fabulous creatures a foot long, with fiery death-dealing eyes and breath

baulk — disappointment, thwarting

Bedlam — Bethlehem Royal Hospital for the insane. Open to sightseers for 2 pence entrance fee

Billingsgate — coarse talk

'The Blue Posts' — a tavern at 59, Haymarket

bob — rap, jerk

bonaroba — harlot

bottom — the lower part of a ship; hence the ship itself

bow strings — a string with which the Turks strangled offenders

bowed on her knees to every stick and stone — Catholic observance of shrines

branches — Restoration theatres were lit by candles held in chandeliers and branches from the walls

brethren of broad hats and narrow bands — Quakers

broil — quarrel

Brother Bay — the Poet Laureate; currently Dryden

bubbies — women's breasts

bumper — a full glass, particularly of an alcoholic beverage

bushel — measure of 8 gallon capacity for corn or fruit

buss — rude or playful kiss

cannic — canonical. Hours in which marriages could take place legally — 8–12 a.m.

cap-à-pied — from head to foot

catechise — question

Catiline's Conspiracy — play by Ben Jonson

Cato . . . Hortensius — Cato Uticensis gave away his wife Marcia to Hortensius in 56 BC. When Hortensius died in 50 BC. Cato is said to have taken her back

caudle cup — cup used for spiced warm gruel with sugar and wine especially for invalids

Cerberus — monster that guarded the entrance to Hades, a dog with three heads

chaplets — wreaths

chymistry — alchemy, trying to turn base metal into gold

cit — citizen

clack — tongue

clothes-press — wardrobe

coffee — was thought in the seventeenth century to have medicinal and dietary properties

commonplace book — notebook for keeping notable passages, platitudes

condign — severe and well deserved

consign — hand over

contagion — infectious disease

cordial water — aromatised and sweetened spirit

corrector — legal adviser

Court of Orleans — French Court of Louis XIV

cross — wrong

cross-question — crossword

Cuckolds' Haven — a well-known point in the Thames, on the south side opposite Limehouse Pier

cuffs — foolish old men

cullies (verb) — cheats, deceives

cully (noun) — dupe, fellow

cur — contemptible scoundrel

deflixion — deviation

demi-culverin — small firearm, cannon

derogates — detracts

Diana — Roman goddess of the moon and the hunt; a virgin

docity — gumption

Doctors' Commons — College of Law at Benet's Hill, St Paul's Churchyard
dog (verb) — follow
dornex — stout, figured linen
drubbed — cudgelled, beaten
dudgeon — small dagger
duenna — chaperon
dunner — importunate creditor
dunning — demanding payment
Mr Eccles — John Eccles, resident composer at Lincoln's Inn Fields
edification — spiritual benefit
eight parts of speech — elements of a sentence: noun, adjective, verb,
    adverb, pronoun, preposition, conjunction, exclamation
ela — sharp of *la* in Tonic Sol-fa
eluded — escaped
Elysium — abode of the blessed after death. State of ideal happiness
The Emperor of the Moon — very successful farce by Aphra Behn
encomium — highflown praise
English Geneva — gin distilled from grain with juniper berries
equipage — outfit, servants, etc.
except — unless
extempore — impromptu
Fanus — ancient Italian god represented with one face on front and
    another on back of head
Mr Finger — composer of popular songs
Finsbury hero — Finsbury Fields was a popular site for archery
flabber chops — fat, puffed-out cheeks
flaged — flapped feebly, grew languid
flagitious — grossly wicked
fly — familiar, demon
foments — fosters
fortune de la guerre — luck of war
France and Philip — Philip V was first Bourbon King of Spain
Gargantua — giant of medieval legend, famous for his huge appetite;
    anti-hero of Rabelais' *Gargantua and Pantagruel*
geometry — magic
George in Whitefriars — tavern in Dogwell Court, within the privileges
    of Alsatia
glasses — carriage windows; mirrors
go snacks — go shares
'good Trebonius' — 'Though last, not least in love. . . good Trebonius'
    Julius Caesar, III i, 189
Gordian knot — an intricate problem
grandee — nobleman of the highest rank
grannum — grandmother
greensickness — anaemic disease of young women

guinea — obsolete English gold coin, valued at twenty-one shillings
gutling — guzzling
Guy of Warwick — old slang name for a sword, rapier
habiliments — clothing
hackney coach — coach let out for hire
half in kilter — half spirited
Haunce in Kelder — unborn child in the womb
hautboys — oboes
Henry the Eighth — production of this Shakespeare play by Davenant
    in 1663, famous for its extravagance
Mr Hodgson — singer
hoiting — giddy
Horn Fair — men would go to find cheap prostitutes at the fairs. At
    Horn Fair, parties sailed from London to Cuckolds' Point (Haven)
    then, wearing horns, walked to Charlton where Horn Fair was held
horns — cuckold's horns
hot cockles — lecherous
Mrs Hudson — singer reputed for her interpretation of the works of
    Finger
Hymen — god of marriage
imprecations — prayers
imputation — censure
indentures — deeds under seal
inexorable — unyielding
investing — being besieged
jantee — elegant, nautical
jiggiting — jumping about and fidgeting
jilts — skittish, flighty young women
Joan Sanderson — air to the Cushion Dance
jointure — property settled on a woman at marriage to be enjoyed
    after her husband's death
ladies of quality in the middle gallery — the middle gallery was
    frequented often by ladies of the town
laid in lavender — pawned
langoone — kind of white wine
leads of castle — frontage
lighter — large open boat used in unloading and loading ships
litter — vehicle containing couch, shut in by curtains
livery and seisin — law signifying the delivery of property into the
    corporal possession of a person
Locket's — fashionable eating-house in Charing Cross
lubberly — clumsy
lucre — financial profit
mantua — woman's loose gown

meridian — midday position of the sun

Merlin — dramatic opera by Dryden/Purcell, possibly revived in 1695
    and updated

Metridate, King o' the Potecaries — *Mithridates, King of Pontus,*
    tragedy by Lee

mien — bearing

misericordia — have pity on me; dagger for final *coup de grâce*

moidores — former Portuguese gold coins

moil — drudge

Momus — ridiculous person, the critic god

montre moi votre chambre — pidgin French: 'show me your room'

Morocco — Settle's *Empress of Morocco*

Mr Motteux — Peter Motteux, songwriter and playwright

Newgate — prison

Newmarket Road — road famous for highwaymen

nick — thwart

niggard — one who grudges to spend or give away

nonage — youth

notionary — fanciful

nymphs of Drury — prostitutes

The Old Batchelor — Congreve's first comedy

opiate draught — sleep-inducing drink

Oranges and Lemons — Orangemen, notably the king, William; lemons =
    lemans, illicit lovers

ordinary — place where a meal is provided at a fixed charge; the meal
    itself

pads — robs on foot

paeans — songs of thanksgiving or triumph

parley — conference

pate — head

peach — inform against

perdue — hidden, lost

perruke — wig

pet — temper

philtre — spell to excite love, a drink

phiz — face, physiognomy

pickeer — forage or flirt

pinnace — small boat

pistoles — gold coins

posset — drink made of milk, curdled as with wine or vinegar

pot guns — pop guns

presage — omen

primer — elementary school book

Priscian — Latin grammarian

proscribed — put on list of those who may be put to death
Proserpine — daughter of Ceres who spent half the year in the underworld
    and half on earth
pulvil — perfumed powder
quarter staff — stout pole 6-8 feet long
quean — woman of worthless character
Queen Statira — Alexander the Great had two wives, Roxana and
    Statira, the main characters in Lee's *Rival Queens*
randy — violent
rant — bombastic declamatory speech
recruit — replenishment
refractory — perverse
regalio — a present, especially food or drink
rib — wife
Rosamund's Pond — favourite meeting-place for lovers in SW corner
    of St James's Park
sack — Spanish white wine
St Martin's trumpery — cheap jewellery, forgeries
St Omer's — town twenty-five miles inland from Calais, with a Jesuit
    seminary
Salamanca doctor — Titus Oates, engineer of the Popish Plot, pretended
    to have taken his degree in divinity at the University of Salamanca
salute — kiss
sash — window frame
scanty sand — short time
scour — drive away
scrip — small bag
scrivener — scribe
Sebastian — tragedy by Dryden
sell switches — offering for sale a cheap article in order to interest
    buyer in dearer purchase
Settle's 'Poet in Ordinary' for the Lord Mayor's Show — Settle regularly
    wrote the pageant for the 'Triumphs of London'
shade — ghost
sharper — cheat
sheep-biters — butchers
shees — banshees, female fairies who wail before a death
sherbet — fruit-juice drink
side-face — profile
Sir-reverence under your girdle — the speaker is rebuked for not
    honouring the character's full title
small beer — weak beer
snicker snee — fight with knives
Snowhill — steep road from Holborn to Newgate prison

spado — sword
Spittal sermon — Easter sermon preached at St Mary Spittal
stiletto - small dagger
struck in a maze — amazed
superscription — address
swear the peace — take oath before a magistrate that a certain person
    should be put under bond to keep the peace
taking of Jerusalem — Crowne's *Destruction of Jerusalem*
tale of a tub — inconsequential story
tarpaulin — sea-bred officer
teaster — sixpence
termagant — boisterous woman
There is no other she — play on Elizabeth Barry's famous line from
    Dryden's *Spanish Friar*: 'There is no other *he*'.
Thetis — sea nymph
third day — third performance was the author's benefit
three-farthings — Elizabethan silver coin, ¾ of a penny
Timon the Atheist — Shadwell's *Timon of Athens*
toilet — dressing-table
token — coin or voucher
Tom Dingle — simpleton
top upon him — cheat at dice
toss the stocking — old matrimonial custom
treat — men's favour
trepanned — trapped, beguiled
trim tram — absurdity
Trinculo says — in fact Stephano does, in Shakespeare's and Dryden's
    Tempest
truckle — low bed
tub — contemporary treatment of VD included long sessions in hot baths
twire — glance, peer
an ugly black devil kills his wife — Shakespeare's *Othello*
usurer — a money-lender
varlet — rascal
vial — vessel for liquids; small medicine bottle; a spirit-level
vicissitude — alteration
votary — devoted worshipper
wait — escort
whatever is in the wardrobe — the theatre's wardrobe stock included
    gowns discarded by royalty, among them the coronation gown of
    Queen Mary of Modena
within-side — inside
Wittal — Newgate prison
The World in the Moon — dramatic opera by Settle/Purcell

wormwood — bitterness
woundy — excessively
yare — skilful, quickly

CHECKLISTS

In the following lists the dates refer to first publication; elsewhere in the book, unless otherwise stated, dates refer to first performance.

KATHERINE PHILIPS

Plays
    Horace, trans. from Corneille, completed by Sir John Denham (1671).
    Pompey, trans. from Corneille (1663).

Non-dramatic works
    Letters from Orinda to Poliarchus (1705; 2nd ed., 1720).
    Poems by the Incomparable Mrs K.P. (1664).
    Poems. . . , to which is added Corneille's 'Pompée' & 'Horace' (1667).

Attributed works
    The Crooked Six-pence (1743).

Collected works (1664, 1667, 1669, 1678)

APHRA BEHN

Plays
    Abdelazer, or: *The Moor's Revenge* (1677).
    The Amorous Prince, or: *The Curious Husband* (1671).
    The City Heiress, or: *Sir Timothy Treat-all* (1682).
    The Dutch Lover (1673).
    The Emperor of the Moon (1687).
    The False Count, or: *A New Way to Play an Old Game* (1682).
    The Feigned Courtesans, or: *A Night's Intrigue* (1679).
    The Forced Marriage, or: *The Jealous Bridegroom* (1671).
    'Like Father Like Son' (only prologue and epilogue survive) (1682).
    The Lucky Chance, or: *An Alderman's Bargain* (1687).
    Romulus and Hersilia (prologue, epilogue and song 'Where art thou')
        (1682).
    The Roundheads, or: *The Good Old Cause* (1682).
    The Rover, or: *The Banished Cavaliers* (1677).
    The Rover, Second Part (1681).
    Sir Patient Fancy (1678).
    The Town Fop, or: *Sir Timothy Tawdry* (1677).
    The Widow Ranter, or: *The History of Bacon in Virginia* (1690).
    The Young King, or: *The Mistake* (1683).
    The Younger Brother, or: *The Amorous Jilt* (1696).

Non-dramatic works
    The Adventure of the Black Lady (1696).
    Aesop's Fables (trans.) (1687).

Agnes de Castro, or: *The Force of Generous Love* (trans. from Mme de Brilhac) (1688).

Congratulatory Poem to her Most Sacred Majesty (1688).

Congratulatory Poem to her Sacred Majesty Queen Mary upon Her Arrival in England (1689).

Congratulatory Poem to the King. . . on the Happy Birthday of the Prince of Wales (1688).

A Discovery of New Worlds (trans. from Fontanelle) (1688).

The Dumb Virgin, or: *The Force of Imagination* (1677).

The Fair Jilt, or: *The Amours of Prince Tarquin and Miranda;* with *The Nun*, or: *The Perjured Beauty* (1688).

Floriana, a Pastoral (1681).

The History of the Nun, or: *The Fair Vow-Breaker* (1689).

History of the Oracles and Cheats of the Pagan Priests (trans. from Fontanelle) (1688).

The Lives of Sundry and Notorious Villains (1678).

Love Letters Between a Nobleman and his Sister (1684).

Love Letters to a Gentleman (1696).

Love of the Plants, book VI: *Of Trees* (1689).

The Lucky Mistake (1689)

Lycidus, or: *The Lover in Fashion, Being an Account from Lycidus to Lysander of his Voyage from the Island of Love* (1684).

Memoirs of the Court of the King of Bantam (1696).

La Montre, or: *The Lover's Watch*, or: *The Art of Making Love, Being Rules for Courtship for every Hour of the Day and Night, & the Case for the Watch* (1685).

Oroonoko, or: *The Royal Slave, A True History* (1688).

Paraphrase on the. . . 'Epistle of Oenone to Paris' in Ovid's 'Epistles', with his Amours, etc. (1727).

Perplexed Prince (1682).

Pindaric on the Death of our Late Sovereign (1685).

Pindaric on the Happy Coronation of His. . . Majesty James II and His Illustrious Consort Queen Mary (1685).

Pindaric Poem to the Rev. Dr Burnet on the Honour he did me of Enquiring after me and my Muse (1689).

Poem humbly Dedicated to the Great Pattern of Piety and Virtue, Catherine Queen Dowager on the Death of her Dear Lord. . . King Charles II (1685).

Poem to Sir Roger L'Estrange on his Third Part of the 'History of the Times' (1688).

Three Histories (1688).

To the Most Illustrious Prince Christopher, Duke of Albemarle, on his Voyage to his Government of Jamaica (1687).

Two Congratulatory Poems to their. . . Majesties (1688).

The Unfortunate Bride, or: *The Blind Lady a Beauty* (1698).

The Unfortunate Happy Lady; a True History (1698)

The Unhappy Mistake, or: *The Impious Vow Punished* (1697).
The Wandering Beauty (1698).

Attributed works
    The Counterfeit Bridegroom, or: *The Defeated Widow* (comedy)
        (1677).
    The Debauchee, or: *The Credulous Cuckold* (comedy) (1677).
    The Ladies Looking Glass to Dress themselves by, or: *The Whole Art*
        of Charming all Mankind (1697).
    The Revenge, or: *A Match in Newgate* (comedy) (1680).
    The Ten Pleasures of Marriage, and. . . the Confession of the New-
        Married Couple (1922 reprint).

Collected poems
    Mrs Behn's *Miscellany* (1685).
    Gildon's *Miscellany* (1692).
    Gildon's *Chorus Poetarum* (1694).
    Muses' Mercury (1707).
    Poems by Eminent Ladies (1757).
    Westminster Drollery (1671).

Collected works
    Histories and Novels of the Late Ingenious Mrs Behn (1696).
    Plays, Histories and Novels of the Ingenious Mrs A. Behn (1871).
    Works of Aphra Behn, ed. Montague Summers (1915).

CATHERINE TROTTER

Plays
    Agnes de Castro (1696).
    The Fatal Friendship (1698).
    Love at a Loss, or: *Most Votes Carry it* (1701). Rewritten as *The*
        Honourable Deceiver, or: *All Right at the Last.*
    The Revolution of Sweden (1707).
    The Unhappy Penitent (1701).

Non-dramatic works
    A Defence of Mr Locke's 'Essay of Human Understanding' (1702).
    A Discourse concerning a Guide in Controversies (1707).
    Notes on Christianity, as old as Creation (1751).
    On the Credibility of the Historical Parts of Scripture (1751).
    On the Infallibility of the Church of Rome (1751).
    On Moral Virtue and its Natural Tendency to Happiness (1751).
    On the Usefulness of Schools and Universities for the Improvement
        of Mind in Right Notions of God (1751).
    Remarks on Mr Seed's Sermon on Moral Virtue (1751)
    Remarks upon an Inquiry into the Origin of Human Appetites and
        Affections (1751).

Remarks on the Principles and Reasonings of Dr Rutherford's 'Essay on the Nature and Obligations of Virtue' (1747).

Remarks upon some Writers in the Controversy concerning the Foundation of Moral Duty and Moral Obligations in The History of the Works of the Learned (1743).

Verses Occasioned by the Busts in the Queen's Hermitage in *The Gentleman's Magazine* (May 1737).

A Vindication of Mr Locke's Christian Principles from the Injurious Imputations of Dr Holdsworth (1751).

Collected works

Works, ed. Thomas Birch (2 vols., 1751).

MARY DELARIVIER MANLEY

Plays

Almyna, or: *The Arabian Vow* (1707).

The Lost Lover, or: *The Jealous Husband* (1696).

Lucius, the First Christian King of Britain (1717).

The Royal Mischief (1696).

Non-dramatic works

The Adventures of Rivella, or: *The history of the author of Atalantis, with secret memoirs and characters of several considerable persons, her contemporaries. Delivered in a conversation to the young Chevalier D'Aumont in Somerset House Garden, by Sir Charles Lovemore. Done into English from the French* (1714).

Bath Intrigues, in four letters to a friend in London (1725).

Court Intrigues, in a collection of original letters from the Island of New Atalantis & c., by the Author of those Memoirs (1711).

The Examiner (writer from 1710. Editor from 1711).

The Female Tatler (writer from 1709).

The Lady's Paquet Broke Open (1706).

Letters Written by Mary de la Rivière Manley (1696). Re-issued as *A Stage-Coach Journey to Exeter, describing the humours on the road, with the characters and adventures of the company. In eight letters to a friend* (1725).

Memoirs of Europe Towards the Close of the Eighth Century, written by Eginardus, secretary and favourite to Charlemagne, and done into English by the translator of the 'New Atalantis' (1710).

A Modest Enquiry into the reasons of the joy expressed by a certain set of people upon the spreading of a report of Her Majesty's death (1714).

The Power of Love, in seven novels (1720).

The Secret History of Queen Zarah and the Zarazians, wherein the amours, intrigues, and gallantries of the Court of Albigion, during her reign, are pleasantly exposed; and as surprising a scene of love

> *and politics represented as perhaps this, or any other age or country,*
> *has hitherto produced. Supposed to be translated from the Italian*
> *copy, now lodged in the Vatican at Rome* (1705).

Secret Memoirs and Manners of Several Persons of Quality, of both
sexes. From the New Atalantis, an island in the Mediterranean,
written originally in Italian (1709).

A True Narrative of what passed at the examination of the Marquis
de Guiscard, at the Cockpit, March 8, 1710–11; his stabbing
Mr Harley (1711).

A True Relation of the several facts and circumstances of the intended
riot and tumult of Queen Elizabeth's birthday; gathered from
authentic accounts (1711).

MARY PIX

Plays

The Adventures in Madrid (1706).
The Beau Defeated, or: *The Lucky Younger Brother* (1700).
The Conquest of Spain (1705).
The Czar of Muscovy (1701).
The Deceiver Deceived (1698).
The Different Widows, or: *Intrigue à la Mode* (1703).
The Double Distress (1701).
The False Friend, or: *The Fate of Disobedience* (1699).
Ibrahim, the Thirteenth Emperor of the Turks (1696).
The Innocent Mistress (1697).
Queen Catherine, or: *The Ruins of Love* (1698).
The Spanish Wives (1696).

Non-dramatic works

Alas! When Charming Sylvia's Son (1697).
The Inhuman Cardinal, or: *Innocence Betrayed* (advertised in 1696
ed. of *Ibrahim*).
To the Right Hon. the Earl of Kent. . . This Poem (1700).
Violenta, or: *The Rewards of Virtue* (1704).

SUSANNAH CENTLIVRE

Plays

The Artifice (1723).
The Basset Table (1705).
The Beau's Duel, or: *A Soldier for the Ladies* (1702).
A Bickerstaff's Burying, or: *Work for the Upholders* (1710).
A Bold Stroke for a Wife (1719).
The Busy Body (1709).
The Cruel Gift, or: *The Royal Resentment* (1717).

The Gamester (1705).
The Gotham Election/The Humours of Elections (1715).
Love at a Venture (1706).
Love's Contrivance, or: *Le Médecin Malgré Lui* (1703).
The Man's Bewitched, or: *The Devil to do about Her* (1710).
Mar-plot, or: *The Second part of 'The Busy Body'* (1711).
The Perjured Husband, or: *The Adventures of Venice* (1700).
The Perplexed Lovers (1712).
The Platonic Lady (1707).
The Stolen Heiress, or: *The Salamanca Doctor Outplotted* (1703).
A Wife Well Managed (1715).
The Wonder! A Woman Keeps a Secret (1714).

Non-dramatic works
Abelard to Heloise (1755).
An Epistle to the King of Sweden (1717).
A Poem Humbly Presented to George, His Most Sacred Majesty (1715).

Collected plays
Works of the Celebrated Mrs Centlivre (1761).
Dramatic works of the celebrated Mrs Centlivre (1872).

THE OTHER WOMEN PLAYWRIGHTS

'ARIADNE'
Play
She Ventures and He Wins (1696).

MME AUBERT
Play
Harlequin Hydaspes (1719).

FRANCES BOOTHBY
Play
Marcelia, or: *The Treacherous Friend* (1670).

MARGARET CAVENDISH
Plays
Kingdom's Intelligencer (14 plays, 1662).
Plays Never Before Printed (5 plays, 1668).

Non-dramatic works
De Vita et Rebus Gestis (1668).
The Description of a New World (1666).
Grounds of Natural Philosophy (1668).
Letters (1676).
Life of. . . William Cavendish (1667).
Nature's Pictures (1656).

Observations upon Experimental Philosophy (1666).
Orations of Divers Sorts (1662).
The Philosophical and Physical Opinions (1655).
Philosophical Fancies (1653).
Philosophical Letters (1664).
Poems and Fancies (1653).
CCXI *Sociable Letters* (1664).
The World's Olio (1655).
A True Relation (1814).

MARY DAVYS
Plays
> *The Northern Heiress,* or: *The Humours of York* (1716).
> *The Self Rival* (1725).

Non-dramatic works
> *The Accomplished Rake,* or: *The Modern Fine Gentleman, being the genuine memoirs of a certain person of distinction* (1756).
> *The Cousins* (1725).
> *Familiar Letters Between a Gentleman and a Lady* (1725).
> *The Lady's Tale* (1725).
> *The Merry Wanderer* (1725).
> *The Modern Poet* (1725).
> *The Reformed Coquet, a surprising novel,* or: *Memoirs of Amorande,* or: *A Fluttering Heart Caught at Last* (1724).

Collected works
> *Works* (1725)

ANNE FINCH
Plays
> *Aristomenes* (1713).
> *Love and Innocence,* in Myra Reynolds (ed.), *Poems of Anne Finch, Countess of Winchilsea* (1903).

Non-dramatic works
> *Collected Poems* (1713).
> *The Spleen, a pindaric ode* (1709).

MME LA ROCHE-GUILHEN
Play
> *Rare En Tout* (1677).

Non-dramatic works
> *Almanzor and Almanzaida* (1676) (trans. into English, 1678).
> *Asteria and Tamberlain* (trans. 1677).
> *The Great Scanderberg* (trans. 1690).

History of Female Favourites (1697).
History of the Royal Genealogy of Spain (1724).
Royal Loves, or: *The Unhappy Prince* (1680).
Zingis, a Tartarian History (1691).

ELIZABETH POLWHELE
Plays
   The Frolics, or *The Lawyer Cheated* (1977)
   The Faithful Virgins (unpublished)

ANNE WHARTON
Play
   Love's Martyr (unpublished).

JANE WISEMAN
Play
   Antiochus the Great, or: *The Fatal Relapse* (1702).

A YOUNG LADY
Play
   The Unnatural Mother, or: *Love's Reward* (1698).

FURTHER READING

THE AGE (history, ideas, culture)

Hill, Christopher. *The Century of Revolution, 1603–1714* (1978)
Stone, Lawrence. *The Crisis of the Aristocracy, 1558–1641* (1965/6)
Willey, Basil. *The Seventeenth Century Background* (1942)

WOMEN

O'Faolain, Julia and Martines, Lauro. *Not in God's Image, Women in History* (1977).
O'Malley, Ida. *Women in Subjection, The Lives of Englishwomen before 1832* (1933).

THE THEATRE

Gagen, J. E. *The New Woman: Her Emergence in the Drama, 1660–1730* (1954).
Harris, Bernard, and Brown, J. Russell (eds). *Restoration Theatre* (essays) (1965).
Highfill, P. H. Jnr, *et al.* (eds). *A Biographical Dictionary of Actors, Actresses, Musicians in London 1660–1800* (1973–   ).
Holland, Norman. *The First Modern Comedies* (1961).
Holland, Peter. *The Ornament of Action* (1979).
Hume, Robert D. *The Development of English Drama in the late Seventeenth Century* (1976).
Loftis, John (ed.). *Restoration Drama* (1966).
Miner, Earl (ed.). *Restoration Dramatists* (essays) (1966).
Sutherland, James, *The Oxford History of English Literature,* Vol, VI, 1969.
Underwood, Dale. *Etherege and the 17th Century Comedy of Manners* (1958).
Van Lennep, W., *et al.* (eds). *The London Stage* (1966–   ).

THE FEMALE WITS

Anderson, P. B. 'Mistress de la Rivière Manley's Biography', *Modern Philology,* vol. 33 (1936).
Bowyer, J. W. *The Celebrated Mrs Centlivre* (1952).
Cameron, W. J. *New Light on Aphra Behn* (1961).
Carter, H. 'Three Women Dramatists of the Restoration', *Bookman's Journal,* vol. 13 (December 1925).
Duffy, Maureen. *The Passionate Shepherdess – Aphra Behn* (1977).
Gosse, Sir E. *Catherine Trotter, Precursor of the Blue Stockings* (1916).
Goulianos, J. *By a Woman Writt* (1973).

Grant, D. *Margaret the First* (1957).

Jerrold, W. C. *Five Queer Women* (1929).

Link, F. M. *Aphra Behn* (1968).

Mahl, M. R., and Koon, H. *The Female Spectator* (1977).

Sackville-West, V. *Aphra Behn, the Incomparable Astraea* (1927).

Sergeant, P. W. *Rogues and Scoundrels* (1924).

Souers, P. W. *The Matchless Orinda* (1931).

Wilson, M. *These Were Muses* (1924).

Woodcock, G. *The Incomparable Aphra* (1948).